SEVEN DREAMS

SEVEN DREAMS

A BOOK OF NORTH AMERICAN LANDSCAPES

by

William T. Vollmann

VIKING

SEVEN DREAMS

ABOUT OUR CONTINENT
IN THE DAYS OF
OKEUS
From Whom
(as Discover'd in Heroicall or Heretickall Epistles)
We Stole *Puccoons;*
and Whose Snake-Earring'd Nation
the *** POWHATANS ***
Lost
By the Scheming of our Counsell-Men
Princesse Poka-huntas
(A Country Lass)
to
TOBACCO
(But *gained* DISCOUNT CIGARETTES);
Lost
KINGDOMS
to
Argall
(Counter-treacherously);
AND THEN
in due procedure
*** Bought ***
GOSPEL RADIOS.

As Extracted and Seasoned *From*
DIVERSE RELATIONS
duly Engross'd in Parchment
by

WILLIAM T. VOLLMANN

(Known in This World as
"WILLIAM THE BLIND")

VIKING
Published by the Penguin Group
Penguin Putnam Inc., 375 Hudson Street, New York, New York 10014, U.S.A
Penguin Books Ltd., 27 Wrights Lane, London W8 5TZ, England
Penguin Books Australia Ltd, Ringwood, Victoria, Australia
Penguin Books Canada Ltd., 10 Alcorn Avenue, Toronto, Ontario, Canada M4V 3B2
Penguin Books (N.Z.) Ltd, 182–190 Wairau Road, Auckland 10, New Zealand

Penguin Books Ltd, Registered Offices:
Harmondsworth, Middlesex, England

First published in 2001 by Viking Penguin,
a member of Penguin Putnam Inc.

10   9   8   7   6   5   4   3   2   1

LIBRARY OF CONGRESS CATALOGING-IN-PUBLICATION DATA

Vollmann, William T.
    Argall / by William T. Vollmann.
        p. cm.
    ISBN 0-670-91030-9
    1. Argall, Samuel, Sir, ca. 1572–ca. 1626—Fiction.   2. Virginia History—Colonial period,
ca. 1600–1775—Fiction.   3. Smith, John, 1580–1631—Fiction.   4. Gravesend (Kent, England)—
Fiction.   5. Pocahontas, d. 1617—Fiction.   6. British—Virginia—Fiction.   7. Powhatan Indians—
Fiction.   8. Indian women—Fiction.   9. Explorers—Fiction.   I. Title.

    PS3572.0395 A83 2001
    813'.54—dc21   2001017744

This book is printed on acid-free paper. ∞

Printed in the United States of America

Maps and illustrations by the author

Set in Adobe Granjon and Adobe Caslon, with additional fonts
Composed by NK Graphics
Designed by Carla Bolte

THIRD DREAM

ARGALL

This land was of old time offered to our kings. Our late Sovereign *Queen Elizabeth* (whose story hath no peer among princes of her sex), being a pure virgin, found it, set foot in it, and called it *Virginia*. Such as do manage the expedition are careful to carry thither no traitors, nor Papists that depend on the *Great Whore*. LORD finish this good work Thou hast begun; and marry this land, a pure virgin, to Thy kingly son CHRIST JESUS; so shall Thy name by magnified; and we shall have a virgin or maiden Britain, a comfortable addition to our Great Britain . . .

REVEREND WILLIAM SYMONDS, sermon, 1609

. . . there are few of us who are not protected from the keenest pain by our inability to see what it is that we have done, what we are suffering, and what we truly are. Let us be grateful to the mirror for revealing to us our appearance only.

SAMUEL BUTLER, *Erewhon* (1872)

This book is for Esther Whitby and Robert Harbison,
without whose friendship and guidance
I would probably still be
unpublished.

CONTENTS

The reader is encouraged to use the Chronology and Glossary only as needed while reading *Seven Dreams*. The first gives context to characters and events in the text. The second defines and gives the origin of words which may be unfamiliar. As for the Source Notes, they may be ignored or skimmed; their function is to record my starting points, which might interest travelers in other directions.

LIST OF MAPS

ARGALL-TEXT

THE GENERALL HISTORIE OF VIRGINIA

(1624)

A NOTE TO LIFE'S VOYAGES

THE GENERALL HISTORIE OF VIRGINIA (1624)

TO THE RIGHT HONOURABLE READER

RIGHT HONOURABLE,

My duetie remembered, &c:

I fear to compound my first offense, in penning such slender and tuneless lines as these, by presuming to direct them to yourself, particularly when their subject is a mere Wilderness of insignificant Salvages. For what could bulk more worthy of our puzzlings (save THE ALMIGHTIE Himself), than the hives of GODliness we call *Cities?* And what less so, than Fens & frog-pools? (O darling fat frogs! If witches denied to take you in marriage to be their familiars, we wouldn't need to burn witches!) I incline toward the best, Right Honourable; I'd fain kiss your hand — yet this Book of mine doth drag me down toward the worst. Truth to tell, my own self mires me now. My mind descends and condescends to foulness; the tale I must tell's putrescent with sin — dangerous not to you, Right Honourable, for by virtue of your celestial blood you're proof against infamy's infections, but *I* own no such liquid armor, being chinked 'twixt my platelets with Adam's taint. Therefore, did you give me leave I'd take my leave of *Captaine Argall, John Smith & Princesse Pokahuntas* before e'er their simulacra broach'd your stage! But already I see inferior persons applauding Pocahontas (no matter that some snicker in their sleeves, her dark squatness proving her risibility). She curtseys to well-trained perfection, tossing her admirers .1. glove of white doeskin embroider'd with green silk. And what else may be won of her? — To this Argall's Sailors shout obscene reply e'en as they troll their ale-bowl lip to lip, moustaches rank and dripping. — Argall laughs: No doubt, villains! But my golden goose is not for sale to such as you. Spit other chickens on your Welsh hooks! — O misbegotten Argall, I love thee not; thy doings disgust me. — But hale him away (no matter that this Dream's call'd after him), and the story-hole remains no less fetid with dishonor, contrivance, cruelty, butchery, stooping sneakiness — why not spade our tale entire into a mucky grave? And belike I might long howl in this strain, like some dog that fears to obey his Master's call, yet must, therefore slinks & whirls in cunning crazy circles, approaching his own fear only because he dreads that his fear might approach him. Howbeit, such eccentric navigations will scarce win us bellytimber — not when there's a whole Globe of fears to be crossed! Let's cross it, then.

✳ ✳ ✳ ✳ ✳

Should it please you, Reader, we'll embark at wise-named *Gravesend,* to put period to our English doom. Life at home being death, why not steal resurrection from Salvages? (No matter that those so named remain diabolically unsalvaged, for they know not OUR REDEEMER. No matter that they likewise in His Book have been en-*graved*. And why not? Even our Queen must die — at least 'till the day call'd *Tombsend,* when CHRIST cometh.) Gravesend, end of all graves! If we could but get beyond that Towne, what colorfully immortal careers we'd make! And by GOD's wounds, that's easy! For Gravesend leads everywhere. Just as Swineshead's a reliable locale for flax, and *Virginia's* a most likely place to kidnap Salvages, so Gravesend enjoys her own fame, being dubbed *the Station of Limbo:* terminus for London-Towne (which lieth but a .4. hours' sail away — tuppence by open barge) — O, throughway she is, birth canal bristling with ships, expedient river-huddle stinking of slops and gudgeons,* tavernway for Sailors, tipplers and trulls, merchantway where Astrologers offer lodestones for sale to lost Captaines whose hearts crave piracy and whose sea-boys run a-chasing after scandaled, diseased and lickerish hacksters who do uplift their petticoats for pay. — Why don't the

---

*Certain freshwater fishes (in this case dead ones.)

boys sit patient on their penny-purses? After all, in *Virginia,* where they're bound, Salvage wenches fresh-painted with oil and puccoons will be their bedfellows. — Well, you see, Virginia's virgin to their ears, just as Gravesend's GOD send to all of us whirligig-men and layabouts, us jesting time-servers, unqualitied Adventurers, dilettantes, sharp actors, vendors, ferrymen, Watermen, shipwrights, innkeepers, pickpockets, blind historians and upstart yeomen who swim in *Between-Times,* watching half-shut opportunities wag their jaws. Shall we rush in, to percase be devoured, or rather tread water at a safer distance, slowly drowning? Thus in Gravesend we wait, dear comets, rocking 'twixt land and sea.*

❋ ❋ ❋ ❋ ❋

In fine, time becalms itself; aspirations swither & swelter. The curtain's not yet up; Virginia's unstoried as I sit in my swivel chair, not troubling to consult my reference works. (How *did* the Salvages make their arrows?) They call for Pocahontas to make Salvage curtseys anew; they demand to taste her submission to Argall and our Sovereign. They thirst for tales to flow down their gullets. But stay a space, Right Honourable. Look on Gravesend while you may. She's but vestibule to this Dream of mine. When we exit, 'tis for good — ha! at least 'till we come back again: There's Gravesend for you! None can be divided forever from earth's oozy bosom. Burn'd alive on a stage, like convicted highwaymen, or drown'd in shroud and cannonball like Cabin-boys perished of the pest, yet translated flesh must revert: Bone-smoke comes down at last to besoot the ground, and the waterlogged youths fall not for all time, but find the *Octopus's* kelpy bed. And we ourselves, briefly resurrected from our womb-grave, paddle down the Thames, lay plots at Gravesend, then fall clay-claimed. *That's* for good, now, isn't it?

Still and all, no voyager returns graveward unchanged. As for those Adventurers who sail for Virginia, why, still deeper in them bites the strange mordant. 'Tis law that they die before they perish. Like felon at rope's end, crewman at Gravesend, they're divorced from earth. Once they beach their aspirations in Virginia's clasp, divorce itself darkens into specious uncertainty; the heart meets nothing to which it can give itself; memory falls away from bone. And if haply they make Gravesend again, for an eye-

---

*"If bound up-river," advises a yachtsman's manual from 1993, "it is not very useful to arrive at the lock of Gravesend just before high water so it will sometimes be preferable to lie at anchor in the river throughout an ebb tide. This can be done by choosing a quiet spot about a mile down-river from the lock and just below the *Ship and Lobster.*"

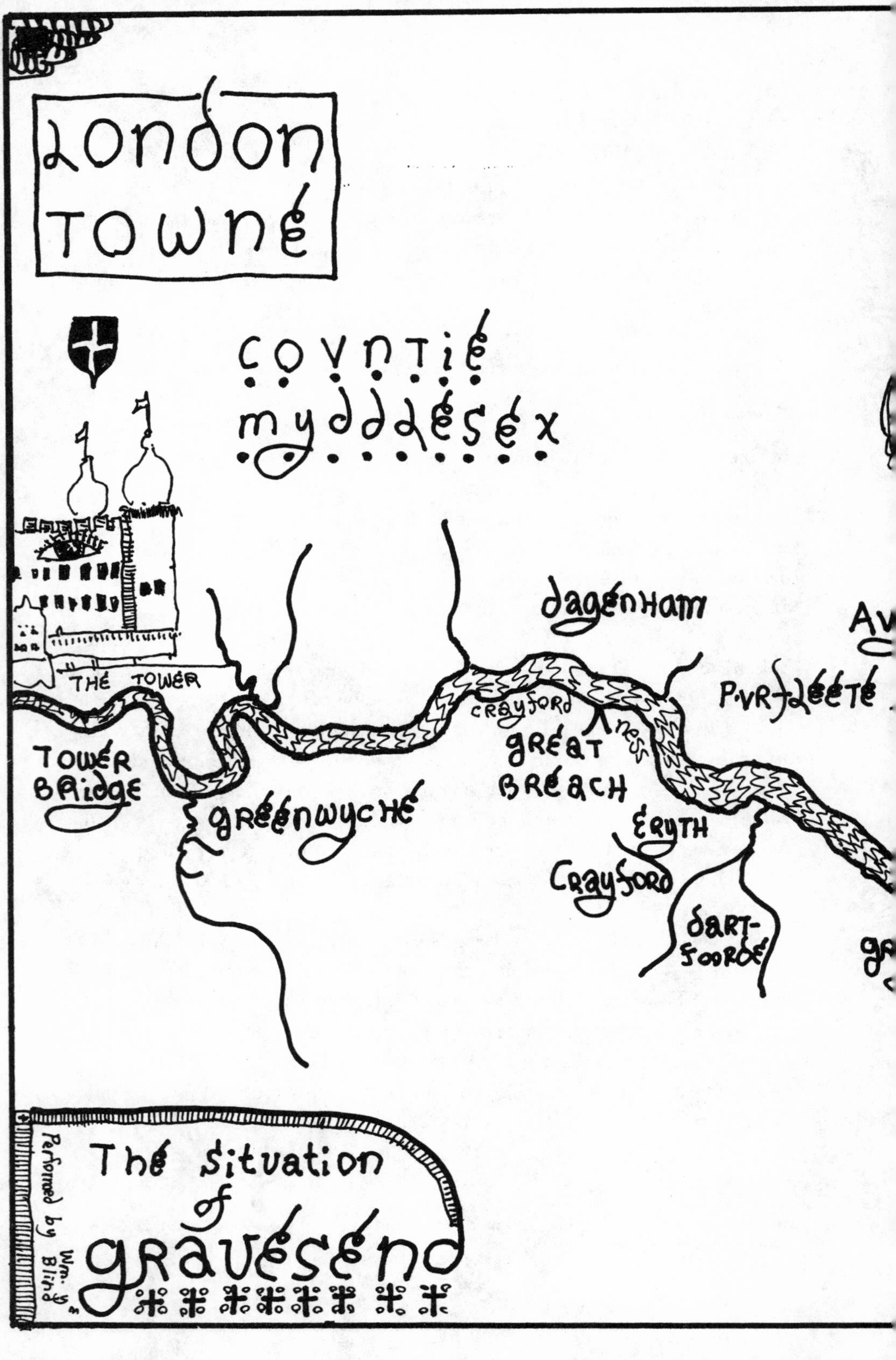

LONDON TOWNE

COVNTIE
MYDDLESEX

THE TOWER

TOWER
BRIDGE

GREENWYCHE

dagenham

CRAYFORD

GREAT
BREACH

NESS

ERYTH

CRAYFORD

DART-
FOORDE

AV

PVRFLEETE

THE situation
of
GRAVESEND

Performed by Wm. Blind

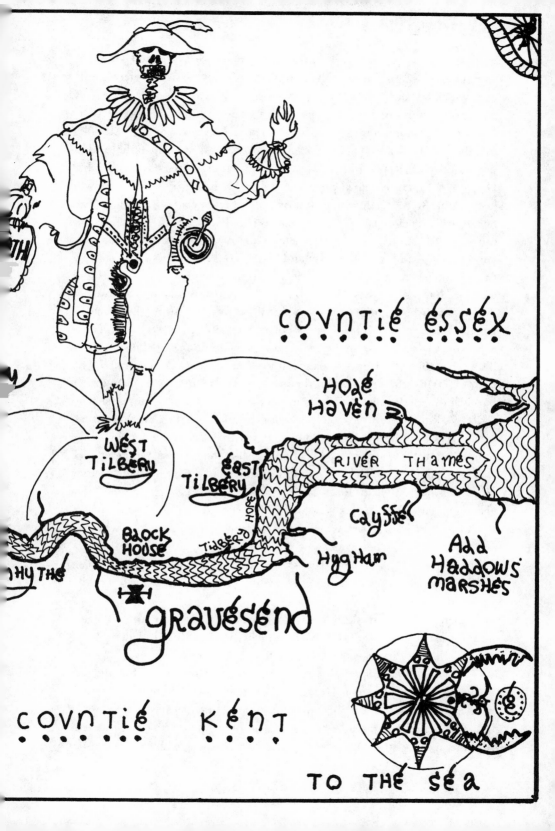

COVNTIÉ ESSEX

HOPÉ HAVÉN

RIVÉR THAMES

WÉST TiLBÉRY

ÉAST TiLBÉRY

TiLBÉRY HOOH

BLOCK HOUSE

CLYSSÉ

HiGHAM

Add HADDOWS MARSHÉS

HYTHÉ

graUésénd

COVNTIÉ KÉNT

TO THÉ SÉA

blink e'en pickpockets stand clear, fearing with a long-clawed snatch to gain not gold, but death. For the Adventurers' faces are as salt-etched mirrors, which do betray the onlooker's own vacancy. *Cain, Methusaleh* & *Lazarus,* who pretended to cheat death in Virginia, all wore leather-green faces at homecoming, & their eyeballs rolled fierce and ghostly like the silver-bluish sea. What did they gain? Ask 'em how many fathoms falls the sea-drop off Ryppe Rappe Bank, or who stands duty today on the .2.nd Dog Watch, and they can answer; but inquire about Virginia, and Cain will keep silent, Methuselah will mutter only that he's never seen anything like her in his entire longish life, and Lazarus huskily whispers: Virginia's another world, she is. Dangers & suchlike, you know . . . the Great Beyond . . . — And his eyes are wet and blank like mussel-shells. What slew those men? Which fate did they choose from the ships at Gravesend that tremble all in a row? Why, I told you — they wed Virginia so as to taste her .5.-foot codfishes, her cherry-trees & hurtleberries, her turpentine sweet as angelic ichor. They read from the Book of Kings: *I dug wells & drank foreign waters, and I dried up with the sole of my foot all the streams in Egypt.* Thus the story of Virginia — and, indeed, of all these .7. Dreams. The theme: Success. But when they returned to bed down at Gravesend, barnacles preyed upon their beards. What faded them? They speak no more. Ask their brethren who yet haunt this place — the new Venturers, I mean. They've been cured ere now in departure's breezes; their Fishwife-lemans swear they've sped to Hell and back, like the Lincolnshire tides. See that salt-stained old jewel? He and his brother sail'd *beyond* Hell to enter Virginia's quim. Quick! Follow to the Cheer-house! What hath their travels taught 'em? They drink wisdom in their rum, then piss it out. They go to Church-yards, or to sea, whichever proves their doom. Sailors, why cast yourselves as lots, when you know you must lose the game? What good's gold in the tomb? Aren't all rewards as this crooked Dream of mine, which hath Virginia's virtues, and therefore twinkles like pyrites, but cannot raise the dead?

A drunkard lifts his skull, turns upon me a sensitive, red-rimmed gaze, and replies: Not true! Death dwells only here. Can I but find a Captaine, he'll save me, for that's his business; he'll take me far away . . .

Very well, dream-sponge, await your Captaine's pleasure for another dozen ale-draughts here at Gravesend! Why *won't* he guide you to immortality? No matter that his nobility's greenish like decayed brass armor-links, his sealed commission speaks but rumors, and your wages prove but promises paid in the currency of desire. In all these many-masted ships crowded together so that they resemble a dead forest trembling on the tide — argosies, shallops, barges, double-masted barks with scarce a pair of stained sails, pinnaces, carracks & caravels, cockboats & ketches, admirals, swift flyboats whose many taut canvases drink in the wind as if they long to be gone — there blooms perhaps but .1. leafy tree in whose bower your good Captaine readies everything. He's rarer than an alligator with a conscience. His name is *Captaine Fortune.* (Drink a round to him!) Nay, his nobility's not verdigris'd at all. But how can one know him, who hasn't served him first? Hurry! Life waits not! Quickly choose him and go! For here comes Death! — There — that's the man to bestow yourself on, for he pities you, and the whores his men haunt say he gives good wages. *(They* know; they've picked pockets, nay, plumbed 'em down to the last shilling. When they robbed the Gunner's Mate they found a gold noble hid behind his balls — that means .6. shillings .8. pence. So tell me they don't cheerily praise Captaine Fortune! His lads will finance their victory!) — But alas, that Captaine's not yet ready; he commands us all to dacker down, and bide yet more at Gravesend . . .

(Death flies o'er, with whirring wings. He's off to London-Towne, to make a plague. Full .15,000. dead, as I did hear.)

Here comes Captaine Not-Death — to wit, Captaine Martin Frobisher in the flagship *Gabriel,* fresh in from misnamed *Greenland,* which is a cold dependency of Cathay. He's fraughted with a dying Esquimau and a lump of fool's gold.* The Queen's alight; he's saved her weeping Treasury! She sends a gold chain, which must forever embrace his neck . . . Tell me he's not Captaine Fortune! He craves to sail back to Greenland again, to clear Her Majestie's last debts. Calling all hands! Sailors, can't you handle a mainsail? He'll pay in jewels of fabulous ice, and for belly-timber you'll have all the Esquimau wenches you can slupper up between your teeth. Make haste! He's provisioning the *Aid* this time; he's signed on Mate and Gunner this very morn; make haste! But, strange Sailors, odd beings, I see that you rub your beards and grin, lurking clear. Damnme if you're not a gaggle of scared pullets! Frobisher entreats, literally impresses, calls you *dainty;* he craves to master you, the better to engraft himself upon the sea. And you disbelieve in his Adventure yet? (Wise-burned souls!) Why duck you down in your nests of tarred ropes wrapped around beams? You prefer to huddle over a pegholed board & play Tick-Tack? Stand clear then! I see his Crewmen crossing yards, reeling in cable about the capstan, weigh-

*As I told in the First Dream.

ing anchor. And off sails worthy Captain Frobisher! He'll never perish.
'Tis said that from a little window of her Greenwyche Palace the Queen
herself waves as he sails by . . .

(Death whirs down and stings a Tavern-keeper. Well, Gravesend reeks
of taverns, so what's .1. the less?)

Here comes Captain Amadas, who serves Sir Walter Ralegh. We'll tell
his biography later, in our "Grammar of Navigators" some hundred pages
on. For now, let's just name him the safest, wisest Captain in the world,
excepting Ralegh himself. (Frobisher? A nobody! You fancy that *he* kens
the true meridian? Why, he's not worth .1. of our Amadas's toenails!)
Something about his salted face, or his strangely menacing mildness, his
neck as graceful as the snaking hilt-guard of a fine German rapier, his —
but how can I define what Fortune is? His patent, like Frobisher, licenses
him to impress any likely men in this haven — to *commaund* you, Sailors,
and if need be to clap you in bilboes of bitterest iron, so you'll serve him in
Virginia. He'll catch you more rapidly than the Slaughterman doth seize
upon his prey. Why flee your red-latticed Tavern-houses to hide? Isn't he
Captain Fortune? He *smiles* on you. He murmurs that Salvages be passing meek, that *Sassafrass* & *Cinnamon* trees will cure your whore-pox;
why hang back from him? — Sign on, bend the knee! All hands to their
proper gear! — O, but now *he's* gone. What pity!

(Death follows him to Virginia, serving sharks all the way.)

A sly Waterman rows in next. He whispers that should you spy any ship
fraught with Spanish plunder (which is to say, *illegal* burthen, by our dear
Queen's command), pray send to him at .1.ˢᵗ blink! You'd think his narrow
bosom could scarce hold any secret, yet he knows where all the graves lie.
He tattles on Captain Amadas, who's but Ralegh's dull drudge, as he
proves by .1,000. syllogisms. Why (sneers the Waterman), Amadas doesn't
even ken where Virginia is! Thank GOD you didn't chance yourself to
him! For pure affection's sake, the Waterman next whispers that his Agent
(nam'd *Maister Fortune)* will do good offices to buyers & sellers of all
commodities. The selfsame Agent dwells under the Sign of the .3. Doves
at Newgate Market. (And, by the bye, Sir, would you lie a-niggling with a
sweet doxy? She's called *Fortuna.* 'Tis but a penny for the narrowest
quim this side of Heaven! The Bawdy-house lies but a musket-shot from
here . . .) Why wait? Isn't this Waterman your truest chance?

No! — Ralegh's fitting out the *Tiger.* I'd lay my coppers on *him!*
The smell of money blows across her weather bow. Why not indenture

yourself to *his* glamor-salted men? Ship on! But mayhap Argall will come and . . . — O, o, o! — Too late! The *Tiger's* gone on the tide . . .

Captaine Fortune's never going to come now. Doom reeks in Gravesend's sickly fogs. We wait.

* * * * * *

Chew cloves, quaff water of cinnamon — again the plague springs out. In London-Towne, thrice .10,000. more crawl groaning down to death. Charnel accumulates, then drips like candle-wax. Just as laboring beasts do turn tread-wheels for their Master's profit, so life revolves for death, swirling & stopping, sailing in & out, until the pest comes whirring down. May sea-breath keep away that devil's-breath! They say that in *Virginia* (e'en though not all's perfect — for instance, you can buy neither butter nor cream in that Countrey*) there grows an herb which can magick mortality into perfect ease, and I myself once glimpsed there an Alp of fool's gold ripe for the digging. So muster your crew, good Undertakers and Adventurers, rig out your fleets and your winding-sheets; get you safe beyond graves' very endings; farewell, G O D speed; may you escape skeletons' applause . . .

* * * * * *

And so you shall — for now I offer cheerier tidings: This is the tale not only of lonely oceans and barbarous Nations, but also (as hinted) of good *John Smith and the Lincolnshire boys,* who wanted but some honest cheese. They'll keep us company this whole Dream through. — *Flood oh!* cries Captaine Smith. Weigh anchor; up spritsail! Ride the swells of eternity!

Our *Almanacke* lays out the proper tide, to wit, *The moone South south west, at Graues end full sea.* From high-water time at Harwich, add an hour for Gravesend. From high-water time at Dover, add an hour and .3.—quarters for Gravesend. — But why spend tuppence on any Almanacke? John Smith stands on deck, and kens sea-science as well as any book! Proof: John Smith *is* but a book nowadays, his bones long since laid down in the muck after every charitable preparation. Squat, rectangular Sailor that he is, he speaks in a rustle & flutter of paper wings which cannot fly.

---

*Milk our Salvages call *Hickory,* because they beat hickory kernels in water to make a white liquor.

Reader, skim bravely o'er his pages now, like a petrel speeding o'er pale-foamed seas, avoiding sharks and Spaniards, 'till looms *Virginia* — she likewise but a paper continent now, inhabited by mere paper tigers — or mayhap I should say paper wasps or hornets, for don't Salvages carry their own stings? Aren't they all born into poisonous cunning? Hideous rigorous reigns their Emperor, Pokahuntas's own father *Powhatan,* who broils Englishmen (so 'tis said), or pricks 'em full of arrows . . . Yea, he knots up dried human hands in his hair! But be comforted; of him likewise naught remains but old paper and nightmare honor. He'd rise up from John Smith's pages to slay us if he could, but from all designs hath GOD excused him forever, his paper flesh tamed, time-tanned, tattooed and o'er-written by letters of the English alphabet, alien epitaphs which he cannot read. He's a ghost cobwebbed with John Smith's words.

And Smith, whom we'll call *Sweet John,* he utters nothing new, being but the husk of his own monument. His pages whisper like the myriad soft lost voices at Gravesend.

* * * * * *

Ten years ago & more I purchased his writings all complete in a triple-volumed set slipcased in burgundy. How long before they too find themselves fetter'd in cobwebs, haled back as trophies to death's dingy prison? Not until I die, I swear! So let them take heart; for the present they've been saved. (The middle volume gratefully whispers: *Your Grace's faithful and devoted Servaunt, John Smith.*) On my shelf they stand gloomily elegant amidst many other tomes about Salvages. Nicely busked up in their box, acid-free (at least for now, until I breathe on them), they lord it over Virginia Watson's *Legend of Pocahontas,* Elaine Raphael and Don Bolognese's *Pocahontas, Princess of the River Tribes,* Grace Steele Woodward's *Pocahontas,* and William S. Rasmussen and Robert S. Tilton's *Pocahontas, Her Life & Legend* — howbeit, try as I might, I can scarce unchain my gaze from this last, for the cover's a pageant of Englishmen round a campfire while, in unlikely relief against the darkness, like the subject of a Weegee photograph caught in the glare of powerful flashbulbs, *POCAHONTAS* herself stands half-draped in a tawny blanket out of some Plains Indians fantasy, showing off .1. perfect, hard-nippled breast as she gestures upward into the night. No matter that she could have looked nothing like this. I suppose she reminds me of a Thai prostitute with whom I once had sexual relations.

Yet I fear that while making eyes at the piquant Virginian wench we've mislaid our lodestone of mercantile confidence, good *Captaine Smith*

himself, whom GOD fashion'd not to whirligig, but to point sweet and
true toward Virginian summers, straight across seas & centuries to reach
blue clouds in a brown pool. Some say the grass-heads rushed into his
brain, baffling him with rays and reflections, but he faithfully, accurately
explor'd many a pudgy blue river-tendril thrusting between alder-lips; his
maps prove it so. See how well he aims! Come magnetic storms he may
equivocate, but *lie* never (except to Salvages). He's Captaine Fortune.
With him we'll win to winegrapes and sassafrass. Another warranty yet:
His .20.th century editor (himself but lately returned to ooze) loved him,
subscribing for stained glass windows in Willoughby Church where John
Smith was christened. Which of those translucent monuments can I remember? (For it's been half a decade since I was there.) I remember —
ooze. The folk of Lincolnshire are half-Salvage themselves, or, as we say
here in London, *helobius hoblobs* — namely, *marsh-dwelling Rustics.*
Granted, Willoughby's not as squishy as some Fen-ridden Townes, but
come a good rain, a sea-tide, a dyke-burst, why won't that Church sink into
ooze as doth a fool's foot in cowshit? — O, but the *windows!* Yes, I seem
to see all sprightly and multicolored from his Adventuring our *Sweet
John* as he's call'd, with the fog of Lincolnshire glowing right through
him; and we've already met Pocahontas, whose Church-glass eyes are black
as Indian plums — and could e'erworthy *Captaine Argall* also be en-
glassed? No, I don't spy him out. (Mayhap he belongs not in any Dream;
he's not Man, but Mechanism; nobody knows him.) Well, *all* of them lie
lost underground now like old Roman coins. To proclaim them in my
Dream is to win them back, salvaging them as GOD did *Israel's remnant,*
namely the Salvages. But only Argall requires proclamation. Pokahuntiss
craves nothing, altho' Sweet John engraves her into his *Generall Historie* nonetheless; and as for he himself, his words, scorning other pro-
claimers, proclaim themselves. They trumpet self-belief. They truculently
clamor: *Idlenesse and carelessnesse brought all I did in .3. yeeres in .6.
moneths to nothing.* They promise to teach how to plant Colonies & destroy
Salvages at a moderate price. They wheedlingly complain themselves into
eternal life.

So here's to his mortal remains! Most skeletons rule but a single backbone, while his owns .3. spines of burgundy. On each gleams the gilded emblem of the Institute of Early American History and Culture, guaranteeing
the *ancientness* of the dead words inside, like the Baker's mark which
gets pricked on each loaf of bread in Lincoln Towne, to guard the buyer
from sawdust-fraud. — Thus our warranty; now, how about the bread?

Hasten; eat up his words. Ship with him, and may he never lose the shirt of Captaine Fortune! For I hear Death whirring down, half-closing wings for to fall on us the faster; his stinger's ready; he's near as inevitable as Argall. Well, well, he's here. On the Virginia Turnpike a car gets front-ended by a truck. The whole front of the car is gone, with small pieces of metal, glass and rubber scattered down the road for **.500.** feet. An ambulance and **.2.** police cars block the intersection, blinking their lights mournfully. The stretcher-bearers unhurriedly carry a litter draped with a white sheet which is already turning crimson in **.3.** places.

*　*　*　*　*

That was why I coveted those burgundied volumes from the very first — for Death assailed me. On **.1.** of his blank charters (my birth certificate) he'd already penned my name. He'd come a-soldiering and a-sailing to find me. He'd come a-riding to smell me out with his hounds of time. How long could I hide? Someday I'd reach my *December,* which is the heel of the year. If only Captain Fortune would haven me within his slipcased works! Let Death hound me then! I'd be Virginia'd safe into words — not myself anymore, true, but signature of myself, as the empty sepulcher doth signify CHRIST. The Book's the thing. Words live beyond life. Word to word I sought comfort from sweet John Smith; I issued counter-charters and licenses of my own; I called upon Vendors of the Word. Just as in a convoy the **.1.**st ship to descry land must shoot off her ordnance and raise the gladsome flag, so, I commanded, ought every Bookseller to telephone me as soon as those **.3.** books came to light — but since I was no Captaine, they stayed out of patience, or else (afraid to attract Death's notice) they ducked my commission like foolish fretting creepers: *Out of print,* they said. (Tush! Don't we all go out of print? Even this very Dream must someday get waterlogged, and give over voyaging. And you, Right Honourable, **.4.** centuries hence where will *you* be? Down, deep down! 'Twixt Gravesend and Virginia swirls many a watery grave.) But **.3.** harquebus shots away, in **.1.** of those tiny cellar-bookstores in the chitterlings of Manhattan's Upper East Side, the pipe-smoking owner, lifting his arm as if to ward off the gazes of Tax-men, engaged himself to try; and **.2.** months and **.200.** dollars later (for I had neither gold nobles, nor French louys, nor Spanish ducatoons), I happed to be a-writing a Dream about the Salvages and CROW-SPIRITS of New York when the telephone sang: *I'm Captaine Fortune, and your ship's in harbor!* — That voice! It did most strangely remind me of a Waterman's whisper; and when I look'd around me with proper sincerity, I saw that I was back in Gravesend. After donning my accustomed funereal spirit, I shouldered a pickaxe, in case any of the cobwebs I was likely to meet had fossilized; then I recited the Anglican burial service and descended into that subterranean bed of typeset virtue off Eighty-First Street, where the Bookseller (himself now buried, as I hear — or did he but go bankrupt?) stood ready with the spoils: — my *Complete Works of Captain John Smith,* duly shrouded in brown paper in a cardboard sarcophagus which OUR REDEEMER had postmarked from North Carolina, bastard latecomer of a State, which was but lately (1662) Virginian territory.

✳ ✳ ✳ ✳ ✳ ✳

About Virginia herself I scarce ken anything. To find her you'd best know the declination of the Sunne and of the Moone. Watermen and great Captaines keep such arcana at hand; but I, mere half-blind scribbler, scarce know my own compass dial. Yet even had I means, how *could* I find her, after the persecutions of Time? She's broken into vertebrae, like the sickle found in Roanoke Fort. She's decayed into pernurious divisions, translated into Counties, States, freeways and naval bases. From her flesh they've lopp'd off *New England, New Scotland, New York, Maryland, Pennsylvania* and *Carolina* (whose wheat yields **.30.**-fold). Poor Virginia! Dig patiently in her, and you may find a tiny white glass bead, a deer's foot, a pouch of deerskin. — Is there value in those? Ask John Smith, who can pen a key to any discovered hoard. He conspires to extend himself a few centuries more, busily remembrance-toiling for hire. He maps her and flatters her with newborn Colonies of English souls. She needs him. Dig, dig! She would not so be mortified, but owns neither remedy, nor miracle now, save him. Archaeologists rape her in her dotage; romanciers misuse her; and at Jamestowne, where her **.1.**st Capitol lies, many a squirrel noses between those stone doorways call'd *Tombs.* (Governor Yeardley might be buried in **.1.** of these, but the records won't tell — they got burned in our recent Civil War.)

So what's left of old Virginia? She lies conquered, her sloughs become but the blank spaces between the chapters of Sweet John's *Generall Historie,* her pickerel-weeds, thalias and lance-leaved arrowheads now but marginal decorations, printer's weeds.

O, but in her day she had fight in her! In her day she shook her bristling tail! Reader, remember this: From 1606 'till 1625, out of **.7,000.** Colonists sent to pickaxe away her maidenhead, **.6,000.** perished! I swear it. (Where are their bones? They lie rotted under river-slime. An archaeologist writes: *No traces have been found.*)   But Captaine Fortune did save us. Virginia, spraddle-legged and weeping, for our sustenance gave up her maidenly ghost!   Then the Colonists swore her full affection, calling her Ole Virginny.   Her oysters lay upon the ground *as thicke as stones* (runs .1. document), so that any gambler or eater could play the husking-game, hoping to discover pearls.   Time further restrained her, assaulted her, then interr'd her beneath her own ooze.   Only John Smith remembers (because he drafted it) the *Map of Virginia,* which, however imperfectly, presents her bygone naked charms of Salvage Townes now o'erwritten by bulldozers & steel beams.

   I know not what to say, when I scan his pages or tread the grass of Jamestowne — both of those my patrimony, from which I've inherited electric ease and genocidal shame.   See a line of a dozen ducks slowly gliding in the still river, as if the heads of ruined pilings have begun to move backwards.   John Smith's statue, benevolent and green, turns its back upon the Church tower, which is the .1. .17.th century structure still standing at this .20.th-century national park call'd after our Soveraigne.   The doorway of the Church-tower, green-rimmed with age, seems to lead not up into Heaven, but *down* into muck and ooze.   Virginia lies lost and silent.

* * * * *

In the Outer Banks, which they nam'd parcel of Virginia* near .30. years before Captaine Smith ever conned Jamestowne, fate is so windy, sandy and immense that currents' local infinities cannot all be foreseen.   Sometimes, however briefly, Virginia gets her own back, even if in a merely allegorical fashion.   Yes, Jamestowne's mainly underwater now, and in the Outer Banks many a gobbet of Virginia's flesh has been stolen by time and the sea, but let me now like a good Undertaker lay out .1. of those allegories — specifically, the eerie tale of *John Harris,* who once upon a time saved his bride from drowning.   After he'd laid her down in the sand and breathed his own life back into her, she opened her eyes, instantaneously experiencing the illusion of being suspended high above our continent or even the whole world, for the isles around him and her were but long low blue fingers on the sapphire sea.   And that world possessed no history, being

---

*Now the Carolinas. In 1700 a botanical Adventurer nam'd *Maister John Lawson* did write: "The Savages do, indeed, still possess the Flower of *Carolina,* the *English* enjoying only the Fagend of that fine Country." Fortunately, progress was being made. In the environs of Charles-Town, "they are absolute Masters over the *Indians,* and carry so strict a Hand over such as are within the Circle of their Trade, that none does the least Injury to any of the *English,* but he is present sent for, amd punish'd with Death, or otherwise, according to the Nature of the Fault."

newborn through her. He carried her home in his arms. Not long after, when they were married and sitting in the porch swing, she whispered that someday she'd repay her rescue, at which he but kissed her and laughed, for she could not swim. Then the years went by, like a long freight train swimming through the forest. In 1933, she lay dying of sickness. His breath could help her no more. Longing never again to be exposed to her former destiny of sinking and changing, she implored him to cherish her within a marble vault into which no ooze could creep. He promised this. Then her breath ceased like golden grass shooting off into darkness. A rusty bell on a concrete block guarded the old clapboard church. No marble vaults hulked there, though, not a .1. Nor had he the means. They embalmed her right pretty for her funeral. Afterward, John Harris went wearily home. He picked up a blackened seagull feather from the lee side of a dune and raised to the sky. The wind whirled it out of sight. Soon it began to rain. A hurricane was coming, the radio said. The next day he sat with the front door open, letting the chilly miserable wind blow rain in his face, glimpsing a lightning pallor behind it all which he knew to be the steady white drive of the breakers curling, turning and smashing though his soul, tiny clots of foam skittering ahead of them as if in fear. A negro boy came running against the wind, his footprints disappearing as quickly as he made them. The boy screamed: *Coast Guard says we all gotta get outta here, Mr. Harris!* Then the boy was gone. John Harris knew by then that his house, like his life and love, was but a fortress of sand, but he did not care. When the hurricane attacked him on that fishy foggy night, he waited for the end of everything. Waves like bygone ladies in long green dresses with ruffled collars came dancing at his door. Their ruffles were lethally cold and brilliant. Their seagull voices cried out: *Love you not me?* and John Harris denied to answer. Black waves shattered his walls and windows, sheared away his roof. To him it seemed befitting. He'd spend himself in the new-coined wreckage of everything. The cold sea began to vomit streams of salty foam upon his head. He shivered soddenly, unable even to perceive the extravagance of the doom which had merely poisoned *her,* but which must obliterate him in a series of orchestral crashes. If only he could simply cease to be! But he would not kill himself; his grief's inertia prohibited that. Near midnight, illuminated by that same hideous pallor of lightning (which now reminded him of his wife's perished flesh), he saw the approach of the wave which would bear him down to death. The wave shouted: *I am Captain Fortune.* It was a mile high at least (for in allegories, "real" scale is treason), and white streaks of salty spittle ran down its crown like fangs as it began to curl over his head, but just then the foundation in which he crouched drench-haired and crazed was shaken when Amy Harris's burial vault, her securest inheritance, massively dense and indrawn like a prey-hunting alligator with its dark legs clenched up its sides and its head in the water, came smashing against the front doorstep (the tradition that it knocked .3. times is surely apocryphal). His heart, virgin-closed in sadness, now opened: Sodden with velvet terror (for the giant wave hung over him), he threw himself onto fortune's cement-lidded lifeboat, gripping the bas-relief angel's wings, praying to live. Yes, his desperately mortal flesh had temporarily overmastered his will-less will! (This turning-point proved nothing other than that he was either more or less than he believed.) Then the wave pounced, almost drowning, almost crushing him. After many a dreary year, it sullenly stemmed itself, leaving droplets like tears of rage in the hollow between the concrete angel's breasts where he'd hidden his head and choked. His flesh was numb. He inquired of himself: Did I choose this fate? Currents took the bait and overwhelmed him in courseless compassless voyaging. *Flood oh!* That corpse-saved man lay upon his wife for the last time while the wallowing barge he'd bought her carried him safe across Currituck Sound. His soul sped far before him, fleeing from his own mortality, so that he no longer knew whom he was. Neither tackle nor crew, captain nor standard, only cargo and supercargo did that ship carry, discoloring itself in no human purpose. At sunrise, the spouses washed up together upon tigerlike wind-striped sand. So John Harris was ferried home to Gravesend. His hair had turned white, but he lived to die a different death. (As for *her* hair, by now it was matted, kelpy, but delicate like Spanish moss.) Thus Amy Harris reclaimed her debt, and—for a single storm-ridden night, at least, she reclaimed him. (Couldn't Virginia do the like?) It's written that when her vault was opened by deputies that day, as required by state law, she was smiling, but this must have surely been some trick of rigor mortis.

✳   ✳   ✳   ✳   ✳

Rigor mortis! In Virginia I've seen birds like white berries, birds like white flowers on the trees — they're all tricked out on John Smith's pages now, with their claws locked forever into g-hooks and r-curves. The black-poxed spade-leaves of lagoon plants and the stenches of dead fish, these verisimilitudinize us all so excellently — and yet I know well that black leaves remain mere black letters, b's and ð's growing down from their vertical stems, tight-budded c's, wild ɟ-vines and ȝ-trees; and as for that fishy smell, sea-mates, it's but binder's glue gone sour, decaying back into Virginian ooze.

* * * * * *

Like every other inhabitant of that pipe-smoker's establishment, the *Complete Works of John Smith* (though they'd slept there less than .2. nights) secreted and exuded the odor of bittersweet smoke, as they do in my library even now a decade later — tribute to Pocahontas's .2.nd husband, *John Rolfe,* who fought hornworms, hanging his leaves in hands of .5. until *Tobacco* equaled *Profit.*   — How can I too profit from Virginia? — Why, by cribbing out of John Smith's tales! My future lies blue and wide. Like John Harris, who on the morning after the hurricane clambered off the beached vault and looked back to see the pale white horizon of breakers, I wish to believe it's possible to turn my back on all I've done and lost. I sit staring out my window at the maples now coming into leaf, and long to give over these failed Dreams, leaving Virginia rotting, living out my bonus of days in someplace fabulous like unknown Spanish Florida where long narrow fishes splash and bubble in the green pool between wall-weeds, and birds peep and creep between mangrove roots. There let me dwell, drinking the strange heaviness of air in those winding ways, forgetting more every day, partaking of but rich swamp water until the hanging branches of mangroves conceal me from myself, and spidery roots protect me from Death. But I have not yet means to travel. That's why I sit here, misusing poor John Smith, who aspired only to be a maritime Merchantman, and failed; his papery husks of plans and expediencies I steal to paper over the skeleton of a narrative which I also stole from him. — Peace. Count coins. — Not yet enough to unrest my oars, says Charon Waterman. Tuppence more! Bide awhile, blind soul; pen your Dream out (we both know how it ends); my fare yet overtowers you. — I dare not reply as I would: Sir, I'm at the terminus, seeking for to play my expenses down. I dig out old Virginia's nakedness for pay. I would be hence from here. I would be gone. I would not die, and to bide here is to die. — Reader, did *you* but give me sufficient pence (and percase a gold noble or .2.), I could escape Gravesend for some safe harbor delivered from all winds. Then you'd never see me more.

Until that day, which in my poverty I'd best never look for, I'll keep a-voyaging in the paper boats of these .7. Dreams, standing off paper coasts until I ken the topography of their wheretofores. Happily my blind spyglass doth help me find Townes, silver-mines, and rivers, so that day by day my *Geographickall* understanding doth ascend toward the Sunne, like steam arising from tropick tombs. And from all my browsing I know this: Into Sweet John's continent lies but a single seemly entrance, that being the very goodly

.**1**. *Volume I,* which bulks .**3**. fingers broad. Herein we Adventurers find ourselves welcomed by John Smith's coat of arms, to wit, his entitlement to worth: — .**3**. Turkes' heads, decapitated by himself! (we'll tell that story when we get to it, and not a moment before). Next falls the *True Relation,* in which he details his famed capture by the Salvages, but forbears mention of how their Princesse, by name .**1**. *Pocahontas,* sav'd his head. That defailment revolts full many a Commentator against him; for 'tis queried: *Why didn't he thank her, when his gratitude flowered fresh? Doubtless the forsworn coistrel dream'd up the lie in after-times, to brighten his braggadacio. Sav'd by a Princesse*

indeed! O, but he pretends himself above his station!
— Against that argument war his defenders thus: Sweet John grew *afeared* to pen what had circumstanc'd him, for (having but lately 'scaped hanging in his own Colonie), he thought *Silence about Salvages was Politick.* Verily, when he'd stood upon his trial in Jamestowne Church, and faced the rope's loop (thinking on camel passing through needle's eye in that Bible proverb), his hopes readied his best apparatus of schemes. His hopes whispered: They may not accuse you of spying for Pokahuntiss's Nation, *if you don't remind 'em,* Sweet John! How could truth touch him then? For in all Virginia he'd found no truth! Sooth, dear Reader, I misdoubt me not that in his ropy hour he smil'd ferociously to recollect his hour lashed to the maple tree but a fortnight before, with all the Salvages pointing arrows because he spied for King James! Then his head had lain on Powhatan's block, until

Captaine   Fortune
(disguised as Pocahontas)
did sweetly salvage him.
— GOD gifts him with
trials everywhere, it seems;
the world cares not for
truth . . . And so, Sweet
John, silence is golden!
Sing not your w e d d i n g -
s o n g (or *prothalamion* as
it be call'd) — especially
since you can't keep your
bride! — Enough: In
1999, as I finger-stroke
these lines upon my
Device Electronickall, the
tale's long since become
but   a   time-foxed
Valentine, which pretends
that the pair did love and
marry together. 'Tis true?
O, Reader, read on!

.2. *Volume II,* made in equal thickness,
contains, amidst other writings of little
harm, his *Generall Historie of Virginia,
New-England and the Summer Isles: with
the names of the Adventurers, Planters, and
Governours from their first beginning
Anno: 1584 to this present 1624,* whose
flesh in part was cobbled out of his earlier
books, & which will be cribbed from by
other compilers down the centuries,
including myself.   Here's where all
Virginian secrets are to be found, including
Pokahuntas's, which is reputed to be as
dark as the Tar River north of Wilson,
North Carolina. The *Generall Historie*
itself is dark with obfuscations as rankly

numerous as swamp channels running around the perimeters of fields. Would I could tell you what this Book means to me! I, William the Blind, do verily believe that if I but con & ken it closely enough, I'll discover what **.20,000.** Readers have never yet: namely, how stood Sweet John's heart regarding that Salvage wench, and what *truly* passed betwixt 'em. Howbeit, his pen's treacherous. He writes self-magnifyingly of his successes, while pricking out the defailments of others in words as sharp-ended as trundle-shot. He's **.1.** with the masterless man who pastes to the door of Saint Paul's Church yet another paper bragging of his own rentable qualities.* But then, mastering himself, he remembers to praise joy-leafed Pocahontas at last, confessing that she did preserve him from her father's sentence of doom. And here in the *Generall Historie* we find that famous reference in Sweet John's Powhatan grammar: *Kekaten Pokahontas patiaquagh niugh tanks manotyens neer mowchik rawrenock audowgh.* To wit: *Bid Pokahantas bring hither* **.2.** *little Baskets, and I will give her white Beads to make a Chaine.* He's Captaine Fortune. He's sudoriferous. He writes no better than he bettered himself (dying impoverished and

---

*But, O, Sweet John, that richly tricked-out title page of yours! How could another masterless man top that? Here lies *Never-Never Virginia* indeed, at whose coast just beneath the title cartouche we discover a lion in an airborne cockleshell — narrow, alert King of Beasts, whose shoulder-ribbons bear a Latin motto which neither John Smith nor I can read. Did that engraver ever scan a living lion? Methinks the beast's less leonine than one of Argall's mutchado'd Sailors who amend their distempers with tipplers, tarts, copesmates and Slaughtermen in the Tavern-houses of Gravesend. Tassels on other ribbons twiddle down from Leo's perch with delicious absurdity, like the tendrils of drunken octopi. Tenderly guarded by them lies a miniature tempest in which a sailing-ship tosses and tilts. If only I had my magnifying glass, I might perhaps see amidst all the stippling of the sea Amy Harris's funeral vault swimming low between the waves. Beyond even Mrs. Harris's reach, where land rises integral, *Tropick Vegetables* do most obscenely erupt, and amongst them we discover many a *Salvage* lurking or disporting himself. *They disguise themselves in tawniness,* writes Captaine John Smith..

consigned to ooze), for his sentences straggle in a wilderness of their own making, in which the meaning doth sometimes hide, like a lurking Salvage. But of all the old Virginias engross'd on paper, his remains the best forested, even though his forests do sometimes comprise but weeds of verbiage. And if we wish to read how Virginia did become persuaded to her new English fortunes (or forfeited to them as one might say), we need only commend ourselves to *The General Historie.*

.**3.**   In Volume III we find .**1.**st the *Accidence,*
.**2.**nd   the *Sea-Grammar* which supplants it and which valiantly explicates how to build and arm a ship from the first orlop up,
.**3.**rd the *True Travels* (wherein he recounts the historie of those Turkes' heads, and hints at certain intimacies with the Turkishe beauty Charatza Tragabigzanda), then
.**4.**th the *Advertisements* with which he seeks to advertise himself, offering sword, shoulders and loyal entrails to any Captaine Fortune who'll bear him back to Virginia (no one will). These texts are followed dutifully by
.**5.**th *fragments* and
.**6.**th diverse *auxilliary documents* concerning death.

(I raise them all to my nose, and smell pipe-smoke.)

And so at leisure I've rounded many a bend of Sweet John's Virginia; I've emerged into sudden lakes which dazzle me with blueness. On a cold Sunday morning, I spied beneath the grey-green sky a solitary black boy in a black hood bicycling to church. Sweet John's words lived invisibly all around him like the Spanish moss upon the trees. Sweet John had written: *The ground is so fertile that doubtless it is capable of producing any grain, fruits, or seeds you will sow or plant* — at which moment he thought, and qualified himself: *but it may be that not every kind of plant will grow to such a perfection of delicacy.* — The requirements of honesty satisfied, he

went on: *All sorts of cattle may be bred here and fed in the islands or penin-*
sulas, safely for nothing. In the interim, until they begin to increase, if need
be (observing the seasons) I would undertake to have enough corn for .300.
men from the savages for a few trifles; and if the savages should be hostile
(as it is most certain they are), .30. or .40. good men will be sufficient to
*bring them all to subjection.** All these recipes the Virginians had followed
amidst the palm-trees, the strips of moss braided and matted by the wind
into strips like shaggy dogtails. And now on that Sunday morning breezy
and clammy with scarcely a spoonbill to be heard, the black boy pedaled
past the Slave Cabin Historic Site. He avoided a dead possum on the road,
ducked under the tree-arms which met over the road with Spanish moss
hanging down; he passed gated mansions and housing developments,
swung around .2. joggers by the Sun Trust Bank. In my car the radio sang:
I hear my Savior calling. And who's He, but Captaine Fortune?

* * * * * *

Across the Thames with its flotsam of wind-corkscrewed sails, our *Sover-*
eign's blockhouse stands like a spool of thread on end. We're back again
at Gravesend, where bristling ships, gunned and masted and beaked, do
comprise a pavement, no matter how queasily queer; but soon each wooden
paving-stone shall take its own road, lurching and tacking, crowned by the
pale and narrow hatchet-faces of Englishmen. They crave to set about their
own *Trve Travels.* Scrupling not to abuse the sea, they would apply
Sweet John's *Sea-Grammar,* and write fresh new chapters of the secret
Generall Histories in which each of them's a hero. They come from
flat green fields like unto Lincolnshire's. They go GOD alone knows
where. Taking the Sunne upon the meridian, they find their declination
from yesterday, and dare to believe they can extrapolate the altitude of tomorrow. Why not? They sail each and every one under Captaine Fortune!
Gravesend cares not. They vanish into life and death. And then what's left
of the watery foundation they were but lately set in? Well, new ships come
in, don't they? (Else where'd Watermen get their wages?) From Gravesend
to Gravesend, travelling due west around the world, 'tis in compass but
.13,320. English miles. Sail all you like! Sail near, and you're nigh unto
Gravesend. Sail far, furiously chasing your own sun, and you'll come to

---

*What a Janus he was! For just a few paragraphs later he said that he required "a company fit for
soldiers to be ready on occasion because of the abuses against the poor savages, and the liberty with
which the French and others deal with them as they please."

Gravesend. *I hear my Savior calling.*   Death, altho' we did entreat him, would not let us out of school.

But never mind my fate, Virginia; you'll hear from me e'en in my coffin, whose very underlid's carven with your name. Virginia, exemplify yourself in flesh, that I might mate with you ere I perish!* Let *Pocahontas* be your embodiment; I swear I'll adore her to her very tripes! Her safety's become my golden jewel. I'll guard her with the counsels of restraint, such as: Never sail to Gravesend — too many turnings of brain's mercantile horse-flesh there for our rustic Princesse! What if she were hook'd? Souls expire at the turning of the tide, and at Gravesend the tide not only turns, but corkscrews, pulled hither and yon by all the scheming malice of men. May she never land at Gravesend, whose fogs choke the world with death!

Indeed tides turn like Kings. Virginia, whom I thought to bury, comes a-vaulted to knock upon my door in every page of the *Generall Historie*. John Harris bites his lip. He can't escape the sea-flung smash. Astonished, he lives on. Neither can *POCAHONTAS* escape Argall — sad, resentful Pokahuntas, who died in England, of an English disease, enshrouded in an English name: *Rebecca.*   'Tis verily a Jewess's name, which for cause her husband chose it — aren't the Salvages descended from the Lost Tribes of Israel? Lost & lost. There's the reason they buried her in Gravesend: What could be farther from anything than the very end of the graves?

✳   ✳   ✳   ✳   ✳   ✳

Three hundred and .72. winters after clay clothed her linen-blurred face, white gulls were floating in the middle of the Thames, on the far side of which stood no King's blockhouse anymore, but a brick building bearing .4. smokestacks of different heights — not as complex as organ-pipes, but they played their tunes of smoke as best they could. Two muddy-footed boys sat upon the river-wall, their fishing poles passively at work. Without emotion they watched a bottle go jigging by. Pocahontas would have grabbed it, I'm sure; because when John Smith .1.ˢᵗ gave her an empty wooden flask, she hugged herself and whispered: *Nowamatamen!* —

---

*Give o'er, Reader. Virginia's heart's not moved to give you gold. E'en her *Sassafrass*   she withholds. Esteeming you not, she offers but herself. Sailors, find another trull. (You'll not be the first to creep defeated back to Gravesend.)   Were Captaine Fortune on hand to open up the vault, he'd surely find some treasure — belike the *Jewell*   on Amy Harris's wedding-ring (holding his nose-wind 'gainst the stench, he quickly lops off the rotting finger of another Yndian territory). Thus do all *Pillagers* and *Historians.*   Ha, ha! My bodkin's out! Quick!   What shall I slash?

which means *I must keep yt* or *I love yt.* The boys did not care. Their minds were engaged in *dead reckoning.* They calculated how best to bring their fishy prey to death.

In a time-puddled shady lot scattered with rusty beams and other rubble, there rose a right worshipful weedy mound of concrete blocks, atop which I got a fair view of the .2. lads' heads and the brown water beyond them, which, cold and flowing like a snake's back, brown-tinged the green and red reflections of boat-bellies; then downriver swam the vista — all the way to Virginia, no doubt, had I but the wit to apprehend it — for the summit of that mound stood passing high above the river-wall. But when I'd climbed as high as I could, I found myself yet shaded by an abandoned building's gloom — utterance of plague's wrathful breath, as it seemed; all had staled into decay.

Another bottle floated out to sea. *Flood oh!*

* * * * * *

One of her many purple biographies cites a "tradition" that Pocahontas died in the last house on Stone Street. Bob, Esther and I strolled there, but it was only a McDonald's restaurant.

No wonder she died, said Bob.

THE PARISH CHURCH OF ST. GEORGE GRAVESEND WELCOMES YOU.

The archway was decorated with broken glass, slate and brick-shards. In the small square window-sockets, glass adhered in ruined bits, like ice.

I'm surprised that there's rubbish, said Esther. And I don't know why the Rector won't answer.

The church's old bricks were red and moss-green, like the bottles floating down the river. Hellebore grew up against the churchwalls. The headstones leaned .2. and .3. together against the outer wall. I saw the green-stained slab of some other young Rebecca there, moss- and mold-patterned like disused courtesy. The remainder of the yard was a rich and empty green.

Of the tower at Saint George's, which was not very high, I remember little but a golden knob above the clock, and the birds living in the steeple. But pray allow me to describe the lower row of segmental arch windows, the upper row of roundheaded arch windows; the spire with its blind windows; the roundheaded pediment behind the chancel (the .19.th-century chancel, that is, not the old lost one in the ooze under which Pocahontas had supposedly been buried). Bob told me that the bricks were of London stock, meaning ordinary yellow clay. We peered at the apse, which Bob considered not an *eyesore* exactly but a *carbuncle,* and he said: This is an atrocity put on later, that little vestry.

In the yard stood Pocahontas's statue. We saw her greeny-white arms outthrust a little down from her sides, her gentle hands peaceably empty, the bare tree behind her with its chirping birds. She was another Caucasian angel, like the "little princess" in Virginia Watson's *Legend of Pocahontas* who never danced naked cartwheels at Jamestowne because that might have offended *you,* Reader, and who cried out to Captaine Smith: *You shall not go! You belong to me, and it is my wish to keep you here so that you may tell me tales of the world beyond the sunrise.* Regarding such language I prefer to requote Bob: This is an atrocity put on later.

Her corpse and coffin had long since been misplaced, for Saint George's burned in 1747, then underwent reconstruction in 1892, and after that no one knew where the relics were. Some say that at the beginning of the .19.th century, body-snatchers stole her bones, which must have partaken of the pale mud-yellow color of Indian pots, and, failing to find a buyer, tumbled them back into the ground in an unmarked place. Come 1907 the *London Daily Mail* announced the discovery of

*** POCAHONTAS'S SKELETON ***

but *alas,* writes Captaine Smith's editor, *the skull turned out to be that of a Negro who was killed by a blow on the back of the head.* In 1923, .10. years before the entombed Amy Harris set sail to rescue her husband, an art critic from Virginia (descendent of those Adventurers and Undertakers who once reckoned latitudes with their most precious instruments) went to Gravesend expressly for to rummage a certain corpse-hole in which old remains had been deposited during the rebuilding of the church. Had the critic found her, what would he have done? Coffined her, borne her back seaward to some brown Virginian marsh crowned by grey and yellow weeds? Locked her into his cabinet of curiosities? All he discovered was a menagerie of human and animal remnants. What power could have swallowed her so thoroughly, but ooze? Indeed, ooze hath a spirit and force all its own; 'tis said that in Egypt by workings of hot sunlight the muck can actually give birth to serpents and crocodiles. Thus the protagonist of this Dream of mine is ooze, here and forever call'd *Oozymandias the King*.

What did you like best about the church, Bob? I asked, since he possessed much knowlege of architecture and was indeed at that time composing a guidebook on English churches.

It didn't seem remarkable enough to recount the details, he said.

It just looked nice against the sky, said Esther. It would have looked very different yesterday; that was a dull day.

✱ ✱ ✱ ✱ ✱ ✱

The taste of muck was in my mouth. Nothing for it but the pub with its homemade ale (a dead rat in every glass, they assured me); now for sandwiches of white bread and powdered cheddar, with onions on the side. Caravel and pinnace, argosy and Argall, John Smith and Pokahuntas, where were they now? In the *Generall Historie?* — *Nay,* in great Heavenhell with King Oozymandias! May we all aspire so high. And thus with my prayers to the ALMIGHTIE for the conversion of all well disposed Salvages, I dare to call myself, sweet Reader,

> Your friend
> WILLIAM THE BLIND.

As I sat amusing myself on the grass,
O, who should I spy but a young Indian lass?

"The Little Mohee" *[folk song]*, ca. 1725

I

SEVERAL
COMPASS CIRCLES

OR,

*HOW CAPTAIN JOHN SMITH CAME
HOME AND HOME AGAIN TO
GRAVESEND*

THE GRAMMAR OF PRINCES (1595–1603)

... the euerworthy gentleman Capt. *Argall* ... partly by gentle usage and partly by the composition and mixture of threats hath euer kept faire and friendly quarters with our neighbours bordering on other rivers of affinity, yea consanguinity ...

RALPH HAMOR, *A Trve Discovrse of the Present Estate of Virginia* (1615)

See Argall, his Jesuit prisoners now unstrung as he hearkens with kindest mien to their plaints (all the while feasting himself with glory, serving himself their hoarded gold with his own hand); see the aforesaid Jesuits falter like poleaxed horses! Granted, Papal fallacies make up the only bellytimber of their minds; straight thought is not to be met with in Black-Gowns; but who could *not* but be mazed and stupefied by Argall? Whatever he says, the poor Jesuits know not what to reply.

See Argall in Rome. (He was never there. But he might have been Pope; everyone paid him such reverence —)

See him discovering the Equator of this world. North Pole and South fall simultaneously before his bodkin. See him conquer Jupiter; see how he sails the shortest route to Hell. He commaunds my map's graticules.

See him en route to *Jamestowne* (a place which well knew what was signified by blood), breaking in the Princess Pokahuntas —

Say, fine Reader: Argall was Fate, and Fate's a serpentine spoiler, that does poison all he bellies through. Argall wrestles hourly with *his* bowelsnake (who by definition is Argall), & I now perform the same, wondering how to unknot my protagonist's writhing history. Shall I strip him down to his last **.1,000.** grimaces? — Better to rear up some easy broomstick-Argall to hang the braincrown on. Then we can spy him everywhere if it pleases us: — ha, ha, see his deeds fairly engrossed in my parchment! Don't you want to be able to *talk* about Argall without actually stooping to *know* him? In case that notion pleases you, here's the full tale in

SYNOPTICKALL FORME

To wit, in the name of GOD:

.1. See Captaine John Smith, schooled in land- and sea-addition, now drawing up his future sums with unsheathed mind-sword penning the runes of blood;

.2. he computes available titles & reverences,

.3. snaps to,

.4. sheaths the sword, then

.5. marches down the flowery field of flattery, picking those vaporously deceitful blossoms which he'll

.6. press on my Lady Pocahontas (see her doing naked cartwheels),

.7. after which he'll pet her 'til *her* heartbloom ripens, ready to be most merrily plucked. *Kekaten Pokahontas patiaquagh niugh tanks manotyens neer mowchik rawrenock audowgh.* Bid Pokahantas bring hither .2. little Baskets, and I will give her white Beads to make a Chaine. (Such medicine he'd ministered to the Lady Tragabigzanda in Turkeland, with results as infallible as hen-bane in a witch's stew. When he'd told *her* the beads of his heart, why, she elevated the Beadsman!)

.8. See Pocahontas sigh;

.9. her soul's belly swells for love of him;

.10. she gives birth to his braggish dreams. —

.11. See her cradle his captured face to save him (as he kens) from her father's axeman.

.12. See her guard & help his companions for his sake. —

.13. Welladay, and whom does she marry? — Not Sweet John at all, but his namesake, the merest cipher, .1. John Rolfe (a person monstrous fit for his place). —

.14. Who activates their nuptials? — Why, Argall, of course! (See Argall stamp upon the dirt as he shouts: If my arms were .2. steel scorpion-claws, how I'd joy to embrace her disregard!) — A chronicler writes: I passe by the benefits of peace in those parts, by reason of his captive *Pochahuntas,* concluded and established. His Norward discoueries towards *Sacadehoc* and beyond to *Port royall, Sancta Cruz* and thereabouts may not be concealed. —

.15. See Pocahontas turn Christian,

.16. bearing the aforesaid Rolfe a pretty young son.

.17. See her perish, aged about .21. years.

.18. *AMEN.* Thus endeth *Vollmann His Synopsis.*

* * * * *

See Spot run. Thus we read in .1.st grade in 1964. I swear the pages of our primers were whiter than our skins! Everybody was white like me. Next year our grammar-books would begin to educate us most tediously in the parts of speech, but in .1.st grade, grammar inconspicuously personified itself within those .2. responsible, all-American children, Dick and Jane, to whom Spot belonged. (Dick and Jane were of my race, yet so pink-cheeked that the spots upon their eponymous dog's snow-furred sides seemed almost fitting.) Now, how did their tale run? *See Dick and Jane,* I remember that. Then Spot began chasing a ball as lovely as the sun: Run, Spot, run. Before the teacher called us to order, I'd already looked at every picture. Even at the age of .6. years I was well aware that ignorance of **THE END** equalled not only seemliness, but happiness; and yet my eyes could not help themselves from reading ahead, perhaps because I had not a friend in the world, as I thought (now I cannot remember whether this notion had been diseased by truth). So I'd already *used up* that primer. The long hour would now consecrate itself to Dick and Jane's thrice-repeated conventionality, not to mention the runnings of Spot, whose every outcome hung over me with insufferable predictability. It was not unlike knowing in advance how the tale of Pocahontas would turn out. And as the intoxicatingly serious smell of our new crayons, books & pencils departed for Heaven moment by moment, I began to suspect that Dick and Jane were not having fun, either (Argall sneered: I'll make 'em pay me in craven love!), that Spot himself had been outgrown, indeed, relegated to a primitive illustration of the present progressive, which was why the poor dog, whose brown patches were neither Vandyke nor yet burnt umber, reduced himself to a hysterical mechanical contrivance, whining softly and steadily for Dick and Jane like the seatbelt alarm of a big cool station wagon; and they could not even perceive his crying because it so closely resembled the buzzing of our classroom voices. Indeed, had they heard, it would have made no difference, for they'd been grammar-straitened into exemplars: Dick rarely skipped away anymore from his dutiful yard and driveway projects; and as for Jane, only the tip of her nose could occasionally be seen in later pages, a *pale* nose, I should add, no longer freckled, being isolated from the sun-ball although she pressed it against the steamy kitchen window when she did the dishes, waiting to be visited, just like Spot, who wanted someone to care when he brought the ball home panting. Word for word, that's exactly what we read. Now, what Argall read you may merely conjecture (for I, Dream-

Secretary of the Virgina Companie, have sworn to keep secret all matters treated secretly at the Counsell-table), but in the case of Sweet John Smith all's reveal'd: *Machiavelli* became his Bible. And here's his tale.

* * * * *

See John Smith of Willoughby-in-Lincolnshire: quick, hopeful to increase his estate, orphaned of his father, unmothered of her who's just now married with Maister Martin Johnson, so that she can do him no more good; cut off from his inheritance; lurking in the Fowl yard, the Church yard and the Chapel yard, longing to go for a Soldier, a Sailor, anything. 'Tis spring-tide; the Sunne's already far into Taurus. The Rector calls upon Sweet John's guardian once more. Sweet John comes across him weeding the graves.

He awarded me no encouragement, my boy. I can send you out to be an apprentice Draper, along with the other yeomen's lads. Naturally they prefer younger hands, of .6. or .7. years . . .

O, your charity would be a burthen upon me, Sir, says John Smith so bitterly.

The Rector rounds upon him. — Is it true what they say of you, John, that you ran away from your Master?

The lad swallows stubbornly. — No, Sir, 'tis not. We parted as friends; he understood that I could not stay with him, because he had no means to send me to sea . . .

Had no means? *Had no means?* The greatest Merchant in Linne — had no means?

He — he *would* not.

O, he *would* not. That perhaps I can believe. And tell me, pray, how did you expect to learn the craft of Merchantry, if your Master kept you not at his side?

John Smith's face is wine-dark with rage.

And now I remember, the Rector goes on, how when you were but .12. . . .

Thirteen, Sweet John debates him with surprising pertness. There's a difference, you know, 'twixt .12. and .13. (The Rector strains not to smile. John Smith can reason like unto a man, but for all that he continues smoothchinned, or *wench-faced* as they say in Lincolnshire.) Yes, Sir, 'tis true; I sold my books & satchel & all that I had, seeking to get to sea, but my father stayed me. I hearkened to him and begged his pardon; I'm not afeared to say that.

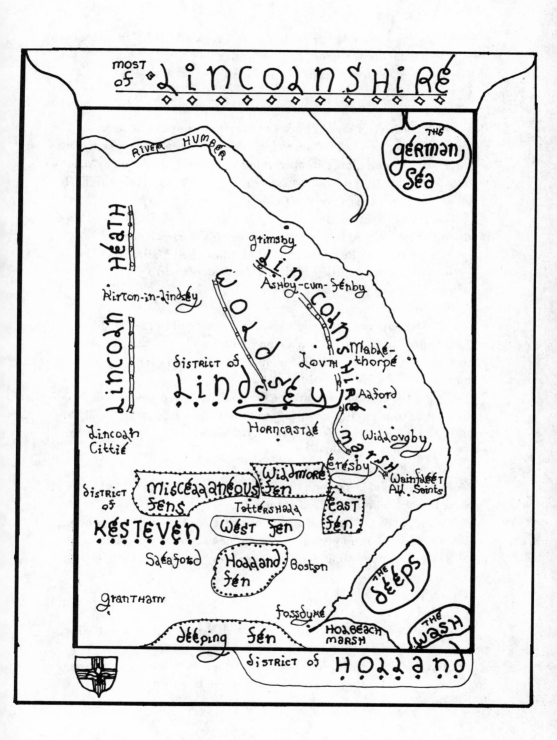

And now your poor father is dead. You've reached the age of self-commaund; what do you aim to do?

The young man's fists clench. — Go to sea.

✳   ✳   ✳   ✳   ✳

Be not rash, the Rector says. Think you to grapple down some lucky star? Chew your pride; accept this chance! Maister Hordley means very well. Or if you host some prejudice 'gainst becoming a Draper, I could send to Maister Hayward in Saltfleetby-Saint Clement, for we like each other well. I misdoubt me not you'd thrive as a Tailor —

A Tailor! says Smith in disgust.

Enough, boy! Would you rather starve with masterless men?

Excuse me, Maister Reverend, but what tidings had Maister Mettham?

Well, he consulted together with your new stepfather; I can't say they made excuses; I know not how it truly stands.

And the auction?

Yes, I disremember seeing you there. Were you still in Linne? I know not what persuaded me to bid on a trunk with iron bands, which I'm told your father was proud of. Would you like me to give it to you?

John Smith clenches his teeth.

Tidings of the auction, yes, says the Rector drily. Ten pounds of the proceeds went to your mother, according to the terms of your father's will; **.5.** pounds paid the Auctioneer's fee; & then **.10.** pounds I think passed to your sister. Why were you not there?

My Master denied to give me leave —

Mayhap with cause. Your brother as I deem took nothing —

Since he swears himself seized of the farm —

As for you, Maister Mettham informs me that you forfeited your bond to your Master, so . . . You must mind you this news comes secondhand from him. 'Tis really not my affair, John — come now, you must not put on such a poor countenance —

Maister Prestwick said —

Yes, what did he say?

He said that my father's goods and chattels remaining were valued at more than **.75.** pounds.

But they didn't sell, did they? Ready money's more convenient, Sweet John; 'tis not so easy to go about with **.75.** pounds' worth of beds & cupboards on your back . . .

Do you make sport with me, Sir?

Never! 'Tis only that I find this a dreary subject, which I'd lighten if I could. But you've set your snickle to trap my jest & trip it down. So I've no mind now *not* to end. Have you aught else to ask me, lad, or may I go my way?

Sir, pray tell me but this. Does my father's farm belong to me?

The Rector is somewhat at a stand. Over and over he's labored with all the tools of tact to bring sweet John his doom. Why then does the youth continue so imploringly?

Sir? What else did they tell you, Sir?

They claimed your legacy was extinct.

✳　✳　✳　✳　✳

The boy begins to run — no, no boy, full **.16.**; as I've said, even the Rector, whose name is Maister Sadler, admits him to the age of reason, hence calls not after him. He goes a-running beneath the long leaves and white crowns of chestnut trees. They say that the noise made by a cantering horse's hooves is *Butter and eggs, butter and eggs.* John Smith listens to his heels as he runs, and they sing out *Come back, come back.* Belike that is what he'd hoped the Rector would say. Disguising himself in resoluteness, he runs through the Town-field gate, and bites his lip hard, forbidding any water to prick his eyes; he goes a-running through the Old Field where 'tis said there used to stand Saxon ruins (but somebody pulled them down just before the end of Popish rule). *Come back, come back, come back, come back.* He throws himself down between **.2.** stones, in a mossy place as warm as any sunsoaked dog's head. After all, the estate's not yet settled. And mayhap he can go to law, if need be ... — But what Barrister would take his case? Condemned to leave his parish, it seems, and, when his time comes, never to be buried under his father's stone! (For he *will* not become a Draper.) Just as Soldiers too oft enter a tavern, & take the Inn-keeper's meat & ale without paying for it, no matter to what courtesy their Prince might have sworn them, ungracious Circumstance likewise robs us *sinkeepers* of hope (which is our heart's food), in apparent despite of all ordinances of the GOD of Lambs. Owned John never bosom to suck on? Well, his mother raised him up full delicately, but now he must profit himself without help, so that the world seems to go against him. Dangerous days, he thinks! But are not all days thus? — Nay, these are the years for the ease of Slaughter-men, when beggars choke the high roads, while Her Gracious Majestie (old, sick and yellow, with hardly three teeth left in ner head) continues to set favorites against foreign Princes while spinning her phony marriage-webs. She gobbles marzipan chessmen, arraying herself in black velvet and necklaces of pearls. They say that Ralegh's in the Tower disgraced, because some fawner inflamed the Queen with tidings of another Elizabeth (not that Her Majestie more than played with his hopes for so many years; why *shouldn't* he give o'er & marry?) — Now Ralegh's free; he sails for El Dorado, to ransom back his honor with gold, but returns silent and unsure. O, he's undone, and she sports with Essex's well-curled hair, goes on offering her teats undauntedly like a sleek Milch cow! But woe to him who sucks! Ralegh yields himself and supplicates yet again; the Queen quills him a poem on scented paper:

> Ah, silly pug, wert thou sore afraid?
> Mourn not, my Wat, nor be thou so dismayed.
> It passeth fickle fortune's power and skill
> To force my heart to think thee any ill.

— because he'd bought tolerance with the forfeit of his Admiral's share from that Spanish cruise: The Queen wants a new dress. All the same, his honor's still in hock; & he learns not to come a-riding to Court, nay, not for more cold years. On his last morn .2. decades later, when at King James's pleasure he must face the Headsman's axe, Ralegh's granted leave to confess his heart; and amidst the other railings and boilings of his discontent, he does cry out that the Queen clothed him ever in the blame of her own oppressions, that she was unjust, tyrannical, & above all *greedy*. — Fancy this! The old man literally standing upon the scaffold, who in a blink will become mere dissevered carrion, opens the Treasure-house of his entire life's rancor, and for a final jewel doth wear this wrathful word: *My Lords, she took all my Spanish pearls in a Cabinet unto herself, without giving me so much as .1. pearl . . .* — Ah, silly pug indeed! — They say that Essex visits the Queen's bedchamber of mornings; they say the Queen's played with the Treasurer's hunchbacked son — all lies; she'll die a virgin — they say she flies into a rage now when she sees her face in a mirror; they say Irish rebellions trouble her sleep (in his summertime of favor, Ralegh was wont to help her against those); they say Spaniards have laid siege to Calais, which is her very last foothold in France. And the Under-Sheriffs march thieves to the gallows every day, and harvests fail, and wretches wander high roads and low roads because rich Lord Merchants have enclosed the commons on which all men's sheep once did graze. The Queen, be it said,

cries against this, being flickeringly compassionate to her inferiors, but what can even she do? The Justice of the Peace arrives; he binds the Enclosers over to the Assizes; but nobody pays him for his pains. The Queen would help him (if someone told her), but, engrossed in those Dutch, Spanish & Irish wars, she needs wealth as much as any Justice of the Peace. Where will her money grow? Damn that Ralegh, for he discovered not El Dorado! Damn him, I say! Waging war requires wages, shiny pennies for her tender Soldier-boys; she'd better sell off more good Crown lands . . . Who buys those, but rich Enclosers? The poor men cry, pointing out their thinning sheep. They have no living now. But where can the Justice of the Peace find his living? The Enclosers offer silver coins. (Think you then; how'll speed their suit?) Mistake me not: I allege that the Justice of the

Peace is and always has been honest. He spurns the bribe, calls the Enclosers traitors & Catalines; he knows them; he's seen them raise the price of
corn in famine-times. He conquers: The Enclosers must pay fines. So the
yeomen give him thanks. They boldly come chop down the palings (even
John Smith's father did it once, and by GOD's grace my Lord Willoughby
never found out); the commons are common again, and everybody's calves
fatten on the sweet grass. But the Enclosers nimbly counter-move. They
raise the lease-rents which they call home from those selfsame yeomen.
Lease for .20. years or .3. lives, it's all the same; time comes leaping o'er the
field-ditch and your lease is up! Now it's not .4. silver coins at Easter and
.5. at Michaelmas anymore, but .7. and .8.; the Enclosers will make their
fines back sooner or later, and then they'll try again. *Enclosure is for the
good of all England,* they say. They can prove that common pastures are
inefficient. They'll fence them off again and grow corn. If there is more
corn, then prices will go down, so all Englishmen will benefit! 'Tis true
prices are *up* of late, but that's merely because the yeomen continue resist-
ing them. Thus the Enclosers explicate. In Lincolnshire they're called *Undertakers and Adventurers;* they Undertake to drain the reedy, fishy
marshes, to benefit the realm: Newborn babes will be no longer trapped on
sedgy isles all winter, in danger of dying unchristened; muck will become
translated into hay — and all that the Undertakers demand is a portion of
the new-improved land! Of course they're vilified by the yokels, the rustics,
lozels, hoblobs, coistrels; the lower orders, the stinking breedlings known as
Fen Slodgers, who sabotage all dykes, and fill in new sluices and sewers
by night. Never mind: The Undertakers post armed Sentries. So what if
the Fen Slodgers ruin an embankment or .2.? The Undertakers will prevail. And their cousin Enclosers — to steal a line from John Smith's book,
*all these for any thing I could perceive differ little in language or any thing,
though most of them be Sagamos,* and Lords of themselves . . .* Our Enclosers hector, spend & scheme. The Queen does not believe them. No matter; they'll wait. King James will succeed her. And if he doesn't play along
(he does), maybe King Charles will. So what if Charles loses his head? Someone must be King next (how convenient — another Charles). They raise the
rent again, and the Rector collects his .1./.10.th in kind. They wait, and while
they're waiting, John Smith arises from between his .2. stones in the Old
Field, spruces up his pale sad face at the brook, and sets off to see his lass,
Maister Reese Allen's daughter Cicely (which name signifies *Grey Eyes*).

*Sagamores; Indian chiefs.

* * * * * *

The Allens, who dwell at Belgreave not far beyond the Church, are **.1.** of the most ancient families in Lincolnshire — "good substantial persons," they're called; but of late their fortunes have turned evil. Reese Allen's father, old Maister Humphrey Allen, was a very bilious and passionate soul, famous for his rages; 'twas said of him that the most piddling trifle could inflame him, and that once inflamed he became like unto the wasp, which can never calm itself save by discharging its venom. Being of such a disposition, he made his best friends amongst *Lawyers,* whose pleasure it e'er shall be to preserve the client's anger hot in his innards. When the Lincolnshire Rising broke out in 1536, Maister Humphrey (then in his youth) told the rebels he had no time to quarrel with the King, being occupied e'en in warring with his own neighbors. So at least he came to no harm in that treason, praise be to OUR REDEEMER. Strange to say (for Physicians claim that rage consumes), he was a rotund, kedgey sort, like a cannonball; his balding head also tended toward the spherical, and it bobbed most righteously through Fen-floods of his own making. He lawed himself to death, as we all said; for the costs & charges were monstrous great; and in the end he lost a case about hayments, and was assessed to pay costs. After this he resolved to remove from the parish which he swore had mistreated him so badly, and despite the remonstrances of his son and other relatives he persisted in this design, old though he was, but where he purposed to go I never learned. Then his son Reese, which is to say Cicely's father, sought once more to dissuade him, at which he became incensed, and fell down dead of an apoplexy. This Maister Reese Allen (as Sweet John well kens) wears a reputation as an egg-walker, as is no wonder, for having been raised by so irritable a parent, he can say with the old proverb, *Blessed are the peace-makers,* for which cause he's so smooth and mild that he scarcely stands up for his rights. Cicely's mother used to upbraid him for this, but she died of a fever. Now that she's gone, everybody's fonder than ever of Maister Reese Allen, who will do almost anything he is asked, no matter how greatly it may be to his disadvantage. Not **.5.** years ago, for instance, he sold Bright Meadow to an Irish Draper, altho' 'twas his fairest pasture, and had been in the Allen lands almost since the Conquest; & this Draper, a wicked, drunken fellow, loves to boast when he's in his cups that he got Bright Meadow for almost nothing, and (what's more) hasn't entirely redeemed the debt! Nonetheless, whosoever marries Cicely will have a substantial fortune in money as her portion. Maister Allen pays for the wine at Easter Communion; he keeps a turret of

his manse just for storing all the silks and cutlery; on holidays his Cicely refreshes herself from bottles of cinnamon-water. So belike he's even richer
than he seems. Grey-Eyes thus counts more than a few suitors — foremost
among them Maister Ralph Nightingale, a waggish enough fellow.   In
Willoughby-Towne he has the by-names of *Buzzard,* & *Rook,* & *Calf,* &
Swindler. But he also has lands, herds and money. — John Smith, on the
other hand, we know for but the merest Woldsman. Howbeit, his father's
line is anciently descended from the ancient Smiths of Crudley in Lancashire; his mother comes from the Rickards at Great Heck in Yorkshire . . . From them he keeps a shagreen box, with a ring inside.

✳   ✳   ✳   ✳   ✳   ✳

Cicely is well tucked up, as the saying goes, in a fringed petticoat, a stom-
acher of tuffed mockado, and a new pair of yellow gloves. She I name a
most proper, comely, tender maid, and ingenious in her learning, for she
can read a little in the Parish Bible, and sometimes pens letters for her father. John Smith enters hopeful of her hand. He's just now delivered himself of a prayer & a Psalm. He bows respectful like, or, as we say nowadays
in England, he *makes a leg*.   He presents her with a bouquet of frog or-
chids. He asks after her cows. He asks after her father's health. Maister
Reese Allen smiles graciously, for he likes Sweet John and pities him. Let
the maid bring ale forthwith for our fine young visitor, who replies: *Your
most humble Servaunt.* Cicely has just purchased a singing-book which is
bosomed with many fine melodies, among them an old lay of Sir Thomas
Wyatt's but recently set to music, which goes: *I am as I am, and so I will
be . . .* — John Smith attends less to the words, which seem to him somewhat dry and problematical, than to Cicely's voice. Yet those words will attend him all his life. Her eyes (those lucent bodies) gaze mildly upon him,
so that he's encouraged to believe that indeed she might tarry with him all
her life. But soon (as he fears) she might well ask him a question he cannot
answer, or Maister Reese Allen might say: How stand your affairs, Sweet
John? Were I to give you Cicely with her portion, what have you by way of
jointure? — Accordingly, the suitor scrapes his heels nervously on the
floor. He heaps up the fire for Cicely. From this act there may well come
an afterclap, for the selfsame Ralph Nightingale whom he's crossed and
who not half an hour since bade Grey-Eyes good morrow, has already
bored a hole into the topmost log, filled it with gunpowder, and then
pegged the hole shut; now he lurks behind a tree, waiting for the onrush of
his own glee — fine bang 'twill be!

A round or **.2.** of Tick-Tack, which John Smith wins. A round of Lurch with Cicely, her father coughing benignly o'er the game. A glass of cinnamon-water for health. Now the dreaded conversation approaches its beginning. Run, Smith, run. The Court of Sewers is in session. He hears the summons in the clearing of Maister Reese Allen's throat, sees it in Maister Reese Allen's grave, judgmental sitting-back. Most gently and gingerly the pretty Cicely sets down her virginal, enfolds her book of music back to closure, smooths her skirts. The corners of her mouth upcrook in a secret smile. Meanwhile, sweeping cobwebs from his mind's seat, the young man speedily reviews his legacy, disregarding the Rector's news. On the death of his father, his brother Frauncis had gotten **.2.** tenements and **.1.** close in Westgate Street; his little sister Alice receiv'd **.10.** pounds, a featherbed with linen sheets, & half of all the pewter & brass. She's engaged to be married. Frauncis, altho' younger, has now already wed. As for Sweet John himself —

And how stand your affairs, my dear lad?

My father left me his farm, which I hold in copyhold to Lord Willoughby, the bridegroom begins.

In copyhold, yes. But copyhold, John — well, 'tis not the securest estate.

And I own **.7.** acres of good pasture lying in the territory of Charleton Magne.

You, or Frauncis?

Maister Allen, 'tis not what —

'Tis true you mean to leave the land?

I —

Talk is, you aim to go to sea.

I wish but to increase my credit, Sir.

Well spoken, Sweet John! says Maister Allen, while Cicely giggles at him near-unmaliciously. And perhaps you'll get cast away among infidels, and have many adventures. But surely —

Do please tell us **.1.** maxim of the sea! whispers Grey-Eyes.

Delighted, the boy recites: *The head of the Dragon, is the place where that the Moone doth come ouer the line Ecliptick, from the South part, vnto the North Part.*

The head of the Dragon! Father, whate'er does he mean?

. . . But dear GOD, John Smith has not yet proposed! Behailed by nervousness, he's entirely disremembered. Out with the ring now, the sweet ring in the shagreen box! Oho, he's fiery-faced now! And Cicely? He durst not send her his eye's scalding kiss! He takes out the ring and can utter nothing.

And ready money you have also, no doubt? continues Maister Allen, searching him out. I will not give my daughter to a poor man. Nor would you ask her of me if you cared for her. Tell me, how much did the auction of your father's goods bring in?

Despairingly, he gazes into Cicely's face. She returns the look with .1. of cool interest.

Soon I shall know more, Sir, he brings out.

Silence witnesses him.

But mayhap 'twould be more proper to invite Maister Mettham to call upon me, says Maister Reese Allen finally. After all, he executed your father's will.

Desiring praise, which Hobbes grants is laudable, the boy extends his ring in an agony of muteness. Grey-Eyes turns to her father. Sadly he shakes his head.

I am wholly thine, the boy mutters, willing Maister Allen out of existence.

The fireplace explodes.

*   *   *   *   *

See John Smith, come on foot to entreat his worshipful guardian, Maister George Mettham; witness John Smith speaking smooth & lowly words, John Smith with his hat in courteous hand. He makes a leg. Almost at once they are in a shouting-match.

You spurned your 'prenticeship with Maister Sendall, and now you want to try my indulgence again, commences Maister Mettham. Your philosophy is all arse-end up! I s'pose you recollect that Maister Sendall is related to me by marriage; he took you in only as a favor to the family. And you make no accompt of this! You demand to go to sea! Frankly, John, your wit's a knife so blunt you could ride bare-arsed to Lincoln on it! I hold here a letter from Maister Sendall, assuring me he'd infallibly have carried you with him to London-Towne at the very least, had you but been patient and applied yourself to the work. But no! You still don't know a debit from a diocese! And yet you must declare off! *It's off,* you say. *I'm through,* you say. *I must go to sea!* And now you come to me. *Sed stultit damno vix sapit inde suo.** Do you know what that means? (You were never o'ermuch a scholar; 'twas all your poor father could do to keep you in school . . .)

---

*"Yet the nincompoop hardly learns even from his loss."

Will you speak to Maister Allen for me, Sir? Cicely and I are to be married —

The DEVIL you are! I certainly shall not. You are in no condition to marry. If you like I shall send a letter to Maister Sendall, apologizing for your behavior, and asking that he agree to take you back —

I shall never go back to Maister Sendall, Sir.

Well, John, says his guardian drily, you are not satisfied with me, nor I with you. I see a remedy, which is that I will pay you what money I have in the house, & then we shall be quits forever. Do you agree?

What sum do you propose to give me, Maister Mettham?

What you are worth.

John Smith leaps to his feet. — What I am worth, you say! And Cicely — I — Then pray give me no less, Sir . . .

Am I to grovel before your stripling rage? Now that you threaten & sulk, I reckon yet less of you than before. To me you're worth .10. shillings thruppence; & if you raise your voice to me again I'll give you but .5.

Why, you maddock-ridden old tyrant!

Ramming his hat onto his head, Smith takes his departure. But the next day, young Thomas Mettham, aged .9. years, brings an envelope to his croft. Inside he finds .10. shillings in good money, and a short note:

Mr. John Smith, Esq.

Dear Mr. Smythe —
In keeping with our agreement, we are now quits.
Kindly do not communicate with me again.

> Yours very truly,
>
> GEO. METTHAM.

The messenger-boy's catching gawp-seed with his mouth, as the saying goes. To excite such astonishment momentarily disimprisons John Smith's heart. Then, pressed & walled back into deformity of soul, he sits, hates, tells his guardian's screed again & again. Thomas Mettham, shy and simple, longs to read it. John Smith presents it to him, saying quietly: Such oft is the share of fatherless children.

* * * * * *

See John Smith a-riding, with a sweet red and blue caddis on his horse's mane (borrowed in truth from his brother Frauncis), to pay a call on Maister Perigrine Bartty, .2.nd son to his landlord, that Right Honorable Peregrine, *Lord Willoughby de Eresby* of undying fame — 'though today much gout-ridden — touched yet deeper by that disease, in fact, than by religion; for religion is not the complaint he'll die of. As they say in Lincolnshire, *mere pity wouldn't preserve his life,* nor has Sweet John any of that to spare, much as he admires his noble Lord. (They say that gout comes from high living, a peril to which John Smith's immune.) But, goutish or not, this Lord Willoughby has e'er been an uncowardly Christian man. Back in '64 the Bishops reported him to be *earnest in matters of religion.* 'Twas true. He reported to London-Towne on several seditious Parishes which (according to evil Popish practice) did light candles on Candlemas Day, or hid their images of saints instead of smashing them. Many rustics did cry out against him then, but he pressed on, being a dutiful & literal *Iconoclast,* & so the Queen's injunctions got carried out e'erywhere in Lincoln Diocese. Moreover, many times has young Bartty (finding Smith a useful sewer or cloaca, into which to spew his stories) told him the tale of how his father was challenged to a duel in Holland while utterly lamed and palsied with this same distemper. — No matter, returned Lord Willoughby, if I must fight, I'll do it with a rapier in my teeth! — But Smith forgot to ask how the duel turned out. — As a result of his personal style (or, mayhap, in cause of it), Lord Willoughby lives .1. of Queen Elizabeth's own men — high distinction even to drunken dreamers such as John Smith — and also distant kin by marriage to Maister George Mettham. Sweet John will never learn that his guardian has troubled to write Lord Willoughby a letter asking him to help his ward in any way that he can think of — for people are rarely as we believe them to be. There being no post in Tudor times, the missive waits a week or .2., until Ralph Nightingale, in arrears with his rent, goes a-riding with a grace-offering: a jury's dozen of slain ducks most fat & soft. O yes, he says, the missive may journey with him, safe in his breast pocket. (For while Nightingale can cipher, he can't read; if he could — and if he dared to unseal the paper — he'd trample the name *John Smith* down into the nearest bog! Welladay, he doesn't.) When the recipient has perused it, unimpeded by Nightingale's muddy bloody finger-smears along the edges, when he's accepted the ducks most praisingly, and sent the bumpkin home, he ponders, does old Lord Willoughby, considering how he might best render John Smith assistance.

He remembers the father well. George Smith was a loving and faithful tenant. In his will he'd specifically abjured his son to honor Lord Willoughby in all affection, & 'twas to the selfsame Lord Willoughby he'd left the best of his .2.-year-old colts in token of his dutiful goodwill (the others went to Frauncis). And George Smith's father before him, though a commoner at Louth, where the Lincolnshire Rising practically began, took no part in it. ('Twas Willoughby's ancestor, my Lord the Duke of Suffolk, who put that rebellion down, striking heads from shoulders like splinters from chopped wood.) No, the Smiths have always continued loyal to their betters, which goes not disremembered by him who now sits outside in his riding-boots, stroking a pair of hunting-dogs on their heads, his finger tracing the long shallow skull-grooves beneath the fur as the hounds sigh in pleasured squirmfulness. A sunny cloudy day. In his decision on John Smith's case, memories of war make an immense under-hum, as of Lincoln Cathedral's sounding bells, which for a full minute after the last toll leave the air buzzing like a swarm of bees. Back in '87 he'd been Viceroy to the Low Countreys. In '89 he'd led an Army of .4,000. from the Normandy coast to help the French King gain back his right. The outcome was successful, 'though collaterally rather than directly. Willoughby (I say it frankly) enjoys foreign quarrels, whose alien slaughter, grief and turbulence makes for a spectacle — and yet the pleasing thing is, that renown earned there is fully transferable! (So he'd fain believe, having entered this World as an exile.) The life of a fighter always thrilled him. Thank G O D he's never failed Her Majestie! As for John Smith, why not study how far the lad can go? To forestall his capabilities would be cruel of a certainty; and, besides, troubled souls may become troublemakers. Then, too, 'tis pleasant to indebt George Mettham to him a little further. Thus Lord Willoughby's unmuzzled calculations.

Bartty, I would speak with you.

Aye, Father. Shall I on some errand?

John Smith was formerly your playmate, as I believe.

I've permitted him to carry my sword & target —

Is he quick?

Wondrously so, Father; indeed I hope he can turn it to profit . . .

Have you heard aught evil about him?

No, Father, aside from some small greed o'er his inheritance — a weary business, as they do tell me.

Ah, says Willoughby, giving the young man a pointed look, inheritances hatch out the worst in decent people.

Bartty blushes, then says: You think me jealous of my brother?

Now Lord Willoughby feels embarrassed in his turn. After all, 'tis scarce young Bartty's fault that Robert was born first. To Robert must go land & title. Families which forget this rule subdivide themselves into nothing. He shakes his head, gives the hounds another pat, and says: Fear not, son. A good wedding-match for you I'll commaund. And Robert surely —

I swear I begrudge him not!

I know it. And sure you know in my affection you're anchored?

Yes —

Well, look after Sweet John, would you?

Gladly, Pater, the lad replies, much relieved to exit.

This Peregrine Bartty fellow owns both a watch which chimes and a soul bursting with secular humors. Had the Court of Sewers gotten hold of him and drained him, no telling what he would have become — belike a hard dry entity like Maister Mettham — but the Court of Sewers has enough to do with all the Fens — decades yet before it can slupper up many drops of Lincolnshire. Bartty fixes his eye on those ducks Ralph Nightingale brought in. Won't they be nice fried in their own yellow lard & rolled in a heap of sea-salt? That's Bartty for you. Well practiced in the exercise of weapons, he loves nothing better than martial sport, followed in more or less discretion by a little wenching, which his father indulges, construing it more becoming for him to sow his oats now than to wait upon the cold raw rakedom of a vicious middle age. Accordingly, despite his lack of a portending Earldom, Bartty remains sincerely unembittered by life. All that he craves, and more, GOD gives him. Loves he best *sweet ducklings* and *fat wenchen,* or 'tis it the other way around? The answer to that riddle I disremember, but .1. secondary quantity which does pleasure him is the service of his myriad yokel squires. And here I might explicate: John Smith and some other boys occasionally play at swordsmanship with Bartty at Tattershall Castle, a transaction from which neither party emerges the loser; for the youths gain knowledge (my Lord Bartty being well taught) & also respite from their melancholy idleness; while Bartty for his part enjoys toying with these yeomens' desperate loyalty.

I can see you're in despond here, says Bartty when Smith appears, hosed & caddised as described, and most well pleased to be summonsed. — You know, I've bespoken you to my Aunt Susie. She has sworn to do her endeavor to help you, and I believe that soon you shall have a suit of armor. Would that please you, Sweet John?

With all my heart, Lord! More than I can say —

Good. But you must sign a writ of forfeiture upon your father's farm, because you'll no longer need it, and your brother does. Ready cash I think is more your line. After that we'll speak with Captaine Duxbury, who's raising a force against the Low Countreys . . .

* * * * *

See John Smith in Roane (or *Rouen,* as the Papists would say in their outlandish French dialect); see him in Haver de Grace. Patent peril, fortune at last! With the Spanish Armada crush'd not even a decade since, how could we English not possess us the globe entire? (For when Spaniard faltered, can pagan Turke do otherwise, if we but call upon the ALMIGHTIE?) Essex, Howard, and Ralegh have smashed Cádiz! The Sunne's in Gemini, & the Queen's in ecstasy. 'Tis war-o'-clock and suppertime, feasttime of a bloody century like all the others. ('Tis likewise the very year when *Virginia* opens her womb to be delivered of Pocahontas.) And Sweet John thrives & trusts most wholesomely, safe not from death, but Draperdom. Agile, level-minded, thick-skinned, cheery-hearted, uncraven soaker-up of strategems, he instantly commences to win praise. (Why not? Captaine Duxbury seeks to please Lord Willoughby.) Sweet John thrills to wake by bugle's *Trarintra-rarara.* His eyes are greedy for to see. Captaine Duxbury teaches him marching, shooting, arson, murthering, mangling, burglary, signalling, torturing, bomb- fashioning, & many another worthy trick, shouting: Hang all, you common block! No grinning like a simpleton! E-*quiv*-ocate! Deceive the enemy! Why, your intentions are as naked as a trollop in the

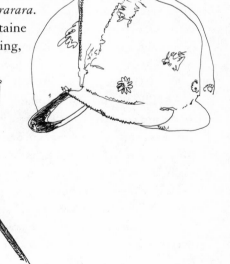

bawdy-house! When you mean to come at me *this* way, feign *t'other* way! Not like that, lozel! I do declare, your brain lives up your arse! Up with you, John, *up* with you! Where's your bodkin, man? Always carry a bodkin! Then you can stab them treacherous Spaniards in the back!

Captaine Duxbury holds him in high affection. Sweet John's never felt so blessed. O, this life smothers down his loneliness.

He's paid in Dutch ducatoons, which his copesmates teach him to bite, to be sure of the gold, and which for a jest they name *Salt fish*. Sometimes the Muster-master doth say: Her Majestie's forgot you, lads! at which they all threaten mutiny. Then the gold gets found. A Harquebusier earns .**10.** pence a day; a Pikeman earns .**8.** pence. Sweet John gets .**13.** pence; for 'tis all at the discretion of the Captaine. And 'tis a miraculous marvel, how quickly those Salt-fish can swarm themselves into a populous school, by the time Muster-Day comes round! When a Soldier dies, Captaine Duxbury bids 'em keep silent; he pockets the dead-pay, but buys the other men a treat. When a battle gets won, why then, here come more snap — Dutch pullets, Spanish velvet, & whate'er else can be pillaged. Sweet John learns how to scavenge, forage, threaten & extort, to get such prizes. Armor-plates jingle o'er his heart most merrily; he's gone for a Soldier in truth! Most every day he receives a pound & a half of good wheaten bread, a quart of strong beer, & sometimes pork or mutton for a treat. Salt fish likewise they give him, the genuine kind which stinketh.

Captaine Duxbury says: Sweet John, I'll tell why these Spanish coistrels* sail'd here. Be not an ass — unclench that salt herring from betwixt your teeth! Does that food relish you so much? In Spain they'll pay .**10.** shillings a quintal for it! But here to buy 'em 'tis much less. So they would control the revenues & commodities, whereby lieth the way to riches . . .

Aye, Captaine.

An' I'll tell you another thing, by my faith. All these Countreys hereabouts are ruled by *Live Patents,* which being Christians we must regard. I've never seen a .**1.** of 'em, an' damn me if I know if seals or ribbands hang off 'em, nor whether they're swaddled nor where they're locked, but whene'er we go against 'em, no matter if Her Majestie doth commaund us (GOD's wounds, I mean no treason, for I'll e'er follow her), 'tis nonetheless a *sin.* A Soldier, a sinner, why, I swear by my codpiece they're *sin*-o-nyms! But the Spaniards, knavish black-bottom'd fiends altho' they be, at least own enough wit to seize on waste territories of Salvages, whose *Dead, Hea-*

*Rascals.

then Patents may be safely disregarded. O, Sweet John, I'm half gristle and half carrion nowadays, but were I stripped back to your stripling years, what deeds I'd do in *Peru, America* and those places! *Riches,* lad! But Time's a cutpurse, that doth steal our substance —

Captaine Duxbury sets great store by a French innovation call'd *Drilling,* whereby amidst the urgencies of trumpets and kettle-drum's a Soldier's taught to pick up his feet right fearlessly, and march *.1. and .2., .1. and .2.,* no matter whether the sky doth storm with bullets and can-nonballs. Thus in good order they may rank, march and skirmish. Sweet John marches *.1. and .2.* with a will. 'Tis easier than hay-mowing in Willoughby, and the drilling-ground's neither mucky nor slimy; moreover (say the olden Soldiers), when there's drilling 'tis no time for fighting, so that praise GOD we keep our teeth yet another day; nor do we spy any sights to render us aghasted. — I fancy that to John Smith these words re-main but incomprehensible wonders.

Every Soldier who drills must learn his place. John Smith's place is: *.3.ʳᵈ from* Left, *.21.ˢᵗ* Rowe. Run, Smith, run. He dwells in a manse com-prised of Soldier-flesh. Captaine Duxbury drills them into figures. Such Geometricall proportions as they make may not prove so far removed from those of Saint Helena's Church in Willoughby, which is laid out like a head & shoulders prone upon the ground. For what's society (queries antique *Plato*), but a giant man whose atoms are made of men? What self may contrive falls now to uselessness; self's but limb or corpuscle to Captaine Duxbury, who, bawdily tender or politick-ally aloof as pleases his conve-niency, leads them whither they know not.

The new man learns that a share of plunder is call'd a *snap.* A *.1.*-eyed Soldier advises him: 'Tis all well *now,* John my lusty-blood. But when the murthering starts, then pure gold *Salt fish's* never nourishment enough. Not JEHOVAH Himself could recompense my eye! So I pay myself, lad-die, an' you must do the same. And as you love good fellowship, why, *share* your snap, be't roast chicken, Church-plate or maidenhead.

How can maidenhead be shared?

Well, if 'tis but lately plucked, the dregs bide passing sweet, so we'll none of us blame you.

Easy duty that! the boy laughs, longing to be ruffianly, but the blood's aflame in his face.

If it proves truly easy for you, Sweet John, why, then, you're an honest fellow, and GOD keep you warranted in your place. Only hold faith; dis-remember us old Soldiers not, for someday you'll be as we. Do ye promise?

I promise.

Ho, then here's a taste of snap for ye, my brave young lad. In my tent you'll discover a fine wench, with breasts like unto round Churches. Don't mind her screams —

* * * * * *

Reader, did I tell you that this Kingdome call'd *Fraunce*   keeps custody of her tongue up Rome's arse? A demiculverin-shot past Captaine Duxbury's drilling-ground, some Nuns in their Convent do embroider white leaves & snowflakes on blue tulle. Sweet John's never seen the like. His eyes pop with horror, and yet the Nuns smile on him friendly-wise. Their altarpiece rises like unto a city of gold! He would purchase some tulle of them, to bring home to his sister, but he fears she might be unnerved by the Popishness of it. He gets fond of the Nuns; he can't help it; they pray for him . . .

* * * * * *

Finished in France (peace having unhappily settled there), see John Smith marching joyously through *Holland,*   a Fenny Countrey of dykes & wastes not unlike Southern Lincolnshire — but he's a Woldsman, a high-lander; squishy ooze can't pull his soul down! Or has he already sunk and drown'd? He swims & swarms within Captaine Duxbury's Army, a-feeding on both kinds of salt fish as before. Yes, name him fishy! For just as chavender-fish do thrive in a fast stream, so John Smith in his proportion seeks good Adventure, thirsting for swift currents and for deeps, longing to be .1. of those luce-fish who inhabit the great waters. Clad in fresh Dutch wool, he wars with a will, making mouths at Spaniards & recreants.

See John Smith on stilts — another trick he's learned in his home Coun-tie. Captaine Duxbury shouts with joy.   — In Lincolnshire their puling lit-tle bastards are born on stilts! he crows to the Reviewing Officers. — Do your best endeavor now, Sweet John! Go fire that house!

The farm is on a mucky island in a sea of muck. Nobody imagined that Soldiers could come here. See John Smith striding in all rapidity of cheer upon his long skinny wooden legs, burning torch most magisterially up-raised. No one bides at home but an old man, whose mouth gapes in a soundless scream as Smith fires the thatch.

See him send his blade a-riding through a Spaniard's throat. See him shoot a pitchy arrow to burn a Spanish ship. See him fire a musket charged with langrell-shot: .2. half-bullets connected by a chain which stretches taut in flight to garrot a man or take his head off. Proud and great rises Captain Duxbury's love.

* * * * * *

See John Smith, back in Roane, sick unto death from that French fever called *the purples,* which hath now cut down so many Englishmen. The hospital stinks of chamber-lees. Galleons of fire sail behind his eyes. The enemy spurs his innards. This spells true war, the struggle of all life. His heart's own beat is but *the purples'* sounding drums. Serious this fight, this battle within his blood for which Captain Duxbury did not train him. Ten shillings from Maister Mettham. Jests from the Rector. A forfeited farm. Mayhap Frauncis will bid him stay. Mayhap he'll marry with Cicely. He craves to slay another Spaniard for Captain Duxbury. Where fell his Dutch ducatoons? Somebody has taken them. He must rise up to go a-searching. Boldly pounds his heart, which hights the enemy's battering ram, smashing through his skull's keep beat by beat. He cannot rise. Aching from dawn till darklins, his courage passing ruinous, he longs like all to thrive, but death stands knapping at the door. He denies to answer. They carry out another stiff — delegated to feed French worms & maddocks. Jocund chestnut-blossoms crown the leaves all about; John sees them through the doorway; and then *the purples* does more murder: another Soldier (young enough still to be wench-chinned) croaks, slobbering spittle the hue of crushed raspberries. After carrying that .1. out, they seal up the door to contain the pestilence; he spies his chestnut-blooms no more. How long does he lie there? His pustules burst, and *the purples* laughs in his ear. He pisses out his life. Most weakly he defies and breathes on. Just as the history of South Lincolnshire is largely the records of the Court of Sewers, so the history of John Smith at this stage must be an account of his channels, scuppers & drainages, whose chapters, as unwholesome as they are monotonous, drag on almost by stealth. It's the Queen's birthday, half-anniversary of *the purples.* He hears the other Soldiers shooting off guns. The trumpet howls *Trarintra-rarara.* — If I continue in life, he says to himself, mayhap I'll go to London and petition Her Majestie to take me into service. The worst she can do is hang me . . .

* * * * * *

Sick too long . . . past the march . . . discharged! Captain Duxbury says he's no use, no spleen left in him. He's conquered *the purples,* but no matter; defeat sits upon his shoulders. No more marching up stairways as white and gold as candy. And as the enemy does approach, John Smith sets himself forward . . . no, that's ended. Nothing left but a beggarly creep back, rattling in his weary armor. — *Cush! Cush!* as they say to call the cows home in Lincolnshire. O'er the *Straight of Callys* to the Lizard he sails by merchaunt ship, *Cush, cush, cush.* The Navigator shews him how at .80. fathoms deep the sand comes up black upon the sounding-tallow, and at .64. fathoms the tallow brings up white sand & white worms; that's how Mariners ken they're nigh unto the Lizard. Sweet John smiles back at the man, but can hardly speak. He abides no more above his hope's horizon. How the Rector will sneer! And Frauncis . . . Back first to Gravesend, longitude .20. degrees .14. minutes, latitude .51. degrees .31. minutes as men do reckon it these days, then down the Long Ferry to London Towne. O, but how the Watermen do straddle and scutter about on the quays, seeking to ferry him to Sheol, to sell him passage to whores' Heavens, to win him preferment to crewmanship on some ruffianly argosy! — Maister, I swear it'll cost ye no dozen gold angels, a spadebearded Charon whines; but John Smith misdoubts him not that Charon would knock him o'er the head, so, denying his company, he locks his hands in his pockets, and sets off to find him a stagecoach. All the while he's thinking: Why not bide in London? For he dreads to return home. Nay, no soul's his friend e'en though they keep a college thereabouts call'd *All Souls* (in plain fact 'tis in Oxford); his lone hope's Lord Willoughby. But he hath not heart e'en to try him, to see if he stays just now in London-Towne. He's *shamed.*   Repairing to a red-latticed alehouse, he drinks himself into opacity. And now that creep. His Countie is cool and wet and emerald. Clouds paler than sheep draw away light with their pale fat fingers. See him in Wainfleet-All-Saints, once a Roman port. Now from the draining of the Fens, mud is choking it.* No cargo to call for anyway, except corn & sheep, and the Taxmen already take those. Only Fen Slodgers 'scape the scathe — they possess nothing to be taxed away. See John Smith in parley with a Justice of the Peace, who questions him to discover whether he be vagabond. He swears oath neither to linger nor beg; he drops Lord Willoughby's name. (In Roane he'd been told by letter that Lord Willoughby got made Governor of Berwick-upon-Tweed. Sweet John penned his respectfulest congratulations, but never received back any answer. Then he got *the purples.*) See him in earnest

---

*"This parish," explains Wheeler's nineteenth-century history of the fens of south Lincolnshire, "is in the Lindsey division and under the jurisdiction of the Spilsby Court of Sewers, but its general drainage system is intimately mixed up with that of the East Fen and the Fourth District."

entreaty with a Baker who cares not to return him petty silver after he buys bread with a Dutch ducatoon. — Spanish coin it is! cries the baker — and then the proverb: *Wicked money, Popish monkey!* — The Under-Sherriff comes. John Smith is commaunded to shove along. With rust in his steel elbow-joints & nothing in his bindsack he marches up the Roman road to Burgh-le-Marsh (a lucky little town, for it stands upon a hillock above the ooze), then follows a mucky horse-path to Gundbye, arrives late under night clouds, sleeps inn-less to economize (because after *the purples* drained from his mind he never did find most of his ducatoons), awakes in the small hours, feverish & shivering. Could it be *the purples* again? But that sickness's knapping he likewise denies to answer. — What a stench! Is it but his own misery? Moonlight's his only match to strike vision's spark. Can he see? The clouds gape open; the round marsh-face called *Luna* peers down through the wound. O, and it's the gallows-tree he's chosen to sleep under! Gundbye he never did know well. But he'd never thought to conclude such a hideous error. And whose bones are these? The last felon to be hanged in Willoughby, unless he disremembers, was one Henry Hatchett, who was arrested by the Under-Sheriff for stealing horses. And these ribs, nail-claws and sinews, how did they fall foul of Gundbye? No matter; his slumberousness is more charged than his curiosity. He's a Soldier now; he's seen bones. The grass feels soft like ribbons. Throwing the corner of his cloak over his nose, he shades himself again with sleep. By dawnlight, having prayed, he's already on the trudge to Willoughby, his home, his prison, his nightmare repose. John Smith's a moth who's beaten his wings to pieces.

✳ ✳ ✳ ✳ ✳

In William the Conqueror's Domesday book one finds this typical entry:

> In *WILGEBI* Tunne had II carucates of land taxable. Land for IV ploughs. Roger, Gilbert's man, has II ploughs. IV freemen on one-half carucate of land have II ploughs and meadow, XXXX acres; marsh, XXXX acres; woodland pasture, CXX acres, underwood, LX acres. Value before 1066 £IV; now £VIII.

Ah, Wilgebi! So long since we named you that! And the .4. freemens' .40. acres of marsh, what happened to those? For they've been centuries now at work a-draining the Fens — half a thousand years, in fact. They've been continuing what the Romans started. And the woodland pasture? All cut down. And the underwood? Only J E H O V A H knows — J E H O - V A H & the Court of Sewers. And now Wilgebi is Willoughby, waiting to snickle his staggering steps. His mother embraces him weeping, but must return to her daily round as Mrs. Martin Johnson. His brother Frauncis bids him stay, but coolly, as he deems. — What news? he asks Fruncis, who replies: News? Why, I'll tell you. Between Easter and Michaelmas the price of wheat's gone a-down .12. shillings! Did you ever hear the like? — He stares at Fruncis. Around him life passes with the strange tiptoe-ing of sheep. He oils his armor and rolls it neatly under the bedstead. All think him a sort of vagabond or rascal, altho' he works most cheerfully and unsparingly with Fruncis in his thickly emerald-bladed field which stretches to the horizon under a wall of chestnut trees. He never calls upon Cicely. One fine afternoon not long before harvest he gets his summons to .6. days' labor maintaining the Parish's bridges & ways. Sending his sub-mission, he takes up bindsack; Fruncis's goodwife Anna has already put some belly-timber in it: bread, flitch, a little early corn. He prepares not grievingly to sweat, for he has this virtue among others: he's no niggard with his strength. At the meeting-place, the Bailiff chalks their way. Ralph Nightingale is there — he who was Cicely's other suitor. That one's never made confession of his trick which exploded the Allens' chimney (a miracle no one was hurt), and Smith does not know 'twas he. Nonetheless, the sight of Nightingale drags him down. The road which they've been called upon to mend begins at the foot of a stately oak tree on what used to be Gallows Hill — since become a commons where we let our sows & boars graze up acorns, altho' sallow-faced Lord Willoughby is said to be scheming to En-close it for gain. (Smith will never believe this of Lord Willoughby.) Next comes Bright Meadow, once the Allens', now the Draper's — a stunningly yellow field of rapeseed. Ralph Nightingale strides always at his side, jest-ing & jeering. John Smith pays no mind. With spade & basket he spreads new earth, then gravel o'er the marshy muck — not that Willoughby is so prone to such; John Smith had not the misfortune to be born in some stink-ing Fenny town — Friskney or Stickney, for instance; Bardney or Sibsey (whose drainage lies under jurisdiction of the Boston Court of Sewers); Ful-ney or Gedney — each of which was in Roman times an island. He loves Willoughby as he loves Lord Willoughby. Here lies his life. The other dig-gers, longing to wander in their fantasies at least from the mucky work, re-quest him to amuse them with war's brimstone. A *Cannon-Royal,* a *Cannon-Serpentine,* a *Bastard Cannon* — he explains how to shoot them all. Being still young, his follies disport them as would not the stinking ec-centricities of a hoarheaded old tramp. Besides, they know him; he comes

the GERMAN SEA

Grainthorpe

Saltfleet

Utterby

North
Cockerington
South   Grimoldby   Saltfleetby
Cockerington   St. Peter
Louth   Theddlethorpe
                    Manby   All Saints
                                                       Mablethorpe   DROWNED
                    Legbourne   Thorpe   CHURCHES
Little Cawthorpe Withern
Cadwell   Woodthorpe   Maltby le
                                     Aby   Marsh
Scamblesby
Ruckland   Bilsby   Huttoft
Belchford   Tetford   HILL HUNDRED   Alford   Mumby
                         Somersby   Brinkhill   Hogsthorpe
Hemingby   Mawthorpe
        West Asbby   Bag Enderby   Harrington   Willoughby
Horncastle   Hagworthingham   Addlethorpe
                        Raithby   Partney   Orby   Ingoldmells
                   Hundleby   Gunby   Skegness
                               Eresby   Great Steping   Burgh le Marsh
        Bolingbroke
                 Kirkby   Thorpe St. Peter
Mareham   le Fen   Stickford   East
                                                Fen
Tattershall   Stickney   Deeps   Wainfleet
                                                         All Saints
Dogdyke   Friskney
        Wildmore Fen   West   East
                                    Fen   Fen
East   the deeps
Lindsey   The Fen   COUNTIE
                                                       NORFOLKE

Capt. John
SMITH
as engraved
in his
generadd
Historie

& goes as he finds occasion, but surely he'll marry in Lincolnshire at last, if corn prices and sheep prices dive no more down. They laugh at him, yet listen eager-eyed; percase he's visited some easy Countrey where with a mere *Cannon-Petro* or *Basilisco* one could take all the gold one's pockets might hold. Then no more work, and no more death. On the .3.rd day, that stretch of road now in fair repair, they find a family of wretches living in the Goblin Hole — foreign *Welshmen,* it would seem, pilferers from the Fens & marches. They've even built themselves a cottage. It's a marvel no one's seen them before. But now somebody remembers how his chickens have gone a-missing, and somebody else remarks his dearth of hen's eggs. Ralph Nightingale begins to abuse the Welshmen, crying out 'tis loiterers such as they who raise the poor rate. Nightingale is sick of paying his taxes for the likes of them. Why don't they go back to where they came from — or, better still, to the DEVIL? Or is the DEVIL where they came from? — The other men laugh, leaning on their spades. Only John Smith keeps silent. His blood makes sincere ebbings of compassion; he would bid the aliens stay and prosper, but stands walled and remote like unto Lincolnshire Cathedral upon its hill. Ralph Nightingale runs for the Bailiff, who presently arrives, stares down the beggar-family, and shows 'em steel. They stand, as if confused about some point. Their baby cries; the matted-haired, mud-streaked mother does not hush it. John Smith, clear-lessoned Soldier, shews his neighbors how to fire the house.

* * * * *

See John Smith at Saint Helena's Church, because it is a Sunday. The Rector, L. Sadler, remains in possession; his life and tenure have another decade left to run. Smith can never scan him without anger now, remembering that conversation which they once held about his inheritance, after which he went a-running. Mayhap it's his shame at that which angers him most. (He knows now never to run or courteously entreat.) Someone, probably his mother, has laid a bouquet of ladyslippers before his father's tombstone. He strolls emptily around the Church yard, inhaling the terrible shadows of its yews, then approaches the heavy oaken door, now ajar, beside which Frauncis & Anna stand quizzically waiting for him while the others pass in. Anna is big with child. Soon the croft will be more crowded than ever. Sweet John hefts the strange black iron polyhedron at the bottom of the Church knocker and follows his relations inside. He wipes the muck from his boots. The Church-bell ceases tolling. Reverend Sadler sermonizes well, like unto some glib scoundrel in plague-time who turns a dead body out of doors before it's discovered, to keep his house from being sealed up, but Smith doesn't listen. His fancies go a-blobbing for eels. Almost up at the high ceiling, **.10.** tiny arched windows have been set into the side of the Church's heavy skull, **.5.** on the left and **.5.** on the right, and white spring light comes in through them as if from afar. See in sable attire our Rector, the aforesaid Maister Sadler, firmly astride his pulpit like a little crofter's boy standing bareback on a worn and broken horse soon destined to be meat. He reads from the Psalms: *Then they cried to the LORD in their trouble, & He deliver'd them from their distress; He brought them out of darkness and gloom, and brake their bonds asunder.* The Rector explains how this verse stands. — What hight our distress in these difficult days? 'Tis pride, I deem, that most revolting revulsion of the soul, when, contrary to GOD, we struggle to vomit our afflictions out. Ah, fools that we are! The self's but a qualmish pill that must be swallowed. How can we seek to change our state, which GOD assigned each of us before birth? Dare we to say our LORD & REDEEMER means not well? Dare we despise the chance which He gave us every one to thrive and prosper in our own stations? Think we to run from our MASTER's side? — Such runs the Rector's dribble and drift, a current not pleasing to John Smith, who, seated beside Frauncis and Anna, not far from the pale yellow octagonal fount where he was baptized, chokes upon the cold and moldy smell of his Church, a whitewashed, double-pillared affair whose tomb-traps yearn never to let him go. — O, 'tis a potent old Church, Saint Helena's — her snares and snickles date back long ago. She infused herself with Willough-bydom from the very beginning, her first Rector in 1227 being the earnest and determined T. De Willegby, said to have dug the foundation-hole out of the ooze with the work of his own hands, followed in 1268 by P. De Wilueby; then in 1290 came H. de Willoughby, succeeded in 1306 by P. de Wylughby and in 1323 by W. de Colleby; after which there were no Willoughby Rectors until 1501, when the last representative of the family, E. Willoughby, accepted the position. There have been none of them in charge of the Church since, mayhap because from Eresby, which lies less than a day's ride away, at the halfway mark between Willoughby and the East Fen, they've removed their ancestral seat all the way to Grimsthorpe Castle, a strangely statue-ridden edifice beyond the East Fen, southwest of Wildmore Fen and West Fen, across the Witham River and southwest again through Aswardhurne Wapontake, also known bluntly as *the Fen* — o, 'tis a hard ride to Grimsthorpe if a man would go crow-straight! (harder still if he would avoid the ooze, and traipse dainty along high roads;

for on high roads lurk highwaymen) — then south by southwest almost out of the Countie; past the Deer Park depicted prettily palisaded in Speed's *Atlas,* and there you are in Leceistershire — a long remove for the Willoughby de Eresbys, to put it frankly; and some will say they've changed lands because that belt of Fens 'twixt themselves & London made 'em feel hemmed in — which is but a fanciful way of putting it that they found these parts too provincial for their liking. Shall we simply note that on his progress our lamented King Henry VIII stayed at Grimsthorpe (which in anticipation of his arrival got expanded outward as rapidly as the skin of any puffer-fish), but never at Eresby? He misliked the Wolds & Fens. John Smith would drain the marshes of his own life, if he but knew how! Only Lord Willoughby or young Bartty can help him therein, as he deems. Just as the cunningest thieves will yet succumb to Popishness, by consulting with Astrologers to learn when they'll be hanged, so John Smith must make his Landlord his idol, in default of any other. The Rector speaks on. John Smith inhales coldly bitter air into his nostrils, bowing his head in that crowd of patient bowers in the whitewashed Church. His prayers strive to swim out of the high bell-openings, but drift melancholically, lethargically down, oozing back into his face like the Rector's breath. Sad light swarms through the clerestory windows. Across the aisle he sees his guardian, Maister George Mettham, piously bowed. In an instant, John's hand is upon his dagger and he actually starts to rise. The Rector gestures from the pulpit, which is angled and chiseled out of the same scratched yellow stone as the fount, with .4.-petalled flowers cut deep into each facet of it, green-stone atop it, surmounted by a winged stone Angel leaning toward the parishioners, bearing on his back the lectern with the Reverend's sermon upon it, beside which a candle rises high.

The Rector leads them in a prayer for the health of the Queen. John Smith aimlessly gazes until he finds, far off, his mother seated beside Maister Martin Johnson.

*   *   *   *   *

Right honorable Reader (& all your well-willers besides), mayhap you wonder just how it is that Frauncis and Alice did rather gloriously of their father's will (or, if I may put it another way, his will did well by them, which is why he, the late Maister George Smith, yeoman, was what I mean by a well-willer); whereas John Smith, eldest son most legitimately begotten, failed to enter his own material utopia of cupboards, disbenches, brass pots, calves, oxen, and the farm itself, which he was to have on his mother's remarriage. Much as he loved to blame Maister Mettham, the truth was that since Frauncis would soon have a wife, being engaged to the sluggish girl of his fancy, one Anna Oseney, from Mareham-le-Fen (she herself was, I believe, distantly related to the Metthams), and John seemed of no mind to settle there in Willoughby or take up any useful trade, the brothers had agreed that Frauncis could have the farm, at least for the time being, and John could have whatever cash accrued from the auction of their father's miscellaneous chattels. Alice of course needed a dowry, and got it. Most of the cash remaining sank like pebbles into that stagnant legal pond called *Escrow*. The truth was that Maister Mettham truly had paid the boy quittance out of his own pocket. Frauncis for his part had perhaps been too quick to accept his brother's kindness, which so suited his convenience. He and his Goodwife watered fields with their own sweat, until the farm seemed fully their own — especially since John, who said nothing, seemed always so restlessly disgruntled. Rooted yeomanry would have been little to his liking. Then came the writ of forfeiture which he had signed upon Bartty's advice, so that he could buy his armor. What he did derive was a room to bide in at the farm (to wit, his and Frauncis's old nook; Frauncis and Anna slept in their parents' bedcloset now), the loan of a horse whenever he needed it, meals cooked by aproned Anna (though seasoned, mayhap, less with salt than cross impatience as he flittered away the years, coming & going, helping Frauncis bring in the corn, but more often riding, shadow-fencing, dreaming). The world said he'd made not such a bad bargain.

✳ ✳ ✳ ✳ ✳ ✳

His friend Bartty, which is to say my Lord Peregrine Bertie, summons him to go a-riding down to Old Hammond Beck. The Court of Sewers in Boston wants to drain more Fens. Its Commissioners commaund a new outfall for the beck, requiring three-quarters of a mile of ditch-digging. They'll call it *The Adventurers' Drain!* Soon enough, the Under-Sheriff's early morning drumbeats will be summoning diggers there. Smith kens not, cares not, what concern it is of the Willoughby family. Mayhap 'tis Willoughbys who'll gain when those Fens get enclosed . . . No matter. Cheery vassal, he sets out on a fine Willoughby horse to deliver a letter from Bartty to the Commissioners of Sewers. The letter is sealed. Smith takes care to preserve it spotless in his breast. The horse gallops: *Come back, come back.* (Bartty has enjoined him never to go faster than canter-pace.) He's thrilled to the very liver of him to be rushing alone on his Lord's errand. The Willoughbys will remember him for this.

Very good, my lad, says the Commissioner. You may go.

* * * * * *

See him a-reading in Maister George Mettham's *Almanacke* (which he'd filched) how to become a Mariner. *It is necessary and convenient for the Seafaring men, to knowe the Prime or golden nomber, & by the golden nomber is knowen the Epact, and the Epact sheweth the age of the moone. And by the age of the moone, you may knowe what a clock it doth flowe in any place that you do knowe, what moone doth make a full sea.*

* * * * * *

Maister George Mettham, again betterhearted than John Smith will know, sends to my Lord Willoughby, who has presently, as it happens, loaned himself from Grimsthorpe back to Eresby Manor, for nostalgia's sake. Al-tho' Berwick-on-Tweed may seem a jewel to be Governor of, yet the old man must ride back & back to all his seats, to spy out whether in his absence they be abused. They say Eresby keeps quiet, but he would see to some business with his vassals. Young Bartty also likes it in Eresby; for he can moon about the Willoughby Chantry just east of the Church's greenstone tower, plotting out new great Adventures: in this count him Sweet John's twin. So many .14.th-century family effigies! Kights & Ladies & panels of quatrefoils bordered by fleurons, O, they sing to Bartty on those muddy summer eves, telling him he's .1. of them, sound fruit from the tree. That's why he loves their monuments. The Willoughby emblem's a monk flanked by .2. wild men. Which member of that company does Bartty long to be? Is it he or his brother Robert who's the monk? John Smith is of the wild men, of course . . .

Once more the father reads, sighs, lifts hand from hound's head, and speaks: The lad cannot be blamed, that he got *the purples!* His dis-charge was honorable. Play pimp to his wanderlust again!

Bartty grins — he's all grin! — inveigles Aunt Susie on John Smith's behalf, goes out a-hunting, tups a wench, summons John Smith, knocks on Smith's armor, beaming in at him with contemptuous love . . .

* * * * * *

See Smith in harness to Maister Perigrine Bartty. They go a-riding toward Horncastle, then breast Sleaford's flat brown sea. Bartty canters ahead on the good road, *butter & eggs, butter & eggs,* while Smith on the old grey leads the baggage-horse, whose pustulent legs sink into the muck. The baggage-horse, we might as well admit, was once the best of the late George Smith's .2.-year-old colts, which he left to Lord Willoughby in his will. With endearing boyishness, Bartty o'er-galloped & ruined that horse a year or .2. since. His father made little noise about it. Best to allow the lad to grow up in his own good time. Besides, the horse was gratis. Once a colt, then a gelding; in future, meat for hungry Soldiers and vagabonds. Smith strokes the gelding's long nose, picking clover for him as he goes. At close whiles Smith must downleap, unburthen him, lead him out of treacherous ground, then pack on Bartty's goods once more. Run, Smith, run. Bartty awaits him behind a little windbreak of trees, his mount most impatiently prancing. A light drizzle sparkles on the fields. The path is as the grand aisle in some Church, wending them between the .2. long facing rows of haybricks like pews, leading them toward the pulpit and the organ-pipes of destiny. John Smith cranes, but ahead spies only farther distant towers of haybricks.

Bartty is collecting rents and other debts for his father. He wears a shirt of fine white linen chased with blackwork embroidery of flowers and bumblebees, but his life's wet and almost rank among those fenside Bell-Churches and High-Churches. He longs to be in France. Smith does every service he's told to do, maintaining high and silent joy. Bartty leads a wench behind a tree. Holding the horses, Smith hears them winnicking with mirth. Now Bartty's shirt hangs from a branch like a white ghost.

Back athurt the sea! And so Maister Bartty comes into France, with Sweet John dogging eagerly behind. Robert, who will someday become Earl of Linsey, awaits in Orleans.

Smith kens him well (Robert being but .3. years younger). In his excitement, he recollects what never happened: himself with Robert, fishing for chub where the stream flows under a shady tree; Robert hooking more and more of the finny spoils; what a fine supper the Willoughbys will have tonight! At last Robert's hook breaks, and John Smith presents him with his own . . . And yet it was actually Bartty who'd stood beside him fishing (and Sweet John's hook which broke — and Bartty kept the fishes), Robert being even then a gloomy boy whose only resemblance to his father lay in his martial manliness — nay, my Lord Willoughby is never in a cross-grained humor even at his most goutish! — whereas Robert belongs to that Army of souls tainted by some sorrow whose secret never comes out. Smith, whose objective life must be counted worse, never gives o'er his cheerfulness for long. Why then does Robert remain a Sad Knight armored by sarcasm of the eyes? Lord Willoughby's biographer writes: *I had thought of proceeding farther, to look into the life of his son, Robert Earl of Lindsey; but this will lead me into so melancholy a scene, so unhappily ended, that I believe I shall not have spirit to undertake it.* Does this signify the death of Robert in the Civil War, a death offered up for the sake of a soon-to-be-decapitated King? Robert will be old then — nigh unto .3.-score years. And Sweet John will already be, as his epitaph reads, *Interr'd in Earth, a Prey to Worms and Flyes.* Why should that biographer construe Robert's case as *melancholy?* Mayhap more than death did filch away that life. For as soon as he comes into Robert's presence (having first waited with the horses, since Maister Bartty deserves to greet his brother alone); as soon as Robert's face swivels his way, Sweet John remembers what he'd disremembered; and all sweet success which he had looked to anneal in the chemistry of the future Earl's affections, all hope precipitates into woeful ash. Yet he steps forward & drops his leg in a zealous bow. The future Earl extends his hand, just as he used to do at rent-time, and the other boys must put into it apples, nuts, or whatever other dainties they might have garnered; and now once again (as it appears) John Smith must pay some forfeit, be it only the clasp of beseeching friendship, shunning his own fears and certainties as he entreats that he's monstrous ready to do anything, be anything. Robert inquires: O, but can you buy horses? I need ones who's expert at buying and selling for the Army. — I prefer to fight at your side, Lord! (thus John Smith). — Robert answers: Sweet John, be not angry with me. There are no battles at present, except in Ireland. — In all Gentlemanly condescension he leans forward, stretches out his fingers, lays them on Smith's shoulder. — Your service is needless, lad. We'll send you back to your friends . . .

* * * * * *

CHRIST's wounds, but Robert mislikes him not. A biographer, having listed many fortunate turns in Sweet John's life, renders up this sum: *None of these helping hands can be identified in documents, yet it is surely worth mentioning that Robert Bertie or his shade seems to be standing by at nearly every event in John Smith's eventful life.* Those words were printed near about .4. centuries after Robert did ask him if he could buy horses. In the same *Biographickall Directory,* Robert's brother Bartty, to whom Smith preferred to turn, appears not at all. Did Sweet John know not his friends?

* * * * * *

The future Earl and Bartty (the latter passing sorry; Bartty's round face almost blubbers!) have given him his liberty in Paris, where he scouts around desperately for new benefactors. He is very emulous; he doesn't want to hear again that cow-call of *cush, cush!* As the .19.th-century drainage engineer William Henry Wheeler once wrote: *The Fens have obtained a world-wide notoriety; and a general, though very erroneous, impression prevails among those who do not know the country, that this part of Lincolnshire is a dull and dreary land, to be avoided by all except those whom necessity or the call of business compel to visit its unattractive scenery.* No matter that the impression is, as Wheeler insists, erroneous; no matter that Sweet John counts himself Woldsman, not Fensman, for Willoughby towers several feet above the level of the tides; to him all Lincolnshire's but a slough of poverty and failure now. He denies to go back. See him trudge the cobbles of Paris. Maister Bartty hath a friend, & this friend hath a cousin, by name Maister Hume — a most philosphic appellation, which puts me in the temper of true empiric. Maister Hume says: Could I but establish you in life! Yet my funds permit it not. However, do you wish it, you may deliver these letters to Scotland for me. Nay, lad, look not for anything to come of it. But take these dozen guineas . . .

* * * * * *

See John Smith at sea, embarked from Ancusan to Lethe, which is no Greekish river of disremembrance, but merely the port of *Edinboro,* city among the Scots. This ship is hulled with great rakes forwards on, in the French style, which make her keep a good wind, but her head pitches in the gathering sea. The Purser mutters (bad bird that he is): *Seagull, seagull, sit on the sand! It's never good weather when you're on the land.* A sickly qualmishness creeps among sailors & passengers. Like the rest, Sweet John gets fits of the vomits. He's mastered by such sharp aches deep down to his very chitterlings as a Convict drawn & quartered might endure. O, to be a Soldier, rather, marching safe upon the land, following Captaine Duxbury's plumed Officers! Howbeit, in his youth he's not yet reserved himself to any .1. thing. If soldiering be not politic, 'tis better to learn the Sailor's life. Straightaway he commences to study the names: the *Boulspret,* the *Misen maine Mast,* the *Parbunkel* . . . Laughing, the Sailors teach him everything. When they wink or beckon, he leaps to assist them.

He would be confirmed for some far-faring occupation, & forget this unease within his guts . . . But a storm boils up at twilight off the Holy Isle of Lindisfarne. *Sheet close aft!* cries the Captaine. *Tie the helm!* The weather growing yet more dangerous, they reef sail & drop the kedge anchor in good time, but the gale becomes insatiable. Sweet John's afeared. The Captaine sings out to drop the sheet anchor, which owns **.4,000.** weight — too much for weakened men to budge in a single thunderclap. Before they get it o'er the side, comes a wild crash that bruises their very bones: The ship has driven against a rock. — GOD save us! croaks the Purser. — Raising the scuttle-hatch, Smith hears rushing water. — *To the pumps!* yells the Captaine. The Coxswain & **.2.** Quarter-Gunners stagger down to the hold, puking. The Mate's nowhere; the Trumpeter's lost his instrument. Sweet John knows not where he should go. The others run for the boats. By Heaven — to the pumps! There he does his best endeavor. But water begins to squirt rhythmically out of the scuppers. Comes a horrid crash; they've struck another rock. The ship near o'ersets. He hears smashing noises in the Galley. The **.1.**st boat has filled with pilgrims, & they've cut the ropes. Better 'twould have been to lower her heedfully from the davits, but her panicked passengers smell their own death & cannot wait. She strikes water stern end **.1.**st, o'ersets, spills screamers, not all of whom come up again. Night loses the living & the dead. The few at the pumps give o'er, come a-fleeing onto deck. The Captaine (whose outline Smith can barely spy, thanks to the rain) sprints to the Round-house and exits with the log under **.1.** arm & a sealskin wallet under the other. Here's the Mate — he's roaring commaundments in the Gun-room, but the roar of water drowns him. What o-'clock is it, what tide? The Almanacke sayeth: *The moone South south weast, betweene holy Ilande* and Tynemouth full sea.* Mayhap this ship can beach even now, if the tides be right. But the Helmsman's flown the Steerage-room. The Mate shoulder-seizes him, but he twists away, leaping into the **.2.**nd boat just as the men in her cut the ropes; & she drops thunderously into the night, whose foggy atmosphere resembles that of the Press-room at Newgate Prison, where Felons who fail to confess at their trial are stretched, roped and pressed to death in darkness, o'er a dismal portion of hours and days which never divorce themselves from night; and now the Swabber catches himself in the cat harpings, and shrieks because the Captaine and some others will not await him in the final boat, and e'en as John Smith comes running, leaving the Swabber to be

*Lindisfarne.

hosted by that spider call'd Death, the Boatswaine cuts the ropes; and *after* the splash ascends the Captaine's faraway ironic commaund: *Man the boats!* Smith has Maister Hume's letters, and he has his dozen guineas, so, believing it time to get shut of this fair-weather ship, he jumps into the sea — or, rather, commits himself to that black and misty night in which he's briefly suspended like a hanged man, and then he's caught in cold and nauseous billows — *an o'ergrown sea,* they call it when the billows are this high. He swims for his life. His armor drags him down, but not o'ermuch; it weighs but .17. pounds. Unable to doff it, he swims & struggles. Now he hears ahead of him *the rut of the sea,* which is to say the evil crashing sound of surf; he can't yet spy any rock-teeth. He's numb. Endurance cannot suffice: How can he outwit this ocean? But he takes heart; didn't he trick the Rector's sentence of doom? His flesh proves wise in fishy rock-dodges (altho' the sea doth coldly choke in his mouth); somehow he makes shore, where lanterns do waveringly shine.

Your Captaine's drown'd, boy, says the Lieutenant of the Garrison. Many others got also swept to death. — And he explains with a note almost of pride: We have very dangerous shoals here, off Lindisfarne.

✳ ✳ ✳ ✳ ✳

Altho', sweet Reader (thou Redeemer of my Mortgage), John Smith was destined in his life of sacrificial tears to visit many rare Countreys, not even excepting the delights, astonishments & deserts of the Mountaines of the Sunne in *Affrica,* & the Mountaines of the Moone as well (some of whose peaks comprise themselves of iron, some of crystal, some of silver, & others yet of gold), yet of all the treasurous vistas he e'er did see, he held *Lindis-farne* almost as dear (as I verily believe) as any memory of Pokahuntas or the Lady Tragabigzanda. 'Twas nigh unto .4.-and-.20. hours after his swim that he lay a-sleeping in a little cottage by the Priory. When he awoke at last, and aspired to rise, a fearsome weakness, almost as mocking to his miserable soul as the importunities of *the purples,* attended him, and again he swooned. He awoke to the smell of ocean and horses. 'Twas quiet. Two rescued Mariners lay snoring. He staggered out to make water, and found half a dozen coffins upon a trestle. The Carpenter was making more. That dark green grass of English Townes, carried still farther into relief by the whitewashed Churches, now escaped his eye. A falling stretch of paler green led him, like the marching hedges, to the sea. 'Twas low tide. Blue pools lay upon the mud, the liquid metallically sheened like mussel shells. Feeling faint again, he sat down upon the bleached salty grass.

The rocks from which the Castle rose were pink with sea-flowers. He could not see the wrecked ship. The Carpenter said she had utterly sunk.

* * * * * *

That night he went out. He listened for a long time, and heard nothing. Then he heard water, low and far away. It was only for the first few moments that he had felt joyous about his escape from the sea. Then a fog of strangeness oozed o'er him. He was drowning in the mucky Fens of a bad dream. Into his mind crept the words: *I am as I am, and so I will be.* He did not know where they came from. Birds chuckled in the Castle wall.

* * * * * *

The people of Holy Island spared not to express their kindness and pity. They themselves seemed lonely; most ravenously they disturbed his peace. He'd have preferred to dwell within his own leaden self, for the sea did whisper like a sullen Sibyl that no matter how heroically he essayed to better himself, 'twould e'er end like this, or worse. He strove to strike her off, wearying himself anew. But wherever he did go, the sea followed. And the Holy Islanders would press their bread & double beer on him. He gave them thanks, but hungered not. When could he escape to continue his *Trve Travels?* Not now. Why then, he must be circumstanced as G O D willed.

Their accents, not quite Lancashire nor Edinboro, made him to crave for Lincolnshire, altho' he'd sworn never to return there. The Carpenter went on knocking together coffins. He walked down to the strand and saw the Purser's corpse come washing in. 'Twas afternoon. A full moon hung above the Castle. He went a-plucking flowers, as he once had done to bring to Cicely. Nettles and flowers, wind and wool, creamy clots of it in the low-grazed grass; sea and clouds; there stood the World's full sum. Did he seek for more, he'd get tricked.

At darklins the Castle grimmed behind a scramble of creamy clouds. The moon lurked lost. — So you have clouds such as these in Lincolnshire, do you? an old man asked, most pridefully strange about his clouds.

I disremember.

Come, lad, take belly-timber with me . . .

But John Smith withdrew behind the long walls raised against the sea. He cleaned his armor with vinegar & sand, then oiled it. He did not yet ask: *What will become of me?* It continued monstrous calm, the isle being full well reckoned up by the words *Emerald grass, sapphire sea.* No matter where he went, he ever discovered the high scarp of the Castle. He commenced to run. *Come back, come back.* But he could not run away from it. Well, 'twas a passing good sea-mark.* From afar he watched as someone belonging to the Castle let down the hard-tarred teeth of the porticulis.

* * * * * *

What else do you want? the woman said. Her gaze burned him like a stinging nettle.

She brought him fresh butter on a tray.

The moon, with all his golden etchings on his face of palest cream, bobbed silently in the sky. For a moment he recollected Maister Reese Allen's late father, Cicely's grandfather, the litigious old Prince of Fools with the round face, and he laughed, inhaling a smell as of new-mown hay.

The woman was staring out the window. She said: I was a-wondering about that brown cloud.

There was no brown cloud. He said: Would you kindly come walking with me?

No! she shouted. I deny to come!

* * * * * *

As they strolled along he began a-shivering between his shoulders — spine-chilled, most likely, from his swim — and took her hot hand in his cold one. Nettles sparkled in the moonlight along the stone wall, beyond which lay grassy marshy darkness, then something resembling a lake — in fact 'twas a finger of the insidious tide, which lay still out, so that Lindisfarne became for that eye-blink no island. He read a secret so hurt and forlorn about her cracked face. Sometimes Sweet John did look at women and thrill with the seducer's power; he kenned when they wanted him, and should he act upon that knowledge with good confidence, he e'er discovered success. Thus far he'd gained, from going for a Soldier. *Tenderness* reigned chief among his jewels. She stripped off her dress, laughing in the cold wet wind, and led him inside a half-open ruin near the sea. The smell of grass was in his nostrils. He could see white breath-clouds coming out of her and mixing with his own, dissipating insouciantly in his hair.

She said she kenned his Countreymen well, for but a year or .2. since, .300. men from Lincolne Countie had lain in Holy Isle for a night. They

*Beacon.

were bound for Ireland, they'd told her, to put down the rebellion there.
John Smith would have come likewise, had he not been already a-soldiering
with Captaine Duxbury in France . . .

In the night sky there dwelt a single cloud like an immense brain, with
the moon in the center of it. After a long time, from far away, he heard a
single sheep *Baaaa*-ing, then the sound of destiny slowly approaching on
heavy clubbed feet. This was the clanging of his heart.

* * * * * *

Northwards, the sky yet lived unbled of its last pale blueness, altho' 'twas
almost midnight. Long gropings and bleedings of the cloud-brain defaced
it. What had he dream'd? He lay full steeped in contentment. (Sweet
John, would I were you! For I'm no longer so young that a tumble may as-
suage my all into symmetry.) — She awoke, rose wordlessly from his arms,
dressed in a twink, and walked away without glancing back. Enchanted
yet, he attended her going in an almost suffocating ease.

He looked down, and thought he'd fallen into the sky; for in the dark
wet grass, tiny constellations gleamed. He plucked a star. 'Twas a miniature white flower, ball-shaped, soft and yielding against his thumb.

* * * * * *

When John Smith has gotten health back into his fists, he finds passage to
Scotland on another ship (whose Captaine does him this service gratis, out
of pity) and so delivers Maister Hume's letters. O, the Scots thank him ever
so kindly! Have a dram of our Usquaebach, darling Sweet John! Don't ye
find it a most savorous liquor? — Unfortunately, they have neither money
nor means . . .

* * * * * *

See John Smith at Berwick-upon-Tweed, calling upon the Governor, my
Lord Willoughby, with a letter of news from Bartty and Robert. Hear him
knapping on the door! His narrow-faced old benefactor, whose beard
curves and tapers unto a steeple's point, will feast him hugely, thank him his
energies, wish him luck, then make him more luck than his wishing. 'Tis
easy for him to raise Sweet John out of low estate! But mishappily Lord
Willoughby has gone a-riding to London-Towne.

* * * * * *

From Gravesend west to London, 'tis but a few river-twists. (Dodge the double-oared wherries of my rival Watermen. How ruffianly they do appear . . . !) First, up-river yourself to Northfleete, which lies close — aye, name her the western wall of that charnelly Church-yard of ships & bawdy-houses call'd Gravesend. At Northfleete, no matter how Pocahontas fears or feigns to sail, the river wriggles northwest, then back southwest again to Greenehyeth, kissing the old abbey at Stone where Papists once angled for passing souls with their heavenly catchpole. Now we angle with pure English tools — and *ha! ha! ha!* We've caught Pocahontas! Tubercular clouds gather o'er her breast. They'll find a way in; they're English; PROVIDENCE proposes them. Refusing to be misled by the double-forks of Cray Creek which spread south past Crayford and Dartfoorde (for *John Smith's* on board to subdue confusion), sweet Reader, passenger of this ungainly Word-barge of mine, pray continue westward past Eryth, wriggle northwest again, bypassing the Great Breach and the northbound creek which serves Barkynge, & so on you'll sail past Plumsted, Wolwych, thence by convenient tides up another tickle where *.2.* more creeks divorce each another at West Ham; you need not entertain those destinies, either. (But could Pokahuntas have been a-rowed into *.1.* of them, percase she'd have outraced her time.) West Comb, Greenewych Stairs, another creek at Diepford, another northern jog to Stepney, and you've arrived at the bristling spires of *London Towne.*

Neptune's disciple and homecoming prodigal, John Smith doth make this voyage again and again — each time deploringly, for *uprivering* signifies *inlanding,* which signifies deafeat. *Cush, cush!*

* * * * * *

See Queen Elizabeth at Whitehall, the oval eyes shining in her milk-hued oval head, her white breasts a downturned heart to balance the immense butterfly-wings of lace and sparkling pearls which rise from her shoulders, her throat cushioned by lace, her snaky red tresses bursting from her skull like flames.

She goes to her chamber, removes the red wig. Her Ladies-in-Waiting begin to undo the lace. She must change her habit; soon there'll be a masquing-show, with many boats & lights; and the velvet gown Ralegh gave her's better for that. (A maid fumbles with a pin; the Queen boxes her ears.)

And what about that man? yawns Essex, lounging in the doorway.

Which man? Are you snooping again, naughty boy?

I brushed by him twice. That vassal of Willoughby's, that log, that post, that importuner. Day and night he waits without. He's kept us company since before Cain knew his sheep! And I'm beginning to abhor him.

My poor, poor boy . . . You're in a pet, I see. Come help me with my dress.

Shall I send for the Knight Marshal?

And my glove. Hath he made water at my gate?

By my faith, he's a Waterman of the basest sort, pissing out lurid pleas and conveyances from his eyes, but I stooped not to learn where his cod did point when he —

What's his name?

John Smith. He craves some boon; he won't go away.

O, send him about his business, says the Queen. (Fie, my tooth aches!) These yeoman slupper up too much of my time, much as I love them. Give him a shilling. They can all be hanged, I say!

* * * * * *

See John Smith, that friendless hang-head, creeping poor and woebegone back to Willoughby, Towne of his birth (hence noblest Towne in Lindsey Riding, indeed in all Lincolnshire — so I, *Pokahuntas's* debtor must claim), Towne of holly hedges, Towne of dead dreams. — Sweet reader, do you know where Willoughby is? On your map, pen out a CHRISTcross thus: *horizontally* from Hogsthorpe all the way west to Sutterby (which is as far as Frauncis Smith ever travelled), then *vertically* from Thorpe to Maltby-le-Marsh — a place not percase of low estate as 'tis said by evilwishers in Thorpe (who I misdoubt me not are dressed in blue like servants), but certainly of *sinking* estate, for Maltby's cottages are as lumps of sugar which sit upon corn-mush, and hence will slowly drizzle down to Hell before our backs be turned. By my faith, the Court of Sewers has scarcely finished its mission in that Towne! — Thus our cross, in which Willoughby lies but pinglingly northeast of center. (Is the center of Lindsey the center of the World? So they say, in Lindsey.) — *There are people who feel the dead level of the Fens depressing,* writes the .20.ᵗʰ-century author Arthur Mee; *to such as find their chief delight in the rolling hills, flat lands seem monotonous . . . The uplands called the Wolds, which have already been referred to, have the greatest variety of scenery, enhanced by wood-lands in the valleys.* John Smith is a Woldsman, as I never tire of stating; what company need he keep with Fens?

* * * * * *

Cicely has married with Ralph Nightingale, his mother relates. (No doubt Maister Reese Allen poured well from his drinking jug.) 'Tis said that in her bridal dress she resembled a spring chestnut tree, a mountain of leaves and flowers, for she was both fair and well garlanded. To this tale he returns scant answer. Now she must feed upon a crustier diet than was her wont, for Ralph's affairs grow passing waterish.

His mother is passing ill. He feels uneasy in her new husband's presence, altho', GOD knows, he wishes them but the best . . .

His sister Alice dwells distant, in Sloothby. When he calls upon her and her spouse, he discovers a babe; .2. more, he learns, did not thrive.

His brother Frauncis continues wedded and happy on the farm. Frauncis bids him stay, but not in sincerity. Wheat prices have dropped again, Frauncis says, to .24. shillings. Distrained by the loathsome flatness of his circumstances, John Smith yet squeezes out of his gullet by main force a question about the price of oats, which Frauncis answers enthusiastically, buzzing about commodities like a bottle-fly. — But 'tis not Frauncis's fault! he cries out deep within the dark mews of his heart. 'Tis but my own failing, that I can hardly listen or understand . . . — Gazing up with a start, he finds his brother staring back in cold irritation cousin almost to hatred. Frauncis has e'er been well aware when a body doesn't listen . . .

Again he visits that yew-ridden Church yard, avoiding the Rector. This time there lie no flowers on his father's grave. He hears a milkmaid calling her cows: *Cush, cush!*

Frauncis roots & wallows in domestic happiness. Sweet John withdraws. Goodwife Anna with her chores and children his idleness affronts.

✱ ✱ ✱ ✱ ✱ ✱

Master neither of himself nor even of his catalogue of schemes, he goes a-riding to call upon the Willoughbys at many-chimneyed Grimsthorpe. Bearing in a leathern bag Frauncis's rent-money in ready coin ('tis the reason Frauncis lent him the horse), he gallops past Bullingbroke, seeking to flee the anxious dread which rides his own shoulders. Mayhap the Rector's sermon on pride indeed approached the mark . . . The horse's hooves beat out the rhythm *Pen and ink, pen and ink.* Run, Smith, run. Lord Willoughby's the only chance he can think upon.

He transects Wildmore Fen at good speed, stops to water his horse in sight of Tattershall Castle where Bartty oft has played with him at fencing, and continues southwest: Billinghay Dales, a willow bank, then marshes and water-parsnips again in Kyme's low ground. He stops at a farm to inquire after the lady's pig-prices, to help Frauncis . . .

Grimsthorpe's hung in bunting for some occasion, but he has no time to inquire. He must parley with my Lord Willoughby. But Willoughby's at Berwick-on-Tweed. Where's Bartty, pray? O, but Maister Bartty's at Court! He turns in his nag at the horse-field, then slowly, slowly enters the main hall, his head wilting down. He'll hold out, though; he'll drown not in the ooze of shame.

Robert, the aforesaid not-yet Earl of Linsey, greets him coldly, wearing a white doublet, a black-feathered hat, a scarlet cloak with fine gold braids. His head comes floating on a great lily-pad of silk.

Rob. All hail, renowned herdsman, mire-man — nay, I forgot, good *Wolds*-man — come to seek your fortune anew, your tools my energies.

Sm. [making a leg]   I beg my Lord's pardon.

Rob. My pardon's not the first thing you've begged.

Sm. If 'tis such a burthen to you, Lord, to help me, why, then, I'll —

Rob. By Heaven, Sweet John, have you built yourself a life out of any save shifting shapes? I begin to wonder in my soul what could nourish you.

Sm. I swear I'll learn me in time better to avail myself —

Rob. [aside]   What doth the lout not avail? My family's gadfly — GOD's wounds, he follows me to France! He rides here time upon time; he . . . John, I know you love me honestly, but *what more must I do?*

Sm. 'Tis not my ingratitude which supplicates you yet again. You yourself did say there were lacking good French wars to send me to —

Rob. O, now he chides me with what I did say! John, Sweet John most silly and never villainous, I would impart you this news: Father returns in a fortnight-odd, and he loves you for *your* father's puppy. Would you wait on him? Enshelter yourself here; feed at our charge, until you may conjure him.

Sm. I humbly thank you for your good intent. And, may't please my Lord —

Rob. Let me guess. He craves a boon. What would you now?

Sm. I would educate my hours, did you grant me leave. For in France I did bethink me to learn somewhat of *Politick,* and can you lend me some discourse writ upon that subject, I'd most gratefully —

Rob. Now the ass would sing, & the serpent go erect! Ha, ha — your humor slays me, John! 'Tis true you drive me to a smile! G O D be with you, for you'll go a-*Politician*-ing. What medicine would best cure your simplicity? Let me dream on 't — but no! I'll filch him my brother's *Machiavell!* 'Tis a downright volume, and meet to teach you to be right mischevious. O precious! What *will* Father say?

[*Exeunt.*

Marry, here's the short of it: 'Til he can get new Worlds, John Smith craves a hiding-place. In his entire Countie of Lincolnshire (whose shape resembles an end-tweaked kidney), has he no refuge? Higher in the Hill Hundred, out of smell of the Fens, away from the Rector, in the direction of Lowthe, where he first kenned Continents at Grammar-School, he builds a bower in the forest, *ensheltering* himself on Willoughby lands, as Robert did invite him, and yet discreetly distant from the aforesaid Robert, who, true to word, lends him Machiavelli, & Marcus Aurelius for dessert. Bartty's home from Court, snickering about all the wenchen whose skirts he did explore. Lord Willoughby's home and at leisure. Sweet John's accordingly summonsed, to eat of venison with them, and drink their most excellent sack. O hearty-powered Landlords, may all my betters be as you — moodish or wasp-tempered, it boots not, so long as their sack doth waft me to princely drunkenness! — He comes to order at their table again & again. Not only are the Willoughbys indulgent by temperament, but he entertains them, like some legless abortion shewn for tuppence at a fair, or — more to the point — a scarecrow aspiring to be King. Gawp-seeded listener to Lord Willoughby's stories, fervent hand-kisser to Lady Willoughby, he bustles to burnish his loyalty, since that's his best and only adornment here. For in all respects else he's outshone. Herewith, his out-shiners: **.1.** Lord Willoughby wears a high collar embroidered with flow-ers (call it a neck-meadow) which supports his long, weary face; he's always ill now. He's discoursed with the Queen again, and gives off rays of high nobility. **.2.** Peregrine Bartty, now likewise returned from London Towne, dresses more sprightly than his father. Having missed the primo-geniture, he breathes less extraordinarily, but can frivol and fritter most awesomely. **.3.** As for Robert, that moody elder son bulks stocky and round of face; his moustache is wider, his beard more squat than that of the father; upon my soul I do believe he'll go parti-bald in middle age; and yet, uncomely though he may be, he possesses a shiny suit of armor to dress in. Similarly guards he his soul armored, self-call'd, locked; he keeps company with none. — What of Sweet John? He (who like most beggars will e'er open himself most un-Robert-ly, pleading, demonstrating, shewing his CHRISTly wounds) now goes most martially a-riding upon Frauncis's old nag, round & round that borrowed woody pasture which he haunts. Of-times now doth Peregrine Bartty, beset by the limits which Robert's fore-birth compells him to dwell within, invite yon yeoman-lad to play at horses at Tattershall Castle, which rears blocky and narrow, with its .2. pairs of turretted towers drawn in as if against a chilly wind. From any pane in its .5. rows of windows, Robert may be glimpsed staring out ironically. (His sister and his mother more frequently show themselves abroad — in the Court-yard, at least.) Now 'tis high summer, a season well disposed to mo-tions, projects, plots, ambitions; but the Castle continues compact and with-drawn upon its isle of lilacs, the moatsides bristling with dandelions and tall wet grass. The horse-hooves go *hammer and pincers, hammer and pincers*. Now Bartty's a-galloping most warfully; Sweet John must needs do the same. O, would he were alone in his bower! But he must e'er make strip-shew his affection (when he forgets this, Machiavelli reminds him). As for galloping, 'tis easy; Captaine Duxbury taught him how. *Pen and ink, pen and ink*. He watches and warrants the pleasure of his Lord. Bartty shouts: *Hyaaaaaah!* then unhorses him, so that he sprains a shoulder. Well, 'tis lit-tle enough to pay for a future of golden angels. Bartty's horse-groom runs to help him up. — Sportive Sweet John, I *love* you! Bartty shouts. — I thank you for it, he replies, essaying not to groan. GOD's wounds, but his shoulder aches! Bartty names him sturdy; he's yet young enough to take the compliment to heart, instead of coolly understanding that by this means the other doth shuck off his own remorse, at having play'd passing rough. Were Bartty a woman, Sweet John might opine: What piquancy hath this pepper-box! How charmingly she sports! — But since Bartty doth rather stand up to piss, he ought to be less superficial in his understanding. (Thus orates his angry shoulder.) Returning painfully to his woody bower to eke out the Dog Days, John Smith, blobbing for refinement, decides to engage a man of his own. He too may commaund when he plays at Soldiers! May-hap he's but a salt-butter yokel, as the Willoughbys believe; yet he's learnt of himself (and Captaine Duxbury) the science of Captaincy, befriending a half-wit, with whom he games half-jestfully at knights and squires. *Butter and eggs, butter and eggs.*   He sees himself in *Affrica*   making discoveries, in *Transylvania*   slaying Turkes and Tartars; it's a moist green afternoon and he lies on his stomach in the grass, munching berries. So *this* is how one becomes a Prince! Nobility of soul, treachery of heart — nay, treachery's brainbound, when 'tis statecraft, not lovecraft. Machiavelli also says: Set your enemies **.1.** against the other. He says: Equivocate. (Shades of Captaine Duxbury!) John Smith turns the page wide-eyed, leaving a purple fingerprint in the margin.

✳ ✳ ✳ ✳ ✳

His half-wit seeks to kiss him. Sweet John laughs and boxes the boy's ear. The boy squeals. In a joyous flurry, remembering his Soldier days, he strikes the boy again. But then he's shamed. He mislikes him this game of punishment.   When he fired houses & spitted traitors for Captaine Duxbury, he did it e'er with a leaden heart. Into his soul rise the words which Cicely used to sing: I am as I am and so I will be.

The half-wit scutters off, soon returning with a peace offering: a capful of berries . . .

✳ ✳ ✳ ✳ ✳

Self-beseecher and hearkener to those beseechings, he remembers his duty, and rides home to Willoughby-Towne for a week, to help Frauncis bring in the hay. Ralph Nightingale, so they say, hath burnt a fertile hillside out of carelessness, and the Rector preaches thrift on Sunday next. Staring at Cicely, John Smith sees her almost giggle right there in Church.* Mayhap that fire was some new misborn prank. Was she in on it? Passing mischevious bride! Less headstrong's his desire for her now, for in France with Captaine Duxbury he's had his whores, trulls, tarts, punquettos, &c. Shall we say he's many a time sheathed his sword? Moreo'er, his shoulder continues to ache whilst he's a-sickling in the fields. He hath not leisure to pine for wenchen. He imagines every stalk of grass to be a heathen Turke, which beheading in a sweltering sweat, he doth but increase his own powers, so that when he returns to war, he'll be full ready to make the enemy weep blood. Swish, swish, & in a trice he's sickled West Field! Frauncis finds his help right good. Altho' to all others it seems that John continues like a vagabond in his unguided days, yet he himself smells change a-coming. Truly this shall be his last sojourn in Willoughby. Soon 'twill be corn sea-

---

*"The village is on the edge of the Marsh," writes that architectural eminence, Nikolaus Pevsner, "and the church partakes of the Marsh character; i.e. it is Perpendicular in style, and all of a piece."

son, and Frauncis will call on him to lay up the silk-tasseled ears in the bing,* but Sweet John'll be flown to war by then! He's impatient — O, how he longs to be away! *Come back, come back.*

Frauncis's sow's now a-brimming, or *in heat* as they say in some parts. Frauncis would borrow a boar of Maister Reese Allen. Just before the Queen's birthday he sends John to ask of him. But John dreads to go. He's afeared that Maister Allen will ask of him where his affairs do stand. Still more he's *shamed* to call upon the father of the bride he lost. So he delays; good Machiavellian, he *equivocates*.   Now back to Tattershall Castle, for his shoulder's well healed with all the labor.

There's danger of a Spanish landing, Robert says. The Irish are a-rising in rebellion. Corn prices are up (nay, he heard that already of Frauncis). Plague in London Towne again. A fly drones in Smith's ear. Captaine Duxbury, says Bartty, was lately slain at the Battle of Nieuport.

✳   ✳   ✳   ✳   ✳

I perceive you're passing loose-ended, Bartty laughed.

Not so much, Lord. But I do engross my strength, I hope for some purpose. You know I humbly desire to try my fortune —

Aye, John, and how would I know that, did you not prate of it from the head of the year to his very heel?

Maister Bartty, I entreat you —

Passing sweet it is to be entreated, John, but look you, I must to London-Towne today. A certain maid would have her womb be sanctified by my balm. Do you understand me, sport?

I —

So meet me in September by our family tombs. 'Tis a whimsical spot, I trow, but, G OD's wounds, if you're not a whimsickall fellow! And I'm right *quim*-sickall, and must bequim me now, before my balls run riot —

✳   ✳   ✳   ✳   ✳

According to Clausewitz, who wrote a good .2. centuries later, in War there stands nothing of greater importance than obedience. In this respect, one must admit, John Smith wasn't washed entirely clean of sin. But he did possess that other gem of character especially prized by Clausewitz, which is *b o l d n e s s*.   What to believe? Clausewitz goes so far as to say that idi-

---

*A rat-proof box used to store corn.

otic rashness itself, while a fault, ought never to be deplored as much as other failings. If the brave Soldier loses his head too soon, why, good faith! commaund his copemate to stuff gunpowder where the brains were, tamp bullets into the eyesockets, and then 'tis a fine cannonball we've made of him! Howbeit, some may dispute that notion. In my time, for instance, our President went merrily a-bombing Yugoslavaia from the air; but he feared to lose a single Soldier, in case our Citizens would denounce him. So he did mislike all rashness. Reader, how do you vote? Those strange patches upon the face of the Moone get call'd by some pedants *marrings,* while others apostrophize them as *strewn roses.* So, John Smith's as he is, but *what* he is, gets crystalled most variously in the beholder's eye. In faith he'd already crystallized himself! Machiavelli's disciple now, he swore to be both lov'd and fear'd by those whom he'd commaund; & if he could choose but .1. manner in which to move their hearts, why, then, he'd as lief be *feared!* And he believed that boldness could make a Wilderness out of Palaces, and could likewise translate Wilderness into new Palaces again. How he long'd to ask Lord Willoughby's opinion! Robert he'd likewise ask, but Robert lived passing snappish. And Bartty mayhap knew more than he told, but with Bartty no question got answered save with a jest. Sweet John knew that since his own education was not sound, his innocency might well misapprehend the paragraphs of wise *Machiavell,* but who'd correct & sanctify his reading? Never mind. He'd lurked in the bower a good month, and then discharged his half-witted Squire. He took in the corn with Frauncis. The Book was done. Time now for glorious *Politick.* Riding toward Eresby (or Spilsby, as 'tis now called), down the gently tilted plane of meadows, he resolved to wait at the tombs of the Willoughbys until Bartty rode thither to lay his promised wreaths. 'Twas more than well, thought Sweet John, for here he need not be muzzled by fear of Robert. Guided by Machiavell, he'd express himself in breaths of admiration. He'd ask most yokelishly about London, whose brothels (so Bartty said) bristled with armed Guardsmen all around, but those fellows ne'er dared slit Bartty's purse, for he (that is to say, Bartty) knew how to thee and thou them (being after all of high degree). Sweet John recollected how Bartty once complimented Mistress Cicely on her rubious lip . . .

Just as one catches eels by bragging up and down with a red-wormed pole, so John Smith would wave his cause in Bartty's sanctimonious face . . .

* * * * * *

Skendleby, Scremby, Ashby . . . *Come back, come back.*   Trees o'erhung the horse-path. He followed immense walls of lilacs. The sheep were as clouds in the swirling green skies of fields.

✳ ✳ ✳ ✳ ✳

He waits patiently in the Chapel of the Willoughby de Eresbys, glaring at sarcophagus effigies recumbent in armor with praying hands. The heavy-ruled windows with their many diamonds of wavy glass in between isolate him from the white summer evening. The stone Willoughbys sleep on, with stone lions at their feet. This grand dark Church of Saint James is much grander than the Church of Saint Helena in Willoughby. Every day the Rector places new wildflowers in the skinny-legged stand before the pulpit, whose CHRIST-carved crow's nest must be reached by a curving stair. The Rector thinks John Smith mad. Every day the young man comes and waits.

How long must you tarry here? he demands at last, exasperated unto itching anger.

John Smith unshutters his lip and speaks: Until I receive means to depart Lincolnshire forever.

You're monstrous hopeful, I ween. But what do you hope for? And what complaint have you 'gainst Lincolnshire? Man, don't you know your own happiness? Why not return to your place?

Never.

Never's the word I speak on *your* fine plans, Sweet John. You're but an earthworm tunneling through your native soil. Give o'er; resign yourself to GOD. Cush, cush; you'll never find means to leave Linconshire . . .

A horse draws nigh — Barty's cantering horse, tapping out *Butter and eggs, butter and eggs.*

✳ ✳ ✳ ✳ ✳

See Smith among the .4. French Gallants: Cursell, La Nelie, Monferrat & the great Lord Dupreau. Everyone kens the great Lord Dupreau. Don't you? John Smith doesn't. — Yes, my Lord, he speedily proclaims, we do know of you in Lincolnshire. — Mayhap the Lord Dupreau can help him crown himself. Strange friends sometimes bring gold. He himself owns ready money now — shillings, farthings & the odd gold noble, all squeezed out of Maister Bartty, who's thus favored him once more. — Where to, Sweet John? Why, to France to become a Machiavellian Prince!

He can ride a horse like a Gentleman now; he acquits himself right well with lance, pistol, battle-axe & falchion. The Sieur Dupreau makes much of these accomplishments, murmuring that lineal honors may be transferred e'en to yeomen, should a fellow's valor be great enough.

Would you ride with us to Duchesse Mercury's, lad?

O yes, in GOD's name!

'Tis well, for she'll write us all letters of favor to her husband, who's fighting for Emperor Rodolphus in Hungaria . . .

Smith trusts himself to be the only soul who's read Machiavelli. Besides, Duke Mercury must ken my Lord Willoughby; for they fought on opposite sides 'til Henry was crowned King of France. They'll undoubtedly prove war-friends. The Sieur Dupreau like cherishes a singular acquaintance with Lord Willoughby — how lucky, how profitable for Sweet John: — Neighbor ships creak around them as they lie ambiguously there at Gravesend. A Waterman would sell John a pair of trulls, but he, calling to rememberance a painful pox which he got .1. time, bids the ladies keep on their skirts. — Wise lad! cries the Sieur Dupreau. The more I see of you, Sweet John, the more I admire you! — John hangs his head and smiles. He can hardly wait to meet Duke Mercury.

Stretch forward your main halyards! the Captaine does shout. Hoist sails half mast high! Boatswaine, anchors aboard! — And England dwindles away. — *Flood oh!* cries John Smith. (So much and more he now knows.) In good order, with good weather, they cross the Channel, or, as sea-dogs call it, the Sleeve. Then 'tis south they go, not north, heedful never to float into grappling range of the Low Countreys, for the Spaniards still hold those to their Popish hearts. Up lateen mizen again; up sprit sail! On a dark night, round about the .2.nd hour of the Middle Watch, they drop anchor at Saint Valleries sur Some. The .4. Gallants whisper to the Captaine, who then most privily summonses the Purser to the Wheelhouse. Now 'tis time to fetch the trunks of the passengers ashore. The sea is rough. The .4. Gallants, being gallant, are right willing to assist in rowing. Prince John would also row, but they tell him 'tis not needed. — Never fear, says the Sieur Dupreau, you'll find labor enough in Hungaria, when we must dig, sap and counter-mine 'gainst the Turkes! — Cursell and the well-practiced Purser's Mate now stow the .1.st round of baggage in the dinghy's forebeak, where it'll be well contingency-shrouded beneath an oiled sheet. Most tenderly of all do they tuck Smith's trunk into that bed. O yes, 'tis locked, and Sweet John hath the key! And what's within? A red cloak which he got of Captaine Duxbury, all his money, courtesy of Bartty; a leathern drinking-bag, his spare sword, a parchment with wise phrases

copied out of Machiavell, spare breeches, iron gauntlets borrowed of
Robert, letters of introduction from my Lord Willoughby, a blanket, an oil-
skin cap, a certain misfortunate shagreen box with Cicely's engagement
ring still inside, a mirror, pen and ink, and .4. fine cheeses from his brother
Frauncis — marry, most everything but the clothes he wears (mail-shirt &
best sword hid beneath). — We'll await you on the beach, young friend
(thus Lord Dupreau). — And the .4. Gallants row into the fog, singing,
with the Purser's Mate saturnine betwixt them. The boat returns not until
the following evening, for the seas were monstrous high. Depreau? Well,
he's long en route to Amiens, and Smith's trunk with him. Run, Smith,
run —

* * * * * *

See him now in the forest, starving and weeping. A Farmer brings him
home, feeds him bread and cheese, and next day he's cold again. He feels .2.
weights of deadness inside him: .1. within his heart, which is as lead, and
the other deep in his belly, a great stone of gall and tears. More tears. He
swallows tears, which turn to ice in his throat. He essays to swallow.

* * * * * *

Here sits Cursell, no longer .1. of the .4. Gallants, shivering in a copse near
Brittany. The Sunne would be in Scorpio, could we but see the Sunne!
Wind hurls away all rain-ruined leaves. Sweet John hath no compass.
Where is he? Whom will he discover? Lovers may never meet again, but
the ways of enemies oft do intersect: This proves some corollary about
gravity. Without a word comes Sweet John, filthy, skinny past admiration,
his eyeballs burning ever deeper into their sockets, as though they would
brand his brain; and he draws his sword. Dreamily Cursell does the same.
Metal rings on metal, then metal thrusts through squeaking leather,
squishes into flesh, grates loud and hard on bone. Wrenching his blade out
of the fallen man's belly, Sweet John thinks he hears something and looks
up; a crowd is watching from the windows of a ruined tower —

* * * * * *

Being most splendidly refurbished by the Earl of Ployer (who fondly remembers Lord Willoughby's mother), John Smith of Lincolnshire makes
his tour of French Duchies & Provinces, certain once again that the Rose of
Sharon shall bloom for him. What an excellent charger he has under him!

Pen and ink, pen and ink. What happy meals he eats! The Papists have a way with pigeon pies. Captaine Duxbury used to say, 'tis 'cause they conjure fresh young birds to death, by *instructin'* 'em about Heaven! (But now where's poor Duxbury, but mess'd in his own pie of mud and worms? Soon 'twill be a year since he was slain.) And their wine's passing better than at home, altho' the beer isn't. Silver dishes of turbot & venison, most scrupulously, nay, solemnly prepared, whisk themselves before him like the fruits of faith. Now 'tis time for wine-boiled turtle-hearts & candied humming-birds' tongues. *Trarintra-rarara.* The Dauphin and Sweet John get into a drinking match, which Sweet John wins, for still he eats and bibulates as if Dame Famine were at his heels! To console the undone Dauphin, he (most monstrous clever and worldly) compliments French *maidens, Castles & guns,* 'till everyone loves him again. I misdoubt me not he learn'd that trick in his Machiavell! Now the Dauphin, asham'd to have been thought ill-humored, presents him with a sword fancifully Damascened, engraved & runneled with gold; 'tis far richer than any John e'er had before. He makes his bow of courtesy, thanking the giver well. *Your most humble Servaunt.* For an eye-blink it seems to him that he need but shew his sword to all he meets, and he'll be treated as a Gentleman of quality e'er after. Indeed all do congratulate him, raise the glass, sing martial airs, and wish him good fortune in that cool yet flowery way which Frenchmen have.

Truly 'tis but a short road from your head to your heels, John, remarks the Dauphin, and for that my admiration stretches all the taller. And now you're geared & outfitted (if not full-grown), pray tell us where you do incline.

I would to war, he replies, to repair my financial defects. If not, mayhap I'll discover new Kingdomes of gold . . .

The Mademoiselles all agree that 'twas bravely said! They enrich him with many gazes and smiles. Meanwhile the talk does turn to certain strange Countreys now possessed by France, to wit: *.1. Canada, .2. Hochelaga, .3. Baccalos, .4. Labrador, .5. Terre-Neuve* & ever so many more. Sweet John's never heard the like, for Lord Willoughby and Captaine Duxbury dwelt only on *Peru* and other Spanish dominions. Leaning eagerly forward, he inquires of the company: And have your noble Countreyman found gold, in keeping with their desires? — Tis near certain they shall, the Dauphin replies, for has not treasure shewn itself in all regions else of this New World? And New France, 'tis so vast, how could there not be gold?

O, the Dauphin's thrummed together a right golden tale. And 'tis true
(as a French maiden whispers in Sweet John's ear, he longing only to tup
her) that Frenchmen are planting CHRIST crosses at Gaspé, with .3.
fleurs-de-lys on every escutcheon, praying: Good JESU, may this Tree
blossom here and bear good fruit! — But as yet they've discovered nothing
in Canada excepting Salvages and codfish. Sweet John therefore throws
o'er that fabled Countrey and embarks for Italy, thinking with the spoils of
galleons to furbish him anew. Life will never be but easeful anymore . . . !

* * * * * *

The weather worsens. They settle their top-sails, but 'tis a nasty swelling sea.
Most idolatrously do these French Sailors cross themselves; he's never seen the
like! (Silently he offers up a prayer.) Now they take in the spritsail. Quick!
Down foresail, for the gale doth blow! Tallow under the parrels! He'd aid in
the labor, but most threateningly do they forbid him. (True Christians own
bad credit here.) In his kidneys he apprehends evil. All sails they now braid
up close. Rain fusillades them. The passengers are shouting — some sick
with fear, the rest angered into ferocious oppugnancy against the *Huguenot*
(as they call Sweet John). The sea's nowise as fierce as off Lindisfarne, but all
souls from Crewmen down to Pilgrims' wailing babes forbear not to devour
themselves in panic, fearing their SAVIOR's summons, the more they cry
aloud to Him. Discord, reasonlessness and desperation all do seek for an object. Will they make the Captaine their prey? He knows not what to do, but
creep backward by degrees . . . A thunder-bolt. The women scream. The
Gunner and the Gunner's Mate lash tight all the ordnance, crossing themselves at every knot. The Captaine's a-praying on his knees. The Boatswaine
kisses a CHRIST cross. The ship pitches. Frantically they strike their top-
masts to the cap. They drop anchor, huddling off Savoy's unseen coast. A
wiry lunatic little Sailor, the kind who stilletto-strikes from behind, commences shrieking in Sweet John's face, gesturing at the lightning-flashes, then
at him. (What's his speech? Basque, belike.) Nay, nay, John tries to explicate,
in truth I'm no DEVIL! But he can do naught to comfort or convince (in
part because he kens the *Frauncish* language but indistinctly). They roar
as cruelly as do bears in the baiting-pit. O, would he were among friends!
Back to solid Willoughby he'd fare now if he could, to plant himself in good
order, like an ear of corn. He pities himself. Near about darklins, the Captaine turns his back. And in a twink these Papists, believing that Sweet John's
presence imperils them, rush upon him and cast him o'er the gunnels. —
Swim, Smith, swim! — As wolves do pounce upon sheep, so falls the waves

on him, to take him for their prey. But he knows fate hath reserved him for a waterless death. 'Tis not as cold as that night off Lindisfarne . . . But his armor's heavier. Now he sinks under, and commences to gurgle and strangle away his life. Off Damascened sword! It sadly glitters for a twink, like a reddish-gold carp-fish, then disappears into the murk. He must not sorrow for it now. Still he drinks the sea. Off cloak, off brigandine vest — O, pity! And in an eyeblink, that faithful plated skin's gone likewise to the bottom, mayhap to grace some martial Merman. Once when he was a-fishing for luce in Lincolnshire not long since, he discovered a silver coin, then lost it in the ooze. Altho' the metal of that quick-sunk find (or *Jewell,* as I almost did call it), did give off a light so furiously, yet in the black carrion-muck of the pond's bottom that radiance was extinguished more speedily than I can tell, which prov'd the reason he could never again turn it up, altho' he searched near about .1. hour. So 'tis the same with his brigantine. More strangely than his sword, and instanter, rushes it below sight. He would bethink him he cares not; in t'other case he'd infallibly drown — and yet he'll never again possess the like of that sword, and *Maister Brigandine* had clung e'er his faithful friend. Well, someday he'll find another. Adamantly, armorlessly & optimistically he swims, he knows not whence in that rainy darkness. Sweet John's wondrous constituted. If need be, he'll swim a day or even .2., should the currents keep him off Savoy coast. By good hap he nears haven in but .4. or .5. hours. Rain and salt bedim his eyes; he pants; his mind's a dullness. Yet, harking to surf-sound, he breasts himself forward, gasping in the odor of orange trees. A leaf floats against his hand. To example himself to spend more strength, he minds him of the Lindisfarne woman he frigged. Mayhap some dainty French maid will take him in tonight. 'Swounds, where's this? He spies neither Tower nor Citadel — nay, not e'en a rush-light. Crawling cold and sodden onto Saint Mary's Isle, he keeps sufficient vim to kill a wild sheep, which he devours, dipping the raw and bloody meat in the sea for salt. Then he drains the ocean from his boots. It rains all night. The back of his neck prickles with clammy cold. He sits on a boulder by his dead sheep, staring at the ocean with bloodshot eyes. By GOD, he's a vengeful young fellow! But in the morn, while cold and foggy swells roll out of the bitter sea onto the dark rocks of this island, rocks so cold as to stick to the skin of his hands, he spies .2. ships a-coming. For pity & charity they take him on, and so he sails with them all the way to *Barbaria* where narrow and angular islands smolder in a molten sea, thence to *Alexandria, Scandaroone, Cyprus* & various other Realmes all bloodied by *Politick.* Just as a seal's whiskers curve backwards in parallels like ribs, so this narrative dwindles now back into art-ful invisibility for many a month. Altho' in his *Trve Travells* he possesses us of certain stepping-stones, yet his equivocations wing us too speedily betwixt 'em, so we know not exactly how he put on the strangeness of manhood. O my Sweet John! Here you gloss yourself in secrecy. Drenched in the sunny blue sweat of the sea, you feed on foreign experiences, and your blood's touched. Your parts of nature develop themselves to perfect sinew. Expert Sailor and Pirate as you become, you swim your own flood-tide, strengthening 'till all the burdens you bear do creak and frolic disregarded like cockleshelled-ships on the shoulders of a full sea! Words & death come more fluently from your mouth. You practice right tunefully to play the melody call'd *Machiavell. Trarintra-rarara.*

* * * * * *

With a box containing .500. gold chichqueenes (his share in their victory o'er a Venetian carrack — his .1.ˢᵗ sea battle), he proceeded to Rome, where he chanced to see the Pope crawling up the holy stairs. Did I mention that he'd hid another .400. chichqueenes in his pocket? Did I explain that while passing through the Countrey of Siena en route to Rome he'd met Robert & Peregrine Bartty, both wounded in a battle of honor, and that he'd bought them physic and sweet wine from his own riches? — Forsooth, the chick did hatch! said Robert, not without admiration. Young Bartty lay snoring and bloody on the pillows. His helm's gilded crest had been split by an axeblow. He'd done credit to his vows. Sweet John slept that night on the floor of their lodgings, and in the morn requited o'er all the coin they'd lent to him. In truth, to the Willoughby brothers 'twas not much, that money ventured to the salt-butter yeoman; and yet it touch'd their hearts that he was fiery to repay his debt. Yea, he conceiv'd himself to be monstrous well-ensconced in their crystalline order. With mirthful trembles of the lip, they listened while he proclaimed his doings: *We gave her a stiff broadside, my Lords, then our stern, then t'other broadside full of murther-shot, 'till that argosy did yield her entire with all her silks, velvet, & cloth-of-gold . . .* (Bartty was itching to burglarize a certain *placket,* or petticoat-slit, of which he'd heard prick-tickling tell. What cared he for other men's conquests?) — Thus John Smith felt himself to be a person of quality, and when he got to Rome, the Pope with all his sumptuous feigning could not scratch the adamantine armor of his self-admiration. (By the way, he'd seized himself of new armor in truth — no matter how. So he'd held up his head well-beseemingly when he met with Bartty and Robert. To him they were all .3. perfect Soldiers like unto Greekish heroes — no matter that

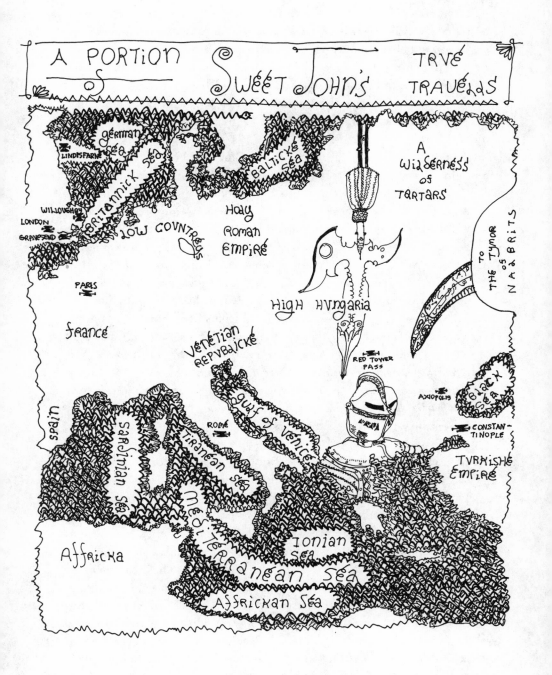

their armor translated them into sumptuous black-and-gold bumblebees, whereas *his* (pluck'd off a dead Moorishman) comprised but a half-corroded old brigandine vest, whose mail-plates rattled and dangled from the sweat-rotted cloth to which they'd once been sewn. Now he would eye Rome's pageant. He wandered through an immense curved and multi-tiered fragment call'd the *Colosseum,* of which he'd never heard, & did marvel at the ambition of those ancient Roman Kings — again, no matter that they'd all now sunk into ooze. Sure England would have her Empire, too — .1. to last more than **.1,000.** years, with GOD's help! He mis-doubted him not Signor Machiavell had promenaded in this very spot, as-sembling his own edifices of many-columned Reason as he gazed upon Reason's decayed shells. By my faith, Sweet John would do the like!

Why were so many Roman Emperors o'erthrown? inquires Machiavell, doubtless reflecting on these aforesaid shells. *'Twas murtherous hard to render satisfaction both to Soldiers & people, for the people did love peace, hence loved the* unaspiring *Prince, whereas the Soldiers loved the* warlike *Prince who was bold, cruel, & rapacious.* And thus, once he chose whom to offend, either Soldiers or people rose up against him. What to do? (See John Smith, wide-eyed in his bower in Lincolnshire, ruminating on this very question — but briefly, for he must comb his horse, and ride to supper at my Lord Willoughby's.) Why, 'tis simple: *Give satisfaction to the* Sol-diers, *caring naught for injuring the people. Which course was necessary, because, as Princes cannot avoid being hated by someone, they must do their best endeavor to 'scape the hatred of the most powerful.* Then should the rabble rise up, of a surety the Soldiers will put 'em down — and rape 'em, plunder 'em, sword-spit 'em even, that they may learn their lesson! — Passing witty, my Machiavell! — But, should you proceed thus, dear Prince, guard your authority o'er the Soldiers, or you're lost.

This Rule full explicated why the French Captaine had suffered him to be toss'd o'erboard off Savoy. Necessity made him choose: Offend his Countreymen, or offend John Smith. John Smith comprehends, nay, com-passionates him. 'Twas pure *Reason's* part to do as that Captaine did.

He sat in the *Church of Sainte Iohn de Laterane* to hear the Pope say Mass, and he understood scarce a word save the Paternoster. But 'twas a splendid occasion, and he felt constrained to grant (as he never could have done at home in Lincolnshire) that this Congregation did good reverence to OUR SAVIOR, after their idolatrous fashion, surrounded by beauteous *Gems, Magicks, Lanterns & Wonders* which he relished well. Gilded saints did gaze wooden-eyed upon the crowd.

To improve himself & his Undertakings he did **.1.** day stroll from the *Therma Diocletiani* all the way to the *Hippodromus* (discovering every soul he met to be deep-mired in Popish servitude — another victory for Machiavell). Yet Rome herself, with her Churches and CHRIST-crosses, her Soldiers in patinated bronze armor chased with gold and silver wires, pits, Monuments, trulls, fields, ruins, robbers, beggars & Pilgrims, had now commenced to disquiet him, for he trowed he shared the air with ghosts. Beneath him ran the labyrinthine *Necropoli* or *Catacombs,* discovered a mere **.20.**-odd years since. He forbore to descend to muse among her sarcophagi, as sad-eyed vassals & Tomb-Pilots invited him to do. What if they outed the candle, and stabbed him in the dark? He must earn his living now; 'twas no time to take bootless chances. So he tempered his brain to make of Rome no Eternal City, but rather a *Way-station* to fortune, a species of Gravesend, in short, whose Watermen ply every Traveller with stupendous chances. And so it passed that near upon the altar of that same murky Church of Saint John, perfumed willy-nilly with Popish incense, he made his salutations to *Father Parsons,* an English Jesuit of renown, whose name had oft invoked itself amongst Papist traitors in Lincolnshire — moreover, Lord Willoughby himself once discoursed at dinner against the man's dangerous cunning — and belike 'twas this self-same Father Parsons who lit a prayer-candle on Sweet John's behalf, penning him an introduction to a certain Irish Jesuit then lurking in *Austria* (which Countrey our hero reached by way of *Albania, Ragousa* & other barren places); here again the tale dims, Sweet John's footprints having collaps'd into the hungry charnel-mud of centuries, yet I can near-precisely say that 'twas through Father Parsons's Irish minion that he won preferment of *Baron Kisell, Generall of the Artillery,* & so for glory and other wages he did set out at last to fight the Turkes.

* * * * * *

Caniza was cut off from communication, thanks to the aforesaid Turkes, who'd establish'd themselves about the walls in a great stranglehold, but Sweet John (who now prov'd as smooth as fingers gliding o'er the grooved backs of Church pews) taught to Baron Kisell a code he knew for sending messages by means of **.3.** flames, then added to that service by confounding the enemy with *Fireworks* trick'd out like unto the muzzle-flashes of myriad imaginary Soldiers, so in the end that siege was raised, and half the Turkes either slain or drowned. *Trarintra-rarara.* Thus John Smith was made Captaine of **.200.** and **.50.** horsemen — a title which he proclaimed to the end. Someday he'd be a Cornett; he'd carry the colors! He acquired a snake-hilted German rapier from a dead man. He seized himself of a Turkishe saber upon whose hilt were plated certain verses of their *Qooran,* or *Devil's Booke.* Within a week's space, he'd gambled it away. Conning a smoke-stained map whose Townes & Secrets were everywhere marked by wavy letter Xes (resembling the cattle-brand for Stickney Towne in Lincolnshire), he kenned his opportunities infinitely and unshakeably culvertailed like **.1.** ship-timber to another; he'd *lead* the campaign if he could, and chop up these ungodly Turkes! How fast his heart did beat! Dark birds speckled the evening sky as he cried out, seeking with jibberjabbering gestures to explain the plot to his brother Mercenaries, who hailed from all parts murtherous & heathenish and who shrugged. All they had in common was rape. He rode on with Duke Mercury's Army to *Alba Regalis,* where on an auspicious midnight the signal was given: Sweet John fired the match of his **.1.**st pyrotechnic missile filled with gunpowder, brimstone & quartered musket-bullets! So those Turkes fled who were not roasted, and their Pasha got taken prisoner. *Your most humble Servaunt.* Now see Captain Smith in Transylvania; see him kill **.3.** Turkes in single combat: to wit, *Turbashaw, Grualgo & Bonny Mulgro.* With his Damascened sword (yes, he'd obtained another of those) did he cut off their gorecloaked skulls, which were duly impaled on lances for a parade of **.6,000.**, and when *Sigismund Bathor the Emperour* came to view his troops, he gave Sweet John a coat of arms in whose shield gazed **.3.** grinning Turkes' heads —

* * * * * *

After the good hap e'er comes ill. 'Twas in the vale of Veristhornes, which lies in Wallachia, that the Turkes & Janissaries o'ermatched the Christians, and slew near **.30,000.** The Sunne was declining out of Libra. Smith was wounded, and lay among the bloody bodies until the corpse-robbers found him. Thinking undoubtedly to extract some ransom, they disarmed & disvested him, staunched his bleeding, rested him in slack chains — and then, when he was somewhat healed, tied him to a cart's arse and sent him down the white alley of sand to Axopolis* to be sold for a slave.

* * * * * *

See John Smith, neck-chained to **.19.** hundred others, trudging deeper and deeper into the Kingdom of S A T A N, there to serve out all his days. Who

---

*A Danube town about a hundred miles to the east of what is now Bucharest.

now owns his Damascened sword? The Turkes laugh and beat him. Crag-isles furred with forest, here and there a toothy castle wall, a tower, a river-sail — all of such a piece with the other marches of Hungaria (not to dispraise them) that they cannot pleasure him. A prisoner of the Turkes, wound up irretrievably in their bloody devices! (But even now he smiles to remember how he refused the Rector's good offices so long ago in Willoughby: Better a slave than an apprentice Draper! Besides, he'll wait his turn, take the unpaved road of opportune escape.) Queasing on his closed thoughts as he tramps eastward, in all that multitude alone but for his bleeding wounds, he drowses, dreams of fishing in the pond that lies at the bottom of the Old Field. He'll catch a fine supper for Cicely. No mat-ter that her wedding-ring's been lost forever to the .4. French Gallants. He knows a place where eels lurk under the hollow roots. And roach-fishes . . . He'll roll a ball of paste between his palms, and ease it onto his tiniest hook . . . And now the Turkes do stop to observe their month of *Ramadan,* during which from sunrise to sunset no good Mussulman may eat or drink. So they disallow their Christian slaves even from tasting water, no matter whether they suffer from fever or grievous wounds, and many die lying in their neck-chains. But John Smith does always watch and help his fellow slaves to find the shadiest ground, so that on his own chain of .20. souls, none perish. All around him he hears the high-pitched cries of raped boys, but closes his eyes to win back dreams of roach-fishes . . .

* * * * * *

The hands of .2. Under-Sheriffs raised him to the block (or, as I might call it, the very Tabernacle of the $ANTI$-$CHRIST$); there he reeled, and blood squirted afresh from every scab on his arms & legs, as does pus from a boil; and the sky glared the color of blinding dust. Then they beat their *Tavu-lulcu,* which is the Turkishe drum. Now to try his strength the Turkes lifted another slave up to the block — a great Negro, fat as a July fish! — and by diverse gestures which they made, Smith grew to understand that they wanted him to fight with this fellow, who'd never provoked him or done him any harm. The Negro uttered words in some strange & churlish language, 'though he grinned at Smith most cheerfully. — O yes, it's danc-ing on the green that we must do, said Smith, and (altho' it ached him in his immortal soul to play such tricks) he struck the Negro a blow in his chitter-lings whilst he was still smiling. Thus did our hero honor Maister *Machi-avell.* And the Negro, he folded up like a hinged Bible! He hissed, and his eyes rolled up. (Captaine Duxbury, you did teach John well.) The Turkes

shouted, but were they pleas'd or did they but give order for his funeral?
Sweet John stood alone, waiting — waiting a good score of miles inside the
crowd of white yearling goats that churned the sand and peered o'er each
other's heads; a dozen miles within the wall of sheep dirty white & black;
encircled by tall camels. When the Negro began to struggle to his feet,
Smith tripped him and smashed him down. Then he rolled him off the
block with his foot.

He waited. He was no boy anymore. He'd learned how to wait now.

'Twas Bashaw Bogall (whose name means *Grocer*) who bought him as a
present for his faire Mistresse, one *Charatza Tragabigzanda*.

✳ ✳ ✳ ✳ ✳ ✳

See John Smith panting through his mask of sweat as the Broker leads him
away, .17.th man upon a chain of .30.. Constantinople's walls have swallowed him. Mosques bulge like unto jeweled bubbles 'twixt the trees. One
by .1., the new-bought slaves are unhooked to be pulled down into their
various pits of servitude. Sweet John trudges ragged and clinking, but not
much bowed. He's ready & eager for grace. He's prayed this morn as e'ery
other. The wretch behind him treads upon his heels; the wretch before
sings a sad song in an unknown tongue. They stop again. The Broker un-
locks Smith's ankle-chains and slaps his buttocks, not unkindly or lewdly;
he knows that Smith cannot hark to Turkishe words, and therefore shews
his intentions & expresses his commaund as he would with a bullock or a
lamb, urging him forward. Obediently, Smith falls out of ranks. Two boys
mock him from the doorway of a Bowyer's shop. Veiled women with bundles of straw on their heads slowly cross the road, gazing down most shyly.
A small boy trips him, but the father comes running, shouts and shakes the
child, then gives Smith a piece of Turkishe bread. Smith smiles and bows
to thank him, though all Turkes are idolators. Hoping confidence fills his
stomach, bite by bite. Far away, back home at Castle Grimsthorpe, he'd often seen upon the railings busts of crowned Saracens smiling haughty and
serene beneath cockeyed moustaches; each of these represented the crest of
my Lord Willoughby. Those ironwrought Turkes had seemed easy enough
fellows to deal with — and now he possesses .3. of their heads on his own
crest! Besides, he kens Machiavelli . . . The Slave-Broker snickers at something unknown. Mostly the Turkes evince sparkling humor today, it being
their grand festival called *Coochick Bayrum,* when their *Ramadan
Month* is done. But now the sputum-splashed sidewalls narrow, and
thus proportionately Sweet John's courage. He gazes about him wide-eyed,

marching at the end of the Broker's iron leash. His own death grows in his breast. He sees wooden stands of meat, red with yellow fat. He remembers what some drunken lozel once told him in High Hungaria: *The Turkes are cannibals!* Could this be the flesh of Christians he sees for sale? Is it their aim to eat him? The Broker brings him to a door, which is a plate of green copper like unto ancient armor, and the door opens and inside stands another slave and behind him Tragabigzanda's mother, an ancient dame (or *Beezel* as we say in Lincolnshire) who, seeing Smith, quickly pulls a fold of yellow cloth over her mouth with .2. fingers; and then Ladies like unto monarch butterflies do swarm & flutter laughingly about; and in the coolest shadows dwells Tragabigzanda, wearing a robe decorated with purple & orange flowers. She sits cross-legged on a carpet drinking tea. The cup glistens dully in her hand. Slowly, very slowly, she looks up.

✳ ✳ ✳ ✳ ✳ ✳

See John Smith . . . well, let's see John Smith. How does he appear? Arctic-whiskered, large of forehead, with twinkling eyes. He puts hand on hip, t'other hand on the pommel of his sword, preferring not to scrape ungracious bows. Such is his portrait. And even though his eyes do not twinkle now, and his hands are chained, and he has no sword, Tragabigzanda, Greekish-blooded, smiles and covers not her face. Her mother reproves her.

Sweet John bows low & murmurs: *Your most humble Servaunt.*

✳ ✳ ✳ ✳ ✳ ✳

See Tragabigzanda as doth the Turkishe sun, in a hat as tall & narrow-tapered as the spire of a Church. She *will* guard her whiteness. She wears silver bangles on her arms, and a necklace of silver at her throat.

✳ ✳ ✳ ✳ ✳ ✳

Semi-impeachable sources in the British Museum report that the harshly tuneless clamor of bells which issued from that crowded ruined tower in France at the exact moment that Cursell fell to the ground, striking like unto the very clapper of a bell — that all the rusty tones and warped echoes were scattered somehow by the *breathing* of those who watched. I long to say that Tragabigzanda's quick soft respirations likewise softened the rattle of Sweet John's chains! But did they? We cunning between-the-lines Readers suspect that in time she blessed him by her gracious embracing, that she meant to make an Officer of him, in order to marry with him in all honor as soon as she would be of age — *marry with him?*   quite so, for in that halcyon epoch of Turkishe grandeur, even a slave could hope to whip others, were he only patient through his years of ambitious submission. (Thus, so the Rector had sought most unsucessfully to explain, runs likewise the Law of Drapers' Apprentices.) — And was John Smith to be whipped, then?   Perhaps I do anticipate the entertainment o'er hastily. Know this: Tragabigzanda's intentions prov'd better than the best — and he encouraged their further engorgement with the most delicate feats of fishery (to catch gudgeon, take a small hook, then crucify the least red worm, lowering him gently down to the bottom where the finny prey doth live). Nay, 'twas not he meant to trick her, nor set a snickle for her heart; he but sought to *soften* her heart; most materially did he need kindness . . . Once he kenned (if only a little) how to twist his tongue in Turkishe jibber-jabber, he began his accustomed wenchwork by exploding the fable of Bashaw Grocer, who'd verily claimed, poor man, in the cloyingly ardent letter which accompanied his walking gift, to have gained possession of Smith by besting him in single combat. — 'Tis G O D's truth, my Lady, that I never spied this Bashaw until they sold me haggling & bragging on the block in Axopolis, and he pinched my muscles!

Tragabigzanda sighed in amazement.

* * * * * *

Having tumbled the aforesaid Grocer out from her affections, he grew more ardent (in the snatched moments he could steal from his drudgery); he was but craving help from her finer nature.

Her mother sent him for wood. Seeing how melancholy Tragabigzanda became whilst he was away, she permitted him to wait upon them both . . .

He could scarcely comprehend any syllable they said.

In his mind he compiled his meaning as he had leisure, calling to remembrance every Turkishe word he knew; these mouth-Soldiers he impressed into double & triple duty. He told them more tales of his piracy and doughty deedsmanship, expressing with his hands what his syllables could not, so that the mother covered her mouth with her sleeve, and laugh'd.

* * * * * *

She recollected some few *Italian* words which she'd learned while still a girl in Greekish Trebizond; he for his part remembering diverse syllables from his sojourn in Rome, their courtship did now commence to go *Allegro*.

* * * * *

Tragabigzanda fed him on *Samboyses* and *Muselbits* (which are great danties to these heathens, and yet but round pies). Out of fear that her mother might sell him (as she explained), she sent him to her brother, to better learn the language, and thence by laborious degrees to comprehend what it was to be a Turke. How began *that* adventure? From a cobalt-glazed penbox cunningly painted with flowers and surahs she withdrew a quill, and, prettily biting her underlip as she peeped at him, ground the inkstone in the water-dish, then wrote a letter with many a Turkishe flourish. John Smith knew that this writing must concern him, since his Mistress did snicker at him as she wrote, clapping her hand over her mouth to modestly bewray her mirth. From her he feared nothing, so he sat in patience, striving to appear gallant like a new coin, in order that her winsome tricks might best advantage him. What did his own heart utter? Sad to say, hearts oft think upon themselves. It loved Tragabigzanda — but it loved her best *afterward,* in Virginia, once peril had been long englamored into story. It tried to compose itself after the fashion of Maister Bartty, who continued as popular with women as mockado cloth. How could Sweet John's heart sow for its own harvest? Beneath the Arabic-blazened lamps of silvered glass in Tragabigzanda's house, a servantmaid washed his hands in an ivory bowl which was inscribed with longtailed purplish characters of their devilish writing. Tragabigzanda placed the quill in his grip, clasping her fingers around his, with fluency equal to his own as he did inscribe in the spot where she directed:

Captaine John Smith, free man of England, all glory to the Almightie.

Thus he delivered himself, to what bargain he knew precisely not, but in this World, aren't most promises made in ignorance?

On the day of his departure, she dressed in silken garments embroidered with gold and pretended to go a-weeping o'er the graves, as is the custom in those heathenish Countreys, but then she slipped away before the others could miss her, found John Smith, & kissed him on the mouth.

* * * * *

See John Smith sailing, captive, by way of *Sander, Screwe, Panassa, Musa, Lastilla,* then *Varna,* prescript town of sea-halts, where

Turkes do love to stop in the brass-lamped Mosques to pray according to their diabolical ceremonies. While he stands chained to a horsepost, .2. small boys throw stones with Satanic accuracy. The .1.st rock numbs his shoulder; the .2.nd strikes the crown of his head, raising a bleeding lump; when he turns away to guard his face, the .3.rd smashes him on the back of the neck, as idle Turkes of all ages watch, just like the spectators leaning against the railings of each of the .3. circular levels at the Globe Theatre in London, paid sluggards, never interfering with the staged murders of Lords' lives & Ladies' hearts. A dirty beggar child looks on, his cheeks dirty, his fingers twitching. When the .4.th stone thumps his ribs, Sweet John gives o'er his silent petitioning of street-Turkes, and bawls out full lustily, until subsequent to the .7.th stone his escort rears angrily out of Church, and the boys run gigglingly away to 'scape the whip. Back to the ship, doubly chained. He remembers how he used to go hawking with Bartty. On days when he'd rendered good service, Bartty sometimes allowed him to lock the hawks' ankles back in the silver varvels. See John Smith carried past the *Twin Capes* & the *Strait of Niger,* and so on deeper into Tartaria — but with such high hopes (Maister Hobbes writes that *hope* is desire accompanied by a belief that the desire will be fulfilled, whereas *de-spair's* the same desire, but with no prospect of fulfillment) — in a state of happy hope, as I say, so that his heart painted itself with flowers like the finest brocaded silk — Tragabigzanda is his! — and, what is more, has written to her brother that pretty epistle in the Turkishe language, asking that he use him fairly & well; soon he'll be considered a very Turke indeed, a Prince of Turkes! . . . and then he'll marry Tragabigzanda (as he now hath both pride & yearning to do, for methinks his fortune lieth that way — moreo'er, he would taste her Secret) . . . but when at last they'd reached the stony Castle of Nalbrits, the *Tymor* her brother, who wore a jade-handled knife inset with gems, sat frowningly down to read her lines, while Sweet John perforce must stand, no matter how dolorously heavy his chains; and at strange intervals the Tymor slashed his person with stern & angry eyes. Steeling himself to courtesy without abasement, he stared back at his new Master, remembering the flowers that Tragabigzanda liked: Tulips, hyacinths, lotuses. How did that letter put his case? Could he only read, speak, and steer the meaning into safe port in the Tymor's mind! Had she sheltered him beneath the wings of her love, or cruelly sported with him after all? Or (as he preferred to believe) did her affection wax madly be-yond maidenliness? Sure a kiss is a compact of faith! (Her lips were as pink as the sea-thirt flowers on the steep rocks of Castle Lindisfarne.) Laying the letter down, the Tymor clapped his hands with a noise like slamming doors, and call'd out a commaund whose echo fell flatly sullen into the stones; then for an after-clap his *Dragoman* came running, stripped Sweet John entirely naked, shaved his beard & head to monkishness, and riveted an iron collar about his throat so that he could barely breathe! To the encumbrance & mortification of this *Neck-bilbo* (as it might well be called) was welded another, in the form of a tall cross-rod which rose from the back of his choker like a plume of iron grass, curving most artistically high above his head, to embellish him in the manner of those *Branks,* or *Scolds' Bridles,* which he'd spied while marching through the German regions of Hungaria — a sight so strange & cruel (though doubtless wisely legislated, for the good of that Commonwealth): there he'd seen women being punished for shrews, who went about adorned with birdlike masks of heavy iron, or helmets fashioned to resemble pigs' heads; or weirdly ridiculous face-cages with heavy beaks or ears, all designed by their unrelenting weight to reduce those insolent hussies to obedience; and while at the sight he'd pitied them, still they must have been cross-grained and quarrelsome, or the Magistrates of those parts would never have condemned 'em. Now he too was punished after the same fashion: — the weight of that iron tusk or fang which he bore half strangled him ('though it was in no way comparable to the *Heretics' Forks* & *Dead-weight Collars* which they use nowadays in Venice). He became crazed.

* * * * * *

Seyyid Lokman, court poet of Murad III, who died but a handspan of years before Sweet John became a slave, once wrote the following lyric: *His hero's moustache was like fresh basil on a rosebud; his lips were pistachios.* Thus I envison the Tymor. Tragabigzanda was beautiful; why not let her brother be handsome? Suppose he was a dandy; mayhap he liked women & boys; belike his favorite pastime was listening to his Muscians play the *zurna* & the *tavululcu;* perhaps he preferred drinking with his young Pages. Of .1. thing, however, I am sure: he loved gardening — not as much, perhaps, as Mehmet II, who slit open a Gardener's stomach to recover his favorite cucumber, but surely enough to upbraid his vassals when they did not remove every weed — for he was liberal, but somewhat unforgiving.

* * * * * *

Month past month he was laboring in the garden with his best effort, but the Tymor ran to him shouting and began to beat him. Sweet John abhorred him more than his own death. The Tymor screamed in his ear. The Tymor kicked him in the mouth. The Tymor's face was as hellish as a glass-blower's oven. At the vortex of the pain, rage and shame that exploded from him, Sweet John grew calmer than Fate. There was a reaping-hook lying by. He seized it, and in .1. furtive blow smashed the Tymor's skull.

* * * * * *

What must Tragabigzanda have thought, when she heard the news? And Sweet John, did he e'er muse on her more than fancifully, & calculate whether he should have seen matters through, to become a Turke? Our knowledge of the girl herself's cropped down to this: He found her beautiful, like unto a very *Jewell* of gold. He'd gifted her but with her brother's Dead-March. Did he never love her as *you* love, Reader — or, loving her, did he misapprehend her brother's earnestness to set him properly on the cockaded path? Did the Tymor hate him for a desperate Christian who must not be granted his sister's maidenhead? Had Smith stayed, labored & borne, would he have been but translated into corpse-manure for the Tymor's cucumbers? Had Tragabigzanda dispatched him eastward for a test he failed on account of his excessive self-love? Or was it meant merely to revenge herself on Bashaw Grocer, whose lie she would punish by breaking the toy he'd given her? Had her mother insisted upon the apprenticeship, in order to separate the lovers? Had that kiss comprised a promise, an exhortation to hopefully endure — or fatality's seal? Which of those now long-perished persons devised most murtherously? This labyrinth, in which we Readers may discover our retroactive delight, not being ourselves confined in it, offers more than .1. moral exit. But whether Sweet John took the Tunnel of Callousness, the Tunnel of Righteousness (miscall'd *Analytic*), or the Tunnel of Misinterpretation, in any case the consequence prov'd the same, and he fled the Countrey of his slavery, looking o'er his shoulder: Run, Smith, run. *Come back, come back.* Motives rarely shine certain in his case. We are left only with the wavering sense of something which might have been, and was ruined.

* * * * * *

There was a song that he sang to himself as he wandered across the plains of Tartary, with the collar still on his neck. Cicely used to sing it as she played upon the virginals. The words were half a century old, and they went:

I am as I am and so I will be
But how that I am none knoweth truly.
Be it evil, be it well, be I bound, be I free,
I am as I am and so will I be.

There were other verses, which he disremembered. He sang this stanza over & over until his lips were rivelled with thirst. He never thought of Cicely.

ARGALL (??–??)

This angel-devil thus shrined in my heart,
This dragon having got the golden fruit,
My very soul to him I did impart.
SIR FRANCIS HUBERT, "The Life and Death of Edward II" (1568?)

What and where was Argall during this time? I don't rightly know.
He penned no *Generall Historie,* to petrify his tracks! Commerce's
votary, he set out to die rich — no time to consort with Printers down at the
Ink-man's Church-yard. I read that he was born in 1572 in Bristol-Towne.
Another history doth make it 1580; a **.3.**rd, 1585. He might have died in
1633, or 1626 — at any rate, by 1641, & doubtless in hope of his body's resurrection. But with Argall nothing's doubtless. He glimmers in the marges
of this Dream, doing unpredictable deeds, then vanishes again.* He sings
bland songs. Just as air may invisibly contain within it clouds, lightnings,
rain, storms, &c, yet shew nothing of itself to our eyes, so euerworthy Argoll
doth hum & sweep ubiquitously over all. See him hard at school, yea, 'midst
schools of gaunt sailing-ships with their squarish standards forward. Argall *will* get his trade. — I scarcely ken whence sprang his success. Sweet
John was no less avaricious, and more bustling, but Sweet John . . . Could it
have been that Argall came into the world untainted by Fens? Is he
craftier? Luckier? I misdoubt me not his family owned means. His father
was *Esquire of East Sutton* in Countie Kent, as they do say; his
mother was a Knight's daughter. He himself would be knighted someday,
altho' for deeds or blood I judge not. Compass'd all about by success; he
hides himself in it; he lurks in it like unto a very *Sharke.*

Enough. From Bristol-Towne can a fellow smell the sea? I was never in
that hive. Let's look it up in Speed's *Atlas.* 'Tis somewhat inland, I see, in
Countie Gloucestershire, bestriding the river Avon in many a nested curl of

---

*John Smith's biographer writes that "the name, Arkil in Danish, seems to have meant 'eagle,' but
this is uncertain and relatively unimportant." There you have it.

red-roofed houses; but close enough to the Ocean to have absorb'd the bulk of the Irish trade, & the codfish merchauntry also. Maister Speed doth encomiumize: BRISTOW *is one of the greatest and famous Cities in England . . . Ther is no dunghill in all yᵉ Cittie nor any Sinke that cometh from any house into yᵉ Streets but all is conveyd vnder ground . . .* So too with Argall's life & education: 'Tis achieved most subterraneously. Nobody ascertains him. His mind gnaws, foraging 'mongst those long skinny hulls-and-masts which resemble the skeletons of fabulous fishes from the time of Genesis — picked clean now that e'erworthy Argall has dined! Never mind. There'll be more.

Perhaps he learns a little law there in Bristow. How else could he have become Deputy Governor of Virginia so wisely? He learns Adventuring, Undertaking, & Enclosure. — O, but who kens what he learns? I just now married another book which whispers that he never was born in Bristol, but (which rings more plausible) at his good Pater's equerry, *the manor of East Sutton, near Maidstone, Kent* — another Countie entirely, which comprehends at its northernost marge a certain stinking terminus of lives & dreams, call'd *Gravesend.* In that case, Argall might as well be Gravesend's *Genius loci,* or *tutelary spirit* as I'll write less Greekishly. Well, well. Maidstone's but a broad-steepled red Church (so Speed delineates it) hid betwixt a river-vein & a diagonal range of hills **.1.** of which is labeled *Vintners.* Does Argall grow up sancitifed by the scent of wine-grapes? I search most toilsomely for *the manor of East Sutton,* but descry it not. Did Maister Speed Adventure there for a glass of milk, & find himself turn'd away? Or was it hid behind the pregnant Church? Percase my eyes blear. 'Swounds, this Thames-topp'd Countie wearies me! It's utterly encharneled by Gravesend . . . Lift up mine eyes, O LORD! Where's Captaine Fortune? I stray to a dense-rigged ship whose sails are puffed fat by a westerly breeze; she's sailing scudding seaward from Gravesend, percase to Adventure or to Undertake somewhat. Could Argall lie already aboard her with his estates roll'd up under his arm? That must be why I can't discover *the manor of East Sutton.* With Argoll gone, it folds itself into the ground, like those rickety gypsy booths from last month's fair. On this atlas-page Speed shews us Canterbury & Rochester, together with **.7.** coats of arms — none of them Argall's. I'm mazed, poleaxed, stupefied. Argoll's trick'd me again.

He hunts for worlds, & sluppers them down. He speeds infallibly on his chase. He navigates doubtfulness into solid land. He's the trump of fate.

He's our Shepherd, our monster, our cornerstone. He expedites. He em-
balms sugar-fancies into codfish-cash. Singing softly wherever he goes, he
binds Salvages according to our necessity. Harbors spring up at his touch;
Virginia dies, & returns unto life an English maid. Now where is he? My
servile eyes cannot spy him; he's embodied Absence; he's a fist in a cloud.
Altho' I named this book for him, I can't compass him. I'm conquered.

So pray allow me to keep on with the history of *Captaine John
Smith.**

*Unlike most authors, who demand a long and weary perusal from beginning to end, I never for-
get the convenience of my readers. My books are unfailingly brief, and I never swerve from my
point. Hence my titles, misses, and blind languishments of words.

THE GRAMMAR OF BACKSTABBERS
(1605–1606)

As we should expect, this caste-like status group operated not in a traditional but in a charismatic setting.

ARTHUR SCHWEITZER, *Big Business in the Third Reich* (1964)

*A*fter sundry miserable wanderings, that youngish Soldier return'd to England (thanks to the charity of his fellow Christians) with scant honor-timber to show for himself, excepting **.1.** his coat of arms, which warm'd him more poorly, by my faith, than **.1.** of wool or leather; **.2.** his pension from a foreign Emperor which I don't suppose he could collect (the mails being irregular in those days), and **.3.** his commission confirming him in the rank of *Captaine over* **.200.** *and* **.50.** *horsemen.* And 'twas monstrous disconvenient to get that much, for he had to journey out of his way. — O, but why do I carp? For his erstwhile Emperor (Sigismund of Hungaria) did pay him **.15.** hundred ducats, when he stopp'd by. (John kept that treasure well hid 'twixt the plates of his brigandine vest.) And (panoramas being eye-riches) he saw *Leipzig, Dresden, Wittenberg, Frank-furt, Paris, Whore's-Quim, Angiers, Bilbao, Gibraltar, Tangier, Marrakesh,* and *Tenerife* (where he again turn'd Pirate), so that he filled & fulfilled himself with diverse new strangenesses. He learn'd how to navigate by the Guard Starres, and when to salute a Spanish Lady, & why one must attend the *Zenith,* where all meridians meet. How fared his **.1500.** ducats by the end? Had Captaine Fortune added to, or subtracted from 'em? No doubt in his piracy he made such shift as he could, to enlarge his means. But how *fared* he? — Neither wisely nor well, I trow; otherwise he'd have stayed Pirate! Instead, with his spirit be-clouded by poverty's breath, he did wash up again at Gravesend, where various Watermen now commenc'd to remember him, and hung admiringly upon his arms-coat (which delineated **.3.** *Tvrkes' heads identickall and*

riven clean; dark-eyed, white-teethed & mvtchado'd they were, capp'd with
the ovtlandish headgear of those heathen Covntreys; and 'tis meet yov know
that those **III** *exotickall Brain-boxes fac'd sideways most tastefvlly vpon a*
green shield bisected by a red chevron like vnto a stream of blood; then vpon
this shield perched a shining helm, fitting throne for a bird that clvtched a
lvcky horseshoe in his beak; and all this was flovrished very richly abovt
with red & white tassels), so that he must dispose of his Water-fellows with
too noble a coin. 'Tis expensive to be famed in Gravesend. Now he's
hounded and hunted by smallpoxed tipplers. Looks he to 'scape them for
newness? Reader, bide with him more murky-fathomed moments. Virginia's almost on him. Father Christmas will tuck into his double-locked
Counsell-box the title deed to a Virginian Towne entire, once the Salvages
there should be removed. But that's yet .**1,000**. labors away. Return to
Angle-Land's Fenland he must. How could OUR REDEEMER permit
aught else? How could OUR REDEEMER's springloaded pit-trap call'd
Gravesend disgorge *any* of us living dead for more than a space? Worthy
Lazarus, and JESUS even, how long did they walk this dirt after their re-
births from within it? JESUS went up, and Lazarus down; hence John
Smith, bred in the Fens, must return to ooze. — Welladay, he hires his
Watermen, arming their envy with his III Tvrkes' heads, & up-rivers again
to *London Towne* (longitude .**19**. degrees .**54**. minutes, latitude .**51**. de-
grees .**32**. minutes) to see about new employment.

   Upon entering that city (which is shapen like unto a bent bow), he spied
a shackled band of robbers being marched off to be hanged. Above the
noose each head would soon nod like the fat yellow dandelions of
Willoughby. He knew it all. Striding away, he found a public house, where
he had a pint. Not half-bad, but his stomach snickled him into buying other
stuff. A Captaine he was, but O so hungry! The candle-flame flickered
over the dark continents of his kidney pie, and some trollop with a sweet
voice was singing and pounding on the table, and a man was laughing and
a man was sneezing. Near the door, .**2**. young Gentlemen sat a-smoking
the Salvage herb call'd *Tobacco,* which Sir Walter Ralegh so greatly affected. These coistrels cared not that the leaf came from *Spanish Amer-*
ica, so that the sum they frittered upon their vice did but swell our
enemies' coffers. O, they joyed in their smoke-tricks! They performed *the*
slights: — to wit, .**1**.ˢᵗ *the Gulpe*, .**2**.ⁿᵈ *the Retention,* then .**3**.ʳᵈ *the Cuban*
Ebolition. Sweet John laughed at their waggishness. 'Twas a blot upon
'em, to be sure, but what had he to do with Gentlemen's consciences? Their

smoke did most prettily tickle his throat. He'd already inhaled the like during his sojourns of Piracy.*

Commaunding another toddy, he began to dream great dreams. He'd be a Prince. The shadows of his fingers, huge & stubby behind the candle, grabbled upon the wall. The candle had wings like unto an Angel. The flame pulsed and bowed like unto a white egret's head. The fireplace was very black. He regarded the snail-spirals of grease upon his plate and thought upon ooze.

The repast proved dear. He slammed his tuppences down in a pet and went out. His heavy bootsteps tolled *Come back, come back.*

All was altered by the tides of time. Her Majesty the Queen had given up the ghost (out of melancholy, they said, at being forced to treat with the Irish rebel Tyrone), and *James of Scotland* was now King. (He'd denounced *Tobacco* as *this filthy novelty.*) Better not try the Palace again, thought Sweet John to himself. 'Tis said the King's miserly. Percase I'll found me a Colonie in *Ireland* . . . — but then he heard that the Salvages there were devilish & hateful, perfect miniatures of Tyrone. — No matter: Sweet John knew how to burn & slay! 'Twas the way of the World. Ireland lay miraculously green, a drunkard said. A bankrupt Captaine muttered about hoards of Irish gold. Sweet John grew passing hot to hear. Lord Chichester was Viceroy there now, 'twas said. Alas, he own'd no acquaintanceship with Lord Chichester. That Irish Jesuit to whom Father Parsons had introduced him might serve his turn . . . — but nay! 'Twould be deadly dangerous, to consort with Popery in Ireland. — Percase I'll sail under *Ralegh,* he calculated, longing for Captaine Fortune — but a wily Waterman told him that Ralegh lay in the Tower again, on suspicion of some Spanish treason; in his despair this Ralegh had e'en (fearing not GOD's judgment for such an act) stabbed himself in the breast — failing, however, to deeply engrave the wound. 'Twas rumor'd he cultivated Tobacco in his prison, to pass the time.

So Sweet John searched for new honeycombs. — Percase I'll join *Sir Oliph Leigh* in Guinea. Percase I'll . . . —

John Smith, having seen about his employment indeed, having seen that there was none, returned by stages to Willoughby in Lincolnshire, *.1. of the most brute and beastly shires of the whole realm,* as our late King Henry

---

*See how a travel'd mind doth travel itself to a standstill! Too many sights & comparisons roost upon its lodgepoles.

had memorialized it; Countie Lincoln where the trees were still partially
bare, it being springtime; their branches reached up toward the sun like
unto the veins in bloodshot eyeballs. With the Fens in their season of flood,
his road proved monstrous difficult. Indeed, as he everywhere was told, the
dykes of the East Fens had been overthrown by rain, so that filthy waters
sped over *Leake, Leverton, Benington* & all those Townes, tickling
hogs, sheep, cows, chickens and people down to a cold and gurgling death.
'Twas said Friskney was islanded again, as she'd been back in Roman times;
Black Dyke was overthrown. The Fendike bank between Saint Marie's
and All Hallows still held but for how long? My poor Countie! thought
Sweet John, strangely sad and guilty that he'd been away. As for The
Deepes, now they were truly become *the deepes;* mayhap they hid *Mermaids* and *Alligators*, altho' only OUR REDEEMER knew ... When
he got to Wainfleete All Souls, the Under-Sheriff impressed him to mend
the embankments for .3. days, which he did with a will, entertaining his
fellow diggers with relations of the Turkes. They ask'd him if 'twas true
that those heathens worship'd SATAN, and he said that they did. They
ask'd him how relished the Turkishe maidens' Secrets, at which he smil'd
and would not answer. An old Papist pray'd him to discourse about Rome,
which he granted. One night in his inn he shewed some men his coat of
arms, with the .3. Turkes' heads; and mouths dropped open; they all gathered gawp-seed, as we say here in Lincolnshire. He had wanderer's eyes by
then; in faraway parts he missed his home Countie, but as soon as ever he
came back, life nauseated him, which showed in his sad, sunken gaze. On
the .4.th day the Under-Sheriff released him with thanks. He passed the
farmers a-rowing to market in their little cock-boats, or *shouts*. None
smoked *Tobacco* yet; Lincolnshire lay e'er behind London-Towne in
those fads. Dyke by dyke, ditch by ditch he went northwest, until he could
roll his soaking stinking breeches back down again and tread upon firmer
ooze. Ahead he spied Saint Helena's Church where he'd been baptized.
The Rector was plucking weeds from between the tombstones — still Reverend Sadler, older than ever, ensconced in Willoughby most immortally.
He stood up to serve the stranger a long slow look from which any recognition had decayed; John Smith therefore ungreeted him. The Rector's eyes
grew anxious. Was this some dangerous cutpurse or vagabond who was
tramping nigh? *Come back, come back, come back.* Sweet John was almost upon him now. Half asphyxiated by his own despondent rage, which
itself was half stifled by the pressure of dreamlike associations, he stopped.
He could not e'en curse. His lack of civility (we need not say "misliking")

evidently accomplished its own work of associations within the Rector's discrimination: this sullen, ill-kempt young Soldier who denied to say good day & who seemed to know his way around Willoughby — why, he could only be . . . Remembrance flooded the pale and marshy cheeks with recognition from both eye-ponds. Was he weeping? Nay, 'twas but the wind, which tickled the old man's rheumy nature. He cleared his throat, his gullet working to prepare the words *O it's you then, John* or *Back from the wars again, John?* or *You look a sight, John* or *Back to bide with us awhile, John? Why can you never find your happiness?* or *Welcome home, John* or *Welcome home forever, John*. Inhaling that strangely clean smell of muck as he watched the cloud-darkenings on shimmering emerald fields, the prodigal fingered a thick oily chestnut bud. In the end the Rector likewise uttered nothing. Onward limped our Captain Smith, his wrists and ankles scarred from the Tymor's chains. His mother lay dead of a fever, 'twas said. O'er in Sloothby his sister Alice had also perished, leaving her husband with another infant, called Alice for her sake, whom they counted to be a most attractive child. Another babe had slept in the Church yard almost a year now, beside his .2. brothers. Ralph Nightingale had been killed in a fall from a horse; Cicely was now married again with a Sow-gelter from Harlescott, by name one *Edward Bellowes*. She'd grown stout, Frauncis said; John would see for himself next Sunday in Church. Her baby did thrive. Cicely's father, old Maister Reese Allen, remained in life. Sweet John, suffering from a monstrous appetancy to shew off his coat of arms, call'd upon him at Belgreave, *Pen & ink, pen & ink*. As he waited to be shown in, he felt uneasy; he could not have said why. But Maister Allen arose; he took the younger man's hands in his. Already Sweet John was thinking to himself: I'll tell Frauncis that Maister Allen took good notice of my approach. And he smiled. They greeted each other most merrily. Because the company of Cicely could no longer be his object, he remained unswayed by the tuggings of diffidence. It seemed to him that his late experiences on the Continent comprised an inexhaustible wealth; for he failed to forsee himself in those wearisome ancient people who tell the same tale .20. times. Captain Fortune was with him: John's stories were not yet exhausted. Indeed, Maister Allen had become more convinced than ever before of the immense importance to England of *Navigation,* and so he wished to learn whether we might easily wrest the *Affrickan* trade from Spain (Sweet John assured him that we could), and whether 'twas too late for us to pluck a city of gold from *America* (Sweet John promised him that it wasn't). — I believe that we should wait upon our most politic opportunity, said his host, who'd waited upon everything for his entire life. Sweet John won a game of Tick-Tack, lost at Lurch. He did not want to be cautious. But now, by means of a channel as well-smoothed as Fossdyke Drain, the water of words had flowed, from the necessity for delay in implementing any new measures all the way down to reminisences of the discreditable olden times. Maister Allen could remember when the Papists adored ashes on Ash Wednesday and palms on Palm Sunday, as if those things were GODS. And these ceremonies had occurred not only in Lincoln-Towne (which lay far enough away to be almost an alien demesne) but in Willoughby itself. Well-travel'd altho' he was, Sweet John felt justified repulsion towards these mental pictures. A pagan Willoughby! 'Twas eerie. A pagan Rome or Constantinople was natural. Besides, he long'd to speak on about himself. His host surveyed him from shrewd and tired orbs inflamed like setting suns, listening to all his tales. Of his commision and coat of arms he did remark: I see you're well fitted for martial affairs, my lad. Cicely was e'er fond of you. She . . . Now pray tell me again what pass'd through your soul when you discover'd yourself at single combat with .3. of those heathens? — Maister Allen further inquired of him (since John had visited several Catholic Countreys) whether the Papists were really behind the Gunpowder Plot to blow up our King. John was sure of it. Pouring him a cup of cinnamon-water with his own trembling hands, Maister Allen smiled sweetly.

In the yew-shaded Church yard he found his father and mother's graves both covered with creepers, which he cut away with his dagger and his bodkin, as the Rector had not yet gotten to them. The rolled golden glove of a cowslip flourished in a field across the way. He plucked it up and laid it on his mother's stone, which bordered the monument to Maister Martin Johnson. He took a broadcloth cloth & scrubbed his father's grave. Why didn't his brother keep it clean? But Frauncis had a son and .2. daughters, all of whom did thrive. He scarce had time to wink, so he put it, squirming his fingers and ducking his brother's eye; his business took him monthly to Alford, where he did much trade with merchants from Sloothby and Hogsthorpe. That was how he'd chanced to see their sister Alice so often, while she'd remained in life. Wheat prices were back up to .32. shillings, he said. He'd sown more wheat this spring, but a flood had marshified his fields, and he feared the grain would rot. The Parish had appointed .2. new Alms Collectors, and he didn't know how much they'd assess him. And had anyone informed Sweet John that there'd been a murrain almost as severe as the sheep-rot of '86? (No, John replied. That was the .1.ˢᵗ he'd heard.) Well, Frauncis had lost half a dozen lambs, and must now work harder than e'er to repair his loss. Speaking of which, Frauncis had heard from the Mayor's lad in Alford that the plague had fallen again upon Lincoln-Towne. Was that true? (Yes, said John.) Had he come that way? (No, said John.) Forgive him for asking, but had he lent out his clothes to anyone near there? He didn't want Anna to take sick. Under any other circumstances she'd gladly mend them, of course. As John himself could see, she was big with child again. — Soon, in fact, she was delivered of a .**3**.rd daughter, who would also be nam'd Alice. One pays nothing for christenings in Lincolnshire, but after the birth of a child one must give the Rector .**4**.*d.* to have the woman Churched. John felt that he ought to pay, for once again he was levying a burthen upon Frauncis and his family. But he himself did not want to put the money in the Rector's hand. He counted out the .**4**. coins and gave them privily to Frauncis, who thanked him . . . Never mind, replied the Tymor's slave, accompanying them in all love to sit beneath the dank high ceiling of Saint Helena's, where he himself had been christened a quarter-century previous. — Welcome home, again John, the Rector said, as if they hadn't met. 'Pon my word, you look well summered. — Little Alice Smith cried when the Rector sprinkled her from the fount. Frauncis, fresh-scrubbed beside her, beet-red and oafish, was grinning with pride. John Smith prayed that this baby might live. He prayed for Frauncis and Anna's happiness. He watched his despair rise up to the ogivearches which ended those .**2**. dank colonnades the congregation sat between.

Lord Willoughby had died in Berwick — O, .**4**. years since, it was, John, said Barty, upon whom he called at Grimsthorpe Castle, riding up on a borrowed horse of Frauncis's (Anna had grudged the loan). — 'Twas the gout that did for him. He died a tremendous ugly death. Nay, you won't find him here. He wanted to be buried at Eresby. And Aunt Susie said . . . — Barty kept talking. He sported the diamond ring which his father had gotten from the King of France. Seeing him possessor of so proud a gift, the visitor thought upon Robert, the .**1**.st-born, the heir, and asked if he still made war in France? — Nay, said Barty, swallowing. He's married and gone to Spain, to be the King's Ambassador. But I— I mislike to talk about him here, for he loves me not . . . — Forgive me, my Lord, said Smith. We were playmates at school. I meant not to clamor to your distress . . . — Nay, quoth Barty. Now tell me where thou hast been, dear friend. And then we'll go a-hunting, eh?

For a keepsake Bartty did engift him with leathern-bound old *Machi-*

avell. Sweet John had already heard that the bower wherein he'd read that volume stood now enclosed by proud rich men; and the half-wit who'd brought him berries had died of plague.

As ever, he felt humiliated in Bartty's society. Bartty was generous; he'd favored him with many a boon, but—

Bartty said: How stand your fortunes?

Better than before. Howbeit—

I misdoubt me not. Listen, you. Robert bides yet in London-Towne with his bride, as I trow. He'll sail from Gravesend round about the heel of April, when some Spaniard comes in. He might pull you up from the ooze again, if his stomach's willing.

I thank you, Sweet John said, loathing the conception of any further interview with Robert. Surely 'twould be better to return to *Affricka,* which he could easily do . . .

Again he dared to visit his now very aged guardian Maister George Mettham, in defiance of the ban that had been put upon him, and was gratified to find that he'd risen sufficiently in that Gentleman's esteem (like unto the Arabian bird call'd *Phoenix*) to be received. Maister Mettham had grown shiny, pockmarked & grey like unto a cannonball. He poured out a dram of aqua vitae for his guest. He'd once gone for a Soldier himself, & so discoursed with much knowledge upon the *Italians* with their long blow-pipes. Sweet John shewed his coat of arms, which Maister Mettham monstrous cordially praised, repeating: Well, well. So you've been within demiculverin-shot of those infidels. Tell me, John, whether it's true their eyes are aslant? — But when Smith turned upon the matter of his visit, the old man turn'd passing hard-mouthed: — I've told you many times that whatever inheritance your father might have left has been spent on death-duties and other sums. The **.10.** shillings I gave you came out of my own pocket. But you have no gratitude, do you? *Mettham gave me some measly groats to be rid of me,* he says. *Mettham never loved me or did anything for me,* he says. *Mettham took my inheritance and hoarded it in a hollow tree,* he says. You see, I know what you say. I s'pose you want another **.10.** shillings. Well, you won't have it, d'you hear? You dare to spread slanders about me, & then disremember that I have ears! As the saying goes, *A bitch that is in haste brings forth blind puppies.* Now take your unsightly person and your **.3.** Turke's heads out of my house.

It was time to try something else. Fortunately, it was just then that Sweet John happened to discover

THE CHARTER OF VIRGINIA (1606)

James, by the Grace of God, King of England, Scotland, France, & Ireland, Defender of the Faith, etc.: Whereas **Our** loving & well-disposed subjects, SIR THOMAS GATES, & SIR GEORGE SOMERS, Knights, RICHARD HACKLUIT, Clerk, Prebendary of Westminister, & EDWARD-MARIA WINGFIELD [whom I, William the Blind, must warn you, Reader, will prove to be John Smith's flim-flam Nemesis], THOMAS HANHAM, and RALEIGH GILBERT, Esquires, WILLIAM PARKER and GEORGE POPHAM, Gentlemen, & diverse others of **Our** loving subjects, have been humble suitors unto **Us,** that **We** would vouchsafe unto them **Our** license, to make Habitation, Plantation, and to deduce a Colonie of sundry of **Our** people into that part of AMERICA commonly called **Virginia,** & other parts and territories in AMERICA, either appertaining unto **Us,** or which are not now possessed by any Christian Prince or people, situate, lying, and being all along the sea-coasts, *between .34.° of northerly latitude from the Equinocktiall Line, and .45.°of the same latitude, and in the Mainland between the same .34.° and .45.°, and the Islandes thereof adjacent or within .100. miles of the coast thereof:*

... **We,** greatly commending and graciously accepting of, their desires for the furtherance of so noble a work, which may, by the Providence of the ALMIGHTIE *GOD,* hereafter tend to the glory of *His Divine Majesty,* in propagating of Christian religion to such people as yet live in **darkness** & MISERABLE IGNORANCE of the true knowledge and worship of GOD, and may in time bring the infidels and savages living in those parts to human civility and to a settled and quiet government, do, by these **Our** letters patent, graciously accept of, and agree to, their humble and well-intended desires.

Reader, if you do wonder what lurk'd behind it all, well, the answer's within reach. The afore-mentioned RICHARD HACKLUIT, Clerk, Prebendary of Westminister, had already written a tract proposing that public stock be raised to pay for the discovery of wild places such as Virginia (a Countrey which like Lincolnshire is most infested with rain). Many reasons and causes were suggested for that endeavor, the most fundamental of them being: *It would savor too much of affectation of a popular state to levy monies without imparting some convenient portion to His Majestie.*

LETTER FROM A LEFTHANDED MAN
(1585)

He is well paid that is well satisfied.
SHAKESPEARE, *The Merchant of Venice,* (1596–97), IV.II (Portia)

*F*orgive me, cheerful Reader, if I do now pause to tell thee that my late Lord Willoughby knew all about Virginia ages ago! About the time when John Smith was born, my Lord accepted into his household (in keeping with his policy of befriending the friendless) **.1.** *John Stubbe,* Gentleman, of Norfolk, who for scribbling a pamphlet entitled *The discoverie of a gaping gulf* paid with his right hand, which the common Executioner struck off at the wrist. For he'd dared to urge that Her Majestie unjilt the sad-eyed Duke of Anjou. Although 'tis true he'd **.2.**nd-guessed his betters, actual treason left no thwart-marks upon the thoughts of Maister Stubbe (who was but windy and foolish rather than ill-intentioned), and there's the reason Lord Willoughby saved him. Meek walked his new guest, and O so silent. But at night, while others slept, he did weep. And so a pair of years pass'd by. Robert was in those days scarce a babe, who did chew and suck upon his mother's dress, gazing at the world with nervous eyes. One day Maister Stubbes, gazing upon him, comprehended with all his soul: *This child shall be my Lord. This child shall be my life.* And, withdrawing himself apart, he did vow to the ALMIGHTIE henceforth to exist in quiet, obeying all authority set over him, for only thus could he hope to escape being snickled by dangerous thoughts. Just as in Willoughby the rich dark fields seem paler green when one leaves them and they dwindle into a cool spring evening, so his former ambitions dimmed & dewed, then were painlessly gone. In that season my Lord Willoughby was not much at home. Upon him among others had descended the duty of calling up a muster of Lincoln Towne against our Spanish enemies. But **.1.** day he came a-riding home just in time for supper. My Lady Willoughby ran to the doorway, smiled upon him and said there was beef with mustard. He gave his horse to the Groom-servant and washed his hands. All sat down. He knapped his knuckles on the table, as was his wont, and .2. varlets carried in the trenchers, which smoked and steamed most savorously. Lord Willoughby smiled. Stroking his hound's head beneath the table, he spied out Maister Stubbe, saying: John, wouldst thou care to offer thanks? and while all bowed their heads, Maister Stubbe did pray aloud in a trembling voice. He was only now learning to feed himself with his left hand full gracefully. In after days he applied himself well to serve his Lord, yet continued cheerless (or, as the Watermen say at Gravesend, he bore slack sail), so for his better encouragement my Lord Willoughby did send him on many an errand to London-Towne, to distract him and return with news. Mayhap this explicates why Stubbe curl'd his hair, as if he were a Courtier; he must needs mix with such persons. (Or did he still pretend to excellence? They say his wit stayed e'er too courtly for his station.)

One rainy day round about CHRISTmastide of the year of our redemption 1585, when Lord Willoughby chanced to be attending on King Frederick in the Realm of *Denmark,* a letter arrived from the aforesaid Stubbe regarding the return from Virginia of Sir Richard Grenville's ship. (To this Sir Richard I'll introduce you presently.) And the letter did say: *I thought not unfitt to send to you, that you might in those northest Countreys know also what is don in the Southwest. The speech is diverse touching the commodities of that voiage.* Exitus acta probat. *And yet in the meen whyle been ther endeavours honorable and praiseworthy to themselves and the land. Barbican, London, 'From your lordship's own howse'. JHOHN STUBBE, scaeva* — which latter appellation signifies in the Latin tongue *Lefthanded,* and which accordingly made Lord Willoughby smile. — By GOD, my fellow's got his grit back! he cried, and for mirth's sake shewed the signature to the other English Ambassadors.

I, William the Blind, suffer from my own vulgarity, being unlearned of both the Greekish and Latinish languages; yet this I do conjecture, that in naming himself *Scaeva,* Maister Stubbe did allude to .1. centurion of Julius Caesar's who was call'd the same, and who ador'd his Master and General so much, that he sacrificed his life for him in battle. Now, in truth, as Stubbe well knew, the best way to trick my Lord Willoughby's heart was to pretend one's identity with such examples: Lord Willoughby loved his vassals the more as they declared themselves so. In fine, the signature was worth more than the news. *Virginia?* He had no desire to go there. Of course he might have designed to Adventure in de-Virgin-ization, going shares with other Undertakers, gambling for Salvage or Spanish gold.

Howbeit, Lord Willoughby e'er preferred to keep an eye on his own business. He was no London-Towne spendthrift, gambling away .**100**. pounds for the hope of .**1,000**. *Virginia?* Mayhap a swindle, a sham, a shuck . . .

The following year came a plague in Lincolne Towne, which did most gruesomely abide until 1587. (That was when Lord Willoughby received his royal appointment to fill the dignity of the disgraced rebel Leicester, so that yet further tasks did enweb him according to his means.) Meanwhile the sheep were perishing of the rot, and many more drowned in floods; once again the Shepherds must carry their animals to Lincolne Towne Market in cock-shout boats. In the Wolds by Willoughby Towne 'twas better than in the Fens, but scores of dependents even there call'd on my Lord Willoughby for help. He laid by no time for Virginia.

The Grammar of Navigators
(CA. 500–1607)

It resteth I speake a word or two of the naturall inhabitants . . . that you may know, how that they in respect of troubling our inhabiting and planting, are not to be feared; but that they shall haue cause both to feare and loue vs, that shall inhabite with them.

THOMAS HARRIOT, *A Briefe and true report,*
Of the new found land of Virginia (1590)

Sweet Reader, for me to tell all principal Relations of Virginia in this little space, would be e'en the same endeavor, as for the rich man to ascend into Heaven through a needle's eye (as the Proverb doth say); nor 'tis it utterly needful to track the spoor of every historical personage, like unto some Hunter a-creeping after wild beasts in that forest call'd *Library,* whose leaves once graced living trees, which being cut down and transform'd into wood-pulp, then became Memory-Trees, whose fruits do wither into forgetfulness, and then cometh the second autumn, when yellow pages fall away.

So let us but name names: .1. King Arthur, who was everywhere, and .2. Malgo, who was nowhere, not to mention .3. that Black Sorcerer call'd Friar Nicolas of Lynne, who in 1360 flew to the North Pole by witchcraft — here I but steal names out of Captaine Smith's *Generall Historie,* and even he confesses he kens these personages not. Yet he did get 'prenticed to a great Merchaunt in that selfsame Linne, so we must give him credence regarding the Black Sorcerer's existence; no jackdaw caws falsely about its own nest. And if indeed Friar Nicholas visited the Arctick regions, then why not credit him likewise with the *Discoverie of Virgina,* a Countrey warmer and easier of access than any Ice Kingdome (and so fruitful, besides, that we'd better use the name *Vagina*)? Why not allow Friar Nicholas the honor of drinking first from the brown swamp-udders of Roanoke?.4. 'Tis .4.thly claimed that Madock Prince of Wales erected a Colonie somewhere in Virginia, *but where this place was,* Smith cheerfully adds, *no History can show.* **.5.** Fifth came **.1.** *Christopher Cullumbus,* about whom I was told in school, *He discovered America,* but did he? For Greenlanders, Yndians, & other such birds had already flown there. So now already dear Virginia hath **.5.** Gallants, who lie dead, lost and fabulous, like the **.5.** medieval Churches sunk beneath the sea between Skegness and Mablethorpe. Lincolnshiremen sail over them, a-coming and a-going from their Countie's silting harbors, but only when the tide lies sweet at her stillest ebb can they see the spires reaching upwards from the ooze. (I know not what else to say of those heroes, for I wasn't at their side; their deeds stand as fanciful as Pocahontas's statue.) **.6.** Near a century after the aforesaid *Cullumbus,* our own Sir Humphrey Gilbert (whose face was as long and narrow as a grave) upped his spritsail, sailed to a certain northern Countie of Virginia not yet call'd Canada, & met with a grand isle, **.1.** *Newfoundland,* whose best peninsula points still farther northwards like unto the very finger of GOD. Thirty-six other ships of all Nations were already there, sluppering up whales and codfish. Craving novelty, Sir Humphrey dreamed himself into a world just made, inscribing his footsteps into uncovered sea-mud between angled boulders around whose bases brown water bloomed as trickily as Time itself, and frilly kelp quivered as the wind blew cold. Here his Factors, Servaunts and mutchado'd Sailors did erect a pillar inset with the arms of England, so that he took eternal possession of the place for our gracious Queen. Being already an accomplish'd Soldier in Ireland ('tis said he took **.30.**-odd castles there, burning corn & slaughtering the Rusticks), he comprehended the necessity of laying down firm laws. Thus he proclaimed the penalty of ear-lopping for sedition, & head-lopping for treason against Her Majestie. He announced the sole validity of the Anglican creed. And then, his work being done, OUR REDEEMER called him: Off that coast he drown'd in a storm, so that he died at least not thirsty. **.7.** The very next year, which was 1584, his half-brother *Sir Walter Ralegh* kissed the Queen's arse, as his enviers said, for from her he received his own Patent of Discoverie (Sir Humphrey's being necessarily defunct along with its possessor), which he immediately applied, commanding *Captaine Philip Amadas* and *Captaine Arthur Barlowe* westward with both their ships & minions. (John Smith was but a bratling then, not yet orphaned, smiling and reaching upward at the cows' eyes.) Let's name these **.2.** *Well-metall'd resolute Adventurers,* schooled in expressing the Queen's authority, for they'd been Soldiers in Ireland, destroying nests of Irish rebels. So they weighed anchor, and off they did sail:

Ushant — the Canaries — Porto Ricco! Stealthily they trespassed upon the Spanish dominion of *Florida,* whose hot ooze was divided into pools by strangler-fig islands and the many-fingered hands of upreaching ferns. Captaine Barlowe spied an alligator snaking almost silently through the blackness between water-weeds, leaving only bubbles behind, & he sang out: We're in the DEVIL's Countrey! — But the Pilot answered: Good Admirall, they devour Christians and Infidels alike!, at which the aforesaid Captaine Barlowe needs must laugh. Then safely northward they skittered, avoiding *Saint Augustine* (a Spanish Towne, whose Magistrates might have condemned 'em to be burned or hanged), and so they came into *Virginia.* This Countrey (percase you haven't heard) is a Paradise of wild grapes and tractable Salvages, who will give you all they possess, for a handful of beads & suchlike trash. And if they'll give all, why not take all? Following the example of the late Sir Humphrey, our .2. Gentlemen now established their pillar on shore, with England's device affixed to it upon a dish of lead. And so these Salvages likewise became instant vassals of Her Majestie (a blessing which they ought to have approv'd). The sun lay low above low islands at that hour, and the pale gold hairs, called grasses, which bend and bristle out of sand dunes, found themselves kissed by the ocean's wet and foamy lip. And grasses bristle there still, as I myself have seen, yet the pillar's wracked to nothingness by the long cold centuries, altho' I search'd for it near about .15. minutes. — Now I wish I had leisure to tell you every proceeding of that voyage, but the moral was simply this: Hoping for gold, the Captaines yet returned with but a pair of naked and ungilded Salvages (their skinnes being already yellow), not to mention other commodities, for example *Tobacco,* which did assure their Master (the aforesaid Sir Walter Ralegh) of the goodness of the soil. The Salvages had spoken of mountains like unto a caravel's .3. shark's-fin sails, and beyond these at a distance of .7. days journeying an Ocean which must surely be the Chinese Sea. The future: Easy rubies from *Thibet,* emeralds from *India.* Spain's evil grandeur will be by us erased. And Ralegh so successfully flirted in the Queen's ear, that she knighted him at Greenwyche upon Twelfth Day. Then he call'd to him all the silly rich men he'd cozened, saying: Now our prologue lies past, so let's commence to change our fortunes. Buy me ships and soldiers, lads; Virginia herself shall make good return. And if not Virginia, Spain! . . . — at which all the silly young Gentlemen laughed for joy, seeing behind closed eyes fat, square-sailed Spanish galleons wallowing full of South American gold and silver: prizes all in those days, lawful prey. Therefore in 1585 set out for Virginia .8. the self-

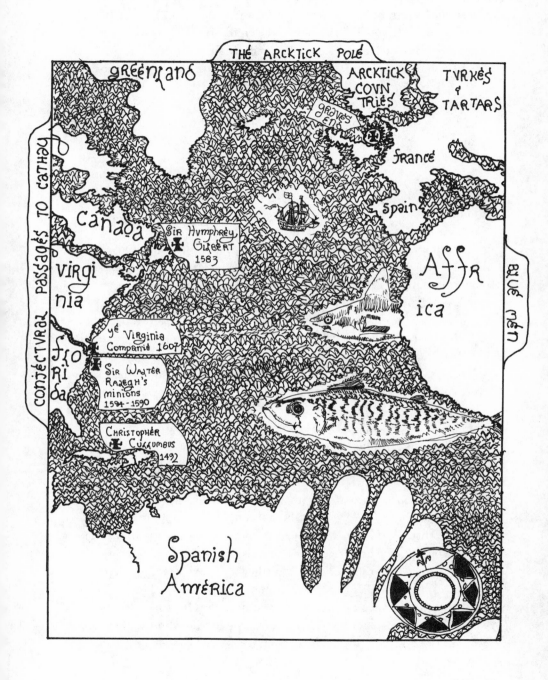

same pair of Captaines, now commanded by *Sir Richard Grenville* in a fleet of .7. ships of war, bearing commissions in Ralegh's name to make laws, execute & pardon miscreants, and e'en impress Sailors for service out of diverse ports or havens in England, all of which indeed they did. My Lord Grenville (the same who achiev'd mention in that letter from Lord Willoughby's lefthanded vassal) had Adventured in Irish wars, yet lost more than he'd gained, for which cause he found himself forced to mortgage his estates at Buckland Abbey. Not wishing to sink still deeper, he jumped at the Virginian gamble, hoping for the golden roll. With him rode half .1,000. men, gamblers all. Whenever they committed some misdemeanor, Lord Grenville did shout: *I'll make dice out of your bones!* For this they call'd him Captaine Fortune. I know not whether they departed Plimouth-Towne or Gravesend, but we may be sure they enrichened many a Waterman, Tavern-keeper & taffeta-skirted drab before the last hogshead got lowered in hold. Then away they did speed. What an easy voyage it prov'd! Only .1. pinnace sank, and a mere .4. or .5. souls perished otherwise (the strangest case being that a fellow who was washing his arse in the beak's-head chains when a *Sharke* did devour his leg). At Porto Ricco they burned a forest to spite the Spaniards, then pillaged .2. Spanish frigates. — Now for the next throw, lads! cried Lord Grenville, & they cheer'd, upraising their caps. 'Twas gambler's weather. Into Virginia they caroused, breasting the *Outer Banks*, that long low smoke-blue line which as they came closer developed a grey middle between the green over- and underlinings of foliage, and this center grew and grew into an infinitude of the late spring's naked bones. Here lay *Roanoke Isle,* compact brush-stroke from a fat brush, painted of both dark grey and yellow-green shimmers on the light grey sea. And now the ships swam into sight of the English arms which the .2. Captaines had erected the previous year. — Captaine Barlowe, how much water doth this inlet draw? asked Lord Grenville. — Ten foot, Sir. — Then hither, friends, he did commaund, tapping his spy-glass 'gainst his fist. By GOD, we'll Roanoke ourselves! — Captaines Amadas and Barlowe .2.nded his conception, for thus sea-locked the Colonists might be preserved aloof from Salvages, 'till they'd waxed strong enough to no longer fear 'em. — Salvages, O yes! Have I told you of those creatures? They dwelt e'erywhere, in houses shapen unto the shells of turtles, houses wearing square scales of bark. Just as in England he who wanders on the heath must beware of cutpurses, so in Virginia he who Adventures and Undertakes had better take his heed of these strange beings, whose smiles (so

I've read) may conceal malignancy. — So the arrivals did beach their Colonie circumspectly, and commenc'd to fortify themselves. Howbeit, their Machiavellian spiderweb throve not, altho' they hoped & waited for tender flies or bumblebees to surrender to their sticky wiles. Reader, may I tell you why? *Because Argoll was not there.* Altho' the palisadoes rose up in good order 'gainst the conspiring Salvages, yet Virginia's clime slipped past all Sentries, sickening and killing, concealing herself in bad water. Chew cloves, my Undertakers; quaff water of cinnamon! You might as well fight sickness here as in Gravesend! Argall could have saved them; Argoll could have shot the bullets of success at mosquito-winged Death himself; Argull could have slain all idleness, carelessness & Yndianness; but since Arkill wasn't there to coin new strategems, alienness belapped them round; strange animals screamed in the night. To briefly tell the tale, our .2. Captaines (or sub-Captaines as I should say) set forth to discover the Countrey thereabouts, & ascertain the loyalty of surrounding Kings. In reason they should have retained the high commaund they'd enjoy'd in the previous voyage. But, feeling utter hopelessness unless they should depose Lord Grenville & set themselves up as joint Virginian Kings, which to them relished far less than gambling on some future golden chance, should they bide patient till they came ashore in London-Towne, they prov'd wise enough to obey all instructions. The Sunne was high in the House of Leo when they marched out of Roanoke Fort. Off they went, spying out the Salvages (who are longhaired like unto Irishmen), and in the even **.A.** reclining in the houses of Werowances, **.B.** slapping flies, **.C.** watching the Rusticks dance around circles of wooden poles whose tops had been carved into the likenesses of men, women & devils, **.D.** tupping red-painted wenchen whose quim-holes were always plucked baby-clean, **.E.** inquiring about riches, & **.F.** offering round tiny drinks of their well-sugared sack, for which the Salvages loved 'em. Then they returned, having failed to meet Captaine Fortune. — Which is their Emperour? demanded Lord Grenville. — My Lord, they have none. We must treat with the lesser Salvages. — At this news their Commaunder grew passing discontented, believing that these Yndians but hid their Sovereign, to multiply the labor of the English. And he wrapt himself in nervous pacing, not knowing the way to pluck Virginia's maidenhead. To him this whole World became but a long insomnia of coasts on which half-dreams made flittering haven, then stood off again, searching for sleep. As for Captaines Barlowe and Amadas (to say naught of the Soldiers & Sailors), none of them felt easier than he. To improve their destinies they hoped yet to discover a wat'ry Passage to the Indies, thereby extending the harmony of the World. For their captive Yndians had *promised* 'em this. Did their introitus lie here, or behind 'em in Florida, or up north in Canada somewhere? Again & again they questioned the Naturalls, but what replies they received merely mazed them further in the murky bog-mires of *Ambiguity*.   —One morn some insinuating Salvages did say that up the river of Moratoc lay a mine of a wondrous metal, in a Countrey call'd *Chaunis Temoatan*. Then all the Soldiers clamored to go there, for to pillage & win their fortunes. The Sailors were well-agreed; likewise the .2. Captaines; and e'en Lord Grenville did think it politick, to accomplish some discovery which might please Sir Walter Ralegh. But when they ventured there, they found neither mine nor metal, for the sake of which *Chimera* they nearly starv'd. All the more reason to ensconce themselves in their established advantages! Therefore, when the Yndians of .1. Towne in those parts stole a silver cup, which they denied to render up, Grenville envoyed Captaine Amadas at the head of .11. men to bring them to justice. He knew the way; 'twas a place call'd Aquascogoc, whose wenchen (or *squaws* as they call 'em) had proved especially agreeable. — It grieves me to see how they betray our friendship, Captaine Amadas told his men. Now we must pay 'em quittance. — They closed down the bevors of their helmets, so that their faces were gone. Now they possessed but naked metal heads crested on top like Salvages' wild hairlocks. 'Twas a different game from guestmanship they were about to play now. But had they refrained, 'twould have made no difference: Good Undertakers know that dice transform themselves from maidens into swords & back again; & howsoever they are, so must the round be played; if not, all's lost. At Captaine Amadas's watchword (which was *Sword)*   they burned every house to the ground (the people being fled), and decapitated every ear of corn. — Now, said he, they will know that they must fear as well as love us. — For so they had e'er done in Ireland. And Lord Grenville for his part was satisfied that honor had won that contention.* But *Autumn*   loom'd like an unkenned coast. Leaving the Colonie to thrive as best she might, Grenville weighed anchor for home, pausing to profitably spoil a Spanish viceadmiral of all her gold, silver, pearls, ginger & sugar, wherefore Ralegh smiled what was call'd his *profitable smile,*   and the silly rich Gentlemen who'd subscribed to the Adventure began to consider themselves infallible

---

*Altho' in a secret letter my Lord Sir Walter Ralegh had advised that no Soldier be allowed to rape, harm, molest, pillage or conscript yᵉ Salvages, silly old Wat wasn't here, & moreover, had himself done worse in other Countreys.

Prophets. (Moreover, off Newfoundland the **.2.** Captaines did capture **.17.** fishing-ships, which they plundered at their pleasure, and besides they took **.4.** Brazilmen and **.1.** French ship which was homeward bound from *Guinea.*) — This hour sways unto us, the Gentlemen said. And Ralegh did send self-congratulatory word to old Queen Elizabeth with her long pearl-paved shoulder-wings. We may be sure he neglected not mention of that golden Countrey call'd *Chaunis Temoatan.* What did Her Majestie think? After her disappointments with Greenlandish fool's gold, perhaps she reserved her joy.

* * * * * *

Masters, I implore you, pay your Servaunts faithfully at Midsummer and Christmas. Navigators, disremember not by what small quantity your Compasse doth alter. Care for your inferiors, good Reader, and e'er keep watch to see which way your course doth go. These rules I refer to the judgment of all men, to be followed in steadfast weather or overcast. If only Ralegh's greedy Adventurers had kept sight of them! But, lost amidst the sickening complexities of wind-tortured water, lusting for *Chaunis Temoatan*, they took no care to make tractable retainers of those *Naturalls* call'd *Salvages.* Well, to be sure, they were monstrous busy with *Navigation,* an art whose practice may yet prove invaluable for the transportation of our English commodities. They made excellently bold discoveries; 'pon my faith, they commenc'd to see how the land did lie in Virginia* — and I wonder how *did* she lie, and with whom? In his own middle age, Captaine John Smith ranged through his memories and wrote: *The bounds thereof on the East side are the great* Ocean: *on the South lyeth* Florida: *on the North* nova Francia (which signifies Canada): *as for the West thereof, the limits are unknowne.*

* * * * * *

In 1586 sail'd back to the gaming-table **.9.** Lord Grenville — only to find his Colonie abandoned, thanks to Warres with yᵉ Salvages, which had interrupted the supply of Yndian corn. ('Tis a common disturbance, when Salvages continue unsubjugated.) Altho' the Colonists had shifted their friendship from **.1.** tribe to the next, kidnapping Salvage Kings or expeditiously beheading them, yet they could not gain tranquility. For, as *Saint*

---

*For instance, here's a Virginian topographic rule: *A swamp without trees is a pond; a pond full of trees is a swamp.*

Machiavell doth warn us, altho' *All armed Prophets have conquered, & the unarmed ones have been destroyed,* yet there must be a true *preponderance* of arms, triple *.6.*'s at least when the bony dice of death get thrown; for *The nature of the people is variable, & whilst 'tis easy to persuade 'em, 'tis difficult to fix 'em in that persuasion. And thus it proves necessary to use such measures that, when they believe no longer, it may be possible to make 'em believe by force.* The Colonists enjoy'd insufficient numbers & ordnance for that. In the end, they all voyaged home with Sir Frauncis Drake. — SATAN's bollocks! shouted Grenville when he heard the silence; and upon his cry did take wing a whole flock of blackbirds, hovering like uneasy clouds over the pale green marsh beyond the trees. — What could he do, save leave *.15.* brave men, well-provisioned, to hold Roanoke Fort 'till more Colonists might be fetched? Homeward he sailed in a rage, and scarcely did he recover all his trouble, altho' he stopped to sack and pillaged some Spanish Townes upon the Azore Isles. When he met his mates in London-Towne, he opined 'twas infinitely less tedious to go a-chasing Irish rebels in the rain. — But in the year of our forgiveness 1587, Ralegh, still hoping otherwise (and wishing for what could never be, that the Queen might permit him to go himself), dispatched *.10.* a certain *Maister John White,* Irish Gentleman, along with *.3.* new ships, *.12.* Assistants, and *.150.* Colonists, together with their wives and children, to re-found the Colonie upon its own ruins. (Where were Grenville's *.15.* place-holders then? Sweet Reader, their empty houses now crawled with melon-vines, and of them nothing could e'er be found, excepting a single skeleton. Amidst the detritus, Maister White spied faint Indian trails winding beneath the moss.) Ralegh of his politic kindness had granted each Settler at least half *.1,000.* acres of good Indian land, so that the throw appeared quite golden. Here lie the men of 1587, some of them: *George Howe, John Burden, William Waters, John Bright, Richard Berrye, Anthony Cage, Griffen Jones.* And some women: *Wenefrid Powell, Elyoner Dare, Alis Chapman, Emme Merrimoth, Joan & Jane, Elizabeth Glane.* All of them hoping for to plant themselves point by point, & to become wealthy Rusticks, they made good landfall, & clung to earth. From them for a promise-token was born *Virginia Dare,* the *.1.*st English child to open eyes in America. And she was baptized; she'd grow up a clear-voiced young chorister.

Governor White did commaund his Colonists to fall to, & lodge themselves in all speed before Salvages or Spaniards should besiege them, but very likely some Soldiers were gold-hungry or wander-thirsty, & others weak, for they failed to labor in as good array as when seasoned Sailors lash

JOHN WHITE   ROGER BAYLYE   SIMON FERNANDO

sail-clews to the lower yard . . . Maister White himself, his eyes enchanted by the new Countrey, pass'd too many days in painting watercolors, and not sufficient in strict & careful Government; thus before the new-cut palisadoes had been raised safely up, a swarm of Salvages did murther George Howe while he essay'd to catch crabs for his dinner, so the English in reprisal did attack a Salvage Towne by night — mistakenly butchering some few who'd remained their friends. (Yet methinks 'twas not entirely Tragickall, seeing that for our sake *all* Salvages must sooner or later be removed.) And now since the Colonie found herself islanded in the same perplexing sea of wars as in Grenville's day, the well-disposed Salvages (if indeed now any remained in life) scrupled* increasingly to render corn to their English Lords. Marry, marry, matters arrived at such a pass that Governor White himself must sail to England for belly-timber. Of his character 'tis said he was weakly generous, and melancholick. His daughter and granddaughter kiss'd him farewell — not piteously, for they could survive yet another year; yet nervousness did glisten & glare within his heart as bright as any *Tiger's-Eye* or suchlike malignant jewel. The Captaine wanted to discover a more sailable passage over America, but White begged him in G O D's name not to fritter away any days in discoveries, for the sake of those on short rations in the Fort. At these words, a grizzled-grey osprey did shriek. The voyage prov'd close-fogged and tempestous. Wafted into Ireland by mistake, at last he reach'd Cornwall, where, flummoxed by boisterous Watermen, he stood amazed by the mercantile hum he'd half forgot, then set off to gain Ralegh's ear. That Gentleman continuing yet in Royal favor, 'twas but a merry matter for him to grant Maister White leave to fraught himself with stores, & set sail, even tho' at that time the Queen had commaunded that all ships stay in their harbors, for fear of Spain. ('Twas now 1588, the fateful year when Spain and England must join full quarrel.) **.11.** But while White might have been Governor in Vrginia, at Gravesend he counted for but a Rustick. Of the **.3.** ships which lay ostensibly at his beck, not **.1.** would agree to fraught herself with any new Colonists, nor even with a single Servaunt to Maister White, whose excessive mildness every Captaine could spy out. Nor had he time to complain to Ralegh, because they were determined to sail to almost upon the turn of the tide. For the love of his dependents at Roanoke, the unfortunate Gentleman betook himself aboard. *Flood oh!* When the spritsail went up, and the flagship slipped toward the open sea, Maister White yielded himself unto

---

*Hesitated.

his most resplendent hopes, but, alas, his fleet turned pirate, chasing French and Spanish ships (since Virginian Salvages own no gold, except perhaps in *Chaunis Temoatan*). 'Twas not long before they came to harm. They slunk back into port with their sails transformed unto scorch'd rags well-enough cannonaded to see the moon through. Virginia lay unreal, like upon a theatrickall Tragedy. On what roots & grubs must John White's people now be a-feeding? Or were they dead? Maister White lay down at an Inn near Gravesend. He stared at a spider upon the ceiling. In dreams he saw his granddaughter's corpse screaming many-mouthed from crimson wounds. The Salvages laid her beside the carcass of his daughter, then after dancing most diabolically did hurl them amidst the golden-dotted shimmers of a slough where the long skinny shadows of branches and the reflections of branches were equally black, black on the black water shot through with green algae-particles. But there was no hope yet to disprove that vision — for a *Great Armada* of Spaniards now essay'd to invade England! Virginia could scarce be thought of. In a letter he did say: *Yet seeing 'tis not my .1.ˢᵗ cross'd voyage, I remain content.* **.12.** In 1589, after GOD's winds had dealt Spain a crushing vanquishment, he gained acquitance anew to depart England. But the Sailors laugh'd at this dreamy Water-colorist who'd mismanaged his Colonie into such a nebulous state. He heard & was shamed. I misdoubt me not they'd have succored Roanoke with more vigor, had my Lord Grenville held commaund! But he'd long since given up the Undertaking. Dispatching **.110.** boisterous Soldiers & Colonists to found a Plantation in Ireland; he explained 'twas steadier return than Roanoke, altho' no less barbarous (for Irishwomen do *keen* like unto beasts when we slay their rebel sons & husbands). And Ralegh, agreeing with Grenville now, sent **.114.** more to Ireland. But Maister White continued on his previous course, being impractically loyal. He scarce could sleep; he feared new bad dreams. — What hope do you have? asked the Captaine, & he would not answer. — Burning & pillaging Spanish possessions to good success as they went, they gained *Havana,* then *Florida.* Maister White did say to the Captaine: Sir, I dub you *Captaine Fortune.* — And now, entering *Virginia*, they neared the Outer Banks in a twink. 'Twas darklins. Discovering smoke & fire on the shore of Roanoke, they grew heartened, and shot off their ordnance, singing English ditties in loud brave voices. There came no reply. John White pass'd that night sleepless. At daybreak they conveyed him ashore. The Colonie had grown yet more watchfully palisaded than e'er before, with curtains & flankers very Fortlike, yet when he slowly enter'd the gates, knowing already that his hopes

had done him but villainous service, he found himself standing in a mere irregular grass bowl not quite shoulder-high. The houses were utterly and
mysteriously perished into weed-grown ruins, and his own trunks and
chests, which he'd so carefully buried, lay open and ruined, & his armor
rusted entire. For in Virginia, Lord Time conquers us more rapidly than in
England, having Tropick Weed-Soldiers, Salvages & Rain-Ordnance to call
upon. Gazing round at the forest pressing in, Maister White felt like unto
the occupant of an open grave discovering his own mourners. — Fellow,
make much of it! laughed the Sailor-lads (who cared litle for Colonies). —
On a palisade post he found the word CROATOAN pleasingly
carved. He begged them in GOD's name to sail for Croatoan Island, but
they would not, for they longed to go a-pirating, and moreover, having by
accident lost near every anchor & cable they possessed, they feared to detour
on errands merely *Altruistickall,* so of all those Colonists not .1. was ever
seen again.*

∗ ∗ ∗ ∗ ∗

All hopes of Virginia thus abandoned, writes John Smith, *it lay dead and
obscured from 1590. till this year 1602. that* .13. *Captaine Gosnell, with*
.32. *and himselfe in a small Barke, set sayle from Dartmouth.* Of this same
Captaine Gosnold (who was a Gentleman come out of Countie Suffolk) I
principally recall that he return'd home nicely fraughted with cedarwood
and Sassafrass, then lost it all to Sir Walter Raleigh, who still owned Virginia with all her merchandise, and so, sweet Reader, we learn the vanity of
earthly things. — But enough of this Gosnold's merchaundizing; what of
his explorations? Well, he saw yellow water in the ocean, .200. leagues
west of Saint Marie's in the Assoris Islands; and doubtless he did make
other discoveries of equal magnitude. Hearing of these, .14. his cousin
Bartholemew Gilbert, that famous Pirate & Vendor of spurious jewels, then weigh'd anchor for North Virginia, where somewhere round
about Canada he got murthered by the Salvages call'd *Yndians.* (This
tale Sweet John doth prudently leave out of his *Generall Historie,* for
fear that Virginia's other suitors might get discouraged.) After poor Captaine Gilbert sailed .15. *Captaine Pring,* who accomplisht nothing

---

*In 1700, Maister John Lawson journeyed through those parts, and was informed by the Hatteras
Salvages that some of their ancestors had been book-learned and white-skinned. "We may rea-
sonably suppose," said he, "that the *English* were forced to cohabit with them, for Relief and Conversation; and that in process of Time, they conform'd themselves to the manners of their *Indian*
Relations. And thus we see, how apt Humane Nature is to degenerate."

known to history, then **.16.** *Captaine Weymouth,* who rhapsodized over the Countrey's currants & spruce-trees, and while trading knives and combs for skins did levitate a needle by means of a lodestone-touched sword (*this we did,* writes **.1.** of his Gentlemen, *to cause them to imagine some great power in us: and for that to loue and feare us*). Captaine Weymouth himself did love the Salvages at first. They were well-mannered, loyal, submissive. But **.1.** day, when they pretended to invite him for further trade, he sent his subaltern Griffin in a Canoa, to see how the land did lie. And Grffin returned all in a fright, whispering: Captaine, Captaine! 'Tis certain they have nothing for truck nor trade; and by the LORD GOD ALMIGHTIE I did spy **.200.** and **.83.** murtherous Salvages all armed, and longing to lead me into a narrow defile . . . — *These things considered,* his Gentleman continues, *we began to ioyne them in the Rankes of other Salvages, who have beene by Travellers in most discoveries found very trecherous.* Accordingly, Captaine Weymouth did send his men to parley with **.5.** likely Salvages, on whom they suddenly laid hands no matter how they struggled. Fraughting them in his ship's belly all the way to England, he fashion'd of them a brave spectacle for human beings to see. Did they have the wit to resemble the convicts in Newgate crying from their holes: *Half a penny for* CHRIST *His sake?* — Not at all. The tale saith that once they grew resigned to the loss of their freedom, their sunny tractability returned. O what mercy of GOD!

(Captaine Weymouth later fell under suspicion of being a Papist, as indeed he was, and so they arrested him for fear he meant to turn over Virginia to the Spaniards. And this precaution prov'd wise, for I read in some pamphlet, which I did buy last Friday at the *Sign of the .III. Salvages,* that on the **.18.**th of August 1607, he shipped himself to Spain, in order to betray his friends.)

And now at last 'twas time for **.17.** the voyage which we must now relate, since it concerns *Captaine John Smith,* who'd invested full **.9.** pounds sterling in the Companie — and it doth likewise concern the aforesaid Captaine Gosnold (number **.13.** if you forgot), who found himself cousin-in-law to Bartty and by the same token to scarlet-cloaked Robert — *viz.;* my new Lord Willoughby whom King James now created *Knight of the Bath.*

* * * * * *

Robert extended his pale sad hand, saying: Sweet John, I ken you can cut off Turkes' heads as quick as e'er a Fen Slodger uproots my cabbages, but can you slay freakish Salvages like unto Captaine Weymouth's?

I beg my Lord's pardon—

I need a man who's expert at cowing Salvages.

Percase I can do that.

Percase? Only percase? Modesty's the Mire-man's mark. Gosnold, what do you make of him?

By my faith, Sir, he's a brave Soldier!

Obedient to Robert's advice, he visited Captaine Weymouth's Salvages & wrote down diverse words of their language. A *Werowance* was a King. *Cuffewh kenneaunten mata mechik* signified *I understand you a little but not much.* (He'd oft said as much to my Lady Tragabigzanda.) Over & over did he move his lips in those circumlutions, altho' the strange syllables much dogged his way. *Cuffewh ken* . . . The Savages smiled upon him most mirthfully. Truly they were loving creatures. He long'd to meet with them on his jolly march. *Netoppew* did signify *Friends.* As for *Ka ka torawincs yowo,* that meant *What call you this?*

He made acquaintance with a certain ice-dreaming Dutchman, by name *Henry Hudson,* & from him did learn surveying & cartography. He prayed for Captaine Fortune to come.

After that, he lived quietly at home with Frauncis & Anna, waiting for a year, until Captaine Gosnold gained his patent. Sweet John joyed to hear of that. He weeded the West Field in a flurry, as if all thistles were infidels. Then, being named & nominated to the fleet as he'd hoped, he set sail with that Companie.

✳ ✳ ✳ ✳ ✳

. . . We lost Roanoke, 'tis true. The Salvages gained that victory. But **.1.** of our most worshipful propagandists, Maister Thomas Harriot, publish'd a relation describing Virginia's many good things, and before his *Finis* he stoutened up our hearts — or, if you prefer, he indulged in **.1.** of those fits of foreshadowing which appear either vulgar or absurd in novels: *If there fall out any warres between vs & them, what their fight is likely to bee, we hauing weapons and deuises else; especially by ordinance great and small, it may be easily imagined.*

THE GRAMMAR OF GENTLEMEN (1607)

... a Man was in his Opinion, as likely to Repent sincerely in the last Fortnight of his Life under the Pressure and Agonies of a Jayl, and the Condemn'd Hole, as he would ever be in the Woods and Wildernesses of *America;* that Servitude and hard Labour were things Gentlemen could never stoop to, that it was but the way to force them to be their own Executioners afterwards ...

DANIEL DEFOE, *Moll Flanders* (1722)

*O*n the .26.th day of April, 1607, they made land at Cape Henry, which yearns toward England as much as doth any other eastern outreach of our continent; and John Smith, disremembering already the sadnesses of that voyage (for in Guadeloupe they'd made a gallows to hang him, thanks to the malice of certain persons who faulted his eager strivings), stared at the mudrimmed Chesapeake, whose inward parts might give upon some fabulous maze of rivers, .1. channel of which, only .1. (ah, he did not expect to discern it right away) might refresh him with Fortune at last, like unto this lovely American Sunne which rose each morn from the muck —

They no longer confined him in the Store-room or the iron-sheath'd Bread-room, being at such a remove from anywhere, let alone from lovely ENGLAND (hearing which name I seem to see Lincolnshire, where Mareham-le-Fen's small whitewashed huts with their moldy grey thatch render eternal allegiance to Tattershall Castle's blocky narrowness), and so he sat in bitter idleness upon the capstan, long-bearded and bereft like unto some Jeremiah or suchlike Prophet cursed with eloquence.

Stained by that charge of mutiny, he was disallowed (altho' he did humbly entreat) from coming ashore with his betters: — to wit, .1.-armed old *Captaine Newport,* who'd sail'd many times a-pirating, which was why he'd been made Admirall of all these Adventurers; *Captaine Gosnold,* he of the .**13**.th voyage, who bore the white ruffled yoke of a Gentleman (indeed, he was now Vice-Admirall), and yet despite his excellence had several times stooped to comfort Sweet John in captivity; *Captaine Archer, Captaine Ratcliffe* the Sub-Admirall, *Maister Percy, Captaine Kendall,* & the other various *Cat's-paws* of that fleet, who with their *Rowers, Soldiers, Sailors* and *Servaunts* did number .**30**. men, if we include inimical *Maister Wingfield.* This old Soldier now bawled out: *There he lurks!* at which all did crane upwards from the pinnace to discover how Captaine Smith stood on the foredeck of the *Susan Constant,* blinking and rubbing his wrists, which were still raw from the irons. — Guard him well! cried Wingfield. O, for he's a rarely crafty Jack! — But the Marshal clapp'd his prisoner's shoulder, murmuring: Never you mind, Sweet John. Soon they'll confess you're as innocent as sugar-candy. — Captaine Smith did thank him for his love, and e'en smiled; but how in truth might he be feeling? Mayhap, like unto a small boy in London-Towne, disremembered by his parents, so that he sits him down upon the reeking dirt of the Globe Theatre, where a forest of legs bulwarks Shakespeare's actors and actresses away from his desperate eyes. He hears the scream when *Titus Andronicus* stabs the *Empress* full in the heart, whereupon all the Play-goers roar in tumult, overtowering him; *he,* poor boy, lacks sight of what's transpiring! His father could lift him on his shoulders, if he would; but the crowd's so rankly o'ergrown that the lad can't even find his father's leg, much less tug at it. And now *Saturnius* murthers *Titus* — another marvelous bloody event, *but he cannot see!* E'en craning on tiptoe he cannot see! And so the little boy beseats himself once again in the dirt and cries. — To be sure, Sweet John, unlike the boy, preserved his hopes of translating himself into a principal Actor (mayhap a Prince), before the next change of scene. He'd not altogether spend himself in quietness, O no! He'd snatch his welfare back! Indeed, he anticipated Fortune's imminent change. Meanwhile, it seemed he must wear endurance for his habit. Disgrace would *not* kill his heart. Hadn't the *Tymor's* irons been heavier and more perilous than any with which he'd been gifted by his Countreymen? Hadn't he conquered *the purples?* Neither shipwreck nor Rector could end him. Sure he'd 'scape Fate's latest accidental judgment . . .

* * * * * *

Now these are the names of the children of Israel which came into Egypt, begins the .2.ⁿᵈ Booke of Moses, call'd *Exodus;* & we can read the name of every man. Then this Booke call'd *Exodus* continues: *And Joseph died, & all his brethren, & all that generation.* Next in the tale we can read that new generations burst out of the charnel clay, as if they were blowflies, or any of the other innocent vermin of death. Yet these were men and women like unto ourselves; they had souls. Their children ran about plucking bog-orchids or helping their fathers ferry pigs to sell in Lincoln-Towne. And they knew not the dead grandfathers from whose loins they'd come, and whose flesh had now become grass. *Now there arose up a new King o'er Egypt, which knew not Joseph,* tells this *Exodus,* which line signifies to me that not only had the memory of that dead generation so utterly decayed, that their bearded old faces lived no more behind any survivor's eyes, but the very Government they laid down, with its myriad ordinances of cleanliness and uncleanliness, of covering and uncovering, of righteousness and hatefulness, was now become a dead letter like unto the place-name of any Salvage Towne engraved in Sweet John's map of Virginia. O you thick black appellations! Your ink runs together; your meaning is perished. Of the Powhatan tongue we now ken but a dozen words or maybe .2. We've pillaged the rest; we've spoiled it in both senses, like the corn which Sweet John would soon extort from the Salvages, and which got burnt and rat-eaten by mistake. For now he could extort nothing. Hidden and beslimed by disgrace, he sat alone, while scarce anyone but the Marshal compassionated him. But GOD heard his groaning. Sweet John bore his trouble as best he could, praying to JEHOVAH; and he remembered how in this self-same Booke call'd *Exodus,* Moses labored patiently for his father-in-law until GOD invited him to the *Land of Milk & Honey,* which Virginia surely was. And altho' Sweet John had sometimes done evil as a Soldier & a Pirate, yet Moses himself, before GOD appeared unto him, secretly murthered an Egyptian who was oppressing .1. of the chosen race.

* * * * * *

Captaine Gosnold became by chance .1.ˢᵗ to plant his heel on the soil of this *Virginia.* Brown grass crawled across the dunes in ragged stripes, as if compris'd of devilish fire which could burn that white sand. The waves sighed: *Come back, come back.* But Captaine Gosnold would not. His fellow Adventurers followed in close array, armored in such color as their means permitted: — Gentlemen in gilded metal, Soldiers in brigandine vests whose links were already rust-greened by the salt air (I warrant you they kept their weapons at full cock), Sailors in blue jerseys and sealskin breeches, Reverend Hunt in his white prayers; & all march'd warily inland (remembering the fable of Roanoke), but spied neither Salvage nor any other chimerical agent of King Oozymandias, to whom we all must pay our forfeitures. Therefore, Virginia'd prove not trial, but treat! (The fat Trumpeter crow'd *Trarintra-rarara.*) Already the Sailors were jesting hard stale greenstone jests about puccoon-crimsoned Salvage slatterns who'd unlock their thighs for a ha'penny (as was claim'd in every Tavern-house at Gravesend). Tup 'em once, and you'd be cured of your pox for life! — The Gentlemen for their parts invincibly expected to descry gold-glints 'twixt their feet; for hadn't Spaniards met with such luck? (Dear gold! Turn it **.1.** way & it shines; turn it t'other, & it gleams; both ways it flickers, flaunts & flantitants itself!) They hailed from the living graves of mortgaged families, undercush'd 'neath *Debt*'s headstone, hence half-maimed into that ruthless ambition whose fantasies are the merest corpse-gases. Only Captaine Fortune could save 'em. **.I.**   Captaine Gosnold, for instance, lusted only to 'scape creditors now that Sir Walter Ralegh had thieved away his cargo of Virginian cedarwood & Sassafrass. More Sassafrass might do the trick. But this *Cape Henrico* could requite him only sandily. Northern Virginia would have better served his turn. The Naturalls there had paid him beaver-skins & goblets of good red copper in exchange for trifles. They'd e'en (for pure affection) helped him dig up that soon to be confiscated Saxifrage. He'd said as much in London, but these 'Venturers had been shipp'd hence under that lesser pygmy of a Newport rather than himself, & so he wavered betwixt jealousy & fear of being denounced for ingratitude. For now, he must strive to be Newport's friend. Longing to swarm ahead for to enrich himself, he grew passing weary when he thought upon the morrow's morrow, when all Adventurers must disembark at Gravesend, & face the Tariff-takers. — **.II.**   As for Captaine Newport — sober fellow, grizzled sober beyond corroboration! — his most precious hope was that these wastrels might found their Plantation as speedily as a horse-thief gets hang'd, so he could get back to that selfsame Gravesend to improve his lucre. For no matter how long or short ran his Admirall-ship, the Companie paid him the same. He'd skippered the *Little John* back in '89, supposedly for to seek the Lost Colonie at Roanoke, but damnme if there wasn't some pleasurable piracy on the way. 'Twas then a hurtled war-chance pluck'd off his arm. In '92, thanks be to Fortune, he'd burned .4. Spanish Townes & pillaged .19. Spanish ships. But now thro' cravenness of King & mistake of GOD we lay at peace with Spain. Home then. Home to Gravesend's secrets. He was but Merchaunt to this crew of dreamers. They'd dream; he'd slupper up wages, & in the end he'd prove the richer. So he e'er did mean to persuade himself. Grizzled, yes, hence without the excuse of innocency, he yet Adventure-diced for luck! The coastal air rang deliciously in his nostrils. O, but he was happy to rest a twink from the sea! He smiled, not kenning that he did. — .III. The Soldiers, being more practiced in sacking & pilferage than Sailors, tricked down their woman-thirst to .2.nd place. In their regimental traditions, the red copper crowns of Werowances had long since gotten translated into gold. — .IV. And Maister Wingfield prayed to be made President; while .V. the cowards astern of him longed only to bide alive. — Thus we see how Captaine Fortune must wear e'er a different mask for each member of his crew.

(Reader, knowing as I do the dissensions soon to attack the Colonie, 'tis difficult for me not to depict these souls as the merest satirical worms. And now that scarce any chalky residue of their skeletons remain in Time's ooze,* they seem insignificant compar'd to Sweet John, with whose *Complete Works* I've dwelt these many years. Virginia's but his map to me now; from blind heights I gaze down upon her crudely wriggling rivers studded alongside with fish-shapen trees & Salvage houses; I find a deer, a Salvage running with bent bow; a naked redskin wench full erotically engrav'd; but where are Newport, Gosnold, & their fellow helmed 'Venturers? They're lost; they lurk in nothingness like unto Argall.)

Sandy-lonely lay Cape Henrico. 'Twas a windy, windy day, so that broken crabshells instantly became bowls of sand, and the sand itself formed moundlets downwind of half-sunk driftwood or shell-shards which crunched beneath the landing party's boots. Virginia welcomed them with rainbows in the sunny sea-spray, hosts of cloud-fingers in the sky. Enfreshened by sassafrass breezes, they cried out in gratitude, interpreting themselves back into Paradise. But their Admirall, kenning not whether these beatitudes were true or false, uttered a commaund, at which his Soldiers formed themselves into a square around their betters, with muskets facing

---

*More marvelous by far than cities of Mexican silver or Peruvian gold I find the panther-hearts well-fortified in great men's skeletons.

outward. Passed a moment, a quarter-hour. Still no Salvages! Was Virginia wrongly famed? Captaine Newport was already softening like unto wax. But essayed not to be slack in this Countrey of phantasmickall mysteries. What price must they pay today? In piracy, war, or for that matter Undertakings to raise up new Plantations, 'tis meet to wait and weigh, till we discover where the dreadfullest quadrant doth lie — and the wealthiest. So longwhiles the Adventurers paused in that strange wind which blew them nothing foreseeable. Then, at *Trarintra-rarara,* within their articulated Fortress of plebians the Masters did kneel, to pray for glory, dominion and riches. The cold sun spied on them between grass stems.

'Twas Reverend Hunt, I trow, who led them in these devotions, he himself having particular cause, since on the voyage he'd nigh unto perished of the vomits. (Nor should I mock him for it, having undergone the like.) With all his heart he thanked OUR REDEEMER for their safe transit of the ocean, for the *Navigation* through whose agency they'd perfectly achieved their direction, for the tranquility of this day which smelled of seashells; &c, &c, &c. But the Gentlemen would have preferr'd not to bide sodden upon their knees — what if Salvages attacked? And Reverend Hunt must himself have considered the danger of such bloody mischances, for his oraisons prov'd obligingly brief. In *Finis* he opened his Book, whose power engluts the whole universe, and read from the chapter call'd *Genesis* a certain happy admonition of our GOD: *Be fruitful & multiply, & fill the Earth & vanquish it; & rule o'er the fishes of the sea & the birds of the air, & o'er every living thing that doth move upon this Earth.* Then once more he prayed for JEHOVAH's help. All rose at his *Amen,* the Gentlemen hungrily awaiting the meat of the matter, which was that the offices of the Colonie be conferred. Maister Wingfield thought he had the best chance, for in Ireland he'd known Lord Mountjoy personally. Captaine Gosnold's hopes were builded upon equally plausibly justifications. But Captaine Newport, who as Admirall remained Commander-in-Chief *pro tempore,* thought .1.st to grant his weary Sailors the enjoyment of that day, to drink health back into their bones. (In truth, by hidden ways Virginia continued to work on him.) So, until nigh upon the hour of darklins (which in Lincolnshire is call'd *The blind man's holiday)* they gamboled 'midst the flowers and sweetwater brooks of Virginia, hunting turtles & berries, bathing, drinking their fill from each stream, laughing at the buzzing caws of a treeful of wood storks, discovering each other's likenesses in brown water-mirrors at the edge of a carpet of lillies and cress, e'er accompting themselves safe. Meanwhile, the Gentlemen took their own pleasures, discovering with interest how the white hilly sands of the place did resemble their own *Downes of England.* — Attend the trumpet-blast! Captaine Niuporte had commaunded 'em, but 'twas such a cheerful day he could muster no heart to sound it. He was a jolly fellow now. The Soldiers snoozed beside their guns. Some e'en removed their brigandines, to clean the plates with vinegar & sand.

Gosnold, what think you?

I know not.

On your voyage did they hide aloof from you?

Nay, Admirall, I remember how full .11. *Canoas* did swim to greet us 'pon our isle on a lake. But 'twas not until the .2.nd day after we landed; I misdoubt me not they .1.st conferr'd with their Werowances, or *Saga-mores* as they call 'em up there—

Where might they be now?

In those trees, or mayhap behind yonder sand-ridge, awaiting the issue.

'Tis but .60. miles to Roanoke, as my chart doth read—

Aye, dear Admirall.

Think you they exterminated that Colonie?

Maybe the baser sort could have brew'd such a crime, I know not . . .

Now Captaine Radclyffe did whisper in Captaine Newport's ear: What an ocherish-bronzy glint I spy in these sands! Come with me! Think you this means *gold?*

Then Newporte, who'd privateered so long & furiously in quest of that excellent substance, fell instantly intoxicated with assurances of wealth. He long'd now to stay & explore Virginia, until they'd ravish'd all gold-mines forth from her belly. The brownish cast of dirt which Ratcliff had shewn him seem'd proof of gold & copper ubiquitously mingl'd, just as a resplendent Nobleman may sometimes stoop to embrace his prettiest Servingmaid, altho' she be not of his degree. My Lord Gold! My Lady Copper! What shall your mating bring forth? Palaces for me! And so poor Newport joined the Gentlemen who already fantasized thus, & they tramped the shore, in that state of mind 'twixt sleep & dreams.

Did you e'er question any Spanish Assayers? asked Ratcliff. For they out of all the World must ken which dirt's most precious.

Nay, & I regret it. Indeed I know not whether they ride in galleons at all, or stay at home in Spain. Next time I seize a Spanish ship I'll spare my prisoners 'till I can learn it.

& think you there's gold only in *their* dominions?

Too cruel of GOD!

As I have leisure I'll press out Gosnold's secrets. Why'd he return here, did he not ken some gold-field in Virginia's clay?

Nay, you o'erwile yourself. Gosnell's an honest dullard—

Or more cunning by far than we've discovered. Leave him to me.

Ratcliffe! Mark how something doth glister 'mongst those pebbles there—

So sped the sand of full .16. Glasses, or (as I the landbound Historian or *Tortoise* must write) .8. hours, *viz., .2.* entire sea-watches back to back. O, drink another Glass of Time, dear Captaine! 'Tis Virginia's loving-cup. How doth it relish? Unlike unto your daily fish-water, at least. Gravesend gapes; your tomb fills with the waters of prophecy, so kneel down — drink, drink! Drink away another measure of your life! Have you hopes of your piracy's resurrection, good Admirall? Then drink in GOD's name, shake off these irrelevant Colonists, & speedily Gravesendward wend! Or do you dread to reconfine yourself within your reeking fleet? Then linger you here, & should this sandy finger of Virginia seem yet too widely empty, which is to say both .1. visible & risible to Spaniards & .2. like unto a waiting grave, why, then, drink another sip of cursed-blessed Time. No fear — you'll be no wiser than before!

Accompting up his Adventurers, Newport sent to all sentries, the *All well:* Neither Salvages nor DEVILS. A speculation began to cross him then that the creatures had utterly removed themselves, or perish'd of a pestilence. Howbeit, GOD's fire between the trees did warn him of the day's *Finis.* Seiz'd by prudence, he made as if to beck the Trumpeter, but a kindly new breeze now blew outwards from the land, which state of wind is call'd by Sailors a *Sea-turne,* & (as our Newport well conceived) would prove convenient to impel them back to their ships. The men did implore him to extend their respite more. So, fancying himself in soft reach of his fleet, he dallied a further quarter-hour. Sand glinted in a sun-ray. Was it gold? (For this delay Maister Wingfield would later accuse him secretly, *that he was prov'd but a Sailor, who kenned nothing of earthen matters,* Maister Wingfield being as I said well-steeped in marching Soldiery.) Black walls of trees stained the twilight. The sky continued blue, and more transparent than ever. Everywhere, tawny deer were leaping, their hindquarters rising and falling as they went. At the Sailors' prayer (they being passing weary of codfish), Captaine Kendall fired his snap-haunce at a fine doe, but missed, & those animals ran away like unto rocking horses. Then at last Captaine Newport call'd upon all souls to rank themselves in

good order, which commaund was well, for in that twink, as they breasted
the long expanse of dune-grass (red blotches of grass bezeling lavender
pools beneath a flesh-colored sky), arrows came like locusts out of darkness,
hissing & rattling down.   At .1.st they believed 'twas merely some gust
which rattled dry stems — how they long'd not to know that Virginia had
thus betrayed 'em! But a Sailor screamed; he'd been arrow-pierced! Salvages rose up invisibly all around like sprites or unkenned monsters whilst
the Adventurers rush'd bewildered.   Captaine Newport did shout; the
Trumpeter sounded *Retreat.*   Now the darkness was o'erhung by hor-
rors which essayed to drown them like unto sea-waves.   Every man grew
pale, and knew not his own brothers.   Never was there anything that could
be seen, till the rising moon betrayed their armored breasts each to the other,
silvered simulacra of an *Alligator's* squarish scales. Again the Trumpeter
blew *Retreat.* At once, hellish arrows came a-hissing and a-rattling, so that
the voyagers feared to follow his call, hiding belly down in the cool moist
sand, struggling to get their guns to full cock. — To the pinnace! cried
Captaine Newport. — Some began to scuttle shoreward, but then new arrows came a-whistling down. Maister Wingfield (who'd encounter'd similar treacheries in Ireland) loudly strove to rally 'em, but e'en he knew not
which vantage to attack. Altho' they discharg'd their pieces in all directions
except waterward, they wounded only darkness, their bullets hurtling into
a sphere of all-encompassing, hence almost characterless malice. — *To the
boat!*   cried their Admirall again. *Run!* — They ran, sinking in beach
sand to the ankles. Dark shapes gibbered. The beach lay empty and ominous indeed, with the sea-grass thrashing in wave-foam. Now before they
could e'en inquire of that Sailor (who was nam'd Matthew Morton) how he
did, another feathered missile whispered dryly out of the night, to sting
Captaine Archer in the arm. Meanwhile the darkness bled with hideous
cries: *Whe, whe, yah, ha, ne, he, wittowa, wittowa!* — Captaine Newport
discharged his pistol, but without doing the enemy any hurt that anyone
could ken (percase because his lack of an arm unsteadied him). Suddenly
the arrows ceased. And the Salvages withdrew into the forest, mocking &
jeering most wantonly.

✳ ✳ ✳ ✳ ✳ ✳

That instant prov'd the beginning of the Englishmens' *twinkling fear,*
which in the coming years (nigh on half a century) would leave some irritable, e'en hate-stain'd; and exhaust the rest. *Twinkling fear* would steal their

appetites, dragging their eyes e'er back and forth inside their heads as they spied for foemen. But as yet they scarcely comprehended how high they stood upon the Hangman's stage. Their mental series ran: **.1.** Ambuscado, **.2.** Counterattack, **.3.** *Finis.* The black ocean stared at them from between the horns of adjacent dunes.

Some were for pursuing the Salvages through the darkness in that very moment, but Captaine Newport forbade so rash an action; for he suspected how the *true* series might flow: **.1.** Ambuscado, **.2.** Counterattack, **.3.** Counter-ambuscado; and so on until *Death.*

And now it doth grow too still, said his Rear-Admirall, that afore-said Captaine Radcliffe. Who can tell how many might be crawling nigh unto us this instant with their bows 'twixt their teeth? Soldiers, keep watch! Captaine Newport, as I do live, methinks we imperil ourselves —

Wise words. Sailors, to oars.

They withdrew, defering their revenge. By lantern-light they gathered upon the *Susan B. Constant* to complete their desecrated ceremony.

* * * * *

The Purser of the *Godspeed* bore the box of dignity. The table was a plank across **.2.** barrels. Just as we call the tools of a shoemaker's craft *Saint Hugh's bones,* so let us now call the tool of the Virginia Company *our President!* All the assembled Gentlemen watched **.1.** another like unto lynxes as Captaine Newport broke the seal and unlocked the oakum-wrapped box. *Trarintra-rarara.* Then Captaine Archer (his arm now bandaged) drew out **.1.** by **.1.** the slips of paper on which the *Counsell for Virginia* had been nominated. And the Gentlemen smiled faintly as they got remembered or not; they unjailed their breaths in silent puffs. These were their names: *Maister Edward Maria Wingfield* (a well-propertied old Soldier was he, who knew how to ride with his sword at his side); *Captaine Bartholemew Gosnold* and *Captaine Christopher Newport,* both likewise already mentioned in this Relation, *Captaine John Martin* (a decently retired Pirate, whose father had been **.3.** times the Mayor of London-Towne), next our Under-Admirall, *John Ratcliffe,* he who'd worried about the stillness; & *Captaine George Kendall,* against whom both Radclyffe and Martynne would soon be a-hissing — and a certain *Captaine John Smith* of Willoughby-in-Lincolnshire. When Captaine Archer read out the name of this last, the Companie grew passing silent.

* * * * *

Concerning Sweet John's appointment, the tale runs that his old jousting- & jesting-mate, Maister Barty, had actually made truce with Robert to help him, then call'd the yeoman to a supper at which he said: And I spoke once again to my Aunt Susie. Do you know, she's monstrous fond of you. And she can twist my step-uncle around her little finger. Isn't that excellent?

Yes, my Lord—

Dost please you?

O, so much! You're passing kind to me! And I hope—

The corn chills on your plate, Sweet John. Eat now. That's where your business lies . . .

You see, good Reader, Maister Barty's step-uncle, the .1. who tupped Aunt Susie and oft followed her advice, was the very reverend Knight *Sir John Wingfield,* who just happened to be son of the .2.nd cousin of Maister Edward Maria Wingfield, who'd invested much treasure in the Virginian Undertaking, which might have been why Edward Maria Wingfield had been appointed to the Counsell-list! . . .

* * * * * *

Now the Drummer drummed and .6. of these .7. brave hearts were called up (Captaine Smith naturally being forbidden to take his position) — fine Gentlemen all, I should say, chosen to rule over .8.score other fine Gentlemen few of whom (unlike those .6. or .7. Masters) had done a day's labor in their lives, for they would have no vulgarity. So the Counsell got sworn in most famously, and from their number they elected a President — that is, *Maister Edward Maria Wingfield,* who did promise by the holy Evangelists to betroth to them his best endeavors.

Neatly poised in all his ways, a calculating, premeditated sort of Generall, this Maister Wingfield took pains to dandify himself like unto Lord Mountjoy, the previous Viceroy of Ireland, whom he admired. Mountjoy had known exactly how to disarm the angry pride of loutish rebel Earls. Apparelling himself far more gorgeously than they, inviting them to parley over little silver goblets of delectably warm'd spirit, he transform'd 'em from foemen into awkward Rusticks beholden to his kindness. Wingfield had several times found himself likewise seated across from the stately Viceroy, but in place of the clammy atmosphere of ornate intimidation, our visitor met with fatherly affection. Against Irishmen, a silver'd refreshment-service warn'd of superiority. But when a liveried Servaunt did prefer up a mirror-metal'd goblet, filled almost unto brimming with sweetly steaming grog, into Wingfield's hand, that gesture reified cameraderie's honor. Indeed,

Lord Mountjoy had been capable of the most delicate attentiveness, whose sunbeams gilded Wingfield's hopes & thereby enchaunted his ambitions into courage. In a word, he felt understood. Not once in Ireland had he been tortured by the *twinkling fear*. Whenever others in private did question any judgment of their Generall, Wingfield spoke up sharply to defend him. The grand project of Empire was just commencing in those days; fools ridiculed it, but Lord Mountjoy revealed to Wingfield the secret caverns of national will, from which English Soldiers & Colonists would in coming centuries be hatch'd & let loose upon the World. Wingfield listened. He believed. He drank deep of his Generall's optimistic firmness. Corn-destroyer, Towne-burner, Lord Mountjoy taught a generation of Soldiers how to crush rebellions down. Under him, Generall Carew slew .12. hundred Irishmen, not to mention women & children unaccomptable. Meanwhile, Mountjoy parleyed with more rebels, & cut down their corn. This got results. He receiv'd the Queen's compliments. In 1601, when Kinsale got conquered at last (a worthy victory, which would lead to the entire subjugation of Ireland), Wingfield of course was almost at Mountjoy's right hand. Together they routed those *keening* varlets & their Spanish instigators! Each casualty was necessary, each reprisal brief. On horseback Wingfield pursued the Spaniards nigh unto their ships, until they sailed away forever. Leaving his disorderly Under-Captaines to pillage where'er they could, he hasted himself back with the sober remainder, & prov'd nearly in time to be at Mountjoy's side when that Conqueror entered the gates of Ulster. I should add that Wingfield's hero-worship did not partake of the merest atom of jealousy. His idol was too generous, too good. How could any man resent a Presence which would advance him according to his merits, meanwhile regaling him from silver goblets? The lesson which Lord Mountjoy did teach was: *Pardon all who utterly submit unto Authority*. Any rebel, murtherer or cattle-thief who came to him on bended knee, Mountjoy spared as *Politick* gave him leave. He allowed those Irish pagans license to continue their Papist idolatry — for what would be the use of inflaming 'em against us, when our Government could not yet garrison itself sufficiently for to permanently correct those errors? At his intercession, the arch-rebel Tyrone was spared from the gallows in 1603. Wingfield's conclusion, that mildness was politic, could not unfortunately be express'd through the same ardent givingness at which Mountjoy excelled. He was a lens, which refracted all he said & did into melancholick, anxious dignity. Moreover, being now decayed in years, his imperiousness rang peevish. Like most of us, he cut a less fine figure than he believed.

All made their President a low leg, as the saying goes, which homage he was passing pleased to accept. And 'twas most misfortunate to Sweet John that Wingfield got that dignity, for just as in olden times each Sheriff practically ruled his Countie, so 'twould be here in this new Shire of England call'd *Virginia,* since London-Towne lay so far a sail away. Wingfield prevailed & reigned. All Virginia was his. And Wingfield hated Sweet John.

✳ ✳ ✳ ✳ ✳

See John Smith in his dull brown shoes the color of mud puddles. See the President in his shiny boots & gold-striped knee-breeches.

Hold you patient, 'til we decide your case.

What course have I else, Maister President?

LORD's sake, you seem ready to catch me by my throat! I misdoubt me not some faultless Angel proclaimed your sovereignty o'er us all—

None announced any dignity which I did not full well deserve, replied John Smith, gazing near-bedazzled at the shining gold threads in his President's clothes. And 'tis a great grief to me that I—

'Tis true you're on the Counsell-list. But we must .1.ˢᵗ investigate & prove you clear'd of mutinous conspiracy, 'fore we can do more. I take this precaution because a certain Gentleman hath communicated to me—

My conscientiousness is known, Sir.

Likewise your contentiousness. You have the makings of a leader in your own station—

Yes, my Lord, and I am assured of that fact.

. . . Could you but stop uttering oaths against your betters—

Now I almost wish I'd—

Pray tell, do you mean to denounce us more?

I denounced no man whose brain was no block. I denounced only cretinous *policy.*

Wingfield blots a letter. Then he seals it with wax. Gazing mildly at Sweet John (whom he ne'er hath invited to sit), he in mildest accents inquires: At Guadeloupe?

Yes.

For which reason we silenced you, knave!

That you did, Maister President. But 'pon my faith, it now appears that our Masters would I'd *kept* my voice.

By all means, had it spoken submission.

But when the Helmsman kens not his compass—

Stop your mouth!

Sir, I *swear* 'twas not of you I spoke, but of certain so-call'd Navigators who bring their ship too near the shore —

Ha! By so saying, the guileful coistrel doth confess it! You would mutiny. You would murther me and the entire Counsell. You grow beyond impudency into full dangerousness . . .

Maister President, I have the same rights as you. The Companie paper says so.

You lie, stinkard. Though we're equally Counsell-men, were we in England I'd think *scorn* that you should be my companion.

I have the same rights as you!

＊　＊　＊　＊　＊

On the following morn, with dawn glowing orange like molten glass, our passing upright President Wingfield again convened his Counsell (excepting only the said Captaine Smith), and there on deck he swore obedience to King James, which he then required of each of his Counsellors. They flew a flag in the main shrouds. From the sacred box they removed the *Instructions Given By Way of Advice* which their Masters in London had composed for their good. These well-wax'd lines they read aloud, learning that they must after discovering a safe port for English commerce follow all grand rivers which bendeth Northwest, for that way they'd soonest meet *China* and the *Spiceries.* They vowed to do this. Then at their President's beck they forsook the icy glassy sea. Laborers & Sailor-boys remain'd at the beachhead, pegging fast a new shallop's water-ribs while whitecaps broke out upon the sea like some pale pox of idiocy.

Captaine Gosnold?

At your service, Captaine Ratcliffe.

Now how can we lay us down to sleep? These Yndians fear'd not our ordnance.

I agree. 'Twas as if they'd faced down guns before.

I know not how we may overawe 'em. Was it thus when you sail'd here **.5.** years since?

Nay, for they lov'd us. Think you they—

Remember Roanoke, said Radcliffe.

But—

Sure all these Salvages joined hands to slaughter our Colonists! They being but carelessly fortified, it took but casual sleight to vanquish 'em. And they being vanquisht, how could guns, or any toy else, inspire Salvages to fear us? I tell you, Captaine Gosnold, we'll never get leisure to disport ourselves here—

Until we find gold.

I've thought the like, Radclyffe did quickly say. But 'tis *copper* we'll get better hope of—

But *gold* brings Soldiers as dung doth flies.

Think you we'll discover any?

I foresee none.

But you allowed that otherwise—

That's why you said 'tis best not sleep. — Ha, ha! Ratcliffe, you grow pallid; I but o'erstate the case, for to make a jest! Fear not; did they slay a single man of us?

✳   ✳   ✳   ✳   ✳   ✳

'Twas now the heel of the Morning Watch. The President (who was both brave and straight-statured as befitted a Generall, & whose very elbows were coutered up in shining metal joints) march'd at the fore. Soldiers flank'd him with their snaphaunces at half-cock. Others carried pikes.

He'd already sworn ne'er to lead his followers into novelty by night. Easy to prove himself superior to Captaine Newport in that respect! In Ireland he'd brought home all his Brigades & Regiments, no matter what ambuscados the Irish fiends did plot. Here too he'd wisely wear his commaund.

Reader, if you've e'er visited the great harbor at Gravesend you'll have surely discerned how the sides of the proudest ships are studded with fend-bolts, to save 'em from being grazed or galled 'gainst their fellows. Wingfield's strategem was now to guard himself with so many dignities that other creaking vessels must be foil'd from harming him. For thus had Lord Mountjoy done. If Wingfield had fewer fend-bolts at his disposal (and these more meanly metal'd), why should we tax him for it? Here's what he possessed: .I. His noble blood. .II. His office. .III. His cultivated aloofness. .IV. His purse. He'd Adventured more heavily in this Plantation than any soul else; to him 'twas therefore very natural to expect immediate returns of wealth. Meanwhile, the treasures he already enjoyed ought to ensure the obedience of others. .V. His vassals. Canny comfort-worshiper, he'd carried .2. Man-servaunts with him to Virginia; the .1.st of these march'd briskly behind in his train, unarmored, while the .2.nd remained aboard to guard his luggage. (What he kept there in his Cabin on the Gun-deck many an idler had wondered without result; for the door stayed locked.) And as soon as the Colonie was establisht, he plann'd to appoint himself Sentries, Watch-men, Heralds & the like, the better to keep all others off his flanks.

It never occurred to him that such measures might work according to his disadvantage. The fact of his substantially generous Undertaking of cash was attested by the receipt he'd obtain'd from the Virginia Companie. The fact of his election to the highest dignity, & the corresponding fact of the Commission which was now his to execute, were likewise indisputable. Other facts, the disputable ones, he conveniently disputed, or, better yet, ignored.

None sat more securely (at least in his own estimation) at Captaine Fortune's side than did Maister Edward Maria Wingfield. Of new Countreys & Continents, 'tis the same as of new Townes — namely, that alien chances hang myriad like unto sweet wild grapes (else why should we have come?), whereas alien obstacles do not exist, for we've never yet seen 'em. The old Beggar cries for but .1. penny; with that he'll save himself sure! The Lover 'tangled in his own lies would start afresh with a new sweetheart — *then* by his faith there'll never be quarrelling more! As for President Wingfield, 'twas with him a *Credo,* that money planted anywhere in Virginia's ooze must instantly blossom into glistering thickets of itself. For Virginia was an immense commons virginal for the Enclosing; he'd do it by degrees, leaving considerable parts for the common Salvages until they should be subjugated, upholding the Salvage Nobility in all reasonable claims, & rewarding his Colonists with nice fat parcels to farm on. 'Twas possible they'd discover a salubrious spot for a Fort this very day. Or mayhap they'd find gold mines, or indigo, or something fabulous enough to be exhibited at London fairs. And for Wingfield's sake, Reader, I do hope so, for whene'er he got baffled in his projects, he fell easily awearied.*

Just then Ratcliffe craved leave to seek gold, which the President granted, instructing him, however, to stay in sight & with his pistol well-charg'd. — Dig with good spirit, he commaunded, & may Fortune permit you'll enrich us all.

---

*He was a type less common then than now, so that he stood out in his own epoch with novelty's bold colors. As a boy he'd been a dilettante, equally bored by his collections of butterflies and of sea-shells. Now he thought that every possibility of life, from love to money, was easily exhausted. He fancied himself monstrous wise to see these limits, which were but his own.

I shall revenge my poverty on this gentle ground, laugh'd Ratcliffe in reply. I'll open up her belly with many wounds of Discovery.

I doubt not. Take .4. Soldiers.

Aye, Maister President.

But nay! Bide awhile.

Sir—

We know not the odds. I would not write to London-Towne: *Dear
Radclyffe's been slain by bloody Salvages.* At my side! And you, Soldiers,
beat the drum! Bugler, to your duty!

Trarintra-rarara!

Pray, Maister President, I would—

Captaine Newport!

What would you?

Admirall, that mode of adress is not agreeable to me.

Pardon me, Maister Wingfield. 'Till yestereven you did defer.

Say no more, but now you must school new habits. I'd ask you: Where
lurk these Salvages?

'Tis what I inquir'd of Gosnold not long since.

And what said he?

He knew nothing, he replied.

Well, then, of your judgment where are they?

Everywhere, to be sure.

Do you fear them?

Those trifling bow-twanglers? Nay, not when Spanish galleons stay
'pon my will! Yet—

Maister President?

Aye, Soldier!

Shall we turn this way or that way?

That way. Newport, do you concur?

'Tis .1. to me.

Then, Soldier, you did hear my commaund. Bid that minion sound the
trumpet.

Trarintra-rarara!

Good Newport (resumed the President), I agree they cannot hurt us.
They're like unto those rascals who engrave their names 'pon the moldering railings of Saint Paul's—

Well, they publish't themselves in Archer's arm, true enough.

A moment ago you said you did not fear them. You're changeable
enough in truth . . .

Nay, I *mislike* 'em. For Archer aches, & my Sailor-boy looks to die.

These are no gaping casualties, Newport. Never fear; we'll avenge 'em once we're planted & fortified.

And yet my conscience sorrows at them. For 'twas I who misread the peril. But if you would discover fear, parley with Ratcliffe. He's the fellow who would have turn'd us back for England, when we found not Virginia in the **.1.**st twink—

He cast no ballot for me.

How do you know? That ballot was secret!

O, laugh'd the President, but I *know.*

Ratcliffe would be about his gold now, Maister Wingfield.

Tell him he must hold him steady 'till my commaund.

'Twas passing breezy, so that the Gentlemen must grip their hats to keep them 'prisoned on their heads. They had no conception yet of the malodorous heat that would come once summer was born from 'twixt Virginia's thighs. To them the clime seemed but mild; they'd conceived no dislike against it; 'twas warmer & easier than their Irish Colonies. And so they marched along, with their long guns resting crosswise upon their backs, pointing right or left. The sand of their brave Kingdome, almost pure white, was grabbled by the wind's fingers and sped over itself in long ghost-wakes like unto dust-trails fuming & twisting in parallels at right angles to the snappish waves. The President, pleas'd to his very stomach, felt Destiny's kiss. They ascended a low, sandy hillside which had once been a dune and was now dense with twisted oaks and pines whose foliage appeared strangely greyish-green in that cloudy, vaporous air. The trees ominously rattled in the wind. Ahead grew vines like snakes and snakes like vines. Now the *twinkling fear* returned to **.1.** and all. Their gazes rushed nervously from within their still living skulls which at any twink might be arrow-split like unto Captaine Archer's arm. But they could not forbear; they were Colonists; they were addicted to dice.

Approaching the forest as carefully as if every leaf were a green knife, they marched full **.8.** miles, yet, as before, they found no sign of Salvages until at last, round about the end of the Forenoon Watch, they discover'd a solitary fire from which those heathenish creatures had fled, leaving oysters roasting on the coals. The English did eat, altho' the *twinkling fear* was shading their souls with a darkness as dark and glassy as holly leaves.

* * * * * *

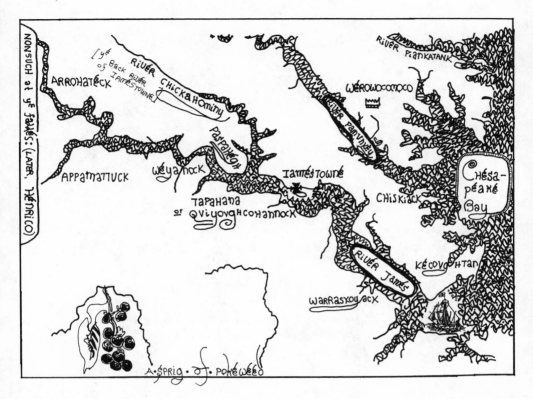

On the map:

NONSUCH at ye IAMES: (LATER, HENRICO)

ARROHATECK

[ye Back RIVER of IAMESTOWNE]

RIVER CHICKAHOMINY

RIVER PIANKATANK

WEROWOCOMOCO

APPAMATTUCK

WEYANOCK

PASPAHEGH

RIVER PAMUNKEY

IAMESTOWNE

CHISKIACK

CHÉSA-péaké Bay

TAPAHANA or QVIYOVGHCOHANNOCX

RIVER James

KÉCOVGHTAN

WARRASXOYACX

A·SPRIG·Of·POKEWEED

At Cape Henrico they did fashion a great CHRIST cross out of unpeeled Virginian timber, & the Laborers rais'd it up at at the Counsell's commaund. The Counsell-men knelt (hemmed in most safely by their armor-beetled Soldiers). Reverend Hunt did pray a goodly prayer, into which he incorporated the following homily from their *Instructions by Way of Advice,* to wit: *Euery Plantation which our HEAVENLY FATHER hath not planted shall be rooted out.*

THE GRAMMAR OF COLONISTS (1606)

My thanes & kinsmen, henceforth be Earls . . .
SHAKESPEARE, *Macbeth* (1623)

*P*resident Wingfield & his cousin Captaine Gosnold fell into a dispute most wrathful as to where they should erect their Cittie. Sweet John, still unseated on the Counsell (his submission being denied), turned away & split his sides with bitterly barren paroxysms, while others laughed likewise, until Wingfield call'd for order, with his hand upon the rapier in his belt. (They already call'd him deluded, like unto a Sleepwalker lost in a *Magick Circle of Dreams*.) Just as meridians do grow togetherward in the extreme north & south of this Globe, so Government (& for that matter consciousness) likewise distorts itself when we get too far from England. Their vigilance turn'd to mutual envy, & their longing to house themselves on new earth became *twinkling fear*. 'Twas dry sport to be here, the Sailors said. Where sang the wenchen & pretty Church-bells? They felt made fools of, deceived almost. Captain Fortune had changed himself, & crept away with every last sea-sparkle of gold, so that sense likewise fled from their Adventure, as if they'd come to on the floor of a Gravesend Tavern-house, bruised & begrogged, disremembering why or whom they'd fought. Now they saw that Virginia & London-Towne, 'twas all **.1.** All Gentlemen were asses, all Captaines diabolical.

Clear away this Publicke, commaunded the President, & then the idlers (including John Smith) must disperse. But the Counsell did linger there upon the beach almost as if to entice the next ambuscado into being. And their quarrel went on, just as in my own time rain falls e'er upon Virginian graveyards.

* * * * * *

Their *Instructions Given By Way of Advice* urged them to discover some strong island **.100.** miles inland where the river-course narrowed, so that enemies might be fusiladed from both banks. *When You have made Choise* *of the River on which you mean to Settle be not hasty in Landing Your Victual and munitions but first Let Captain Newport Discover how far that River may be found navigable,* so they sent sorties up several narrowing brownish-green channels which stank like the sea. Flood oh! (The broad trunks of oak trees were braided with diamonds, like rivers and rattlesnakes.) The President grew passing enthusiastic. As for John Smith, of course he was not allowed to go on any of these sublunary voyages, but stood at the gunnels of the *Susan Constant.* The river which they'd already christened *James,* in token of their Sovereign, seemed of best estate for their purposes (being the **.1.**ˢᵗ they'd found). What a fine roadstead it was! — wide like the sea, bluish-grey (at that hour) like the sky, grand enough for any frigate or vessel of war . . . easeful, also, should they need to retreat discreetly inland, to hide from the Spaniards of *Florida* — an ominous southerly Countrey (so I've read) where many, many alligators lie **.1.** upon another by the reeking water's edge, submerging their heads or baring their teeth in long yellow upturned curves of stupid viciousness.

Captaine Archer loved a certain isle whose sunny meadow rose gently to a knoll of blond grass overlooking that bleached blue creek befriended by low trees — in all, an airy, open, pleasant place wealthy in timber, squirrels & turkey-eggs; so they called it *Archer's Hope,* but the President said him nay, because the James ran too shallow there to moor ships close. What if Spaniards did steal betwixt 'em and their fleet? O, they'd be in a sickly disposition then! Captain Archer sat shrugging. He was applying crushed nettles to his arrow-wound.

Next, Captaine Gosnold prais'd the advantages of Cape Cod, & grew cross-grained when the President said 'twas not to the point.

They argued over their unbuilt city for a night and a day, until Reverend Hunt prayed for concord. The *twinkling fear* reeked within them all. Their armpits darkened with expectations of death. As Sweet John's friend Maister Barty would have said: *I can see that you are in despond here . . .* — And dark herons with ominous long necks passed silently o'er that river now constellated with dead white fish bloated almost as round as stars.

Where *would* the Countie seat arise? The President did summon all his Counsell-men (excepting John Smith) to a banquet served upon silver plate, and over this constellation of metallick *Jewels* they drew charts, & fix'd on a river-girt place to call *Jamestowne;* for it offered an excellent depth of water above the ooze; &, moreover, promised security 'gainst storms, neap-tides and spring-tides. — By my faith, but this isle is swollen with baleful humors! Yet they did not know this, but rejoiced, like unto some poor boy who finds a wet cold shilling-coin in a Church yard, & never scruples to think what skeleton-hand it might have come from.

* * * * * *

See John Smith gnash his teeth as he remains yet virgin to Virginia. The Marshal bids him lure patience into his bosom — good & necessary advice, which he essays to follow. To himself he mutters: *Cush, cush!*

What sayeth his Genius, all-knowing *Machiavell?* Closing his eyes, he murmurously recites the lesson: *As the circumstance of becoming a Prince from private station presupposes either* Ability *or* Fortune, *'tis manifest that .1. or t'other of those .2. qualities will quell many a difficulty.*

'Tis clear I possess Ability, not Fortune. For my luck's tides run e'er on the ebb. (Thus reasoned our aforesaid Captain Smith.) What doth the Mentor advise in such a case? O, I disremember not! *Those who by valorous ways become Princes, acquire their Kingdome with a struggle, but they keep it with ease.* 'Tis a comfort. I must but labor goodhearted, and bide my turn—

Then a worm moves within his heart, and he remembers how he'd stood prisoned equally in irons and hope before the *Tymor* in the stony Castle of Nalbrits; & e'ery time the Tymor did scratch him with a disdeignfull gaze, or curl angry fingers round that jade-handled knife, Sweet John bled another drop of confidence, shriveling & shrinking down into a pale corpsedoll which could scarce rattle its own slave-chains.

All who would be Tymor o'er me, beware! For I stung .1. Tymor to death already with a reaping-hook . . . — Nay, there's treason! . . . And yet, didn't *King Sigismundus of High Hungaria* grant me .15. hundred ducats for my own merit? And my Countreymen would hang me! And e'er they wrangle & blunder. I swear I'd bare myself to *any* authority, were it wise & accurate. But these Gentlemen fail to use me well. And I've labored past enough for tyrannickall Turkes—

* * * * * *

On the Royal Counsell back home sat .14. Gentlemen. He knew the .7. London men would be against him for the reason of his birth. The .7. West Countrey men would not be for him, because he wasn't from there. Should he devise a letter to them, or . . . ? — 'Twould take months or longer before Captain Newport returned a reply. And what if he obtained from it neither succor nor grace?

* * * * * *

The World did shrink in upon him 'till 'twas but a coffin's-breadth. All other souls moved outside the World. Here came Captaine Newport. Sweet John would express his opinions to him, & yet could not. The coffin-World clammed him down. He sat dull-eyed, a-yearning for to speak, yet wearied, bound. Far away, the Colonists & the Yndians buzz'd ambiguously.

* * * * * *

Just as a rascal may strive to appease the Night-Watch in London-Towne with jests or pretensions to high birth, in order to avoid getting jail-clapt, so this hairy little John Smith would clothe his malicious insolency, but Wing-field saw right to the bottom of him. He had thought himself free, in coming to Virginia, from all such self-willed diminutive annoyances as that yeoman. There was nothing innately unkind about Wingfield. Indeed, how could he have been elected, had the Counsell considered him ungiving or cruel? They call'd him *the amiable old Gentleman*. But Virginia was his own precious toy, which he'd purchased for a generous price. Now he'd play with her as he listed. John Smith was like unto a Beggar, or even some vile footpad, who snatches a Gentleman's arm, then cuts away his purse with a dagger-strike. Wingfield would not have grudged him his littleness, had he made due submission, but he e'er did spoil the yielding through a self-willed *urgency* approaching actual challenge. Confessing his own fault, Sweet John sometimes commaunded himself to dacker down, & make a leg, but he felt passing old to obey himself in that, having now survived full .27. winters of his age. Hadn't he bowed enough already to silly Maister Perigrine Bartty, that muck-riding ruiner of colts & Servaunt-wenches? And here was President Wingfield as haughty as if he did stand in the grand aisle in some Church! Sweet John held a patent from King Zigismundus! Why need he permit this President to bridle him? For he too was passing o'eranxious to wed Virginia . . .

* * * * * *

At the close of these Assises, they proceeded toward the afore-mentioned Jamestowne. Sweat oozed down into their nostrils, & wormy vines groped up the sides of trees. Sailing along the northern edge of Cape Henry (which in Sweet John's map bears much of the brunt of rays hurled in each direction by the compass-sun), they cross'd the river-mouth to reach Poynt Comfort, which of all the Counsell only Sweet John had not seen before. There some of the Gentlemen landed in the new shallop & prayed. (John Smith remained dispermitted to go ashore.) Come the **.1.**st bell of the Afternoon Watch they did fly the signal-flag from their flagship, & those praying Gentlemen re-embarked. They weigh'd anchor. A cannon-shot of consecration! Now the Adventure commenced in truth. Sweet John's heart uplifted. He'd found & save the Colonie . . . Running to the beak-head for to see, he spied the waiting introitus, birth canal of Queen Fortune, who, shifting face & sex, drops us every day into an unknown World. (Come, Soldiers! cried the happy President; on we fly!) Between these elastic walls they ascended, and so entered what until now had been call'd *the Powhatan River.* Many a bold-engraved river-wriggle lay ahead on Sweet John's map, for this fissure, this kinky hair, this twirling water-root grew all the way through Powhatan's Empire, then up the Falls to the Countrey of the Monacans. But how could our grave Undertakers ken aught of that? They'd not gone far in. And (as I've said) 'twas the very **.1.**st time in these parts for Sweet John! (He kept silent now, misliking the unsteady fashion in which they shortened their sails. He considered himself a better Seaman than Captaine Newport.) — Nay, tis several bends farther, he heard a knowing Sailor say. On the south side, in forest as green as that jewel-stone nam'd *Emrod,** they spied the villages of Salvages in this order: *Chesapeack, Mattanock* just past the **.2.**nd inlet, *Mokete, Warraskoyack,* then *Mathomauk* where the river narrowed and made strain to go northwest, subsequent to which it bent, wriggled and congealed. On that low wide promontory, or sometime isle, which Captaine Newport had mark'd, they swelled up their courage, then, furling sail & bending their cables to the anchors, they landed, there to build their Jamestowne. (Again Reverend Hunt guided them in a prayer.) Did I mention the baleful humors of that spot? I the *Ignoramus* (as historians are commonly called) make it my doctrine that 'twas unwise for a **.2.**nd reason, lying as it did in dangerous proximity to the low Towne of *Paspahegh,* whose Werowance was rumored to be warlike; but belike Wingfield was correct in his homing, for in those early days, before plagues, guns and fires killed the Salvages, what place was not infested with 'em? And, as he claimed, they were so weak that we could defeat them with *Eggshells, eggshells, eggshells.* Moreover (so he said) whereas Ireland was a nest of Spanish-

*Emerald.

paid traitors, at least these Yndians remained within a degree of animal innocency, so that betwixt kindness & firmness we might win 'em o'er. It did seem that this landing might well grow over time into a most splendid and sumptuous Seat. But John Smith, struck right away by its marshy noisesome lowness, heard a crying-out from within the mew or cage of his heart, because in running so far and far away he'd 'scaped not the doom of his birth: here lay the Fens of Lincolnshire all over again — merely warmer and oozier in a rotten stew . . .

✳ ✳ ✳ ✳ ✳ ✳

Yes, yes, he was a Woldsman, but you know, in olden times all Lincolnshire lurked more or less under water, like unto *Holland* of old. Marcellinus wrote to Rome that the British Salvages, *not dwelling in the towns but in cottages within Fenny places, compass'd with thick woods, having hidden whatsoever they had most estimation of, did more annoyance to the wearied Romans than they received from them.* In those days the water and ooze was often waist-deep. Sweet John own'd swamp-water in his very arteries.

✳ ✳ ✳ ✳ ✳ ✳

So they cut down trees revengefully, and raised their tents between the stumps (like unto those poisonous vermin which first gnaw holes in our flesh, into which can obtrude themselves; then, having both shelter and leisure, destroy our kidneys, bollocks, brains &c in their good time). Around themselves they dug a deep ditch. And then those who had *not* tents, or could discover neither patience nor affection for their tent-mates, dug holes in which to sleep — not so deep, nor oozy; line 'em with clean marsh rushes and you have a bed just as in England — no lice until the .2.ⁿᵈ night! (See John Smith a-soaking rushes in a grisset full of grease by day, that he might burn them for light in the even time. O, but he's provident! See John Smith curled in his hole like a vagabond, trying for to read, pinching mosquitoes to death. He strives not to compare this burrow to his bower in Lincolnshire.) Jamestowne, this was Jamestowne. Someday they'd plant orchards, but not tomorrow — no, nor next year, by the DE-ITY! Dark cypress-wands combed themselves across the swampy mirrors and pools streaked blue with tar-oil, while the .3. low ships of the fleet lay a-stinking & creaking in the slimy water from which all souls drank. Soldiers rolled out the powder-kegs; rats escaped from Ratcliffe's pinnace—

✳ ✳ ✳ ✳ ✳ ✳

Well (to make open proclamation), they relished life not. Gentlemen must dwell in excessive propinquity to their Servaunts, Soldiers, Blacksmiths & other vassals. They all ate slimy, maddocks-ridden biscuits & cried: *O, but for a tuppenny bun!* — The Lincolnshire boys (among them John Smith) went blobbing for eels* as they were wont to do in the home Fens; Sweet John for .1. was expert at that sport When he'd gained enough belly-timber for himself, he gave the surplus to his friends. His fellow Counsell-men supped from the Store-house (from which he continued disallowed). Every eve at darklins they withdrew to Wingfield's tent to drink well-sugared sack.

They spoke but seldom of their *twinkling fear.* But on the very .1.ˢᵗ night, when Sweet John's pit was but half-dug, Salvages had come sailing close in their Canoas, altho' they fled when the Sentry gave the alarm. Four days later, from marsh grasses higher than their heads emerged the Werowance of *Paspahegh,* attended by .100. armed Salvages (many of whom had tattooed themselves most heathenishly with rings and circles). 'Twas on his dominions that the Adventurers had seated themselves (altho', after all, Jamestowne Isle was o'ergrown with trees, so these Yndians shouldn't claim it). This Werowance (or *King* as I should say in good English) was painted black. His name was *Wowinchopunck.* Sweet John thought him very dangerous. He'd horn'd his face like unto SATAN. He swore that he welcomed them; indeed, his Bow-men dragg'd a fat deer for a feast; but soon .1. of his Courtiers essayed to steal a hatchet, no doubt for some bloody purpose, & so a brawl erupted, and those Yndians exeunted in a rage. Where they'd disappeared, reeds waved on & on, with the river oozing through them. And all did wait in dread, lest they return murtherously by night. Already some Soldiers had commenc'd to say that Paspahegh-Towne ought to be annex'd & dissolv'd, like unto the Papist monasteries now thankfully defunct in England. For from such near quarters could come only further mischief. Naturally, that pestiferous Sweet John Smith (who falsely claimed to be Captaine of .200. and .50. horsemen) did offer to capture the Towne for the Colonie. But the President commaunded him to silence, he having not yet been found guiltless of his crimes.

* * * * * *

See John Smith, a-trying for to warn our President of his fears. *Sure* the King of Paspahegh must hate us! We've settled on his lands. 'Twill be most

---

*"To catch eels with a ball of worsted and worms." — Campion.

Politick to stall him, until we've fortified. After that he can rage his worst . . .

But the President disdains to answer.

* * * * * *

See John Smith a-lying in his hole. Full miserable now, he takes this resolution: I'll gainsay my President no more. To win out, I'll kiss e'ery hand!

He brings to mind a certain Low Countrey wench whom he'd tupped solely to make his fellow Soldiers love him. In those days he'd craved any place, e'en a mean one. (His place was *.3.ʳᵈ from Left, .21.ˢᵗ* Rowe. He'd never disremember that.) 'Twas behind the Lazar-house in Haver de Grace that the business was done. Captain Duxbury sat at supper. Altho' he would have shewn her respect & friendship, yet they'd nam'd her *Spanish trull,* no doubt for good reason. He seized her while she stood amazed, then threw her down right there in the street. Her doleful lamentations were most wonderful to hear. O, he did repent him then; he would have begged her pardon had not his brothers chaunted pell-mell, pounding their feet upon the cobblestones in time with his raping. Should he fail to cobble together his purpose e'en to mercilessness, the Army might leave him behind, to struggle alone in the ooze of life. Afterward they call'd him *Good Knave, Spark,* & *Sport,* and were cheered to be his copesmate. For an entire warp* of weeks they paid his Tavern-house scores.

Now in Virginia, overcoming different scruples, he must again enter darkness if he would keep his place. This time, 'tis the darkness not of crime, but *meekness.* He must render up his submission to the President. Later, he'll repay all courtesies committed.

* * * * * *

But he sent his peitition for an interview with the President, & was refused.

* * * * * *

After the misery of the voyage, Maister Wingfield enjoyed the solitude of his own tent. The rawness of the settlement distrained him from repose no less than did the cares of his Presidency. As yet, their Virginian lives remained but speculative. But the Counsell and his Servaunts would host his commaunds in flesh, until all did thrive. His *.1.ˢᵗ* care must naturally be to array the Government secure. Captaine Newport he trusted above all — because

*Four

Captaine Newport would soon depart. And if we wander ahead a few centuries to the night when *Stalin*, having murther'd *Comrade Kirov* for fear of his popularity, did thereupon immediately enshrine him to be an Ikon, then we can see writ large the anxious turnings of Wingfield's mind.

Before his door-flap, a Sentry uttered his salutation. 'Twas halfway through the .2.nd Dog Watch.

What is it? said Wingfield.

Maister President, the Admirall doth invite you to sup with him tomorrow.

Send my assent.

Maister President?

Speak.

That unhappy Captaine Smith doth inquire—

Away with him.

Aye, said the Sentry, embarrassed.

And send for Captaine Ratcliffe.

They say he's—

I care not for what they say. Send for him now.

Aye, Maister President.

* * * * *

Soon 'twill be but you & I, & Gosnold, Martynne & Kendall, said Wingfield.

Aye, for a fact, replied Captaine Radclyffe complacently. Now, if we could but get Archer on the Counsell—

The President was silent. Then he said: No doubt it weigh'd heavy on his heart, when he did read aloud all .7. names, & none were his.

Shall we play a hand of *Security,* Maister President? For I do love to play that game.

Perhaps we'd do better to play the game of *Jamestowne.* Or do you prefer to fold?

Never! I'd lay all my coppers down on you!

Well, I'm pleas'd to hear you rest friendly to me. And the others?

I'll make a clean breast, said Ratcliff. Gosnell doth speak against you, but mildly, being your cousin. Archer awaits his opportunity. Kendall hath twice to my knowledge visited Captain Smith—

The DEVIL!

Ha, ha! I grant you he's a goblin indeed, Maister President.

And Martin?

O, he's too sickly to play any but a pawn's part—

Him then I love.

Gosnell points always to Archer's wound, as if 'twere like unto the very *stigmata* of JESUS. He says it proves we must drill our Colonists into Soldiers —

May his sayings stick in his throat! He's 'gainst me, too!

But it may be true, what he doth croak—

Forbear with your *Remember Roanoake*. Don't you see he would unseat me?

For what purpose? He voted you in.

Which proves nothing, said the President, shooting him an ill look.

Virginia having been uninhabited since the creation of the world, it had been easy until now to joy in his own reign. But now, on this night so heated that their very swords & guns did sweat, he fell victim anew to the *twinkling fear*.

＊ ＊ ＊ ＊ ＊

At his commaund they stripped the sails & sea-anchors from Ratclyffe's pinnace, so that none could desert the Colonie in her.

Back in '88, when Spain's Armada threaten'd us, Sir Walter Ralegh warn'd the Queen that e'ery Soldier must be issued **.10.** pounds gunpowder, half a pound of match per day for **.16.** days, & a pound of lead — which came to a cost of nearly **.600.** pounds sterling! Against Salvages we might not require so much; & yet our English armories lay far away . . .

He set Radclyffe & Martynne (after Newport the only men he trusted) to counting out the ordnance, & they discovered that some had already been stolen — for trade with the Salvages or for directer treason he knew not. In any case, he knew not whether weapons might prove more perilous in the hands of Salvages or Counsell-men—

＊ ＊ ＊ ＊ ＊

Remember Roanoke, repeated Radcliffe.

His timorousness had become a byword, & so 'twas sport to torment him.

'Twere best you shook off your sloth & found gold, said Captaine Gosnold. Then you'd be palisadoed about with greedy Soldiers—

Gosnell, you drone always the same tune, laugh'd Captaine Archer. His arm was already much improved, the tree-gums & nettles of Virginia happily proving better e'en than frankincense for healing.

Gosnold fell silent, but Radcliffe said in a low, rapid voice: I've heard tell these imps can shoot flint-headed reeds through Spanish armor at a **.100.** and **.50.** paces. And so, unless we fortify . . .

Then the President, not without eagerness, did commence to pace, &
said: Their true bent's obedience, as must come out. I rate 'em well.

Captaine Archer mischeviously murmured: *Remember Roanoke.*

Nay, I forget Ronaoke not. But that Colonie got builded out of baser
metal than our own.

'Tis true, said Captaine Gosnold. Moreover, I've heard that at Roanoke
Lord Grenville began too early to be rigorous with the Naturalls. He burnt
their Towne for a minor fault, which turn'd 'em dangerous.

Aye, cried Archer, and when t'other day they gave me my wound, how
minor stood *that* fault?

Ratcliffe said: Good Captaine Archer, we must not so, for Maister
Wingfield's now our President. And, looking toward autumn, I see no
safety, save in unity, patience, and good usage for all authority's forms.

I'm amazed my mild words could have cross'd him! But I beg pardon.
Now tell us, pray, what shall be our policy?

You're not on the Counsell.

But I *may* be, if we—

Radcliffe laugh'd. — You also would remove the little yeoman?

O, 'tis not up to me. But should he prove mutinous in truth—

I misdoubt me not you've made him your enemy, laugh'd Ratclyffe.

Enough of him, said Gosnold. Cousin, pray inform us of our policy.

To the Salvages? asked the President.

Yes. Is the last oyster devour'd?

It shall be *Fear 'em not.*

The oysters?

Gifted but with lowly fantasies, scarce kenning fire, kenning not the veriest wheel, how can they *not* be o'erswayed? Whether they kneel today or
tomorrow, I guarantee they shall; for in Virginia we'll enact our dreams
into prodigies and Forts to nullify their humors.

'Tis a wide and roomy strategy, quoth Radcliffe; but Captaine Gosnold
said: Then may I reckon that we'll enact our Fort without delay?

In silence, Captaine Archer gazed upon a squirrel which leaped in long,
shallow arcs, with an acorn in its mouth. There were .3. oysters left.

* * * * * *

Near Smith's hole there dwelt a Yorkshire boy nam'd John Asbie, who
nightly moaned (most clownishly): How long, O mightie JEHOVAH,
'fore I can once again sleep my undermeal in a bawdyhouse?

Sweet John did laugh and say: Here at Jamestowne, lad, you save your cost. Moreover, you're safer 'gainst the pox!

Marry, Captaine Smith, I seem myself to be a drowning man. I would go home to my lechery—

Now your fooling begins to stale. Come, play a round of Primero with me. We'll need .2. partners—

Captaine Smith?

How would you catechize me, boy?

What book keep you there?

Why, 'tis my Machiavell. I got it cheap in Lincolnshire, for in Virginia 'tis not easy to go a-borrowing books of one's friends.* Would you hear what he doth say?

Is he lecherous?

O, most dexterously so, but only for *Politick*. Here. He shews us how to divide Virginia into convenient parts. On this page he doth say . . .

* * * * * *

See John Smith come to supplicate Reverend Hunt as privily as may obtain. Maister Hunt doth say: I assure you that the President takes your case most excellently to heart. When the Fort's full-builded into tranquility—

Sir, he disobeys his own oath, to follow the Counsell's writ. I feel myself to be such a stranger under this Government—

Patience, my friend. Speak not thus mutinously, when you stand already arraigned of mutiny. I'll be your spokesman again in good time. Surely you comprehend we must all live in good accordance here!

Aye, Maister Hunt, but 'twas understood that when I came here I'd —

I'll tell you a thing, Sweet John. Have you e'er loved a lass?

Aye.

As have we all. What was her name?

Tra . . . Cicely.

Well, I loved, & did marry with my Elizabeth. And what a maid she was. All her behaviors did enthrall me with ecstasy. *'Twas understood*

---

*Actually, the Willoughbys had proffered it to him. Strange to say, the gift occurred at Robert's beck. Bartty thought 'twas out of pity, for after the decline of those earnest summer days of Sweet John's in the reading-bower, Robert had shouted: I tell him to give over, and he dreams! Give over, I've said to him, and he begs another courtesy of me! Wants to be me, Bartty, or be you — worse yet — or percase just have what we have . . . Poor stinking yeoman lad, sometimes for him I've cried my truthless tears! Let's give him Father's Machiavell! We know it cold; we need it not — let him play Sovereign to his dreams!

when we swore our vows that we'd dwell in happiness together for always. And shall I tell you the afterclap?

I'm right sorry, Maister Hunt . . .

O, she continues in life, never fear. But she lives commonly defamed for her incontinency with John Taylor of Heathfield. That's the reason I embarked me here to Jamestowne, altho' to do it I abandoned my .2. young children, whom I cherish with every beat of my heart. And I'm indifferent if I see not England again.

I agree, says Sweet John, 'tis a pitiful case.

And now you're wroth with me, for my grief doth interrupt your suit. Nay, lad, I meant it not so. Think only this: HEAVEN bids you bear yourself with a dry man's dignity, no matter what rain HEAVEN sends you. 'Tis an uncomfortable time, I know. But wait carefully upon your Fortune.

Year upon year I wait, Maister Hunt.

So do we all. Then comes death. John Smith, wilst thou pray with me? Aye.

Let's pray together this prayer. Are you ready? *The LORD is my SHEPHERD* . . .

✳ ✳ ✳ ✳ ✳

But 'tisn't *prov'd.*

Nay, Maister President. But look you: This *Virginia's* so excellent & vast a Countrey, that it must be rich in many things. And can we discover gold—

Such hopes have I, that I fear almost to number them.

They say you've Adventured near .1,000. pound in this Colonie.

Not so much, but enough, for which reason I was chosen President. We would all of us reap quick profit in quiet. This golden earth with which you fraught your ship, if the Assayers discover true color in it, then Jamestowne will become James Cittie in a year, & you and I both rich.

Ha! A toast to that!

To riches, glass 'gainst glass! (O, 'tis most excellently sugared sack.) But now I'd pick a bone with you, Captaine Newport. Your Sailors hath laden you with so much *Sassifrax* root that I fear me the price must sink in England. I believe they took .2. tons at the least . . .

No doubt. They too would get rapid wealth . . .

But they're the Companie's Wage-men, enriching themselves at my expense, & with my tools, to mine own detriment. Well, no matter. If your dirt proves golden for a fact, then—

May GOD have it so. And 'twould advantage us all, Maister President, if you'll dispatch Adventurers to make more discoveries ere I return. For there may be richer gold-mines on the way to the *Chinese Sea.* These Salvages are colored like unto Chinamen, so they must surely be the outlying vassals of His Celestial Majestie. Whatever you may find this year could prop us up. And I'll essay to wheedle us more support when Lord Salisbury doth summons me—

Urge it all the way from Plymouth unto London-Towne.

✳ ✳ ✳ ✳ ✳ ✳

Sometimes they smelled smoke from far away when the Salvages had been burning grass, perhaps as a signal to assemble their wicked *Bravos* and *Idolators* for battle. But at other times the air smelled of flowers or of the perfume of cedar-trees. The Colonists strove not to further lay waste one another's affections, lest their entire Undertaking fall extinct. Some even showed joy; their city had begun now, even thus, amidst the red oakleaves of last year & the hard white pebbles. For their Church they stretched an old sail between .4. trees, in which shelter Reverend Hunt gave them Common Prayer each day in the morn and again at darklins, and likewise each Sunday .2. sermons. Here the Counsell met, there being no more stately place for their quorums. Someday they'd improve GOD's house more solid-like, but not now. First 'twas time to keep consideration for their own houses. Those with forethought (such as John Smith) had dug & palisadoed gardens near their holes. All felt distrained by urgency; soon Captaine Newporte must go, leaving 'em alone here in *Virginia* without help. They reloaded the ships with clapboard from the forests, to make some try how profitably that might vend in England; they fashion'd nets for fishing, but little enough they did for their defense, since the President would not permit it. Even musket-practice they must do in secret, so nervous he was that any drill or exercise might culminate (as he thought) in unseating him. They'd already rolled into place their demiculverin on its squeaky wooden wheels. The barrel, longer than the height of a tall man, now pointed firmly out upon that river of sky-blue mixed with milk, & they aim'd it downstream, ball-ready in the event that the Spaniards would find them. But 'twas more than half for show. Every time you fire a culverin, there goes .14. pounds of good black gunpowder! A musket ball eats not quite

an ounce of powder. A demiculverin, of course, burns something in between. But how much powder sleeps in the casks in James Towne? And
how long will it preserve itself fresh? The aforesaid Smith (as President
Wingfield knew) comprehended little of these economies.

A white veil of cloud drifted in from the sea. And on the other .3. sides
pressed their jail-bars: dark and narrow trees in endless profusion, amidst
which lurked Salvages. — Pointing to the *Instructions Given By Way of
Advice,* Wingfield insisted, not without reason, that their .1.ˢᵗ care must be
to build a Store-house or Magazine, in which to land their victuals. Meanwhile Captaines Newport and Gosnold had been commaunded in those
same *Instructions* to march inland with pickaxes to search for gold or copper or any other minerals which they might find, for the Companie's grizzled Undertakers back in London must get their profit. How then with a
divided force could his Colonists raise up walls? Wingfield hatched better
worries.

Ratcliffe was the basest member of his conclave, & snickled his gratitude
by fanning his jealous fear; by that same process of transference through
which husband & wife become like one another, Ratcliffe for his part grew
pregnant with Wingfield's suspicions; so daily the hand & the tool blended
into .1. spiteful object. Captain Kendall, true man and Councillor, entreated Maister Wingfield even on his knees (so rumor said), until at last he
got rewarded with a grant of right to build a half-moon bulwark out of
tree-bows for the protection of the Fort, but nothing further; and even this
must be at his own pain. Captain John Smith grew heated with pity for
him (or, as some say, with ambition), & joined him in that labor each
evening when his own duties were done, digging with a turf-spade, whose
edge is keen almost like unto a pickaxe's; & this went on until the President
did summons him.

How now, Sir? asked the yeoman with grating courtesy.

Smoke darkened the palisadoes into silhouettes. Wingfield scraped at
the wall with his fingernail, and the dirt crumbled, smearing his finger. —
Worse than a Lincolnshire croft, he said in disgust.

Sweet John bit his lip. He essayed to take heart. He reminded himself
that large ships often fall behind in good weather, but forge ahead in bad—

You dig perpetually with Captaine Kendall. Whose grave do you dig?

I dig for the security of all of us, Maister President, I promise you!

If you feel secure, then why so pale? smiled our President in triumph.

Sweet John twisted his heel into the dirt, remembering how he'd stove in the Tymor's skull. To himself he thought: Your *Security's* but a game you play with Ratcliffe—

Silent, eh? said the President. What sick worm of peevish treachery turns 'neath your pate? GOD's wounds!

If you would, Sir, I'll begone, altho' I know not where—

And until now methought your sly endeavors were carried out merely in a threapening* spirit, when now I see your hard, most masterless contempt . . .

John Smith, no longer so youthfully brashful as to misknow where duty and safety lie, makes a leg & chokes out: I beg pardon, my Lord —

You beg pardon, yet beg leave to quit me; you begged in Ireland like a vagabond without a license! You'd pack up, would you? O, I know your game, you scurrilous Lincolnshire manure-hound! How many of your rebellious begettors was good King Henry called on to string up? I should have strung *you* up in Guadeloupe! Ratcliffe, come hither! Yonder knave begs to quit us! In a twink you'd dispraise me in London Town with facts most freakish, or with wry intimations of your face would spread your stinking tales . . . Aye, you 'scaped your gallows in Guadeloupe, but there are several distant errands I might set you on; therefore —

* * * * * *

On the .2.nd-and-.20.th day of May, by his own inclination and that of the President, Sweet John buckled on his new-regained broadsword and set forward in company of Captaine Newport & a score of others (especially *Soldiers,* who are squat and bulky underneath their pointed-headed morions), to discover the river to its source. The tide swiggled up; *flood oh!* he happily cried. — A diamond surmounted by a cross is the brand of Hagnaby Towne in Lincolnshire (kissing cousin, I should add, to the brand of Butterwick Towne). But how many diamonds had they ever seen there? Ha! John Smith would fill their mouths with the gawp-seed of amaze, when he shewed 'em true Yndian diamonds! — And they departed right cheerfully, for by law they could keep all the gold & silver they discovered, saving only a .5.th part to be tithed to His Majesty, and likewise all the copper they could find, excepting the merest .15.th part. (Moreover, how would His Majestie know what they hoarded away?) Captaine Newport for his part could smell gold somewhere. (He always could.) And so they fell to re-

*Contradictory.

connoitering just where the land did lie. At that time they still had great stores of flour, or *dumpling dust,* as 'tis named back home in Lincolnshire. Accordingly they remained starched, stiffened & dignified in the collars of their souls; and, falling subject to no desperate motive, could relish themselves in most worthy ease, spying such pleasant & best compacted groves as might have been acceptable to Greekish philosphers. Virginia loved 'em; American summer set her snares and snickles for their hearts. Clinging ivy clothed the forests in green sheets of mail, just as it doth in High Hungaria, where a man may fight Turkes in sight of the long red fish-back of a hill-castle's palisade, then run into the foliage & be safe from all revenge.

Everywhere they found Salvages most joyful and tractable, who danced & feasted them on strawberries. Captaine Newport chucklingly requited 'em with needles and beads. Altho' the Adventurers found no gold, they discovered many a fertile meadow of which they would gladly have become seized. (But the far-seeing *Instructions Given By Way of Advice* warned: *You must in no Case Suffer any of the natural people of the Country to inhabit between You and the Sea Coast for you Cannot Carry Your Selves so toward them but they will Grow Discontented with Your habitation . . .* Therefore, they had to wait until they could run those Naturalls out.) They marveled at the rounded-roof'd longhouses airy & open, each doorway scaffolded with poles to which bark curtains could be lash'd to keep out bad weather. Bemused they gazed upon the butterflies of fringed leather about the squatting people's buttocks. Bear-greased Salvages these all were, oiled & ointmented with the root or berry of some herb to tawnify them. Sometimes they plastered themselves with feathers. The men in some freakish humor oft painted their bodies black & yellow. As for the wenches, many owned snakes or flowers tattooed on their fat brown teats; and when Captaine Newport didn't see, why, in return for nailspikes and other trash they gave his Sailors many a treat. That ever moderate wencher, John Smith, for his part asked for no more than to suck the sweet cornleaf juice of Salvage Pastry-cooks, which regaled him wondrously well.

The land inclined gently upwards, as it doth at home going westward from East Fen to West Fen to Lincoln Towne. At the village called *Arrohattoc,* which comprised full many connected nokes & virgates of land (and Smith thought: how meet for my future pastures!), the Werowance called them to a banquet of mullberries, fishes, & suchlike dainties, following which he presented them (most conveniently for themselves) with a guide who swore to bring them to the Emperour of all these parts, by name *Powhatan . . .*

The Grammar of Emperors

To understand Pocahontas, one must first understand the Powhatan culture from which she emerged, a culture of dark superstitions and devil worship, a culture of easy cruelty and primitive social accomplishments. Although Pocahontas was exceptional within this culture, . . . she was not immune to it.

GRACE STEELE WOODWARD, *Pocahontas* (1969)

In the cruel and brutal world of mid-seventeenth-century England men were hanged, drawn and quartered for having the wrong ideas . . . an elderly clergyman [was] tortured and sentenced to death for having in his drawer a sermon which had never been preached and which he had no intention of publishing.

CHRISTOPHER HILL, *Change and Continuity*
in Seventeenth-Century England (1991)

*S*entinels with canoes gave the alarm. He called his Cronoccoes for advice. He knew them; their minds would prove as divided as his. It hardly befitted him to express irresolution, especially now in his ancient age. His subject Nations were already restless. What would these Cronoccoes propose? Ambuscadoes had failed. Nonetheless, he disdained the other turning, which was to welcome these *Tassantasses** with a dance.

A warrior came running from Paspahegh to warn him that the Tassantasses had shot magic at them, killing several warriors. The counterattack had not succeeded. Smiling faintly, he threw the man a bead.

He was cutting arrow-reeds as long as his arm. Bearing them back to his great house, he squatted by the rearmost fire. He must guard everything when he would rather lie in the laps of his wives. Why must this trouble sting him after all his other wars? But he'd soon unvex himself, once he'd adorned his judgment with darkness.

Scorning the smoky company of women, other men would have kindled a blaze in one of the pits outside, but not he. They had friends; in his posi-

*Strangers.

tion he could have none. He must be on hand for all, but only to give, take, judge, listen, command, reward or punish. Solitude cleared his mind. Yes, in the darkness his mind glowed like a jewel. What should he do? Hunching his shoulders a little, he glared into the fire. Soon he must paint his face, come forth and decide.

One of his wives had been tending the hearth; she fled. She feared him overmuch. Moreover, he found her not as beautiful as at first. Perhaps he'd bestow her on Wowinchopunck, who was now Werowance of Paspahegh. Surely the Paspaheghs deserved to be heartened, now that the Tassantasses threatened them.

He was rubbing the reeds with grease when his Cronoccoes began to arrive. Now all his wives appeared at once. Their faces and shoulders were already painted. Softly begging his pardon, they began to carry out mats to the sunny meadow by the second brook. Winganuske, his favorite, was grilling a deer outside. He sent Ottopomtacke and Appomosicut to prepare more walnut milk. The rest began to bring trenchers of fresh bread.

Without looking up, he asked his brother Opitchapam, whom he'd hosted now for two days, to smoke a pipe with the guests until Uttamattomakkin and the other priests were ready. Although it would have been more appropriate to welcome them himself, he remained unready in his mind. They would complain. But before him they'd say nothing unmannerly. He held them all in his hand. He would give them copper crescents. After each of them had spoken, he'd hold a dance to make them dizzy with delight. The People would sing. There'd be another feast, with his Cronoccoes all seated round this very fire as he reclined above them with his loveliest wives. He'd smile on them all, and pretend to bite at their bait.

Opitchapam, who was in equal proportions unmanly and understanding, left him to his silence. He grimaced for unease. He must conclude on something now, before he passed the pipe. Sweating in the smoke, he prayed for cunning in all things. Then he stared into the hearth's red womb. His hands knew their task so well that they never needed to disturb his eyes. His fingertips dipped in and out of the gourd of bear-fat, then caressed those smooth-plucked reeds, enriching them with life even as they felt for crookedness or weakness. Once each reed was softened through, he held it close over the coals and bent it straight. Then he set it down on a scrap of deerskin to cool. Again he prayed. A flame flicked upwards like a snake's tongue.

He could hear the people singing songs now to welcome the guests.

Winganuske, who alone would have dared, lifted the screen of mats and stood before him.

Has Uttamattomakkin sent word?

No, husband.

Go feast the visitors.

Although he could scarcely see her there in the darkness past the fire, he was well aware of the anxious manner in which she turned away. She lifted the curtain of hanging mats, and vanished. Again he hunched alone, and no VOICE spoke unto him.

Most of his arrows would be perfect. There was one which he disliked, he knew not why. Casting it into the embers, he watched a yellow mane of fire rise up along its backbone. Bear-fat oozed out of it and sizzled. Then it twisted itself into black brittleness. It was a thread; it was a ghost; it was gone.

His daughter Mayachanna, herself now a matron, came respectfully before him. He arose to embrace her. From her presence he knew that her husband Uttamattomakkin was prepared at last. Smiling, she ran to help his wives make more walnut milk for the guests.

He painted himself crimson. Winganuske rushed in to bedeck him with pearls and coppers. He donned his mantle of raccoon-skins. Then he convoked a meeting in the Wiochisan House.*

The torches were all burning high. Uttamattomakkin greeted the others in silence, with his face black-painted. With him were four other priests from Uttamussack, two priests from Pamunkey, a priest each from Paspahegh and Kecoughtan (those towns lying closest to the Tassantasses), and the three priests of Werowocomoco who stayed ever in this Wiochisan House. Thus there were twelve of them in all. Beneath their black paint, their skins were already blackened with smoke, for like women they spent much of their lives indoors. Four of them went behind the mats to speak with OKEUS. The ones who waited heard Uttamattomakkin crying out in the magic language, and then they heard a low, muffled, bear-like grunting which might have been OKEUS's answer. Now Uttamattomakkin called out sharply, and the other eight priests rose and joined their comrades.

The others waited silently with lowered heads. Something sizzled behind the mats. They heard singing, and then all fell quiet. The priests emerged, sweaty and faint. They sat down by the fire.

*A temple to OKEUS.

Uttamattomakkin said: He spoke.

Powhatan gazed at him.

Uttamattomakkin said: He told us that the prophecy you know of will soon come true.

Powhatan frowned angrily. But there was no hurrying the priest.

Uttamattomakkin said: He said that we must bring one of these Tassantasses to this Wiochisan House. Until then we must not call Him, again.

Now the nervousness mounted above their chieftain's heart, so that he wondered whether it would gnaw him down to death. OKEUS had said nothing that was clear. As ever, Powhatan was alone. On him lay all the responsibility.

No one knew where the Tassantasses came from in those forest-like ships. He was informed that they were a wandering Nation, not very numerous. They appeared and then vanished, sometimes for many winters. But each time they came back, they were closer on his dominions. And so it had begun to seem to him that all his life he'd faced down their evil, although in fact he forgot them whenever they were absent. He had far greater dreads of the Susquehannocks. Yes, he'd dreamed bad dreams of the Tassantasses. They'd come to spread plagues and make slaves. But the Monacans were still more dangerous, and Uttamattomakkin had recently warned him against the Chesapeakes. They were all worms; he must fear them not.

A wind-breath caused the walls of the Wiochisan House to creak back and forth. The smoke-holes danced above them.

So, said Powhatan.

One of his Cronoccoes, his son Parahunt (a valiant boy, whom he must reward), spoke to him thus, saying: Let us dispose ourselves against these rovers. We'll devour their lives. If we fail, that's the time to be their friends.

Wowinchopunck of Paspahegh said simply: I curse them. They weigh down my dominion. Let there be an end to them.

The high priest of Uttamussack said: They have appeared. They will come here. They will come to Uttamussack. I see it.

All fell silent.

Opitchapam finally said: If fortune favors them, I would learn their secrets.

But his other brother Opechancanough, a great Werowance much in the people's esteem, began to speak in a different way. Opechancanough said: I was young when they built their houses at Roanoke. Parahunt, you weren't yet born. I went there when the Island Nations alerted us. I saw these Tassantasses. Then we agreed: This year they must perish. So our People joined the Island Nations. The Tassantasses slept unready. They had no friends because they were murderers, so no one warned them. None escaped except for some children whom we adopted. Now they come back again. Must we kill them twice?

(Parahunt smiled angrily.)

Opechancanough continued: We can neither frighten nor instruct them. OKEUS has not declared. Who are they? Where is their Nation? What is their magic? We must discover everything about them. Then, with divine help, we'll destroy them forever.

Uttamattomakkin, he who kept the shrine of OKEUS, spoke thus: I like what Opechancanough has said. Let us bid them come unto us. Then we'll study what manner of beings they are.

Powhatan smiled grimly. He knew they'd all do as they pleased.

To Opechancanough he said: I will not receive them. If you see fit, brother, then by all means stay and await their coming. Feast them at your expense. Learn what you can; tell them nothing.

Because they still looked at him expectantly, he said: I have seen the deaths of all my people thrice, and not anyone remains living of those three generations but myself. I know the difference between peace and war better than any in this Nation.

* * * * * *

He spoke privately to Wowinchopunck, advising him to endure his injuries. In good time, he'd help him revenge himself upon the Tassantasses. Meanwhile, he promised him a wife.

* * * * * *

The Tassantasses grew hair around their mouths, like the Keyauwee Nation to the southwest. They behaved as erratically as women. Laughable, yet treacherous, they possessed many good things. (He kept a musket barrel and a brass mortar which Opechancanough had pillaged from the dead at Roanoke.) He preferred not to meet them, for they figured in several of Uttamatommakkin's doleful prophecies. They'd slain the People and their Werowances alike, for no reason. They ruined cornfields. Wherever they came, People sickened & died without remedy even of OKEUS. They captured warriors and took them away. Just two summers since, they'd be-

gun to trade, then suddenly murdered the Werowance of Rappahannock . . .

* * * * * *

Now it came to Powhatan's ears that the Tassantasses had already proceeded all the way to the head of the falls, called *Paquachowng*, where
his Nation ended and Nation of the Monacans began. Fearing that they
might league themselves with the Monacans, he sent urgent word to
Opechancanough, who promised yet again to feast them if they crossed his
way on their return to the island where they dwelled. Powhatan knew not
whether they ought to be used or destroyed. If they would teach him how
to kill at a distance, with their diseases and their thunder-sticks, then perhaps he could exterminate the Monacans.

* * * * * *

And so Captaine Newport's Undertakers did dine with Prince Opechancanough, & Captaine Archer afterwards wrote in his relation: *There is a*
king in this land called great Pawatah, vnder whose dominions are at least
20ʸ severall kingdomes, yet each king potent as a prince in his owne terri-
tory. These have their Subiectes at so quick Commaund, as a beck brings
obedience . . . He thought he'd met Powhatan, but in fact he met Parahunt,
who was there to spy upon the Tassantasses . . .

The Grammar of Virginia

I would banish all minor questions, assert the broad doctrine that as a nation the United States has the right, and also the physical power, to penetrate to every part of our national domain, and that we will do it — that we will do it in our own time and in our own way, that it makes no difference whether it be one year, or two, or ten, or twenty — that we remove and destroy every obstacle, if need be, take every life, every acre of land, every particle of property, every thing that to us seems proper; that we will not cease till the end is attained; that all who do not aid us are enemies, and that we will not account to them for our acts.

GENERAL WILLIAM T. SHERMAN, to General H. W. Halleck (1863)

The people vsed our men well vntill they found we began to plant & fortefye, Then they fell to skyrmishing & killd 3 of our people.

Thus runs the postscript of a letter from Sir Walter Cope to my Lord Salisbury, in the year of our redemption 1607, which is to say the very first year of the Colonie. Thus, if you will, a précis of this entire Dream. As for the **.3.** who perished, well, they weren't quite the last. Burn'd alive or perish'd of the pest, cannonaded or flayed, the multitudes became Captaine Fortune's treasure. He flew o'er, with whirring wings. Then he swooped, but not for long. He was off for London-Towne, to make a plague.

The Grammar of Lovers (1607–1608)

... impressed by Smith's self-confidence and by such supernatural instruments as a pocket compass, Powhatan seems to have invoked an Indian custom and adopted Smith into his tribe as a subordinate werowance. A ceremony followed in which Powhatan's little daughter Pocahontas played an unclear role.

      PHILIP L. BARBOUR, "Brief Biography of Captain John Smith" (*ca.* 1980)

*S*ee Smith run. At Jamestown, .17. men got pierced by arrows, groaning o'er their green wounds, and .1. Cabin-boy sped entirely out of life. So Jamestowne presses on her occupants with all the stiflements of a Church-vault. Who's our enemy? Some say 'tis that black-faced *King of Paspahegh;* others, distraught with rumors wherried in by Yndians come to trade, blame *Emperor Powhatan* (whom none of us hath seen) or his brother *Opechancanough.* And Sweet John lies dessicated, dis-Counselled, drain'd of all his war-juice. Would they but resurrect him into potent grace he'd work most cheerfully to save 'em all! He can't ken their policy. When the battle came, he lay festering in the pinnace at the President's order. Fearing now he'd bide convicted forever, he gnashed his teeth & gripped the gunnels in despair when bowstrings commenced to twang. *Whe, whe, yah, ha, ne, he, wittowa, wittowa!* After all his *Trve Travells,* to be con-signed to watch the battle as if he were a yokel gaping at Shakespeare's plays, well, 'twas worse than being trapped at Gravesend, watching Cap-taine Fortune sail away! The pity was, he knew just where & how to shoot; he would have made those Bow-men look to their own fears — yet not a single Salvage got skullduggery's reward, for thanks to the President all the guns were locked in their casks. Likewise enclosed in grief, Sweet John waited unto the morrow. He sought to busk himself up in silvery prayers. At last, being wearied out with the folly of this Government (or, as I should say, the lack thereof), he requested an interview, which the President de-clined. Therefore, crunch-treading o'er oyster-shells between the trees, Sweet John went privily to Captaines *Newport, Gosnold, Archer* &

Kendall; for he no longer cared whether he might be re-indicted for treasonable sayings. What had he won him, for all his hire?

'Twas hot & stinking at James-towne, like unto summer in Spain. They gave thanks now for their long, greasy locks & beards, which kept Mosquitors from stinging 'em, in those parts, at least. Pest-ridden and starving, their complexions asheen with that poisonous yellow hue call'd orpiment, they'd become so riddled with the *twinkling fear* that they durst not go into the forest even for wood, but stripped the deserted houses of their perisht fellows. Mangy exiles they, their resolution (whatever they'd had) melted to frogspawn. This was what he opined to the aforesaid Niuport, Gosnell, Artcher & Kendal, who hearked in friendliness (I'm surprised to tell); and he also quoted to them wise *Machiavelli,* who warns that when Princes think more upon ease than upon the wars to come, then they'll surely lose both titles and estates. What if our Colonie were already lost? Scarce .3. barrels of salt pork stood unbroached; all tuns of beer were drunk or burst, some wine-barrels leaked (or did coistrels drink 'em up by night?), and very likely this *Virginia* would have at them with her inclement season just as did (for instance) *Transylvania,* a Countrey whose winters he remembered as direfully as doth the child the fire which burned his hand, so let us have a care, Gentlemen, &c. Thus spake Captaine John Smith — truly a Captaine, no matter what his enviers said, *Captaine over .200. and .50. horsemen* — and the other .4. Captaines listened as though they rightfully conceived of his words. — Aye, said Captaine Kendall. I fear our General's in his dotage. — (But Captaine Gosnold whispered low to Captaine Newport that 'twas plain John Smith was motivated from greed for some preferment . . . — to which One-Arm replied: Then, by JEHOVAH, he's brother to us!) So these .5. together pled of the President for a meeting with the Lincolnshireman. Came another refusal (a thing unseemly & most indecent) — on which occasion Generall Wingfyld also said: Why give ear to John Smith? For 'tis proved, as a thing beyond question, that he begged in Ireland like a rogue, without a license!

Howbeit, just as at tithing-time the Husbandman himself picks out the first .2. lambs to yield up, but the Titheman chooses the .3.rd, so it befell that the .3.rd initiative in this matter came from the President himself, who got prick'd by a revelation not long after the Cabin-boy's funeral. What was he about? Not .1. of his soul's prophecies had been fulfilled! It may have been what his Sentry saw that undid him — an uncanny sight of dappled leaves resolving into painted foemen & back again, e'er & restlessly, like unto waves of shape-shimmers just beyond the half-built walls. He grew amazed; he let out a hideous shriek. When Maister Wingfield heard the tale, he thrilled with the *twinkling fear.* Scarce .3. days before the battle, a painted Yndian canoa had come to James-towne, & from it had leapt a messenger from King Powhatan, promising Maister Wyngfeld specially that all the Salvages would now bide e'er friends. But Captaine Archer (he who'd usurped Sweet John's place in the Counsell) did murmur somewhat about *that subtle old Poughwaton.* And Maister Wingfield grew afraid. — It may have been the shrilling of Death's imps, those *Mosquitors,* which haunted the President in his tent so that he could but scantly sleep, &, arose sick-eyed to inhale days which choked him with their syrupy weight. For he did feel ill. His tabulations of traitors grew as muddled as the Sentry's sight. Attainted with fever, he could scarce raise his head from his chest, & yet his eyes, which longed to rest, servilely followed any insect's flight. Baited by the little yeoman's threats, he dared not crush him, on account of his nomination to the Counsell; & now apathy, corroding vigilance, inclined him to a truce with his own race. — For whatever cause, our President could finally scent around him the hyperintelligent malice of so many Salvages on this fine morning arrayed with its Werowances and Weronesquas — to wit: (I) *Parahunt,* also call'd *Tanxpowhatan* because he was .1. of Powhatan's sons; on the border with the Moncans, he had .50. fighting men; (II) *Ashuaquid of Arrohateck,* with .60. warriors; (III) *Coquonasum of Appomatuck,* with .100. warriors; (IV) *Opossunoquonuske,* sister to Coquonasum, whose small village, namesake to his, possessed .20. fighting men; the English were to burn this town in 1610 and murder some of its inhabitants because the aforesaid Opossunoquonuske did to death .14. woman-trusting Englishmen after a feast; yes, Reader, they'd soon treat her with small shot; (V) *Kaquothocun of Weanock,* who could summons .100. fighting men; (VI) *Ohoroquoh of Cecocomake,* a cater-cornered village in the Weanock province; he had .50. warriors; (VII) *Oholasc,* the Weronesqua of *Coiacabhanoauke,* or, if you prefer, *Tapahanock,* or *Quiyoughcohanock;* how many Soldiers stood at her beck only she & Powhatan knew (her son was *Tathcoope;* he'd soon be Werowance; the previous Werowance had been named Pepiscunimah, but he stole a woman from Powhatan's brother **Opechancanough**, so that finished him); (VIII) *Tackonekintaco of Warraskoyack,* whom the English would capture in 1610 along with his son *Tangoit;* they'd bring him to the Lord Generall, with whom Tackonekintaco would contract to exchange .500. bushels of wheat, beans & peas for an indefinite quantity of copper, beads & hatchets, after which, the transaction being completed to the satisfaction of at least .1.

party, Tackonekintaco got his son back, leaving a nephew as his hostage; and just off Poynt Comfort, where beside ragged jumpy whiteness of almost played-out waves, beside salty sand-bubbles popping, a fat brown crab galloping underwater in a lagoon, fog halfway up the hills, beside foam so pure, beside paisley-flecks of foam on the brown waves the Lord Generall succumbed to a hankering to pick silk-grass, at which Tackonekintaco's nephew leaped overboard, forgetting or miscalculating the weight of the fetters on his legs, so that he drown'd, in consequence of which the aforesaid Tackonekintaco, quite unreasonably blaming the Lord Generall, renounced his bargain, compelling .2. companies of men, .1. under Capt. Brewster & the other under kindly **Argall**, to raze .2. towns of his to the ground; this Tackonekintaco at any rate commaunded .60. fighting men; (IX) *Weyhohomo,* the great Werowance of *Nansamund,* together with his .3. lesser Werowances (X) *Annapetough,* (XI) *Weywingopo* and (XII) *Tirchtough,* controlled .2. hundred fighting men; (XIII) black-painted *Wowinchopunk of Paspahegh,* who on the .9.th of February 1611 would be spotted "skulking" in Jamestown, so Governor Percy would send Ensigns Powell & Walker to get him; not succeeding in taking him alive as ordered, Ensign Powell would stab Wowinchopunk twice with a sword; and we can't accompt how many men Wowinchopunk had, but a goodly number of them shot arrows on that day until they could retrieve his corpse; (XIV) *Pochins,* another son of Powhatan's, who ruled at *Kecoughtan;* (XV) some person or persons unknown on the *Chickahominy River,* who controlled .3. hundreds of men (later 'twould come out that the Chickahominies had no Werowances at all, which was why Powhatan long'd for to devour them up); (XVI) **Opechancanough** the afore-mentioned; (XVII) *Kequotough,* (XVIII) *Toughaiten* and (XIX) *Ottahotin;* all .4. being Powhatan's brothers in *Pamunkey,* and the latter, our afore-mentioned Ottahotin, ruling his subdomain of *Kiskiack;* he controlled .50. men; they, .3. hundred; then there was *Werowocomoco,* the capital as we might say, with .40. fighting men; and doubtless more at **Powhatan**'s need; (XX) *Ohonnomo of Canaunkack,* with .100. men; (XXI) *Ottondeacommoc of Mummapacun,* with a hundred men; (XXII) *Essentaugh of Pataunck,* with .100. men; (XXIII) *Vropaack of Ochahannauke,* with .40. men; (XXIV) *Keyghaughton of Cassapecock,* with a hundred men; (XXV) *Weyamot of Caposepock,* with .3. hundred men; (XXVI) *Attasquintan of Pamareke,* with .4. hundred men, (XXVII) *Nansuapunck of Shamapa,* with .100. men, (XXVIII) **Powhatan** again, when he lay at his secret Towne of *Orapaks,* with .50. men; (XXIX) *Opopohcumunk of Chepeco,* with .3. hundred men; (XXX)

Attossamunck, a Tanxwerowance of *Baracanos,* with **.10.** men; (XXXI) *Pomiscutuck of Voughtamund,* with **.70.** men; (XXXII) *Werowough of Mattapanient,* with **.100.** & **.40.** men — the total comprising **.3.** thousand, **.2.** hundred and **.20.** fighting men, as well as we can know. And I beg you, Reader, not to censure my imperfection, should these details have been too curious for your liking. President Wingfield, at any event, had not such Arithmetic at his beck; but perhaps in breathing that humid Virginian air he began to suspect that he might be inhaling the respirations of many, many Salvages who crowded & watched him. In short, he was galvanized (let's not say paralyzed) by the *twinkling fear.*

Powhatan wore the crown. Could he but treat with Powhatan, all would fall under order. A commaund from that rusticke Sovereign, & no ambuscadoes would molest our troops! 'Twas why he strove to remain lenient toward the Yndians as long as he could: Without mildness, how could he send out Envoys? Once he better conn'd the lay of the land, he could march along to accept submission from each Salvage Towne. In other words, what his Critics did take for folly was truly politick. But Powhatan sent him no Ambassador.

In the night he commenced for to have bad dreams of Salvage murther & destruction. No doubt that the Salvages held sway in the white river just beyond his authority; no doubt they could each night disturb his rest!

And so Sweet John won the point. On Wednesday the **.10.**th day of June, at the wise beseechings of Captaine Gosnold & Captaine Newport together, the Marshal of the Counsell (having frisk'd him for weapons) permitted him to step forward, drop his leg in all courtesy to these assembled Gentlemen, & take the place to which he had been instated so long before, so that poor Captaine Archer, dismissed by Captaine Fortune, got expelled from his unlawful seat, & necessarily became Sweet John's enemy. What of that? Sweet John was at last a Counsell-man! He felt himself to be monstrous strong of might now; he aspired for to be President — in G O D's good time, of course, let not G O D believe he wasn't satisfied . . .

Yet still Maister Wingfield delayed in swearing him into the seat he occupied. O, he was present, but only as a sad ghost (which perhaps he is now as I compose these lines). Again & again (altho' he would have flung it from him) he seemed to traffic in that spiteful memory of the day he'd called upon the Rector in the Church yard of Willoughby, pleading to learn how matters stood with his inheritance. Every triumph had 'scaped him, with the single exception of that coat of arms graced by **.3.** grinning Turkes' heads. (They laughed at that device here in James Towne. They agreed that he'd invented it from his own phantastickall phantasies. They call'd it his *signed patent to Virtue*). Sitting with his superiors in President Wingfield's tent (whose flap had been shut, for fear of Salvage arrows, so that 'twas as dark within as the nook behind hogsheads in an alehouse), he raged to find himself *disallowed to speak!*

Maister Wingfield's white laid gloves came a good .6. inches up the wrist; & were embroidered with floral abstractions comprised of metal thread. Sweet John would have joyed to possess such gloves. Disallowed to speak!

At his left hand, Captaine Newport whisperingly bade him be patient. Sweet John smiled upon the President, hating him.

The President peeled off .1. white glove, the better to scratch a palm. — What news? he said.

First, regarding your health, Maister President, quoth sickly Captaine Martynne, we should dearly like to know—

My health's at fault, said Wingfield. 'Tis natural in Virginia. What news?

Being foeman-compassed . . . began Captaine Archer, sitting in the corner.

You all irk me . . . Your panic's shameless . . .

Do you need physick, Maister President?

Nay, but my head . . . Now hark. I'll suffer no more conspiracies. Remember your oaths, or I'll do execution.

At this, Captane Kendall did bristle & say: 'Pon my word, Maister President! We all of us supposed you an amiable old Gentlemen until now! Every faction thought to make you its tool. 'Twas the reason you were voted into your chair. Now, if you would try my patience, by all means badger me with your new-granted powers, but I can sail away to Gravesend tomorrow if I list!

GOD rest you then, said Wingfield through his teeth, as the other Counsell-men did roar at Captaine Kendall.

Finally Captaine Ratcliffe said: We're content to be loyal, Maister President.

Thank you. Now, what news?

I must haste me back to London-Towne, said Newport. My men commence to eat your stores, since our own grow foul. 'Tis most seasonable to go, but I misdoubt your Colonie's strength . . .

If there truly be, as our *Rustickall friend* there assures us, no hope for the Colonie, then we might as well embark our boats! laughed the President in a soft low voice.

That's hardly Captaine Smith's position, Sir.

Captaine Niuporte, pray tell me, which follies shall be licensed, should John Smith become President?

(For who said that Edward Maria Wingfield could not read minds?)

At this jest the Counsell-men did laugh.

Sweet John uprais'd his hand, meeker than a lad at school.

Disallowed to speak, yes, but 'twas finally his moment equivalent to that twink of time in alehouses when tipplers did say to Argall: *Hold up your dagger-hand!;* now by dint of all his war-tricks he'd save the Colonie, rendering such service that at last he'd be freed from that cage in which he'd been born. Excitedly, he commenced for to explain, *Butter & eggs, butter & eggs.* He stood ready to do service in full sincerity —

＊　＊　＊　＊　＊

As he went on explaining, his mind's eye, desperate to spy out superiority in its superiors, persuaded itself to see, not President Edward Maria Wingfield at all, but instead a dead man, a kind man, my Lord Willoughby who always sat with hound and dagger by his side.

＊　＊　＊　＊　＊

Go to, said the President, worn out by his inferiors.

Then Sweet John began:

.1. He set them to deepening the triangular ditch within whose bounds they reposed; within this moat they planted better palisadoes of stout oak logs, which they bulwarked behind with ooze-weighted earth. **.2.** At each meeting-point of ditches they raised a bastion, so that they might be upon their guard against the Salvages. **.3.** They culvertailed the timbers like unto those of a well-built ship: Plank lock'd into plank, & the whole grew more invincible 'gainst assault. And Sweet John knew not that month by month he was performing the same within his own heart. — **.4.** See him dry out besogged serpentine powder in the sun, so that it's good to feed a gun with again. (Reverend Hunt prays o'er them all.) **.5.** See him catch another monstrous sturgeon-fish, to improve that rotten, sodden barley of which all must eat. **.6.** See him lead the rabble in a marching-tune which he'd learned of the late Captaine Duxbury years before. (How doth it run? Reader, that tune's been lost.) He would have pleasured in more martial exercises, e'en if only to commaund for practice, & wave his sword, at which his underlings must fall upon some straw Salvage all together. *Trarintra-rarara!* But of a certainty 'twas not to be thought of; Ratcliffe &

Archer already complained that *he continued on with his improvements, as if he regarded the Colonie like unto his own!*

.7. From his personal store of dainties, which he'd not spent unto now, he bribed the Blacksmith to shape new round-shot & crossbar-shot, trundle-shot & langrell-shot. Any means to an end, good Reader! .8. He persuaded the Carpenters (who were clad in muck-grey, and who wore flat dark caps) to inspect all drinking-barrels & affirm the staves, before more casks leaked wastefully. .9. For the demi-culverins, Sweet John coaxed them to fashion half a dozen cases of wood, tailored according to the measure of each gunbarrel. Within these hollow cylinders he poured bullets, nails & other such gifts, for of case-shot he'd obtained right good knowledge in the Low Countreys; with his own eyes he'd seen how .1. such missile could wreak marvelous slaughter 'gainst the Turkes. Someday he'd fire his guns here; he'd carry the colors! .10. Turning now unsatisfied to that triangular ditch of his, he commaunded that it be deepened still further, until it became almost of compare with the moat at Tattersall Castle. Rain would soon belly it full. *What cheer, mates?* he called down, lowering the drinking-jug; and they replied: *All well, all well, good Captaine Smith.*

They having dug to their uttermost (altho' within any mass of souls there is always to be found at least .1. of a malignant sort, just as e'en the Apostles did have their Judas), Sweet John next besought the President to open the Colonie stores, and serve out .1. some Olde Holland cheese, .2. a dram of aqua vitae for every head, & (with permission of any worms & spiders) .3. a piece of white biscuit. This favor Maister Wingfield at .1.ˢᵗ refused, for not only did he disenjoy to raise his enemy's esteem in that fashion, but, half-poisoned by new forebodings, he wondered how long 'twould be before Captaine Newport returned from England with the next supply. Howbeit, Sweet John sweetly entreated him to note how the poor men were all skinny and weak, until he was box'd into playing the kind-hearted Machiavell.

The unmann'd Colonists rushed to watch the vault be opened. They shone upon each other their disease-rimmed hopes, & thought now to be saved. Sweet John stood there at the President's side, so that all would know 'twas due to *him.*

The Magazine's shackle padlock had already commenced for to rust, the clime being so moist that surely by the time the Sunne completed his full season's turn, to unclose the lock would no longer be convenient. (So salty-wet indeed coursed Virginia's breath that e'en the Gentlemen's armor, whose rivets had been tinned or coppered for longevity, began to rust.) The Marshal struck many a gallant stroke with his sword, until the lock swung free. The President entered, then grudgingly becked Sweet John beside him.

Within the Storehouse oozed the pissy reek of rat-work, which shocked both men unto the *twinkling fear,* but the President whispered: Why nurse their dread? — Sweet John nodded rapidly, like unto a boy at school. The President trusted him!   — Happily, many biscuits remained preserved; more happily still (for the moment), only Sweet John believed in winter. Generall Wingfyld bawled out for the Marshal to roll out a barrel for the people . . .

At the distribution the whole Colonie grew joyous, so that it seemed that unchristian *Faction* had slipped his biting grip. Indeed, our little yeoman now felt strong enough in his *Politique* to bring suit against the President for slander, whereby he was declared innocent of any plot to murther the Counsell, and the President got adjudged to pay him **.2.** hundred pounds in goods! Then he got sworn into his seat in the Counsell at last, murmuring *Your most humble Servaunt;* & together they took the communion of peace.

✳ ✳ ✳ ✳ ✳ ✳

The attacks occurred by night, or whenever stealth might give them advantage, as was the case in *Vietnam Americana,* when our soldiers could never tell apart *Hostiles* and *Friendlies.*   Indeed, Sweet John misdoubted him not that the same Salvages who visited with them by daylight shot at them at darklins; there was no knowing. On the **.25.**th of May, while Newport, Sweet John & that crew were off discovering the falls, came **.200.** Yndians straight to attack the Fort, and shot arrows into the tents — nay, **.1.** e'en passed through President Wingfield's beard! This time, at least, our Adventurers with their snaphaunces & matchlocks did shoot down many Salvages dead, whom their companions, finally retiring, carried away on their backs, & buried in the forest with many doleful chauntings whose meaning no Christian could sign. They came on again, but with more fear, & musket-shots sent them scampering away as if they were but dogs. The President now agreed with Sweet John's saying (which was truly a wise rule) that for the nonce they must be prepared to fire upon these creeping murtherers on sight. For indeed they came back again & again. On the **.30.**th of May they rose up like demons from the long grass and shot Eustace Clovell, Gent., with half a dozen arrows, so that he came running into the

Fort shrieking with his guts bleeding out, then died. So we all grew somewhat hardened 'gainst these infidels . . .

* * * * *

On the .**15**.th of June, when the Sunne abode in the princely sign of Gemini,
Captaine Newport raised sail for England, at which the company remaining dwindled into wretched homesickness; yet that was as felicity in comparison to the new flux which fell upon them all within .**10**. days of his
going; for being now unable to trade sub-legally with the Sailors for extra
measures of ship's-biscuit, they must subsist on water & wormy barley.
Seven Salvages did present them, 'tis true, with the carcass of a fat deer,
which was the transubstantiation of their compliments; when Smith asked
whose devising kindness this was, they replied: *Opechancanough's, of
Pamunkey,* for which he heartily thanked them (since Maister Wingfield
their President had not the wit to do it). Howbeit, this deer was only a
species of treat, which lasted but a day among so many — and mayhap
'twas sent by Opechancanough solely to give that wicked Salvage opportunity to inquire about Captaine Newport's whereabouts: — without him
and his big cannon our Colonie might be exterminated. (*Remember
Roanoke,* warned Ratcliffe.) They requited the aforesaid Opechancanough with a hatchet, which doubtless gratified him, he being said to be
intelligent (for a Salvage).

As for Maister Wingfield, still hoping to make his fortune (or at least to
please his Lords in London), he issued instructions to scour diverse rocks
and crystals for gold, which all performed with such greedy dispatch
(though unsuccessfully) that they scarcely found leisure to drop a food-seed
in the holes they made. Sweet John warned of doom, but he was much too
tiresome. Besides, he could scarcely Undertake to pay the Colonie's expenses! Only Virginian gold could do that. (Pray to Captaine Fortune!)
What would their self-spending be for, did they fail to buy themselves into
a richer state? Hurry! Life waits not! Here comes Ratcliffe with more
gold dirt; he's happy now; he lays by his worries for an hour; once Captaine
Newport returns, bears back the essay to London-Towne, & returns again,
dry Radclyffe will be anointed with honor! Calling all hands! Don't tell
me Captaine Fortune's not here! Even the Cooper in his blue apron now
neglected duty for the sake of these quixotic riches; barrels sprang leaks; the
Malmsey ran out, and no one stemmed that luxurious tide—

And meanwhile the illness increased; everywhere in that moist atmosphere was the very stink of sickness. Radclyffe fell too sick to spade up any

more gold-holes; the President's disease seethed in his bowels; Captaine Gosnold lay a-groaning on the sweltering ground. Around their Fort, shell-fungi grew on the treesides as thick as mushrooms on a skewer, and some said that the venom from those devilish vegetables did attaint them .1. and all; but if 'twas true then they might as well despair, for in Virginia there stood far too many trees to be bested by a few undernourished Englishmen. After the .1.st month, suspecting the slimy river at last, they made a well .7. fathoms deep, from which they drank their drink of brackish water, but by then how many had already been poison'd? Whereas formerly it had taken but .2. men to cut and carry a sapling-pole from the forest, it now required half a dozen, and these staggered puking and beshat themselves.

On the .6.th day of August, John Asbie became the next to end his days, for he farted blood in great agony from his chitterlings. On the .9.th perisht George Flowre of a most hideous swelling. On the .20.th, Captaine Gosnold relinquisht his ghost, at which (he being of high degree) they did o'erspread his coffin with a black pall, & fire off all guns as they committed him to the ground. 'Twas the Forenoon Watch. Pewter-colored clouds roll'd in from the river. Sweet John sorrowed to lose the only Gentleman in Jamestowne who was his friend. In short, he sorrowed for himself. What forfeit must he pay now in subservience to the President's Damascened follies? Captaine Newport was gone; Captaine Kendall, who'd muttered *Sheet close aft!* when they wrapt poor Gosnell in his shroud, now seemed mistrustful of Sweet John's purpose; Radclyffe was e'er dangerous; Captaine Archer hated him; how could he spare any tears for Gosnold's clay? He must now seize himself of other friends. (In fluctuating times, Princes get rapidly advanced.)

* * * * * *

What paper have you there?

A warrant, Maister President.

And how doth it run?

It runs, that we the Counsell do herewith depose you and expel you from the Counsell.

Wingfield gazed at his reflection in his silver candlestick. His silken vest was slit in a pattern of raindrops. He said: Maister Radcliff, now by J E - H O V A H I can work up no surprise to see you here. Indeed, will you not be the new President? So I infer from all I know of you. Maister Martynn, I forgive you full well, you being but a tool befitting these others. And Maister Smith, your vengefulness hath its reward at last, which I misdoubt me not you'll enjoy in fair humility . . .

We think you unworthy to be President or Counsell-man anymore.

It pleases you thus to say, *Yeoman* Smith. Welladay, you've eased me of care and trouble. But I do recollect that Jamestowne hath **.13.** Counsell-men. You are but **.3..** Do you proceed lawfully?

If we do you wrong, Maister Wingfield, then we must answer it.

Bluntly and brutishly spoken, Sweet John! Thus have you forsaken His Majesty's government as set down in the *Instructions,* and made of it a triumvirate. So be it. I am at your pleasure; dispose of me as you will without further garboil.

Confine him in the pinnace, quoth Ratcliffe.

In the Gun-room or the Bread-room, Maister President?

The Gun-roome's better bulkheaded . . .

I do protest the necessity, said Wingfield, but Sweet John strode close, drew his broadsword and with an ugly smile repeated: If we do you wrong, then *we* must answer it.

* * * * * *

They took all the prisoner's books &c from his Store-chest. He sued Master Crofts to get back his copper kettle at least, but lost, because he was too proud to swear an oath that it was his.

I see that I am made good prize on all sides, he said.

Maister Wingfield, I pray you be more sparing of law, until we have more wit, or wealth. Laws are good spies in a populous and plentiful Countrey, where they do make the good men better, & stay the bad from being worse. Yet here at Jamestowne, we are so poor, as laws do but rob us of time that might be better employed in the service of the Colonie —

* * * * * *

But already Sweet John was discovering that the Adventure remained no less Enclosed in turpitude after the Government was changed, that Radcliffe had but played him for a pawn, to help himself become President.

In Lincoln Town the Maltsters & Brewers are by law distrained from buying corn until the **.2.**-o'-clock bell, so that Citizens may first get their share. And in every Commonwealth, wise sovereignty ought to enact such decrees; otherwise rich rascals must infallibly overreach the multitude. Under the reign of Ratcliffe, alas, 'twas not so. Those who fished the river and caught sweet sturgeon, kept it but for themselves. The key to the Magazine turned for Radcliffe & his friends, but not for other inmates of that Colonie. Thus Sweet John believed, at least. Just as Captaine Archer, who'd been arm-wounded by arrows on that **.1.**st Virginian day so long ago now, longed to apprehend the Salvages in their wrongdoing, to expose the destestable secret actions of the Salvages, so our Lincolnshireman yearned to prove the corruption of this Government. Never loving authority, nor trusting in its wisdom (still less now since he'd escap'd the Turkishe Hordes), he soured, reading his Machiavell.

✳ ✳ ✳ ✳ ✳

When they fired salvoes across the newest grave and began to shovel in the oozey clay, then they most frequently heard Salvages jeering and making sport of their lamentations: *Whe, whe, yah, ha, ne, he, wittowa, wittowa.* (This reminded Sweet John most incongruously of the utterances made by Tragabigzanda & her fellow Turkes, when they went *a-weeping o'er the graves.*) Oftentimes a feathered arrow whizzed among them, and the enemy shouted and then there was silence. Thirteen-year-old Nathaniell Pecock, **.1.** of the Cabin-boys, gave up his ghost that fall, on the very day that Ratcliffe placed Maister Wingfield under guard, proclaiming: *Now that I am President, no more sheep will die for the Shepherd's selfishness!* — doubtless rightfully, for they died of other causes. — Their provisions were all gone, & the sturgeon had left the river, it being past their season, so that all the Colonists found to eat (aside from their verminous barley) was scuttlefish, by which I mean sea-crabs. These they procured only at a distance, and with danger and labor unsuited to sick men. President Ratcliffe's guards had interrogated Maister Wingfield at some length, to discover where he might have hidden his remaining dainties, but nothing was learned (undoubtedly, thought Sweet John, because Maisters Wingfield and Radcliffe had already devoured 'em all together).

'Twas the morrow of Nathaniell's death. The Carpenter lay now too diseased to build any more coffins; Nathaniell must be buried only in his shroud. After the mucky clay had covered Nathaniell's face, and dunghill-flies settled brassily upon his grave, Sweet John knelt down to pray. To GOD he whispered: *Love you not me?*

✳ ✳ ✳ ✳ ✳

What was the result? He writes it in his *Generall Historie* most coyly: GOD *the patron of all good indevours, in that desperate extremity so changed the hearts of the Salvages, that they brought such plenty of their fruits, and provision, as no man wanted.* But then our English ate those dainties all up, & they starved.

* * * * * *

Burnt offerings, abominations, covenants, spoils roasted with fire — so runs the *Ancient Testament,* which we ourselves (who've fallen out of literalness) get call'd upon to allegoricize. Take a pause, Reader. *The Counsell sacrificed unto Sweet John Smith.* What do we really mean? — Why, quite simply that (seeing the way the wind blew) the Counsell now appointed him *Captaine of Supply.*

But he sat alone, rubbing specks of rust off his armor with a handful of river-sand. Then he garnished e'ery plate with some oil he'd borrowed of the Blacksmith, James Read.

Radcliffe would not acknowledge his myriad services. How now? Helpless, fetid, Enclosed, he schemed to get Ratcliffe neutered in his authority like unto .1. of those castrati who sing in velvet in Rome. But whene'er Reverend Hunt did sermonize, Sweet John fell into shame, that his heart could move so unchristianly. He wiped the muck from his boots. He readied himself for the next gambler's chance.

He sent word by a knowing Salvage unto Prince Opecancanough, to for charity's sake send 'em some corn. Opechancanough replied not.

Time to get belly-timber by force! He promised he could do it. But the Counsell said him nay.

He played Tick-Tack and *The Irish-Game* with Thomas Emry. He caught fleas by means of a stick dabbed with blood.

They buried the dead at night now, so the Salvages wouldn't see. A Guard stood ready with his matchlock. (I miss the tolling of the bells, said Thomas Emry. Doesn't seem like a true death without 'em. Seems heathenish, somehow . . .) At dusk, the deer would come near the graveyard, pattering and crunching in the fallen leaves. But after George Cassenden killed a fawn they became shyer. The men were sad, for that meat, slight portion though it was, had relished well . . .

* * * * * *

More perished, & more, e'en though some of the afflicted had purged themselves with black hellebore brought from Europe, and others essayed cinammon-water, which reminded Sweet John of old Mr. Reese Allen back in Willoughby. This train of thought brought to mind fair *Cicely* of his former enamorment, she of the cinammon-breath in whose honor he soon

with naked *Pocahontas* would play Tick-Tack, Lurch, & Ruffs. O, undoubtedly they were all lonely for the night-creaks of Captaine Newporte's
.3. ships which had once been tied to the trees without the Fort, & now
might well be safe at Gravesend, unless they were chasing Spanish prizes,
or storm-sunken to the bottom of the sea . . .

Dost recollect the great plague in Lincolne Towne? he asks the other
Lincolnshire boys. They're all seated (like unto Salvages) upon the ground.

O, too well, Captaine Smith (thus Thomas Emry). I was full **.10.** years
old—

And I but **.7.** But old Mr. Reese Allen in Willoughby got such a scare from
it that he could never leave off telling me how it was. He served cinnamon-
water daily in his household, I trow to keep off those bad vapors . . .

It's vaporish that I am this eve, Captaine Smith. I'm feeling so sad.

* * * * * *

He search'd for an issue of fair water, there to make another well, for he
misdoubted him not that the river they drunk from was somehow tainted
with disease, yet could discover no convenient place to make his diggings.
Salvages shot arrows at him. He saw no remedy but to terrify 'em once the
Soldiers grew stronger (if ever they would). Meanwhile, nobody would
help him terrorize. Men failed day by day. And Reverend Hunt would
have them be ever a-praying down upon their marrybones — but now
Reverend Hunt fell also sick. Swet John knew not what he should do. That
putrid lazar-house in Roane was much in his mind; that where he'd lain
near a-dying from *the purples*.   Here 'twas like unto *the purples* all
over again, what with the groans of the sick night & day, so that scarce any
in the entire Colonie could sleep, which wore down the strength of the few
healthy men, priming them for the new plague. 'Twas Sweet John who began to call it *the seasoning,* for he misdoubted him not that could any
man but adjust himself to the new clime & strange water, he might live.
And he thought it sounded more cheerful to think & speak in such a way.
But he himself could hear Plague's wings a-whirring as in London-Towne.

He hung fresh ferns & grass-bundles daily around his tent, to keep away
the seasoning's breath. Soon all others did the same.

A man screamed. Another man cried out: *O, sweet Maister! Help me,
Maister!* — Then that man died a-vomiting. The whole Fort stank of
vomit, death & dung.

* * * * * *

When the Salvages again denied to bring corn, meats, fruits, breads and berries, & the bloody leaves began to fall, Sweet John found himself summonsed before the Counsell by President Ratcliffe, who addressed him as follows: — I do fear me, dear *Captaine of Supply,* that you've lost us all our labors, by driving away those who would have been our friends—

Phantastickall President, whate'er do you mean?

Temper your tongue! Why, your fury 'gainst these innocent heathens is a by-word! You wall 'em out, you threaten for to slaughter 'em; you—

A by-word, Maister President? Or should I call you *Sicklemore?* For I hear you're the merest counterfeit impostor! 'Pon my faith, I'd thought your by-word was *Remember Roanoke!*

Counsell-men, hark unto that gallows-bait varlet! Soon we'll be snow-bound, and then what if the Starving-Time should come again?

Snow-bound, you say? quoth Sweet John. I would never have known it, Maister Sicklemore, when all season long you've been drying your backside in the Sunne like unto a flitch of bacon —

Here there rose to Heaven a most argumentive din, which if I were diagrammatical would be indicated thusly:

but soon Sweet John got reduced to propriety, and craved the President's pardon, which was given, but only on condition that he set out, without delay & of his own accord, to obtain more provisions from the Salvages by way of trade.

* * * * *

See John Smith and his henchmen at the village called *Kecoughtan.* They are not far from Poynt Comfort; their shallop rocks uneasily in the great Bay called *Chesapeack,* which Sweet John has scarce begun exploring & delimiting e'en in his dreams. (He thinks to himself: 'Tis a convenient harbor for fisher-boats.) The weirs of the Salvages rise like unto picket fences in this inlet, & trapped fishes swim within them helplessly. See the birds flying everywhere, excited beyond rapture at this great concatenation of fishes fat & thin, fishes with waists and fishes without, fishes long and unswerving like torpedos, guiding their hammerish heads steadily towards various non-existent escapes; stingrays, sturgeons, perches and trout mingle anxiously in the shallow water, and the Salvages are spearing them. Wading solitary with spears, they stab downward into the sky-blue water, never missing; or they glide predatorily by .3.s and .4.s in their vessels of hollowed-out logs, which we call *Canoas;* they stab and stab, until the canoes are packed with silver slimy fishes whose dead bodies lose immediately the iridescence which Mistress Pocahontas still carries at this stage of her legend.

See the shallop enter this scene; the People desist from fish-harvesting; they draw together with spears in easy reach.

On shore, past the stinking mound of fish-guts and horseshoe crabs where the fat dogs wallow, fight, vomit and goggle, see the Salvage females with their children gathered. The women are plump, and their teats flop down. They seem for to smile at Sweet John, but he has never believed in smiles since the night of the .4. French gallants. Behind is the village called Kecoughtan. Bark houses form a circle about a central fire, inscribed in a circled palisade. Beyond, cornleaves hang from the stalks like dogs' panting tongues.

Sweet John rolls up his hose to the knee and leaps into the water. He scorns to wear his armor, but the broadsword hangs at his belt, and he carries a fine snaphaunce on loan from President Ratcliffe. The others in the shallop wait with half-cocked muskets, ringing hearts. He picks his bullet off the leaden sprue and loads it in the caliver. The Salvage fishers grip their spears more readily; on shore, a woman giggles nervously (the other wenchen are blank-faced now; the children stare). Some ancient men are peering through the gaps in the palisadoes, their bows half-drawn. Sweet John splashes through the muck, with fishes scattering around him like unto dreams & watermelon seeds. Raider, provisioner, he's ever skillful. O yes, for this very cause he was in his youth Captaine Duxbury's darling . . . He draws toward the line of canoes. Above his head he hath a secret in his left fist. Now let the fingers blossom open, Sweet John, for 'tis the time: Show 'em your white beads (*Roanoke,* they call it). He makes as if to offer them that treasure; then eats air, and points to the village, which lurks behind its plum-trees (those small blackish plums of theirs* relish much better than do the hedge-plums of England). He touches his belly, points to

*The "plums" were actually mullberries.

his men in the shallop, eats nothingness again. — *Nettopew, nettopew!* he insists, but neither he nor the Salvages truly believe in this ideal or diseased friendship to which he refers (nobody cries *friend* unless he's not); indeed, they commence to laugh at him most scornfully. He's nothing; he's a famished man.

A Salvage wades toward him, never looking at the living fishes between his feet. He is old, and wrinkles rise in parallel disdains on his forehead; even the grey stubble that tops his shaved skull seems to shrug at Sweet John. Black feathers dangle languidly from his ears. A striped feather rises from the single strip of hair that runs down the middle of his head. His birdlike face, bony and sunken-eyed, regards Sweet John with what the latter deems to be menace. Deerskin fringes hang limply down his chest, stinking with sweat & grease. From within his robe the man pulls a deerskin bag of pounded corn. He takes a handful, holds it out, & points to Sweet John's musket in exchange. All the women laugh in nervous ringing bursts which echo across the water and seem to agitate the fishes still further, for they begin to wheel and whirl, and form themselves into a circle of tortured motion, swimming round and round a central nothing most colorfully.

Sweet John folds his arms, forbearing to be insulted by this clown. He says: *Mowchick wayawgh tawgh noeragh kaquere mecher,* which signifies: I am monstrous hungry. What shall I eat?

Again the Salvages laugh uneasily.

He rushes back to the shallop (which in shape is hardly less simple than a Salvage *canoe*). He speaks a word to his men. They cock their muskets and point them at the fishers, who snatch up spears most threateningly.

Mowchick wayawgh tawgh noeragh kaquere mecher! shouts Sweet John.

They laugh.

Fire! comes Sweet John's commaund.

At once his terrified Soldiers let fly, without even aiming, and the muskets shout.

The Salvages run into the forest screaming. The canoes float upon the water; in .1., a half-dead fish flops in agony, reaches the water he desires, and dies there, frozen-eyed in a cloud of pink.

The Soldiers & Sailors row straight onto shore. — Powder down the barrel, my lusty-hearts! shouts their little Lincolnshire Generall, & they reload. Walnuts & fishes lie a-drying on hurdles of reeds o'er fires. Laughing,

Sweet John snatches up a strip of half-jerked meat & serves his bearded mouth. He marches toward the barken houses, which he knows will now be safely silent. — Ready, boys? Forbear to curse me, or I'll . . . .*1. and .2.*, *.1. and .2.!* Behind me, now!

They follow Sweet John, who happily declaims: I killed *.3.* Turkes in single combat! Now let these Salvages send their best Bonny Mulgro! and he laughs aloud, but the men do not laugh.

*   *   *   *   *   *

Upon his return, the boat well laden with captured Indian corn, President Ratcliffe met him with much the same expression of astonished delight as you, dear Reader, might discover on the face of someone else's baby were you to open your eyes early *.1.* morning and see him pissing artlessly all over your new carpet. — Well done, Smith! cried Ratcliffe. I hereby forgive your sundry earlier offenses!

*   *   *   *   *   *

After this, Sweet John found his extortions greatly in demand, since the folk at Jamestown no longer had to reflect whence their next day's corn might be derived; they riotously ate, & wasted as they saw fit, which grieved the procurer's heart, but not so exceedingly heavy that he broke out of the trap or mouse-wheel to which he had been confined: he'd bring back the corn and be welcomed; the corn would be spent, then all would look to him to be their savior once again. (Experience recapitulates Machiavelli: When you take a Turkishe town, slaughter all in arms & set their grinning heads on stakes all around, just as the Turkes would have done had they seiz'd the victory. You flay the enemy's pickets alive. On the high seas, you can do what you like with the enemy's ship, not least rifle it. In Ireland, kill the Irish rebels. — But Sweet John forbore to be so definitively cruel.)

He grew weary; his sweetness grew still more variegated, like unto Indian corn; but his fellow English ate, & the Yndians commenced to fear them more respectfully. At the beginning of September the black-faced *Werowance of Paspahegh* (he who'd earlier assaulted them) returned a runaway boy to mark the peace. Radclyffe was well satisfied, but Sweet John knew 'twas but Machiavellian *Policy,* for didn't the Salvages' corn-pits now commence to get devour'd? Doubtless they preferred to have the boy feasted at the expense of their *Friends.* Still, 'twas better to receive this pretended friendship than their arowheads! Of course this change in them came entirely from his own travels, dangers, miseries & encumbrances. 'Twould be too much to expect Captaine Radclyffe to acknowledge that—

The way from James Towne to Kecoughtan grew now almost as familiar to him as from Willoughby to Burgh-le-Marsh. Kecoughtan had no more corn; the inhabitants begged & wept most piteously for him not to starve them any further; he essayed other Townes yonder. Each time he expected full well to be rewarded for his pains, it being so patent that he was the .1. man of discretion and courage in that Colonie. No longer scorned, he'd rise above the temporizing proceedings which had so far comprised his life; meanwhile his hopes made the corn come in, and Ratcliffe laughed.

* * * * *

Your obedient Servaunt, cries Sweet John in a sprightly voice, making a leg to the Counsell.

So we'd have you be, laughs the President. Now be seated. What news, Captaine Martynne?

None, Sir, for I feel poorly in my belly this day—

Captaine Archer?

The Sentry tells me a Salvage did shoot at him, when he went for to shit—

Is it come to that? said Radclyffe in disgust. Upon my life, I see there's no news. Captaine Smith, when go you out again?

Where must I make shift to haste me now, Maister President?

Take note, Counsell-men. His tongue doth e'er drip with grudges. Smith, I care not a Milk-maid's pox for all your humors. We need more corn.

The Salvages have none.

In all Virginia? But you know not all Virginia, dear *Captaine of Supply.* I'd have you go past the Falls, to discover the Monacans—

But —

O, so you have no stomach to that? Belike the Chickahominies still have corn.

Nay, Maister President, for I already did harvest their treasury.

And have you explored the River Chickahominy unto its womb?

Maister President, I entreat you, such errands are more fit for summer, when we can live in ease upon the land—

What's the hour? said Captaine Archer. Time for a nip of spirits, Maister President. Come, pay him no sense; dole out a gulp and I'll dole you my reasoning!

The bold spirit drinks bold spirits, scoffed Captaine Kendall.

* * * * * *

See John Smith wand'ring to and from the Fort, the rattle of whose thatch roofs gets lost in the cold winds. He cuts firewood with his broadsword & wonders: Now how can I get a living? — See him a-sitting upon his bunkstead, with a candle-lantern at his head, and herbs hanging to dry on the walls. Every morn he calls his mates to prayer & a Psalm. There's a rat in the Cooper's shop. The Carpenter's whittling pegs on his wooden bench. Sweet John dreams his not yet bygone dreams. Some eves he plays Lurch with Thomas Emry, who's another good Lincolshire lad although he hails from the fennier Towne of Sibsey, near Stickney. Ooze reigns in those parts; Emry well kens how to tell neap-tides from spring-tides, for without such knowledge, how can any yeoman's son hope to row home from pasture in winter? Unlike John Smith, he's never in the least distempered by his own science. Home's oozy? All right, let's live in ooze! He's come to Jamestowne not because the climate's healthful, but because his eldest brother will inherit the farm. He's in a mew, or cage, called *Virginia,* and there he'll flutter about until Queen Mammon grants him better vestments in which to worship King Ooze in Sibsey. Sweet John has been to Sibsey thrice — once in winter to collect a steed from some debtor of my Lord Willoughby. Emry, who's .1. of those people who must play omniscient about every event which every occurred in his home Towne, claims to remember the trembling horse (which had to be put down, Bartty's stupid smile twitching into defiance). All that had been back in Queen Elizabeth's day. To Smith and Emry, her reign now seems a grander time than ever it was, simply because it's over, sinking ever farther into the dirt of time. They call her *Old Gloriana.* But Sweet John hasn't forgotten the miserableness of his errand, his despisement of Bartty (who was fecklessly thankless), his muddy trudge home. Life is mucky sometimes, agrees Emry. He tells a tale of .2. pallbearers back in the .13.th century who were carrying a dead body from Stickney to Sibsey Church-yard, when Nordyke Causeway proved a treacherous isthmus only, and the waters drowned the living & the dead.

Reason, I hope, will better fortify your causeway against such accidents. Sweet John, tell me something I don't know!

Ehm, replies Smith, picking through his Treasure-house of Novelties. Well then, have you been in the Low Countreys?

What about 'em?

The *Dutchmen* use mussel-shells to wipe their arseholes! he cries triumphantly.

They *what?*

I've seen it.

And why, pray, did you set out to watch Dutchmen wiping their arseholes?

The talk soon swivels onto Lincolnshire farm women in their long grey dress and white aprons, and Thomas Emry says: I pine for honest wenchen — or even percase dishonest ones. What think you of the Salvage trulls?

Beware, my lad. Beware their treachery.

But I do pine for a woman in my bed, John.

So do we all.

All indeed, yet I particularly.

As for me, I do literally dream upon the Holland cheese I once sluppered up in the Low Countreys . . .

* * * * * *

Having drain'd his goblet of acquae vitae as well & profitably as e'er a Dutchman drains a Fen, Captaine Kendall said: Now speak plainly, and say what you will. I know you, whether your name be Ratcliffe or Sicklemore; I know your greeds & mincing exacting courtesies. What would you courteously exact from me?

Ratcliffe, seeing that his moment had come, replied: I want Archer on the Counsell, to share our burdens, & to counterweigh Smith, whose rash insolencies —

Yes, but what shall I have? Sweet John's nothing to me. A tart sells her quim for a penny; I'll sell my vote to pay for my ravenous prayers!

I have little enough to pay you, Captaine Kendall. If you wanted pennies you should have stayed in England.

Where we'll soon be again! laughed Captaine Archer, drunk on the President's generosity.

Bite your tongue, fool! cried Ratcliffe.

Ah, so you mean to steal away even yet! cried Captaine Kendall.

And why not? Would you wait upon Sweet John to feed you with Yndian corn? 'Tis more than perilous here, & we've gained no sure gold yet.

But the Salvages—

Remember Roanoke.

By my arrow-wounded arm, I'm the man who should say that! said Captaine Archer.

(And here, Reader, I want to tell you that altho' some were cool to Captaine Radclyffe, yet as many considered his the greyest brain of prudence that ever sat upon a President's eyes, for they feared no less than hated Virginia, & expected only to be buried there if they could not soon 'scape. He'd promised them all a place on the pinnace should he accomplish his scheme; now that autumn was full and red and the pumpkins, turkeys, geese & other dainties were heaped up in Salvage larders, the declaration of now had become the question of when. Therefore they harked to the President whatever he said, lest when the time came the pinnace might prove too small to hold them all.)

Where's Sweet John? Kendall inquired then.

What, do you fear him?

Never.

He's rigging out the shallop. I'll dispatch him in a twink to wherry us more belly-timber—

Ha! And then I'll come for supper, Maister President! Commaund becomes you. Well, I give way. You can have Captaine Archer on this Counsell. I care not.

My thanks. Martynne, will you copy that vote?

I cannot form my judgments so instantly—

Pay you heed, Martin. Captaine Archer sits here with us. Would you—

Nay, Archer, come be elected to our Counsell & welcome.

What will Sweet John say? whispered Captaine Martin.

He'll have no leisure for speech, since I'll send him forth to wander again on his *Trve Travells* . . .

*   *   *   *   *   *

I have spoken long with Captaine Smith on the subject of his discoveries and I am not pleased. He has failed in the requirement that we gave him to discover the head of Chickahamania's river . . .

Indeed, Maister President, but we ought to excuse him, for he has saved us from hunger once again, and that is more valuable than any number of discoveries.

Than *any* number of discoveries, Captaine Martin? Suppose that there are gold-mines that way!

Why, then, they'll surely abide until we've eaten.

Sluggard, what made you an Adventurer? Should the Spaniards force a way, what will you say then, while you swill Smith's supply? (So saying, Ratcliffe cocked his head brightly and cracked a nut between his teeth; the noise, which was almost as loud as a pistol-shot, made every Counsellor blink.)

Let's summons him, then! cried Captaine Archer. Enough of this; my brain aches—

Once more, said Sweet John when he entered, you've refused to seat me, & kept me waiting under guard, as if you deliberate my fate. What's your pleasure now, Maister President?

Think you that I but maze my considerations about my own pleasure?

Yea, Sicklemore, as I do thrive!

Well, *there's* a nice judgment — listen to him! Not **.1.** of us can repress this coistrel's disobedience —

By now all the Counsellors had risen and were shouting in wrath at Sweet John's impudency, as they thought it, in the meanwhile not displeased to be donning robes of righteousness; at that moment each man believed Smith to be the enemy, believed himself to be the Colonie's sole support (it *must* be so, since his breast glowed with such anger); as for the President, he was forgotten from such equations.

Captaine Smith, said Ratcliffe then, I forgive you; I excuse you, but you must discover for us the head of the Chickahamania River without fail.

Very well, my Lord Sicklemore . For me that's a trifle; 'tis my pleasure to serve 𝕹𝕬𝖀𝕴𝕲𝕬𝕿𝕴𝕺𝕹. But let me press upon you this caution in return: I've met with all the Sailors this day, representing to them your aims and arrogancy; you may conclude your designs to abandon the Colonie yet **.10.** times more, but I hardly think you'll get much beyond the open sea . . . Well, am I dismissed now, Gentlemen? Expel me forthwith, that I may be about your errands—

Out he went; & Ratcliffe said to the others, well satisfied: Now he'll lose himself for days and weeks in that winter woods . . . !

And when the meeting was adjourned, he gathered together his faction, and they crowded into the Magazine each Counsell-man with his own bung-straw, so that in spraddle-legged crowds they might suck a little more from the casks of spirit . . .

* * * * *

See John Smith in the December forest, poling up the Chickahamania River in a barge outfitted with plates of woven bark to absorb enemy arrows

like blotting-paper. Oh, he's in the evil marches now, in the wilderness far
beyond Jamestown's bounds and borders. December is the month to bleed
horses, the month to dig away snow from the vetch-fields because the hay
begins to lose its virtue; but in Virginia they have no horses, no cows to eat
vetch or hay — none but wild beasts, & shivering miserable men.   In
Jamestowne Fort they're splitting fire-logs with beetle and wedge. Those
who can, lie close against the hearth. Sweet John cannot. Clad in a stout
leather buff-coat he is (in Hungaria's mountains, winter froze a man worse
than this; & Transylvania's 'graved equally cold 'pon his memory-tablet).
Underneath, a vest of frozen armor-plates. Of his Soldiers we retain the
names only of those who are about to be murthered: *George Cassen, Jehu
Robinson,* & *Thomas Emry.* Methinks there were .3. or .4. others; they
lived to die of unknown causes, having endured for reasons as unknown;
and got buried in unknown graves unthought of by all the young belles &
fat sweating boys in sweatshirts who in this my century do stream past the
fountains of Virginia. Let 'em live now. All (as we may well credit) are
afeared — homesick also, as I wot; Emry mumbles: I would I had hold of
my old cat's tail. I would I had hold of our shithouse door. — Poor Emry!
He's as white as seal-blown bubbles! Sweet John spies this well, and consequently feels himself almost a Turke of cruelty (for these *Saracens* do drive
their poorest troops into battle with rawhide whips). Enough; he'll hide his
heart.   No fault his the vulgar Sicklemore's swept them out into such
weather; no fault his the evil Salvages! By GOD, they'll do as they're told,
and do 't well! For the discover of this *Riuer Chickahominy* (also call'd *The
Back River of James Towne*) may forseeably prove of inestimable use to
𝕹𝖆𝖚𝖎𝖌𝖆𝖙𝖎𝖔𝖓. Moreover, his troops go provisioned adequately, if
not well, with a budgebarrel of fine-corned gunpowder.   Their
snaphaunces lie ready to hand; they all claim to be good Musketeers. No
matter if they look to find painted goblins creeping from behind the
trees . . . Robinson, formerly a masterless man from Shropshire, was born
with the .2.nd sight (which Smith does not believe). Every minute he sees
another fairy. Sweet John cries: Surely you must been suckled in some
Popish conclave, for you reek of superstition! — Beg pardon, Maister
Smith (thus Robinson, not truly sorry). — 'Tis a sin, you know! chuckles
his bearded little Captaine. A *dangerous* sin, like unto setting up a May-
pole . . . — Beg pardon, Maister Smith. — The river narrows until icicle-
hung trees are raking their bow on either side; a milk-skin of ice crackles
around them; now branches clasp each other across the water and Sweet
John sets the men to work with hatchets: Smith and Cassen on the port

side, Robinson and Emry on the starboard; and the troops are sniffling, hewing listlessly. Maister Robinson sees goblins, 'tis true, but his fear's half tarred o'er with untainted, free invulnerability, because Wingfield's been deposed, and 'twas Wingfield who'd charged him with seeking to desert Jamestowne in the shallop; Robinson's won a judgment of **.100.** pounds against him for slander! No **.1.** can harm him. A branch whacks him on the forehead. He throws up a hand like a child bewildered by light, at which Sweet John sings out: Chop away now! You must satisfy me! and Sweet John is monstrous happy, & a certain tune which Radclyffe joys in humming has gotten prisoned in his head, so he commences to invent a ballad of his own to invigorate his companions:

> I am as I am and so I will be
> But how that I am none knoweth truly.

and raises his hand in a theatrical stroke which severs another branch, e'en as the Soldiers do sing:

> Be it evil, be it well, be I bound, be I free,
> I am as I am and so will I be.

but now this giddy toy of his conceptions, conceived from sad wisps of Lincolnshire fogs, dancing slaphappily from slack thought-threads, becomes *Tragabigzanda* with her dully shining silver bangles! Her memory wounds him now. He repents that he murthered her brother & mistrusted her. Her glamorous maidenhead he'd paint upon his coat of arms if he only could, right below the **.3.** Turkes' heads. Truly, he would he were a Turke, be he only in Tragabigzanda's arms! — Or Cicely's . . . but Cicely is . . . Upon my life, poor Sweet John's stuck; he cannot complete the rhyme; and Cassen kneels to peer ahead (he's looked for just such an excuse to rest his blistered hands, and who can blame him? he hath no more than a single evening left to live!) and in a doleful voice calls: Nothing but trees & more trees ahead, Sir, & skeletons of dead winter trees!

O cries Sweet John in disgust. You're all as soft as a lot of learned Doctors! Steady now!

They laugh in sobs, hanging their heads.

Captaine Smith, kindly give us leave to rest. We feel but poorly . . .

Rest? 'Tis nothing but rest I hear, rest and more rest ahead, & skeletons of dead winter rest! What did you sail to Virginia for? Rest, fairies & hobgoblins!

Master, let us breathe—

Straight on! Spy you not all that ooze to the larboard?

Robinson, seeing his Commaunder to be in good humor (the only man on that barge to be, surely), sees fit to try the trick that they know: Dream us a tale to hearten us, Captain Smith! I'd hear about those **.500.** gold chichqueenes you won from the Venetian carrack —

So it's wrapped in myself you think I am! laughs Sweet John — and maybe 'tis true such a blanket keeps me warm . . . (He pours out a toddy for all from his drinking jug, which is green and cracked.) 'Twas my **.1.**ˢᵗ sea battle, when the Venetians played the fool, not seeing our impudent speck on the horizon — here's more of that ale we stole from President Swizzle-bones . . . They had half **.100.** Greekish girls on board for slaves, & were sunk fast in them as they'd soon be sunk fast in the sea! We struck hard, getting our prize. The Greekish girls we landed at a nunnery . . .

A nunnery, Captain Smith! You told us a pleasure-garden . . .

Maybe it was. That's how I met Tragabigzanda, after I slew those **.3.** Turkes in single combat. She had royal blood, to be sure, & promised me that I might reign over all the Turkes, had I but patience . . .

For a slice of a moment he saw her brother, his master, the *Tymor* whom he'd slain, frowning in his peaked helmet of iron with inlaid silver blossoms and letter-snakes from the glorious Koran; for the first time he took notice of the man's sad, preoccupied face. Maister Barty once read him a tale of how the Turkes took Axopolis, a century and a half past. Smashing in the doors of the Hagia Sophia, they topped a crucifix with a janissary's cap and bobbed it up and down in mockery of the terrified Christians, then raped girls and boys alike on the very altars. So Master Barty had read, and Sweet John believed; but 'tis true that many vassals of the Tymor's wore the Cross without molestation. What if he'd stayed & become a Turke?

As he stood in the boat exuding silence, Cassen, Robinson and the others accompted him to be relenting. Once again they pressed him to rest. Easy now, his eyes shining like unto a lion's, he gave his consent, that **.1.** they should swing the barge around, & embay her at the previous bend, where they'd seen a wide landing, & **.2.** all the other Adventurers would bide in it with the kedge-anchor down, while Sweet John with a chosen pair of zealots would push on in a canoe; by rote he requisitioned **.2.** more Salvages at Appamatuck; he'd pay 'em in beads now or later . . . — But you must not go ashore, he commaunded earnestly, you must promise me that, you being but ignorant men untrained in the ways of Salvages & all their cunning subtle dangers —

Aye, Captaine Smith! We swear by the very CHRISTcross!

They'll bring you to ruin, I say!

Never fear, Master—

Sweet John thought he saw them wink. A horrid idea now shot its way into his heart. — Hath Sicklemore slipped you secret instructions? Beware, for I'll not be deceived!

Why would we deceive you? quoth Emry. Finding his Captaine's scowl still unsmoothed, he added: Leastwise would we sneak for that .2.-faced President!

Sweet John laughed. — Two-faced? The man's queerly half-faced — no, I say quarter-faced, for he spies the .4. directions cunningly, twitching in all directions with his Ratcliffe cheeks; meseems those twitches pull his face asunder . . .

As soon as he'd sailed beyond kenning them, they embark'd on their debate. 'Twas the .4.th hour of the Morning Watch, with the sun hardly up. George Cassen saw no reason to freeze in idleness when they could descend upon Appamatuck and pillage there. He spoke of cornbread, roast turkeys, raw squaw-venison until their mouths watered; the mildness of Sweet John's government left no respect in them, & they had not the capacity for love. Percase their Captaine was somewhat to blame, for his talk of Greekish girls had inflamed their worse natures, just as the fetus, the young soul, is pricked & excited into life by the seminal worms. So they set out on the DEVIL's business.

* * * * * *

What do we actually know about the Salvages of Virginia? One of our abundant dead Presidents — to wit, *Maister Thomas Jefferson* — sought most assiduously to help us. Unfortunately his Indian vocabulary, which occupied a trunk of grandeur, was stolen, and the thief upon forcing the lock was so vexed by finding not silver, but mere wearisome sheafs, that he threw them all into the river. Jefferson picked them out and dried them, but they were ruined; the ink had effused away. As for his surviving observations, which never spied water, here is the most significant of them:

It has been said, that Indians have less hair than the whites, except on the head. But this is a fact of which fair proof can scarcely be had. With them it is a disgrace to be hairy on the body. They say it likens them to hogs. They therefore pluck the hair as fast as it appears. But the traders who marry their women, and prevail on them to discontinue this practice, say, that nature is the same with them as with the whites. Nor, if the fact be true, is the consequence necessary which has been drawn from it. Negroes have notoriously less hair than the whites; yet they are more ardent.

George Cassen was attempting to investigate this question in all its ramifications when the Salvages took him in hand. He was enjoying a little look around, a little wander as he called it. Truth to tell, he had not gotten monstrous far. He'd led his companions creeping down .1. of their forest lanes like unto a gang of masterless men, and then they rose up around him resembling goblins, deerskinned against the winter, shining with walnut oil, and a great grim Salvage who wore a dead rat for an ornament in his ear-hole grabbed George Cassen, who roaringly grappled with him as the Salvage laughed & the dead rat swung by its tail and then another Salvage almost naked seized him by the hair and he heard his comrades fleeing and had scarcely time to despair or rage before a .3.rd Salvage leapt upon him. Now they were all grown around him into a hedge of menace, upraising fine fat war-clubs of maple wood inset with stones, & a man with a red-painted bone in his ear took out a knife, smiled and began to sing, softly & with great hatred (George Cassen could smell his meat-breath) the song which all the men of Jamestown had heard every day of that summer & fall from the tree-shadows just beyond the bounds of the Fort:

Mattanerew shashasewaw crawango pechecomn
Whe Tassanttassa inoshashaw yehockab pocosack
Whe, whe, yah, na, ha, he, he, wittowa, wittowa.

They tied him to a tree at the place called Appocant and cut off his joints .1. by .1. with mussel shells, searing the cut places to keep him alive a little longer. Whenever he screamed they smiled down on him in disgust. Questioning him to their hearts' content, they learned where Captaine Smith had gone. They slit his belly open and unreeled his guts like nightmare fishermen; they burned him inside there, too (maintaining their throttling hold on his life), then sliced the skin from his face; he was still alive; so they set the tree on fire and watched him burn, right down to his marybones. That was their happiness. Having accomplished their desire, they set out with .3. hundred bowmen, conducted by Opechancanough, half-brother of Powhatan and King of the Pamunkies.

* * * * * *

Meanwhile our good Captaine Smith, having now achieved the head of that river (although I have yet to head off my own naked unstudied discourse), discovered what he and Ratcliffe had separately well imagined: — namely, that here lay neither crock of gold nor Fountain of Youth, but only marsh, oozy under ice, into which he sank to his knees while the Salvages smoked *Tobacco*.   Robinson and Emry commenced for to whine again; they were hungry, they said, and wanted sleep.   Remembering his own wood-wanderings after the .4. French Gallants had robbed him, Sweet John longed to strike these .2. or at least shout: I bore my pains and miseries; now you do the like! — Instead he smiled upon them, charged his musket with bird-shot, and set off to hunt them up a supper of wild geese. One of the Salvages agreed to remain with the men, they being as inexperienced in woodcraft as they were unsure of their courage; departing with the other Salvage, he saw them rheumishly essaying to build a fire. 'Twas late after-noon. Sleet danced in the air like gnats or midges; tree-boughs groaned; ice grated & snapped freakishly.   Sweet John was monstrous happy.   The deeper his Salvage led him into that swamp (the sun glancing dull & red upon the ice), the higher did his sense of freedom exalt him. His distance from Emry and Robinson was now sufficient for their panicked horselike screams to fail, though the screams grabbled and slipped between the trees, seeking his ears, weakening as their utterers weakened; arrows pierced their bellies, buttocks & throats. They fell into the campfire, writhed and died. The arrow-shafts began to burn. As for the Salvage who'd overseen them, he took part in the merriment, being a subject of the .1. whom Hamor calls *that subtill old revengefull Powhatan.*

Sweet John's distance from the fire was, as I said, sufficient to isolate their dying, yet hardly so great that an hour had passed before he found himself beset by killers (or aerial spirits as poor Robinson might well have believed) like unto the crowds of spectators leaning over the railings of the Globe Theatre for the .5.th act of *Shakespeare's* latest melodrama, his exeunt or extinction to be their entertainment! Belike .2. hundred of them there were, so it seemed to him — well, mayhap fewer; no matter; he was but .1., to which lone tally he scorned to add his Salvage. Before that worthy could leave him in the lurch, Sweet John, seeking to prolong his own breaths, threw him down into the ooze & knelt upon him; then he lashed him se-curely to his arm with both garters, in order to be possessed of a living shield to stare at him as the snow fell down upon his hair. — *Love you not me?* the Salvage moaned. — Aye, there's a fair thought, laughed Sweet John, you positively indict me to love. — The other Salvages now came yelping towards him, painted red or black or white like unto the most terrifying bugbears, and when he spied them nocking their arrows he turned to face

them, with his captive in between him & them; — how like you this, Sir
Buckler? he queried mockingly, and the arrows begin to sing through the
twilight. Sweet John perceived at once that his precaution had been wise,
for they seemed to avoid injuring his prisoner as much as they could; thus
no arrow greeted him between his eyes, but his coat and trousers, already
stiff with leather, brass, & frozen ooze and sweat, began to weigh him down
like unto pennies on a dead man's eyelids as arrows pinked him and the
shafts rattled together. Otherwise they did him no hurt, until he made the
error of turning a little sidewise, in order to shorten his Salvage's lash; then
at once an arrow stung his thigh; the head was in an inch or more — no opportunity to dislodge it. — And I'd thought it bedtime, he muttered to
himself. — He was still almost cheery. These fiends were as nothing to the
Turkes. He began working his way backwards toward the campfire, dragging the Salvage, who stumbled; he embraced him tightly, knowing himself
to be embracing life, and the Salvage shouted something in terror and dug
in his heels but Sweet John grappled an arm about his throat and jerked
him sharply backwards, wondering when an arrow would find that arm
(which he promptly slid lower, locking it hard against the Salvage's chest),
and to maintain his spirits he shouted aloud: I mean to live until I'm as
wrinked as an oyster! but it was getting monstrous dark & much colder so
that he could no longer see the spaces betwixt the trees where the Salvages
lurked. At last his companion no longer struggled with him, only scuttled
backwards in time with his dodgings when the arrows whined. His thigh
had begun to ache but he did not stop, holding the Salvage ever more tightly
and tenderly in his retreat. For a moment he suffered .1. of those brief
cracked confusions which assault us as we get older; he fancied that the Salvage was Tragabigzanda and he was with her caressing her face and bosom;
the man turned to him smiling & Sweet John saw that he had been stroking
him after the fashion of Salvages (or *Naturalls,* as they be sometimes
called), who do exactly that when they mean to show love or friendship;
shaking his head, he minced back & back, the Salvage clinging to him almost willingly now, so that again Sweet John became confused and thought
that he loved him. A Salvage came howling at him, and he shot him dead.
Back and back; faster now since they were about to rush. Biting off the end
of the next paper cartridge, he scuttled to the rhythmn of *butter and eggs,
butter and eggs.* He ducked behind a wide mossy oak with his lover, who
screeched uncannily while he poured powder from the cartridge into the
flash-pan. Run, Smith, run! The lessons he'd learned from good Captaine
Duxbury in the Low Countreys undaunted his heart. He shut the pan,

emptied the remainder of the cartridge into the musket-barrel, snapped a bullet off the sprue and flicked it in, rammed it deep with the scouring stick, lit his match, cocked the tarnished cock's-head, presented at a parti-colored nightmare face & shattered it like a rotten pumpkin. Screech and screech. Faces glared at him in the dark; they must be more than near if he could see them yet so clearly. And yet he still had no notion of laying himself down like unto a slave. His teeth tore open the next cartridge. Fortune had not despised him so far, not even in this blackness; but just as the Hangman pulls the cap down over his patient's eyes, so it now grew yet *darker,* which confounded him in his heart, altho' he'd not confess it. He said to himself: Now by my faith I can slip away! — but he knew all the time that if he tried it, they'd soon find him out in all his blinded blundering. Open the pan; dribble powder in. He was running backwards now, his Salvage embracing him for comfort as they scuttered back matrimonially, Sweet John never knowing when dead-iced tree-fingers would scrape his cheek or whether he was about to mislead his shoulders into some ambuscado. Powder in the barrel. Break the sprue; ball in the barrel. One more Salvage he killed with a musket-burst, and various others he wounded bloody, yellow balls of flame rushing out on white smoke-twirls, so that they screeched most dolefully in that darksome evening of ice and ooze. When would he achieve the canoe, & why didn't Emry and Robinson come to his help? He drew his dear Salvage back, but then the ground grew too smooth. Ice breached him into gruesome muck, & his Salvage with him. In Lincolnshire the Fen-dwellers 'scape such broils by wearing stilts; John Smith had none. Cold-strangled, an ill-used instrument, he stood coughing, his musket wavering in his hand; it must be again as when he was sold a slave among the Turkes.

Tell them I surrender and yield myself, if they swear by their OKEE to do me no hurt; otherwise I defy them and will kill as many as I can.

His fettered friend, pockmarked and dear, repeated these words in the Powhatan language.

They regarded him from the bank of the river, speaking rapidly amongst themselves. 'Twas pitch-black now; he could scarcely distinguish their silhouettes. Nor could he feel aught below his waist. At least he'd be no coward; there was no use in that —

They say 'tis well, his Salvage said.

He raised his musket high above his head, to make them see, then flung it from him so that it smashed down under the ice & went to nothing. He felt sorry. He stood shivering for a moment, his Salvage shivering against him, unseasoned perchance into sickness, and then he came out to them. (How monstrous strange to be marching along without feeling the ground at all, save by a dull distant vibration in his excruciating bones!) They denied to touch him yet; there was always that .**1**.st moment when a man came among his enemies, when servitude's vile usage lay still entreasured in the future, coequal with the free life before. Their painted faces considered and weighed him as he strove to undo the lashings that associated his Salvage to him. His fingers disremembered the ways of knots. His foes had to do it. Then he stretched himself out on the ground to die. His gaze he'd already forsaken; he knew not whether his Salvage had joined the others or vanished into the dark, which was soft and girlish like unto ooze. He sensed himself being lifted. When he opened his eyes they were at the campfire in whose embers Robinson and Emry lay sizzling; a Salvage dragged them out by the hair, and then others dragged him by his elbows so that he must look down at those corpses. — Fine work, quoth Sweet John, indeed you are a lot of Gentlemen. — They uttered something, and he replied what he would soon so often say to Pokahuntas, namely, *Cuffewh kenneaunten mata mechik,* which signifies, *I understand you a little but not much.*

Now they fell to assisting the aforesaid Captaine Smith. They removed his clothing mail-heavy with ice and arrows; gently they drew the arrow from his thigh, rubbing his arms and legs until the blood began to come back; he felt their warm calloused palms gliding urgently upon him; he schooled himself in their eyes, which he could not understand, and watched their faces darken and flicker. Was he condemned? They had beaten the ice from his clothes and dried them over the fire. He drew them on, skipping a little to warm himself, whereupon they laughed.

Which is your Captaine? he said. Show me your highest Werowance.

Comprehending that word, they led him in good order to the aforementioned *Opechancanough,* King of Pamunkey. Sweet John smelled the walnut oil on their hair.

Well, my Lord, so again it is you, said he, defiant so as not to be fearful.

Opechancanough smiled in hate.

I am Captaine Newporte's dearly beloved son, Sweet John essayed. Murther me, & he must revenge me well.

Slowly, Opechancanough ground his teeth.

From around his neck Sweet John took his ivory compass. He put it in the King's hand. He looked him in the face and said to him a very useful saying, which Pocahuntas would also often say to him: *Thacgwenymmeraun,* which means *I give yt yo^u gratis.*

Opechancanough shouted: *Nowamatamen!*   — Sweet John did not know what this meant.

He repeated that phrase which Captain Weymouth's Salvages had once taught him in London-Towne: *Cuffewh kenneaunten mata mechik,* which signifies *I understand you a little but not much.*

Opechancanough regarded him, curled his lip, and turned away.

Send me then to Axopolis, most dear Lord Ambassador, he shouted. I'm fain to be Tragabigzanda's again. I'm half a Turke already!

Opechancanough held the compass by the fire. He uttered some words in his lowly Salvage dialect, which discolored Sweet John's brain with terror between his ears. Then in silence there came upon him as suddenly as a crime, as smoothly as a copper knife slid out from the sheath, a stern grave Salvage of louring height, who wore in the piercement of his ear a yellow and green snake half a yard long, and the snake surged and bucked and wriggled most nauseously, and kissed the Salvage's lips with its tongue; that man took him by his left hand; and a man whose shoulder-length hair was black and glistening with grease-light took him by his right — most disdeignfully as it seemed to him; and all the other men (their hair shaved close on **.1.** side, and left full-length on the other, with a great coxcomb or skull-crest of hair in the middle that flourished like unto tufts of evil black grass) swarmed behind him to be his escorts, as the Soldiers do in England when some great stout fellow is led out to be hanged. Sweet John wondered if their aim might be to sacrifice him to their Devil, OKEUS, to Whom he'd heard they did great reverence; and he wondered how that yellow and green snake made shift to live in this biting weather (for serpents, as we all know, love best to burrow in moisty darkness); and he wondered why GOD had chosen to inflict upon him so many perilous misfortunes, although he continued hopeful of increasing his dignity & estate; and to undaunt himself he recalled to mind how he'd slaughtered those **.3.** Turkes; and he decided that if he was able he would offer to fight **.3.** Salvages in single combat, in order to save his life — this being but a chancy plan, but the best that he could think of; and so now that he'd resolved himself to firmness he felt much eased, as behooves a man who must soon struggle for his life.

* * * * * *

They lashed him most tightly to a maple-tree and hemmed him in all around, cocking their bows and aiming their arrow-tips at his face. His state being remedyless (or at least not in his own power), he brought on board his humming brain all his memory-crewmen of other narrow scrapes; these did as they were told, swarming most helpfully to keep his brain humming, most dispatchfully: shipwrecks, Turkishe duels, and the gunpowder pranks of Ralph Nightingale kept him fair, so that he gazed upon these murtherers with calm eyes cold with hate. Opechancanough, marking this, raised high the compass as a sort of signal, and the other prostrated their weapons at once, like unto the most wonderful worshippers.

* * * * *

Now he was almost happy, explicating the compass to Opechancanough. Signing for his hands to be unbound (which they granted), he gestured at the compass needle, then pointed at that *North Star* which standeth upon the tail of Ursa Minor. Opechancanough glared. Sweet John indicated the compass needle once more. He wished to inform them of the miracle of *Magnetism,* and, should he accomplish that, to tell them how well he himself could reckon the declination of that North Star, who dwells ever in the longitude of Aries. Opechancanough turned away, and they bound up his hands again.

* * * * *

They slept beneath a dishonest moon, he being passably well secured. He dreamed of Lincolnshire, where the leaves of beech trees curve gently down like unto scallop shells. He and Cicely were dancing the garland.

* * * * *

In the morning (grim and chilly morn it was), they led him breakfastless just behind Opechancanough, .1. stout Salvage gripping each of the prisoner's arms, and a .3.rd close on his heels behind, and .6. on his left hand, .6. on his right hand, marching close about with their arrows nocked. He prepared himself to be ready. He said to himself: At least I'm making discoveries. Through chattering teeth he mumbled prayer & Psalm. And they came to the towne call'd *Orapaks,* which comprised .40. houses more or less, each dwelling being simultaneously squat and high-rigged, like unto a ship; and all the women and little ones did gawk to see him, like unto yokels from Sloothby or Mareham at a fair, and the tiny Indian dogs did howl. Then the Salvages danced in a circle, squatting and crouching most strangely, so that he was amazed.

* * * * *

When he'd been a slave amongst the Turkes, and the screams of the raped Christian boys stained every chained night from Veristhornes all the way to Axiopolis, he'd owned scant hope of retrieving himself, and could merely pretend his soul back into Countie Lincolnshire, which he did love the more as he forgot its ooze. As for the screamers, he could only comfort them and himself by whispering: In after times, this shall be reckoned. — But at least he hadn't felt alone, not until the Under-Sheriff raised him to the auction block. Now the absence of fellow human cattle barred him from resignation, which is a stench that doth exhale from slaughter-herds. Contrariwise, his perceptions did sparkle and skitter anxiously, like unto grains of poisonous gold. If he saw his chance, he'd kill Opechancanough as he had the Tymor, and flee; if not, he must smilingly submit without showing fear. Alertness prickled over him from head to toe like unto the stings of verminous insects. The Salvages kept him in a lodge under strong guard, every day feeding him upon capacious trenchers of bread & venison, which at least proved they did esteem him. Each morning, after he had done praying, .3. pygophilous half-naked Salvagesses did come, to learn how he liked his breakfast. Still remembering what Captaine Weymouth's Yndians had taught him, he smiled, stroked his beard, and sang out in their brogue or dialect: *Love you not me?* Then these wenchen laughed, licking their lips, so that of a sudden he suddenly wondered (just as he had done in *Turkemania*) whether they meant to eat him. They grew horrible to him then! One day a girl whose plaited hair was blacker than a flock of marsh-hens at darklins-time brought him back his cloak, for which he was monstrous thankful, the weather being cold, and he began to point about his prison, asking about each object he saw: *Ka ka torawincs yowo?* — which signifies: *What call you this?* The girl laughed and answered him (altho' he sometimes disremembered her replies, for their dialect stayed not easy 'pon his tongue). Her face was tattooed with a black spider's semblance. Because she licked her teeth as wantonly as her sisters, he thought to be bold, and pointed to the base of her belly, inquiring: *Ka ka torawincs yowo?* — He was remembering his success with Tragabigzanda. If he could but get this hellish wench to fall in love with him, his life might be secured. — She regarded him for a long space with what seemed to be neutral eyes, opened her mantle of black fox-skins (whose possession proved her to be of high degree, for a Salvage), then shewed him her Secret, which (just as President Jefferson writes) she'd most strangely stript & peel'd of all its hairs, so that it resembled the quim of a little girl, and said unsmiling: *Muttusk.*   (Her thighs were tattooed with the likenesses of flowers &

snakes. Presumably she'd long since spent her maidenhead.) He rapidly touched his heart, then turned the palm of his hand around to reach toward her, saying: *Neckaun,* a word which a Salvage in Kecoughtan had taught him and which means: *Child.*   (He prayed GOD would give him acquittance for his bad behavior.) The woman grinned & seemed very happy. Regarding him almost fiercely, she squatted down before him with her legs spread and with .2. fingers opened the lips of her quim. He placed his hand upon the parted fingers and said: *Mowchick wayawgh tawgh noeragh kaquere mecher.* I am exceeding hungry. What shall I eat? — The woman chuckled, and snot flew out of her nose. Because she might own the power to save him, he found her inexpressibly dear. All along the walls, his great grim Salvage guardsmen laughed.

✳ ✳ ✳ ✳ ✳

Every morn & every darklins he did inquire of them: *Tawnor nehiegh Powhatan,* which signifies, *Where dwells Powhatan?*

They would not answer.

✳ ✳ ✳ ✳ ✳

Where is Captaine Newport? Opechancanough queried him.

Not far. He will revenge any injuries I receive. I'm his dear son — Opechancanough waved a hand in disgust.

He essayed to give Opechancanough a .2.nd demonstration of compass-magic, but while explicating the greatness of English arts he heard the interpreter use the word *Marrapough,* which signifies: *Enemies.*

✳ ✳ ✳ ✳ ✳

And here I should write that when Sweet John .1.st glimpsed Opechancanough (whose name means *He Whose Soul Is White*), he felt a strange eerie sense of destiny, which he'd never felt before his whole life over. Opechancanough was Futurity. Sweet John felt that; he knew not why—

✳ ✳ ✳ ✳ ✳

Shall I send word to Jamestowne Fort?

You cannot go there.

No need, Lord Opechancanough. We English can speak to one another by means of these marks.

All the Salvages placed the letter earward, but could hear nothing.

What does it say? questioned Opechancanough.

It says that you treat me kindly and that I continue in health, he cunningly replied, so that they need not revenge my death.

They turned the paper round and round, until .1. of them bit it. Ever he heard them jabber the word *Pawcussacks,* which signifieth, *Guns.*

It is well, said Opechancanough finally.

Then Sweet John sealed the message, as if it were the charter of an ancient guild of craftsmen in Lincolnshire.

* * * * * *

When the Salvages returned with an answer from Jamestowne, which John Smith read out in a brassy voice and the interpreter translated, then were all his captors awed and amazed, for they knew not the art of writing, and what the letter from the Counsell said agreed with the report of the Salvage messengers, so that they thought Captaine Smith to be a Sorcerer or something like. (The father of a man he'd shot besought him then to heal him, but Sweet John replied that he needed a magical water which they had only at Jamestowne. So the warrior died.)

Mustering up new files of strangehaired Footmen, or Servitors, or Slaughtermen (he knew not which), they removed him northwards to a village in the realm of *Toppahannock,* where Pocahontas would later live in lawful concord with Maister John Rolfe, & there certain stout Salvages (which he now knew were call'd *Cronoccoes*) were for putting him to death, to revenge the murthers there committed by a previous English Captaine, but Sweet John being shorter than that violent Countreyman of his, they kept him yet alive. He felt weak. He yearned to know his end. But his destiny resembled the night sky in May, when no man in Countie London can spy the .7. Starres.

* * * * * *

Now they were come to Werowocomoco, which means *King's House* in the language of these Virginians; and he supposed that they'd conduct him into the presence of *Powhatan his Majestie.* — But which Majestie was he? For among these Salvages they have a King of the Head, *Ningapamutla,* and a King of the Teeth, *Vneghiawmdupmeputs,* & diverse other such notions. — In truth, Powhatan was all of these and more. Would that I had whomever he loves most at my truncheon's length! (Thus Captaine Smith.) All who displeased him or trespassed against Powhatan's laws he commaunded to be baked & broiled in the coals. Yea, and he was also called *Ottaniack* and *Mamanatowick,* meaning *Great King.*

His real name was *Wahunsenacawh*.   His inheritance was *Powhatan, Ar-rohatec, Appamatuck, Pamunky, Youghtamond, & Mattapanient*.   All his other Countreys and Dominions were his conquests.

John Smith determinedly insisted to himself that inside the skull of the very meanest man was a church whose eye-windows admitted the light of GOD; the candleabra of intellect blazed more or less brightly, and the bone-ceiling was impressed, or not, with patrician reliefs; but there was always spaciousness, measure, proportion, worthiness, *life*.   How much more, then, must rational goodness glow within the skull of a King!   Americans from my century believe such notions to comprise mere brainsickness; and Sweet John himself, had he acknowledged his own utterly rational tremblings, might have called to mind the example of the *Tymor,* who, noble-blooded though he was, had shown no more kindness than the Turk-ishe street-wastrels who threw stones at chained men.   And yet, if he believed perhaps too optimistically in Powhatan's sovereign mildness, he was no worse off in any case, for not despairing.   Powhatan would murther him now, or not.   Why not hope to smooth away this King's hate?

Big grim men with muscular breasts squinted at him & never stopped looking.   *Your most humble Servaunt,* he replied.   But he denied to make a leg to them.   Naked, shaveheaded, snotnosed wenchen hid behind their mothers, gasping as though they'd been bewitched.   A baby screamed itself speechless in rising & falling squeaks.   He tried to throw .**1**. of them a white bead.   A dog snarled.   A warrior shook a club in his face.   His heart rang out like unto young Maister Barty's chiming watch.

* * * * * *

Powhatan's greatest Palace was long and narrow as a dog's jaws.   (Closing his dizzy eyes, he strove to remember his Machiavelli, brought up all the treasures of strategic experience from his mind's cellars, neglected not even to see himself once more playing Lurch with old Maister Reese Allen.   He rarely lost at those games.)   They pushed him down into a squat in the outer room, leaving him to wait there hemmed in by his tall and frowning guards who stood gripping war-clubs.   Would Powhatan prove yet crueller than the *Great Turke?*   The baby screamed on & on.   All sensations clawed at him & breathed upon him, so overpoweringly close that e'en behind closed eyes he could not but see the pores of their scaly skin.   Something wicked would slay him.   Every sound was a hook twisted into his ear.   When he shifted himself against the rough bark wall, the rasp of it almost deafened him. There was something which he should be doing to save himself, but it was unsearchable. He remembered the Rector back in Willoughby, who'd essayed to guide him into safer humbler courses. But why be a Tailor or a Draper for wages of .3. dozen shillings? He'd been spared that. He smelled smoke, corn, & chamber-lees. Behind the wall he heard a fire, and calculated and conjectured as to whether they were warming coals to a cherry-hue in order to cook his flesh.

Now they brought him in before Powhatan, whereupon the Salvages shouted crashingly, and the Queene of Appamatuck, whom he'd met last summer in company with Captaine Newport, presented water for him to wash his hands, which proved that they valued him as a Werowance — an estimation he applauded, as it meant that he might yet keep his life.

(But the Queene cast a sneer his way, which proved equally formidably that he was doomed to be eaten up.)

He prayed most inwardly to GOD: Do not turn away from me Thy most loving and merciful eyes.

As for Powhatan, he who reclined upon the throne of mats, his authority was as that of Lincoln Cathedral, which cannot be taken in all at once: .1.st the wide square hooves of its many stone Church-legs meet the petitioner's lowered gaze, which then (when commanded to do so) rises up the Cathedral's flanks, those being greyed and browned by time, like unto a smoked cheese; then come the black and slate jigsaws of stained glass windows, from which the interior's greedy darkness has deprived all color, so that they resemble fragments of seashells pierced together most cunningly; above the rounded points of those long glass bullets, traced successively larger by multiple labia of stone, come the tarnished brass or copper panels incised with .6.-petaled flowers, or the stone petal-ribs inscribed within stone squares, and then far away rises the true rising, and after all this the eye has only begun to approach the great Tower with its glories of grilles and birds. So it was with that Emperor, whose feet, at .1.st, were all that John Smith dared to regard from his lowly distance across the fire. As for his Guards & captors, whose malice already brought him nigh unto trembling, e'en these hellish spiders louted and toadied before Powhatan.

He lay at his ease upon his royal platform behind the rearmost fire, mantled in long-tailed coonskins sewn together, with his .2. freshest young concubines on either hand. His men & women formed nested walls along the house-flanks.

William Strachey called him wrinkled, & unbending, & tall, & clean, &

THE MEREST
PORTION of
LINCOLN-
SHIRE
CATHEDRAL

cruel, & sad; said he had grey hairs and skinny shoulders; said that he had a few hairs on chin and lip. Sweet John later wrote: *He is of parsonage a tall well proportioned man, with a sower look.* O, but he was grey! Grey like unto Lincoln Cathedral's walls, grey as the stone walls of Northumberland!

Sweet John gazed upon him well, to see whether he might possess magick-all charms or images which could do him hurt, but saw nothing, so that he conjectured that even this Prince of Salvages disliked images as did the Turkes, or else (such was his benighted nature) knew not how to fashion them. Perceiving no DEVILish toys, he began to grow more sprightly — indeed he needed to drink what cheer he could, being Captaine Fortune's pawn.

✳ ✳ ✳ ✳ ✳

In that place they feasted Sweet John upon fishes, fowls, venison, corn & other dainties; but, as e'er throughout his captivity, he must eat alone, while the Salvages observed him in silence. Altho' suffering from fits of the *twinkling fear,* he solicited himself to fill his belly right up to his chest, because he knew not whether they'd starve him now, or hunt him naked through the snowy forest, or wring away his life. He could hardly disremember the smoking corpses of his Soldier-friends. In the Book of Job it doth say, *Naked came I from my mother's womb, & naked shall I return;* but Sweet John said to himself: I'm not return'd yet! — and if today these DEVIL-stained hearts decide to return me, at least I can glut my last instants with decent belly-timber.

He felt himself to be like upon a specter in another man's dream. He longed to pray, & durst not, for fear 'twould incite these Salvages against him.

But then already his nervousness began to pass off. 'Twas the merest carbuncle in his heart! So many of these tedious ceremonies he'd already borne; doubtless there'd be more. Therefore, his life was infinite.

✳ ✳ ✳ ✳ ✳

See John Smith in that longhouse as the Emperor & his snakelaced Courtiers debate his doom. Sweet John comprehends no word. O, how he pities himself! They speak on, each with passion, yet never interrupting any other as an Englishman might do.

Sweet John stares straight into Powhatan's face. 'Tis as if he's been condemned to relive his introduction to the cruel *Tymor* of the Turkes! But toward that Tymor he bore himself perhaps with o'ermuch humility. He gazes at Powhatan with a stern readiness for the impending ordeal. He's awearied; he scarce cares what Powhatan might be thinking, so long as he, Sweet John, can gain safe harbor . . .

* * * * * *

Now see a troupe of great grim Salvages rolling in .2. anvil-stones (or chopping-blocks), each of them about the size of the *Bluestone* in Louth, which used to be a Druid altar; as a boy, he'd passed it e'ery day when he went to Grammar-school. Neatly & almost silently (he supposes they get much practice) they convey these instruments down the entire length of that Rustickall Palace. They halt before Powhatan's fire. They join the stones neatly together.

His heart pounds with fear until he believes he'll choke. He's sick with fear. He almost vomits. 'Tis as if someone were punching him in the stomach. His future's like unto black water between marsh-spines. Seeking to bend their intentions, he gazes more imploringly now into Powhatan's face, which is yellow like unto a lightly smoked buckskin. But the Emperor's not clement. So his eyes go a-blobbing for friends. They find none. See Powhatan's bravos & Slaughtermen now arise from the walls, with war-clubs in their hands.

* * * * * *

See John Smith. He entreats for his life. Powhatan laughs; his Assassins all snatch Sweet John, & hale him to the stones of execution, no matter how much he struggles & shouts. Draping his writhing body across the .1.st stone, they slam down his head 'pon the .2.nd. He cries out to the Emperor: *Netoppew,* which signifies: *Friends.*

Opechancanough sits near Powhatan. Opechancanough smiles in happy hate.

A Salvage's hand muffles Sweet John's mouth. He bites at the hand. The heel of another hand slams into his temple.

They roll him upon his back, so that in the flame-light he sees a swarm of war-clubs upraised. He cannot see the Emperor anymore.

Behind the hand he tries to say: *The LORD is my Shepherd. I shall not want.*

* * * * * *

See a little squaw come a-darting from Powhatan's side. She wraps her arms about Sweet John's head; she lays her cheek against his. He comprehends nothing.

* * * * * *

They permit him to rise. Dazed, he clutches the wench's hand.

* * * * * *

Powhatan takes up a rusty English hatchet from between a concubine's feet. He gestures at Sweet John, who believes he's being commaunded to fashion more hatchets for the Emperor. He nods.

Powhatan now gestures at the girl-child who's saved him. Sweet John peers at her for the .1.ˢᵗ time. Shaveheaded in front, she sports long black tresses plaited near about as tightly as chains of beads. Nobly confident (which perhaps beseems her blood), she gazes into his face. He can't accompt her now. His heart's not yet sure it's yet allowed to beat. How could he discover her face, let alone remember it?

She is wearing winter skin-clothes with the hair on them. At her throat she wears a stone bead with a round carven face which gazes upon him with deep-sunk eyes. He fears it, & her. (She herself hath glistering eyes.) What if she proves tigress?

She smiles upon him. Now he fears her not.

About her wrists she wears English beads & bells, which Powhatan must have taken in tribute from the other poor Yndians. 'Tis manifest they come from the stores of the *Susan B. Constant*. Again Powhatan gestures at Sweet John. He is to make more of this trash, & give it to the wench. He smiles and nods.

* * * * * *

. . . And into his ear she whispered: *Mufkaiuwh*. This word he did not know.

* * * * * *

She seemed to him like unto a very jewel of gold.

* * * * * *

Legend being strangled rather nourished by any abundance of original fact, it is unremarkable how rapidly our .2. best sources, John Smith and William Strachey, pass over Pocahontas. Strachey indeed mentions her only twice in his *Historie of Travell into Virginia Britannia* (1612); and the .1.ˢᵗ reference is such as to make us think that there might have been more than .1. woman by that name, or else that her life was even stranger than we know; for he says that *Pocahunta,* a daughter of Powhatan's, is now married to .1. of the Salvage Captaines, by name *Kocoum,* & has been for .2. years since. Could this be she? Strachey writes explicitly that she visited the Fort in times past; but many of the Indians would have done so. And the matter is clinched by the other reference, which *must* be to the Pocahontas we strive for, & there she's called *the before remembered.* Here it is in full, the more precious for its glancing illumination on that person, for it makes of her a beautiful ephemerality, as specific and simultaneously unknowable as, say, an eidetic image which I once had of faces kissing: they slide along each other, so that .1. mouth kisses only the mouth of nothing, while the other kisses a cheek; and the faces are pale, Roman-nosed; I will never understand why I closed my eyes and saw this:

> Their younger women [says Strachey] goe not shadowed amongst their owne company untill they be nigh eleaven or twelue returnes of the leaf old (for so they accompt and bring about the yeare, calling the fall of the leafe *Taquitock*), nor are they much ashamed thereof, and therefore would the before remembered *Pochohuntas,* a well featured but wanton young girle Powhatans daughter, sometimes resorting to our Fort, of the age then of 11. or 12. yeares, gett the boyes forth with her into the markett place and make them wheele, falling on their handes turning their heeles vpwardes, whome she would follow, and wheele so her self naked as she was all the Fort over, but being once past 12. yeres they put on a kind of semicinctum or leathren apron (as doe our artificers or handicrafts men) before their bellies and are very shamefac'd to be seene bare . . .

Can you see her now? I think I can, as soon as Strachey, who struts like unto a bird, finishes peering down his nose in an ecstasy of prurient horror & withdraws from the scene. As for Sweet John Smith, he minds not her lewdness — he e'en laughs! — for, as they say, he's like unto to some pranksterish lad tiddley-bumping his neighbors' windowpanes.

Would you love this child who could cartwheel so rapidly that her long black hair, now unplaited for play, bloomed in the air like the upspread fingers of a hand for the instant that she rested upside down on springy palms? Now the arms shoot upward and she touches nothing but air, screaming with laughter until Strachey, longing for to write another passage of his *Historie,* stuffs up his ears; her muddy heels whistle down backwards and her hair falls down like a skirt going up, leaving the hairless girl-slit and the well-ochered buttocks; it brushes her flat chest, passes her shoulders, spreads like a cloak upon the muck — but not at all! — for by this time the jacknifing body has whirled almost a quarter-turn; the buttocks are highest, the hands still the lowest extremity of the upside down **L**, which is already *before* we speak an upside down **V**, founded equally in air by hands and by feet; her hair, never quite touching the ground, has begun to whirl weightlessly up again like those longstemmed waterplants when the tide rises; the feet squash down in the muck and she is screeching with glee and rolling onward, toes up, head back, arms outstretched; and again she is as we saw her, or maybe infinitesimally previous, her palms not yet having touched? — The mystery of the circle has never been solved. We observe that the caged squirrel in his wheel grows successively older with each revolution; and yet there is a .2.nd kind of time, which the Jesuit Adventurers in Canada, for instance, had to recognize,* because whether their Stream of Time was imagined to flow upstream or downstream, in either case an inconsistency resulted; only by supposing the current to go both ways (as it once had, according to the Iroquois) could they square their circle within some watchful palisado or other; we, who are removed from all the events in this book, ought to be bold enough simply to *take* the circle in love as our time, granting that Pocahontas gets older, granting also that each completed revolution is a return, so that each instant lives again and will live as long as the naked child continues her somersaults. Because each circle may be subdivided into an infinite number of points, the number of instants is infinite. In some very real sense, Pocahontas will always be here; she is in every turning wheel of the taxicab. It is probably also true to say (although here I am less certain) that because the circle closes, between every delighted smack of palms into the ooze Pocahontas is going forward in time and backward in time at the same moment; or rather that forward and backward do not apply: — what seems, in fact, to happen is that as the next cartwheel begins she gets older, and by the time she is no longer commencing but ending her circle she has become younger but grows ever less young until as her palms slap mud again she has become as she was and therefore will always be: Somewhere in the course of her circuit she has simply reversed time. — But this statement, like the sterile Greek paradoxes, is surely the result of an error on my part, because Pocahontas lies dead at Saint George's Church. Nonetheless I see that bright brown-red face, the girl whirling with even greater agility than the Cabin-boys whose continued lives depend on monkey-speed and confidence among the rigging of the *Godspeed,* so Poca-

*As explicated in the Second Dream.

hontas wins cartwheel-races with them all until they give over, at which she grins and coaxes them to begin again, crying: *Love you not me?*

* * * * *

According to Strachey, *I love you* is *Nouwmais* in the Powhatan language. This transliteration might be pronounced *new mace,* or possibly *noah maize,* or *no umma is,* or any variety of ways. Her face blurs more than ever when the phrase does. Nobody knows how she spoke. But I am sure that when she said *Love you not me?* she said it in a way that the English could understand; for she was constantly with them in those days & they had taught her to say it; thus in seeking that alien Indian face and finding a blur we make for ourselves an English face, like unto the face of the Church-yard Angel in Gravesend.

* * * * *

It was because he was not unstudied, having learned much from Wingfield, Ratcliffe, the .4. French gallants and the *Tymor,* that Sweet John quickly spied out how desirous the child was to please. — 'Tis always of interest to hear a baby's first word. Whether he says *Mama* or *Dada,* that is how his lifelong partiality is evinced, as we assume, and maybe even correctly. In the case of our budding young Sweet John, the Indian word which left his mouth before any other was *Netoppew,* which means *friends.* (Captaine Weymouth's Salvages had taught him that in London-Towne.) The .2.nd was *Marrapaugh,* which signifies *enemies.* Thus armed with carrot and stick, dauntless Smith commenced, as I said, to learn their grammar a little, which he considered to be a most glorious action. He learned to accompt & to name commodities and weapons, grew adept at juggling their syllables on his tongue (for in Hungaria and France as in Afrique and the Turkishe Countreys he'd marked full well that an Undertaker could never attain his end unarmed by the shinings of local words); in his list of politic phrases we find the following:

Kekaten Pokahontas patiaquagh niugh tanks
manotyens neer mowchik rawrenock audowgh.
Bid Pokahantas bring hither .2. little Baskets, and I
will give her white Beads to make a Chaine.

* * * * *

For her part, the child grew in her knowledge of the English tongue full speedily; it was a wonder how so many words did bewray themselves with all their fluent meanings into her ears.

What are these?

Beads. I pray you say it, dearling. *Beads.*

Bees.

O yes, beads.

From where?

From my Countrey. Someday I'll take you there, sure. I'll show you my brother Frauncis, and introduce you to his Goodwife's fat backside, and you'll study grammar in Louth . . . But they'll have you cover your quim there, mayhap. Never fear, I'll buy you fine dresses of silk & satin . . .

Bees, she repeated, and when he gazed at her he seemed to spy a deer's ears raised, face frozen, straining to ken what it had heard.

* * * * * *

Mowchick, she said.

Pray allow me to guess, smiled John Smith, stroking his beard. I trow—

Mowchick! she impatiently repeated, touching first her mouth, then her naked brown stomach. *Mowchick wayawgh tawgh noeragh kaquere mecher!*

O, he said. Is it belly-timber you'd be wanting?

He stroked the child's skin, which was soft and shiny like unto milky-brown swamp water.

* * * * * *

She taught him a certain gambling-game involving reeds, which he comprehended to be of ancient favor in her Countrey, for many did gather round & play with him after that.

Her half-brother Nantaquas proved likewise most kind.

* * * * * *

He taught her how to play Tick-Tack and Lurch. In the army under Captaine Duxbury in the Low Countreys, a Salopian (or *Shropshireman,* as they're sometimes called) had taught him how to play *Cats and Dogs.* He tried to instruct Pokahuntas in that game likewise, but she would not play it, being but a young unbroken girl.

He said: Tell your father to provision me against my going with **.20.** baskets of dried oysters, & with mullberies, acorns, wheat and beans . . .

She laughed, and ran off into a crowd of black-and-yellow-painted men,
.2. of whom backward-gazed at him, pointing to his broadsword, which
Powhatan had restored unto him with all his other property . . .

* * * * * *

She desired to play. Plaiting up her hair, she sat herself down with him by
the hearth-fire. She was wet; she'd just swum with the other Salvages in the
ice-skinned river. Sweet John felt monstrous cold, but she, all in a sweat,
flung off her furs & began to prance naked around him, turning droll cartwheels & other Salvage tricks, which brought the mirth of exasperation to
his lips. Yesterday he'd been a convicted enemy, doomed to death; today he
was a girl-child's plaything! O, his life seem'd transitive in truth, a passing
stay at Gravesend . . .

The skin of her body was speckled with summer like unto the waterlily
tubers that those Salvages stewed. Her eyes were shining like unto black
cherries.

* * * * * *

. . . And she ran a hand through his hair and whispered to him *Mufkaiuwh,*
which was a word that he did not know, so to help himself remember it he
murmured it aloud twice in this wise: *Mufkaiuwh, Mufkaiuwh,* at which
she hugged him still more tightly with her cheek against his and then he did
not have to guess the general significance of the word that she had said.

* * * * * *

He stayed among them deep into the Sunne's wanderings through Capricorn.
Powhatan's toadies all gave him good cheer now. He knew how to be emulous. Their mirth grew unGODly; they pretended that he would dacker
down with Pokahuntiss, & sport with her as doth a man with a whore . . .

* * * * * *

Sweet John meant to hold her heart fast with only a slippery hitch, that cunning rope-bight which comes free with but a pull. He meant not to break
her, never to harm her.

She laid her hand upon her heart, then upraised her hand toward the
Sunne. Therefore he did the like, but afterwards laid his hand between her
prepubescent breasts, at which she smiled.

* * * * * *

In the Church at Willoughby there's a little hatchway inside the big door which opens only for weddings, christenings and funerals. So it is with Fate's innermost door. Let's pretend it now doth gape, for this joyous wedding with Pokahuntas which will admit John Smith to glory at last.

(Dear Father, when will you fashion me those bells & beads you did promise me?

(In good time, child. I must .1.st gather my materials at James-town . . .)

Tragabigzanda lov'd him, but he could not stay to taste the proof! Pocahontas loves him, and by means of it the Colonie shall get a living. Could that *Yndian* maid be bought and sold for black silk ribbons? Nay, though he'd present her, if he could, with an Englishwoman's white under-shirt embroidered with a garden of blackwork (back in Willoughby, Cicely Bellowes surely owns .1.), he means not to deprave himself or her, by means of bribes. Her love is *his*. She's his Fate. Her door has opened of itself, to serve John Smith's most dreadfully needful turn.

✳ ✳ ✳ ✳ ✳ ✳

They set out through winter forests as eerie as the rigging of ship-crowds at Gravesend. Powhatan had strok'd his breast most tenderly when they bade each other goodbye. And Pokahuntiss appear'd passing sad . . . Between the trees were stars which watched him without pity. 'Twas hellish cold, and thorny vines groped at his chest and ankles as he trudged with his Salvage retinue through the darkness, hearing the polysyllabic moans of ghosts. His shoes sank into the cold ooze beneath the snow. An icy twig snapped loudly and painfully against his shoulder. Searching for the Fix'd Starres to know where he was (for should they murther him not, why then, he'd surely return unto Werowocomoco for purposes of chaffering, marrying or assault), he uprais'd his eyes nearabouts .15. degrees to discover the *Lion's Taile* in Virgo. Yes, he gazed up at the weak spring crowns of trees, scanned the twinkling stars, and heard the silence grow & grow until an unknown bird called twice, mayhap 'twas the device of an enemy Virginian. He listened to the darkness growing fearfully about him.

Strange Salvages! In the Low Countreys when he went a-soldiering there'd been many a sinister fellow who blackened his face and armor the better to rape and pillage, anonymous to all save G O D; these murtherers were called *Swart-rutters*. His blackguard honor-guard seem'd self-evidently comprised of Swart-rutters now, with their hangdog glares and puccoon face-paint. Was this but the final plot of Powhatan, to have our Sweet John convey'd into the night forest and done away?

Full wearied (such was his fear), he strove nonetheless to shew e'er a sunny, manly face, as he'd done amongst the Turkes. His conductors spoke to him, & he replied: *I comprehend thee a little, but not much.*

He marveled how they did turn most childishly off their path from time to time, to look for clawmarks of bears on the trees. Sure the bears must be a-sleeping now! But maybe they could track 'em to their snow-hid dens, he knew not . . .

* * * * * *

They slept that night in almost-ruined Salvage crofts at Paspegh. Sweet John lay so excited to be near home that he could scarce sleep. He prayed: *O LORD, Thou hast brought up my soul from the grave, & preserv'd me alive, so that I not go down unto the pit.* Long before sunrise he'd arisen, prayed, & set his face toward James Towne. With half-smiles, his **.4.** Salvages did set out. 'Twas but an hour's struggle through snow and grey thickets (the path proving very good in places), until he'd returned most proudly to the Colonie which anew he had saved. Yea, here lay James Towne — already half-eaten by the wilderness, as it seemed; for old leaves lived in the grey roof-thatch, and branches had fallen athwart the chimneys — percase some spark could take dangerous root; he liked this ill. But he'd utter his plaint on some other occasion. He stood watching with his Salvages. And did his Countreymen watch? Already he'd arrived within demiculverin-shot, and no man challenged him. He spied no Sentinel save that icicle'd Fort itself, with the bare trees all around.

The palisadoes had begun to weather. The gate was shut. Did they fester there in sleep, or in fear?

Striding thereto, he knapped & rapped upon it with an irritated mien.

Who goes there? shrieked the Sentry of a sudden.

John Smith. God save you, Gentlemen.

* * * * * *

Granted, then, as I have proved, that his rotten motives break beneath the weight of questioning (this was, of course, Ratcliffe speaking), Captaine Smith must go upon his trial. And a speedy one it shall be. Gentlemen Counsellors, I call on you to judge and sentence him *today,* executing our charge upon him before nightfall without fail. He's not merely shamed, but *dangerous* —

O GOD! he shouted. And shall I now be impeach'd for *this?*

Look you, Gentlemen. He appeals his very fault, wallowing in mucky lies. Base-coined yeoman fabler that he is, he e'er wrongs us, seeking to depose us in his heart. Contention's bastard, political adulterer, he sallies out to his curs'd *Friends,* who nock arrows at us night & day, scheming to deprive us of our Colonie, so that, being weak, we must sequester ourselves 'twixt these walls! Captaine Smith, where's George Cassen?

Dead, Sir, as you well know.

See how he struts like a gamecock, uncrestfallen, regardless of our reproach! *He will not confess his fault!* Where's Jehu Robinson?

Dead and murthered, Sicklemore. What would you expect? For 'tis as Maister Wingfield said: I'm no true man, but an idle beggar, that in Ireland did beg without a license. I wink'd and flinch'd at gun-flashes; I never did help your Colonie—

Hark, he denies it not! And Thomas Emry?

Have at me, Maister President. Expir'd like the rest—

What 'venomed pride this little yeoman has! He puffs himself up like unto a corpse diseased with dropsy! He distends, nay, distempers himself *beyond* all temperance. Did we give him leave, he'd go out to the wilderness to fetch here his Salvage allies—

John Smith whispered almost piteously: How can I make good, when you e'er think ill of me?

✻ ✻ ✻ ✻ ✻

For a blink, Ratcliffe himself, who hated almost beyond telling this spleenful fellowman now well handcuffed and clamped at the ankles with cold stout bilboes, did believe in his intentions, and would have resigned all proceedings if he could; but once the Doctor prescribes a purge, how can he countermand himself? Better that the patient dies — for should he falter, they'll trust him with no patients more! Could John Smith but beg the Counsell's pardon for his misdemeanors, percase Radclyffe might save his face, and Smith his head. If not, how darkly poison'd the man's rancor must ooze! He'd turn against the Colonie sure! A Condemned-Hole .10. fathoms deep and fenced with iron would scarcely preserve him undelivered from his Salvage pandars, conspirators & intermediaries . . .

As gently as he could, he said: Think upon yourself, Sweet John. How can you be in the right, to contemn authority?

But what must I sue for? Am I turn'd Turke, that I must crave and beg? The pains & perils I've swallowed, why, somehow they've translated away all my obsequiousness . . .

Pray you now, man, *pray* and pray *consider* how you sink yourself into newfound perils which denying you do but increase! Make us your gravest suit, or you'll be *hang'd* this moonrise! Can't you revoke your pride to save your own life?

But who will prosecute him, Maister President? put in Maister Martynn. We dwell at the Antipodes here; we have no lawyers for such a serious matter —

Upon my honor, but you disremember Captaine Archer here! He studied law at Gray's Inn —

Oh, *Captaine Archer,* laughed Smith. Pardon me. You might as well hang me without the earnest malice of your Captaine Archer—

Hang you? cried Ratcliffe, galled raw by the prisoner's scorn. Listen, Gentlemen! He already begins to speak of hanging! He knows his guilt. (Marshal, look you well to him. He's the King's prisoner.) — Now we expect your full & speedy answer. How did the Salvages solicit you, once they'd murthered your wards? Surely you were foreadvised, and led the monsters to their bloody work, else how came you back again?

Maister Sicklemore, you are e'er the enemy of doings you cannot see.

Captaine Archer said: Delay no more time, Smith, but return your answer suddenly.

Have I no friend here?

None.

I —

For the last time, answer!

I've become his son—

Whose?

King Powhatan's—

O, baser and baser! He forswears his allegiance to our King, and pandars his services to Salvages who roasted his own men—

And what would you have had me do?

Hark! He confesses himself!

Gentlemen, I deny any treason—

In this dank desert of trees, began Captaine Archer (now appointed to the Counsell by Ratcliffe's **.2.** votes which overrode Martin's solitary nay, Kendall being lead-ridden and buried,* Sweet John un-Counselled to be

---

*In those times it was common for the Counsell of Jamestowne, and especially its President, to call the Master Recorder to them within almost every space of hours, to frame some indictment against those they ruled, whipping and beating them, sometimes even hanging them. (For entertainment's sake, or because 'twas *Politick* (best to blame our predecessors before the people brand *us* guilty!), Captaine Archer, who was now appointed back unto the Counsell, haled Maister

cast in the jailhouse), which we find peopled by the *Lost Tribes of Israel*, 'tis fitting that their former or so-called *Leviticall* law be invoked.

Hear, hear! said Radcliff, who for all his passionate words incongruously remained as immobile as some Werowance who sits upon a mat of reeds.

'Tis a canon of said law (continued Captaine Archer) that *Blood must pay for blood,* especially in cases of wilfull rebellion when our suspicions are umpire over the protestations of the accused — may GOD comfort him now! For how can he deny it? He levied English lives as tribute for his stained glory! I read out from our Letters Patent: *Yᵉ offences of tumults, rebellion, Conspiracies, mutiny & seditions in those parts which may be dangeous to the estates there, together with murther, manslaughter, Incest, rapes & adulteries committed within those parts* shall be punished by death, *and that without yᵉ benefit of yᵉ Clergy, except in the case of manslaughter.*

We cannot dispute that, put in Captaine Martynn, for our Masters wrote it. And now, John Smith, when you left Maister Emry & Maister Robinson, what disposition were they in?

Disposition? Why, they were disposed to sleep. Just as *you* were, Maister Sicklemore, while I took my needless pleasure in discovering the Countreys around us, building and entrenching this Fort, and such unnecessary fooleries. Did you not say that an *egg-shell* would be sufficient against our enemies, or was that Maister Wingfield?

Mayhap it would have been, villain, save that you delivered us over to their devouring. GOD comfort you. Your cunning has bewrayed us all.

And again they commended him to the Marshal (whom for a jest they call'd *Lieutenant of the Tower*).

Wingfield before the Counsell on every conceivable occasion, threatening & accusing him for having starved them, to which he replied in a faint voice: It is said I did much banquet and riot; I never had but **.1.** squirrel roasted, whereof I gave part to Maister Radcliffe then sick; yet was that squirrel given me . . .) Thus their sport. And so **.1.** day when President Ratcliffe did beat James Read the Smith with his own hands, for what offense nobody knew, such bad dealing had long been smoothed by habit into the semblance of mild reason; but James Read did strike the President back again, for which he was sentenced to be hanged. *Now* the aforesaid Read had need of quick-witted cunning to preserve himself from an early grave! Entreating for a private audience, which was granted, he whispered into the President's ear, or yielded himself up to sing on command, some tale about Captaine Kendall's mutinous doings, this being much the same strategem employed in after centuries in *Russia* by the citizens of *Iosif Stalin* and his Counsell: When arrested and condemned, save yourself by slandering others. Stalin, being more rigorous in his noble sovereignty than Ratcliffe, condemned the newly accused, but prudently upheld the indictments of their accusers also, for he would have no villainy. Howbeit, James Read was permitted by Ratcliffe's regal graciousness to redeem his life, and so poor Captaine Kendall found himself arraigned. (Reader, I suppose our President thought it politick to kill him so as to thin out the Counsell.) Ratcliffe pronouncing judgment of doom upon him, he defiantly said that he was no Ratcliffe, but only a Sicklemore, and had no warrant or power for any such act, and so Maister Martynn cried out the sentence, and they shot him.

Defiant again, he said: You did commaund me to explore the Chickahominy River to its source. Before you murther me, I must faithfully report that beyond the sandbar 'tis navigable for full **.38.** miles, should the vessel's burthen be **.6.** tons or less . . .

The articles against you have been prov'd.

* * * * * *

By then he had learned the precise meaning of that name she had called him when she held him at the block: *Mufkaiuwh,* the flower of a fine thing.

* * * * * *

And so GOD have mercy on your soul! shouted Ratcliffe.

They sued out a writ against the said Smith, and sentenced him to be hanged; but Captaine Newport (who very easily might have dawdled at Guadeloupe, indulging his crew in the killing tortoises & alligators for their larder), arrived that day on the *John & Francis,* and saved him.

THE GRAMMAR OF TIDES (1608)

The womb was first my grave; whence since I rose,
My body, grave-like, doth my soul enclose:
That body (like a corpse) with sheets o'erspread,
Dying each night, lies buried in my bed;
O'er which my spreading tester's large extent,
Borne with carved antiquities, marks my monument;
And o'er my head, perchance, such things may stand,
When I am quite run out in dust and sand.

WILLIAM AUSTIN, "Sepulchrum Domus Mea Est" (before 1634)

At dawn they were sitting in a circle, still cold from having been in the river, and then her father rose up and cried *Bowh, waugh* and the women lay down. The men thrust firesticks into the earth. Dark whittlings of smoke rose slowly into the chilly, glowing air. Amonute felt comforted by the tiny points of flame all around. The SUN must see these lights which her father was giving to Him. She lay still and safe. The dirt was cold beneath the reed mat. Now all the men began to stamp their feet so that the SUN could hear. The morning changed from orange to yellowish-white. She became very happy; she knew not why. At her father's command the rhythm ceased. When he raised his hand they brought river stones and beat them with sticks.

Her father was skinny and old now. Although in this season all the People grew thin, he shivered more than others. But she would never have dared remark on it. He remained strong enough to do anything.

Her father clapped his hands. Amonute arose to gave thanks. After the MOON died twice more, they could begin to plant corn again. She longed to drink the sweet green cornstalk juice. The days would be long and warm then. No one would be shivering. Her father's discomfort would be ended.

Today he appeared so tired and old! She dreaded his death.

The boys were roasting mussels on the fire. They grinned and pinched her for sport. Soon would come time to give them unto OKEUS. Then she'd not see them for nine changes of the MOON. They'd be men after that; they'd play with her no more. Amonute snatched a handful, and craved more, but was afraid they'd tease her. So she ran back to her father's house to eat from the stewpot, which today contained many fishes seasoned rich and bloody with deer-guts. She ate her fill there; there was plenty.

By the palisades lay a grindstone which the Tassantasses had given them. Whenever she saw that, she remembered her other father, the one into whose ear she had whispered *Mufkaiuwh*. She was angry with him, because he had forborne to return. But her father had promised to send him food. She hoped to have a long enough life to go and visit the Tassantasses many times. Perhaps if she prayed it of him her father would let her go . . .

She also wished to see her mother in Rapahannock, the one whose breasts she'd sucked. Her mother was proud that her father desired her to live with him, so Amonute felt the same, but today she'd woken up sorrowful, remembering her mother's house. She was too young to go alone, and no one would take her there.

But her uncle Opechancanough was coming soon to hunt deer with her father. He often traveled to Rapahannock; he was her mother's kinsman. Perhaps he had seen her.

Amonute went with her plaited-haired sisters to cut reeds. It was the place where Nantoquod had slain a fat bear last autumn. In the canoe her sisters and mothers talked only to each other until she said: When does Uncle come?

Soon, they said laughing.

And soon enough he came, all the way from Menapacunt. As soon as she ran to him, he said: Your mother does well. You have two brothers now, not only one.

Amonute was happy. Her mothers Otterniske and Oweroughwough both laughed. She ran to give her uncle an oyster-shell for him to dip up his stew from the great pot. Smiling, he caressed her head. She grinned anxiously; although she loved him, in him she ever sensed some fearsomeness.

The next day some of her sisters came running and cried: Your father commands you!

Amonute ran, pleased and afraid. She ran through the ice-skinned reeds which embristled the ice-paned river-curves all the way along that mussel-studded ooze.

Her father was sitting on a rock stringing his bow. Her uncle Opechancanough was there beside him. He no longer wore her other father's magic needle around his neck. Perhaps he'd given it to Uttamattomakkin to keep in the temple. She rushed to serve them both water from her turtle-shell cup. Laughing, they waved her aside.

Her father said to her: Your other *Father,* how many hatchets has he made me?

She hung her head.

Well, should we have bashed out his brains?

No, she said faintly.

Ha, ha! her father laughed. My little bear shows her teeth!

Uncle Opechancanough grimaced. He said: Now I begin to think you love those Tassantasses . . .

Such faces as their I've never seen before, the girl whispered.

They laughed again, not quite approvingly. Amonute felt cold. At last her father said: I must keep my promise to provision the Tassantasses. But it ill befits me to go to them. Daughter, since you love them, go play with them, and bring me back some hatchets—

Thank you, father. I shall go, & come back unto you—

Not long after, they found her on her knees, resting her hands on the Tassantasses' grindstone as she sang a song.

THE GRAMMAR OF MAIDS

None other pain pray I for them to be
But, when the rage doth lead them from the right,
That looking backward, Virtue they may see,
Even as she is, so goodly fair and bright.
SIR THOMAS WYATT (before 1539)

*T*hey were in straits in James Towne that winter, the state and condition of their hearts as cheap as clinch-nails; for from hunger they did have a most grievous smart. Yet slightly oftener than every week did good Pocahontas now come with corn (and once even venison) from her father King Powhatan. Gentlemen who could scarce be troubled to pare their nails made haste to salute the plaited-haired wench. And President Ratcliffe, although he blustered of *that fantastical Powhatan, that would be my check-mate,* did use Powhatan's daughter with near obsequious courtesy. Just as when one plays the game call'd *Primero,* each card holds thrice the value proclaimed on its face, so the Jamestowne gamblers made shift to accompt the girl at more than her ill-favored worth. Sweet John kenned full well she was but messenger and spy, no more, yet thought 'twas wise to pretend her upwards into a Heaven of greater power, since all knew she lov'd him: He who must needs get ahead in this World, is better served by embroidering the affection of a great Lady on his standard, than by attainting himself with the reality of some snotnosed wench. (Thus writeth *Machiavell.*) Moreover, he pitied her condition with all his heart, and whene'er he saw her his breath grew heavy-fogged with guilt, for her reproachful eyes did recollect him of his lies.

(She'd fashion'd him a basket made of cornhusks; she said 'twas the work of her own hands. He kiss'd her forehead.)

He'd sworn to be her playmate for e'er! No matter that desperate necessity had fathered his policy; Pokahuntas had taken no hand in his oppressment; yet it was to her he'd lied. What to do then (since he scarcely could unsoil himself) but at least placate and reverence her with offerings to her high birth? Moreover, 'twas certain 'twould please King

Powhatan, who'd be King not many years more, did the English but win their game.

Sometimes she came from Paspahegh, with the black-painted Werowance of that Towne and his great grim fellows. They might appear with a fat deer on their shoulders, or e'en a Bruin, that did dangle his bloody claws down the back of a Salvage who wore other claws in his transpierced earlobes. As spring wore on, and the river opened, they came by canoe. At other times Pokahuntas came overland from GOD alone knows where, her companions all strange — lordly men prying about (no matter that they carried baskets of corn). The President would have preferr'd to receive 'em outside the Fort, dislading them of their edible credentials, then discharging them forthwith, but Sweet John pled almost ragefully or tragically that such conduct would insult the King's daughter, whose love for them might straightaway translate to hate (as is oft the case with scorn'd women, he whispered with a wink).

We must heed him now, the other Counsell-men advised. (Smith was off a-playing Lurch with the Princesse.) The Counsell sat in the President's half-roof'd house, drinking sack out of the wide cone of a Chinese cup on which a landscape had been figured in blue. A pair of gold handles further distinguished it, & inside 'twas white as the white of an egg! It had been Wingfield's, before that Gentleman got deposed.

Heed him! exclaimed Ratcliffe. (Pass the cup, Captaine Archer.) What, has he cooed likewise in your ears, you unmanned *Pokahuntases?*

No, Maister President, but since we could not hang him last time, best allot new rope for him to mistake himself in.

I like that! 'Tis true, the varlet must soon enough reveal his o'erstepping; 'tis in his blood; he *cannot* but dance out of his proper place. Well, let him dance when the gallows-trap drops.

And (should 't please you, Maister President), we require corn. May his wench keep us in life 'til spring. *Then* . . .

Your policy likes me well. Come April we'll end this business. Captaine Newport shall trade directly with Powhatan, and hold his friendship, 'til we all make our fortunes with gold!

Spoken statesmanlike! Captaine Archer did cry, and the other Counsell-men concurred. (For in their Counsell John Smith brought up the rear e'en yet, like that shark's-fin triangle of a sail which in a pinnace always travels last. No one cared for him, he being but a Lincolnshire yokel.)

Then Ratcliffe was full contented to give Sweet John and Pokahuntas quiet pass.

But let me speak .1. speech, prayed Matthew Scrivener (a new Counsell-man of good towardliness). If 'tis true Powhatan's daughter bears his mandate, as Smith would have it, then shall we not make her our gamepiece, should he fail to bear us loyal love?

Oho, what novel metal you've coined! said Ratcliffe. Do you propose to detain her?

Aye, Maister President — not now, but if need proves. Sweet John's the lime-twigged bait. Bid him allure her here whene'er Powhatan defaults; then we'll seal her away, until the Salvages do our pleasure. What say you all?

Then the Counsell agreed 'twas excellently reasoned and conceived. But Ratcliffe compelled them to swear an oath to say nothing to Sweet John, lest his pricksome pawings of the wench did mislead him into pitiful scruples. Nor was her imprisonment meet — for now. So they pledged each other and pass'd Wingfield's cup.

Pokahuntas came near e'ery week, as I said. They devoured the young maid's bounty. When by accident the Colonie did burn, her father sent them raccoon skins, which they employed to warm themselves whilst raising up new houses. So by degrees the Englishmen lost their dread of death, at least for that season. One-armed Captaine Newport own'd it politic to return the Salvages' favors full measure, at which John Smith demurred, saying: I know not whether we'll get advanced in Powhatan's affections by reason of the gifts you send (his affections being mercurial), yet sure we'll get correspondingly empaupered.

From your manner of speech, I see your head's grown swoll'n since I sav'd you from the rope, Sweet John.

I seek but to save our credit here—

Think you I liv'd unexposed to *credit* 'till you got whelped?

Forgive me, Captaine, but what if they come to ken that beads and hatchets are but trash? Then how shall we pay for our living here?

We needn't pay for it long.

'Tis mere prudence to—

O, but Adventurers aren't *prudent* men, John! Let your dice fall with a merry heart, & if you like not the result, why, play another game.

Machiavelli saith—

I'll tell you a fact of *Policy,* Sweet John. At Court they care not o'er-much for your Colonie, whether it doth thrive or starve. I told 'em there was gold here, so to save you. Now help me get gold.

I misdoubt there may be none.

Then we'll up spiritsail & leave this Colonie! Without gold what man would plant himself here? And if there's gold, then we'll quickly get the means to conquer all these Salvages. So let's sow coppers in e'ery furrow, & keep our Undertakers well disposed. Come on, man, don't look at me so sourishly! If this time I sail home fraughted with nothing, think you my Lord Salisbury will send me here again?

Truth to tell, Captaine Newport could not believe that Virginia engross'd no gold whatsoever in her womb. He yearned to make friends with Powhatan. By easy means he won the Counsell's ear, and via Pocahuntas did envoy many bushels of gewgaws, each time asking for to meet with that Emperor. So it came about that in the month of February, Pokahuntas did say to Sweet John (after he'd allowed her to vanquish him in a round of Lurch): Father, be not afraid to enter my other father's Countrey, for now he waits upon you to keep your promise, and live with us, lest it be said of you Tassantasses, *they lie much.*

Sweet John hung his head.

Fear us not, father, the girl whispered earnestly. Believe you not I love you?

And in his ear she whispered *Mufkaiuwh,* which is to say, *A Flower of a fine thing.*

He opened his arms and the bear-greased little body leaped upon him. Almost frantically she kissed his lips. Doubtless the poor child was starved for kindness, her father the King owning so many wives and children . . .

I promise I will tell the Counsell, he said.

But methinks you'e a great Werowance, father, as you told us in Werowocomoco. Did you lie?

Nay, Pokauntas, I lied not. 'Tis unfitting to symbolize the tale to .1. of your years, though I comprehend full well you speak and hear for King Powhatan . . .

I must home to my father. What shall I say?

Bide a moment here, my child. I speak with . . .

(He *would* not name Ratcliffe, who'd essayed to murther him, as his kin. As for Radclyffe's cronies and swingebreech dandies . . .)

With Captaine Newport, he said at last. He's my father—

(And wasn't that true, in a manner of speaking? Newport had preserved his life from the halter. Newport had given him life.)

Bidding Jefferey Shortridge amuse her, he went to the President's house, where he found Ratcliffe and Captaine Archer a-playing at Primero again. Ratcliffe (who was e'er lucky in his cards) did hold .3. Kings & a Jack, while Captaine Archer stayed literally at sixes and sevens.

And d'ye remember good strong merry-go-round ale, Archer was saying, that savors of sweet woody brownness, and spins the head like unto a child's painted top?

O, full well I remember it. We're down to our last kilderkin of piss-dyed beer. But you, Sir, have lost this hand. Captaine Smith, what would you report?

Pokahuntas bids us to Werowocomoco, Maister President. Powhatan would guest us—

Ha, ha! Your Princesse soon will have handsomer suitors than yourself, Sweet John! Will you despair when she throws you o'er?

What shall I tell her?

Why, that 'tis concluded we shall come with our best Officers. Tell her to prepare accomodations for half a hundred—

Maister President, 'tis too many! Powhatan will not—

I misdoubt me not your custom of *few and fast* were better, Smith. More convenient then for Powhatan to pare us down to the marybones, and roast us . . .

O, I'll set a good face on it, was all Sweet John replied.

$$* \quad * \quad * \quad * \quad * \quad *$$

When he peeped in on her, she was waiting for him, sitting just as a pregnant woman sits with her hands clasped over her belly.

$$* \quad * \quad * \quad * \quad * \quad *$$

Could we establish once and for all Sweet John's true dealings with Tragabigzanda, we could be surer how he regarded Pocahontas. Is somersaulting Sweet John but completing the circle to slap his weight again on the same soft thing? Despite her grief for herself, her father & her People, there's not yet any grief *fixed* in Pocahontas's face, as there is in the Bootan Hall portrait of .9. years later, when, pale and flabby-cheeked, she gazes patiently out of the gravestone of lace that yokes her neck; her slender fingers are likewise pale. (Did John Rolfe her husband direct her to scrub the last residue of ocher from her skin, or did she bathe in milk like royal Ladies in fairytales, or is she already ill, or did Rolfe, taking the Artist into his private study, explain what for the sake of the family *must* be painted white?) She looks frightened, dyspeptic, bloated with strange food, resigned. Bursting from the lace which chokes her wrist, her white fingers clutch vacantly at the darkness under her scarlet cloak. There is really nothing to be seen of her bodily self but that groping hand and the head severed bloodlessly in darkness — a shadow of pink on the cheek, the full lips unnaturally red. Her **.1.** hand, the right, dwindles into strangulation in its translucent crown. No elbow — only darkness and then the empty shoulder-sleeve. From the left shoulder-sleeve, darkness slithers, bisected by a streak of somber gold. Her breast is darkness; the cut-off hand tears at the black stuff of it, writhing amongst gold buttons, trying to find something there: her heart, her nipples, her shoulders, her armpits (there John Rolfe never kissed you, Pocahontas), her naked brown body now a woman's, the body impassioned like any fullgrown body to give itself, thereby enslaving itself to another body enslaved within it; the brown body is naked beneath another brown body; the brown body robes itself and dances with others round the circle of posts; it raises **.1.** knee, letting the foot hang down, and shouts: *Whe, whe, yah, ha, ne, he, wittowa, wittowa!* while the warriors leap and stamp; it sings and brings its wrists against its sides; it pounds its breasts singing *Whe, whe, yah, ha, ne, he, wittowa, wittowa!;* a feathered warrior waves a branch. The People dance round, and the carven faces on the poles stare into the inner circle where **.2.** warriors embrace a naked enemy, tying him to a high pole most tenderly; the brown body caresses its vulva and there is nothing but joy. As the fire burns for, under & within that mutilated man, the brown body has an orgasm which replicates any instant of naked cartwheels. — But this other instant, when the brown body is gone, and the face, the sad face gazes from darkness (a tiny earring glitters like silver night) — there's another moment entirely. The death of the sad face will be *its* reiteration. —Still another point on the circle, we might believe, is the moment when she pities, and gains leave from Powhatan her father to succor the strangers with deer-meat and berries; but this moment is due to Sweet John, or at least due to her *feeling* for Sweet John; and so it lies at a negligible distance along the circle's circumference from that other moment, the orgasm of the brown body; yet perhaps it lies not so far from the death of the sad face, either; perhaps the circle is much smaller and more wretched than we might want to believe.

✳ ✳ ✳ ✳ ✳ ✳

Having now escaped anew from these metaphysickall whirls, let us hoist sail, raise anchor, &c, thereby continuing our relation of the doughty *Captaine Smith,* whom we now see in the Cooper's shed with the Princesse of the *Yndians,* or *Naturalls,* by name **.1.** *Pockahoontis.* 'Tis said she looks wondrous pensive at her friend, whom Ratcliffe has named *that pa-*

thetic cum-twang. The snow-crust is thinning and coarsening. Last year's grass pokes palely through it. Birds laugh from their nests. She would go a-walking with him, but he hangs his head and says her nay.

She will depart with her Ladies and attendants at dawn. At twilight, with the stars creeping out like spiders, he reads to her from his *Almanacke,* thus: *And now by this rule you may know the rising and setting of the Moone for euer . . . That for euery day of the age of the moone, the moone goeth to ye eastwarde* .1. *point and* .3. *minutes, and* .2. *daies* .2. *pointe and* .6. *minutes.*

He understands it most mechanickally. He'll never comprehend it to perfection in his very blood, as doth euerworthy *Captaine Argoll.*

*   *   *   *   *   *

Smoke blew in through the windows of the cool dank Church (which was scarcely but a tent, & soon would be a barnlike shed of divinity, constructed on forked poles). The Counsell met there when the President's house was indisposed. Sweet John sat through a sermon, wondering whether Powhatan hated him, because he did not return with Pokahuntiss to Werowocomoco. Percase the Salvages would shoot flaming arrows to fire the roof.

Spring rain, and his floor was ooze.

*   *   *   *   *   *

He was thinking to himself: Who can the powerfullest Prince of the Salvages be? Be he Powhatan? Doth *Opechancanough* hide behind him? Powhatan, then or Opechancanough? Or what about this OKEUS? Mayhap he's no DEVIL, but a subterranean King. I must learn (altho' I swear I'll never tell Ratcliffe) through whom to obtain the cession of this Countrey. For Machiavelli saith, that the new Prince must destroy the most powerful in the Countrey, and exterminate his lineage, then leave all lesser Lords and Princes to be his friends . . . — These rarities of uncertainties greatly teased his brain.

*   *   *   *   *   *

Let me quote again, if I may, from the Letters-Patent of Jamestowne.

*Euery person and persons being our subjects of euery the said Collonies and Plantations shall from time to time well entreate those saluages in those parts, and use all good meanes to draw the saluages and heathen people . . . to the true seruice and knowledge of God, and . . . all just kind, and charitable courses shall be holden with such of them, as shall conforme theselves to any good and sociable traffique . . . whereby they may be ye sooner drawne to the true knowledge of God, and y** Obedi-ence of us, our heires and successors, and under seuere paines and pun-ishments as shal be inflicted by y** same seueral Presidents and Councells of y** said seueral Colonies . . .*

✳ ✳ ✳ ✳ ✳ ✳

See John Smith, ferrying Captaine Newport to Werowocomoco in obedi-ence to great Powhatan's summons. 'Twould have been better by far to dis-allow the odious little yeoman's presence, but this time he's needed; he alone hath been guested by Powhatan. Next time they can leave him to hew cargo-timber as befits his station. Meanwhile they'll keep that revelation dark unto him. He misdoubts his future not; he's like unto a child. — *Flood oh!* cries this Captaine Smith. He's in the .2.-masted *Discov-ery,* which is Newport's ship; he dreams she's his. Near a dozen Gentle-men swell their Undertaking into an excellent Exploit: to wit, *Nathaniell Powell, Anthony Gosnoll, Anas Todkill, John Taverner,* and diverse others, whose names can be read in the *Generall Historie.* A bargeful of Soldiers wallows behind.

(Maister Radclyffe stays at home for to helm the Government. Already his ambitions do work at raising up a Presidential Palace, which will be trapezoidal like unto a foretopsail; here he'll literally enlarge & engross his office, so that the Counsell need meet no more in the Church, or in Maister Wyngfyld's old tent. Indeed, this Palace will prove so well appointed as might perhaps serve to become the capitol of *Virginia Britania . . .*)

They pass Newport's other Sailors a-tippling sullenly upon their ships. Then down river they speed. In a twink they've rounded the cape at Ke-coughtan, whose Salvages scutter away at their approach, fearing further exactions of corn. Captain Newport sings out: Keep it, varlets — *until the harvest!*

Aye, Smith answers, to that they've already consented.

To every article, Sweet John? And was the lawyer there? His name's *Demiculverin,* and he's got largish balls. Ha!

Now northward, paralleling a horizon of breakers as puffed up as thistleheads — into the next river's mouth! 'Tis a grand harbor Powhatan possesses here, perhaps the best in the entire Plantation. Sweet John explains: Gentlemen, you'll soon see how the water narrows to but a mile's width. I believe 'tis full .4. fathom deep at flood tide, so that it could berth any argosy or man-o'-war . . . — O yes, Sweet John kens it all! In snickering whispers he's already been named *the Waterman of Jamestowne,* who for his glittering aspirations deserves but to shuttle his betters from London to Gravesend, until the worms do haste to their feast of clay.

Amidst the many underlings and Adventurers of Jamestowne who keep them company rides that newish Counsell-man *Master Scrivener,* in part to spy on Sweet John's doings, as the latter knows full well, this entire Counsell being a nest of false forswearing and treachery, as if he's fallen once again among the Turkes! Percase his many perils have hardened him against his superiors, or chilled him full cold. He cares not: Jamestowne and Werowocomoco seem to him the same, and in each place some *Tymor* akin to Tragabigzanda's brother bides ready for to enchain his neck . . . This World is hollow! He owns scant patience more. And what cares he, or .1.-armed Captaine Newport, for Powhatan's summons? Jamestowne must have corn. So be it. They will go, grabble, trade.

Look! A flock of ring-necked geese! The half-starv'd men commence to shoot, but too soon, so that all but .2. or .3. birds are safely startled away—

The river runs east & west. Captaine Newport wears full armor. John Smith wears his rusty old iron-scaled brigandine vest, which Bartty gave him after he 'scaped the Turkes, and which he always calls his suit of armor. Passing the rotten roots of toppled trees, he directs the pinnace deeper up river, in accordance with the barbarous explanations of a hired Salvage. The snowy muck of spring swamps burns behind his eyes. He writes down every compass bearing in his book, thereby following the dictates together of his prudence and of the *Instructions Given By Way of Advice,* which warn: *if that Your Guides Run from You in the Great Woods or Deserts you Shall hardly Ever find a Passage back.* (See an old Salvage house, sere & crusted with dead twigs and grasses like a bird's nest.) On the bank, a Sal-

vage frowns upon them, ugly like unto some DEVIL-toad, then skips back into darkness. I once read in an old Almanacke, that the principal duty of a Navigator is to know where he is. Welladay, and how to do that here in *Vir-ginia?* Rivers and streams, to be sure, make faultless landmarks, but what of this darkness to starboard and larboard? *And as for wooddes and hedges with such like,* the Almanacke sayeth, these *are not to be marked, because suche things may be cut or felled downe, and so youre marke is lost: Wherfore hylles, vales, cliftes, and Castels, with stepels and Churches, are the beste and most surest markes, that may or can be taken, and are better than hedgrowes, wooddes or trees.*

Through a spyglass, Captain Newport seeks despondently for gold-glints in the sand. Back at Gravesend it had seemed manifest that he could swear any oath to his Masters — tomorrow wouldn't he have means to redeem it? But just as Jailers are naturally choleric men, so our Lords are naturally severe; Newport can already see himself wandering unto Lord Salibury's presence with uncertain step, gall'd by his own fears, & behind him come his fellow woebegone Sailors to entreat for their pay; Lord Salisbury will greet them in a rage, screaming: Your faces prove how well I conceived your purpose! — Dear Reader, for Captain Newport those will prove most cumbersome days.

'Tis a grey day of grey vines and creepers in Powhatan's Countrey, the season still naked & in arms. Along the shore, ferns have begun to bud, 'tis true, and the coarse stalks of some unknown herb to stick up from the leaves, but most trees remain skeletons. Captain Newport is saying: What shall we do with him? — Crown him King, my Lord; crown his ferocious vanity. (Thus John Smith.) — And what will be his strength today, I wonder? says Newport; Sweet John, perceiving that the Captain but soliloquizes, bides silent.

Powhatan's Countrey is flat and marshy with many bearded, grizzled pines casting their pinish pall. Powhatan's Countrey smells of ooze, pine needles & dust. A most breezily blue-grey afternoon it is, and the river streams; leaves stream as laundry will someday stream, .4. centuries later, in the era of Rick's General Store; the wind clicks twigs against each other and the river murmurs, and it begins to drizzle while the grey pines and cypresses weep with vines.

What a weary, gloomy place! cries Captain Newport with a scowl. He'd rather spoil some Dutch ship for candles & double-beer—

The slatey sky has become pale yellow like unto the sandy floor of a Salvage's house, and everything softens in sheets of rain. Skinny blurred trees shoot upwards in an opposing grey rain. The rain turns to hail for a moment, knapping at everyone's skulls, and then becomes rain again, hissing with glassy delicacy, like a shy woman urinating into a puddle, slobbering down upon the reddish-brown marsh grass which in the time of Rick's will become red fields. Again hail skitters down. Sad grey creeks shake sluggishly down leaf-choked gullies. Salvages spy upon them from among the black seedheads of rain-slicked grass. Grey sky, red leaves; raindrops like fat caterpillars strike Sweet John's cap . . .

Among tall, lonely old pines the grey river hooks its last finger-joint inland, sinking itself into a plain of grassy ooze. They cast anchor so that the pinnace lies aloof from shore (for that's only wise, this *Virginia* being sometimes very shallow & silty). Captaine Newport secretes himself within the cabin, as though he were some lethal chess-piece best reserved for emergencies. Mayhap he's a-hoping Sweet John will stumble. (That surmise, now, 'tis desperately true. *Pokahuntiss* hath puffed up the yeoman too much, as Ratcliffe said; the Counsell can scarce deal now with his moonish conceits.) So 'tis loathsome little *Smith,* with his wide-brimmed feathered hat, his broadsword & musket & powder-bag always with him, who now bawls orders (for all the world like some comical Drill-Sergeant in the Low Countreys), bustling and strutting, as if 'twas to his own hearth they were acoming. Newport thinks to himself: What if that lozel slupper'd up Pocahontas's maidenhead last December? What might he do next, if he owns that credit?

At least he's forgotten no jot of Mariner's drudgery, for they embeach the barge right faultlessly, tying her to a scaly pine whose roots bore and grapple in the muck like a handful of banded grubworms. Then 'tis ashore they go, with Sweet John .1.st, aping some great Generall.

A Salvage clothed only in leaves stands where the river-muck is speckled white with freshly opened clamshells.

The Salvage utters syllables as uncountable & unaccountable as the ripples of any creek.

✳   ✳   ✳   ✳   ✳   ✳

Netoppew, replied Sweet John, which signifies: Friends.

The Salvage spoke again, another long hemorrhage of syllables.

Sweet John said: *Cuffewh kenneaunten mata mechik.* I understand you a little but not much.

The Salvage spoke.

Sweet John declaimed with a virtuoso's graceful confidence: *Kekaten Pokahontas patiaquagh niugh tanks manotyens neer mowchik rawrenock audowgh.* Bid Pokahantas bring hither .2. little Baskets, and I will give her white Beads to make a Chaine.

The Salvage gazed upon him unspeaking.

A pox on him — a *Spanish* pox! cried Maister Taverner impatiently. Turning to the Salvage, he made as if to shake him by the shoulder and shouted: Where is thy Master, man? Where is King Powhatan?

The Salvage smiled grimly. Turning away from that river now lost in rusty plains of marsh grass which concealed cold dark ooze, he led them down a wet avenue of warped trees. O, but 'twas an evil forest, haunted by Powhatan's Slaughtermen! Salvages by the dozen came a-gathering in — tattooed murtherers, fettered with a fiend's disfigurements. Most of them wore feathers erected in their hair like unto the horns of DEMONS. The Englishmen looked them o'er with dislike & fear, fearing to see their own ends looming now. Rain slapped upon the pine-needles into which they sunk to the ankles at every step. Dreamily, Sweet John touched a pale bark-striped tree. (He did think it most convenient now to meet with Pocahontas, who'd feast him & single him out before all others.) A bow-bent sapling had accumulated on its underside droplets which clung like a string of strange small eggs. Maister Scrivener trod upon it, and Sweet John watched all the eggs break.

* * * * * *

He felt within his heart all the familiar old motions of hope & dread intermixed. Fearing not to advance from this outer zone of Salvage footmen to the more worthy sphere of *Emperor Powhatan* himself, yet Sweet John did fail & falter just a little to know for a fact that the tall, grim old man now was aware of his coming, & awaited him in the smoky darkness of his Salvage Palace. Sweet John tasted dread in his throat. But he must not show it.

* * * * * *

Now 'tis time to cross the Salvage foot-bridges, which creak precarious above the ooze. Sweet John reserves a Salvage or .2. unto himself, to be hostages in the rear, should be bridges prove traps, as he mistakenly apprehends. See how the Soldiers of our Colonie do march forward, lowering helms, probing their way with their halberd-tips. Booted and jack-armored, they weigh down the narrow planks near to forfeit. O those grinning English with their guns over their shoulders! They strain not to vent their terror. 'Tis Sweet John's apprehension that .1. of 'em might discharge his snaphaunce or bastard-musket by accident. He cries out: *Is all well?* but they answer not. Reader, you might construe each of them to be alone, like some solitary traveller peering over his shoulder for highwaymen as he

trudges the infamously dangerous road from Dover to Gravesend. Methinks that's why I hear no snatches of old songs on their mutchado'd lips;
they fear their mouths will all too soon be stuffed with mud! And, poor
Soldiers, how correctly you fear, for now as I sit writing, what remains of
e'en your skeletons but a fragment or .2., scarce larger than a horn-button?
As Ecclesiasticus saith, *That which is, is far off, and deep, very deep; who
can find it out?* I know not what lies beneath the earth. And our Soldiers
and Gentlemen fear to know. But at last, the bridge-logs (or sticks as I
should say), qualified by rot, reject their burden! *Plash! Ploosh!* How
the Gentlemen curse, and the Soldiers scream affrighted! But their good
Shepherds the *Salvages* do with scarce a smile engage to pull them out, until they're come to oozeless ground, safe — altho' their armor's bemired.
Meanwhile a canoe doth come to ease the way of Captaine John Smith,
whom Powhatan still half-lovingly names *My son.*

Raindrops seethe upon the river, torturing its skin into a pattern like
treebark. Maister Todkill utters something, but to Sweet John his words
are but weary blurs of color like the uneven rhythmn of raindrops.

✱ ✱ ✱ ✱ ✱ ✱

At his commaund they did form up **.II.** by **.II.**, and march'd behind him
.1. *and* **.2.**, **.1.** *and* **.2.**, for John Smith kenned the way. Now they heard
all the treacherous little dogs begin to howl, and they smelled the dung & offal of the Indian town, which relished no better in their nostrils than the
filth of James Towne; and in the meadow-field outside of Werowocomoco
came Powhatan's wives already painted red and clattering with copper,
among which decorations canny Maister Scrivener spied Spanish coins with
their irregular edges as if some child had gnawed at them, and he whispered from the side of his mouth: Spaniards must lie dead hereabouts! at
which Smith squash'd a mosquito that had stolen blood, and answered:
Then the Salvages must be our friends.

O yes, Sweet John, as long as they have corn. But are these whores for
sale?

Let them welcome us thus if they would. I trust not such Amazons . . .
— And he remembered that Salvage wench he'd frigged last winter when
he was captive in the Towne of *Orapaks,* that spider-faced girl in the
mantle of black fox-skins. He wanted her again, but dared not seeks
her before his Countreyman, lest he be despised & arraigned for a traitor.
And Pokahuntas, he'd looked upon her **.10.**-year-old quim likewise,
when she shewed herself in her innocency; but he scorned that meat, for

she did but play. Percase when she turned **.12.**, which is the marrying-age in England . . . Reckoning of such sports did draw him on, just as in dark English forests the glaze-worms do shine without actually illuming one's way.

✳ ✳ ✳ ✳ ✳

With their guns ready they did march **.II.** by **.II.** through the palisadoes, e'er fearing treachery. The Salvages commenced for to sing most welcomingly. Bundles of corn & dried oysters reigned upon woven platforms like unto the stage 'pon which an attainted felon is hang'd back home in England. Veritable hillocks of Yndian bread lay awaiting them outside Powhatan's Palace (which, to tell you true, seem'd to have shrunk since he last spied it — for now he stood in no peril of his life). His Countreymen licked their lips. How they craved to eat with the Salvages, sharing their trenchers of steaming corn!

('Twas evident that this bounty issued from Powhatan's private Storehouse, for the common people appear'd extremely thin.)

O yes, here came little Pocahontas a-running to see her special friend. Naked she did leap upon him, and wrap her arms about his neck. She strok'd his breast. Pulling his beard, she shouted: — *Nowamatamen!* which signifies *I must keep yt,* or *I love yt.*

Captaine Newport's crew, some of whom came freshly poxed from whoring at Shoreditch, did lick their lips to spy her naked quim, but Ratcliffe and Newport together had convoked an assembly beforehand to threaten 'em with death did they so much as solicit that Salvagess, for without her, he said, they were *all* dead. — Fie! For that I care not a fart, said **.1.** Gentleman, unlacing the points of his codpiece & scratching his balls. Death's no worse than this cuntless life! — Now here loitered other Salvages wenches dressed in little more than puccoon-paint, so that these envious persons bethought themselves of riper quims than hers; and yet at Pokahuntas they ever sniggered. Sweet John heard their jests, & was shamed. Yet what could he do, but also merrily laugh, so that the Salvages might continue ignorantly unoffended?

✳ ✳ ✳ ✳ ✳

In the long dark house where Sweet John had nearly got his death, Powhatan sits upon an embroidered leathern pillow, warmed by a pair of luscious wives, while **.20.** more line the house-walls with red-painted pulchritude, each of them necklaced with white seashell-beads. Powhatan smiles. He feasts the Tassantasses with bread. He pretends to be glad at their coming.

The Queen of Appomattoc washes Sweet John's hands & dries them with turkey feathers. Her mantle's quillwork as sharply ornate as the parade halberds he remembered from the Armies of noble Hungaria. He would o'ergaze her further, but fears for to render Pocahontas jealous. (There she is, sitting in the darkness behind her father. Around her neck she wears a little leathern bag well stitched with shell-beads. How he'd love to fill it up with toys & dainties for her!) Anyhow, 'tis now best to give attention to his dear *Father,* the Emperor.

So you have kept your vow, and come to dwell with me as my loyal son, he addresses Captaine Smith, who blushes, mortified.

Receiving no reply, he frowns, and says: But where is your other father Captaine Newport?

He comes tomorrow morn.

And why do you call *me* father no more?

Pray excuse me, *Father,* that I did but forget myself in the presence of my Countreymen. Once you grant me the Towne & lands of Capohosick, as you did vow, then I can keep you better in my memory.

Powhatan gives him a sharp look, while the Gentlemen of the Colonie do struggle to constrain their mirth.

Sleep here, he replies at last, then withdraws to another place — Pocahontas, too . . .

*   *   *   *   *   *

Captaine Newporte came next morn on the flood-tide, conducted by the industrious Captaine Smith, who warn'd him once again not to ravel out overmany gifts & presents. — Then be on the watch to help me, Sweet John. — *Your most humble Servaunt, Sir.* — The day being clement like unto spring-tide, the Salvages would that the ceremonies be held out of doors, to which their guests must accede. Three grim old men ornamented with red-dyed deer-hair laid out mats upon the ground, and so the English did sit down. — What doleful wails they do make! whispered Master Scrivener. I trow they have been at their idolatry! — Now arrived great Powhatan unsmiling, with the same clean sad round face that Smith remembered, and with him came all his Cronoccoes and others of importance (like ghosts, they smelled of smoke & old leaves), and his wives vanished into Werowocomoco and presently returned with trenchers of some Salvage stew, with deer-meat, cornbread and boiled roots mixed all together.

Newport had to confess that it relished well, although he would have pre-ferr'd more salt. Then the Salvages gave to them of the herb *Tobacco,* which in truth strongly grates and tickles against men's throats, so that Mas-ter Scrivener begged to forbear, but Smith told him that he must inhale it for courtesy's sake, which he did. All the while Powhatan did smoke his pipe in quietude, like a foreign ship standing aloof at sea.

Now the Salvages began to dance. And they did skip, leap about & turn cartwheels, in the manner of some bewitched hogs which John Smith once seen in Countie Essex, altho' hogs can but grunt & whinny, while these Sal-vages howled as if they were so many wolves or DEVILS. Lost in their own frenzies, or exaltedly stretching out hands & rattles as they stamped in their circle, the feather-crown'd dancers made both Master Scrivener and Captaine Newport afraid. But Sweet John warned 'em to shew no fear, so they smiled, not tamely, and rewarded the painted, beast-furred dancers with beads & such trifling jewels. Powhatan watched them sidelong, his face painted red and blue, and his ears behung with mussel-shells, and he appeared to be very ill pleased.

Such is his nature, good Captaine Newport. (Thus John Smith).

He loves us not?

Pray treat him in friendly wise, and—

Think you I cannot scrape by with these ill-favored Salvages? By heaven, Smith, those Turkishe moonbeams swelled your head!

As you will, my Lord. Can I never win you to acknowledge that I labor only for—

For your weal's engrossment?

In a Salvage's long black leftward locks, a raccoon's jawbone grinned at Captaine Newport like unto the sawback sail-array of a caravel rigged out for merry gales, and he fell silent.

* * * * * *

Then through the trees he spied darling Pocanhontas winnicking with mirth. He longed to marry with her.

* * * * * *

The famous *Nonpareil,* growled Captaine Newport with a grin. — And she's yours, I hear. She means to have you, John.

Smith is silent. An immense hemisphere of cloud commences peeping over the trees.

Has she had you?

I see you envy my estimation among the Salvages—

They say gold's tested by a stamp, a woman by gold, and a man by woman. How will you endure your test, my lad?

* * * * * *

Now John Smith did gift his so-called *Father* with a greyhound, a hat, & a suit of brave red cloth, at which all the Salvages joyed. The Trumpeter played a *Trarintra-rarara.* Then Smith said: King Powhatan, craving your fair judgment I am come to remind you of your promise, that you did grant me the Towne of Capahosick, to be mine own.

And you did swear to bring me a pair of cannons.

O, those demi-culverins? Did your vassals not tell you, Powhatan, that altho' I gave 'em license to carry them away, yet they could not?

Seeing all the English grinning at these words, Powhatan saw how he'd been tricked, and grew more sour than before. Then he said: So be it. Regarding Capahosick, my *Son,* I'll give it to you just as soon as your men lay down their weapons as do my subjects.

Then John Smith must confess that he too had been stymied . . .

* * * * * *

Captaine Newport now presents Powhatan with a boy jestingly nam'd *Thomas Salvage,* whom he swears is his son, in order that the Salvages may keep and preserve him. Of course Thomas is in truth but an expendable spy, sent to learn the Salvage language and all their secrets. Canny Powhatan doth reciprocate with a lad call'd *Namontack,* given with much the same protestations and purposes. So far it goeth to the contrary of the game *Primero,* where (as I said) each card must be estimated .3. times more highly than its face proclaims. The boys are but satellites; new boys can be made.

* * * * * *

In the hour before darklins, Powhatan's mud-pools lie ashine with the same dull white light which glances off copper knifeblades. A messenger from Powhatan's brother, tall King *Opechancanough,* comes to visit the Englishmen with many a smile. Captaine Newport says: Methinks he's a good honest fellow.

Trust not in Salvages, Smith whispers most earnestly.

Why goes he so sad away?

He's moved by our multitude, my Lord. He would we were all in Hell.

Oho, now I recollect how that Opechancanough importuned me to sleep in Pamunkey last year, but I mistrusted his intentions. Percase he fears I love him not. Quick, John, we'll suture up his varlet's melancholy. Send after him, and gladden his Infidel heart with a hatchet or a red matchcoat . . .

Opechancanough I know well. 'Twas he who nearly murthered me.

Many persons share that distinction.

Sir, he'll never be our friend no matter how wide he grins. He kens our purpose here.

But we mean *him* no inconveniency. Now my heart begins to clench against the knave. Who's he, to scorn me in advance?

His villainy I ever suspect. He's a very cutpurse.

* * * * * *

King Powhatan departed them until the morning, and they entered a house which was squat and wide like the sails of a Spanish galleon. Captaine Newport stared about. This selfsame *Pokahuntas* (though she owned but .10. or .11. years of her age) did cause them to sit down near the fire, and her Serving-women drew off the Englishmen's stockings to be washed, then those same kind maids cleansed the Englishmen's feet in ewers of water heated warm upon the fire. Now Pokahuntas and diverse others of the better sort began to roast venison o'er the fire for them, dressing it and tending it with their own hands.

He observed that Pocahontas & all her maids did cover their noses with their hands & laugh most wantonly, so he asked her the meaning of this, at which she replied: Your Countreymen stink much.

* * * * * *

Late at night, when 'twas time for the English to quarter themselves, those selfsame women, fresh painted with oil & puccoons, waited for to be their bedfellows. Pocahontas came to be his bedmate. He enclasp'd her tight, & that was all. Her breathing was as soft and silent as the footfalls of a huntress who creeps on pine needles over sand.

* * * * * *

On the following morn, Captaine Newport then did say and swear that they needed victuals, and in particular corn, wheat, beans and peas.

Powhatan said: Captaine Newport, it is not agreeable to my greatness to trade for trifles in this peddling manner. I esteem you also as a great Werowance (here he smiled bitterly), and am sure that you wish your greatness to remain likewise unvexed. Therefore lay down for me all your commodities together. What I like, I will take, and in recompense give you what I think fitting to their value.

At this Captaine Newport did smile somewhat, being full sure of his capacity to overawe the skinny-shouldered old Salvage with such a plenitude of nearly worthless toys as to gain .20. hogsheads of corn, but Captaine Smith did say: You whom I must call *Father,* I pray you comprehend his intention, which is but to cheat us, and do what we would do to him . . . — to which the Admirall made reply: Sweet John, amend yourself. Obstruct me no more.

'Tis customary in Ireland & the Low Countreys for our Generalls to permit their Captaines to set the chaffering-price. For we best know the Naturalls of those regions—

Captaine Smith, I've sav'd you from the gallows twice. Now fall silent, or I swear to GOD I'll clap you up by your heels.

So it fell out both as Captaine Newport desired & as John Smith prophesied; for Powhatan took what he listed, whilst in exchange gave the English scarce .4. bushels of corn. Then Newporte sat shamefaced, like unto an Under-Sheriff whose felon hath escaped; while Sweet John's soul grew equally transparent, burning with the fire call'd *rage:* — After all his labors and extremities, e'en now he was valued as no more than trash by those he had saved & saved; so that for an instant he could see down into his pit of old age, when his powers of cunning, endurance and strength had eroded entirely away, while still he'd have hoarded up neither goods nor honor for reward. But, remembering how he'd rescued himself even from his slavery among the Turkes, how triumph had been his in the .3. duels now engross'd upon his coat of arms, how the darling *Pokahuntas* had saved him from her father's executioners, he marched home again unto his mood of goldenness, & tantalized Powhatan with some blue beads which Captaine Newporte had disremembered to present. At .1.ˢᵗ the old Salvage afforded these baubles but the coolest glance, but Captaine Smith hastily snatched them away, as if to return them to their befitting darkness, as if here were some *Whore of the streets,* who doth shew men her Secret only by glitt'ring glistening glimpses, in order through scarcity to price up her charms (which in truth half the human race possesseth). For he who would succeed in this chaffering-match called life, must puffingly o'ervalue himself, while robbing others of their best commodities. Thus Sweet John explain'd unto Powhatan that these blue beads (which back in Willoughby his own brother's wife would scorn to wear) partook of the sky's substance itself, which was why only the brightest Kings of all Countreys could don them. Powhatan composed a sour grimace, as if he doubted the like. But John Smith did lay his hand upon his heart, and upraise his hand toward the SUN, to swear his faith, at which Master Scrivener whispered to Captaine Newport: See how he hath fallen into Salvage idolatry. Then (Powhatan being full grasping & jealous of his Salvage dignitie) was the bargain struck: For scarce .2. pounds of those beads, Powhatan, greedily stroking the grey hairs on his upper lip, did pay .200. bushels of corn, and e'en more. Some days later, Sweet John did pull the same hoax on Powhatan's brother Opechancanough, the same who'd captured him in the bogmire last December. These spoils they conveyed to Jamestowne in triumph, but a fire broke out in the Store-house and reduced all to scorched black granules in the likeness of gunpowder.

* * * * * *

Departing, he call'd to him young Pokahuntas, and did give her near .3. dozen beads, to make her a chain. Doubtless her father would give her more.

* * * * * *

Before I continue my near-blindish narrative with Sweet John's subsequent travels & travails, it may behoove me to relate some trifles concerning that visit to the Countrey of Opechancanough. For just as a certain *Argoll* doth o'erhang this tale with an invisible ubiquitousness like unto GOD's, so the aforesaid *Apachankano* lurks behind his half-brother, portending only, not instigating (as far as we know) during Pocahontas's lifetime. Argall & Opechancanough are twins. They reify the struggle near as purely as do Marxian quantities. History renders 'em greater than themselves. Understanding Reader, have I your leave to grant 'em both the masks of Greekish Fates?

Opechancanough, then, dwells at *Menapacunt,* a royal Towne yet more conducive of Sailors' puns than *Gravesend* herself, altho' her earth offers a more eternal slit. In the future, a more dire & dreadful time, Opechancanough will withdraw & secrete himself at *Menmend,* a Towne as yet unbuilt (for these Yndians, dear Reader, must change their residences every .10. or .20. years, when their cornland's exhausted); & this place will be reed-hid (for fear of yᵉ English) upon an isle or peninsula in the midst of *Pamunkey Swamp,* that oozy wilderness of water which bubbles as black (so they say) as all the crepe in London-Towne when our late Queen had her funeral. And will this *Menmend* mend his fortunes? For that, Reader, you must wait until the end of this Book (or else look around you, & make your own prognostication). As for Menapacunt, 'tis a more open & sightly place, pleasantly seated upon a high hill of ancient soft sea-sand, so that Opechancanough & his wives, children & subjects may gaze out upon the riverine marshes which run westerly. Sweet John kens this place well. When he was a captive, Opechancanough had march'd him here in quick order, to preserve him from the vengeance of an angry old Spear-man whose son our hero had slain.

Opechancanough with his women & children did meet them at Cinquoateck, where the Powhatan's other brother *Opitchapam* did dwell. This Towne also prov'd oozy (for Salvages, like carpfish, eels, & tenchfish, all love muddy ground). Pamunkey Kingdome commenced here, in the delta 'twixt marrying rivers. Being well apprised of their guests' coming, the people incorporated themselves into a dancing-ring, & whirled about with many outcries, so that all the Adventurers save Sweet John gathered gawp-seed in their gaping mouths. — Fear not, he said, last time I surmised they'd execute me; yet this is but their way of shewing pleasure at our coming. — Some Soldiers did grumble discountenanced that they misliked it to see him so at ease here, as if he were himself become half Salvage to bewray 'em, but, having all earned personal shares in his wrath before now, they knew to keep their voices low.

Now Captain Newport strode most jocularly ashore, having reenshrouded his mind with the thrills attendant to a Gambler's chance; he'd conceived the notion that since Pamunkey lay farther upriver from the half-known sea, 'twas more likely that gold-marvels could flourish there, environed in the clammy marshy shade like unto skunk cabbages, so that perhaps e'en the sunlight of reason couldn't penetrate to dissolve 'em into dreams. He had but to win the confidence of this *Opechancanough,* or *Apachankano,* or whoever he was, to be told all secrets. Indeed he'd come to wonder (his thoughts travelling on a course parallel to those of the Soldiers) whether this grimy Fen Slodger from Lincolnshire might himself be apprised of a hoard of *Jewells* somewhere beyond these mulberry trees. Wasn't it thanks to him that Sweet John's little heels now kicked muck instead of gallows-air? Should the man succeed in poisoning the Salvages' minds with disrespect for all Englishmen save himself, why then, he'd become far too indispensable. This fear was what motivated Captaine Newport's strategem of o'ergenerosity to the Salvages. Not for the merest twink of time was Niuporte unaware that Powhatan had cheated him;

Opechancanough would doubtless do the like. 'Twas of no moment; could he but undermine their all too evident affection for Sweet John (paying double to substitute himself within their hearts), *then* he could find out where the gold was hid. *Remember Roanoke,* croak'd Ratcliffe. Newport remembered Mexico & Peru, where Adventurers got rich. When eyesight stands at variance from dreamsight, 'tis natural to go Adventuring in misty places.

✳ ✳ ✳ ✳ ✳ ✳

In short, to both Admirall & Captaine this Towne call'd *Cinquoateck* was a sort of Gravesend. The former considered it a merchantway to gold; the latter, an *Ante-room* to corn. And so they both did bear themselves passing wearily (longing to sail direct toward their hopes) whilst the Salvages danced, *Butter & eggs, butter & eggs.*

Captaine Newport was constrained to ride in the pinnace, to save his dignity, while Sweet John & his new toady Maister Scrivener did walk with *Opechancanough;* 'twas but a mile by the straight path to the new feasting-house which that aforesaid King of Pamunkey had caused to be erected especially for them. Upon Captaine Newport's arrival the Salvages engifted them with .6. trenchers of their bread, & a corn-bean pottage besides. Naked & near-naked wenchen of all ages brought strings of smoked mussels — a rare sight, which reminded the Adventurers of the saucy Onion-girls in England who swing their wares upon a rope. Opechancanough's Cronoccoes orated incomprehensibly at length, after which all regal'd themselves on creamy green-white walnut-milk. Then the 'Venturers went to bed, where, as always, they got mirthful entertainment with red-painted flesh. Sweet John alone in the smoky, red-embered darkness (he'd pluck'd his own pleasure quickly, the better for to play the game call'd *Security*) did smile upon the heaving double shadows. 'Twould befit him to omit those from his *Generall Historie.* Captaine Newport partook not, for he slept in the pinnace with most of the Sailors, fearing treachery. This circumstance relished Sweet John well. He misliked for anybody to outface his boldness.

His trull had been a girl of the King's own household. She told him her name, but he could scarce comprehend it. Her hot shoulders smelled very pleasurably of smoke & walnut oil. Remembering an endearment which Princesse Pocahontas had taught him, he whisper'd into her ear, *Mufkaiuwh,* at which she seem'd well contented. Passing anxious not to be later ridiculed, should his Countreymen hear him sporting as they did, he clapt his hand o'er her mouth just before she spent herself. Closing his eyes, he pretended he was mating with Cicely.

Next day he gull'd the King with blue beads, as hath already been related. After they finished that sport, there was dancing &c, then another night they quartered themselves upon those most delightful Salvage wenchen, & on the last day, Opechancanough did most lovingly bid them farewell, sending them away with more venison than they could carry.

* * * * * *

After that misfortunate fire did eat up all that Sweet John had so painstakingly won, half the Colonists perisht, some by cold, others by sickness, & the rest by starving. The weather turn'd cold again. Only .3. houses remained unburnt. Many men froze their feet. They held no feast for Lady Day* (altho' perhaps that was to the good, such occasions being remnants of Popery). April† came with the Colonie in scarce better case, for the Sailors had spoil'd trade with the Salvages, by parting too readily with tools, bells &c in exchange for corn. Captaine Newport should have sailed unto England long since, but he & his crew continued to leech away at what cornmeal remained, because they feared to return home until they'd obtained a proper cargo of *gold*. At that Admirall's orders, Sweet John was disallowed to meddle in their diggings & pre-assayings, he having become so insufferable in his carping self-conceit. In Willoughby-Towne they'd now be celebrating Easter-Tide with many fine cakes (as he well remembered) & then commencing the Cattle-Fair for selling old heifers & calves. Full well he recollected how in his boyhood his mother of her kindness oft did give him to eat of good things — most e'ery morn a mess of honey & cream; then meat if Father gain'd any profit at the fair. He'd .1.ˢᵗ seen Cicely at one of these Easter markets (altho' he might have frittered away his more ancient memories of her.) She'd been nicely busked up in a blue dress. For a twink he was seiz'd by violent grief, which then drained away, he kenned not where. Perhaps the Virginian clime produced such infirmities.

And now Captaine Newport did lade up his ship with fool's gold, aspiring to gain on earth the riches which he could scarcely expect to be granted him in Heaven, and so on Sunday the .10.ᵗʰ he upped spiritsail, and voy-

---

*March 25th.
†This was the month (tho' the Colonie knew it not yet) when New England got pared off from Virginia by letters patent, so that poor Province first commenc'd to shrink.

aged down river for England, bearing **.I.** the Convict, Maister Wingfield, who had no heart to stay anymore in Virginia if he must lie in jail. **.II.** Captaine Archer also bore him company, since he was excluded from the Counsell. **.III.** As for Powhatan's *Son* (or mayhap merely his spy), that boy call'd *Namontack,* he too sail'd off for London-Towne, to learn whate'er he could. — *Flood oh!* cried the Lookout. Then the *John & Francis* (which you may be sure, wise Reader, was not call'd after Sweet John & his brother) began to dwindle. So again Jamestowne stood alone.

* * * * * *

On the very next day a Salvage well ocelated with antimony-paint did come from Powhatan, demanding: *Casacunnakack, peya quagh acquintan uttas-antasough,* which signifies, *In how many daies will there come hither any more English Ships?* But of all the Colonists, only Captaine Smith could comprehend.

What does he say, man? cried the President, almost beside himself with unease.

Sweet John told him, then said: They think to learn whether they can attack us.

Do you truly think so? 'Tis a challenge we must answer, for I remember Roanoke. Bid him begone never to return.

To the Salvage, Smith did reply: *Kaskete,* meaning, *ten daies,* with which the Salvage seemed toweringly ill satisfied. He did quit the Fort in a rage, while John Smith laughed.

* * * * * *

Next Pokahuntiss skipp'd in with many Servaunts, bringing **.20.** turkeys from her father. This he joyed at, 'till following her departure some tall Salvages arrived to demand **.20.** swords in return. The President lying asleep in his half-built Palace, they made their request to Sweet John, who alone could parley in their brogue (howe'er imperfectly).

I care not to requite Powhatan's gift in that fashion, he replied, full nervous to the bottom of his chitterlings.

Then Powhatan, who's now both your father & ours, will surely call you *Niggard,* for Captaine Newport did return us gift for gift in just that fashion.

Let Powhatan name me what he will, & pray remind him that I have full means to defend myself and to revenge mine own insults & injuries . . .

The Yndians look'd on him reproachfully. He was shamed, but trusted 'em not.

* * * * * *

After this, they began trying to steal swords & weapons wherever they could. Their subtle old King stood no doubt behind it; for among these Yndians the greatest proportion of each subject's harvest goes into Powhatan's treasury. How would gentle Machiavell reply to such thieveries? 'Twas evident. Sweet John caught .7. bear-greased blackguards, locked 'em up tight in the hold of the pinnace, & then, recollecting that in Lincolnshire 'tis the Constable's duty to whip all vagabonds apprehended, until their backs be bloody, he gave them all a great beating, after which (when he pretended that he would now shoot away their villainous lives) they confess'd that at great *Powhatan's* orders they'd meant to kill all the English. So 'twas prov'd that his so-called Salvage *Father* was like unto those .4. French Gallants! Well, well. Nothing would e'er surprise Sweet John more. Caring not what the Counsell did say about his so-call'd *Cruelty,* he set out to reduce all these Yndians unto the most craven, crawling fear & obedience! He flogg'd his prisoners. He flogg'd 'em again. Finally Powhatan fired Pocahontas off to James Towne, to speak the soft words of his mouth. Then Sweet John complied to release those Assassins, solely for the sake of Pocahontas, so that by these .7. lives Powhatan was requited for the life his daughter had spared that winter's day in Werowocomoco. Next time he'd scruple not, if necessity caus'd him to snatch Powhatan by the throat—

Father, I swear my other father kenned nothing of this thievery . . .

Nothing? But is he not *Emperor of Virginia?* Nay, nay, child, matters cannot be ordered so. E'en in my own Countie Lincoln, the High Sheriff must answer for all his Under-Sheriff's misdemeanors.

Father, I see that you speak as you see fit. I must not contradict you.

* * * * * *

See John Smith a-laboring with all his might to upraise again that scorched & wasted Colonie. See him threaten all idlers with whipping & with hungry nights (unless compelled they would not labor e'en for their own good). Having accepted by now that his President & fellow-Counsellors were but wet powder, he engaged the Carpenters & Laborers together in crews to raise better houses — for despite the miserable winter scarce any Undertaker had Ventured to move out of the tents, these having grown commodious both by habit and by the deaths of half their occupants. 'Twas

Sweet John who carried the heaviest beams on his own shoulder, in order to encourage his men the better (for he had few subalterns, now that William Garrett the Bricklayer and Edward Brinto the Mason both lay coffinless & wormridden 'neath the mold). 'Twas he who shored unto durability certain foundations always sinking in the oozey ground, he who sang songs with any and all at night to help them expell sickly airs from their lungs; so it fell out that his inferiors came to love him well for these condescensions, while those above him (especially Ratcliffe) despised him yet the more, seeing him working like a dog, & therefore calculating that he had but the worth of **.1.**

He had less leisure than e'er before, so who can find it remarkable that he paid fewer addresses to young Pocahontas? — though 'tis true he'd generally find time to slip her some treat, such as a piece of velvet, which would of a surety soon get ruined by the greasy way she lived; or a yard of good red lustring silk (a material much beloved by women; indeed it had advanced him much in Cicely Allen's affections back in Willoughby). — No, in faith he did the child no harm! Be that as it may, when a young man does his courting, to entreat a lass to accept him as her spark, he must give her his attention in equal part as he offers her lace, linen or Dutch Holland. Pokahuntiss, belike fancying herself curbed (though we know *not* which thought-flowers bloomed in the bone-room beneath her lustrous scalp), began to lessen her visits, for which he was truly sorry even though she'd sometimes stared at him for half the day, he striding hither and fro to assist Old Vere in binding thatch, to coax William Rhodes and William White to forbear with **.1.** another as Christians instead of coming to blows, to plead with sulky Gentlemen not to go searching for gold, copper or *Sassafrass* root just yet, to raise up the mud-wattles of new houses with his own hands, while the brown body continued to follow him, craving to prove & digest his love. Doubtless she expected somewhat of him, which as beneficient Prince he'd grant if he could, being well fond of her, for all her lowly Indian courtesy. He gave her another slew of pink ribbands (which he'd had to steal from the Store-house, President Radclyffe being so ignorantly and perversely opposed to these necessities of politics and trade).

Our father doth bid me ask of you when you'll come to make him hatchets, as you did promise him.

O yes, so I did. Shall I visit him now? I fear me this season we're in bad straits to go a-visiting—

Nay, 'tis an incovenient time for us also, for now we all do purge ourselves with *Wighscan* root, so that at Werowocomoco lie many sick . . .

Come and kiss me, child. That's a good lass!

Father, when will you fashion those beads which you promis'd me?

Why, since you mention it, I must confess to you, darling Pokahuntiss, that I made some yestereven. Ho, you, Raymond Goodison! Run quickly to the Store-house, lad, & fetch me a farthingworth of beads of the very whitest quality. Nay, 'twere best not to burthen our President with so small a matter—

Father, do you come from under the ground?

Nay, dearling, what childish folly! What Turkishe heathen told you that?

I disremember.

Then 'twas but your fancy. You, Richard Milmer! Hoist that beam higher, or I'll deem you an idle twangler! Christopher Rods! Did you break your shovel again, lad? Mercy! Don't stand there gathering gawp-seed! Go cut an oak-branch & I'll shew you how to refurbish the handle . . .

Father?

Yes, child.

Father, do you love me?

Casting his eyes about (to ascertain he would not be ridiculed), Sweet John did lean forward to tickle her up & down with his beard, then whispered in her ear: *Mufkaiuwh,* at which she shriek'd in delight.

✳ ✳ ✳ ✳ ✳ ✳

There was always some albumen or other essential substance lacking in the ooze which they dried to make walls; no matter how they baked it & thickened it with grass, it would crumble from the dwellings; but .1. day Pocahontas threw a piece of bone into their mud-cauldron, after which the ooze congealed into building-bricks of the best temper, & they never suffered from that trouble anymore. Whene'er Sweet John glanced sidewise & spied her he fell doubtful of something left undone, he knew not what, so that he could not take good pleasure in his efforts. (He slipped her a parcel of lace.) Did it have to do with her or with the Journeymen raising roofbeams from wobbling ropes? — When .1. rope frayed, Pocahontas brought another — for all the women among those Salvages can weave grass most cunningly on their thighs.

She sometimes wore her deerskin apron, as I should already have said, since the dark down had begun to grow upon her secret — so much he'd seen, and warned the men away from her, as 'twould be the greatest misfortune to assault or molest such a *Nonpareil,* be she ripe or not. (Several Soldiers in particular were like unto wolves.) There is reason to infer that she misconstrued this forbearance, misunderstood what we all misunderstand when our friends avoid us, so her visits declined, as I did say, and at night the enemy began again to shoot arrows into the camp, singing *Whe, whe, yah, ha, ne, he, wittowa, wittowa!*

* * * * * *

On that dull evening ruled by pines (.5. thousand .5. hundred & .70. years since the creation of the World), muck & ooze were sparkling in the sunset. A pine tree spread its arms above John Smith's head, the cones hanging down; he sat upon a patch of grass where no one had shat, and gazed at the progress of an armada of ducks whose heads and necks were as massive coathooks. The evening smelled like pine needles. 'Twas hot and blue, & the World belonged to him. A blue laziness overcame him; he thought to be safely secure at last. The spring air was already commencing to get heavy. Then he heard the metallic squeaking of birds, and the hot heavy air abruptly became clammy. The Sunne was a cool white Globe in the hazy sky, bleeding white droplets down upon the river.

'Twas a fine evening, as cool as a mosquito on his skin, and the sun had begun to dissolve above the river, spreading & deforming like unto a ball of jellied wax. Twilight o'erran the oozy rushes behind James Towne, and he knew now GOD would never bless his life, that life would go on & on, that he would struggle in this swamp.

The crickets began for to scream.

THE GRAMMAR OF EXPLORERS (1608)

As we are Angli, make us Angells, too
No better work can Church or statesman do.
WILLIAM STRACHEY (1612)

The *Sharke* . . . is the most ravenous fish known in the Sea; for he swalloweth
all that he findeth . . .
SIR RICHARD HAWKINS, *Observations* (1593)

*I*f you live .30. years, my boy, and make any observations upon human
life, you will perceive that the general business of it turns on the getting and
keeping of an estate. — Thus my Lord Willoughby to John Smith, in those
summery days before Tragabigzanda, when our wench-faced stripling-
hero, never dreaming that he might someday fall homesick for the smell of
manure in Willoughby, was conning Machiavelli in the bower (*A Prince
doth not outlaye much upon his Colonies* . . .); and, scaring all foreign foes
from his fancy, thereby warrantized his own future dignity. The Rector
said his legacy was extinct. But good *Machiavell* did whisper: From thy
scabbard, boy, draw forth shining means to take new legacies! — And
when had Machiavell spoken false? Force and craft's innate in things, like
gravity, which e'er draws the small stone toward the larger. The lowly
must likewise kneel to the strong; flesh opens courteously to the keen blade;
and *Maister Simplicity* cannot but find himself bound prisoner to *Maister
Strategem*. Guide yourself by these principles, John Smith, and within the
merest eye-glimmer you'll get the estate Lord Willoughby prates of! From
the Rector's displeasure and his guardian's fury, from Frauncis & Anna,
from old Maister Reese Allen and the daughter who is as she is, he'll redeem
himself with vineyards, argosies, Amazon gold (& why not Amazons?).
Not much longer must he endure to wear the insignificant collar of a low
person . . . — He stor'd up his brain-Tower with several fine suits of armor
fashion'd out of Machiavell's thought-metal, closed the book, then full
cheerfully did mount his caddised steed (borrowed of his brother Frauncis)

to canter through the chestnut trees to Lord Willoughby's, *Butter and eggs, butter and eggs,* there to tuck away another good fine supper, consolation-payment for unemployment on the Continent. Nary a Salvage lurk'd behind any bush, and there weren't many highwaymen in those parts, either, so he had leisure to imagine himself supervening in great wars, dozing & daydreaming in the saddle. At Jamestowne, by CHRIST, no Englishman could ever have ridden so carefree . . . ! Already he perceived Castle Grimsthorpe above the cornfields; the Sentry spied him; the gate lay open, as it customarily did; family statues towered sightlessly; Lady Willoughby smiled on him; he twinkled down to his knees, the more loyally to kiss her hand. Didn't the Willoughbys all love him? Later, when he'd been better scarred by experience, he could scarcely bear to read the engrav'd memories of their kindnesses. They'd sheltered & perfected him. (Gentle comic they thought him in truth, though none but Robert ever taxed him with the knowledge of their opinion. They call'd him *harmless,* and *simple,* a bird flailing in a fuming cloud; they sounded him and found no offense.) Lady Willoughby told him that her husband was in the kennels a-tending to a sick hound. He'd appear at supper sure. Bowing, thanking her, excusing himself, John Smith turn'd in his nag to the horse-field. He washed his hands in an ewer filled with rosewater. At Grimsthorpe indeed all went cleanly fashion, and every Thursday the henchmen laid out fresh green rushes on the floor. Barty haled him into the hall, & he quickly came, hoping that he'd wiped the last dreg of muck off his shoes (he durst not look). Robert sat a-playing with a little silver pistol. (Sweet John hoped 'twas unloaded.) Barty said a new plague had established itself in London; Her Majestie had been advised to close the theaters. (A plague on all actors anyway, quoth Robert, twirling the pistol on his finger.) Barty said the Spaniards were on the march again in the Low Countreys. The yeoman listened beamingly, excited to stand among those who possessed such great news of the World. Presently Robert began most joshingly to quiz him on his Machiavell. He commenced a well-tuned discourse of reply, but ere a dozen grains had sped through the hourglass he discover'd himself interrupted by the young men's sister, Catharine,* who, fresh from the kitchen, challenged anyone to a game of Tick-Tack. Sweet John would gladly have

---

*Arthur Mee's volume on Lincolnshire instructs us that below the tomb of Lord Willoughby, whom Mee envisions as "a proud upright figure in armour with helmet and gauntlets at his feet," "reclines the strangely-hooded figure of his only daughter, Catharine Lady Watson, with the babe who cost her her life lying in a cradle at her feet. She was the last of the Willoughbys to be buried here" at Spilsby.

played, being risen to confidence thanks to his victories o'er old Maister
Reese Allen, but since Catharine was so far above him, he kept silent,
though fidgeting most eagerly. — Pity us! laughed Catharine. None dares
take up weapons! — Listlessly, Robert farewelled his gun & sat down at
the long narrow board; she'd already uplifted her peg. — She games right
well, my Lord, said Smith to Barty, who giggled gratingly and asked:
What do you bet she'll lose? Can she 'scape with life, or must her head roll,
and she be attainted? — Give over, imbecile, growled Robert as he clicked
his peg of destiny in its latest hole. (So 'tis also at Gravesend: peg & peg &
peg again, a-waiting for Captaine Fortune, 'till our ship comes in, and we
sail down forever to the oozy Indies.) Then the clock struck dinner-hour,
succor to all. They took their seats when Lord Willoughby came in. John
Smith did kneel before his worship, swearing he was bound to him in
honor. — Enough, lad. Rise, and good even! laughed the other, not displeased. Sweet John rose. Robert appointed him to sit at the bench beside
the Horse-groom. Then Maister Stubbe their one-handed Servitor did lead
them in prayer, for as Lord Willoughby often said, the fellow owned a
peculiar *praying voice*.   John Smith bowed his head and thanked OUR
REDEEMER for what now arrived on the trenchers: a fat sheep roasted
whole, a dozen large pike-fish from the Fens, boiled ducks with butter,
green beans (it being the season), & ale with which to wet his weezle. Far
away, near the table's head, Robert evinced no appetite. Sweet John, however, tucked in most excellently. He knew enough not to gulp down his
meat like unto some rude wolf, for which dillydallying the Horse-groom
respectfully call'd him *neere a Gentleman*. His heart opened wide its
wings, being swollen with love's joyous blood. Afterward, over honest Lincolnshire cheese, Lord Willoughby invited him close, for the goutish old
man grew oftimes of a tutorial humor (which his sons but resentfully forbore, being themselves already in an educated state of grace). He explained
to John Smith that once his fortune was made he'd best put .3. parts of it in
land for every part in money; and the aforesaid Smith, whispering *well
said, my Lord,* lodged his chin in his hand the better for to listen, being as
he knew practically enter'd on that fortune already — but by then apple-
cheeked Bartty was kicking him under the table. Bartty wanted to go play
with the armor again! He wanted to joust with Sweet John, who alone
of all comers never complained when he got unhorsed! — My Lord
Willoughby, however, was saying that good land came cheap, if a fellow enclosed it. He reminded John Smith, and incidentally Barty & Robert, that
Adventuresome proprietors had been a-draining Deeping Fen ever since

William the Conqueror's time, that Crowland monastery rested secure on a man-built island in the midst of ooze more than **.30.** foot deep, that in **.100.** years mayhap all Countie Lincoln could be oozelessly rich, and no crofter would have to go a-rowing in a little boat to milk his cows anymore. John Smith, 'tis true, saw the other side of the question. His father had brought him up to be revulsion-tickled against Enclosers — but once he possessed his own estate, who could hedge him out? He misliked Undertakers, who sluiced away our birds and fishes, leaving the Fen Slodgers literally high and dry — but 'twas true Fen Slodgers were mere vagrants by another name; and how could he deny that new fields would bejewel the shire, e'en if water-animals had to be drain'd away to pay for it? See John Smith! I myself cannot believe he wouldn't have Undertaken to drain the whole World, did Lord Willoughby but invite him. He must make his fortune somehow. Was that why he sat on so enraptured at table, awaiting absolution from his nothingness? But now he received another kick. Barty, a grown man ('though not the eldest son, not the principal heir, wherein lay the wellspring of his childish dotings) could not sit still! — Welladay, such was John Smith's vice, too — ha! — he'd rather burn his fingers than stay for a pawn. Hence on the **.2.**nd day of June, 1608, when *Virginia* stood in full leaf, vastly out-greening even emerald Lincolnshire in this season, he set forth in commaund of a company of **.14.,** so as to performe his discovery of the Bay of Chisapeack. Belike the congratulations on living unhanged had staled in his ears. Impotent, corrupted by undead accusations, he drew up his accompts, and, after all his calculations had bottom'd, read neither profit nor spoor of land-estate which both Machiavell and Lord Willoughby had promised him. Three parts in land for every part in money — O, and in this uninhabited wilderness he could not even get the land! Radclyffe & Archer stood e'er against him, Maister Scrivener, altho' well-disposed, had proven weak; how could Sweet John arrive at the dignity he full deserved? His fellow Colonists complained he'd grown too serious — peevish indeed, like unto an oer'looked man debating with himself whether to become masterless. I tell you, Reader, such alienated souls do grow malignant. They flourish into vagrants, or e'en highwaymen, who end up getting burned on a public stage. Was it possible that what his enemies insinuated might be true, that he held his Englishness in such low regard that he'd set out to make treason with Salvages? But 'twould also be admitted e'en by those who loved him not that during this new progress of his, searching every inlet, discovering and mapping the aforesaid Bay of Chisapeack as thoroughly as a London drab will inspect her quim-hairs for lice, he was observed to treat with the Salvages in good order, prepared to see *them* treacherous like Turkes, never fully trusting what they said. Mayhap he trusted *nobody*.   After all, the rope's end nearly caught him that time in Guadeloupe already; nearer again it came at Jamestowne; after that, who'd not wonder when he might sway & falter from the gallows of his own luck?   And yet if the insubstantiality of hanging prov'd so hostile to a fellow's neck-weight, how else could he get on in life but by mucking through the very mire he'd craved to 'scape?   Thus he fed upon himself without relief, pacing 'midst the stinking slops and turds in Jamestowne's streets.   Captaine Newport (at that time still almost his friend) had seen him make as though to tear to pieces that parchment depicting the .3. Turkes' heads of his Captaincy, but for lovingkindness persuaded him to forbear. How many years and struggles had Sweet John paid to puzzle out that he must go on like unto the rising grass in Lincolnshire Cathedral's Church yard — with his feats, duels, strategems, alliances, and TRVE TRAVELS monumented, 'twas true, and in that sense recompensed, but only with flat tombstones like cobbles, grey islands in the grass which crept decade by decade round their edges, nibbling here and there in rank bites of greeenness?   That was why in his moment of despair he'd sought to destroy the mocking coat of arms.   But aren't we *all* brought low? (So Captaine Newport had comforted him.)   Maister Wingfield, previously embroidered into Presidential mightiness, next slept shivering, enchained in the pinnace. Him they'd nam'd *Hoarder, atheist, rebel* & *Spanish conspirator.*   Now he was back in London, penning his justifications.   Captaine Kendall's bulletshattered skeleton lay rotting.   Captaine Archer got expelled from the Counsell, and, like unto John Smith himself, 'scaped the noose only thanks to Captaine Newport.   — Yet Sweet John the Victorious could not give over. I am as I am and so I will be. He turned & turned his bootless plans, which glowed within him just as a Glass-blower's molten bubbles fill the world with light.   He'd dreamt that authority had sentenced him to be buried alive, and crowds gathered by the graveside to see him nailed into the gabled coffin, but he 'scaped and they brought him back.   He awoke sweating, tried to bide awake, and couldn't.   Once he was asleep again, they brought him back again, bound him, sealed him in his deathbox, muffled the World from him with a black, black pall.   He could feel himself being raised, moved laterally, then slowly lowered away from all sounds.   He came to rest.   A shovelful of clods thundered down upon him.   His wooden walls had already begun to sweat with ooze.   — He's had a fright, was how Matthew Scrivener put it.   No wonder if he's busked up in sullen dreads . . . — How would Maister Machiavell have calculated up these facts? 'Twas easy: Since President Radclyffe did by statute enjoy **.2.** votes, while Maister Scrivner & Sweet John each had **.1.**, 'twas better for our Protagonist to depart the Colonie for so long as he could, resigning its misgovernance to the aforesaid Ratcliffe, rather than e'er bootlessly to lock horns for the ugly merriment of all. — Gazing out across the waxlike river at the low grey riverbank, he yearned for the trial of strength. He longed to have his achievements measurable & measured. — *Flood oh!* cried he when he saw the tide coming upriver, and off they went. Now the sharp and stubby timbers of the palisade were out of sight. GOD frame it to the best! As in his youth, he was almost enchanted by the upcurving beak of his own morion, the clink of his powder flask.

✳ ✳ ✳ ✳ ✳ ✳

Captaine Smith, in our conquests shall we take prisoners?

For what purpose, lad?

To control their good behavior.

Disdain to do thus. They shall love us.

And if not?

Then they'll fear us.

And shall we discover pearls?

Why not? The Spaniards did.

And gold?

GOD send us all to do for the best.

✳ ✳ ✳ ✳ ✳ ✳

Now at last they did bear out past the wide river's mouth, so that he could see Heaven unhindered by trees. With his astrolabe he took measure of how many degrees the *Arctick Pole* stood above his horizon, that he might learn more of Virginia's declinations, to speed himself & other Mariners more conveniently about. This he did morn and even of every day. He took soundings, seeking to engrave his comprehension upon this grey-green windy world of snoring, chattering trees.

Captaine Smith, I spy Kecoughtan.

Aye, 'tis Kecoughtan, without a doubt. Ready at the helm!

Need we swing aloof?

Nay, fear 'em not. Moreover, at this season they have no merchaundise worth venting to us—

Captaine Smith, they signal us!

Then send 'em a trumpet-blast. Next time we'll stop. We must round Cape Henrico ere darklins.

Aye, aye!

Trarintra-rarara!

And so in a fine lather they did cross the Bay all the way to the *Eastern Shore,* feeling near as free as if they'd returned unto the very creation of this World, when islands were letters in the alphabet of waves. Th'ALMIGHTIE alone kenned what gracious discoveries our Adventurers might make! Dear Reader, in this world of *Women, Wine & Worms,* the fabulous lurks everywhere, e'en 'midst the gentle flatness of Lincolnshire where near Castle Carleton, on the very land which at Bartty's commaund Sweet John had signed away in exchange for armor, there once dwelled, nigh upon .2. centuries since, an actual *Dragon,* who, as I read, *envenomed men and bestes with hys air,* and was slain by Sir Hugh Bardolfe *oppon a Weddensdaie.*   And therefore, Reader, I bid you wait upon this voyage of Sweet John's in all expectation, for what if he could rouse another Dragon from its bed of Virginian ooze, & thereby slay it to prove himself *Heroickall?*

Already they'd discovered *Smith's Isles* (Sweet John being determined through that place-label to engrave himself upon the maps of all envious persons who'd rewarded him not).   The .2.nd-in-Commaund, *Dr Russell,* would have preferred an appellation of homage to our dread Soveraigne, but Sweet John replied: Look you; there's Cape Charles straight off the bow! If you think *Smith's Isles* to be so strange or impossible, why, we'll name some goodly headland after you; just bide a twink!

As you will, good Captaine.

Soldiers!

Aye, Captaine Smith!

How'd you like your names engrafted 'pon our new discoveries?

We'd prefer rum & quim, Sir.

Spoken like Soldiers! Never fear; if you can't have the .1.st, mayhap some red-painted wenchen'll grant you the .2.nd. (Excuse me, Dr Russell, for that vulgarity. 'Tis necessary with Soldiers.) Now, lads, would you pay 'em compliments, so you can coax 'em into bed?   Then you must say *Mufkaiuwh,* which signifies, *A Flower of a fine thing.*

Captaine?

What would you now, Todkill?

'Tis true you speak from *experience?*

Ha, ha! Inquire of the Yndian lassies! Now then! Reef sail!

Dropping anchor, they charg'd up their pistols & muskets with fine serpentine powder. Sweet John appointed the **.1.**ˢᵗ Dog Watch. Then they all
prayed together by a last gleam of yellow grass before night oozed down on
top of the cold sea.

* * * * * *

Morning came to save them from their *twinkling fear.*   He led them in
prayer & a Psalm. 'Twasn't o'erlong before they fell in with a pair of menacing Salvages like unto giants, who gripped bone-headed javelins, &
guarded the place for their King. To the Soldiers, these twain might as well
have been Gypsies, or *Moon Men* as we call 'em back home in England.
But Sweet John comprehended **.1,000.** sunny tricks for to deal with such
personages, & so as quick as Jack can shinny up the beanstalk he'd won
them their admittance to discover the *Countrey of Accomack.*   ('Twould
be good harbor for small craft once the Salvages were dispossessed, but argosies, galleons &c would do better at James Towne.)

'Twas now the **.1.**ˢᵗ hour of the Forenoon Watch. The King received 'em
kindly. *Your humble Servaunt,* said Sweet John. 'Twould be child's play to
make him serve their turn.

* * * * * *

See John Smith sitting bold & cheery upon a mat in this selfsame Werowance's Palace (which proves rude & small in comparison to Powhatan's).
He asks him: Sir, what are you call'd?

Kiptopeke.

Know you Powhatan?

The King's Interpreter (a sly & knowing old Salvage) says: Captaine, 'tis
not meet to question Werowances in this manner.

O, but I myself stand in his brotherhood! Powhatan hath made me
Werowance of Capahowasick.

Kiptopeke inquires of you the reason for your coming.

To be friends. Pray allow me to present him these blue beads. And to
you I offer this Elizabeth-graven **.20.**-shilling piece to be a luck-charm.
Thacgwenymmeraun. I give yᵗ yoᵘ gratis.

Kiptopeke asks if you do serve Powhatan?

To be sure, great Powhatan's my fast friend. He hath granted me the
Towne of Capahowasick forever, as I said; & his daughter *Pocahantas* is
promis'd to be my wife once she hath ripened.

Kiptopeke asks if you would take a wife here in Accomack.

'Pon my faith! laughs Sweet John. I misdoubt me not my Soldiers would jump at that chance, but I fear they're of too low a degree—

Kiptopeke would tell you of a wonder.

I'm all ears. By the bye, Sir, you speak English passing well.

I was kidnapp'd once, replied the Interpreter.

I see you made good use of the opportunity.

Kiptopeke bids me relate to you that .2. children died here recently, & when their parents did visit the platform 'pon which they'd been entombed, they found them undecayed, & indeed so shiningly beautiful to behold, that many other people came to view the marvel. Then some pestilence humm'd down, & of all those who'd gazed upon those magick carcases, scant few escaped.

Aye, 'tis indeed a wondrous accident he tells of.

He would know whether you Tassantasses brought this about.

All things are possible with our JEHOVAH, Sweet John smilingly returns. But pray tell King Kiptopeke that we mean only his good. And tell him we long to penetrate deeper into his Kingdome, to make as many discoveries as we can; for 'tis our occupation. You see, Maister Intepreter, I'm passing anxious to continue on with my *Trve Travells* . . .

＊　＊　＊　＊　＊

See John Smith a-discovering *Russell's Isles,* in observance of his promise to Dr Russell (who smiles, full-tickled). See him at the barge's helm. He steers all safe through a fog the color of watered-down purple ink, listening for *the rut of the sea,* so that they'll not be surprised by treacherous shoals. See him discover *Keale's Hill* in honor of his most quim-thirsty Soldier. See him at *Wighcomoco River,* exposing new Yndians of lukewarm lovingkindness. He's now outside Powhatan's Empire. ('Tis natural enough, he explains to his followers. My own Countie Lincoln's divided into *Lincoln, Kesteven* & *Holland* . . .) The Salvages speak an outlandish brogue whose syllables do rattle & brabble against his ear like unto Turkishe. He longs for to remember it all down.

Captaine?

Aye, lad.

Captaine, we thirst.

And I too, good Jonas! Conceive you my gullet's metal'd otherwise than your own? Nay, look not so grim, glum & sour. I'll teach you a song. Are you ready?

Our tongues are overdry for singing, Captaine Smith. We dislike for to sing—

Why, the lot of you are good for nothing but Spanish punks!* Here's
how the tune doth run: *This doxy dell can cut bene whids . . .*

What air's that? I remember hearing it in some Tavern-house—

Silence! Now sing it out most sportfully, lads, or 'pon my oath I'll send
you down for a salty ducking! Ho, look lusty there, my good Maister
Keale! Don't you e'er drivel on about your doxy dells? Well, stand to! Are
you ready?

> This doxy dell can cut bene whids
> And whap well for a win,
> And prig & cloy so beneshiply
> All the Deuce-a-ville within.

O, but 'tis too irreligious, Captaine Smith! Ha, ha! And did your *Pocahontas* whap likewise well?

Keale, your forwardness will get you hang'd. Now do you sing with me,
.1. and .2., .1. and .2. . . .

* * * * * *

More fog fantastically lost them entirely out of their schemes, for Sweet
John no longer had his compass; he'd given it unto Opechancanough last
winter for his ransom. The Sunne return'd; & he took bearings, reestab-
lishing them unto themselves. Yet couldn't he have decided that their destinies were now committed unto cunning mainlands of islands, where if a
soul denied to wait on Captaine Fortune with a deer's raised alert ears,
'twould be impossible to extract a single spark of success from all that toil, &
in the end, no matter how sunny those might pretend to be those creeks between bush-islands temporarily blue and green, there'd be no Dominion to
be coin'd, nothing but ooze the dark dull grey of a sanddollar's ventral side?
If Captaine Fortune e'er *did* come (calling all hands!), then there'd be
treasure, & farms, & someday Churches & Cattle-Fairs just as at peace-
cloy'd Willoughby. So what then if he gave o'er? Many men spoke unto
him of running away. Some begg'd him to save them, to bear them far
away. They long'd for cherry-trees & Yndian maids. They call'd *him* Captaine Fortune! O pity! He landed 'em. He kicked at the dull, red upturned
bowl of a horseshoe crab's exoskeleton which lay like a slain Soldier's
morion in the sand. He said: Captaine Fortune's not here . . .

*Whores.

* * * * * *

At a point not far from Wighcocomoco they found a pond of fresh water to relieve their thirst, so Sweet John called that place *Poynt Ployer,* after the Earl of Ployer who'd outfitted him in his friendless wanderings long ago in Fraunce, just after the .4. French Gallants had robb'd him of everything. He said to himself: Thus do I requite you, Earl! & felt that he'd given the highest. More and more he seemed to be thinking upon those olden times; his memory would not relent. He cared not to see himself stab Cursell again and again, with the crowd watching from the ruined tower. O, he was bored with his .3. Turkes' heads! This *Chisapeake* did not bore him yet. (Among the trees he met with a deer's round black eyes.) Where was Cursell now? He half expected to see him somewhere in this forest. But all he spied was little secret brooks & waterfalls, and the land went on as far as they cared to sail (they were sickly and mutinous again), and they misdoubted that Virginia must be an island of great size; naturally they never kenned how grand she was; they never realized that her other coast was thousands of miles west, where other waterfalls trifled steadily, making each its own white rushing lines inside the cliff-shadow; & 'twere best that they never knew that, because if they had they might have felt like unto ghosts in the landscape, or they might have wondered if there were a room at the end of the continent, a room of crying horses. Fronting each waterfall was the larger ocean, unmoved by the regular falling of fresh water. The falls seemed almost blue against the wet blackness of the cliffs. The top of the water was a monstrous bright line in the morning sun. Beyond the sea-cliffs, the sky lay open and blue, inviting Spaniards into the interior, where they would look for treasures and find none, not seeing the light inside the shining pink agates at the base of the falls, or the salt-polished quartzes like crystal balls in the sand. Meanwhile Sweet John kept silence, inwardly beseeching G O D for rich discoveries.

* * * * * *

See John Smith wrapt up in a lightning-storm in a place nam'd *Limbo.* Altho' the foremast doth break, he cares not, but laughs & bails alongside his inferiors. In Affricka he's endured worse. He joys in such challenges as these. Omnipotently he holds his men safe. Patching the sail with their shirts, they proceed toward the main at his true signal.

* * * * * *

Discovering a blue glinting of light, Sweet John directed his party around a cape and found a river called *Cuskarawaok* where the Salvages scuttled into the treetops for to shoot down arrows upon them, screeching with hatred; doubtless they had been set to that by Powhatan. — What asses they are! laughed Smith. Drop anchor here where they cannot reach us. — So they bobbed, and Keale spewed for sea-sickness, while Sweet John directed the others to calm the Naturalls by making signals of friendship, which they did, holding up toys, trinkets & trash until darklins. *Kekaten Pokahontas patiaquagh niugh tanks manotyens neer mowchik rawrenock audowgh.* Bid Pokahantas bring hither two little Baskets, and I will give her white Beads to make a Chaine. Next morn, when the sun was well up he landed his 'Venturers bidding 'em bide ready for any business. Now here came the Salvages — merry rustics let's call them, tawny-skinned Fen Slodgers! They bore baskets for the trade and danced most merrily in a circle, but then a lid slipped awry & Sweet John glimpsed darkness inside .1. of the baskets, so that he plainly knew that these Virginians meant only to betray him. Smiling, he becked the Salvages closer, as if he paid mind's tribute to their schemes. When they'd reached the edge of the grass, he raised his hand, and the party fired a stiff volley (the muskets being loaded already with fine lead pistol-shot) — they all fell bleeding, screaming, plaintfully sighing, dying! O Salvages of my heart's treachery, how you twist in upon me like my own guts . . . — Again-ho! — Salvages crept, died & hid, some in a thicket of reeds where a good number of their warriors, as he now perceived, had been lying in ambuscado . . . At evening, round about the hour of Vespers, they approached land again for to fire a few leisurely contemptuous shots into the reeds, but without reply. Sweet John waded forward (the others feared to do it; but for him, ooze was but ooze). On the lookout for arrows, daggers, knives & bodkins, he strolled about the scene of his triumph (another flat tombstone in the Church yard of his hopes), meditating and searching for further signatures of their purpose, but conceiv'd no discovery, excepting footprints, bulletridden baskets, footprints & bloodstains in the sand of Virginia's chagrin & then finally a horseshoe crab like the morion of an ocean soldier . . . Marching his men in good array down an Yndian track, Sweet John discovered a Towne, in whose houses (or *wigwams* as they say here) he placed mirrors & pretty little bells. Meanwhile he deployed his Soldiers yonder, in case of ambushes; there were none. The next day came rushing .2,000. Salvages like unto children at Christmastide. Maybe they were the same he'd conquered, or maybe others. With beads and looking-glasses he initiated 'em all into eternal friendship.

* * * * * *

In the night he glimpsed some unknown creature whose eyes were as tiny as the rivets on a vest of light mail.

* * * * * *

Were his neck to erect itself in entire resolution, which life-course could he most fittingly take? For from every path he'd tried he'd emerged spotted with misfortune, like the *Pard* or *Tiger* of old. Remain here, and he'd be soon enough insulted again, slandered, mayhap hanged.* Return to England, and he could starve in London or rot in Willoughby; he could not importune Peregrine Bartty anymore, were he to renounce the James Towne chance. In the Low Countreys he could not rise; in Wallachia, Hungaria and those other Countreys he'd be surrounded by the LORD only knew what babble and machinations and plottings of Turkes. Best wisdom to bide here in Virginia, once more essaying some great victory; no matter that his heart was not in it. Maister Wingfield had doddered on about gold. Could it lie here in the Chisapeack? Someday he *must* be lucky. If any Salvages had gold he'd act quickly to bereave 'em of it . . .

* * * * * *

See John Smith in search of the *Massowomeckes,* who seem to be enemies of these *Nanticokes* he's just conquered. At sunset the sky becomes yellow behind all the islands. *Tra-rintra-rarara,* my lust-bloods! Our future's dilineated by the silhouettes of grass-heads against this cold red sky. Seeking the aforesaid ogres, Captaine Smith doth next morning (after prayer & a Psalm) lead his Adventurers up the River *Bolus,* so nam'd & fam'd for its red & white knots of clay like unto medicinal Armenian dirt. Dʳ Russell hath employ'd that very substance upon poxed men in a Lazar-house in London, & found it miraculously effective. He's almost confident this earth is the same, or nearly so, as the simple vended by greedy Apothecaries. How happy the Virginia Companie will be, if 'tis *proved* so, & the Adventurers can turn a profit at last! The river narrows. Then contrary currents & breezes do conspire to stop their ascent. Where is Sweet John now? To the south, dusk's green darkness, spattered with pickerel-weed, mosquitoes and the shiny eyes of alligators, wells up beneath the pines and

---

*As a certain English chaplain wrote in his diary in 1582 while voyaging to the Spanish Indies, "to return home enriched with plunder is neither safe nor honest. And after plundering to return home in poverty is an offense punishable by death."

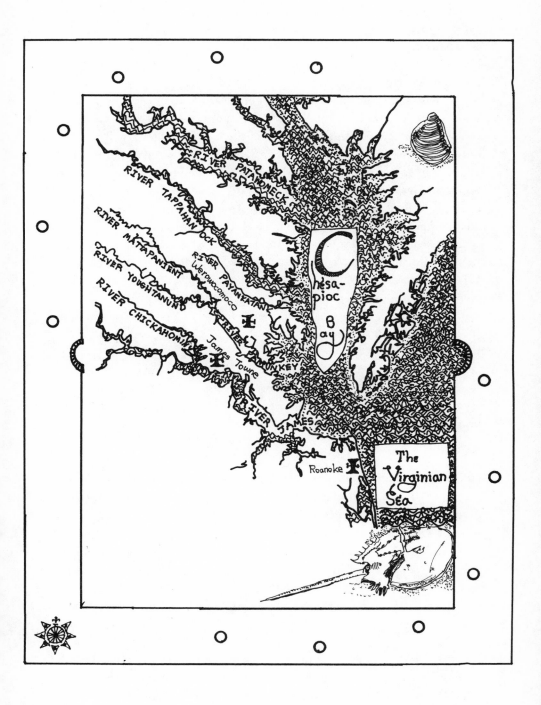

palms like a swamp tide. 'Tis said that life's symbol in those parts is a cypress in the white-webbed embraces of a strangler fig. There the *Spaniards* are debouched. To the north sing grosbeaks green, yellow, black and white in the boreal forest with its unknown tragedies, as when an Algonquian wigwam catches fire from hearth-embers on a windy winter night, roasting a family in their sleep. The *French* abide there now where our continent raises itself into higher ridges, grey walls of mist palisadoed with white birches. To the west? Nobody kens it. John Smith will discover only an infinity of pale blue mountains. And now his men mutiny, complaining in equal part of fear & of maddocks-ridden bread. Four of them falling ill, Sweet John dreads to to be arraigned before Radclyffe's gallows again, & so he yields to their demands. To him 'tis all **.1.** He's dead, or adamantine. Fortune's changes, which flittered by him in his youth with the rapid colors of a masquing-show, do now crawl more wearisomely slow than the shadows of the longest afternoon. He nails another brass CHRISTcross to a tree, to claim possession of all this Countrey for England. Sometimes he cares not what might befall.

(A small gaggle of rusty-helmed men stand alone upon a river-bank on the Virginian plain. Sweet John sniffs the place's oozy reek & feels sad, he kens not why.)

And so it's turn about & hard-a-lee! We'll fall in with the islands! Jamestowne becks like unto Gravesend. Dr Russell sits athurt a sack of red & white dirt. Sweet John disbelieves in Dr Russell's riches, but bites his tongue. Indeed, it'll turn out worthless . . .

✳ ✳ ✳ ✳ ✳ ✳

Chesapeaked back down into Powhatan's dominions, Sweet John & his crew now draw nigh unto the mouth of the river call'd *Pattawomeck* or *Potomac* — a most storeyed watercourse, upon which Pokahuntiss will soon be kidnapp'd, and the capitol of *the United States of America* later builded. 'Tis **.7.** and a half miles wide at its mouth, & **.7.** fathom deep. The men agree to discover it, in hopes that it might lead to China or other strange Countreys. They throw out log & line, to measure the swiftness of its currents. But now in a twink they get assaulted by **.3.** or **.4,000.** treacherous Salvages! (Or percase they number **.30.** or **.40.**.) Sweet John loves nothing better than a fight. He arrays all at their stations, & commaunds 'em to shoot their bullets skipping-wise across the water, to amaze the Salvages without exceeding loss of life. So quickly the enemy do surrender, for which th'ALMIGHTIE be praised. Sweet John sends his doughty *John*

Watkins to be hostage to their King, or Werowance, while he himself re-serves a Salvage or *.2.* as surety for the Naturalls' continued good behavior.

Now tell me, pray, why you thus made your bravados against us.

We were commaunded to it by Powhatan, reply the poor inconstant Sal-vages.

And for which reason did he direct you so?

Because some Tassantasses at Jamestowne did send to him, saying that they abide in his Countrey against their own volition.

Why then do they stay?

Because you compel them, Captaine Smith.

Ha! Most excellently reason'd, for a Salvage. Well, for this time I for-give you, since your own Emperor drove you to it. I must pay *him* my ad-dresses.

(Why hath Sweet John prov'd so forbearing? — Because he's read his *Machiavell.* He owns a strategy to conquer all Virginia, yes, indeed he doth: Just as in London-Towne men break off a bear's teeth, before they set hounds on him in the bear-baiting ring, so the trick with Powhatan must be to detach the diverse Yndian Tribes from his Empire *.1.* by *.1.*, & *then* strike at the heart of his dominions once he's full unfang'd. So he'll work these other Nations loose from Powhatan's jaw. He'll wiggle 'em out with friendliness. That failing, he can always march his Soldiers 'pon 'em, *.1. and .2., .1. and .2.*)

They sail on, Virginia's marshes twitching in the rain. Here & there he spies the dark low entrance to an Yndian house. At *Pattawomeck, Cecoca-wonee,* & other Salvages Townes the Yndians do hatch ambuscadoes yet again, but Sweet John repels 'em. No matter those Yndian Warriors gath-ered threatening-wise 'pon a riverbank, shaking their fists & nocking their bows! (He's so weary of them! How can he disremember the minarets of Constantinople, or noble & beauteous Charatza Tragabigzanda as she guides her quill in his hand across the top of her cobalt-glazed penbox? Some days he's tempted nigh unto cruelty 'gainst these monotonously igno-rant beings.)

But Sweet John spies a spangle of something exotickall in the dirt! Could it be fortune?

And so they do return to double-palisadoed Patawomecke-Towne, whose houses all sport massive corn-cribs as replete as Powhatan's own Store-house. Doubly rich! Sweet John's agog. (Bullets in, lads! he warns. Bide you ready!) They sit themselves down upon bark mats, with their weapons ready at their sides, whilst the Salvages lean upon their spears and survey them not without hatred, then themselves sit on mats a frog-hop away. The King hath painted his face with a silvery pigment, seeing which, Sweet John commences for to dog his own future full as eagerly as he once did in the days of his wench-chinn'd youth. Peru shall be o'ertower'd! Captaine Newporte shall have his mine of precious Jewells! — Why then do yonder damsels adorn their ears with bird-bone beads 'stead of silver-globs? Ask not, dear Captaine Smith! Enjoy thine hopes! — 'Tis a passing joyous afternoon. They smoke *Tobacco*. Soon bread, venison & corn shall come; of that much, a least, we can be sure. Sweet John puts out his flag, so to speak, & gifts all comers with beads & Yndian words. He's passing cheerful now.

And do you hold Powhatan to be your friend?

The King frowns & hesitates, his face all wrinkled up like unto **.1.** of his dried oysters. Better & better! He's Powhatan's enemy, & silver-rich! Maister *Machiavell* loves to make such alliances.

At the King's signal all rise up for to daunce. The air doth reek of their bear-grease, but 'tis pleasant enough beneath the mullberry-shade. Yea, our Captaine's content. His bright-eyed Soldiers peer from side to side, wondering aloud what plunder might be found, should the Towne e'er fall to them. Maister Keale, his favorite, dislikes the Yndians more each day, having unalterably concluded that nothing can be builded 'pon their oozy treachery. He hath his own claims, he does, & no Salvage shall obstruct him from running after Captaine Fortune. But for now, Fortune's personified in this very Captaine Smith who loves him. Therefore he obeys. He'll box up his rampantness, for now. Now all goes as is customarily array'd in Sweet John's cheerful Undertakings: Red-painted wenchen bring the food, then darklins brings the wenchen themselves — what fine girls! — or, as the footpads & murtherers in London do say, *bene morts* . . . 'Neath strings of smoked mussels our Sweet John doth indulge in a spot of pucelage, & likewise his Soldiers (solely for the sake of friendship). His own squaw's a sweet little maid. Her cries of happiness remind him of a tree's squeaking in the wind.

On the morrow he smokes *Tobacco* again with the King, who's passing kind. Sweet John loves him. They sit like unto brothers, on a mat nigh unto a great fat oak tree. The King strokes the plates of Sweet John's brigandine. (Grey iron's better than white, say the Armorers. His, alas, is going rust-red now. If only these Salvages would cease pestering him with arrows, so that he could clean it!) Sweet John reaches into his his belt-sack. He lays out a handful of the glistering earth. Smiling almost sweetly, the

Werowance makes gestures as if he were painting his face, then utters the word *Matchqueon.* Sweet John resolves not to disremember this word for the rest of his life, for it may enrichen him. From the Werowance he now obtains some knowing hostages, whom (considering his own conveniency) he enchains. They mislike this, but he promises 'em that once they've led him back to the Werowance's house, these chains will be their ornaments, to keep forever. So then with many exclamations, I misdoubt me not of pleasure, they guide him some .7. or .8. miles up into the Countreyside, past a black and oily pond shaped like a uterus, & white sky-shimers in a grasshaired creek. There's ooze in everything. His Soldiers play at crowning each other Kings; they're so sure they've beat the Spaniards at last! As the Forenoon Watch ends, they achieve the silvery Mountain digged out with clamshells & other Salvage toys — 'tis the *Womb of Virginia!* — Alas, but this veritable Golgotha of what all hope should be silver, 'tis mere antimony, which (to be sure) may be a good purge when mix'd with wine; and when added to salt & powdered bricks makes a most sovereign balm against pustulent battle-wounds — but, Reader, *it doth not vend for a high price.*

* * * * *

Now see him on the river *Tapahannock,* or *Rapahannock* as some do say. Here King Opechancanough conveyed him last Christmastide, when he was a captive. Concerning this locality I must write that there are many fishes. If we can but dispossess the Salvages, think how easy our living will be!

See him map some dead-end mud-ponds.

See John Smith a-catching fishes 'pon his sword-point. What's this? A rarely triangular fish he's speared! No one's seen the like.

— O! — He's stung with its treacherous tail!

See John Smith swollen & befevered, his teeth clinking and rattling like unto the iron plates on his brigandine vest. 'Tis worse than *the purples,* from which he suffered so painfully in his youth in Fraunce.

A Sting-ray

For a certainty he'll die. They conclude his funeral; he chooses the spot where he wishes to be buried. But (fortuitously) good D^r. Russell hath a certain precious oil which saves him, & so at darklins he eats the stingray for his supper, & names the place of his great peril *Stingray Isle.*

* * * * * *

Scudding southwards past the rivers *Payankatank* and *Pamunkey,* they came to Kecoughtan, where they told the Salvages they'd but lately accomplisht an excellent victory o'er the Massowomecks.   The people thus getting duly terrified into goodness, Sweet John commaunded the barge up river to Waraskoyack & then Jamestowne.   The hysterical Sentry did at .1.st misdoubt them for Spaniards.

* * * * * *

While his Soldiers doff'd their armor at last, then cleansed it by rolling it in a barrel of sand & vinegar until it glistered again like unto new, Sweet John (fearing to un-brigandine himself, on account of President Radclyffe's malice) strolled about the Fort, discovering that most were sick or idle, as ever, & the rest dissatisfied.   Many clamor'd in his ear to save them.   Three cheers! His good friend Maister Scrivener (the only person now remaining on the Counsell, other than the President & Sweet John himself) did opine that now 'twas high time to play the game call'd *Machiavell*.   Accordingly he gathered his faction together, & march'd at their head to the President's half-roofed Palace.   There he shewed himself to Maister Radclyffe, who caused him to be seated.

Now tell me what you did discover.

Void ground only, Maister President.   But 'tis most fair, & I misdoubt me not if 'twere well manured—

You speak ever of manuring, farmboy.   But we need gold, not muck.

Then seek it yourself, you miserable, counterfeit impostor.

Smith, I promise you: Someday I'll see you hang'd.

All complain of your extravagance & cruelty.   I now depose you, Sicklemore, & give the Government unto Maister Scrivener until your term runs out.

Ha!   So now Scrivener's your pawn, just as was I when you deposed Wingfield—

Will you take an oath to be peaceful, Sicklemore, or must I confine you with Maister Wingfield?

I'll see you hang'd!

Good.   President Scrivener, my congratulations.   Let's you & I now appoint more honest Officers than did this scoundrel.

Aye, Captaine Smith, but the letters-patent—

Disregard 'em.   Best we do it now, 'fore I sail again to the *Chisapeack*.

I can see I'd best be guided by your advice, return'd Scrivener with a broad smile. Else you'll depose me, too.

Far from it! I rely on you for an honest Government.

I swear to follow your example, said Scrivener, at which Sweet John recoiled a little, remembering how Machiavelli had warn'd: *Beware of flatterers.* But he'd now fear nothing. By night he'd already taken the following resolution: *I'll ne'ermore divide myself against myself. I'll follow myself with all my all.*

* * * * * *

On the .24.th day of July, Captaine John Smith sets back upon his travels. Martial Undertaker and Adventurer, drainer of barbarism's endless marshes, hoping yet to climb in the world, measuring the rising stages of Gentlemanship which resemble the narrow & narrowing ladders of rigging ascending to the heights of a flyboat's sails, he'll make the Virginian Jest again. To the .12. who follow him, his hopes appear as wide as the James River (which the Salvages call *Powhatan*). Laughingly he mutters: *I am as I am and so will I be.*

A Soldier wails to him: This time we ought to be allowed better water . . . — but Sweet John rages not against him, only chuckles.

The Soldier persists: Pray, Captaine Smith, what shall we drink when you quarter us 'midst the Mosquitors of the ooze?

Why, 'tis easy, man! Drink your own blood! For otherwise the Mosquitors would get most legally seized of it, in each nightly forfeiture . . .

If it please you, Captaine Smith, I'm afeared to come . . .

Why, you twangling little coward! Stay home at James Towne, then, & be hang'd! I have no time for such as you . . .

Captaine Smith, good Captaine Smith! cries a Sailor.

Aye?

Shall we conquer the Massowomeckes this season?

Why, sure, if we bestir ourselves, & find not better entertainment elsewhere. Are you prepared to fight?

That am I!

Then I appoint thee *King of the Massowomecks,* lad, & may thy reign prosper thee! Now to your places! How stands the tide?

Flood oh, Captaine Smith!

* * * * * *

See John Smith at Kecoughtan. Powhatan's son *Pochins* is now Werowance there. Out come the mats again, & 'tis time for that delicious

Yndian bread made of guinea wheat. Sweet John smiles, bows, introduces himself to Pochins as his brother, for hath not Powhatan rais'd 'em *both* up to be Werowance of Capahosick?

The townspeople dance, their faces locking themselves into dreamy masks.

Here his Soldiers would idle away the dog days, there being corn, venison, wenchen & strawberries in abundance, altho' perhaps not serv'd up quite so willingly as in the year before. They stay a good .2. or .3. nights, until the winds turn favorable. Every morning Sweet John leads them in prayer & a Psalm.

Pochins inquires of him where he would go.

To revenge myself upon the Massawomecks, *Brother.*

O, but, Captaine Smith, they're a dangerous people! E'en great Powhatan's affrighted by them. He would guard his corn & women from them, if he could—

'Tis the reason we seek 'em out, to render your Father's old age easy.

Ah, we thank you, Captaine Smith. And you are welcome here, but we would bid you send away your men, for they gnaw up our stores like unto locusts. Also, their demeanor with their guns doth affright our children.

Fear not, Pochins. We'll remain your friends, as long as you give us reason to be so.

That even, Sweet John terrifies them with *fireworks* resembling the rockets he employed against the Turkes.

When he departs the Towne, he scowls & twists his beard, for the Salvages offer him but a meager indraw of acclaim.

By way of *Stingray Isle,* then *Patawomeck River* & the *River Bolus* Sweet John now guides his Gentlemen & Soldiers back up the Chesapeake, whose roof's now proven bifurcated like unto the crown of a woman's womb. He sails closer. Nay, 'tis *quadrifurcated!* The farther he goes, the more widely doth his life expand into summery nothingness. Full well he kens now he'll never discover any Citadel all of gold. (He could have won that, had he but married with Tragabigzanda.) His aims & purposes sail compassless, like unto blue clouds in the white sea-sky of dusk. But so long as he continues thus his *Trve Travells* his heart misgives him not. A salmon-colored inverted mushroom of cloud grows down from Heaven for his fancies to feed on. Jamestowne being a mere prison of small measure, he yearns to play the game of *Liberty* in a wider jail. For that, this *Virginia* proves passing commodious.

✳ ✳ ✳ ✳ ✳

See John Smith at the head of the Chesapeak Bay, now meeting *Massowomecks* in truth. 'Tis the .2.nd hour of the .1.st Dog Watch. The Salvages prepare to attack from betwixt certain hot grassy bulwarks of islands. Near all his men having fall'n sick, Sweet John hides the invalids under a tarpaulin, then mounts their hats each upon a stick (just as when some miscreant's executed in London-Towne, & the Marshal plants his traitorous head upon a pike) to overawe the enemy. The few well men kneel down between these decoys, everyone grasping a gun in his left hand & another in his right. 'Tis sufficient. Terror wins the day against the Massawomecks. Then Sweet John grants 'em bells, & then they trade full happily. He likes most especially their barken shields, or targets, turned out most solidly, altho' of course in a barbarous fashion.

The Massawomecks promise to meet next morn, but never come again — doubtless by reason of their fear . . .

✳ ✳ ✳ ✳ ✳

See him 'midst the Tockwaughs — enemies of the Massawomecks, & therefore his singing, dauncing friends once he doth shew them the Massawomeck war-gear he was given in trade. They've embeached the barge 'midst reddish-brown cattails. Laughing, he mimes his fictitious victory. His greedy Soldiers slupper up fruits, furs, fishes & women's quims.

See him with the Susquehannocks, who stand like unto giants, & who bear .3.-foot *Tobacco*-pipes. They crown themselves with bear-heads; they necklace themselves with a wolves' heads enchained. Amongst them he's small & agile, flickering with the snaky flash of a white ibis's back. Naturally these Salvages reverence him as a G O D, & adore him with the offering of a well-painted bearskin. When through an Interpreter he informs them of his conquest of the Massawomecks, they weigh him down with chains of white pearl. Wouldn't it be most excellently *Politick,* to fight alongside 'em in their Warres? Then they'd be his faithful allies, to supply him with corn; his Colonie would lie no longer at Powhatan's mercy.

They sport iron hatchets. It seems they've received these toys in trade with *Maister Champlain* up north in Novia Francia. Sweet John longs to plumb the watercourses 'twixt here & there. He promises the Susquehannocks he'll return next year, to accept their subjection to the King of England, an honor for which they send up shrill oraisons of gratitude.

* * * * * *

In his deepest penetration of the Susquehannocks' Countrey he did stop to survey & name *Peregrine's Mount,* in honor of his dear friend Master Peregrine Bartty; & he also did name a *Willoughby's River.* For a space he stood, and altho' his Soldiers & other followers did conceive that he sought to spy out Salvage ambuscadoes, in fact he was remembering how he once lay at his ease in the field just outside the moat of Tattersall Castle, a mossy stone for a pillow, watching Robert and Peregrine Bartty come a-charging at each other through the kind of tall grasses and leaf-laden trees that walled off his world in a way most excellent for dreaming; soon, perhaps, Robert would tire of the sport, and then John Smith could spring through the Queen Anne's lace to accept the lend of a sweaty steed. Young Bartty sometimes had days when he could not get enough. He'd gallop down upon Sweet John in high delight, *pen and ink, pen and ink,* striving to unhorse him once more. The yeoman comprehended well enough that at intervals not quite corresponding to the chime of Bartty's watch, he must let him succeed. That was the way to retain the luster of good-humored friendship. Later, bruised and thorn-pricked to irritability, he'd withdraw to the Church of the Holy Trinity to lurk amidst tombstones, reading the whitish lichen-clouds upon their blanked grey skies. An old stone said:

S CRED

To h M mory of

but to whose memory it was sacred to could no longer know.

* * * * * *

He explor'd the Patuxent River, promising the Naturalls there to punish the Massawomecks utterly ere long, then return'd into Powhatan's Empire. (The Chirugian *Anthony Bagnall* did dress his infected stingray-wound.) He discovered yet more of the pleasant Tapahannock. Leaves like lolling green dog-tongues panted the breath of summer. A mosquito raised a tiny white welt on his hand.

* * * * * *

Now see him in a battle with the Rapahannocks, who'd sought to ambush him for being friends with the Moraughtacunds.

The Moraughtacunds warn him not to continue onward, for since they've entertained him with berries, green corn & delicious wenchen, & since (moreover) the entertainers have stolen *.3.* wives of the Werowance of Rapahannock, why then, how could Sweet John be anything to these Rapahunnocs but an enemy?

He brushes this aside on *.2.* grounds: *.1.*^{stly}, the Moraughtacunds have argued thusly out of selfish interest, for they would engross the monopoly 'pon the English trade in these parts; & *.2.*^{ndly}, 'tis but dangerous folly to bow to the admonitions of Salvages. His Soldiers and Sailors stand patiently around, like horses in a stable. The sweat shines heavy and slimy upon their throats. — Are you ready, my lusty-hearts? Get in array now! *.1. and .2.*, *.1. and .2.* 'Pon my soul, mates do ye grow afeared? Listen to the Word of GOD: *The LORD bringeth the Counsell of the heathen to naught. His Counsell standeth fore'er; blessed is the Nation whose GOD is the LORD.* Now here we go: *.1. and .2., .1. and .2.* — And so they river-cross unto the Rapahannocks & stand ready with their ordnance at full-cock. The river's almost as lush as *Florida* to the south, where the trees rain beards of Spanish moss. Sweet John warns the Helmsman not to get entrapped in the great spiderwebs of the Salvages' fishing-nets. The Helmsman swears to avert all. As for Sweet John, he longs to commaund the flat snout of a gunship with its inset cannons. 'Twould be rare sport to terrorize all these Salvages to the very death! But that's not Christian. He must keep courteous, respecting all civil bonds. Anas Todkill agreeing to be the hostage, they send him ashore to spy out any ambuscadoes, meanwhile fraughting aboard the barge a certain Salvage in return, who sits a-glowering at James Watkins his keeper. Now from the shore doth Todkill cry *Treachery!* at which the Salvage wriggles overboard, & Watkins shoots him true, exploding him, attainting the water with his dying blood. At Sweet John's commaund all the Englishmen let loose a volley so that the Salvages do shrill & fly, like unto a horde of venomous insects. From the oaks do near about *.1,000.* arrows come humming; but (by a clever strategem) Sweet John hath previously armor'd his barge with Massawomeke shields, which stop all such Yndian projectiles right well. Moreover, his Soldiers manfully withstand everything. So in the end good Todkill gets sav'd, & many Salvages slain, so that the oozy woods are slimed scarlet like the gates of a Lord-Mayor's house. Then the Soldiers go a-running in search of plunder, but discover nothing except a blood-dyed quiver all rolled up like unto some papyrus from ancient Egypt, with arrows inside it . . .

On the morrow they sail harmlessly past another ambush, then induct the Werowances of *Pissassack, Nandtaughcund* & *Cuttatawomen* into their love. O, he joys to play the game call'd *blobbing for Salvages.*

* * * * *

See John Smith in parley with a wounded prisoner from the tribe call'd *Manahoacs,* an outlandish Nation yonder outside Powhatan's dominions. These Yndians having ambushed our Adventurers near the falls, Sweet John did stand to his own defense, & so the Soldiers fir'd many a volley of shot.

Why did you attack us? asks Sweet John.

They say that you are a people come from under the world, to take our world from us.

How many worlds do you know?

Only this **.1.,** which lieth under the sky that covers me.

Laughing, Sweet John doth requite him & his crawling Kings with English commodities . . .

* * * * *

See him now return'd (with all his men) into the Countrey of the Rapahannocks, whom upon receipt of Sweet John's threats do agree forever to be friends, supplying the English with corn on demand, & giving up forever the **.3.** royal women whom the Moraughtacunds have stol'n. Now Sweet John makes those damsels serve the cause of concord. The King of Rapahannock he allows to take back his favorite. The **.2.**nd Sweet John doth kiss away to the King of Moraughtacund. The last he presents to his busy little Salvage vassal *Mosco,* who's already prov'd very loyal (for an Yndian). And so Sweet John's scored another victory.

* * * * *

See John Smith at darklins, a-tramping for to seek his Destiny. 'Tis near the end of the last Dog Watch. In the boat, his home-lorn fellows loiter, a-dreaming as e'er of food & wanton Salvage maids. All the Soldiers are soaking rope in vinegar and watered gunpowder for to make a match. Sweet John's commaunded 'em to prepare for war. The

Gentlemen are gaming at Tick-Tack. Why hath JEHOVAH summoned 'em all hither? Sweet John's incomprehension burns him. Where's Grace? Where's Fame? Where's Bounty?

The twilight's suddenly broken by what he .1.ˢᵗ thinks to be a patch of snow. Then his eyes untrick themselves. 'Tis a huge congregation of egrets already asleep, so that he can see only their slender necks and the white bodies beneath, like closed white buds of immense flowers drooping from long stems . . .

✳ ✳ ✳ ✳ ✳

See Sweet John at the head of all his crew, sailing up the river call'd *Nandsamund,* after the Nation which inhabits it. I do believe 'twas these very Yndians who ambuscadoed our men at Cape Henry last year. So let's look out for mischief. O, but the Salvages do sing & daunce so innocently! A Salvage rides in their barge, to direct 'em to his house, which standeth on an Isle of Corne. Ducking through the low, dark doorway, Sweet John scatters toys within, so that the Nandsamunds much love him. Here come his neighbors, who affirm that their Towne stands higher up the now ominously narrowing river; none will come aboard to be Sweet John's hostages, & so, suspecting 'em to be corrupt like unto all Salvages, he doth ready his men for the fight. (Treachery? laughs a Soldier. I'd lay my coppers on it! — His face grows ugly with the *twinkling fear.*) In the tightest bend of that stream, which is darkly o'erhung by trees, come arrows from both shores, buzzing like the DEVIL's flies. Moreover, near .7. or .8. canoes of warriors shoot at them from behind. Altho' Anonthy Bagnall gets hat-pierced & sleeve-pierced, the arrows (or, as I should say, *Yndian missiles)* do no hurt, thanks to the Massawomeck targets. *Fire!* commaunds Sweet John. A volley clears the Salvage canoas. A few bullets more, & the shore-lurkers do retire into the forest darkness. So now Sweet John doth lead his men to gather up all those heavy, squarish *Cannows* which the fleeing Salvages have leaped from, & they commence to destroy them, for such manufactures seem most difficult for Salvages without iron tools. Indeed, in a twink the Nandsamunds send desperate embassies of peace, which he scorns, saying: You have assaulted me, who came only in love to do you good, & therefore I shall now burn all your canoes & houses, destroy your corn, & forever hold you my enemies, until you make me satisfaction.

Then the Nandsamunds commence crying & wailing, agreeing to all. — *Canoa, canoa!* they call to him — for without .1. of those, how can they ransom themselves?

Keale, do you set a Canoa adrift towards them. They can swim for it. Now listen up, all you Salvages! You want peace? Then you must give me all your King's bowes, & a great chain of pearl, & additionally **.400.** baskets of corn. If not, I shall ruin & destroy all your Canoas. (Men, keep hacking 'em up! Do your best endeavor now!)

For you see, dear Reader, our Sweet John's like unto a Countie Sheriff, who can seize himself of any felon's goods, in order to remit them to His Majestie.

The Nandsamunds agree to e'erything. They own not **.400.** baskets of corn, but offer up to Sweet John whatsoever they have, dipping desperately into their King's House, & he promises them to return for the remainder. (See Sweet John's sweetness sloughing off like grime.) And so, as e'er, our English do depart good friends.

❋ ❋ ❋ ❋ ❋

Back unto the River James they sail. Cape Henrico, Cape Henrico! How dark trees & grass-tufts do pox your white sands! Sweet John havens there, to shew the Nandsamunds he fears 'em not. (Snot-green jellyfishes, foam on their mouths, quiver flabbily in the wind.) He sets his Soldiers to refurbishing the great CHRIST cross which the Counsell had rais'd up in that time when Wingfield disallowed him to take his seat. *Bitterness* remains Sweet John's ordnance.

'Tis September now, almost the end of President Scrivener's term. But no doubt the living's better here than at Jamestowne. The men would go to quarter themselves at Kecoughtan for yet another night; they talk endlessly about wenchen-bubs, until Sweet John's full disgusted. He warns 'em they've eaten up their welcome there. Then it's Warraskoyack which they would go to, for Keale & Todkill, having both been there before, commend the belly-timber of that Towne.

Have you no care for your own home? he asks 'em sternly. What if they have need of us?

Sicklemore hath need that you should make him a servile leg, Captaine Smith. But ne'er fear; we're with you to the death! Besides, he's deposed —

At this mention of President Ratcliffe, Sweet John slowly smiles. Then he gazes into their eyes & says: I'll never bow to them at James Towne anymore.

THE GRAMMAR OF BLACKGUARDS (1608)

... there is no friendship to be had with him that is resolute to do or suffer anything rather than to endure the destiny whereto he was born; for he will not spare his own father or brother, to make himself a Gentleman.

THOMAS NASHE, *Pierce Penniless his Supplication to the Devil* (1592)

On the .10.th day of September, as the Sunne prepared to exit from the house of Virgo, Captaine Smith did accept the Letters-Patent of the Counsell of James-town, and thus became President. Into his hands at long last fell the Counsell's seal, which bears on .1. side the King's coat of arms, and on the other his likeness. Nicely busk'd up in his brigantine vest (whose plates he'd polished unto gleaming), he took the oath. His voice rang high & clear. Next, Matthew Scrivener read out the President's commission, in order that all men might remember their duty unto authority. The trumpet sang *Trarintrararara*. Gunners shot off all the demiculverins (which they'd never done for his predecessors; Sweet John had many military friends). When the echoes perisht to the last degree, Reverend Hunt uttered a prayer. He smil'd. He whisper'd in the new-anointed's ear: Remember when I told you to have patience? — Sweet John stood an Undertaker now in truth! The shallow, broken time of life had ended. Aye, he stood seiz'd of all this: — sea-grass as grey as old barn doors, algae-lipped ponds, grey marshes and brown rivers all around. Wheat & barley, oats & rye, foodstuffs for all England could grow here, to enrich him & our King! Almost wanton in her fertility, his Virginia . . . The breeze played with his hair. Maple-leaves pelted his breast; red needles hung from dying pines. No more need he fear the Colonie might be undone! Rather would he undo the Salvages. He'd discover & thwart their every ambuscado! He'd stay the building of Ratclyffe's Palace. (Radcliffe? O yes. Smith's pawn Maister Scrivener had arrested him for mutiny, as told. He went not without scoldings & wailings, yet lock'd in the Bread-room of the pinnace he abode as quietly as some Virginian *Cray-fish* which hath been trapped 'neath a glass bell; after many bristlings & clickings the monster gives o'er everything, lapsing into a statuette of itself.) And Sweet John march'd towards his next conquest. What faith he had in himself! He'd erect & fortify a Towne 'twixt the Susquehannocks & *Canada,* to interdict the French trade. He'd find *China* if 'twas to be found. He'd throw more dirt over Jamestowne's Burying-ground (which in truth had begun to stink, with so many of his Countrey-men lying there dead.) He'd grant the living good dwellings like unto his Father's grass-shagged house (which was now Frauncis & Anna's). He'd persuade the idlest Gentlemen to plant corn & other vegetables, to 'scape dependency on the harvests of Salvages. Poor Salvages! He thought upon 'em with a certain tenderness, as he would have any weak & wild creatures.

With a surplus of food, his Adventurers would no longer have to be robbers, beggars, or o'er-assiduous friends. The Salvages would respect 'em more, & Sweet John's dealings with Powhatan could comprise themselves in a purer amalgam of Christian charity & Machiavellian *Politick.* If only Frauncis & Anna were here! They'd translate that waste-marsh yonder unto a Bright Meadow of money-seed. Their self-interested drudgeful industry was what Virginia needed. Or had my Lord Willoughby remain'd in life . . . No matter — Sweet John stood on hand! He'd cajole his troops, or show 'em steel! He'd repair the Church, re-wall the Fort unto a more convenient pentagonal shape, & set more trained watches of Sentries; he'd drill every Colonist in marching and shooting according to the perfect forms which he'd learned in the Low Countreys . . .

Men followed him with their bloodshot squinting eyes. Men rush'd to have a peep, whene'er he did unlock the rotting Store-house. Men sat helpless. Some misliked & condemned him, I fear, because he was the only President who wore neither gold stitching nor golden points in his clothes. But his favorite Bravos did ring him round most loyally. Keale & Todkill strutted e'er about, seeking drones to report unto their Captaine. O, how the Gentlemen loathed 'em & the greasy Rustick they served!

✳   ✳   ✳   ✳   ✳

'Tis Saturday (a day layered green, grey and yellow by the forest hills), and the fat Trumpeter sounds his *Trarintra-rarara.* Every Colonist (excepting only he **.I.** hath the excuse of illness, or **.II.** serves that instant on the Watch, or **.III.** haps to be nam'd Radclyffe) must hie to the meadow past the West Bulwark, there to practice marching *.1. and .2., .1. and .2.* 'Tis the way to o'ercome all enemies, including Salvages. The President doth say so. He marches them *.1. and .2.* with a will.

Yea, see John Smith with his hand clenched around his broadsword's pommel within the basket-guard (which resembles the hollow, long-jawed skull of a badger, ferret or stoat). He stands upon a flour-barrel so as to lengthen himself. He's already nam'd the drilling-ground *Smithfield.*

Bide a twink, my lusty-hearts! he doth shout. I'll make you a mark for to shoot at. D'ye spy yon tree? 'Tis the enemy. Powder in your flash-pans, now! Powder down the barrel! Bullets in! Ready?

At a distance stand more than **.100.** Salvages all silent, their hair shaved strangely close on the right side, & full length on the left; thus runs their Salvage fashion. Snakes writhe in their ear-holes, & in their coxcombs Sweet John can see a number of those marvelous blue beads thro' which he sav'd Captaine Niuporte's prestige last spring. These Yndians glare & brood upon the Colonie. That they mislike him 'tis sure. Should he express his apprehensions to his *Father* King Powhatan? Nay, 'tis more likely they're Powhatan's spies. No matter; both sides can well perform their vigilance . . .

Strike the match! he cries. Watch how Lieutenant Percy accomplishes it, for he's a very knowng Gentleman. Now cock your pieces at my *mark!* Steady, lads. Present — *arms!* Ready — aim — *fire!*

At the ragged volley, some Salvages take to their heels most gratifyingly, while the rest (who've paid previous Saturday visits to Jamestowne) bide sullenly silent. The tree, instantly folded 'pon itself, sways back & back, then falls. The Salvages turn murmurously to **.1.** another. How runs their speech? Presumably they plot against him . . .

Well shot, lads! he cries. Now again. Keale, roll out another good fat pumpkin there. Can all of you see it? 'Tis your *foe.* Powder in your flashpans! Do your best endeavor now!

✳ ✳ ✳ ✳ ✳ ✳

An idle Gentleman refused to drill anymore.

Why then, man, you'll be dining with good Duke Humphrey. Did you e'er take cheer with him, in Saint Paul's Church?

Nay, & I deny to be commaunded by lowly little —

Well. Here's the tale. They who have neither farthings nor other persuasions gather round his tomb e'ery eve, to meet their fellow vagabonds, and go blackguarding in company. Do ye crave to bash my head in, laddie, and rob me of my purse? We're far from England now, don't disremember that. I have the same rights as you. In fact, this commission says I have more. I'm Helmsman here. Go sup at Duke Humphrey's, and may thy confederates grant thee courage. O, poor fellow! You'll eat no more in Jamestowne . . . !

Then that Gentleman did agree to drill.

*　*　*　*　*　*

He summonsed the Counsell unto the Church. Excepting Matthew Scrivener, they were but temporary Officers appointed until Captaine Newport should return, the ancient Counsell-men now being deposed, departed or dead. Lieutenant George Percie was the most illustrious of his pawns — in short, another dreamy & disdainful Gentleman. At least he never complained. Keale & Todkill he would have admitted, but fear'd that the other Gentlemen might revolt, to be thus rul'd by their inferiors. So he'd filled up that chamber with Patentees & rich young sons whose only recommendation was that they were too languid to be his enemies.

'Twas the .1.st bell of the Afternoon Watch. They took their places with bad grace, fearing his news. They were pale & a-hungered. Radclyffe (who in his own way worship'd *Machiavell*) had invited his Counsell-men to vote an extra allowance of provision for themselves. Sweet John would never do that. Nor did he keep any sack to pour out to 'em, as previous Presidents would have done. He'd given the entire cask to Dr Russell, for the comfort of the sick. They could hate him, or not. He was not the weak, cajoling species of Prince.

He sat down & admonish'd 'em thus: Well, my good lads, grace to Captaine Newport's follies at Werowocomoco, we must soon either pillage or starve. Did you know Powhatan's rais'd his price again? Today a basket of Yndian corn's worth more than a basket of good red English copper!

But, Maister President, *Kemps the Salvage* did swear—

Pokahuntiss herself told me this. Her father's argument runs thus: He can eat corn, yet not copper. Hence copper's good for naught.

Ha, ha! laughed Maister Scrivener. 'Tis most excellently reason'd, for an old Salvage!

The President glared in wrath.

Tup her again, Sweet John! Then your father-in-law will down the price!

Sir, I'll thank you not to mock me in my dignity.

(O, what an irascible little fellow this yeoman had prov'd to be! The Gentlemen laugh'd behind their hands—)

* * * * * *

Lieutenant Percy!

Aye, Maister President?

I'll send you out to chaffer with them at Kecoughtan. Deal direct with Pochins their Werowance. He's Powhatan's son. If he's absent, remind his Cronoccoes of the promise they gave me last autumn, when for pity I did refrain from burning their idol. Take Kemps or Machumps to speak for you. Tell 'em they must trade, but seek to content 'em with our commodities.

Should they deny me, I'll soon amend 'em.

I like your spirit. In season you'll come with me to the Chickahominies. — Now, Maister Scrivener!

Ready for your example, Sir!

I'll dispatch thee to Werowocomo, to persuade Powhatan into fairer exchange. Methinks he'd tax me with traducing him did I accompany you, for altho' he invested me with the dignity of *Werowance of Capahowsick* I denied to settle there, for the love I bear you all . . .

Maister President, I'm afeared—

Nonsense! Th'only thing to fear at Powhatan's is a surfeit of venison! Off you go!

Aye, Sir.

Now, lads, when Captaine Newport arrives, I'll call upon you all to help me resist his follies . . .

He trail'd off. He realiz'd that none of 'em would stand with him.

* * * * * *

He barr'd the Salvages from entering Jamestowne unescorted now, for they e'er did seek to filch English arms & tools. (Reader, I'll tell you how it is with creatures such as they, who refuse to comprehend our supremacy. At .1.st they seem but friendly in their rustick fashion. Then quickly familiarity swells to insolency, as if they were those pesky Fiddlers who follow men into Tavern-houses, in hopes of hiring out their twangling "Musick." Next by stages insolency becomes theft.) Only Pocahontas (whom he call'd his *Little Chickling)* remain'd subject to no such rule.

A flask hung on a bare dirt wall. Morion and chain-vests glittered sleepily in the Guard-house. Breastplates shone like grey lakes.

A long grey line of riverbank ran around the world.

The plaited-haired girl having not yet arrived at the Fort, Sweet John sat rereading his Machiavell. Reverend Hunt's sermon was done. The men curs'd, drowsed, or jawboned about Captaine Fortune. They agreed that he came not to those who watched not. So they watch'd; they hop'd. If they ran away to Powhatan, he'd feed 'em at his charge, after which they could surprise him, & ransom him for gold. Or they could run away past the fall line, to the Countrey of the Monacans, whose Werowance (being nearly unknown to them), must surely own gold. Or they could pilfer from the Store-house by night. Or they could make off with the pinnace, & set sail for England.

Jamestowne was Gravesend again. Argoll lay aloof off another Continent; Virginia's hymen, altho' stretched drum-taut, abode unstained. On the river, the idiot glare of the autumn Sunne diffused itself into bloody foam. Sweet John's expectations of his *Chickling*'s visit began to similarly dissolve itself unto annoyance. He felt the more impelled to promenade his thoughts thro' the Italian divine's pages, in order to weary them into some kind of accord with her ominous non-appearance. *Love you not me?*

A Prince doth not outlaye much upon his Colonies, for with little or no expense he can send 'em out & keep 'em there, explain'd this Signor Machiavelli, *and he offends a minority only of the Citizens from whom he takes Lands and Houses to give them to the newe Inhabitants; and those whom he doth offende, remaining poore and scattered, are ne'er able to injure him; whilst the rest being uninjured are easily kept quiet* . . .

As true as words 'graved upon some tablet! cried Sweet John to himself, squashing a loud Mosquitor upon his ear, skipping down a line or .2. to his favorite part:

Upon this, one has to remark that men ought either to be well treated *or* crush'd, *because they can avenge themselves of lighter injuries; of more serious ones they cannot; therefore the injury that is done to a man ought to be of such a kind that one does not stand in feare of* Revenge.

To Sweet John this signified, *Give 'em beads, or else exterminate 'em.* But he granted that in this case wise Machiavell didn't apply. He enjoy'd an insufficient power of men to exterminate the Salvages; & giving 'em beads — too many beads — had compris'd Captaine Newport's folly. That was why he long'd to make the Colonie sufficient unto itself, so that he could avoid begging to the Salvages e'ery month for belly-timber. No matter. Pocahontas lov'd him. He awaited her with pleasure. (Why wasn't she here?) A feather'd Salvage had promised him that she'd come today. If not today, then tomorrow. Tomorrow'd serve him another of those autumnal Jamestowne dawns which smelled most anciently of leaves & wet waste ground. Upon the Princesse's arrival (which each time confirm'd the peace), he'd send Lieutenant Percy out to Kecoughtan. Maister Scrivener continued to be afeared; he'd coax Pocahontas to gambol with him; she'd beguile him with another naked somersault—

He clos'd his eyes. 'Twas all thankless, like unto the time he'd gone a-riding for Bartty all the way to Old Hammond Beck, & gained nothing for his pains. *Men ought either to be well treated or crush'd.* An upturned letter **U** with a single vine-shoot boring out horizontally and rightward — thus the cattle brand of Revesby Towne in Lincolnshire. *Come back, come back.* And yet Revesby's not so vine-grown as all that — as for instance *Virginia* with her fine and pleasant suckles, yea, suckles and snickles — suckles *are* snickles; ivy of longing had long since commenced to o'erwrap John Smith, who thought himself well satisfied with his situation; he'd make his home here, ruling and reforming the Colonie to its good (if he could but dissipate all their cowardly and venomous disputations). A letter **U** overturned and surmounted by a cross — that's the cattle brand of Leake Towne as decreed long since by the Court of Sewers. He'd upraise the crosses of his dread Sovereign, King James, all across this land, snickling down all Salvages into obedience to CHRIST'S power. The hooked-anchor brand of Boston Towne would signify his ploughing & foundation-sinking of farms into all these yet treed wastelands which soon he'd render treelessly fecund.

And, honestly, there's another Signe or Symbol to be upraised here: The ancient cuneiform symbol for a vulva consists of a letter **Y** whose trunk continues upward between the two upraised branches. This is likewise the cattle brand for Lusby Towne in Lincolnshire. 'Tis the brand of Pocahontas's secret. GOD save her, she thinks him fully as sweet as the black sugar from the abdomen of a roasted ant.

✳ ✳ ✳ ✳ ✳

He call'd a Salvage unto him & said: How fares Pocahontas?

The Salvage replied at length — to which poor Sweet John had to say: *Cuffewh kenneaunten mata mechik,* which means, *I understand you a little but not much.*

Keale, go bring Kemps or Tassore from the dungeon-hole. They speak English more eagerly.

The Salvage laugh'd & said: *Maangairagwatonu.* — Sweet John knew not what that signified.

When comes she to James-towne?

The Salvage gazed upon him very earnestly. Then he said: *Nay.*

What, she won't come? But I've waited day upon day . . .

The Salvage flicked his eyes. Whirling, the President spied **.3.** of the man's copesmates, a-trying for to filch some tools. He raged. Gripping the edge of the table, he said to the Salvage: *Kekaten Pokahontas patiaquagh niugh tanks manotyens neer mowchik rawrenock audowgh.*   To wit: *Bid Pokahantas bring hither .2. little Baskets, and I will give her white Beads to make a Chaine.*

✳ ✳ ✳ ✳ ✳

Anas Todkill comes a-running. Captaine Newport's fleet's in sight! (News from England: Pot-ale's more than a penny now; the times grow dear.) Now see John Smith within his Presidential tent, preparing for to receive the **.2.**nd Supply. What would Lord Willoughy have done? Why, he'd have held a banquet at a long table, replete with Servaunts to carry in the trenchers of roast beef &c. Barty & Robert would be there to greet the guests. And . . .

Ha, Sweet John, I see you've won the throw. Wingfield & Ratcliffe broken both, Archer out of commission (he sends his *halloo),* & you in the Presidential saddle — 'tis too rich!

Good even, Captaine Newporte. 'Tis near about time for our Reverend's service. Would you care to come?

How could I deny to do that? Now tell me. Where's the gold? I hear from Lieutenant Percy that you've squirreled it all away — ha, ha!

He jests. Or you jest. I continue conscientious—

Just as ketches, flyboats & pinnaces sport ever the same long twinned diagonal descending from foresail to stern deck, so Captaine Newporte doth comprise himself of unchanged warp, no matter how grows or shrinks his official dignity. Hath he been made Admirall again? Sweet John cares not. He scorns to extend himself in any fashion unto this would-be underminer of all his Adventures. O, a shame it is that he's disallowed to blast nasty Niuport with spleen-juice! No matter. He'll bite the lip. He'll enforce himself upon himself as best he can. 'Tis a President's part to act thus.

Come, laddie, where's the gold?

Captaine Newporte, I'm as ill apprised of that as you.

Never fret. We'll find it. I have a private commission **.I.** to discover the Monacans, **.II.** to find the South Sea to China, **.III.** to bring back gold, & finally **.IV.** to succor the lost Colonists of Roanoke. Are you with me, sweet little President?

Madness!

Frankly, they do begin to say of you in London-Towne that your Colonie's a cesspit for money. For this **.2.**nd Supply they must pay me near **.1,000.** pounds, & you've not return'd 'em **.100.**! Moreover, they allege on your part certain cruelties—

Cruelties!

Toward the Salvages.

O, what strange Gentlemen! I—

Naturally I'd stake all my coppers on your *forbearance* to the Naturalls, my dear Sweet John, & to Lord Salisbury I did express as much.

I —

For instance, you're passing kind unto Pokahuntiss—

Look you, Captaine Newporte. It may well prove *there's no gold in Virginia.*

Then you & I are bankrupt men.

*   *   *   *   *   *

Now in consequence of this **.2.**nd Supply, Jamestowne hath suddenly gained near about **.120.** persons of various stripes — Glass-makers, Soapsters, Assayers, e'en **.2.** women, namely *Mistresse Forrest* (who's already wed) & her pink-cheek'd Maid-servaunt *Anne,* who doubtless will get herself married quick as a twink, as folks do calculate . . . They all crave to eat. They hound him for Yndian corn. They're like unto helpless relations at a rich man's door. What's Sweet John to do? Winter's whirring down to sting them. *He offends a minority only of the Citizens from whom he takes Lands and Houses to give them to the newe Inhabitants,* but 'tis scarcely Christian to turn the Salvages from their houses. Now day & night dreads come a-knapping on his door. He can scarce decide what to Undertake. His faith in his own luck hath weakened at the root. Yet he'll never forget misfortune's consequence. Haunted by the clammy limitations of Willoughby, the Rector's indifferent face, his weary supplications to Bartty & Robert, half-crazed with recollections of unrest at Bolingbroke Castle, whose long plough-grooves sped in a million parallels toward the horizon, he feels his belly clench. He's President now, but that Office hath prov'd precarious to both his predecessors, so he must strain to make his success complete. He must become a *complete* Prince without further delay. To do that, he'll Enclose & Adventure anything; he'll flitter from Towne to Towne to get provender for his Colonists, as if he were their Servaunt; he'll wring the Salvages out of their cornfields forever, & drive 'em into the ooze. He bides confident (e'en as President Wingfield once did) that he can discharge his place right honorably, to the benefit of the Colonie. He'll soon incorporate his ill luck into stone.

But now upon Newporte's authority they do reinstate malignant *Ratcliffe* to the Counsell! Additionally, they install .2. pawns by name *Captaine Waldo* & *Captaine Wynne*. Matthew Scrivener, ere now obedient to Sweet John in most things, begins to incline unto these baleful Dissensionists (as is only to be expected from a wench-chinned youth).

They toll the Church-bell. The meeting's convoked. Full wrathfully doth Sweet John inquire of his new Counsell: How are we to feed so many souls come winter?

Why, 'tis easy, Sweet John! (thus Captaine Newport.) If you fear to do it, I myself shall sail the pinnace to Werowocomoco, & from Powhatan, after I crown him—

Crown him?

— Gain .20. tons of corn!

✳ ✳ ✳ ✳ ✳

'Pon my honesty, GOD loves to stuff our mouths with gawp-seed, then grin as we fall o'erwhelmed & 'mazed at the wobbly correspondences of this World. For just as *Iohn Smythe* receiveth here his dignitie, so forsooth the Companie of Virginia hath already decided to coronate Powhatan King! Here 'tis in Newport's *Instructions Given By Way of Advice.* Do those Gentlemen then reverence His Virginian Majestie? Fie on you, to even ask so! Don't you ken that Powhatan's naught but a sour old Salvage? Captaine Smith knows the reason for that copper crown (now arrived with .1.-armed Captaine Newport): — to wit (if I may explicate in a parable) — at Christmas-tide in Lincolne Towne our City Fathers choose half a dozen paupers to receive gowns whose badges bear the City's arms; .1. of these becomes *Master of the Poor,* which is a fine tin hat to wear; and for a good salary of .20. shillings he punishes & expels his brethren who've arrived from foreign Townes. And on the same principle, when I the *Tourist* go to see the Taj Mahal, I hire the first Guide I see, so he'll keep away the rest. Our worshipful Maisters in London Towne have thus resolved to invest Powhatan as *Master of the Salvages,* which is to say their lickspittle *Under-King* to do their need, until the day when their Colonie be so well established and fortified as to disregard all Salvage pandars and vagabonds.

As for Captaine Newport, 'tis hardly his .1.st such commssion. Scarce .3. years since, he'd presented a pair of baby crocodiles to King James, for which act of homage he'd been rewarded with commaund of all the Virginia Companie's sea-voyages. What booty doth old One-Arm expect this time? Maybe *gold*.

Sweet John shrills protest. Powhatan's pride will get puff'd up like unto an adder. The price of corn will rise higher. Jamestowne will tumble further into dangerousness.

He fears only the 'minishment of his own hollow grandeur! sneers Captaine Radclyffe, at which Captaines Winne & Waldo eye their President askance, as if he were a traitor. Counsell-man Scrivener shifts & wavers. Newport yawns. To him, it's all **.1.**

After inevitability doth abrade his scorn, Sweet John begins to cherish wage-hopes. For he cannot forbear to believe that should he execute enough menial commissions with successful dispatch (for instance, leading Bartty's horse prudently through the ooze), then he'll be rewarded with a sinecure's fine dignities, ascending percase from *President* to *Governor*.

On his personal authority (which he's assured doth remain highly esteemed amongst these Salvages) he doth invite his *Father* hither to be crowned. Pokahuntiss's brother Nantaquod takes the message (& with it, a little brass bell for his *Nonpareil* of a sister, she who loves our Sweet John & hath adored his imperiled head with her own hands).

The gate doth come creaking & crashing shut. Our President stands upon a Sentry-tower, watching Nantaquod depart at the head of his retinue. 'Tis an excellently pretty show they do put on, being painted red & black as is their wont, & bearing maple-wood war-clubs o'er their shoulders, as if they go to do murther. The Sentry spits. They stand together a-watching that mass of spittle tumble down toward Smith-field.

Sweet John claps his hand 'pon the Sentry's shoulder. — Prince Nantaquod makes a brave display, says he.

Aye, Maister President.

(Nantoquod stops. He wheels. Loping to the river's edge, he shoots a fish with an arrow on a cord.)

What reckon you of this coronation, my good lad? Methinks we'd have Powhatan's favor much better only for a plain piece of copper! But that scurvy Niuporte—

Aye, Maister President.

Do you mislike him as much as I?

I know him not, Sir.

Sweet John taps his foot, stretches, alters his gaze. Nantaquod's now long vanisht in the marsh-grass. Is all well? He spies the Lookout in his wooden nest on Admirall Newport's flagship. He waves his hand. The Lookout lazily salutes him.

You stand your watch very trustworthy, he assures the boy. What Countie do you hie from?

Countie Kent. My father's a Tavern-keeper in Gravesend.

Well, well. Which .1.?

The Scarlet Peacock. 'Tis ancient—

I never was there, altho' I know it. Gravesend's passing populous, of course, with as many Taverns as Virginia hath trees. Do you oft think upon the place?

'Tis my home, so—

Gravesend, now, well that place sometimes seems busier than the center of the World!

Aye, Maister President.

You being from there (& your father a Tavern-keeper, too), I fancy you've a shrewd head for business.

Umsiling, the Sentry ducks his head. He's near about .15. years of age, maybe a little more.

I've whiled away the odd month in your Cittie, boy, a-waiting for Captaine Fortune.

Did you find him, Maister President?

How can'st thou ask such a silly question, when in the same breath you name me *Maister President?*

Aye, the Sentry wisely replies.

And do you agree these Salvages are free & handsome fellows?

To be sure, says the Sentry wearily.

Well then. If you were President, what would comprise your policy?

Kill 'em all, says the Sentry.

* * * * * *

Thus summonsed, Powhatan yet denied to hie himself to Jamestowne. Unsettled .1.-Arm next proposed to appoint with him some likely halfway spot, much as whores & trulls do meet their clients in the middle aisle of Saint Paul's. But neither did this hold color with the Virginian King's vainglory. Welladay; in the pinnace they sailed for Werowocomoco and accomplished their landing, the grass like brown porcupine quills flashing green or bone-white as it bristled in the wind like rising hair on the back of some alertly dangerous animal. Meanwhile, Sweet John with **.4.** Lieutenants did set forth by land to prepare the way.

✳ ✳ ✳ ✳ ✳ ✳

See our President on the march. He wears his dignity most grandly now — nay, he swells in it; it's like unto the bay arcades of Saint Helena's Church in Willoughby. Nor is dignity the only substance he's clothed in: Yea, Sweet John's like a house unto himself, low and heavy with plates of bark, except that *his* plates be iron. (On the shady Yndian trails, his armor offers GOD the dark corncob reflections of alligator scales.) He'll bring his dependents to safe harbor; he swears it! He's yet prouder and happier than when he used to go a-riding on Frauncis's colorfully caddised horse. Leading his Soldiers without fear 'twixt fern-erupting hummocks, he strides as lengthily & rapidly as his armor's weight permits him. 'Tis the **.3.**rd hour of the Morning Watch. He feels young, healthy; he longs to visit all his Yndian friends! Today he's full confidently persuaded of their love. Why not? Think on Pokahuntas — a loving apparition, 'tis true, & foul the tongue that dares untrick my eye from her! And for his **.4.** men (**.1.** of whom's that selfsame *Captaine Waldo* appointed to the Counsell; 'tis a wise Machiavellianism to bring him along, in hopes of alluring him unto all Sweet John's views), Pocahontas just may summon her Serving-maids. — O yes, there'll be wenchen as numerous as the Fish-wives of Yarmouth-Towne . . . 'Tis chilly this morn, & all the Mosquitors which torment Virginia in the summer months are dead. He joys in this jaunt, craves to stop e'erwhere, & stops not, no matter that the Soldiers do pant & puff, begging him for GOD's love to dacker down. How well he kens this path! *The King's highway* he's nam'd it now, so smoothly doth he traverse it, altho' in spots it's no more than a green and scummy channel between alders. 'Tis the way Pocahontas always takes with her Courtiers, whene'er she goes by land.

His life is new. James-Towne's stink falls behind. He harks back for a last sighting of the isle he rules. White water's oozing around the grass.

His Soldiers beg leave to dissect the domed house of a muskrat, which he laughingly grants. They would replenish themselves with meat. Yet the muskrat (perhaps spying the light which glistens & glisters upon their helms) escapes in a twink. With jesting strategems Sweet John doth restore the men's good dispositions. O, how they'll feast at the Emperor's board! . . . They march on. Vines clutch the sides of trees.

From afar they're greeted by an ibis, a pelican, a long line of birds, tiptoeing and paddling out into the slough to eat worms and fishes. The corroded little breastplates of their armor do rattle and tinkle most musically, & the birds all fly away.

Gazing upward with joyous wonder, he shews his men the many birds' nests like unto the baskets and balconies high up in a ship's rigging, where Lookouts wait on watch, greedy to gain gold for .1.ˢᵗ sighting of land or an enemy's galleon.

And this Pamunkey River which we must cross, lads, O, you'll see how many merchauntable fishes it doth contain—

Aye, Maister President. (Why, he doth prate like unto the vulgarest Waterman!)

'Tis possible they may ambuscado us here, but they've no call to do it. Full cock, lads, & muzzles outward!

Aye, Maister President. Captaine Radclyffe did say—

Let me guess. He said: *Remember Roanoke!*

But 'tis true that Powhatan murthered all them Colonists?

'Tis plausible, at least.

Then when we spy Powhatan's garrison—

Be not afeared; I swear Powhatan will give us a monstrous good meal to chomp down. 'Tis the season of their feasting & sacrifice. Why, last time I saw him, if I don't disremember . . .

How far lies this Pamunkey River, Sir? Because we're a-wearied . . .

Full .14. miles! laughs Sweet John; & none laugh with him.

O, he loves Virginia! His Soldiers reel amaz'd at silver mirror-channels which lie prison-barred by tree-images. ('Tis no very convenient road, he hears 'em say.) Pamunkey River he adores especially; there's a certain creek which flows into it, where he'd love to someday install a Mill-wheel, there to live & grind Yndian corn, once he hath found an English wife to dwell with; & when he's enrichened enough to keep Salvage Servaunts, it's they who'll do the grinding while he sits a-fishing for sturgeon with his unborn children. For now that he's attained the dignity of *President,* he mislikes it; indeed he'd prefer to be the stout yeoman which they accompt him. 'Tis impractical to keep Englishmen happy merely by giving 'em chains of beads! What if he'd gone to dwell in Capahowsick-Towne when Powhatan had invited him? Well, for all that, *Tymor Smith* they might have call'd him — & he'd ken passing well how it relished inside Tragabigzanda's heart & quim. Or Cicely, land sakes, he might've won her anytime, were it not that he couldn't forbear his craving to go to sea. She would have been a good wife, so sweet

& comely, with good money to pay her portion. But too late — he'd left the tillage of an honest life, to become a drudge in this unhallowed Colonie.

His Soldiers stagger on in a sweat.

O, how I would yon bush hung at a pole's end!* cries Captaine Waldo.

Never fear, Sweet John returns him, you'll have good refreshment yonder at their *Weracomoca.* 'Tis the season of their festivals . . .

And here's the river! Across her currents, the palisadoes of Werowocomoco begin to peep o'er the trees, like unto the tines of an immense comb; & then they see the longhouses plaited with bark; & hordes of Salvages come boiling out, ready for peace or war.

Sweet John waves at 'em from where he's standing on the south shore. Gaily he doth shout: *Kekaten Pokahontas patiaquagh niugh tanks manotyens neer mowchik rawrenock audowgh* — which signifies: *Bid Pokahantas bring hither .2. little Baskets, and I'll gift her with white Beads for to make a Chaine.*

Laughing, the Salvages dispatch a Canoa to fraught 'em o'er the water. All the while, his Soldiers do sit a-gathering gawp-seed. Sweet John's swaggeringly proud of himself & all his works. Without him, how could Jamestowne have endured?

Do your best endeavor now! Greet him with courtesy, for all that he's a Salvage!

But the Soldiers do gaze upon their Waterman but coldly.

He hath shrewd eyes, murmurs Captaine Waldo.

Be at ease. This man's been my familiar many times since!

(This careless lie none believes.)

Across the divide they do speed. The Soldiers gaze mournfully backwards, like children at night when their mother withdraws with the candle. Captaine Waldo grips the gunnels hard. Doth he expect for to get drown'd? Perceiving the anxious loneliness of his men, Sweet John knows not whether to smile or scold. So he keeps silent. And in a twink, they've achiev'd the other shore.

He gives the Ferryman a white bead, which is esteem'd among these Salvages as being of middling quality.

And so they arrive at .**III**.-creeked Werowocomoco, which at this season is half-o'ergrown with fat orange pumpkins. An infant begins to screech until it gets red in the face, straining to defecate its panic. 'Tis near

---

*The sign of a rustic ale-house.

about Saint Matthew's Day,* when in Willoughby they e'ery year hold a Cattle-Fair for white meats & for young heifers. Salvages rush about him. They scritch their fingernails in the dirt & wail welcome. He loves 'em, yet trusts 'em not. His Soldiers stand mute & pallid with fear.

* * * * * *

Pocahontas, my dearling! How d'ye do?

Passing well, *Father,* excepting that I see you but scantly. This day I'm joyous that you've returned again . . .

She wore a painted mantle & a chain of some white beads which he did once give her. Her face & shoulders shone bloodlike with puccoon-paint. 'Twas passing strange for to see her not naked. He would have joyed to find her bare. Her fingers were stain'd purplish; no doubt she'd been crushing walnuts to make *Nut-milk* in honor of their coming. The .4. Soldiers frown'd at her in uneasy amaze.

And Powhatan is—

He hunts the deer not far from here. His Cronoccoes run now to give word of your coming.

My thanks, he said.

A little uneasily, she approach'd him & strok'd his breast. He embraced her, but lukewarmly, since the Soldiers' gaze unnerved him.

And how do you fare, at your *Jamestowne?*

No doubt we'll become the *Terror of the World,* he said brightly. But 'tis a state to be builded by scant degrees.

She had much ado not to smile. He felt wrath. Tragabigzanda had perfumed herself from a turquoise bottle. But Pokahuntas was a Salvage, scarce human; moreover, her face was passing ill-favored.)

And have you a new song to teach me, *Father*?

Forthwith he did sing her the ancient rhyme from Lincolnshire's Popish days:

> Ramsay, the rich of gold and fee,
> Thorney, the flower of many a fair tree,
> Croyland, the courteous of their meat and drink,
> Spalding, the gluttons, as all men do think . . .

She clap't her hands.

He now set himself with all his might to pleasuring this innocent Poca-

---

*21 September.

hontas with beads, games & other preordained trifles, all of which she relished most gratefully; then, thinking upon the subject of heartstrings, he
squatted down and she flew into his arms as usual. He stroked her head
and took a single **.1.** of her long black hairs between his fingers and tugged
it out and she laughed; next he gathered **.2.** hairs in his hand without
pulling them, then **.4.**, **.8.**, **.16.**, **.32.**, according to the highest algebra of
Marcus Aurelius; he seized a tuft of hair from her left temple and **.1.** from
her right; by tugging at these reins he steered her face left and right and she
laughed.

(O, then he frigs her sure! he heard a Soldier sneer.)

Now the dearling Pocahontas did speak a word, & Servaunt-maids came
to lead them all to mats on a sunny field (which did comprise their courtli-
est comfort), there to find good variety of vittles. But the Soldiers picked
through their food, searching for sign or spoor of any flower, for 'twas rumored in the Colonie that the Salvages do poison their enemies with the
blossom of a black cherry.

Listen up, you lads. 'Tis an honest entertainment which her hospitality
hath distill'd. Lock away all misprisons.

I'm sad if we offend you, Maister President. Yet we do accompt our own
lives as jewel-like as doth e'ery man—

'Tis cat-lap & chamber-lees which you speak. Moreover, your frowning
foreheads encumber us all. Think you good Pocahontas cannot read a
glance?

Pardon, Maister President, but we fear to be trick'd—

And you, Captain Waldo?

Nay, Sir, I relish this banquet. Moreo'er, by studying about me, I now see
how (should they prove treacherous) 'twould be simple to burn this
Towne—

Enough. Still your mouths **.1.** & all, excepting for to eat—

Now I should explain to you, dear Reader, that Salvages keep no Voider
to clear the table at their banquets; each guest must swallow whatsoever he
can, then take the residuum with him. So the scarce-touch'd trenchers
could not be concealed. Therefore Pocahontas did look passing discontented, that these venom-fearing English ate not more. But at last (they being full a-hungered, & their President urging 'em to it), they did their best
endeavor, from which they suffered no more than a surfeit.

Next they smok'd *Tobacco* like unto so many DEVILS — a thing
which all relished. After this, Pokahuntiss did promise 'em a good entertainment. First her Servaunt-maids (or perhaps I should say *Ladies-in*

waiting) kindled a fire, which set Sweet John somewhat on his guard, for he could not but remember the doom by broiling of George Cassen. Then all those damsels withdrew themselves. The President & his men sat there 'mongst those Salvages, awaiting they knew not what.

Captaine Smith? a Soldier did whisper in his ear.

Aye?

Captaine Smith, I'm afeared—

Act not the part, lad. From experience I know that most of their courage proceeds from others' fear. Look hearty now; be no freshwater Soldier.

Aye, Captaine.

From the trees ahead came horrid cries, louder & louder. What if 'twere Powhatan, coming for to murther them? What if 'twere Captaine Fortune? Sweet John had 'scaped & lost so many futurities — rich-toyed guestings with Lords, oozy drownings off France, Turkishe slavery, Turkishe marriage — that habit now helmed him down & opened his friendship's hands, all in the same twink. He stood confident both to fight & to grasp. As for his companions, their judgment's clockwork had not yet been set to Virginia's tides. Seized only by the *twinkling fear,* therefore, they made haste to capture **.3.** Salvage greyheads who sat amongst them, each with his own prisoner tight-clutched & bedaggered at breast or throat. Mechanickally moved by their panic, Sweet John, needing not to be call'd behindhand (& what if Pokahuntiss *had* betrayed them all?) leapt alert most sensitively; he'd already powder'd his gun, which he trained upon the woods . . .

But from that self-parted wilderness appear'd only Pocahontas, running. — *Father, father!* she wept. *Love you not me?*

What pretends Powhatan? Methinks he means to ambuscado us —

Nay, I swear it! Slay me if any hurt's intended . . .

So at Sweet John's word they subsided themselves, letting the hoarheads go. 'Twas a risk, as he concurred, but in the game call'd *Imperium* we must sometimes act a dreadless part 'gainst the alien gloom.

I'd have thought you trusted me now, she whispered, sobbing now not only with grief but bitterness. The Salvages look'd on, their eyes a-flittering like compass-needles.

Catching his breath, he faintly said: Pokahuntiss, I give you all my blessings and prayers.

She lay continually upon his heart.

Again the woods gave birth. The screechings were now reveal'd to be uttered by full upon **.30.** nubile wenches, arm'd with swords, bows, sticks or clubs, painted as bravely as English ships, & stript nearly down to their

Secrets (which they covered with but leaves). Relieved now, Sweet John smil'd to see his men in such amaze. He explained to 'em that these were like unto the bad women in England who flock to Tavern-houses, in hopes that some lusty Gentleman will refresh 'em on sugared wine. There was nothing to dread.

Daunce & daunce about! How their bosoms do shake! Back at Graves-end they'd never credit this—

When they cameth into my discovery . . .

By the mightie JEHOVAH (thus Captaine Waldo), but they give a man a whopper!

And so Sweet John with his men did quarter themselves most happily in Werowocomoco that night, there in the smoky arbor-houses where men & women lay utterly naked together on the floormats. All the wenchen (not excluding Pokahuntiss herself) kept cooing with candied words: *Love you not me?* And what happened next, dear Reader, I'm sure you can tell as well as I.

As for Captaine Smith, he lay somewhat pensive alone, until his *Nonpareil* came to him. She said: Did you make me beads?

Why, yes, darling lass, I do have here some white beads which I fashion'd for you—

Father?

Yes, child.

I would call thee *Husband*.

O, but you're passing youngish for such sports, my sweet chuck. Wait a year or *.2.*—

I must obey you, Father, said Pokahuntiss.

But soon, naked & laughing in the firelight, she was frog-leaping o'er him. Laughing, he sported with her hair.

＊ ＊ ＊ ＊ ＊ ＊

'Tis a coolish morn. They feed him & his men on fresh venison. Now they tell him that her other father's come. He dreads Powhatan, knowing he'll serve up but scornful courtesy. Yet by virtue of *Pokahuntiss* their mutual tie, he remains Sweet John's best instrument to bring the Salvages into concord.

Helming himself, leading the others when summonsed, he approaches Powhatan's Palace.

＊ ＊ ＊ ＊ ＊ ＊

You did promise to make me hatchets, said this ancient King. Where are they?

Captaine Waldo, kindly do present him .III. good axes from your rucksack—

And your great guns which you did promise me, I discover them not.

Your warriors prov'd somewhat feeble for the purpose, replied Sweet John. Send me stronger men, dear *Father,* & they can hale away all the demiculverins they do list.

At this witticism, Powhatan commenc'd grinning like all the cracks of old pottery.

And now, dear *Father,* we would help thee revenge thy injuries 'pon the Monacans, he began — for indeed, as gentle Machiavell hath writ, 'tis wisest, when conquering the Countreys of other Princes, to embroil 'em .1. against the other.

Powhatan abode silent.

Moreover, continued Sweet John, somewhat disconcerted, we do again invite you to Jamestowne, to receive presents from the *King of the World.* After that we would Adventure to the Countrey of the Monacans with you, to safeguard your Empire & discover new oceans—

If your King hath sent me presents, replied Powhatan, gazing deeply into John Smith's eyes, I also am a King, and this is my Countrey.

O yes, said the President, but mayhap you misapprehend —

Eight days will I stay to receive them. Your father is to come to me, not I to him, nor yet to your Fort; neither will I bite at such a bait, he added almost with a snarl. — As for the Monacans, I can revenge mine own injuries. And as for any salt water beyond the mountains to the west, the relations you have had about that from my people are *false*.

Sweet John was scarce amazed by these refusals. Indeed, they almost pleasured him, by proving how much more he knew than his other supposed *Father* Captaine Newporte. Reader, haven't you e'er known a soul who, marr'd by o'ermuch suffering & rage, commences to joy in what justifies its anger, no matter that it takes hurt thereby? Sweet John's *Trve Trauells* now compris'd a *Black cherry blossom* of their own, beauteous to behold, yet no less poisonous for that—

* * * * * *

Now by water arrived good Captaine Newporte, like unto some bustling Sherriff busily executing a whole sheaf of King's writs! And he came at the head of .120. men. Werowocomoco's many Sentries did shrill out the news.

The pinnace swarm'd with shining Englishmen. Presently some of them came a-struggling through the ooze.

Powhatan for his part form'd up his Salvage musters. Captain New-porte's Sailors disfraughted *basin, ewer, bedstead, scarlet cloak* & all the rest. And those Yndians commenced for to welcome 'em with their doleful scritchings. Only Sweet John cared to see that some struck sullen silent poses, or e'en made mocking mouths. Were these the Bravos who kept stealing his tools? Full changeable they all were, in truth, & the manner in which they tricked themselves out with red paint, feathers & snakes made them seem the more abominable. Yet he fear'd not to couch himself (for now) in Pocahontas's affections. So long as he could persuade her to smile on his will, he feared not these living, glaring implements of her father's murtherousness.

So the Englishmen were all here, each with his gun, no matter how Powhatan did protest. The speeches & dances were concluded. The next trick was to persuade the Emperor to kneel for his coronation.

Perchance you'll *damn* me, if I do not his bidding! croaked Powhatan to Sweet John with a loathsome laugh.

Nay, dear *Father,* 'tis but to enhance your dignity—

But Powhatan in his devilish malice would not, until the English did force his shoulders down. Three stout villains clapt the pennyworth-crown on his pate; Captain Newporte shot off his pistol, & then at once the boats did fire off a fusillade to celebrate the occasion! But Sweet John, gazing intently at the King, mark'd well how at the gunshots he leapt back a-grimacing in fear.

Then they blew the trumpet: *Trarintra-rarara.*

* * * * * *

In consideration of all these benefits received, Powhatan contented himself with giving Captain Newporte his mantle & his old shoes. When the time came to chaffer beads for corn, the trading went much against the English.

* * * * * *

See John Smith a-felling cedar-trees in the snow with **.30.** Gentlemen, whilst Captain Newport (who now hates him) betakes his own choice of Adventurers up river to discover the Countrey of the Monacans, disregarding Powhatan's refusal to be their pawn.

Snow, snow & snow again! Still, shivering is better than being cozened

by Ratcliffe. He sets his Gentlemen to work with a will, *.1. and .2.*, *.1. and*
.2. — & how they curse whene'er they do blister their fingers! Sweet John's
pleas'd to establish the penalty: A bucket of ice-water down their sleeve for
e'ery oath, no exceptions! (The hatchet-rhythmns: *Come, back, come*
back.) — His eponymous sweetness? 'Tis near about entirely gone, as the
ooze of Willoughby someday will be, should the Enclosers & Undertakers
keep steadily to their drainage. He's as good as a Gentleman now. Yet Captaine Newport, & these sneering lace-sleev'd idlers, all deny to make anything of his accomplishments. They hate him. He expected nothing else.
Under his authority they'll undoubtedly do more of benefit than in their
whole lives up to now! O, so many years now they've nam'd him
Climber, & *Creeper,* & *Rusticke,* & *Stinkard,* & *Rebel.* He
would have toil'd a slave for the *Tymor,* had that man not driven him beyond obedience. How many times hath he been corner'd, expell'd, near-
drowned, almost-hang'd, tried, accused? He's got more endurance than
any of his tormenters, & now he's angry, & now he's President.

Years later, in his *Generall Historie,* he'll anxiously write: *By this, let no*
man think that the President & these Gentlemen spent their times as com-
mon Wood haggers, or that they were prest to it as hirelings, or common
slaves . . .

And Captaine Newporte did presently return from the Monacans, having accomplisht near about nothing, & brought back no corn.

✳ ✳ ✳ ✳ ✳ ✳

How doth Powhatan?

Ha, ha, Maister John! I have tidings. Permit me to whisper 'em to you
inside the Church—

Kemps, you sly old villain, what hath your fellow Salvages told you?

You'll reward me, Maister John?

I've already rewarded you sufficiently by striking off your fetters & for-
giving your past thievery. What else would you?

Maister John, I would have some beads or other gifts to appease my relations in Paspahegh, who say I do but spy for the English.

Ha! They say true—

For I do love you, thus to risk Powhatan's wrath, & the anger of *Wowin-*
chopunck my Werowance—

You persuade me, lad. I'll give you a fine hatchet, or—

'Tis rum I'd be wanting, Maister John.

Spoken like an Englishman, you reprobate! Now enough of this. What's your news?

Powhatan hath exterminated the Chisapeacks, said the Salvage with great self-satisfaction.

For what cause?

Because OKEUS did warn Uttamattomakkin in a dream that a Nation from the east would devour us all. The Chesapeakes did dwell eastward.

Well, chuckled Sweet John, 'tis your Emperor's folly, to be guided thus by the authority of the DEVIL! He did murther the wrong Nation. For we *Tasantasses* (as you call us) did sail from the East to take his Countrey, & by GOD we shall do it! Hey, Todkill, dear lad! Treat Maister Kemps here to a deep shot of grog . . .

The Salvage lean'd closer. (Sweet John prepared for to stand aloof & whip forth his falchion, should he be assaulted.) — Maister John, do you remember Roanoke?

How can I not? Radclyffe doth e'er adore to remind us of it, now he's re-turn'd to our Counsell . . .

My Uncle assures me that those *Lost Colonists* did find haven with the Chisapeacks. And now hath Powhatan murthered 'em. Think upon it, Maister John.

O, I know Powhatan loves us not. But he can do us no hurt, Kemps — even if *you* do play the spy.

Maister John, you know I'm passing loyal—

Aye, that you may be, drunkard. Todkill, you heard me! Hasten to un-bung that barrel yonder—

* * * * * *

See John Smith amongst the Chickahominies. The snow thereabouts is tramped down to slush, then frozen again, so that his marching's passing treacherous, but he who's wintered in *High Hungaria* cares not for such trifling inconveniencies. He's ready for to try his fortune! Those of his Soldiers lucky enough to be thus delegated bide faithfully on the .3. shield-armored barges. Sweet John their Generall hath wisely affrighted them by relating the doom of *George Cassen, Jehu Robinson,* & *Thomas Emry.* His policy hath matured: no more will he entertain his troops with tales of Tragabigzanda & her shining silver bangles! Already (thanks to the love of Pocahontas) 'tis whispered he's licentious. But what's more to the point is that he'll not encourage other quim-hunters unto their doom.

Smoke arises like whale-steam from the those reed-scaled, arch-shapen houses, which tremble in the winter wind. The *Caw-cawwassoughes* (as the Chickahominies' Parliamentaries or Counsell-men be call'd) invite him in (knowing they can scarcely do aught else). He enters with half a dozen of his most trusted widow-makers, while the others wait outside with leveled guns. He keeps consonant to all Salvage courtesies, understanding well to inhibit his designs until the tide's high in flood, so to speak. They offer *Tobacco*, which he smokes with thanks, saying, *Your obedient Servaunt.* But only a lone beldam brings food, & there's no welcome dance. The stink of *Raccoon*-guts arises from their stewpot, freezing on his leather buff-coat. With thanks, he falls to, & so do the other men. They've all eaten worse.

Now to the business at hand. Full civilly Sweet John doth outspread his bells, beads & other commodities, but the Chickahominies will not chaffer for corn. They boldly assert that their harvest was oppress'd this year by drought & worms. They do deny his trade with meekly steadfast insolency. 'Tis passing evident now Powhatan's policy is to starve the Colonie.

Nay, laughs Sweet John then. I come not so much for your trifling corn, as to revenge my imprisonment of last year, and the cruel murthers of my men.

He rises up. He helms himself with a clang. — Come, lads! We'll favor these Yndians with a little heartache! — He leads his noble Assassins out thro' the low mat-hung door, & the uncomprehending Salvages watch them go. Outside, he forms up a party. His reserves stand ready behind in case of some ambuscado. Little Sweet John sings out: *.1. and .2., .1. and .2.* 'Tis the cadence of Civilization. He's at the head of *.18.* picked Soldiers. Commaunding them to advance upon the Towne, he speedily brings the Salvages to a more submissive composition. See how they wail & boil! He lights a torch. He raises it high. He touches it to the thatch of the nearest house . . .

They favor him with *.100.* bushels of corn, & another *.100.* for Lieutenant George Pearcie, who follows behind to repeat the whole comedy. The famisht women do weep. The old matrons howl; they shew him their shrunken dugs, as if to say they have no milk for to feed their babes. Well, 'tis a tragedy, all right. Lieutenant Percy says that Irishwomen utter much the same noises when we put their rebel husbands to death. Sweet John pities them a little, but if he'd acted otherwise, his Colonists would have enkennel'd themselves in *Starvation's* grave. Corn-revenued, secure until the next onslaught of time or rats, Sweet John marches his troops back to the barge, *.1. and .2., .1. and .2.* The last he sees of those Salvages, they're a-wandering disconsolately into the woods, like unto straggling Tartars . . .

✳ ✳ ✳ ✳ ✳

Upon his return, Captaines Newport & Radclyffe, being his utter enemies, do hale him before a Tribunal of nonsensickall threapenings, to depose him for having illegally departed the Fort. His bitterness being already so deep, this new stroke adds little to it. He acquits himself, & that right scornfully. He cares not.

He sets Radclyffe & some other particularly hated Gentlemen to splitting firewood with beetle and wedge . . . Observing this, the commoner sort (who all hate Ratcliffe) do all send up to HEAVEN their *Hurrah.* Ratcliffe hastens to complain to Captaine Newport. Sweet John cares not.

Catching Kemps & Tassore in the commission of further misdemeanors, he confines 'em to the pinnace o'ernight, flogs 'em heartily, & expels 'em from the Fort. — They'll be back. Well, it's yet the Princely deed to do. Kemps doth howl when he's whipt— a marvelous affectation in a Salvage, for Sweet John's seen men silently endure far worse at Powhatan's hands. 'Tis our *mildness* which draws forth his musicke . . . . — & yet without him, or Tassore, Sweet John must depend on Pocahontas, who never comes here anymore.

Fearing to leave the Fort again in the midst of such broils, he dispatches Matthew Scrivener to Werowocomoco to trade. But Maister Scrivener gains but *.3.* or *.4.* hogsheads of corn, & comes back aghast with terror, for Powhatan hath menaced the lives of his Soldiers & Sailors. All's not well in Virginia. Sweet John, unmastered by necessity, finds each of his Government's choices to be as dark as an Yndian house.

✳ ✳ ✳ ✳ ✳

He sends Captaine Newport away to Gravesend — & good riddance. He commaunds Radcliffe off the Counsell & aboard the flagship. In a letter to their most worshipful Puppet-Masters he writes: *Captaine Ratliffe is now called Sicklemore, a poore counterfeited Imposture. I have sent you him home, least the company should cut his throat. What he is, now every one can tell you: if he and Archer return againe, they are sufficient to keepe us alwayes in factions.*

* * * * * *

The Counsell meets. 'Tis *his* Counsell again. The Counsell-men will vote his decree. Percy swears to keep the Gentlemen quiet. (O, but Pearcie's shiftier e'en than Nantoquod! He dreams in secret, waking with wandering eyes. Some unwholesomeness doth ail him . . .)

Matthew Scrivener confesses his past errors, after which he's reinstated within the President's heart. Reclaiming the bottle from Dr Russell, Sweet John pours out sack. He's e'er more *Politick* these days. O, & they love him for it! They toast *Our gallant President!*

All hands agree that famine lies ahead. They look helplessly to him.

* * * * * *

See John Smith at Nansemond, come to collect the **.400.** baskets of corn which those Salvages have promised him. 'Tis to no avail they now plead their own hunger & incapacity.

You cannot excuse yourselves for having spent most of what you had, he replies. And I know full well you were commaunded by Powhatan not to let us come into your river—

How know you that?

Why, *Pokauntiss* herself did confess it—

Have pity, Captaine Smith, or we starve.

You shewed no pity, when you sought to ambuscado me last summer. Do you disremember that?

Dear Captaine Smith, our women grow weak, & on us falls sickness.

Tush! Powhatan commaunds you to speak thus. Tell him to feed you & send sick-nurses, after I spoil your Towne.

O, he's a full hard man now, this Sweet John! He *will not* forbear his tithes. He doth bide as straight and stern as e'er he did when he'd been a boy, & sat all night beside his father's corpse. At his signal all Soldiers discharge their guns in unison, just as he'd taught 'em — straight into the air, for he disdains to slay such poor creatures. They screech like unto Hungarian *Vampires*. Then he strides to the nearest house & catches it ablaze.

The Nandsamunds give him all his request, down to the last cake of deer suet. At his coming & going they wail; they scritch their fingernails in the earth. They might as well be a school of sturgeons in the river, watching their fishermen with fix'd eyes. He feels himself now utterly translated unto success. Because he forbears to raze their Towne utterly, they swear by the SUNNE to plant corn specifically for the English.

Well laden, they sail down the snow-rimmed river near about .4. miles & sleep in the snow as Sweet John doth shew them. On their return, by virtue of his Adventuresomeness in **NAUIGATION** they do discover the Countrey of Apamatuck . . .

* * * * * *

Powhatan hath exterminated the Piankatanks, said Kemps.

I misdoubt me if that's worth as deep a grog-shot, dear boy. For (to tell you true) the novelty doth begin to stale.

Maister John, 'tis perilous for me, yet, as you see, I've sojourned back to you altho' you whipt me like the veriest dog—

Then drink. Where's Keale? One of you lusty lads, pour a dram for our pet Salvage . . .

And 'tis likewise perilous for you, Maister John. The Piankatanks dwelt *easterly.*

Which eastern Nations are left?

Only you & the subjects of the Laughing King—

Ha! laugh'd Sweet John. Ne'er mind us. But tell me, do ye pity these Piankatanks?

Nay, for I once filched a wife from that Countrey but she ran away . . .

* * * * * *

He sat himself down within the becreepered ruins of Radclyffe's Palace, & closed his eyes. The creepers themselves were dying, for 'twas cold. He struck a fire. (See him cooking corn in the shell of a turtle he'd caught last summer near Kecoughtan. O, how capitally some turtle stew would relish right now!) At last he'd discovered leisure for to get his fortune. Now what should he do? How best to speed the Colonie, 'twas clearer than that jewel call'd *Diamant,* which they say an eye can gaze through as easily as through air. The remedy: Get corn!

But his own case, now, how misty & how mystickall — how checkered yet!

He approach'd a crisis of the heart which to him remained sufficiently imperceptible to seem a niggling crisis of the mind. When the .4. French Gallants betrayed him on that long ago sea-night, his wench-chinn'd inno-cency got affronted to the point of eternal mistrust, altho' the sweet nature which nicknam'd him temporarily endured, persuading courtesy to clothe his suspicions. That courtesy lay now sepulchred, having been prick'd to death at last by his many humiliations, censures, battles, brawls, & condemnations to the gallows. Doubtless he imagined that he continued agreeable, & when it pleas'd him or somebody toucht his heart, why then, so he was (Pokahuntiss certainly thought him sweet). But the eager acquiescence of that yeoman lad who held horses for his betters was long decayed. At .1. time, Powhatan's declaration that Sweet John had become his son might have actually called forth the latter's deferential love. But what Bartty & Robert both laughingly referred to as *The Tragabigzanda affair* had convinced him that love should only be spent on .1.'s own kind. How ironical, that Sweet John's happy youthful ways had actually borne fruit with that silver-bangled Turkishe damsel! She'd trusted him (that much was clear); she'd presented her fondest hopes to him. And what were those? He remember'd signing his name to an unknown promise as he sat beside her 'neath those lamps of silvered glass. She'd desired him to become a famous Soldier or *Janissary* amongst her Countreymen, & simultaneously (as he supposed) to become a Muslim, in order to increase his own likelihood of Paradise; meanwhile she'd lain ready to proffer the Paradise of her love. The bitterness which she now must feel, both towards him & Christians generally, lay beyond description. But how could he have endured such a brother-in-law as the *Tymor?*   No doubt all mix'd marriages get strewn with perils & difficulties, which was why he'd never again consider joining himself to an unbelieving creature, such as Pocahontas.

When he estimated himself, the accompt prov'd passing base. But he was as he was, & so he would be. Perhaps he suffered from what by then they were all calling *the Jamestowne sickness.*

What if young Pocahantas did lust to take him for her husband? What if her Father pretended to be his? That subtle old Powhatan was the veriest *Tymor,* who, did Sweet John place himself in his power, would traduce or e'en murther him; so he could never accompt himself safe! (Not that his own Countreymen at James Towne were any less treacherous, but *their* plottings he could more easily comprehend in the o'erhearing.)

And so Sweet John lov'd not. Nor was he capable of trust.

He'd filched the harvest of Kecoughtan last autumn. He'd done the same with the Chickahominies for .2. years running. He'd clean'd out the Nandsamunds. Whom should he now fall upon? The King of Paspahegh, he who'd painted his countenance a devilish-black, & horn'd himself like unto BEELZEBUB, might prove a fitting victim. He was counterfeit-faced, JANUS-faced; he'd pretended to welcome yᵉ Colonie, yet essayed many an ambuscado. 'Twould be fitting to punish him by taking his corn. Yet he lay so near that he could easily do mischief. Sweet John had not yet become so unchristian as to massacre a Towne entire, which would have been the only way to guard the colony against that aforesaid *Wowinchop-unck's* revenge. Therefore, Paspahegh-Towne must be spared.

Then he thought upon Werowocomoco, where Powhatan's secret corn-treasuries did lie. Could he but take his Salvage *Father* by surprise, percase the gamble might be his.

His heart beat against it, but he pretended 'twas but his mind.

How'd he be advised by euerworthy *Machiavell?*

Of a sudden he did wonder whether Machiavell addressed him at all. What if that sage (whom we may as well name *Captaine Fortune)* had signed him on only as an honest Servaunt?

Sweet John whispered: *I'm a Prince, I'm a Prince,* & the fashion in which he whisper'd was like unto an incantation.

THE GRAMMAR OF WALNUTS (1608)

... with a lowd oration he proclaimed me a werowanes of Powhatan, and that all his subject should so esteeme us, and no man account us strangers nor Paspaheghans, but Powhatans, and that the Corne, weomen and Country, should be to us as to his owne people ...

CAPTAIN JOHN SMITH, *A True Relation of Such Occurrences and Accidents of Noate as Hath Hapned in Virginia* (1608)

*A*s for Wahunsenacawh, he who was call'd *Powhatan,* he had now made his own resolution concerning the Tasstasses. Uttamatomakkin was incorrect, for the Tassantasses could never be trusted. His Cronoccoes concurred with this. Every handful of days another Werowance sent a runner to complain of their threatening greed. Wahunsenacawh's decision came agreeably. He would crush them up, just as a woman crushes walnuts. She pounds them. She grinds them into coarse, honey-colored sand. Then she pounds them again. She grinds them again. Now they're but oily, sticky powder, a compacted paste of flesh. She dissolves them in water to make walnut milk. Then together the People drink them all down into nothingness.

The Conquest of Pamunkey
(1609–1610)

Smiths Forge mends all, makes chaines for *Savage* Nation, Frees, feeds the rest; the rest reade in his Bookes Relation.

Samuel Purchas, dedicatory verse

*S*ee little Sweet John, standing on the flour-barrel, mustering up his Soldiers on the frozen ground at *Smith-field*. 'Tis time to gather them new belly-timber, he shouts. Stand they ready? *Trarintra-rarara*. *.1. and .2.*, *.1. and .2.*

Some few greenhorns do seem afeared, so he jests: Whoe'er gets murthered by the Salvages, I'll share his pay with all the rest!

Then some do laugh, for nobody pays 'em. The remainder pull sour grimaces. Almost all are feeble like unto Beggars. They're stung & burn'd by frost. They hate Sweet John's guts.

Now, men, I do promise you, if you follow & obey me in e'erything, that we'll secure enough corn to feast upon, & mayhap some venison or suet. 'Tis for your own good weal that I lead you there. Moreover, Powhatan himself hath invited us . . .

But they glower at him. O'erpassing their wrath, he says: Dear Maister Hunt, prithee lead 'em in a little prayer . . .

✳ ✳ ✳ ✳ ✳ ✳

See John Smith in his accustomed *Discovery Barge,* which hath now long been outfitted with the shields of the Massawomeckes — his conquest-trophies from last summer. The armor-plates of his brigadine vest do glister in the icy sun. 'Tis *.4.* days after their cheerless Christmas-tide. Soon they'll all starve, can he not persuade Powhatan to chaffer with him on advantageous terms. 'Tis an evil season, to be sure. They're all red-leaved with bloody apprehensions. He hath half a dozen Soldiers on board at his commaund, amongst 'em *Todkill & Shortridge,* who did him such excellent service 'pon the *Bay of Chisapioc*. Beside 'em, half a dozen Gentlemen stand ready to battle — or at least to eat up Powhatan's vittles. Kemps (or

Light-fingers, as he's unlovingly call'd) will translate. Meanwhile, in the pinnace (Captained by William Phittiplace, & Generalled by Lieutenant George Pearcie) ride altogether **.15.** men, counting those **.2.** Commaunders. Sweet John's dispatched **.14.** more by land, ostensibly to build Powhatan the *Royall Residence* which that Monarch's requested.

More snow is coming. He's o'erseen the fraughting of the pinnace. He's laded the barge with a whole barrel of gunpowder, just in case. Matthew Scrivener will stay behind to be his Deputy. Reverend Hunt marshals everyone in another prayer. Sweet John runs back up the demi-culverin's Tower, to give the Sentry final admonishments. Halfway through the Forenoon Watch, they cast off. — *Flood oh!* cries Maister Shortridge like unto a rooster. For a twink, Sweet John's passing exultant. He's launch'd at last from the dreary dry-dock of James-towne. He remembers how Adventurous it was when he **.1.**st ran away to sea . . .

But Jamestowne's still in sight, & some Gentlemen are already muttering against him.

Hold faith! he shouts. Do ye promise?

They fall quiet. No matter. Don't they cry out day & night for his support? The whole Colonie's like unto an infant blaring for food!

✳ ✳ ✳ ✳ ✳

By now it had long since come to this, that whene'er Sweet John did sail to guest himself upon Salvages, he **.1.**^{stly} demanded child-hostages, then **.2.**^{ndly} took all bows, arrows & spears within sight, as well as the fur-cloaks in which other weapons might be hidden. Then whene'er they did refuse, he was forewarned of their villainy. (But there was **.1.** who came for whom he felt nothing but trustful tenderness. This was Powhatan's daughter, Powhatan's dearling.)

Being short of belly-timber, they passed a few nights among the Warraskoyacks, whose Werowance continued loyal. For the sake of courtesy Sweet John did therefore *hire* fullgrown hostages by way of guides. They march'd off in company with a stout Soldier of his, to seek survivors from the Lost Colony of Roanoke, so that on Captaine Newport's return to Jamesowne there'd be no complaints about the President's idleness. Moreover, he e'en left Samuel Collier his page to study the Yndian tongue. So all went passing merrily at Warraskoyack, & they ate up the King's provender without stint. Kemps promised to spy out his corn-pits, but fail'd . . .

Captaine Smith!

Aye, Shortridge, what tidings?

Belike he's an intelligencer for the Salvages!

Who? Kemps?

Yea, upon my faith! And he struts around as big as a bull beef—

So long as we have rum, he'll harm us not.

Just now he spoke insolently to me.

Well, he's ape-drunk. Ne'er mind him, lad. What else would ye?

We would fall upon these Salvages, for our security, &—

Restrain those passions! They deserve our love.

Sir, our raw-gall'd hunger will not heal. We fear for to starve—

I warn thee: *Outrage 'em not.*   We'll purchase belly-timber at Powhatan's, if there's any metal in my heart—

Another meal of venison! The King did throw a morsel into the fire, for a sacrifice to their DEVIL, call'd OKEUS. Then he utter'd a sort of grace, just as Powhatan always did. Sweet John thought 'twould not be hard to convert 'em unto goodness.

Trust Powhatan not, warn'd the King. Above all, grant him no opportunity to seize on your arms, for he hath sent for you only to cut your throats.

Sweet John thank'd him, thinking: If he denounces another Salvage to me, it could be his honesty, or it could be that he wishes but to embroil me with my subtle old *Father,* for his own 'vantage.

Both parties expressing their faithful love, Sweet John next embark'd his flotilla for Kecoughtan, where for near about a week they did feast on those Salvages' venison, oyster, fish, corn-bread, &c. Rounding Poynt Comfort, they did the same at Kiskiack, solely to take those Yndians down a peg. (In Yndians the very name of servitude will breed ill blood.) Some were wearing blue beads. How did they come to possess 'em? Did Powhatan hand 'em out? If so, then doubtless they were his spies. If not, then they must have obtain'd 'em through illegal chaffering with the Colonists, in which case they were equivalently insidious. No matter! Sweet John stood watch!

*   *   *   *   *   *

See John Smith at Werowocomoco. O, what cold & wicked darkness he's embark'd them all into again? Or, as a poetaster once wrote:

> What may move the mouse to bite the bait
> Which strikes the trap that stops her hungry breath?

All the Gentlemen do complain, excepting only Lieutenant Percie, who's so proud & pale & silent. Sweet John's barge shatters a channel thro' the river-ice as far as she may, then grounds 'pon freezing ooze. — Trim course now! Forbear on the broadside! Now hold water! Kedge anchor down! Shortridge, do you signal to the pinnace — good lad! Bend your cable — no, t'other way. Ready, boys? I wish I had a dram for all of you, but we'll seize our cheer at the Emperor's, never fear. Nay, forbear to frown at me in that fashion, you idlers! Would you rather starve at James-towne? Prepare yourselves! 'Twill be a marvel unto these Yndians, for they e'er sneer that we're afeared to bathe! Behind me, now! — And he leaps unto his waist in the nearest ice-hole, with his gun & sword held high. — Look sharp! No slacking, lads! — He marches 'em right through that black water & muck. He's a Prince; all must follow 'pon his heels. They murmur against his fantastickall ambitions. — *Maister John Russell, Gent.,* being passing fat & weak, doth almost give up the ghost, but Sweet John brings him round with a dram & some slaps betwixt the shoulder-blades. Now they all stand there disconsolate upon the bank (excepting only the lucky remnant, whom he's assigned to be Guardsmen for the barge & the Pinnace). 'Tis hellish cold! Their trousers hang black with frozen mire. Laughing full sportively (all the while pitying the misery now iced upon their faces), Sweet John leads 'em through a brittle confusion of sticks & leaves beneath the snow, until they arrive at the palisadoes, where all's silent, as if the Yndians mis-like their coming.

Sweet John knaps upon a paling. He doth shout: *Kekaten Pokahontas patiaquagh niugh tanks manotyens neer mowchik rawrenock audowgh!*

In silence, a squadron of grim tall Salvages comes onstage. Doubtless they've prepared all for their Emperor's advantage. Could it be that Powhatan seeks to juggle him down to death? No matter — at his leisure, Sweet John can beat them all right out of Virginia! His Soldiers stand with ready-barreled harquebuses. Their burning matches glow yellow in the shivery darkness. The Salvages do well perceive these marks of his suspi-ciousness. So they glower at him, & he slams his hands unto his hips & glow-ers back. In them he perceives a certain greatness. Could he but fuse them unto his own troops, think what conquests he might undertake! He'd con-quer the Monacans in a twink, & then — well, 'tis not the time to dream too precisely. — *Netoppew,* he shouts. This signifies: *Friends.* — The Sal-vages make mouths at him. Then they escort his army to some abandoned crofts of theirs which lie without. These houses are fireless within, which among Salvages signifies ill fortune. Frowning, Sweet John commaunds his minions to gather wood, strikes a spark with his tinder-box, & soon has the hearth a-blazing in each of their lodgings. His men commence for to smile. They strip off their trousers & hang 'em o'er the fire to smoke & drip & stink. Meanwhile, the Salvages stand tall & silent without, with their arms folded o'er their hearts. Sweet John thinks to himself: 'Pon my faith, they do resemble Lieutenant Percie in his pride! — And he laughs, telling none the reason.

To their hosts he cries: *Mowchick wayawgh tawgh noeragh kaquere mecher,* which means in good English: I'm passing hungry. What shall I eat?

Wait, replies a Salvage. And presently some Serving-maids do come (but dourly) to bring them roast turkeys, venison & bread, for which they're all thankful unto GOD. The Salvages depart. While Sweet John eats of the vittles, he sits o'erwatching how his men fall to. That terrible, silent hunger of theirs would drive 'em to anything. They plunge their faces into the meat, collecting gobbet-taxes with their teeth. They're desperate.

Pocahontas comes not. Hath her father denied her the privilege for his own reasons, or hath her affection now staled into misliking? This thought near about panics him. Without her merrily flittering presence, her relations will succor him no longer. How can he disremember that chopping-stone onto which they'd forced his head last winter in this very Towne? Verily, he considers their solitary guesting to be a token. Just as winter's wind may be foretold in a twinkle of stars, so Pokahuntiss's absence doth proclaim some proximate evil.

'Tis already near the end of the .1.ˢᵗ Dog-Watch. Sweet John appoints Sentries in all the houses, then retires. Long after midnight he opens his eyes to find his house's Sentry adoze. For a jest, he annoints the back of the man's neck with snow. The Sentry starts. He screams. E'ery man starts up with weapon in hand. Sweet John smiles kindly. He admonishes 'em all on the needfulness of vigilance. Then they all sleep again.

He opens an eye. The Sentry sits awake and sullen.

At dawn they hear the Salvages at their idolatry in the river, with chauntings & breaking ice a-ringing most strangely in the icy air. They wait. Some men are too affrighted e'en to piss, until Sweet John leads them out. They hear an ancient, froggish voice a-croaking: *Bowh, waugh.* Sweet John explains 'tis Powhatan. Some would seize that Salvage then, but Sweet John reminds 'em that the Counsell hath nay-voiced all such Adventures: They must supplicate before they may attack.

They see smoke. Now Sweet John's compelled to assure his troops that these Salvages will not carbanado them for breakfast.

Back inside, then, to sit around the embers. He sends Lieutenant Percy with .4. Soldiers to fetch firewood. This being accomplisht, they wait again, until the weak white Sunne's climbed full into the sky.

At last several Bow-men appear unto them: Powhatan sends summons unto his Palace. — Ne'er fear, lads! cries Sweet John full lovingly. But bide ready for my commaund . . .

They enter unto the snowy Towne, & between .2. mulberry-trees they spy the scalps of the exterminated Piankatanks all stretched out on a cord, for a publicke *Triumph:* Kemps spoke true. Each black scalp hath its little white crown of snow. Not wishing to affright the Gentlemen, Sweet John says nothing, but the Solders commence for to blare & shout, so that all's reveal'd. Again he commaunds 'em to hearten themselves.

Into the Palace they file, winding through mat-hung recesses as they're bid. The Salvages gesture them down. Soon they're breakfast-feasting on mats 'twixt the smoky fires. The Queen of Appatamuck is not on hand for to dry Sweet John's hands with turkey-wings anymore. Pocahontas continues absent. — And where's the Emperor? — Why, in the rearmost nook, as usual, surrounded by Masquers of sundry sorts . . . If this long House of his were a ship, he'd be a-lurking in the rung-heads! His mind being refresh'd with these irrelevancies, Sweet John smiles inattentatively upon the fervent orations of the Ancient Salvages who always greet strangers on such occasions — for Powhatan's inattentive, too! Powhatan, splendid in his deerskin mantle pattern'd with *Roanoke*-shells, gazes sourly above the smoke. Powhatan's rigid. Powhatan mislikes him. Powhatan, sitting between red-painted wives high on his bunkstead, offers a *Tobacco* pipe in silence. No more doth he name Sweet John his *Son.* Therefore, Sweet John forbears to call him *Father.*

Still you fail of your promises, says this Emperor then. Where are the great guns which you did vow to give me?

Why, come to Jamestowne, great Powhatan, & you're welcome to hale 'em away 'pon your own shoulders—

This time the old Salvage grins not at the jest. Coldly he doth inquire: When would you be gone? I have scant corn in my Treasury, & my subjects keep e'en less. I did not send for you . . .

Powhatan, how chanced it that you grew so forgetful? Look! There's your man who did send us your invitation—

Now Powhatan laughs full merrily, & one of his loveliest Concubines, by name *Ortoughnoiske,* doth fan him with a turkey-wing while Sweet John gazes watchfully on.

You came for corn, he says then. Why else would you enter here at this season?

Aye, 'tis for that we trouble you, & also to inform you that the Chickahominies & the Nandsamunds did deny to render up what they'd promised, so we—

About these matters I stand well informed.

O, & did their insolent Courtiers come to you with tales, or did *Wowinchopunck of Paspahegh* come perchance a-tattling?

'Tis not for you, Captaine Smith, to inquire into these matters. Nor have you shewn befitting respect for me.

Powhatan, I would tell you—

For .40. swords you may take .40. baskets. I have spoken.

Forty baskets, eh? With or without corn inside 'em? Either way, methinks, that chaffer's somewhat niggling to my taste—

Powhatan smiles not. Neither do Sweet John's Soldiers, who hunker there on the mats, devouring cornbread with .1. hand, gun or sword in the other.

Drawing himself upright, Sweet John doth say: Powhatan, altho' I had many courses to have made my provision, yet believing your promises to supply my wants, I neglected all to satisfy your desire. I have crowned you, sent you Dutchmen for to build you a house, gifted you with sky-hued beads . . .

While this gets translated, he watches Powhatan's face. Doth that sly old Salvage make any untoward signal, why then, he'll blow out his brains, & fire Werowocomoco!

What your subjects had, you engross'd, he continues, forbidding 'em to trade with us. Now you think that by consuming the time, we shall consume for want. As for swords & guns, I told you long ago that I had none to spare. *You must know that those I have can keep me from want,* he adds with a threatening look, which he's full sure Powhatan apprehends.

Yet steal or wrong you I will not, Powhatan, nor dissolve that friendship which we have mutually promised — *except you constrain me by your bad usage.*

Powhatan smiles coldly down at him & his ready Soldiers. He says: Some doubt I have your coming hither, that makes me not so kindly seek to relieve you as I would.

✻　✻　✻　✻　✻　✻

Reader, can we say here *'Twas the moment?* — Nay, for disremember not that other moment when Pocahontas sav'd Sweet John's life, & the moment

ere that when Captaines Amadas & Barlowe marcht forth from Roanoke
Fort to burn a Salvage Towne for the sake of a missing silver cup. Or if we
but peep into futurity, we'll soon discover a moment alter'd by euerworthy
Argall, which will wrest all tides unto subjection — & then on **.2.** yet more
future occasions, Powhatan's brother *Opechancanough* will change Virginia according to his own strategems.

So there is no moment. Inevitability's a fiction.

Yet after all this I still must say: *'Twas the moment.*

* * * * * *

In the end (denying to lay down their weapons on Powhatan's request), they
do by way of jesting, coaxing, explicating & threatening gain from that subtle old Salvage **.10.** quarters of corn for a copper kettle. But Powhatan continually harp'd upon *This bruit from Nansamund, that you are here to
destroy my Countrey.* 'Twas scantly pleasant for Sweet John to be twitted
with that. Thank th'ALMIGHTIE Captaine Newport wasn't here! Had
he been, Sweet John's enemies would have won further proof of his supposed *cruelty* to these Yndians — a cruelty without which the Colonie
would utterly starve! Seeking now to reassure the grimacing Emperor,
Sweet John said: For your sake only, we have curb'd our thirsting desire of
revenge 'gainst those of your subjects who've violated your sworn promise
of friendship. Had we not thus forbearingly demean'd ourselves, they
would have known the cruelty we use to our enemies, as well as they already know the true love & courtesy to our friends . . .

* * * * * *

Now the winter darkness begins a-creeping back down, & Powhatan sighs:
Captaine Smith, I never use any Werowance so kindly as yourself, yet from
you I receive the least kindness of any . . . — Sweet John smiles & shrugs.
In truth he's paying scant heed. To Maister Jeffrey Shortridge he murmurs:
This Salvage doth but trifle the time, until he can cut our throats. Tell
Maister Todkill to pretend a physical necessity. Then let him sneak quickly
to the boats, to get more men, should we be surpris'd . . .

To the Emperor he says aloud (intending not a syllable of it): Powhatan,
to content you, *tomorrow* I'll lay down my weapons & trust to your
promise.

Todkill hath now slipt out. Powhatan starts horribly in alarm, just as he
did when he was crown'd. He utters a word in the ear of his nearmost wife.
She, pretending for to laugh (but Sweet John marks her unease), whispers

to the Salvage beside her, & so the ripple of Powhatan's intent doth not speedily carry down both sides of his long reed-wall'd Palace. Presently some Yndians commence for to steal away. Just as an incoming tide slyly conquers the coastal rocks with the most tentative or sportive-seemed lickings & foamings, rolling forwards & back, so that 'tis imperceptible how much ground hath already been seized, thus these onswells of ominous absence occur not all at once — nay, their hosts & hostesses bustle as if to prepare another banquet-course; new Yndians appear, old ones vanish — & 'tis the especial errand of the lassies to distrain Sweet John's men from perceiving how the others withdraw. But Sweet John marks it, all right. He's not a-going to get fooled! His heart flies up his throat; soon there'll be another throw of the game call'd *Gambler's chance!* Where's Captaine Fortune now? Percase he's inside the pages of *Machiavell,* whose wisdom Sweet John essays to remember. When should he cock the match of his gun? The smolder will give him away . . . — Oho, now Powhatan himself hath fled, & our 'Venturers grow unnerv'd, no matter the damsels shewing their red-puccooned teats, who flirt near desperately in Sweet John's ear . . . 'Tis dark & cold. They're lost, given over to doom. Jamestowne's far away, the boats remain half-frozen in the ice, & e'en could they reach their Colonie, what could welcome 'em but more cold, more hunger?

Shoving the sluts away, he leaps up, shouting: Strike your matches, lads! Behind me, now! Don't fear Powhatan, for he knows not a **B** from a bull's foot. Aim sideways & low when you come out! If the man ahead aims left, do you aim right. *Vice versa* goes. I'll aim right. Ready? On my mark!

And they're a-running now, *Come back, come back, come back.* Sweet John down flings himself, permitting the low Palace door to give birth unto his bearded, bright-eyed head. Discovering a crowd of Salvages with rais'd war-clubs, he outhrusts his arm, firing his .1.st shot rightwards as he promised. The screaming Salvages do take to their heels. — All well, men! he cries. — He gives their foes another twink of time for to flee, then crawls warily into the icy ooze. The night lies silent.

Come on now, lads! he shouts. Don't shoot!

They form up behind him, as submissive as children. At his signal, all quick-march unambuscado'd thro' the palisadoes, back to where they'd stayed the previous night. This time he gathers 'em in a single croft, to better play *Security.* The barge & pinnace remaining ice-mired, there's no sense in hieing themselves back out there; for they'll be helpless in the ooze should Powhatan's Bow-men seek to pick them off from the darkness. Moreover, Maister Todkill (if he got away) will be returning soon, with men

& weapons. Again they kindle a fire. They crouch there in a stinking huddle, beset by each other's panting breaths.

After a long, long time, an ancient old Salvage doth come creeping, with
a bracelet & a chain of pearls in token of the peace. He sighs: Captaine
Smith, our Werowance is fled, fearing your guns—

Indeed! The old scoundrel!

. . . And knowing you'd summons more men, sent these numbers outside his Palace but to guard his corne from stealing—

Chamber-lees! cries Sweet John in contempt, & all his Bravos howl be-
mirthed.

Now here come an army of Powhatan's Bow-men, ready for to guard the
Englishmens' weapons, whilst the corn's carried to the pinnace.

'Tis a pretty notion, lads, says Sweet John, but I believe we'll take it
th'opposite way round. Men, cock your matches!

The Salvages turn pale for fright.

Now, you Yndians there! Upon *your* backs be this corn-burthen, &
ne'er fear, we'll guard your bows for you — hah!

And so it haps, for Sweet John doth e'er get his way.

* * * * * *

Now they must dacker down to wait upon *Flood oh!* to 'scape safe in the
boats. So they withdraw themselves into their improvised Corps de Guard,
whilst they & the Salvages do mutually pretend friendliness.

The night chills colder & colder. The Salvages do go away, to hie 'emselves back within their palisadoes to sleep 'midst their women & children.

Sweet John sings his men a ditty, to wit:

> I am as I am and so I will be
> But how that I am none knoweth truly.
> Be it evil, be it well, be I bound, be I free,
> I am as I am and so will I be.

There comes a knapping on the door.

* * * * * *

Pocahontas, my sweet chuck! Let her through, boys! And what a fine
mantle you're all busked up in. Now I *know* 'tis cold, when you cover your
pretty little bum—

She gestured him to silence. Indeed, she did appear passing mournful.

Nearly weeping (as he thought), she strok'd his breast. The Soldiers commenc'd their hateful taunts.

They'll bring you cheer by & by . . . she began.

What are you chittering about like that, girl?

My father & all the power he can make will afterward fall upon you all, to—

Now she burst full into sobs, while his men did marvel. Caring not for their scorn, he embrac'd her — no matter that this was hardly so safe and intimate a meeting place as some crypt-chapel. He fed her upon many candied words, until she smil'd through her tears. Then, essaying for to cheer her further, he said in her language: *Love you not me?*

Father, if you would live I'd wish you presently to be gone—

Thank you for your love, my dearling. Well, no doubt I'll find means to congratulate your other father's courtesy. Bentley, gift her with a handful of bells—

Nay, *Father,* I dare not. Should he see me with anything, I'll be slain by fire—

Before he could kiss her again, she'd fled away into the snow, wiping her eyes.

* * * * * *

Years later, considerably after her death, when he thought upon that secret meeting of theirs (indeed, 'twas the .2.nd to last time he'd e'er glimpsed her), there came into his heart's vision a memory from his *Voyages of Discoverie* — namely, a certain *Raccoon* humping its back (perhaps near Pattawomeck), lumbering almost like unto a fabled *Armadillo,* then suddenly hearing Sweet John, turning & flashing its strange masked face. *Her* face had somehow resembled this.

* * * * * *

And so, thanks to their *Nonpareil's* warning, they stand most threateningly 'pon their guard when the Salvage Footmen come to lay down trenchers of well-beseeming vittles. Pleading that the smoke from so many gun-matches doth quease their stomachs, they plead to have 'em snuff'd out. At this, Sweet John grows yet more belligerent. He makes 'em taste each dish, meanwhile berating Powhatan's villainy. So they await high water & dawn. As soon as the Sunne doth rise, 'tis to the boats they go, with they & the Salvages mutually swearing eternal friendship . . .

* * * * *

Now see John Smith sailing full gaily with his fleet of *.2.* ships up *Pa-munkey his Riuer,* meaning not only to get what corn he can, but also to un-hinge Opechancanough's attachment to his brother, & attach him to himself through baubles & favors. Thus doth divine Machiavelli advise. Misfortu-nately, Sweet John owns not riches enough to securely sway that old Salvage who's already King, & moreover heir to his brother's Empire. Sweet John's Soldiers & Gentlemen fall already a-clamoring for to feast 'pon venison & woman-flesh again. — Dacker down! he cries testily. Your sundry greeds do cap my arse! — With these parasites riding on him, how may he hope to present himself as a Prince in need of nothing? Well, the thing cannot be helped, so he'll Adventure anyway. (Thus our plucky little Sweet John, who's never desisted from any scheme for mere lack of armaments or readi-ness.)

And so they drew near Menapacunt-Towne, upon whose strand a crowd of great grim Salvages did gather to lour at him. 'Twas late in the After-noon Watch. He whispered: *Powder in your flash-pans, lads!* Then he prayed in silence. Virginia was turning more sinister week by week, he knew not why. But (studied Soldier as he was) he thought yet to master her. Leaping ashore, he gazed up into the face of the giantest Salvage and sang out: *Spaughtynere keragh werowance opechancanough kekaten wawgh peyaquaugh,* which signifies, *Run you then to the King Opechancanough & bid him come hither.*

A Salvage replied: Opechancanough is a great Werowance. He goeth not hither & thither at your bidding.

Sweet John stroked his beard, laughing at this insolency. (*Wowinchop-unck, Opechancanough, Powhatan, Nantoquod* — he misliked 'em all.) Now his Soldiers had all formed a line behind him with their guns leveled at the Salvages' hearts.

A Salvage came & said: Opechancanough awaits you in his Palace.

Ready, my lusty lads? Behind me, now! Look sharp! Guns at half-cock! Here we go, *.1. and .2., .1. and .2.*

So they marched, yea, they slackly, slouchingly marched, their bellies rumbling with the winter-flux. They marched right into the Towne, whose people chaunted out their customary song of greeting, but this time it seemed to him that several lurked back, whilst others forbore to smile upon him. Surely 'twas not as it had been in olden days, when all Salvages had flock'd round joyfully, dancing, feasting the English on strawberries. But, after all, their new hostility was but to be expected, for the sovereignty of the Countrey was passing from them.

Smiling most pleasantly, Sweet John touched his heart, & said: *Maw-chick chammay,* which means, *The best of friends.*

The Salvages were silent. Many wore coppers in their ears.

His eyes picked out some robust, likely looking lads from the crowd. When he upraised his finger, the Soldiers swung their guns upon them.

Ningh Marowanchesso, he commaunded, meaning (altho' mayhap his grammar was none of the best), *.2. boys.*

The children stalked defiantly forward. He chose a pair who might have been Opechancanough's sons, & offered 'em copper beads to stay with him, but they hurled his presents to the ground.

Maskapow! a child shouted. This signified, *The worst of the enemies.*

As you like, said Sweet John, but I'll keep you just the same. Todkill, take 'em to the pinnace & guard 'em.

Next he did sing out the Yndian words for *arrows, bows, targets, spears* & the like, until all Salvages in sight had been utterly disarmed. He detailed .4. more Soldiers to stand sentry o'er the heap of weapons. Then with his remaining followers he did enter Opechancanough's Palace, where they feasted near about .3. days. Came *Tobacco,* a dance, puccoon-painted wenchen—

(Say, Maister President, shall I call Dr Russell for to poison the King?

(Nay, his smile already reeks poison. Best we bear him, till the Colonie grows in strength.

(Now see! He comes back again!

('Tis his nature, Keale. He ever comes and goes, like the needle on that compass dial I did give him to save my life. So I say he intends secret mischief—)

Captaine Smith, said Opechancanough, I must again express my pleasure in seeing you back again into our Countrey. And do you continue in fear of me? For I remember well that last year your *Father* Captaine Newport denied to sleep in my lodge.

What does he say, Kemps?

He inquires whether you fear him, Maister John. Jealously he harps on your disdain—

Bid him know I've never met the man I fear. And should he move my heart to wrath with his taunts, why, then, I'll become dangerous.

Maister John, I warn you he's proud, and strange—

Captaine Smith, last winter you promised me that your Tassantasses would soon depart our Countrey forever. I speak from my heart; I see your people ever mistrustful; Powhatan bids me speak to you so, for it scarcely becomes his greatness to disturb himself with such questions . . .

Kemps, tell him nothing.

On the day which they'd agreed upon for trade, they came again to the doorway of Opechancanough's Palace, but this time all the other houses were abanon'd, almost as if the Salvages misliked yᵉ English. Sweet John strove to keep his cheer-sails up.

A lame old man gestured them to enter the Palace, & so they did. 'Twas passing smoky within, but not drafty, for like his kinsfolk of this Salvage Nobility, Opechancanough had rich means to commaund that his house be builded of chestnut bark, which hath prov'd to be an armor superior to the *Marsh reeds* employed by the poor Yndian rabble. But in either case, 'twould be an easy, nay, mechanickall action to burn down any hive of these Natives . . . Opechancanough, the aforesaid *King of Pamunkey,* did presently appear, a-sporting a rattlesnake's tail in his hair. His legs were striped with tattoos not unlike unto the outlines of a Gentleman's garters. Sweet John had half-expected him to be wearing round his neck the Compass which fear had constrain'd him to give last winter, being as it seem'd in imminent peril of murther by those Salvages. But perhaps the marvel wore off, or Opechancanough re-gifted that jewel to a nephew, brother or wife . . .

Sweet John bowed, saying: *Your most humble Servaunt.*

They smoked *Tobacco.* But Opechancanough demeaned himself fish-expressionless towards yᵉ English.

Now here came the Pamunkey Salvages at last, passing sour-faced, bearing bows & arrows, & all their corn's o'erpriced.

The Soldiers do gaze upon 'em like unto ferocious bears, awaiting word to shoot 'em all down to death.

Sweet John forms a smile on his face. (To him, as I've said, his own smile's still sweet.)

Opechancanough, says he, the great love you bear with your tongue seems mere deceit by your actions. Last year you kindly fraughted my ship; but you've now invited me to starve with hunger.

O, but I invited you not here to my Countrey, rejoined Opechancanough, passing wittily.

Sweet John fix'd him in his gaze. He said slowly: You know my want, & I your plenty, *of which by some means I must have part.*

With a sinister smile, Opechancanough did say: I'm not amaz'd that you would require this of us. For 'tis plain, *dear brother,* that you Tassantasses cannot supply your own wants.

Did we desire to supply ourselves now at your expense, I assure you we could effect it. Now, King Apachankeno, will you chaffer with us or no?

At this forthright invitation, the King (in whose countenance he seem'd to discover something base & imperfect) did agree to the bargain, & so that day he rendered up his corn at whatever trifling prices Sweet John cared to set.

Now I thank you for your affection, said Sweet John, & tomorrow I would return to trade again.

Gnashing his teeth, Opechancanough said: I know not why you disbelieve me, when I tell you that we ourselves will suffer hardship, should we empty any more of our corn-pits. 'Twas but an indifferent harvest . . .

Still, you must agree to accept our commodities in exchange for corn, should you wish to remain our friends.

So 'twas agreed; but the next day, when they came again unto the Palace, Sweet John had just settled himself down for to chaffer a great basket of corn 'gainst a tiny bell, when portly Maister Russell whispered in his ear: Maister President, we're betrayed, for when I crept out for to piss I did spy many Bow-men & Club-men a-creeping round this house—

How many?

Near about .6. or .700. as I best reckon. But I can't rightly tell, for they gather as thick as a rack of autumn clouds—

Keep heart. They may think to ambuscado us, but I'll compel 'em to unroll their mats for us to sit upon, as do the Turkes their carpets.

And yet the *twinking fear* bloomed in Sweet John's chest: Doth Opechancanough truly own .700. Soldiers? Well, percase some might be Powhatan's. No matter. Powhatan surely wants us dead. As for this Opechancanough, he too would run us utterly out of Virginia if he could . . .

Recollecting that cold night a year ago when Opechancanough's hunters had captur'd him in the ooze, he envisioned full well how they'd lashed him tightly to a maple-tree, to shoot him full of arrows. Nor would he e'er disremember how the King had smil'd in hate. Of a sudden he knew uncannily that Opechancanough was more subtle & redoubtable than Powhatan himself. Sweet John *dreaded* him. Moreover, he loathed what he feared.

Shooting a glance at the King, he saw him turn pale, like unto a guilty murtherer. *Guilty, guilty,* he thought almost happily. Nudging Maister Todkill, he gestured as if he were about to cock his match. Todkill comprehended, looking hastily round. The men commenced for to hark. Sweet John slowly nodded at 'em .1. & all.

Opechancanough would soothe 'em poisonously, but Sweet John rises up, turning his back 'pon that evil King whose scalp-lock glisters blue-black in the fire-darkness, & says with a laugh: Worthy Countrey-men, I could wish good *Radclyffe, Wingfield & Newport*   here, who make these Salvages seem saints, & me an oppressor!

The men swallow air, terrified & ready for a fight. 'Tis politique of him to affect them so.

As for their fury, he continues, 'tis the least danger. And their arrow-points are dull bones; we could ride bare-assed to London-Towne on 'em. Yet howsoe'er they may shoot, let us fight like men, & not die like sheep. Do you promise to be valiant?

Aye, aye, Captaine Smith!

Good lads! — Now, Apachenkano, I see your plot to murther me, but fear it not. I propose a duel on yonder isle, you against me, the Conqueror to take all. Ha! For I'm not afeared! I did once harvest .III. Turkes' heads in a similar case—

Nay, dear *Brother,* I desire only to be your friend, in token of which a great present lies without the door for you alone to receive—

As your dearer brother the Emperor would say, *neither will I bite at such a bait.* Maister Dod, be a good Soldier & discover what kind of deceit this may be. Off with you now!

Captaine Smith, I . . . I'm full afeared—

Now I'm vexed at you, coward. Lieutenant Pearcie!

I'm ready, Sir, & I fancy you'll find no occasion to name me *Coward.*

How I wish we'd fought together in Transylvania! Nay, good Percy, do you, Maister West & the others but hold the house. I'll see to this. Cock your matches, lads! Maister Powell!

Aye, Captaine Smith!

Do you & Maister Behethland guard the door.

'Tis secured!

Excellent! cried Sweet John, flooded with joy. He swarm'd up to Opechancanough, & before that wondering King could divine his intent, he snatch'd him by his scalp-lock, e'en as he press'd a pistol 'gainst his heart! How astounded now grew the Salvage Courtiers! As for Opechancanough, he trembl'd, either with fear or shame . . .

Was this the moment then? That tall, twice-subtle Weronance, now vio-lated forever before his merest subjects, led to & fro like a dog, shame-faced, yes, panicked, ruined in his glory, his heart now fill'd with the bitterest ooze, must live, & live, & somehow warp his way, dimensionless. Sweet John's gamepiece, yet King, a humbled spirit in a Countrey of unhumble men whose vicarious insult in his bad usage could never absolve him out of his own swamp — no matter either that he'd led Sweet John in nearly that fashion last year because none but aliens witnessed that captive's bondage — Opechancanough now must bide forever within his own shell-simulacrum, hiding there, indenting himself, vanishing footprint in his own obscure soul, until he could come out in an ambuscado. To him this was more than *Politick*.

And Sweet John knew it.

＊ ＊ ＊ ＊ ＊

Now see John Smith a-chaffering at ease 'mongst these tigerish Salvages, parading their Werowance e'erywhere, so that they do disarm. Opechancanough hath already yielded up his vambrace, bow & arrows.

The Soldiers complain that corn's but poor tack for hungry men. They would have meat. So be it. He constrains the King to summons a venison-haunch or .2. for them to fraught within the pinnace. After that, it's *Hurrah for Captaine Smith!*   Sweet John knows they'll be cursing him again within the hour—

Upon Sweet John our trusty Opechancanough now bestows many presents, altho' to be sure, he does so making a mouth of sadness. Sweet John engrosses all the corn he desires. 'Tis like unto a fairytale! To the Yndians he saith: The cause I have forborne your insolencies, is the promise I made you to be your friend, till you give me just cause to be your enemy. You promised to fraught my ship ere I departed, & so you shall, or I meane to load her with your dead carcasses . . .

In comes corn & corn, until at last Sweet John & his own Courtiers would sleep. They post a light guard, keeping Opechancanough by them to be their hostage. Presently the walls do shake, as Pamunkey Club-men commence a-creeping in. Leaping up, he charges 'em, & they flee. Opechancanough makes feeble excuses, after which they continue friends . . .

＊ ＊ ＊ ＊ ＊

Hearing a noise, he whirl'd. But 'twas merely some old Salvage, muttering monstrous Greekishly . . .

＊ ＊ ＊ ＊ ＊

See John Smith a-sailing back down the river for Werowocomoco, a-hoping for to get more corn out of Powhatan. 'Tis a fine cold day, with the sky prickled about by those tiny clouds call'd *Hen-scratchings*. Who spies on him from the snowy banks? He cares not. He's thinking how fine 'twould be to tickle little Pocahontas's lips with his beard, & possibly persuade her away with him to James-towne, where she could do him good services. With her beside him, e'en the Paspaheghs must be affrighted into rendering up all their corn!

But hark! What's this? Painted Salvages line the river, with baskets of meat, suet & corn! (A Bow-man holds up .2. wildcat-skins.) 'Tis but dawn, but they've been a-waiting. No doubt 'tis some snare, but he'll try the chance. Why not envarnish his victories with more belly-revenue? He's proud & perfect now, a Prince. As for the Gentlemen, they're gleeful for to see so many puccoon'd damsels a-straddling & shewing 'emselves forth, with their little painted baskets. E'en the grim & bloody Soldiers are grinning. — Here's a taste of snap for you all! cries Sweet John. — Aye, aye, Maister President!

Now they're scritching at the earth & wailing welcome as is their habit. They rise. They outstretch their arms. Altho' no doubt they meditate some murtherous imposture, still Sweet John finds 'em a brave sight. He smiles generously, forbearing to fire upon them until their evil be prov'd.

He comes rapidly ashore with Percy, West & Russell. The Soldiers hide on the barge, behind the Massowomeck shields. This will be good Adventure. Sweet John would fain shout for joy.

'Tis like unto trusting the DEVIL! whispers Captaine West.

O, but we'll not trust 'em, lad, so don't talk posh. Anyhow, there's no such dangerous service ashore, as a resolved resolute fight at sea. Be not afeared—

I'm not afeared!

Then stand to your weapon, Captaine West. Forward!

Pretending to be utterly at his ease, but listening e'er (for he kens well the disposition of Salvages), he presently hears a man say: *Vdafemeodaan,* which means, *Go softly.* Knowing they prepare some new treachery, he stealthily doth hand his weapon.

In a shady ravine whose side is cold mossy granite, red leaves hang dead from maples like unto scalps. He dispatches Lieutenant Pearcie there, out of sight of the Yndians. Nothing could be more good or easy than this! Now here comes Opechancanough with some **.300.** Bow-men. When the

women commence to flitter away, & the men to surround him, he waves to
Maister Percy, at whose secret signal the Soldiers shew themselves & their
smoking, match-cocked guns. The Salvages run away screeching (being
not so valorous as the Turkes); next day Opechancanough envoys him a
pleading chain of pearls.

✳ ✳ ✳ ✳ ✳ ✳

See Opechancanough's subjects, fraughting more corn aboard the pinnace
for Sweet John, altho' 'tis full snowy & cold this season. A hungry-looking,
half-naked old beezum, her dugs as coarse-pored as the sand-hills above
Menapacunt, doth stand spread-armed for to curse him. She's no matter —
& no matter that some food proves poison'd! Sweet John & his men do spew
up the venom with no hurt. The poisoner confesses himself. Scorning to
grant him e'en the credit of due punishment, Sweet John kicks his face,
whilst the Soldiers applaud laughing. But to keep the peace thus endangered by that Yndian treachery, Sweet John demands more corn & more
corn . . .

✳ ✳ ✳ ✳ ✳ ✳

Master Machiavelli saith, howbeit, that *they are Enemies who, whilst
beaten on their own ground, are yet able to do hurte.* For which cause, he
did now commaund his men to retire posthaste from Pamunkey. His boats
were halfway fraughted with corn, so that complaining Gentlemen nipped
at him no longer. He was absolute. And so the English & the Salvages did
part, both sides swearing oaths to continue great friends as they had done
before.

✳ ✳ ✳ ✳ ✳ ✳

See him in the Countrey of Youghtanund. See him in the Countrey of Mattapanient. And his success in both of those Kingdomes I can best testify
from the *Generall Historie* itself: *The people imparted that little they had
with such complaints & teares from the eyes of women and children, as he
would have been too cruell to have been a Christian, that would not have
beene satisfied and moved with compassion.*

✳ ✳ ✳ ✳ ✳ ✳

Back now to Werowocomoco, whence Powhatan's sure to have return'd,
for that ancient Salvage would hardly flee his home's comforts. Just as a

good Pirate will never burn or sink his prey, unless he can .1.ˢᵗ snatch the treasure out, so Sweet John means to coax more corn from that Emperor's secret corn-pits, rather than setting all ablaze. He'll make his politest leg. *Your obedient Servaunt,* he'll say.

But Powhatan's not there. Powhatan will never be there again.

THE GRAMMAR OF OCEANS (1609)

False Love, Desire, and Beauty Frail, adieu —
Dead is the root whence all these fancies grew.
SIR WALTER RALEGH, "A Farewell to False Love" (1588)

$\mathcal{T}$he bleached blue sea, almost swell-less, brought Argall between rocks besieged by subtle ripples. His sails wilted, Argoll sang in a fine soft voice:

Red sky at night, Sailor's delight.
Red sky at morning, Sailor's warning.

He took an hour and divided it into **.5.** parts. The **.5.**th part he put away in representation of the alteration of **.24.** hours. The other **.4.** parts made **.48.** minutes. (Now, a flood tide and an ebb tide do alter **.24.** minutes forwards.) Knowing the Moone to be **.8.** days old, Argull calculated the flow of the tides by putting forward **.8.** hours each of which lived but **.48.** minutes long, and so he discovered that the tide would come **.6.** hours and **.24.** minutes after the tide-time at the new moon, which he knew to have been at half past **.1.** of the clock, because he had been here then. Thus he could look to the flow just before **.8.** bells, when the Lookout would cry: *Flood oh!*

He lurk'd & fished. 'Twas great sport here in the Bay of *Chisapioc*. He'd never seen sturgeons so large.

He was in no exceeding haste. The Companie had sent him to spy things out. The Colonie would be privatized now, under fitting license — for there'd been complaints. Whate'er piddling Counsell or Parliament they might have in Virginia, that would soon be swept away. My Lord De La Warr was to be Governor.

Their timorous route by way of the Canaries, he'd bettered that forever. Running due west, he utterly avoided yᵉ Spaniards. Moreo'er, when Captaine Newport's fleet had sail'd to James Towne, it took 'em **.4.** months. It had taken him by **.9.** weeks so far; he'd arrive in haven before the **.10.**th.

At **.8.** bells **.30.**, the tide now being in her secret ruthless glory, Argal told the Mate to weigh anchor, which command the Mate did shout, and so the *Treasurer* put out to sea in GOD's name. Continuing south-southwestward (.SSW.), Argall did observe the Sunne, and saw that all continued on course. — Brutus, why so sad? he cried out to Lieutenant Turnell. Do you dream of murthering me? For today tolls the Ides of March, and so help me, Brutus, I *would* be deified!

Ay, Captaine Argoll, sure we've already done so. Sure we've GODded you past all honesty; we fear your name!

Ha! Then offer me a crown!

Good Captaine, I have neither crowns nor sovereigns. I have scarce a silver-jacked copper farthing.

Then we must to the Salvages, to snatch crowns off their apish heads. Ho, Cassius!

Ay, Captaine Argall! shrilled the Mate.

Take soundings.

Two hundred fathoms shew me nothing, Sir.

Sail on!

On the .3.rd day of May they did take soundings and find soft ooze a hundred & .40. fathoms down. Argull did smile in his beard, like unto the Astrologers who can foretell (and perhaps hasten) our deaths. And so they came into South Virginia (call'd by the Papists *Florida*), where in places the Spanish moss hung down as strangely white as the reflection of a crane's belly. They tacked. Cape Henrico was .6., .7. & .8. fathoms. They penetrated the James River, about which a good Englishman hath said, *I will not prefer it before our riuer of Thames, because it is* England's *richest treasure.*

* * * * * *

'Tis a sere grey spring at Jamestowne, very still and riverine. The waters remain high. In midsummer, muck will shew itself foully gleaming, in what we men of Lincolnshire call *the Bird-Tides,* because it's when our marshes become somewhat less liquid that the seabirds find it most convenient to hatch their eggs.

The Fort is silent. Men lie sick, as usual. The Church-yard hath engross'd new graves. Sweet John, a-wearied out with the day's business, opens up his Machiavell. He wonders why he doesn't see Pocahontas more.

The Sentry cries: *A ship, a ship!* And the Trumpeter blares his *Trarintra-rarara.*

* * * * * *

See John Smith, most joyously smiling, bow & extend his hand. — *Your obedient Servaunt,* he doth say.

Well, well, laughs e'erworthy Argoll. 'Twould seem we're fellow Soldiers, sweet Maister President! For I serv'd in Berg.

Southeast of Cleves? I was there—

Ah, what an eager face you do put on, Maister President! I s'pose you enjoyed your service?

O yes, Captaine Argoll. And did you e'er meet with Captaine Jos. Duxbury?

Duxbury? Ha, ha! I escorted him safe to the Tower!

You jest.

Then his neck did gush most nobly, once it was attainted & lost virginity to the Headsman's axe.

Sir?

Nay, Maister President, I never met any Captaine Duxbury. Well met, well met! And may your Presidency prosper while it can. For it's *Tick, tick & tick again.*

Captaine Argall, you speak passing strange, whispers Sweet John in a voice as weak as the wake of a sailing-ship in calm weather.

Then it's *Tick again & tick again.* It's *tick again & tick again, tick, tick & tick again* — till Policy's clock hath strook!

On this Ocean of Life we find ourselves a-voyaging on, e'erworthy *Argall's* a princely caravel with many a magnificent sail, while poor John Smith's but a cheap shallop rigged out with sheets stolen from a bawdyhouse. These .2. now stare each other o'er. Sweet John's mastered again by the selfsame feeling which conquered him when he did .1.st meet Opechancanough. He knows not what this sensation should be call'd. It's akin unto fear, envy, sadness, & above all *recognition;* yet it lies in eerie otherness to all these. (Who's spoken unto him in this fashion before? Methinks it's Lord Willoughby's son Robert. And yet Robert discourses e'er in ennui'd tones. Behind Argoll's smoldering eyes burns a veritable *Holocaust of starres,* energy beyond any human limit.) Nay, this strange emotion in his heart, 'tis what? 'Tis a heart-bell clanging *Take heed, take heed;* & yet he comprehends not what safeguard to take.

Never fear, continued Argall. (He wore a black partlett about his throat.) You'll have a new supply fresh from Gravesend. Soon your Jamestowne will be swollen pregnant with amenities, like unto the many Merchaunts' booths upon London Bridge. I swear it, Maister President! Lord De La Warr hath set forth at the head of a great fleet—

THE GRAMMAR OF GRAVESEND (1609)

Malignant Times!   What can be said or done
But shall be censur'd and traduc'd by some!
THOMAS CARLETON, dedicatory verse to *The Generall Historie*

*W*here the river *Witham* meets the *Fossdyke* in Lincoln-Towne, there's a High Bridge (or *Glory Hole* as some call it) which endures from medieval times, bearing gingerbread houses on its back. Sweet John in his Presidential fantasies can veritably see a New World Glory Hole spanning the river just below the falls at *Nonesuch,* where the forest floor is riven with great boulders and rock-ridges all covered with trees. How fine that will be! 'Twill be the gateway unto the Monacan Yndians. Some year not long from now, he'll set the Colonie to building it — e'en though he may be opposed in this by Powhatan, by Powhatan's half-brother Opechan-canough, *He Whose Soul Is White,* or by the silly Colonists themselves. He's not afeared of any. In his recollections, Powhatan's Palace seems e'en smaller than before! (But nightmares fly o'er, with whirring wings.) Soon, quickened unto old Wingfield's semblance, he'll keep faith with victories won with *Eggshells, egshells.*

Yea, Sweet John's on the veriest verge of becoming an *Ineradicable Prince.* Maister Scrivener, Captaine Waldo, & **.9.** others having drown'd in January, whilst he was away extorting corn from Powhatan & Opechancanough, he's gained more authority than e'er before in the Counsell. Soon he'll obtain a proportionately better fame from those grave old Undertakers in London-Towne! Captaine Fortune gave Pokahuntiss into his pocket, & isn't she both good & perfect in her ways? Well, 'tis true he hasn't guested her of late, but whene'er he thinks upon her, he's as safe-aim'd as those who mend their Compasse according to the *North Starre* — more so, indeed, for that orb standeth not always at true north, whilst Pocahontas will go against her own father for Sweet John's sake. Now that she hath commenc'd to ripen a trifle, he wonders how 'twould be to . . .

His Soldiers call on him to pillage Werowocomco, & depose Powhatan forever.

Nay, says the bearded little President, we need only defend what we have, & uphold our allies.

He would continue Christianly if he could. He ne'er hath meant to dispossess those Salvages of their own holdings. Just-spirited, compassionate unto their brutishness, he'll take only so much of Virginia as he requires.

He sets his new *Dutchmen* to making trials at the Glass-house. (He knows that their feigning love toward him doth enwrap a poisonous hatred.) He commaunds the Laborers to dig a deeper well. He makes 'em plant near about .**40**. acres. He essays to prepare a specimen of soap-ashes for Captaine Newport to fraught back home to England, conformable to the instructions of the Maister-Undertakers. In rapid time he completes the erection of his new Block-house. He 'graves each Colonist's name upon a Publicke Tablet, with merits & demerits indicated. He strives to translate all men unto provident persons.

They say his ambition's full as high as Lincoln-Towne upon its hill. They call him *Tyrant,* but so good Captaine Duxbury was also nam'd by grumblers in the Low Countreys. To be a Generall is to compel men 'gainst their inclinations; 'tis all natural. (Reverend Hunt implores him: Be not cross & quarrelsome towards 'em, Sweet John, for *'tis but Nature* that a ship must go e'er contrary to her helm . . .)

Argoll's news hath affrighted him somewhat, but if that proves true, why then, Sweet John will beg leave of my Lord De La Warr to commaund the new Colonie at Nonesuch. Once Virginia's settled & tranquil, he'll see if he can get appointed *Sheriff of Nonsuch Countie.* He'll solve all disputations justly, & take his statutory share of the proceeds. (Captaine Duxbury had meant someday to essay the like in Ireland, but of course death altered his policy.)

✳ ✳ ✳ ✳ ✳ ✳

See John Smith, hopeful, altho' not so much as before, care-tired, dreaming of funerals, haunted by *Saluadge* specters, palisadoed by the pointing fingers of the idlers he's outraged, safety-hungry, lonely, poised upon the instability of his eminence. His Presidency's ticking away. His fears rise rapid & milky like unto the seas at Poynt Comfort.

Send for Lieutenant Percy, he commaunded the Sentry.

Aye, aye, Maister President.

And Pearcie came, with his customary ornate mournfulness.

Sit down with me, my good lad, & quaff this dram of sack. Tell me, how goes e'erything with you & the other Soldiers?

All well, Captaine Smith . . .

Then why that pallid, weary look? For as long as I've known you, your eyes have resembled dusty marbles dropt in the eye-sockets of a skull! Tell me, dear George — nay, now you start at my familiarity . . .

Lieutenant Pearcie sits silent, with his glass unraised. (Well, well; he's e'er thus. And when he speaks, he but dribbles out ambiguities, as if he were some slippery Jesuit lurking outside the law.)

Come now. Here we are, discovering & conquering new Kingdomes for His Majestie! Why then so sad? How may I riddle your unhappiness?

Argall, clangs this unhappy Pearcie. Yea, on his tongue the name clangs like unto a Church-bell!

Argoll! Argull! Why do you all speak that name?

But with the same scornful gloom, Percy repeats: *Argall.*

Hark! Sweet John wakes! 'Tis but the bell after all, summonsing all men to pray. After the sermon's done, he sends for Lieutenant Percy.

What kind of man is Argall, think you? he demands.

I know not, Maister President, for I never saw him until now, & now he's cod-fishing in North Virginia . . .

Yea, he *claim'd* to have upp'd anchor in order to reel in codfish. You think 'tis true?

I know not. But why misprison* him, Sir? For you're an open-hearted sort of Generall . . .

For which compliment I thank you. Mayhap 'tis but this heavy Virginian atmosphere which queases me unto distrust—

Or the distrust of others, Maister President.

Aye, our Renegados do e'er suspect those in authority. Or did you mean something else?

Pearcie's silent.

Tell me at once. To whom are you loyal?

Argoll.

For what reason?

For that he comprises all things in himself—

Now I can see that after all the favors you've received at my hands, you

*Suspect or doubt.

continue to treasure up your own coldness. So be it. Return you then to your foppish *Gentlemen*.

Argall, Argoll, Argull! tolls the bell, & he awakes again! Why doth he e'er dream of that e'erworthy Captaine?

✳   ✳   ✳   ✳   ✳

See John Smith at the Glass-house, coming for to o'erwatch his Dutchmen — for gossip saith that they've commited some errors of idleness & pilferage, which must be verified & 'graved upon that publicke tablet. And how have their latest glass-trials assayed? Should Virginian sands prove purer than the English (as he'd fain believe), why then, he'll have another vendible article to lay before those Gentlemen-Undertakers in London, whose love will sail him onto riches, *straight* on if we accompt not the river-bends. But the Glass-House is silent.

Something clangs within his heart.

The metallic squeaking of birds doth cease, & the hot heavy air falls clammy. What chance whirs down now? The Werowance of Paspahegh emerges from pine-darkness, with his face painted unto its accustomed funereal blackness, & the deer's horns bristling atop his head. Stout & muscular like unto some slippery Wrestler, he glistens with bear-grease. He's Captaine Fortune for a fact. Kenelled in obscurity comes our future from free-hung places in the wet earth. Will he serve our turn? He comes just the same. But with a lucky bullet, we can play a twink longer, until he comes again and we lose. Death comes not here, we pray. Death comes. But Argoll comes not here; the gamble continues possible. Sweet John won't abdicate yet! Nor will he admit that the times when he was Powhatan's *son* are old times now gone into the earth. Wowinchopunck, Powhatan's mastiff, hunter in oceans of reeds, had best not bark at him, or he'll . . . — As do all these Salvages, he wears a great bow o'er his shoulder. Is that a snake aslumber in his hair? And what errand hath spewed him out? Swayed almost into awe by this apparition, as if he'd turn'd a corner & found some yellow-eyed *Panther,* Sweet John hesitates. Indeed he feels the *twinkling fear.* But if he e'er shews it, he's doomed.

Good day to you, friend Wowinchopunck. 'Tis unmeet to discover you here so close upon my Fort.

The King smiles hideously. How much he comprehends Sweet John can but doubt, *Pocahontas, Kemps, Tassore, Nantaquod* & all his other pawns being absent. He advances step by step. His pistol's not charg'd, so his right hand rides upon his hip, ready for to snatch up falchion . . .

Wowinchopunck becks him towards a darksome thicket. Then he speaks a word whose meaning's lock'd away.

Aye, doubtless you would increase your credit in that place, yet I—

Wowinchopunck points yet more strangely. He says: *Thacgwenymmer-aun!* — a Salvage word which signifies *I give yt yo" gratis.*

What would you gift me with? My own death? 'Pon my faith, you Salvages do e'er seek for to murther me!

Sweet John grins & crouches as he says this. The *twinkling fear's* so poisonous within his chitterlings that he would spew.

That glaring-eyed black mask of a face swims towards him. Sweet John shoots birdlike glances thro' the dark & slender trees, but discovers no ally anywhere. Mayhap 'tis not so ominous; he spies only pine-cones at the center of needles, dark green & light green stars . . . — but now, with whirling speed, King Wowinchopunck hath nocked an arrow to his bow now already half-bent & aim'd at Sweet John's heart.

No time to draw his falchion! He leaps on Wowinchopunck, striking the weapon away. They tumble together down. Now they wrestle in pine needles, & Sweet John can gain no 'vantage, for the smooth-oil'd enemy slips e'er thro' his grip. From that dark wilderness, the voices of Bandittos & Renegadoes commence for to chaunt: *Whe, whe, yah, ha, ne, he, wit-towa, wittowa!* — How many duels must he fight in this life? Cursell of the .4. French Gallants, .3. Turkes .1. by .1., and . . . — Wowinchopunck slides & slithers. He's uppermost now. Giantlike, Powhatan's best Champion, he now commences for to squeeze Sweet John 'gainst his breast, & as sweat-drops explode from their locked bodies like unto a fusillado of bullets, they roll; indeed they roll; Wowinchopunck would strategize 'em both into the river, & little Sweet John cannot halt that venture! In they go, into dark water o'er midnight-ooze. Will it be here he must gurgle out his life? Strange GOD! Wowinchopunck's atop him irresistibly; Sweet John cannot get his head into air. He thinks to hear Church-bells. As always in his career, mere endurance suffices not. Blacker & blacker; he's . . . *Mark;* he's won a grip on the Yndian's throat. Quick, Sweet John, squeeze with all thy might! Breath-thirst tortures him, but he clenches with his best endeavor, until Wowinchopunck throws o'er, being strangled almost unto death.

I've said it before: Sweet John's wondrous constituted. So he gains the victory.

* * * * * *

Now see Captaine Smith with his boot 'pon this King's neck. Off with that crown of deer-horns, 'fore it can do mischief! What if Wowinchopunck were to gore him with it, as might a bull in Lincolnshire? (But he merely gasps, his tongue swelling out like unto a hang'd felon's.) Sweet John outdraws his falchion now & flourishes it, preparing for to harvest this new head. When he'd faced those .3. Turkes, he had each time (being sweet) awarded his opponent a courteous salute before the *Coup de grace*. Wowinchopunck he'll not honor thus. For a twink he remembers how it was, with the Turkishe Champions all gorgeously accoutered, the Turkishe Ladies o'er-watching the fight with their faces busk'd up in veils, & his own Army shouting for joy as he slew each Duellist in turn. Now 'tis but a weary parody, without glory when he wins, & with the same foul Death should he lose. Well, he's won. His Jamestowne idlers & Gentlemen will not care. Why tell the tale to any but Jeffrey Shortridge? (Say, what begging eyes hath this trampled King!)

He thinks he hears something. Nay, the Paspahegh Salvages have all run away . . .

Time for the King to get his desserts. Ha! How Powhatan will terrify himself into goodness, once the spies report that they've seen great *Wow-inchopunck's* skull impaled at Jamestowne Fort! Thro' fear these people will now yield up all their treasures & secrets!

But the King implores him with many strange syllables. He hath not the unyielding honor of a Turke. Nay, he's but vicious, greedy & cowardly, like unto some inbred dog. Sweet John hath not the heart to kill any who cringes. (Reader, think you he learnt his mercy out of Machiavell?) Upon his Salvage supplication, Sweet John doth pardon him, but hales him home enchained.

See John Smith a-marching up the Yndian trail, a-kicking & a-whacking his prisoner, for to humble him out of any schemes of escape. Now the conqueror's spirits begin to raise him up into cheer. Little, muddy & triumphant, he knaps upon James-towne Gate with shrill cries, until the Sentry doth stop scratching himself long enough to open.

Call Lieutenant Percy.

He sleeps, Maister President—

Obey my commaund! he cries, stamping his foot.

Here comes Pearcie now, pale & silent, with his gold stripes stain'd by Virginia's corruption.

Guard this King, Lieutenant, for he sought to ambuscado me.

Captaine Winne would have entreated for to hear the tale; Pearcie merely stares, scratching 'neath the ruffles round his throat.

Did you hear?

Aye, Maister President. Shall I cast him in the Guard-house with Kemps?

Give Kemps his liberty. Then—

But I do dread that Kemps in his malice may—

You must not *dread* these Saluadges, lad. They're but treacherous infidels to be managed & led. Now take this Wowinchopunck to the Guardhouse. Flog him not. Feed & water him as he requires, for he's a King.

Yes, Maister President . . .

*　*　*　*　*　*

Having achiev'd so much, he craved to rest as doth a summer's sturgeon drowsing near the surface. Like bubbles his daydreams ascended, prayers of nothingness within nobody's whitewashed Church. It wasn't that he wisht to engross himself on other men's labor as Ratcliffe had done, nor craved he to withdraw from men like some fabulous *Dragon* guarding his hoard (thus Wingfield's example); but his heart had beaten too passionately — neither love-beats nor lust-beats; martially, ambitiously, *Politick-*ally it had clang'd, hasting, dreading, planning, defending & scheming, until the bell-clapper broke. *He felt incapable of feeling.* (Those soul-sensations, which resembled the queasy turnings of sea-foam 'midst the rocks, he accompted 'em not.) The thud of the Blockhouse-gate, the crashing & squeaking of the West-gate, the Sentries' tread on the high demiculverin platforms, the lethargic curses of men, bird-sounds & river-sounds, creakings of trees & rain-song rattlings of tall reeds in evening gusts, these noises now enveloped him in as humdrum a web as any Milk-maid's call of *Cush!* Virginia creeper crept into tent & croft. Yndian canoes passed & repassed on the horizon, wearying his Colonists with *the twinkling fear.* Egrets dove for fishes. He felt himself like unto the Convict he'd been .2. years before on the *Susan B. Constant,* with the same ocean swelling meaninglessly around. Yea, he was empty! For this reason, the glassy-eyed company of Lieutenant Percy attracted him, no matter that Percy misliked his inferior birth. No matter Percy's dark suspicious eyes, his cold gold stripes, his smooth dark hair like unto armor around his head . . . They'd become corpses together.

All was hot & quieted nearly to a half-lascivious doom. He lay a-dreaming of the previous summer, when that plague had whirred o'er Jamestowne &

so many died. Who could disremember how the Salvages had sported at those funerals from behind the trees, shooting feather-tipped death, hatefully laughing, jeering: *Whe, whe, yah, ha, ne, he, wittowa, wittowa?* GOD or Sweet John would punish 'em in time. But in his dream it seemed that Pocahontas attended all obsequies, thereby unfeathering the arrows down to submission. Sweet John too lay dead, a worm-lung entrant unto *Countie Oozymandias.* Yet in the dream (as 'tis customary, Reader, when we 'vision our own mortality), he bided free to perceive himself. A shadow rose, dimensionless and jewel-like. He strained in heart & groin. O'ertaken by the dream-spell, he watcht Pocahontas's approach. Now she spied his yellow corpse. She commenced for to wail & embraced him fiercely (altho' he could not feel her head on his heart), crying as she always did: *Love you not me?*

He awoke sure for a twink that all this had really happened. Then perforce he must laugh, at the chaff with which his mind bestrawed his way.

He must send some beads, if 'twould not enrage her father against her . . .

* * * * * *

More rats in the bing! Again our supply of corn (which we saw Sweet John gather at such hazard) lies all spoiled! Reader, there ne'er before were any rats in Virginia; they came from England. Just as we bear our own deaths within our bellies, so those corn-casks disembarked pre-attainted from *the Kingdome of Navigation.* (Why shouldn't rats seek Captaine Fortune?)

Undoing the hang-lock, he enters the Store-house, which stinks of vermin-charmings. 'Tis a festering emergency within. Unless he snatches more corn from ye Salvages, the Colonie will starve come winter. Ever & again he must sing the same stanza. He's weary; he scarce believes in Captaine Fortune's grace . . .

Nay, he *must* set 'em for to corn-growing, else there'll be unremitting war with the Virginians, which would knock all his ambitions out of ranks. Hollow-eyed's his heart's vision. He's snickled by futility. Men mark the resemblance of his face to Lieutenant Pearcie's. What's he to feed 'em on? *Butter & eggs, buter & eggs.*

* * * * * *

He sent some to Poynt Comfort under the aforesaid *Lieutenant Pearcie* for to fish for their living, but (that Gentleman continuing sick & dreamy), they never once cast their nets under those long white wave-streaks. Empty-souled, they drank their own hollowness.

He sent others with *Ensign Laxon,* to save themselves by eating oysters; they also prov'd idle. (The factionalists who hated him jested most evilly that this Lincolnshire breedling malappointed over them was observing *Pag-Rag Day,* which marks the time when Servaunts pack up their bundles & go back into the Countrey, departing their Master's service; he, being ambitious beyond the bounds of his blood, was now packing his Masters off! The Masters raged against him to their uttermost.)

Captaine West he dispatched direct to the Falles, yet his men scavenged but acorns.

Kemps & Tassore being fetter'd again, he set those *.2. Yndian Felons* at liberty, so as not to be charg'd with feeding 'em. But they, joying in Sweet John's company, desired to stay amongst the English (I misdoubt me not in hopes of *Rum.)* None did his will. He grew afeared of GOD's audit. He long'd for to sleep unvex'd in Willoughby's Church-yard.

In July he summonsed 'em all. He said: Dream no longer of this vain hope of getting more corn from Powhatan. Nor should you dream I'll endlessly forbear to force you from your idleness. If I find any more who seek to 'scape for Newfoundland in the pinnace, let 'em look to arrive at the gallows. The sick shall not starve, but equally share of all our labors; & he that gathereth not e'ery day as much as do I, the next day shall be set beyond the river, & banish'd from the Fort as a *Drone,* till he amend his conditions or starve.

O cruel! they shouted.

He quartered many rascals amongst the Salvages, who e'er since he'd conquered *Opechancanough* y^e *King of Pamunkey,* & in that river-brawl bested *Wowinchopunck* y^e *King of Paspahegh,* dared not complain about anything. But Kemps for a sport did pass on Sweet John's law to the drones, so that those who work'd not amidst the Salvages ate not, & when Sweet John heard, he laugh'd.

In spite of all, he'd furbish up the Colonie—

* * * * * *

But in August comes the *.3.*^rd Supply, a great fleet originally of *.9.* ships whose *.500.* new Colonists are attainted with many Factionalists & vagabonds, Swart-rutters and Fen Slodgers, Criminals, Desperados & masterless men. Eight ships actually arrive, for a *hurricano* in the Bermudas did destroy a vessel. The New Lord Generall's lost with his flagship. Until he should appear, all's chaos at Jamestowne.

Sweet John commences with a smile to receive them into his Colonie, but they respect him not, crying out most wrathfully for *Rome booze,* which signifies *Wine* in the language of Convicts.

I have no *Rome booze* for you, he replies. But should you disobey mine authority, I'll give you another thing. I'll shew you how to *cly the jerk* — by which he doth signify *to get whipped,* for when he did his service in the Low Countreys, many of his brethren were Convicts discharg'd or escaped, so then he kens very well their speech.

He despises 'em all for freshwater Soldiers.

In spite of them, he hoards his embers of optimism thro' the next quarter-hour, until the last boat rows ashore. The Factionalists & Desperados rush gloatingly for to observe his face. Surprise, Sweet John! Here come thine old Undertaking-friends, *Archer, Ratcliffe & Martin.*

* * * * * *

I have not deserved this, he said.

That opinion not all share, *Maister President,* sneered Ratcliffe most scornfully. Now, 'twas you & I & Captaine Archer here, who .1.ˢᵗ created the custom of depositions here at James-Towne. We deposed Maister Wingfield together. Then you deposed me, altho' not by such a name. Think you not I can't play your game to a counterpoise?

I *challenge* you, villain! Where's your commission? Where's the Counsell-seal to prove your acts? I will not yield. My term contains a month yet to run . . .

(The Soldiers stood around laughing.)

So be it, said Radcliffe. Perhaps we'll divert your intent.

Perhaps I'll seize you by the ear, snarled Sweet John.

Just as a muscular sea-wave, striking rock, foams sharply upwards, then dribbles back in scatters of futility, so his aspirations now were grounded by this .3.ʳᵈ Supply. *Policy's clock hath strook.*

* * * * * *

As late as 1898 an Engineer who'd spent much of his life draining the marshes of Lincolnshire could write: *By so precarious a tenure is the Fen land held, and so great is the necessity for constant and unremitting vigilance and care, that with the least neglect, only, perhaps, an unseen rat hole, the waving corn fields may be turned into a sea of water.* This metaphor holds good for life and all its endeavors — no less for James Towne. And now the waters of faction & anarchy came speedily in. The men were ape-drunk & lion-drunk. They got sow-drunk & lay down snoring.

'Twas long since decreed that each Colonist learn his place in the great war-figure comprehended by their President at *Smith-field*. But too many fell sick; the figure could not be maintained. And now the men of the .3.rd Supply denied utterly to drill.

And yet he *would not* dance the recreants from any gallows-end, altho' his lustiest Soldiers, & even that strangely dreamy Lieutenant Pearcie did advise him to it. — He is double mad that will leave his friends, means & freedom in England, to be worse here, said Sweet John. Therefore, let all men have as much freedom in reason as may be . . .

Then they said he'd lost his spunk.

* * * * * *

Now the Counsell seeks e'er to prefer articles against him. He withstands all.

The RUFFIAN cly his nab! they snarl, meaning, *The DEVIL beat his head!*

Radclyffe demands again that he surrender the Government.

Wearily he replies: My Lord De La Warr will be Governor, but my Lord De La Warr is not here. I stand.

He hears .2. rascals a-whispering together 'neath the Watch-tower. They would *bing 'emselves to Romeville,* which means to go unto London-Towne.

He springs upon them, warning: If you return to England without my passport, then you'll be judged as traitors, & punished befittingly.

They laugh in his face.

He claps 'em in irons, but Radcliffe persuades the Sentry to release 'em.

See John Smith, alone & foiled again. What had he won him? Briganti-ning his breast full metallically, he strode thro' the gate to Smith-field for to hunt, & meditate. He strode past the Block-house. Now he was alone at twilight in a swamp, and heaven's pale blue thrilled him with joy as he'd once felt in his bower in Lincolnshire. It was summer again, and he could do wander without limit through the fern-green crystal of his dreams.

* * * * * *

He fashion'd an angling-rod of hazel wood, using the straightest twig that he could find. He left the leaves on the tip until he had thoroughly peeled and stripped it; doing so preserved it from warping. He went a-fishing. The creek was much calmer (so it seemed to him) than the River Witham with its old arched bridge-edge of Tattershall.

Pokahuntiss's brother Nantiquod had shewed him how to take crawfish with half-cooked venison stuck on reeds; but the trouble was that he couldn't get the venison, his men being unpracticed in hunting; nor had he himself the leisure for such pastimes. Well, this .3.rd Supply had gifted him with plenty of rotten beef—

He lay listening to the sounds of the river, & wondered whether the state of this new Countrey would e'er grant him leave to make a pleasure-journey for to discover the river's head.

Well, & why not? After his Presidency was expir'd, he'd lead many new Companies of Discoverie.

Already he'd caught a great fat fish for his supper. In earlier days he would have fish'd continually with all his heart, for to feed his fellow Colonists despite their childish follies. No more.

O'erhung by a rack of purple-grey clouds, he paced & marched. Now he longed for his own Countie's cool green obscurity. *Cush, cush, cush.*

It had seemed so excellently easy to accomplish all, on that day when he'd become President! But now failure stood knapping at his heart. Resolution could not avail him now, nor bravery, generosity, strength. He longed to go a-sailing lightly upon the sea again, with Jamestown far astern. Should he Adventure back to Hungaria? But he quailed now at the remembrance of Turkes, with their tortures which could translate a living man into a skeleton half-clothed with twitching flesh. Moreover, he thought he deserved his .100.-odd Virginian acres. Why shouldn't he go off & claim Capahowsick-Towne, which Powhatan had promised him? 'Twould be his velvet prize. Percase he'd marry with Pocahontas. He'd already kissed her little mouth . . . He'd get his own corn from the Salvages. Maister Percy could do the rest — he & that jury of foul-mouthed detractors at Jamestowne. Meanwhile, Sweet John would sit beneath a *Sassafrass* tree, reading Machiavelli to Pokahuntiss. As he found means, he'd set 'em all to render of that spot a place well builded of stone, like unto Grantham-Towne in Linconshire. Could he hire a demi-culverin or better yet a *Cannon-Petro* from Gravesend, then he'd abide Maister of that Dominion e'en when he fell into his age. (Which reminded him: He must leave his falchion at the Blacksmith's, for it had been nicked in his duel with the King of Paspahegh. Moreover, he must commaund Jeffrey Shortridge, who was cunning at such work, to oil his armor for him. He must set the Laborers to pulling down the creepers from the West Gate.)

He heard a knave say: I saw him a-frigging with that Pocahontas, which is how he got his venereal—

Pock-a-huntiss, did you say? Aye, her very name pocks her with the buboes—

Sickened with disgust at their hatefulness, he stole away to Smith-field. His hopes hung dissected, like unto clouds spied through rigging. To publicly correct those .2. detractors; twould be like unto sprinkling water upon the pitch-and-oil-fire of his shame. To duel with them would be the same.

Jamestowne's vexations had bungholed his ambitions with their dreary clots of dust; he'd drink no more of them. What would be his policy now? Why, he'd go a-blobbing for eels, & these idlers could go hang.

* * * * * *

See John Smith at Nonesuch, laying mutineers & faction-poisoners up by the heels, to give 'em salutary correction when he doth get his leisure. See him solve e'erything in the highest degree. — And now I've redelivered to all parties their former losses, he announces. Thus all are friends. What say you?

They rebel against him. They prove so vicious to the Salvages that he's ashamed. He shouts: *Come you here!* — & they deny to come. Must he fire upon his own Countreymen? His authority's dimpled like blown & trodden sand. At last, copped down to despair, he throws up his hands, & begins to sail back to Jamestowne in that famous barge of his adorn'd with Massowomeck shields. Green pine-clouds o'ercloud brown river-skies. He longs to give o'er. But he won't. He'll fight; he'll never stumble—

* * * * * *

Here comes John Smith limping and halting, as if in some spell of repentance.

* * * * * *

See John Smith a-sleeping in a Boate amidst his kindred snorers. In the dark, a man sits up, driven by some greedish, thick-spittled craving for the Salvage weed call'd *Tobacco.* He tamps his pipe; he strikes a spark. (Sweet John hath admonish'd him never to do so indoors, yet what does that yeoman know? He got his education a-tippling with the Watermen in Temple Lane!) The man most happily smokes. Then carelessly or maliciously he doth o'erspill the ashes of his pipe upon his fellows. Worthy Reader, dost thou remember how long ago in Willoughby, at the commencement of this relation, dastardly Ralph Nightingale did for a joke secrete gunpowder in a log, & blow up Maister Reese Allen's fireplace? Now

Ralph's exemplar, gleeful Death, doth clap his bony hands as the lazy smoker's embers light on Sweet John's powder-bag! (Could it be that our President hath enemies?) See John Smith now instantaneously clothed in black smoke & orange fire. He shouts; he o'erleaps into the night river, to save himself from being sizzled to death — and, O, he's older than he was in other shipwrecked days, when he swam safely onto the rocks of Holy Isle, & when he o'ernighted in the stormy sweels after the Papists threw him off — for John Smith now approaches his .30.th gaunt and long-toothed year. And so by drowning the powder-flames which scorched off a good .10.-inch patch of his belly and thighs, he nearly drowns himself. And then he goes delirious as they carry him back a hundred miles to Jamestowne. His burns swell and rot. Fever attaches shimmering illuminations to the outlines of all objects; & when he closes his eyes he sees pulsing blue holes. This is his true war, yes, just as when he lay almost a-dying of *the purples* so many years ago in Roane. Captaine Duxbury had discharged him then, explaining: Laddie, you're no use; your spleen's been quenched . . . — He screams.

Darling *Ratcliffe* at Jamestowne gains the word from a spy: Smith's assured to croak at last, 'tis said. Ratcliffe convokes Archer and other confederates; they lay their plans to restore the government under which they will thrive.

Now the Boat docks at Jamestowne, & they carry in Sweet John on a plank — burned, screaming man, screaming & screaming. 'Tis said he'll die today. 'Tis said he'll die tomorrow. He faints, so that they're compelled to bleed him. He awakens screaming.

Not dead? Ratcliffe envoys a Pistolman to assassinate him, but that murtherer, thinking percase upon OUR REDEEMER, grows irresolute, and slinks instead to the Cooper's shop, because where a Cooper dwells there must be barrels; where barrels, there'll be grog, percase. So he drinks away his murtherousness, until John Smith wakens again unto his own screaming.

His courage is broken at last. He cannot heal. He shrieks & twists.

From nowhere, Radclyffe and Archer shew authority to suppress his commission. He gives o'er. Ratcliffe orates into his ear: *Thou wilt be hang'd, Smith, ere the tale is told.* — Replying not, he limps aboard .1. of the vessels whose sailing-day cometh just now due, and so forever he quits Virginia.

* * * * * *

His berth was behind a ladder, in the Cook's cabin. Stinking feet thumped up and down an inch from his face. The Sailors did lewdly chaunt: *Now bing we to Romeville,* which means, *Now we're a-coming to London-Towne.* All day & all night they did chaunt it.

Rats squeaked hideously. He set his teeth not to scream when the sea-wallows jostled his wounds.

* * * * * *

'Twas told him by a Sailor that *Maister George Percy* had been serv'd up with the Presidency a twink before they'd departed Jamestowne. Concerning Pearcie, the wounded & befevered man thought chiefly upon **.1.** thing of small relevance: In his youth, when he'd visited Rome, he'd wandered by the shop of an Armorer who fashion'd gilded & fantastically enameled suits of self-defense, but they cost too dear. How he would have joyed to don the finest of those, ere he set off to battle the Turkes! He could not. Yet this Maister Percie possessed armor all shiny & gilded; Maister Percy was a Gentleman . . .

* * * * * *

To torment him they did say: 'Tis sure you're excluded from the Government forever.

Smiling malignantly, Sweet John replied: In *Affricka* I've seen with my own eyes how the *Elephant,* be he great enough, can shake down the tallest Cocar tree.

Smith, you speak full dangerously, like unto some Rustick rebel or dyke-smasher. Defeat yourself, man; cast down your angry pride 'fore you begin to worship it as do we the CHRIST cross —

Pray content you. I speak but of the Salvages' humors —

He'd not yet learnt of the letter which his dear friend Radclyffe had penn'd, for Captaine Newporte to deliver unto the Earl of Salisbury, who personified all those stern old Undertakers who rul'd the World. The letter said: *At our arrivall we found an English shipp riding at Jamestown and Captaine Argall her Commander. We heard that all the Counsell were dead, but Captain Smith, the President, who reigned sole governor, without assistance, would at first admit of no Councell but himselfe. This man is sent home to answere some misdeameanor, whereof I perswade me he can scarcely clear himself of great imputation of blame.*

* * * * * *

Between James Towne and London Towne one must sail clockwisely, southwest from England and then northwest; northeast from Virginia and then southeast. 'Tis how the currents drive us. And it is all round and round, for peasants and for Kings, until life forsakes us; & the fishes go on swimming round, crowned by salt water. John Smith is certain that he'll go round again yet. Three Turkes, the Tymor, Powhatan's axeman, & THE ALMIGHTIE alone knoweth how many shipwrecks had never ceased him, never! And so, now and forever, Sweet John falls home upon the English coast (which in my day sports shades of reddish-brown on old maps) — home in Angle-Land whose many gentle capes and bulges comprise grassy teats of Motherland whose nipples are white churches and plundered, exorcised shells of abbeys from the old Catholic days (every town owns its heavenly tower, but the Willoughbys had grown rich and great after the late King's dissolution of the monastery lands); Sweet John falls home among kindred sailing-ships languidly creaking in the smelly fog, swallowed by the Thames-mouth, where he thinks on Argall, who'll surely speed him back to Virginia with all good commendations. He's resigned his gage. He's done. At the .8.-mile width, with Maplin Sands to the north and the Isle of Sheppey to the south, he thinks on Pocahontas — all the way 'til Holehaven Creek a mile west of Scars Elbow. It was at Holehaven that he once when he was younger rode out a squallish breeze for .8. gruesome days. Pocahontas to Holehaven, then no Pocahontas, but Smallgains Creek, and the Kentish shore, and Yantlet Creek, Holehaven, yes, where his bitterness instigates onto his mind's stage the image of his brother Frauncis's goodwife with her linen coif under her hat — embroidered by herself, of course, and passably so, but why did she long to resemble a Merchauntwoman? Upon his return to Willoughy, she'll pronounce him ineffectual. Why should he fear her disregard? He's her superior to his very chitterlings; he's travelled, saved Jamestowne and cut off .3. Turkes' heads . . . Vange Creek, Mucking Flats, and so on to Gravesend. And Smith comprehends by all faith that (as it sayeth in the Thirty-First Psalm, which he'd never disremembered), *I have passed out of mind like one who is dead; I have become like a broken vessel.* This is the end.

✳ ✳ ✳ ✳ ✳ ✳

It is written that Pocahontas ceased her visits when she learned that John Smith was gone.

II

CHANGES
OF THE MOON

OR,

HOW $\mathcal{P}OKAHUNTISS$ *FOUND*
HERSELF TO BE TWICE
MARRIED

THE GRAMMAR OF MARTIAL LAW (1609)

Of all passions, that which inclineth men least to break the Laws is *Fear*. Nay, excepting some generous natures, it is the only thing . . . that makes men keep them.

HOBBES, Leviathan (1651)

It is as much as if a father should be said to offer violence to his child, when he beats him, to bringe him into goodnes.

THE REV. WILLIAM SYMONDS, speaking on policy to Salvages (1612)

'*T*is prov'd he's belowdecks?

Nearly to the uttermost orlop. Would he were lower yet, in the ooze beneath the sea!

Out of sight's enough. Quick. Let's fix it up. Shall it be West?

He kens too well his price. I crave no such heavy figurehead.

Ratcliffe, tell us not *you* seek your old position! Why, you were worse than our loathsome little Captaine there—

Nail down your tongue, Captaine Martin, for *you* reigned e'er sickly, like unto a husband who cannot tup his wife . . .

Your mutual jealousy scathes *me* not, laughed Captaine Archer, but I know you well enough to see you allied unto marriage, tupless or not, did I but press *my* own claims. Friends, let not ambition divide us. We agreed already that none of us can be President. And Sweet John—

Send a man, to see if he dies.

Ratcliffe, if you buzz & fleer so flightily to our purpose, then there's no remedy. Now, whose Lieutenants shall we be? Shall we be West's?

E'en did he remake himself entirely contrary, so that men call'd him *East,* I'd not vote for that lead Soldier. Percy's softer to our purpose; he melts like wax in any heat. He'll reward us surely with good preferments if we—

By HEAVEN, 'tis true, altho' I hate him near equal unto Sweet John—

Martynn, plague you with fleas! You're a creeping, crying old fellow—

Enough. We have but an hour, ere others act to our offending. 'Tis West, Percie, or some other?

Then Ratcliffye did cough wisely, & say: Dear friends, allow me to unlace my soul. West would bide here; Percy would go. If we persuade Percie to stay, we can unpersuade him, should he not suit us. He'll be sweetly temporary for our devices. After him, we'll convene again.

To the point! cried Captaine Archer. Since we cannot agree for ever, why then, let's agree for this twink. I vote for Percy. There's .2. of us. What say you, Martin?

I pray you pardon me, good Gentlemen. I cannot make up my mind of a sudden—

Martynne, awake! Our hour's slipped nigh entire through the glass!

So I see, & yet I fear we debate but superficially, for—

Your hesitation's dangerous, man. Vote now, for or against. If not—

Come, come, said Martin. Don't flare at me. Think you Percie can be persuaded?

I know not. We can essay him—

And if not Percy, 'tis West, or 'tis not West?

Why, 'tis naked *Pokahuntiss,* you droll fellow! I'm full exasperated now. Your vote!

I — Percie. But West hath—

Done. He votes for Percy. Radcliffe, run now & persuade him, before he boards the ship. He dotes on you. And, Martynne, let's you and I draw up a nice indictment to sting Sweet John's tail in case he lives to reach England. That'll finish him with the Companie.

Ha, ha! laughed feeble Captaine Martin. *Indictment's* better sport than *Tick-Tack* or *Lurch.* My heart indicts him .8. score times at least. Write this: *He expell'd the Colonie to the Oyster-banks, where many did starve.* But how many, I wonder? Put down a score . . .

Who's that perjurer he whipp'd? I would confabulate with him—

✳   ✳   ✳   ✳   ✳

George Percy was now President *pro tempore,* and from the sacred box removed the *Instructions Given By Way of Advice* from London-Towne, whereof he read: *You shall for capitall and Criminal Iustice in Case of Rebellion and mutiny and in all such cases of present necessity, proceede by Martiall lawe according to your comission as of most dispatch and terror, and fittest for this government.* Yet this Government for which terror was fittest, why, 'twas like unto a leaky bark whose drabble-sail's full grimed!

Lieutenant Pearcie felt the *twinkling fear.* Anxiously he pick'd at a gold stripe in his sleeve. He knew not where to turn. The Colonie had scarce any supplies, & without Sweet John to engorge 'em with corn, they must soon be in straits.

Now that Powhatan's pleasure began to take effect, the Salvages would not chaffer. Bells & beads grew worthless at last.

Enlaced in his somber dressings, with a face (said Radclyffe to himself) of a somewhat Moorish cast, good Maister Percie appointed to his Counsell *Captaine Radclyffe,* of course, & that pliantly feeble *Captaine Martynne,* & a certain *Captaine West,* who was my Lord De La Warr's brother. Lord Delaware being en route to take all unto his hands, this device seem'd wisely calculated to obtain his favor . . .

He serv'd out aqua vitae in little silver goblets. His Counsell greedily drank it down.

Like Sweet John, he kenned the need to command absolutely, like any *Generall* of a Fort, there being so many Gentlemen idlers who would not work to save their own skins. He required them to attend him at the beat of the first drum. But he was sick. Moreo'er, once Lord De La Warr did arrive, he'd lose his present dignities, so . . .

He permitted the Church to revise itself back out of rainworthiness. He gave o'er posting Sentries. Week by week the palisadoes & perimeters of the Fort grew creeper'd & decay'd.

✳ ✳ ✳ ✳ ✳ ✳

Men begg'd him for bread.

'Tis the inconveniency of the time, Maister Percie sighed.

Yet they begg'd him again. They were already reduced to culling likely herbs & insects out of the ground.

Go fish for sturgeons to make your living. When Captaine Smith was here, he took over **.50.** of 'em at a single draught.

Sweet John is vanisht, Maister. He'll save us no more.

So our new President did envoy some Colonists of good quality to Poynt Comfort, there to fortify themselves & live by fishing. Last summer, that Undertaking had fail'd. But 'twas not Lieutenant Pearcie's fault. He was too good to be galled by their insolencies. If they would not work, why then, they must look to sink idly down to death. As for him, why should he be expected to o'errule their nature? He was no coward. Neither would he be their nurse.

At his commaund they uprais'd palisadoes; they established a demi-culverin in a Tower; they built a Church on which to found themselves:

Trarintra-rarara. Up colors! And they nam'd their dominion *Fort Algernon.* They fir'd the grass & began to turn o'er the soil for their new Cittie. Then they stopp'd. Lieutenant Pearcie did wearily admonish them to Enclose that land as quick as they could, & try to get in a harvest before the trees fell utterly out of leaf, but they preferred to remove themselves from that labor, saying that under the reign of Captaine Smith they'd been compelled to so many cruel toils that they might as well have been enslaved by Turkes! 'Twas no marvel that they reasoned thus, for the honey-hive call'd *Kecoughtan* lay at but half a mile's distance.

So be it, he said. Then may these structures which you now uprear prove to be your cerements! I shall not stay—

Maister President, your commission requires you to provide for us, & yet you shrug us off —

I care nothing for your plaints. Dare again to delineate my duty, & I'll lop your head. All ready, Sailors?

By your order, Maister President!

Prepare to upsail. We leave on the instant. As for you others, fare well or fare ill, it rides with you. There's no corn occulted in my Jamestowne Store-house; think not I can sound some food-pit to save you—

Maister President, we're afeared—

Enough. Up anchor, up sail!

Flood oh!

And so Fort Algernon was left barren of Government. Near e'ery day the Englishmen did call upon the Werowance of Kecoughtan (a certain *Pochins,* who was half-brother to Pocahontas). The Werowance grew weary of them.

They demanded food; yet this Prince Pochins denied to give it, save at monstrous high prices. (Reader, may I teach you a maxim of *Oeconomy?* Here goes: Just as Sextons get rich in plague years [for 'tis not gratis, you know, to bury a corpse], so Salvages raise their corn-fees whenever the English be starving.)

As for the President, he'd long since sail'd home to James-towne. Let them take their own audit, was what he thought. — O, but he was sick! He was sick!

* * * * * *

See this Captaine West en route to double-palisadoed Patawomecke-Towne. Sweet John claim'd their antimony's but silver, but Sweet John's a discredited knave. Besides, they have corn.

Captaine West will succor the Colonie, so he avers.

Yndian men as brightly painted as the *Susan B. Constant,* Yndian maids most fantastickally tattooed — all these worthies seek for to charm him down. But Patawomeck antimony's but antimony. And altho' near e'ery house hath corn in baskets the size of dog-kennels, the Werowance swears by the SUNNE that he hath but little corn. Enraged at their insolency (& ahungered besides), West doth behead .2. of these Yndians, so that next time they'll better respect martial law . . . He returns without any corn.

✳ ✳ ✳ ✳ ✳ ✳

See dear Captaine Ratcliffe at Orapax, come at Powhatan's invitation to trade. How it doth please him, to be singled out thus! The Salvage messenger had tenderly said, 'twould best beseem all, did Radcliffe himself lead the mission, for so high stood Powhatan's estimation of him. 'Tis a fine meditation 'pon the Virginia Companie, that it takes a Salvage to recognize his excellence! And yet Captaine Fortune doth love to disguise himself under outlandish apparitions, for which reason our hero's no more amaz'd than any other dreamer. Sure there's treasure in Virginia, and Powhatan hath the keeping of it! Won't it be fine to trick the whereabouts of *Tropickall Jewels* out of the old villain? Too long hath restless Ratcliffe lain a-twisting at this Gravesend of a Colonie, whose arbitrary opportunities must be grabbed, if a man's not to wither away like unto some Tavernhouse sleepyhead who awakes to find his Captaine already gone, his ship sunk far under the Atlantic horizon of the World, her sails set for Ushant & then for American gold! Radcliffe will sit patient no longer. All of our Adventurers came to Virginia *to get rich.* How can that be done by lurking here? Sweet John's twin in superannuatedness, he longs to 'scape from Jamestown, & especially from the ruins of his Palace, which too uncomfortably resemble the Mausoleum of his ambitions. Granted, he was never well liked (they despised him for his odor like unto an old woman's smell); & we must give Captaine Radclyffe the credit of never losing sight of that fact. But 'tis hardly his fault he was born a trifle timid & crabbed! He would be more agreeable, did he only know how. Indeed, he seems to have made strides in that direction today; for he's happy — he's thrill-suffused. He cleans & polishes his breastplate, which is far more excellently metall'd than Sweet John's tarnish'd brigandine vest (indeed, I think it's of Spanish manufacture, come down to Radclyffe thro' many queer channels of Piracy). He essays to sing a little tune which he once heard *Captaine Argoll* hum:

Red sky at night, Sailor's delight.   After all, thinks he, the only surprise is that Captaine Fortune didn't come sooner.   He comes full near to pitying Maister Percie, who can't go without the gates . . .

The other Counsell-men have already engross'd themselves in selling off the food from the Store-house.   Truly y^e Colonie's now in desperate case.

At the .$1.^{st}$ bell of the Forenoon Watch he's summonsed to Percie's manse.   The Sentry doth bow to him.   The door opens of itself, with a Servaunt's hand attach'd to it.   Another Servaunt doth pour him out a dram of brandy, which relishes very pleasant.   Remembering his own decked-out days of Presidential dignity, when he had many such Domestics at his beck, Radclyffe can't entirely distrain himself from jealousy; but, draining down the dram-dregs, he reminds himself 'tis now the commencement of his triumph.   He confesses he's grown hardened & enraged.   But Captaine Fortune waits to guide him to immortality.   He longs to take the Salvage air. He'll bring home corn, glory & the promise of gold-mines.   To him the future's so fixed (like unto an intricately carven brass portal) that he's irritated by any hint of vaporousness — for instance, Maister Percy's long, haggard face, which appears to melt & sway with Virginian fever.

Beware of 'em, Sicklemore, for their courtesy doth e'er abate.

Ha, ha, Maister President!   I misdoubt me not I can be more *politick* than Sweet John.   And by your leave I'll take that Yndian *Kemps* for to be my Translator . . .

But Maister Percie falls silent.   He plucks at the silken butterflies at his shoulders.   Suddenly he shivers & pulls the red cloak tighter about his head. Radcliffe shines his teeth in sweetness, pleas'd that he can persuade or unpersuade this President to anything.   Poor Ratcliffe!   What pride owns he else?   Indeed, his pride's cadent like unto the frothy river at the Falles: Pride tumbles into malicious spleen.   Yet, loving Reader, wasn't he fine? Wasn't he wise?   'Twas under his Government that we did .$1.^{st}$ go a-voyaging to Powhatan's Palace for our corn-trade.   'Twas under him that we explored & delineated the Chisapeack Bay.   (He remembers a-sitting at his ease in the foundations of his new Palace [since gone to ruin under succeeding Administrations, as I said], while Sweet John nervously stands before him.   A Servaunt fills a single goblet, just for President Radclyffe, who says to Sweet John: *Now tell me what you did discover.*   Sweet John hastens to relate it all. . . .)   Yea, 'twas under Radcliffe the Wise that we fraughted Captaine Newport's ship with gold-dust.   For this most wounded, this most delicate Captaine John Radcliffe, kenning not the oracles of Saint Machiavell, pays credence to the following syllogism: .**1.** I owned authority.   .**2.** Powhatan

Radclyffe's
Palace

requests me, 'cause in my authority I was excellent. **.3.** I knew my quality all along. How could I have been installed in authority, had I *not* been excellent? **.4.** All men who deny my excellence are jealous fools.

'Tis November-month, when the Sunne doth enter unto Saggitarius. He's at the head of **.40.** men well appointed for war or trade. They're in haven now. They'll live hungerless forever!

But Powhatan (altho' he's donned his tuppenny crown) will not invite them within the new bark-plated Palace where at their ease they could feast & spy him lounging wife-flanked 'pon his leathern pillow. Nay, he parleys with his guests on a meadow **.2.** creeks upriver from the Towne. Virginia welcomes Ratcliffe with red leaves. Radclyffe welcomes *her* with copper kettles.

He would have his Soldiers form themselves into a square of *Security,* but then Powhatan must mislike him. Do Bow-men lurk in ambuscado beyond those trees? Well, in any event the Adventure must be tried now. The pinnace lies bogg'd sideways & out of sight —

Ratcliffe's Soldiers grow afeared, but he bids 'em shut up & stuff their gobs with Powhatan's bread, for at Jamestowne there's not the veriest scrap of belly-kindling to be had. Yet how he longs to pierce through that Salvage Despot's gaze, to discover his purpose!

Near-nude *Pocahontas* is there, of course, her shoulders red-daubed; other wenchen squat behind, well-necklaced with white & blue beads; she smiles on him not; welladay, he e'er misliked that squaw, she proving free with her charms only to odious little Sweet John (now happily vanish'd away forever).

At her father's word she brings an ewer of river-water for him to wash his hands. Advantaging himself, he stares at her unripened bubs. She dries his hands with a gob of feathers.

Kind Princesse, take this blue bead . . . Kemps, do present it unto her, & translate . . .

But she scorns to accept it. She denies to speak. Her eyes are glimmering & glistering. (Strange, she appears to have been weeping!) Captaine Radclyffe feels abashed. No matter; he must trust his own discretion.

He looks around him. He sees blue slats of sky in every pool.

'Tis a cool shady spring afternoon in that swamp. A Mosquitor bites Pokahuntiss, yet she disdains to brush it away.

Powhatan lights a pipe of *Tobacco*. Fearing that it might be poison'd, Ratcliffe refuses to essay it, altho' that cullionly *Kemps* doth pleadingly reprove him. — If only Sweet John were here! thinks Radclyffe. He'd comprehend what to do . . . — He gnaws his underlip, dreadfully unsure. The Soldiers sit tense.

Under your pardon, King Powhatan, I crave to undo all the many cruelties with which Captaine Smith afflicted you. I do beseech you to forgive us, now that he's dead & gone away . . .

Powhatan squints at him .1.-eyed, exactly as a Gunner takes aim at his mark. He says: 'Tis not befitting to my dignity that you come here begging pardon for your trespasses, yet meanwhile bear yourselves distrustfully.

Why, whatever do you mean, Powhatan?

Your Soldiers sit here armed, as if you meant to murther me. I did e'er demand of Captaine Smith to lay down his weapons if he were indeed my *Son* as he call'd himself; yet he would not. In the end he threatened & insulted me, which is why I removed from Werowocomoco. As for my brother Opechancanough, he'll not soon disremember the visit you Tassantasses did pay him . . .

But, dear Powhatan —

Now again you come here like beggars, to take my corn. You were sent here by others at Jamestowne; I've come to know your craft —

Powhatan, you yourself did send for us. As for Captaine Smith, that varlet only pretended to represent the Colonie when he made war upon you. Indeed, had your daughter not spared his life, we'd never have carped, he being but a gallows-bird who twice narrowly 'scaped judgment among us —

You swore friendship to me just now. Did you lie?

No, I swear it again by OUR REDEMER!

Then demean yourself in friendliness. Put by your guns.

'Tis not our custom . . .

You starve. Put by your custom, & live.

We've come but to pay you honor, & —

I reverence you likewise, replied Powhatan with a smile of hate. — Regarding the corn for which you came, I'll give it to you no sooner than you and your men set aside their weapons just as do my subjects.

That Pocahontas flits o'er him her insolent eye. O, now she commences for to tickle his hatred! She hath e'er dealt curtly with him. GOD, could he but tread her down, she'd prove as fine as virgin sand underfoot.

Kemps, says he, inquire of *Sweet John's great dearling* what we should do.

Maister, she doth say, she cannot contradict her father.

He turns to his men. His leg jitters just as a squirrel's tail flickers when he is running, or near about the way in which an autumn leaf falls whirling in the wind. He says: 'Tis now politic to yield. You, Abbots, collect the arms.

Sir?

Stand & obey me.

But, Sir, we're all adread —

Your dreads are nothing to mine. Soldiers! Dislade your arms, & keep the powder, so that our fine *Friends* can do us no mischief —

The Soldiers do whisper to **.1.** another: *Farewell.*

The aforesaid Jeffrey Abbotts now hath ta'en all the harquebuses & pistolos unto himself. Sadly he gazes upon his Captaine. Sadly he doth dredge up these words: *Remember Roanoke.*

Radclyffe turns pale. The Salvages fall on him.

They o'erpower all his Soldiers, smashing their heads with war-clubs & deer-horn pickaxes. They strip him & lash him unto a tree-bole near a fire. Then the Salvage squaws & wenchen do hale the flesh off him gobbet by gobbet, worrying it off his shrieking carcase with the edges of mussel-shells, then with laughter & imprecations sizzling those dainties in the fire. Pokahuntiss is there, staring sadly or indifferently or — soon he cannot apprehend her stare. All around him, the Salvages sing: *Whe, whe, yah, ha, ne, he, wittowa, wittowa.* So perish all his fellow Adventurers, each in his turn. Out of all those **.41.** men, only a certain Jeffrey Shortridge escapes (for we'll not count *Kemps,* he being but a Salvage) . . .

* * * * * *

And now the *Starving-Tyme* did steal upon them at Jamestowne. Near e'ery day they carried blackened corpses out thro' the rotting gates, these sad processions now compris'd of Undertakers in truth, who staggered until they could release their burthens into common pits in that rawly gruesome Church yard. The Yndians watcht. They shot arrows, singing: *Whe, whe, yah, ha, ne, he, wittowa, wittowa.* That winter out of **.500.** men at Jamestowne, only **.60.** did live until spring. Reverend Hunt sermonized: *Why standest Thou afar off, O LORD?* Then he died.

When the Colonists came to him for food, the President dully replied: Well, but Government can't protect our Undertakers in Ireland, either . . .

For CHRIST's own sake, Maister President! We starve!

As do I —

A certaine Colonist did kill & begin to feed on his wife, for which deed he was justly hang'd. Captaine West with **.36.** men did flee for England; & Maister Percie himself was on the verge of abandoning the Government . . .

THE GRAMMAR OF DAUGHTERS (1610)

I can at will, doubt not, as soon as thou,
Command a table in this wilderness . . .

MILTON, *Paradise Regained* (1671)

*A*t the earing of the corn, which is to say *Nepinough,* skinny-shouldered old Wahunsenacawh went to the witch-hazel sapling that he'd killed with fire. It was ready now — no longer green, yet not brittle. Having offered tobacco, he made his prayer of thanks, saying: *By YOUR strength I am shooting deer, shooting deer; by YOUR strength I feed my women, feed my women; by YOUR strength I feed my darling children.* He laid the heel of his hand upon the charred ring he'd made, and almost tenderly eased his palm against the wood until all his fingers were touching it, callused old skin against dead young bark. From the burned place up to the tip of his middle finger, that much would not be fit to use. His father had taught him thus. While the black dog took the white dog by the skin of the throat, he took the knife which the Tassantasses had given him and scratched a mark there, a hand's length above the charred ring. This knife had been fashioned most excellently of that white metal which none of his Cronoccoes could ever find, no matter how earnestly he advised them to search. It cut joyfully, imparting luck. He commenced to saw a notch at that mark. When the gash was deep enough, he crooked himself (a little stiffly, for after all he'd seen near seventy returns of the leaf) and pressed his left shoulder against it. Then he stretched his right arm up the dead young tree as far as he could reach. That was where the other notch would need to be. So he marked it and cut it, softly singing *Whe, whe, yah, ha.* Joining the pair of notches by means of two vertical scorings, he formed the outline of a stave. Wahunsenacawh was cunning at this work, which had ever constituted one of his best delights. He stepped back to measure the stave again, while it remained yet a part of the tree. (The two dogs had run away, scenting muskrats to kill.) All was well. Again he squinted about beneath the falling SUN, plucking at the greyish hairs on his chin. He returned thanks unto the tree. A thrill shivered over him, as it always did at this moment. Then he drew forth his knife again, deepening all four cuts until the stave was born. He pried it out of the tree with an antler wedge. When he held it in both hands, it sang to him. He did not flex it, but set one end in the ground to turn it slowly until he found where the bend was. He uttered his song, *Whe, whe, yah, ha;* his heart was content.

The sapling being so giving in its soul, he cut three more staves for spares. With his steel knife he pried the bark off them all. He smiled. Then he left them to season overnight inside a hollow tree which had often sheltered his treasures. He prayed.

Leaves rubbed together with a noise like tearing silk, a noise made by the Tassantasses. But those enemies no longer disturbed his sleep. It was near SUN set. Fiery leaves flickered, being tree-stars on the boughs; and tree-thighs spread themselves in shimmers in the bloody water. Quietly he returned to Orapaks, while the two dogs played at his heels. Then he led the People in a ring of prayer to the SUN. They made round circle on the ground with dried tobacco, and they sang. They bathed in the river.

After this his Cronoccoes saluted him with good respect, to which he replied asking for news; they had none. The Tassantasses continued quiet. Some had eaten each other. With luck they would all die soon, the Cronoccoes said, but he disbelieved. Although such troubles may come of themselves, they rarely go of themselves. His son Parahunt said that some Tassantasses had approached the falls of late, searching for edible plants. Parahunt's bowmen had shot arrows at them, and they ran away. Hearing this, Wahunsenacawh smiled. He gave his son a copper crescent.

He smoked a pipe with his Cronoccoes. Darkness finished the day.

While he lay down on his platform above the fire, two of his women served him a stew of groundnuts, rattlesnakes, and sweet green corn. He ate, but not much, so that the leavings could fill their bellies.

His favorite wife Winganuske inquired if he was well. He caressed her, but replied not.

Kocoum had killed another deer. A haunch came for him. He sent some of it to the priest Uttatomakkin.

The hearth crackled loudly. Sap sizzled out of a green stick.

He summoned his daughter Amonute and said to her: Cut my hair.

She flushed with pleasure and took up two mussel-shells to tweeze out the hairs from the righthand side of his head as he sat inhaling the young breath that blew upon him. One of his nephews built up the fire, to help her see. Wahunsenacawh turned silent. The man withdrew.

Quick and careful, Amonute dressed his hair, kneeling at his side.

You begin to go to the women's house, he said.

She said nothing, waiting upon his words while she plucked his grey old hairs.

When she had finished, he said: Bring your mother.

Winganuske (for in that season she was the mother who was meant) came quickly with red-painted shoulders, holding his daughter's hand. They stood before him. He said: Kocoum has given me many presents.

Comprehension glittered in the mother's eyes.

He said: Amonute, shave away your plaits. Kocoum will be your husband. Every day you shall dwell with him.

The child was frightened; that he could tell. He smiled at her very kindly and said: You must have a brave man to protect you after I am dead, my darling *Pocahontas*.

✴ ✴ ✴ ✴ ✴ ✴

The brave man kills all his fears. Sickness, old age, death, torture, and the anger of OKEUS, all these he overcomes. But when he becomes a father, he meets an entire army of new dreads who live among the trees, seeking to eat his soul. For no man can protect himself from evil; he who tries overmuch must not only fail, but be called coward. And yet the brave man *must* protect his children — who cannot be protected: Someday they'll die. Let it happen when they are old, and he himself already wrapped in mats forever; then all will be well. His fears swim slow and silent like an alligator submerged unto the eyes.

He gives this baby the secret name *Matoaka,* which a dream once granted unto him. Before others he names her *Amonute.* Yes, he takes her into his arms, raises her up where SUN-arrows pierce the leaves, then names her *Amonute* before the people. At the feast which follows, he's already anxious. Evil always listens. That's why he kept her soul-name a secret. Only he, she and Uttamatomakkin will know it.

The baby laughs among the rotten roots of toppled trees. She comprehends not that evil is watching. (This world is evil, so how could the case be otherwise?) Her feet beat in quick trembles like swamp gas disturbing the wan SUN's image on the waters. Beneath the waters, evil swims. In the trees perch evil SPIRITS, contending over her like birds fighting over fishes, squawking and wailing over her like cats in heat. The father sees. He guards his children; he watches over all his women. Praying for his Amonute, he takes her in his arms and raises her up to the SUN. She smiles. Her fat fingers crawl across his face. She reaches for the copper crescent in his hair. He almost cannot bear his love for her. When she cries, he holds her, knowing that she'll lay her head upon his breast and grow calm. At dawn he opens his eyes. Her eyes are already open. His wife sleeps among the other wives; her breast sleeps, weeping milk. Soon he must send her away, for that is the law when a Werowance's wife brings forth a child. No matter. If Amonute grows well, she can return here to live.

The sleeping platform is smoky and warm. He lifts the baby under her arms so that she stands upon his chest, kicking gleefully with her soft little feet. Her eyes widen. Her mouth smiles. She reaches for his face, shrieking with glee. His knowledge of the wickedness all around her leaves him sickened by dread. The only way that he can overcome these fears is to cease loving her, which he will never do.

*　*　*　*　*　*

In the morning, clammy morning, he returned to the hollow tree. Twigs and vines showered with leaves the bounding deer; but he was not hunting on that day. In a very low voice he sang, *Whe, whe, yah, ha*. But his mind unfixed itself from his task. He was thinking on Opechancanough, who'd be Powhatan after him in fact — for although Opitchapam owned the title, that brother was sluggish in his soul. Opechancanough was brave, vengeful, wise. He must send him summons. They needed to smoke a pipe together, and consider once more how best to destroy the Tassantasses, whom he now not only hated, but feared. He prayed, but his nervous eyes could not still themselves. The forest prickled all about him. A dark bird uttered a groaning laugh.

Not far away, hatchets were beating. Their move to Orapax having been so sudden, the cornfields lay but half prepared. People might starve this winter. The men were killing trees. Thanks to the hatchets of the Tassantasses, they could do in one year what used to take two. So at least these enemies gave back some of what they'd thieved away. He'd told the People to try burning out the roots and stumps right away, even though green wood was more difficult to destroy. Should OKEUS pity them, they might even be able to plant a little corn this very season. If not, he could scarce bear to think upon it.

Again he offered tobacco to the dead sapling which he'd gashed; again he made his prayer of thanks. Then he gathered his makings and set his face for the blue smoke of Orapax which soon loomed before him with its pal-

isades and crooked-ribbed drying racks. His Cronoccoes had no news for
him. Anxiety snaked through his guts.

Everything was blanched yellow inside the house: yellow wood, yellow
floor-dirt, yellow mats and poles. The dark, coarse-furred deerskins
crawled with lice.

All save one of the peeled staves he laid across his ceiling beams to season
further until he might need them. But the one in hand, the first he'd cut, he
tapered with a good stone knife, working in long strokes from the center
down to each tip. This was of all steps the most difficult. As a boy he'd ruined many pieces of wood in this way. Now the work was easy pleasure.
Next time perhaps he might try the English knife. Perhaps not. There was
a danger of slicing away too much. He preferred the milder dependability
of this quartzite blade which lifted long and even slivers. It was smoky-
dark inside his house, but he worked by feel, narrowing the ends to lovely
symmetrical curves like the bows of a canoe. He passed his fingers over
them, and there was no flaw. Then he hung the stave near the fire.

He called Amonute to him and told her to gather a little pitch. She went
out running to obey him, and his heart was gladdened. (She was as sweet as
the oil of white acorns.) He had not desired to give her to Kocoum, but it
was as he had said: She must be provided for, he being old. Then, too, he
had nine daughters by other wives.

He presented her with a blue bead made by the Tassantasses, for which
she thanked him. He laid his hand upon her arm.

That night there was dancing, after which he sat greasing the stave with
deer-suet until it would drink no more. Then he heated each tip over the
coals to bend it, holding it in the new shape with his wiry powerful wrists
until it had cooled. It struggled against him, but he mastered it; it could not
withstand his strength. He roughened each tip with a flint scraper.
Amonute was already boiling pitch for him.

* * * * * *

You are not content? he said to her, a little sternly.

She was stirring the pitch. — It shall be as you will, Father, she said.
She was shaveheaded now. He'd never tell her how much he mourned her
tresses.

* * * * * *

He smeared the liquid pitch on the tips of the stave, and it sank in. That
would keep the wood from splitting. Then he arose. His daughter from a

long forgotten wife was tending the fire. What was the secret name with which he'd gifted her? Grieving that his memory had begun to be destroyed, he walked to the Wiochisan House.

Uttamattomakkin was there with the other priests. Powhatan greeted them well. There was a Store-house in the back of that temple where he kept some of his treasures. He chose a heavy copper crescent and carried it away to give to Amonute.

* * * * * *

Amonute went out into the cornfields to tweeze the new hairs which had grown between her legs. Her soul was as taut as a deerskin on a frame. When she returned, one of her mothers gave her an apron of deerskin to wear. Nevermore would she go about uncovered.

* * * * * *

Now Kocoum came to Orapax and brought her many fishes, for which she gave her best gratitude. He was a tall man from Youghtanund, much grown up. She felt pleased and comforted that he dwelled so near her father. Her older sisters told her that he had slain a Monacan in ambush already, and indeed he wore a mummified human hand as an ornament to his hair. Yet for a knife he carried but a sharpened reed. The next day he brought her a needle from the Tassantasses, which she gave to her father. He smiled and told her to keep it. Then she did not see Kocoum for several days, after which he brought her a bear, not overly fat but still her bear, which she accepted with prideful pleasure, and everyone feasted on it. She had already begun to believe that in him lay her safety, as her father had said.

* * * * * *

Kocoum and her father sat awhile together outside beneath a cornhusk awning. Amonute felt very proud at this proof of her father's regard for her. Her sisters kept giggling and pinching her.

* * * * * *

At dawn she went to river-bathe and pray to the SUN. It seemed to her that her father sang more beautifully than ever. Afterward, when she was eating sturgeon with the others, her older sister Mayachanna (much older, almost as old as Amonute's mother) came to sit beside her under the oak

tree. Mayachanna was the wife of Uttamattomakkin. She promised
Amonute that Uttamattomakkin himself would pray for her . . .

* * * * * *

Kocoum, so she now learned, was the nephew of her uncle Opechancanough. This new assurance added to her happiness. When Opechancanough become Powhatan, which all her mothers believed would
infallibly happen (the incapacity of Opitchapam being less secret than her
father believed), then as niece of Powhatan she'd command almost as much
respect as now. She felt utterly protected by her father's love.

* * * * * *

She did not see Kocoum for some days, and then he came to lay more presents at her father's feet. Her mothers gasped at all the wealth she was
worth: beaverskins, muskrats, puccoons, coppers, antimony from Pattawomeck, long strings of smoked oysters, a single gauntlet stolen from the
Tassantasses, fishes, feathers, tobacco and a living snake. Her father said: I
am satisfied. — Amonute smiled.

In the night time she commenced to think of him as a husband. Of
course she often heard the noises that men and women made together behind their mat-curtains; girls had told her exactly what happened and how
it felt. She comprehended that at first there might be pain, but resolved to
be brave so that he would love her all the more. She'd heard that what a
man and a woman did with each other was the most perfect thing which
could ever be imagined. Closing her eyes, she imagined Kocoum's face
approaching hers. But then a mosquito troubled her, and she forgot all
about it.

* * * * * *

She was of age. Her father lent her serving-men and serving-women to accompany her. Thanking him, she set out for Rapahannock to see the
mother who'd given her birth. It was a long way, but not so long. They
stopped at the edge of each town, peering through the silhouetted trees to be
sure that no Monacans or Tassantasses were there. When they arrived in
Rapahannock at last, there was singing and dancing. Some kinswomen of
hers from Paspahegh also happened to be there. Amonute heard them
speaking of the Tassantasses, but stopped up her ears.

They feasted her on walnut milk. Her maidservants had brought with them a copper kettle from her father's storehouse. Radclyffe had carried it with him that time when her father put him to death. Now his soul was destroyed and hidden. Amonute had not much thought upon him until she saw that kettle. Well, someday she too must die. Everyone gathered about to see that marvelous object. Her mother expressed her gratefullest thanks, which Amonute promised to carry back to Orapaks. They passed the kettle around. Then her new father commenced to cut it up for ornaments.

Perhaps she stayed in her mother's house awhile. Anyhow, some days passed; her serving-men speared fishes. She stripped green corn with her mother.

Two of her aunts remained unmarried, so they lived in her mother's house. Perhaps they were a little jealous of Amonute's marriage.

She learned that she had had a little brother two years previous, but the baby died. No one had wanted to tell her, for fear of making her sad. The little bundle of bones hung from the ceiling.

Her mother sat her down upon a mat of silk grass and said: May good fortune shelter you, Amonute.

Together they began to make treebark baskets. Her mother said: Are you content?

Mother, I'm afraid.

Her mother smiled. — Be brave. Trust in your father's care.

The girl was silent.

And so you begin to cover yourself, Amonute. You're a woman now?

Yes, Mother.

May your marriage give you much joy, my darling.

*   *   *   *   *   *

Kocoum said to her father: Wahunsenacawh, great Powhatan, thank you for this distinction.

Her father smoked a pipe. Then he said: I love this daughter of mine. Take good care of her. I'll come often to Youghtanund to behold her. I am content. Amonute, are you satisfied?

The girl nodded.

*   *   *   *   *   *

She journeyed by canoe with her father, three of her mothers, and many Cronoccoes to Youghtanund, where Kocoum lived. Her mother in Rapahannock did not come. (Perhaps there was some coldness between her and

Amonute's father.) Many ladies came with her, to wait upon her. For this she did thank her father most gratefully.

The land was low and sandy-oozy. She'd never been there before.

Her father was wearing his red-dyed deer's-head crown in the house whch Kocoum's kinswomen had built for her. Her father's face was powdered blue and silver. Kocoum had painted his face red, but soberly, indeed almost drably, for (as he'd whispered into Amonute's ear) he feared lest he be thought to try for greater resplendence than her father. No fear of *that,* thought the girl.

Now the moment had come for her father to give her away forever. Gazing tenderly into her face, he took her hand and placed it in her husband's. Kocoum's father would have done this had the bride been anybody else. But Powhatan was lord of all, so that Kocoum's father waited anxious and silent, knowing not what he should do.

The new pair knelt down. Then her father shattered a roanoke-string upon their heads, so that the white and purple beads came sizzling down.

✳ ✳ ✳ ✳ ✳ ✳

Captaine Smith had once given her singularly large beads like painted nuts. He had said to one of her women: *Bid Pocahantas bring a pair of little baskets, and I will give her white beads to make a chain.* They were more beautiful by far than this roanoke. She'd rushed to present them to her father . . .

✳ ✳ ✳ ✳ ✳ ✳

She gazed almost pleadingly into her father's face, hoping that he would not depart them without a word. But although he returned her look for many moments, he said nothing. At the feast which had been prepared against his arrival he sat likewise withered and silent. She rushed to bring water so that he could wash his hands. He smiled sadly. Or had she somehow angered him? She'd never felt such mournfulness and dread.

Having eaten but little, he withdrew into the Wiochisan house with the priest. Next morning he uttered a quiet command to his men, and then he and they were gone.

✳ ✳ ✳ ✳ ✳ ✳

He returned by slow stages to Orapax, because he desired to confer with his Cronoccoes, and also to collect tribute. The Monacans had not yet attacked

this year. His son Parahunt, whose town lay near those enemies, feared they were preparing some poisonous ruse.
Wahunsenacawh could only advise him to send
out sentinels, which he already knew.

He was stronger than ever. So much did the
Tribes and Nations fear these Tassantasses that
they'd told him: Great Powhatan, we trust
only in you.

That being so, he'd increase their tribute.

About the Tassantasses his strategem was: Eliminate
their Cronoccoes, and they would starve.

He'd already sent messengers unto all his subject Nations: *Starve the
Tassantasses.* If the enemy came, all should flee. Never trade away any
corn. The men he'd slain last autumn had been skinny and shivering. He
promised Opechancanough and the others that he'd hatch new strategems,
so that more Tassantasses would perish. He'd already pitted them against
the Chickahominies.

Uttamattomakkin had fared through the snow all the way to the Great
Wiochisan House at Uttamussack to invoke that long-scalp-locked ONE,
and the invocations had been answered. Indeed, through winter and spring
the Tassantasses dwindled, as his spies reported. With good fortune they
might all die or go away.

(He was informed that a levy of Tassantasses was travelling up river, perhaps to seek another settlement. Raging terror darkened his face, but he
said nothing.)

About Amonute he thought little, for the moment. Having provided for
her as best he could, he felt satisfied. Yet when he arrived in his house and
saw her not, he was sorry. Not so many years had withered since she'd been
an infant reaching out her plump little hands for the light.

He went with Uttamatomakkin to the Wiochisan House to request
OKEUS's mercy. He left many puccoons there, but Uttamatomakkin said
that the signs were not good. Later he took the priest with him to Menapacunt, where Opechancanough feasted them well. Opechancanough inquired what he should do, should the Tassantasses return to menace him.
Wahunsenacawh knew not what to reply.

When he found leisure after gathering in the corn and receiving the
presents of some Chickahominies, he took up the stave he'd made and with
the Tassantasses' knife, which was better than any other for that work, cut

a fine notch just inward of each tip. Then he took a length of deer sinew half an arm's length longer than the stave and wrapped it twice inside the topmost notch. Amonute would have been boiling a deer's hooves in a little water to make glue. Today Winganuske was doing it. Murmuring *Whe, whe, yah, ha,* he knotted the sinew tightly inside the groove, which he filled with glue. Then he hung it up to dry.

The next day he pulled the free end of the sinew down tight into the other groove and the stave bent into a bow's lovely curve. He smiled.

❋ ❋ ❋ ❋ ❋ ❋

Not long into the autumnal season, which is called *Taquitock,* he went into the forest at dawn, carrying his new bow, a quiver, a stone knife from his father and a deerskin with the head still on. He sang: *Here I come forth. Good deer, let me kill you. Whe, whe, yah, ha. Here I come forth. Good deer, give me your life.* It was humid and overcast. He went northward into the Country of the Pianktank, now an excellent hunting ground since he'd gnawed that insolent Nation up, and he watched very carefully when he came to where it was oozy because that was the place where the People had taken many deer last year. A warmish wind blew toward him as he went, which was very good because any deer ahead would not be able to smell him. His hunting-lust was a tall green maple sapling shaking in the wind, drawing its branches together like a bear clapping his paws, tossing and shaking and glittering on every lashing leaf-point. It would not rain for some hours. By then he hoped to have made his kill. The soil firmed as he followed a rise choked with loblolly pines, and on the other side was a stand of rushes which had not been recently trodden down

A dream had told him to keep company with the rise yet a little farther. Oaks rose red, then paled as he came into the strengthening light, until finally they glowed white beneath their high green crowns which now were turning red again for autumn. Hawks swooped in love-pairs from the dark trees, to cast their watchful shadows upon the river. He listened. He overlooked a river which escorted shelves of sand and steps of sand, all of different colors. In the sand he saw fresh deer-tracks.

There was a thick hedge of inkberry bushes with a hidden opening in it which he knew as he knew everything in that Country, so that it formed a natural blind, and on the other side was a creek lined with deerberries. Crouching here, he spied through the branches carefully, and saw a beautiful stag gazing back at him, swishing his white tail. He remained still. The stag was beyond sure range of his arrows. He waited, watched the animal's tremblings die down, listened to him snort, watched him trot slowly toward the far edge of the clearing.

Silently he backed out from the bushes, a wiry old man whose eyes burned blackly greedy. He drew the deerskin over himself, the deer's head masking his face as he saw through the deer's eyes. Then he began to go silently on all fours. The stag had vanished, but he knew that the deer trail curved back around toward him. He nocked the arrow, drew back the bowstring, waited so easily in the treacherous shadows, and the stag came on, then stopped, sniffed, began to forage. The man eased closer. The stag raised his head, hesitated, then began to eat again. Wahunsenacawh was close enough now. The stag looked up, but the arrow came smashing through his ribs and plunged into his heart, so that his belly filled with blood.

THE GRAMMAR OF WIVES, .1.ST PART (1610)

> But let concealment like a worm i' the bud
> Feed on her damask cheek . . .
> SHAKESPEARE, *Twelfth Night* (*ca.* 1600), II.iv.11-12

*A*t dawn when she rolled up the snow-white mat of her marriage-bed to go offer tobacco to the SUN, Kocoum was already sorting through his arrows. He did this perhaps more than was necessary, his arrows being always perfect. Amonute took pains to compliment their straightness. (She marveled how he could even see them by ember-light.) They went to the river with all the others. Although the Werowance of Youghtanund was passing kind unto her, it seemed strange not to find her father leading the People. The songs were different.

As soon as the ceremony had ended, Kocoum went out to hunt. He hunted very hard those first few months, to please her. Almost every day he came with something for the stewpot. She took prideful delight in him.

Amonute was braiding grass into rope. Two of her sisters had come, one from Orapax and the other (whom she barely knew) from Cuttatawomen; they were helping in the work. She knew that this visit was still another mark of her father's solicitude for her. He must know how she felt now, to be commencing in a strange place. They brought gifts both from her father and from her mothers Ponnoiske and Appimmonoiske. They asked insistently how she did, to which she replied that she did well, that she and Kocoum loved and were contented with each other. This was true. And full well did she enjoy to dwell in that house which her husband's kinswomen had made, a pretty house beneath a mulberry tree, the beams well lashed with deerskin and the roots of yellow pine, so that it scarcely trembled when any guest entered. She was happy.

She had made a fine white mat, to keep ready in case her father came to visit. She gave this to her sister from Orapax, asking her to give it to her father.

Her sisters had gone now. Her husband came home. He brought her many fat fishes. Thanking him, she went to weed the corn-fields.

Kocoum killed a racoon, then another, keeping the skins always aside for tribute to her father. She began to wonder why her father took so much.

*   *   *   *   *   *

Her husband had set out to hunt. Amonute followed him, bearing their house. But after several days of this she grew awearied. Her other *Father* had told her that in England a married woman need do nothing but sit at home, preparing feasts for her husband, who works to be her support. She's given *cakes* to eat, & *milk,* & other such dainties, which Amonute could only imagine, having never tasted them. Why could they not be given to her, through whom Kocoum had gained both distinctions and copper crescents? She was Powhatan's daughter, yet she felt lonely and awearied.

But her other *Father* was broken and decayed, they said. He was dead.

To her he had always resembled some lightweight bird who watched her alertly from a wide and unwinking eye, a bird so tiny that a raspberry-bush scarcely bent beneath its body. Flittering and huffing so comically, her *Father* brought her little gifts in his beak.

Bur Kocoum was her dear friend, her support. Almost every day he brought her home some fish or animal to eat . . .

She was sharpening a needle against a sanding-stone. Her other *Father* had given her a better one, of English steel, but that she'd presented forth-with to her new mother Winganuske, to make her glad. She had no qualmishness against bone needles. She sang a little song — a song of ha-tred against the Tassantasses, it was true, but the tune pleased her: *Whe, whe, yah, ha, ne, he, wittowa, wittowa!*   Then it came time to pray unto the sinking SUN.

Her husband was oiling himself before sleeping, as was his custom to keep away fleas. She sang a song that her other *Father* had taught her. Smiling, her husband lowered his face close unto hers. Very tenatively she whispered: *Mufkaiuwh,* which means *A flower of a fine thing.*

THE GRAMMAR OF HOGS (1610)

O my America, my new found land,

My kingdom, safeliest when with one man manned,

My mine of precious stones, my empery,

How blessed am I in thus discovering thee!

To enter in these bonds, is to be free.

JOHN DONNE, "To his Mistress Going to Bed" (wr. 1593-6, pub. 1633)

& Captaine Scott did once attach himself to you? inquired courteous Argall. My elder brother Richard was Standard-bearer to a Captaine Scott in the Low Countreys.

I knew your brother passing well. He reap'd up much brave glory for his heart. Captaine Scott is now my Standard-bearer. And, Captaine Argoll, I misdoubt me not you're comprised of the same metal. You well deserve of any boon the Companie can give you.

Many thanks to your Grace. And is your health in temper this morn?

No, returned my Lord De La Warr. I'm passing aguish.

I'll send a man forthwith, to gather *Sassafrass* for your amendment. Ho! Brutus!

Aye, Captaine Argoll!

Dost thou reverence this Gentleman?

In a twink I'll do as I'm bid, Sir.

Then take the shallop, & fetch *Sassafrass* for my Lord.

Aye, Aye! Sweet Cassius, lend me .2. Sailors, I do beg of you!

Cassius? Brutus? What incomparable names your men do sport.

They have Roman blood, you know, from the days when Caesar bedded Boadicea.

The DEVIL speed you! Caesar was murthered ere she e'er rebelled!

Now I must beg your pardon, Sir, for my jesting. In me there's stuff which patterns me into clownishness. But it keeps the crew companionate. See you yonder isthmus? 'Tis your *James-towne* which lies there—

Jamestown? Why, 'tis like unto a ruin!

But now her wretched roofs & wattles give praise, Argall did soothe, because your Grace has come to put right e'erything. And see you that plain by the western Bulwark, my Lord? When I did **.1.**st arrive, I spied a little yeoman, by name *Captaine Smith,* who was drilling 'em there in marching figures. And he'd nam'd the spot *Smithfield.* Can you credit it? We all did laugh to scorn his yokelish conceit—

I do begin to see your humor's more quizzical than your brother's, Argoll. But you're a brave & able man, I don't deny that . . .

For which observation I thank your Grace. And for the rest, Richard's as merry a trickster as I. He could make e'en a *Dutchman* laugh! But let me inquire of you. The armor you wear, 'tis of true Isebrook steel?

The same.

Most wondrously wrought. And I see from its many dents you know how to fight, my Lord.

You flatter me well.

And 'tis dented only in front, as becomes your honor, purr'd Argoll, with his tongue nicely tuck'd up in his cheek. What could he get from this anxious old invalid? His mirth did glimmer to itself, & Lord De La Warr failed to spy it. *He* wouldn't last long here, as Argol could tell. Virginia would *season* him to death, unless he fled, as the entire Colonie had sought to do merely **.2.** days since—

Lord Delaware was smiling like unto a foul skull, saying: Indeed, I offered the Spaniards somewhat to remember me by, yet found few takers, for they did turn coward . . .

Like unto Salvages.

O yes. *They* we must requite for their treachery. Where do they bide?

Everywhere & nowhere.

Speak not obscurely, man. My thoughts need quiet pass . . .

Well, they dwell in Townes—

Warrens.

. . . But they can vanish behind the trees when we come — & they can appear swifter than the plague! Misdoubt you not, my Lord: They spy us e'en now. — Cassius!

Ay, Captaine Argall!

Reef sails.

'Tis done, 'tis done!

Lord De La Warr bent closer to his interlocutor as he inquired: And 'tis true of them, what your Sailors did say?

To be sure, these lads are oracles. I've trusted 'em to piss wisely in all my chamber-pots . . .

In *Armenia* (as I've heard) the Armorers do empoison the iron of their swords, to fatalize e'ery wound. And your men swore to me that these Salvages do the like with their arrows, which if prov'd would mean us great mischief.

Have no fear, my Lord. No Salvage is so eminent, as your own eyes can prove. See, yonder's the Church-yard, where several hundred English lads lie moldering. — Oho, these gamesters repaired it not. D'you spy that corpse-hand sticking out the bank?

I'm aware that men die, dear Argoll. What of it?

Well, how many of 'em do you s'pose our Salvages killed?

I —

Fewer than our hands together rule fingers! 'Twas but an ordinary pestilence that slew 'em, & their own idleness, for they starv'd instead of planting corn.

So I've heard. Well, Captaine Argoll, by my faith we'll outstare all idlers. Then we'll bring the Salvages to heel. They'll no longer obstruct our business . . .

* * * * * *

In the .2.nd hour of the Forenoon Watch, with the sun hot in his face, my Lord De La Warr did kneel down in the dirt before the Fort & give thanks to OUR REDEEMER that he'd arrived in time to save James Towne. (The starving Adventurers had abandoned their Colonie to the last man before he came. He met 'em in James River. He ordered 'em back.)

Low, steamy forest hearkened all around. He was Governor for life. George Percie's Presidency was ended forever. (Suave *Cicero* toll'd the ship's bells near about .**100**. times.) The Counsell got abolished. And well that was, for self-government breeds factionalism. Red-robed Servaunts assisted him to his feet. Then they bore away the golden-threaded carpet he'd knelt upon. He entered through the South-gate, with his eyes rais'd up to Heaven. The Trumpeter blew *Trarintra-rarara.*

Next, Reverend Bucke, the new Minister, preach'd a sermon of *Thanksgiving,* in which he said: Two ships may hail one another in the night with the same watchword, if the same Admiral they serve. Then they'll be easy in friendship. But without their Admiral, who unifies their signals, they might for fear's sake fire mutual broadsides. Outside *Obedience,* the only watchword's *Death.*

Amen, said my Lord De La Warr.

Now Argoll's cousin *Captaine Scott* did read out Lord De La Warr's commission, & Sir Thomas Gates rendered unto him the keys of the Fort. Cannoneers fired off a thunderation to salvo the day. Argoll, who wore again the black partlett about his throat, did make obeisance to the rest, & his eyes glistered with the solemnity.

Congratulations, my Lord.

Thank you, dear Argoll. Certes this place doth stink like a rusticke dunghill—

To the Colonie assembled that old man did say: Since to me 'tis befitted to rule you, I earnestly entreat you all to amend all these desperate follies I see about me, lest I be compelled to draw Justice's sword & cut off the delinquents. 'Pon my faith, men, I'd rather unsheath it to the shedding of mine own vital blood! So hearken unto me, I advise you, for your own protection; & fear not, for I've wherried unto you an entire year's supply of stores . . .

Applause rang out (in much the same spirit as the Salvages in their exuberancy do sometimes dance about human-headed poles). Lord Delawarr smil'd wearily.

Moreover, if you follow me with sure discretion we'll put down the Salvages . . .

He cough'd.

My Lord De La Warr returned unto Argoll's ship, for as yet no residence had been prepared which befitted unto his dignity. The flagship which pertained to him was getting careened, unbarnacled, and retarred with the best Virginian pitch. He must bear with such necessities. Meanwhile, this aforesaid Argall did certainly keep perfect accompt of e'erything. All brasswork gleamed; not a plank was rotted; the Sailors grinn'd & strain'd to obey their Master. 'Twas all good. He'd enact his Government from here. Here, too, he'd repose his body until illness no longer debased it. Mollusk in the shell, Turkishe woman veil'd, treasure locked in Store-house — these conceptions must metaphorize him, delimiting his physicke. He'd bar himself in. He'd rest. The living brain ne'er doth meet daylight, & yet it hath eyes & hands for to execute its judgments.

Argal having wisht him a pleasant rest, he entered his State-room & lock'd the portal. Then he laid himself down, listening to his scarlet-liveried Guard-servaunts pacing without — a most regular sound which always comforted him like unto raindrops 'pon a sturdy roof. Drowsing, he remembered how it had been when he reposed beside his wife,* whose head turn'd unto the wall when she slept, her lips trembling in dreams, her naked breast rising & falling like unto the sea. Now she lay at home, being for all he knew quite perish'd of the *London Plague,* whilst he lay far away. He loathed Virginia. He trusted no one, excepting steady Captaine Argull . . .

* * * * * *

The Salvages kept aloof. Virginia drowsed torridly. Sometimes he heard Captaine Argall pleasantly singing.

* * * * * *

His own vessel now drew up. 'Twas long & black — a coffinlike flagship, with her masts ornately shrouded. (Indeed, to Argoll's mind she was somewhat o'er-rigg'd. But he buried his opinion in his heart's Church-yard.) Lord Delaware stayed on Argall's ship while they did newly furbish his quarters. Then he chang'd o'er, with his Servaunts transferring his baggage. It would hardly do, for the Governor to remain another man's guest, e'en Argoll's. He was feeling passing sickly. He laid himself down beneath a pall of velvet.

* * * * * *

Like Sweet John, my Lord De La Warr was a seasoned Soldier; he was also noble, being (as I have read) of cousinage to Her late Majestie. Thus accustomed by birth to govern & commaund, he scrupled not to fulfill his commission, which was to draw the Colonie into better order thro' a more rigorous Government. Can we say that Sweet John, himself destined merely to unburthen Bartty's mare & lead her out of treacherous ooze, would have been any less cruel had he continued to enjoy the means to be so? We've seen him to have been stain'd by hot passions. Still, he'd forborne to slay *Opechancanough, Powhatan, Wowinchopunck* & their kindred Kings. Perhaps 'twas why he'd failed. Amongst alligators, he who denies to bite must lose his watery Kingdome. As for Lord Delaware, he march'd more coldly toward his premeditated triumphs. Judging according to his own integrity, he believed for a fact (as the Booke of Psalms doth

---

*Reader, for emblem that Lord Delaware had e'erything which Sweet John had not, I need merely tell you that her name was *Cecily.*

say, *The heathen rage, & the people fancy a vain thing).* Reader, I'm sure of it: Sweet John never could have accomplisht what this other did, for his rabble-flavored blood left him impotent to rein in Gentlemen.

Now all was doomed to succeed, altho' the drumbeat to which our Governor's soul did march fell muffled by his sickness. Brought into formal unison, the Colonists of James Towne grew changed into sweating horses whose bare flesh quivers in anticipation of the lash.

My Lord De La Warr set the idlers to cleansing the streets of dung & corpses. Any 'Venturers with water-knowledge he set to scouring the river for fishes or other food, to feed their brethren (altho' few won near as much success as had graced Sweet John always). He caused the Laborers to erect a Corps du Guard, a Market-place, a cedar-chanceled Chapel, & a better Storehouse whose Dutch-forged locks no villain could pick. He posted laws against mutiny, sluggishness & unnaturalness. He commaunded that everything be done to the tune of Church-bells. The **.1.**st bell toll'd each morning at **.6.** of the clock, which is to say exactly halfway thro' the Morning Watch. And that bell did proclaim that before anything, each Colonist must hie himself to worship. Afterwards, he could eat. Lord Delaware came always there, no matter how gruesomely he had slept. Then when Reverend Hunt's sermon had ended, his gorgeous Servants did wherry him away within a long black litter on gilded poles.

Now the Plantation did buzz with sawing & ring with hammering; Carpenters, Laborers & other Plebeians cut roof-boards, under the direction of white-gloved Gentlemen (who stood well-pleas'd that that Sweet John was gone; ne'er again would souls of their nobility be compell'd to blister their hands). The Undertakers and Adventurers commenced at last to reify their schemes. For the **.1.**st time, Jamestowne Haven was abristle with ships! Masts & shrouds, ratlines & cat-harpings, yard-arms, flags, guns & pennants did all sprout forth from the swaying hulls, wriggling like unto the hairs of a *Woolly Caterpillar.* Gravesend hath resurrected herself here. From her new & no more savory womb, she'll people Virginia; the Salvages shall be o'ercome.

Yea, Reader, life at James-towne grew utterly o'erturned! Perhaps that Lord la Ware kenned the epigraph out of Sweet John's leathern-bound Machiavelli that *he who becomes Master of a city accustomed to freedom and does not destroy it, may expect to be destroyed by it.*

But, altho' he wished to utterly cleanse Virginia down to the last pickerel-weed, the years of his life had already near run their race; so in these unwholesome Tropickall climes he found himself to be **.1.**^{stly} afflicted by the

ague, then .2.^{ndly} distempered with the flux, after which he got strick by
.3.rd the cramp, .4.th the gout, & .5.th the scurvy. Following kind Argoll's
advice, he commaunded the Soldiers to gather him more *Sassafrass* root.
This herb, or rare *Vegeteball,* is a great boon to syphilitics, who pay a
high price for it, so that it stands almost as good as gold. He gorged himself
on it, to see what its properties might be in his own case, but did not improve. His own Servaunt, Docktor Bohun, failed to cure him, even after
administering a dram of the *Eternal Elixir.*

The sudden resumption of Yndian ambuscadoes further endulled his
spirits (between Englishmen and Salvages, peace *must* quickly erode as
quickly as a tombstone in Willoughby). Thoughts swam down the channels of his mind of trees, his mind of mist. He would not be false, or slack.
But he never felt hale enough to prosecute the conquest of Virginia to
the end.

✻ ✻ ✻ ✻ ✻ ✻

A bell rang the .2.nd Dog Watch. He started, all asweat from his nightmares (which partook of the *twinkling fear).* Musquetors humm'd
about him, striving for to steal his blood.

✻ ✻ ✻ ✻ ✻ ✻

In his quicker days, Lord De La Warr had distinguished himself in Ireland,
quelling the tumults there with exemplary cruelties. But such measures
could be applied here only in good season. Pacifiers must have Forts, to
shelter 'em from the revenge their actions invariably excite. So he set the
waged men to building .2. additional Redoubts — .1. near Poynt Comfort
(for under Lieutenant Pearcie's tenure, Fort Algernon had fallen into decay) and .1. at the Falles, which do represent the demarcation between
High Virginia, & *Virginia's Low Countreys.* ('Twas at this latter
site that Sweet John sought to plant his Cittie of *Nonsuch.* He'd failed, of
course.) And so Lord Delaware's strategems blazed up. Lying in his darkened State-room, he received the reports of his modest Servitors at regular
times. So many times he rehearsed his plans for Virginia that when he
closed his eyes he could see the English shires springing up with their joyful
steeples, & himself at rest beneath a golden-'graved stone within some as yet
unbuilt Church. Originally such dreams had been but a means to toy away
the time, but presently they commenced to seem like unto a Ship-wright's
drawings, which by men's labor translate themselves into a fleet of War-
skimmers & commodious Merchaunt-vessels, all well appointed with liv-

ing, creaking truth. Altho' day by day he grew more pallid, altho' he got bedsores, & his voice did dwindle, & his commaundments must be relayed thro' Factors & Agents, yet he wrought in his stillness far more radically than anything which had been accomplished by Sweet John's sprightly, companionate prancings.

Meanwhile, the Colonists most nervously clapt one another's shoulders, seeing how Salvages had set the grass alight.

✳   ✳   ✳   ✳   ✳

Send for Lieutenant Percy, he said.

Aye, Sir.

He opened the Book of Job to where it did read: *He discovereth deep things out of darkness, & bringeth out to light the shadow of death.*

My Lord?

Send him unto me.

The Governor bids you enter, Lieutenant Percie.

Thanks, lad. — My Lord, I wish you fine morning. I'm come to report, as you did bid me—

Leave us, Nathaniel. Shut the door.

Aye, Sir.

Sit down, Lieutenant Percie.

How fares your health, Lord? GOD grant it may soon be amended—

Percy, under you this Colonie plunged to doubtful digrace.

My good Lord! In HEAVEN's name I cannot tell what I should have done else—

Silence. No sooner did Captaine Smith up sail, than you lost West; you lost Radclyffe with near all his troops . . .

Lord, I crave pardon, should I have misdemeaned myself. But Captaine West sail'd home without my leave—

No matter. Your Government must have miscontented him.

Now I do begin to fear I cannot clear myself. The malice of my enemies hath—

Enough. Ratcliffe embark'd for Orapacks at thy pleasure?

He did, my Lord. But 'twas his own folly which undid the flesh from his living bones, for I warn'd him of the Salvages' traitorous cunning.

That was coldly spoken!

His stupidity got exactly requited. Moreover, everybody misliked him—

I'll examine into this matter further. Jeffrey Shortridge did 'scape, as I'm told.

Aye, Lord, & several others who waited safely in the shallop. I fancy me their tales will do me service.

GOD prove so, Lieutenant Percie. You serv'd in Ireland full bravely. Moreover, marriage brings you into cousinage with me. If you've shamed yourself, you'll answer to our mutual relations as well as to Companie & Crown.

As I live, Lord De La Warr, I swear I did cherish mine integrity.

Good. Give me thy hand. Until 'tis prov'd against you, I must trust in your excellent blood. Now let me ask you: Did we give the Salvages aught to carp at, that they attack'd us thus?

That I cannot tell, for who can fathom their minds? But I'll say that under my Government, at least, we proffer'd 'em e'ery chance to be loving subjects to His Majestie. Doubtless their King would have preferr'd not to be reduced to vassalage—

'Tis but scantly to the point.

Yes, my Lord. And we did proceed always circumspectly, within the limits of our Charter . . .

What think you of Captaine Argall?

Why, he's a good Mariner, & a very civil Gentleman . . .

✳ ✳ ✳ ✳ ✳ ✳

You may go. Send for Captaine Argoll.

Right away, my Lord.

Welcome, Captaine, & my thanks that you did come quickly. Now, stand you ready for war?

Yea, by the whites of a dog's eyes — by the whites of my teeth!

Heartily said. We'll reduce the Salvages to doleful entreaties—

Ha, my Lord! These wanton wastrels have made my heart a burning bruise.

Can you get 'em to pay us tribute?

Do the rivers pay tribute to the ocean?

You're a lyrical fellow, Captaine Argull. I half think you'd sing your words, did my Drummer but strike up a beat . . .

Poetic I am, my Lord, just as surely as the Pope is Anti-CHRIST!

But can you strategize?

Nay, Lord Delaware, I'm but an innocent virgin. Altho' I would wed her, *Lady Politicka* denies to do more than buss me on my cheek . . .

Never mind your jests. I know you can fight.

O! (quoth gentle Argall), how I long to see us raise sword!

(In truth he cares not a cheese-paring for this sickly old dotard. The dotard coughs. Argoll hums; he sings. They drink sack together out of little silver cups.)

And, good Captaine Argall, I do appoint you to be *Captaine of y^e .1.st Companie.*

My best thanks, Lord.

Sir George Somers shall be *Admirall of the Virginian Sea,* & Captaine Newport shall be *Vice-Admirall.*

Excellently conceiv'd!

Percie shall be made *Captaine of James Fort.* Do you approve?

Dread Lord, I think you best know his deserv'd estate.

Tell me quick: Was he lackadaisical as President? For I see the men do confide their news to you.

They tell me he serv'd their purpose, Lord. Now, what purpose that was I scarce suspect, but I swear by Cape Henry's white and hilly sand 'tis time true Policy came to Virginia! And here she is, fully person'd in yourself—

I deem you're metal-hearted, Argoll, which fact shall refresh my purpose. Now, regarding these Yndians, who's their King?

Powhatan.

(In those days, Reader, this *Powhatan's* fame came well into England, and thence to Spain, where 'twas written of him that he sent spies every year by land to West India and Newfoundland, such being their ignorant estimation of his reach. For he was a Salvage, a mere Salvage with bolter'd* hair.)

That's the .1. we crown'd? ask'd Lord De La Warr.

The very same.

Disloyal wretch! I'll burn him alive!

You're as merry songster as I, my Lord.

Keep respectful, dear Argoll, I caution you.

Naturally, 'pon my life!

How far lies his new capital?

Some .16. miles.

Can't we surprise him?

Not easily, for he doth keep e'ery night .4. guards in the .4. quarters of his house. Further, Sir, his *Cronoccoes* do stand without . . .

How know you this?

---

*Matted; gobbetted with blood.

From a little yeoman nam'd Sweet John who once tumbled into his clutches. He's the same who—

I remember. How did he get free?

By taking Powhatan's daughter to bed, so they relate, for Powhatan did count him after that a son. But I scarce know how true the tale runs, the squaw being monstrous young. E'en a Salvage might hesitate to give so ill-grown a child to slut-work, I trow . . .

Her name?

Pokahuntiss, my Lord. She's so called on account of her pock-marked, ugly face. Still, they judge her tractable.

(In his heart Argoll can see her very well, for she came to the Colonie several times, when that yeoman was President. Dear Pokahuntiss, your face is like unto a fat orange pumpkin!)

And did she drop the yeoman's brat?

I've heard no news of such.

Worse luck — then there's no cub to seize. But Powhatan's fond of her?

Monstrously so, I swear it by her buttocks! But we know not where she bides now, so to pluck her might prove weary policy . . .

Send out spies. How many Yndians can we trust?

None, excepting that greasy *Kemps,* whom we've now bought to be our villain—

Send him out on that errand. And the King bides e'er within his gates?

'Tis said that when he issues forth, armed vassals accompany him, just as if he were .1. of those rebellious Earls in Ireland . . .

Well, shall we assault him by river?

His Sentinels watch our ships. They'll give the alarm.

Captaine Argoll, you *do* desire to help bring him into amendment?

I stand e'er ready to do your pleasure, Sir.

Then can you amend him?

Ho, but can I! When was I ever denied, e'en by sea-waves and Prince's discountenances? Powhatan I'll un-Prince of all his telltale pride; I'll strip his daughter from his shame.

Captaine Argull, I cannot sound you. You wax hot & cold at once; your very words flare like unto a rushing house-fire. You're passing strange!

'Tis but my manner, Your Grace. It signifies my eagerness to serve your strategies.

Be not untimely to cease playing ape, when my wars bid you play the man. Now to the point: Where shall we strike?

'Tis the Towne of *Kecoughtan* you must .1.st o'erthrow, Lord, & then ask of Powhatan his submission. 'Tis now the season when they sow their corn. Bide a twink, 'till the corn grows high. Then when you spoil it, you'll pain 'em more . . .

* * * * *

See *Sir Thomas Gates* at Kecoughtan, in obedience to the rede of Argoll. (Where's Argull? My Lord Governor hath commaunded him to sail forthwith to the Bermudas, to fleshen & fishen up the Colonie's empty hogsheads with meaty belly-timber.) This Sir Thomas is Lord De La Warr's good Deputy, & in time he'll be Governor. Today let's call him *Executioner of Knaves.* He too serv'd in Ireland, & knows how to cast rebels down to Hell. Indeed, 'twould taint us with unmanliness did he fail to render such service, for the Yndians have murthered another Englishman! At Governor De La Warr's commaund, we've toll'd the Church-bell for the victim, serving up our best dole. We've dug a hole in Fort Algernon Church-yard. Down dropt his mortal substance, there to melt unto corruption in the Virginian summer. All swore to get reveng'd (such being our new brave spirit). His farewell sermon (uttered by good Reverend Bucke) did speak of *An eye for an eye.* And when words do steel us beyond our loving dispositions, why, 'tis honor's part to follow those words.

Just as in Willoughby in summertime the long heavy shadows of chestnut trees grow hour by hour, so crime-shadows have now chilled the sunny peace down unto war. And by our scale or scantling, 'twas all the Yndians' fault! Lord De La Warr, awaking feverish with rage, sees how his *Body Politick* hath swelled. The next night 'tis worse. (Dr Bohun administers a cordial of the Sassafrass call'd *Rhubarbum album.)* Lord Delaware prays. He takes up his dirk from the bedside (& the name of the dirk is *Sir Thomas Gates),* & he envoys it to stab the goiterous zone.

'Tis July y^e .9.th, 1610. The Dog Days have gone; soon the Sunne will swim into the House of Leo. Destiny's projecting taperingly forwards like unto a ship's head! Do the Salvages know it? Nay, sweet Reader; they're on a par with those green pine-beasts which get reflected in brown creeks; they resemble wild grapevines clambering up dead trees. At Poynt Comfort, whose dunes are marbled with white & black sand like unto that Turkish sweet call'd *Halvah,* the Nandsamund Salvages peep at us, murmuring in hate. They won't soon disremember how Sweet John nearly pillaged their Towne — nay, how he took their corn at sword's point! Many children persht last winter, thanks to him. Belike that's why they're now afraid to snipe at us with their bone-headed arrows, singing *Whe, whe, yah, ha, ne, he, wittowa, wittowa!* If they did, might we have been temporarily distrain'd?

Ring round the Towne, my lusty-hearts! Sweet John's not here, but he ne'er was so indispensable as he supposed. Undertakers, prepare Kecoughtan's grave! This day the Future's come a-slavering & a-sucking its monstrous gulf.

They .1.st see a man with a fish-trap on his shoulder. At Sir Thomas's commaund (which follows Lord De La Warr's will & pleasure), they hail him & throw him a bead, for to bait the others. He smiles upon them, crying out: *Nowamatamen!* which in their jibber-jabber doth approximate *I must keep yt* or *I love yt.* — How the murtherers do grin!

Now when our Generall upraises his forefinger a certain dark-eyed, dark-bearded young Tambourine-man commences for to play, with such fervor as to help him disremember why he plays. Upon my faith, he plays so beautifully that out come ye Salvages to drink up his mirth. Can we say they long to be changed? Nay, they foolishly believe that since they need nothing of consequence, Captaine Fortune means to alter them inconsequentially. (They've disremember'd the malignancy of their own OKEUS.) 'Tis comical they are, & strange, & thickly-number'd as summer mosquitoes! Well, 'tis the last day they shall be *that.*

Trarintra-rarara!

Quick! O'er-rush their wooden thresholds! (Mats hang low. Cut thro' the mats!) Prevent these Wormes from turning e'er again; kill all who fail to run away! Kecoughtan lies forfeit forever.* 'Tis a windless blue day, a mindless blue day, with seaweed clumping on the surface of the Virginian Ocean like unto green puddles. And so our resolute English have gain'd yet another Garrison in Virginia. 'Twas as easy as Argoll said. And e'er since then, many good Americans have dwelt there.

* * * * * *

My Lord De la War uprais'd himself. Dr Bohun let blood from his left arm. The patient grew dizzy, & swooned. Dr Bohun administered a cordial.

---

*For spoils they did get corn, *Tobacco* and women's girdles fashion'd out of grass-silk. Reader, if you do wonder what use those men made of women's girdles, 'tis not to the point. This grass-silk is said to be of the same substance from which the Chinese make their damask. As such, it may well excite the Lord Merchaunts of London-Towne to Adventure money in the Companie, in hopes that should .1. of Sweet John's successors but explore a little bit farther west, 'twill soon be possible to chaffer direct for spiceries with the Great Khan . . .

Lord Delaware did open his eyes. His red-habited Attendants carried him out onto the sunny deck. He summonsed Salvages. He sent to Powhatan in all friendship, to inquire whether he desired peace or war.

Tell him that he must give an universal order to all his subjects, to cease their hostility.

Seeking for to gull him, his Salvages murmured that not all warriors obeyed Powhatan.

Not so, he said. I care not to argue that question. He's Emperor. To him's the responsibility.

Powhatan did reply that the English should cease annoying him in his own Dominions. He e'en demanded a coach like upon the conveyances owned by great Lords in London Towne! Then Lord De La Warr was more resolv'd than ever to punish him, just as the School-master must beat the careless amongst his Scholars.

* * * * * *

He summonsed the Counsell to a meeting in the Church. When all were seated, he entered pale & slow like unto a specter. A pair of scarlet-clad Servaunts did support his hands.

He said: Their King refuses to render up himself. He disdains our good purposes. 'Tis time we correct the injuries we've received.

My Lord, we know not how to strike at him —

Lend me your attentions, Gentlemen. We'll visit his crimes upon his subjects, for since he be King, then in him all other Yndians & their deeds must be complicitly contained.

Aye, aye, Lord — a plague upon him!

Slay the Salvages!

Cut their throats!

We'll avenge Ratcliffe, Your Grace, & then we'll—

Abate 'em all unto ooze!

* * * * * *

Lieutenant George Percy was too noble for this World. From the very .1.st, o'ersensitiveness had plagued him worse than Virginian *Mosquitors* on a hot night, his aspirations resembling the lucent jewels of sleep which he could not pluck, for his own fellow creatures fleered about, tormenting him with their baseness. Alive, they reek'd of stupidity. Dead, they merely reek'd. Eternally pale, high-collar'd, he fortified his heart in rich clothes sent him by his elder brother the Earl of Northumberland. Never could he discover the *Ideal Gold* which glisters thrice remov'd from the kind that Captaines Ratcliffe & Newport had sought at Cape Henrico. If (as the Fish-wives do maintain, after years spent unspinning the guts from shining mackerel) we can't thrust out our own inbred corruption without suffering death, then what are we to do? **.1.** We may pray unto GOD as doth Reverend Bucke, but meanwhile shit beslimes our needful bowels. **.2.** Sweet John's strategem is to fling himself into feculence & swim his fishy heart out, hoping for to haven himself on illusory shores. **.3.** Argoll in his divinity dabbles in the ooze, spreading it from here to there, stirring up e'ery stew-pot, then flinging mud in. Some say his joy's to ruin e'erything. Others comprehend there's profit in his play. **.4.** My Lord De La Warr floats en-coffined upon the surface of projects, holding his breath in so that he can float a little longer. **.5.** As for Lieutenant Pearcie, well, I know not what to say. In those days the younger son of any Noble house was of course an unsatisfied, foredoomed type, exemplified in softness by Sweet John's old play-chum Bartty, that ruiner of horses & unwary Countrey-wenchen. Knowing that unless his brother Robert untimely perish'd he could never attain the dignity of being Lord Willoughby, poor Bartty disdained to fight resourceless battles. He idled & gamed. He was **.1.** of those persons whom Lieutenant Pearcie hated. But did our Percy, who'd been marr'd by the same accident of birth as he, necessarily bepoison himself with a draught of the same poisonous infusion? Reader, alto' I'm shamed to write it, *Bartty's heart ne'er 'scaped its lowness,* whereas within George Percie's flesh there dwelt the soul of the Artist, the Philosopher, or mayhap the Mage. What triumphs he was fitted for! How it would have behooved him to be better fam'd & honor'd! We can scantly blame him, that this heart of his ruled strengthlessness. Indeed, envious mouths might term his condition *incapacity.* 'Twould be cruel to construe that this Percy was not a man. Misfortunate swims the fish with insufficient guts! Beauty afflicted him with sadness, for he knew not how to join himself unto her forever. The temporary joinings which beguiled Bartty, or for that matter Sweet John's Soldiers when they guested 'emselves 'midst friendly Salvages, kindled no flame of similar aspiration in Percy, but only a common torch. Soon he'd be summonsed to make more spectacular fires, but for the nonce dread *Imperfections* afflicted him with such sickly queasiness as to make him hate their separate causes. And those, if we commence to accompt 'em up into numerals, they'll prove more populous than all Virginia's Salvages convok'd! Flies of BEELZEBUB, vermin of Hades, they soil what they land on.

I myself (being already corrupted) think life can sail no other way. Because this whole Globe's but a Gravesend, dear Reader, in which we flitter & fool ourselves with dreams of Captaine Fortune, 'tis passing difficult to 'scape harbor-foulnesses: the rotting, stinking hopes, the visions gutted & fried in Tavern-houses (how can our daily path prevent us from crunching our heels upon their little fishbones?), the exoticall loves fraughted in the holds of merchaunt-ships, disladed here to spoil for want of buyers, the Adventures translated into abortions which by night the Midwives do cast down 'pon the streets amongst other chamber-lees, the religious dogmas soured to the point of abomination, &c, &c. Most of us accomodate ourselves to such impurities by learning to deny our sense of smell. But Maister Percie could not.

So he went for a Soldier, thinking that if he could not slay all the grave- & womb-worms of this World, at least he'd symptomatically relieve his anger in a fashion approv'd by the Kingdome. With his arms diagonally upraised like unto sprits on a sailing-ship, he cried out: *Victory!* He was in the Low Countreys at the same years as Sweet John, but his birth spared him from serving under laughable Rustickes such as Captaine Duxbury. By day he charged the Spaniards on a fine black stallion; by night he sported upon his harp, often in the company of Netherlandish Gentlewomen. Commoners saluted him when they cantered past. But to him the cause stood already soiled. His pride shining self-evident, in exactly the same proportion as his self-disdain approximated bravery, he rode brilliantly o'er the keening hordes of Ireland, cutting 'em down when our bugles did blare. And yet the weariness to which he was subject soon persuaded him that all mounds of Celtic fairy-gold had been dug up in bygone years. He denied to Undertake new gambles in that dank green Countrey. For (if I may put the matter plainly) this unhappy Percy lived enthrall'd by a faith in Captaine Fortune which prov'd more powerful e'en than Sweet John's. The Jews, I've heard, look for their *Messiah.* The hungry Colonists gambled on *Powhatan's corn.* Percie awaited PURITY. For since Nature's productions (not least himself) rendered him so miserable, how could he give o'er his supplications (which were all the more addictive in that they were unconscious) to be saved?

And so this project of Virginia infatuated him near as soon as he heard of it. Since he belonged to the well-born caste, 'twas no trouble for him to envoy himself there. Lying on the horizon, Cape Henrico appeared to him like unto a jocundly purple concretion of Heaven itself, adamantine 'gainst disappointments. Then came the landing, when they were assaulted by Salvages, & Captaine Archer wounded in his arm. Already poisoned then &

there by a gloomy indignation against those infidels, Lieutenant Percy would have sail'd homeward with Captaine Newport, had not the prospect of another sea-voyage beclogged his resolution. Hoping to rediscover the horizon's congeniality at Jamestowne, he stayed, supposing that at least the nightmares which had haunted him in England might not discover him here. Darkness & close-work'd foliage might yet shelter him from his weary self-knowledge. But corruption breath'd on him. The disastrous tenures of the .1.st .3. Presidents speedily shewed him that life e'en here on this far-flung Continent continued subject to the same baleful influences of sin & decay. O yes, 'twas unutterably the same, by his sigh-bewasted heart! Jamestowne was Hell, & London-Towne a lethally vulgar Game-board of politics. Sweet John the gallows-bird of Ratclyffe & Wingfyld he despised equally with Sweet John the President. Yndians appalled him neither more nor less than Irish rebels. 'Twas Mosquitors here & Beggar-men there. At length his armor had rusted, & he'd fallen into a mind to return unto England with the .3.rd Supply, but, like all lost natures, his lay extremely susceptible to influence. The oraisons of Radclyffe had convinced him to stay a little longer, & become President in his own turn. If the Colonie lay entirely at his charge, then he might at last be able to accomplish something fine, like unto a Sculptor who gazes down all his completed productions with disgust, yet uplifts his chisel to the latest block of marble with that peculiar optimism known as desperation. But Destiny prov'd not much kinder to him than to Sweet John. The Starving-Time & the murther of Ratclyffe with most of his men, had once again shocked Percy forth from his dreams. When my Lord De La Warr arrived to relieve him of his Presidency, he'd already become a positive wretch to whom Virginia reeked of excrement, blood & guilt.

The dressing down he'd received at the Governor's hands stung almost pleasantly, for at least the gravitational pull of disgrace, if succumbed to, must reward the plunging heart with a brief sensation of voluptuousness before the pit's floor's struck. And then it came to him that since Virginia lay under a new Government, he had another Gambler's chance for moral or spiritual newness. (Reader, if you cannot understand the impulsions of George Percy, keep out of his reach!) He crav'd to be sent forth, to discover the sweetmeats of the Unknown.

Now my Lord De La Warr did summons the Officers aboard his long black ship (which was moored on the south shore of that great river, for the inconveniency of Spies & Traitors). He was white-clad like a Choir-boy at Saint Paul's. Streamers black & gold flew from the yard-arms. After these

Gentlemen had assembled on the quarter-deck, his Servaunts carried him out in a litter. They set him down. He looked ghastly ill.

He rais'd his haggard head. He peered into each man's face. Then he said: Gentlemen, you've all march'd in Ireland. Several served with me. Carrying out our policies there, you've suffered the sight of rebel carcases. On you hath rain'd the shrieks of widows you've bereaved. Sometimes necessity commaunded you to put those women likewise to death — yea, & their infants, too. To starve, scorch, hang & fusilade comprised your duty. To have retained your undauntedness then, 'tis what renders you true Englishmen. Now, this *Virginia*'s an Ireland of infinitely greater worth, for, once taken & secured, she'll supply all our wants for ages. Moreover, as the Spaniards have prov'd, there's treasure here, & I'm assured we're now in grappling-reach of China.

Lieutenant Percie gazed westwards past his Generall's face. He gazed between cedars, where this unknown bank thinned. He heard swans, geese & mallards in the reeds. How could he believe in treasure anymore? And yet there was a mysterious grandeur in what their Generall said, which could not but snare his heart.

Take Ireland to be your paradigm henceforth, Lord Delaware continued, and Percy thrilled to receive this rule, which seemed to emit the curling bluish flames of inspiration.

Now the sickly man uprais'd his trembling hand. He pointed up the river. — As you know, heathens have drawn English blood. But Kecoughtan is ours. Now I'm dispatching you to *Paspahegh-Towne*. That's a nest of rebels, as I do hear. Do not treat with 'em. Stop your ears to their monstrous pleas. Strike 'em at their heads & innards; cut 'em down as you hew their corn. Burn e'erything; leave their Towne a skeleton unflesh'd.

His heavy head fell forward. He rais'd it again & said: Maintain our rights. GOD be with you.

He gestured faintly. The scarlet-liveried Servaunt-men rush'd to carry him out of sight.

Lieutenant Percie gave this speech his deepest consideration. He felt a fierce joy that at last Virginia would be *changed*. Any alteration in the conditions of life must be worth the price. Once again it seemed to him possible to achieve wonders. What if 'twas merely the *twinkling fear* which had prevented him from discovering perfection? Certainly when these Salvages had been remov'd there'd be more leisure to obtain better results. But already, e'en as the Waterman rowed the Officers back to Jamestowne to form up their troops, Percy's hopes had begun to sink. He no longer believed that Virginia could improve herself, or indeed be anything other than an oozy Salvage whore. No matter. He'd continue a good Soldier unto the very last.

His Captaines now mustered the Soldiers silver-helmed with upraised muskets & pikes — full .70. of them there were. How ought I to describe their quality? Well, in their home Counties in England they'd all seen vagabonds flogg'd bloody, & hungry children hang'd for stealing bread. Some few had watched old Goodwives from their own Parish Churches get burn'd alive for witchcraft. They were men without much pity. Moreover, they'd fall'n full awearied at the heat & hunger of James-towne. They lay ready for a change. Moustachio'd & shaggy-haired, wearing rags iron-stiffened by their own stench, they came a-running from their verminous tents, enthralled by this latest throw of the dice. Lieutenant Pearcie wrinkled his nose.

What about Percy's own strictness? The .1.ˢᵗ time he slew a Citizen (this happen'd in the Low Countreys), he feared that the crime would lie eternally upon his heart. But that had befallen a decade since, & wise men adapt their hearts unto anything.

Reverend Bucke did sermonize them thus, after the Book of Psalms: *Yet have I set my King upon my holy Mount of Zion. I shall give thee the heathen for thine inheritance, & the uttermost reaches of the World for thine own. Thou shalt break them with a rod of iron; thou shalt dash them into pieces like unto a Potter's vessel.*

Amen, they replied.

Lieutenant Percie did now cause the drum to beat, thereby summonsing all of 'em instantly unto the colors. The Captaines form'd 'em into Companies, promising 'em all the swag they could loot. They comprised a moving, clattering forest as Maister Pearcie march'd 'em out of the Fort, *Trarintra-rarara.* He drew them up at what used to be call'd *Smith-field,* & then they boarded the pinnace .1. by .1.

'Twas not so ornate as Maister Pearcie might have preferr'd. The *Red Lion* (which is a very famous merchaunt-ship out of Gravesend) hath a lion-figurehead a-rearing from her beak. The pinnace had nothing. Percy thought she'd be much improv'd, did the Carpenter carve out the form of an Yndian squaw to grace her bow.

'Twas the .9.ᵗʰ of August 1610. The Sunne had not yet enter'd Virgo. The Lookout sang: *Flood oh!* And so their sail caught the humid turquoise sky. The horizon lay lower than a man's waist. Limp, yellow-green foliage confused their spirits. Blue flecks of open water twinked between the cress. So they went a-foraging for Salvages, like unto those who forage in the Countreyside for flowers & branches with which to deck their May-pole. The River *Iames* surrounded them with his very low horizon. They found themselves greeted by an osprey, or perhaps 'twas a fish-hawk . . .

Stand you ready for action, Captaine Davis?

Aye, Sir! replied his Deputy. Then he added most cheerfully: I misdoubt me not 'twill be a great annoyance unto Powhatan . . .

Lieutenant Percy laugh'd gloomily. He wish'd that he were at home in Northumberland, being guested by his brother. At his brother's table the service was all of golden plate. The wine was serv'd in goblets of Bohemian crystal which seem'd in its scintillations to represent the Ideal. All lay clean & well-arrayed.

Then most strangely he did remember an uncanny thing which Sweet John, of all people, had once said. That vulgar little President, despite his grasping & boasting, had possess'd a shrewd head. And last year when they'd sail'd up the Pamunkey River to get corn, he'd said: 'Tisn't Powhatan that I fear, but *Opechancanough*. What say you?

The other Gentlemen had laugh'd, for wasn't Powhatan the Emperor? Pearcie had kept silence, as he customarily did around Captaine Smith. Well, well, 'twasn't to the point, so why did he recollect it now?

Pardon me, Sir, said Captaine Davis then, but how doth their King, or *Werowance,* appear?

In Paspahegh, or—

Aye, Sir. For I mean not to let him 'scape—

Well, he's painted all black, with horns on him like unto a DEVIL. So he was deck'd out when I last spied him, at least. But he fled me, & I . . . Now be silent. I must prepare our dispositions.

Most misfortunately, Lieutenant Percie's brother now lay in the Tower nigh unto Sir Walter Ralegh. Those Gentlemen were both of them attainted for treason. One of the reasons that Lieutenant Pearcie now warr'd so zealously in Virginia was to avoid getting tarr'd by the same brush. Therein lay his best aspiration. There was no golden service anymore.

Sweet John's old Block-house had long since fallen astern, & lay buried in a deep grave of piled river-bends. (Lord Delawarr's commaundments would doubtless soon repolish that Jewell.) The wilderness beyond James-Towne lay as dark as the mouth of a demiculverin. Yet once they'd entered it, they discovered it to be a fair-flowered ground, most pleasantly suckled with sweet gums. Lieutenant Percy remembered that .1.ˢᵗ summer in 1607 when they'd gone a-visiting to Paspahegh & Kecoughtan. He remembered those joyous dancing Salvages who had feasted them on strawberries. Captaine Newport was giving 'em needles and beads; Wowinchopunck had been friendly, & his wives both beautiful & lewd. It had all been lovely then.

Now wise Pearcie did cast his ear upon Soldier-mutters & Soldier-whispers, for to learn how martially they stood. Some few appeared fearful of the Yndians' DEVILs & unknown posion'd weapons, which no persuasion could convince them were hollow chimeras. They had Captaine Radclyffe's fate e'er in their blockish minds — no matter that Pearcie'd explain'd that such a doom could come upon only unarmed or unready men. — Other Soldiers crouched jesting & gambling. *Now bing we all to Romeville!* an evil-looker screamed.

They passed closed-in *Mattapanient* (was that the name? or did Mattapanient lie in Opechancanough's domains?) & some other irrelevant Yndian Townes, & already they'd achiev'd the turning where the Chickahominy River flow'd in. *Quiyoughcohanock* & *Nantapoyac* were also lethally silent. Not a single Salvage Canoa marr'd the river; nobody fish'd at the weirs. The people had developed a wholesome dread of yᵉ English at last! Perhaps after today the entire river would be safe—

He strode to the bow, & stared ahead. His eyes sipped weed-froth and weed-foam from atop a pondful of dark swamp-ale.

As they drew nearer unto Paspahegh, his heart commenc'd to thrill. He felt a thirst to try Lord De La Warr's experiment. Sweet John (that Latin-mute stutterer) had remained always o'er timorous for such measures. Could they truly bring Powhatan into some kind of amendment? In that hope-gulf our good Maister Percie cast no faith; Powhatan would ne'er amend until they'd dissolv'd him utterly away. Therefore, what they were about was not *politick*. But he cared not. It was so grand —

At the start of the Forenoon Watch they landed on the south shore, in a strawberry-meadow near about .3. miles downstream of the Towne. At Lieutenant Percy's signal the Bugler *trarintrararara*-urated, then Captaine West rais'd his arm, at which the colors did proudly fly.

Form up! Maister Pearcie commaunded. Let each man ensure that his piece be charg'd. Captaine Davis, is e'erything in order?

We're ready, Generall.

Where's Kemps? Captaine West, he's s'posed to be under your charge.

I've got him tied, Sir! Shall I permit him to speak?

Nay. March him here.

Move thy shitty arse, varlet!   There.   On thy knees before our Generall—

Now unstop his mouth.

Pray have pity on me, Maister George. I always did as I was told —

Hark unto me, Kemps. I hereby charge thee to lead my Soldiers to attain this *Paspahegh* in the slenderest possible time that may be done of a secret. Should we be misled, or the enemy alarmed, why then, Captaine West has my order to lop thy head.

Maister George, I beg—

Have done. Captaine West, ensure this wretch guards silence.

Aye, Sir. Ho, Soldiers! Take Kemps & gag him.

Captaine Scott!

Here I am, dear Generall!

You being Standard-bearer, your task shall be rather to inconspicuate us. You'll sail with me now. Trumpeteer, the same.

Yes, Sir.

Then down standard! Now!

Aye, aye, Sir

Captaine West!

Yea, Master.

Station yourself in sight of shore. Upon our arrival with the colors, fire off your pistol. That shall be the signal.

I comprehend.

As soon as you've utter'd your shot, take .5. strong men & set 'em to destroying Canoas, so that our Salvages can't 'scape by water. When they come running, stand clear. We'll shoot 'em from the pinnace.

Yes, Sir.

Captaine Davis, we're here to teach 'em death. I count on you not to repeal the lesson.

Sir, I hope to gratify you.

For the last time, Lieutenant Percie inspected his troops. Most now seemed as high-spirited as if their mission consisted of nothing more unpleasant than to rape some fine young Irish girls. Well, they were on the mark. Having serv'd under Captaine Smith at Werowocomoco & likewise against the Chickahominies, he considered this enemy to be contemptibly feeble. This action, 'twould be nothing more perilous than sport.

All ready?

By your order, Generall!

Soldiers, take this Towne, or bide fore'er disgraced. *Get me this Towne.* Now go.

Go, go, go!

For'ard march! To Paspahegh, lads! Let's give 'em some bonny lead beads! Ha, ha!

For'ard!

To Paspahegh!

Kemps, my animal, shall I teach thee a phrase? *Kekaten Pokahontas . . .* (Now I disremember some of that babble. How did Sweet John say it?) Bid Pokahantas bring hither .2. little baskets, and I'll shoot her a clean new cunt-hole! Then I'll—

Shut up now! commaunded Captaine Davis. From now 'till Captaine West doth signal, not a word, or yᵉ Governor'll have you burn'd! Silence, you damn'd Hell-dogs! Single file now on this Yndian path. Muskets ahead! Silence & for the last time silence! Now for'ard!

Lieutenant Pearcie stood on the pinnace, guarded by half a dozen out of his .70. Soldiers. He watch'd 'em go. Then he turn'd o'er his woman-waisted Hour-glass.

To himself, he said a little prayer. For, after all, any good Hangman in England doth pray forgiveness of the condemned, before he burns him or draws out his guts.

* * * * * *

The Yndian corn was high, full ready to be reap'd. Yndian dreams had drowsed 'midst those high green stalks; now the stalks were beset by English nightmares. Young pumpkins slept in that corn-maze like unto fat nuggets of gold.

Careful, whispered Captaine Davis, for he guards himself with many Bowmen.

All the Soldiers staggered, half-drunken on the heavy, *greenish* smell of the corn.

Captaine West with his file of men now went their way. In a twink they met a small boy in the cornfield who was stalking a crow with a bow & arrow which his father must have fashioned for him. They most fortunately seiz'd him before he could scream. As deftly as Virginians shuck peanuts, Captaine West slit his throat, so that there'd be no alarm ere Lieutenant Percie's commaund. The child flailed his little fists while he bled. A Soldier thrust a sword into his mouth — thrust clear through unto earth, then twisted. Withdrawing the blade then, he wiped it on the scalp-lock of the twitching little corpse. Meanwhile, the other Soldiers, all pale & ahungered, were munching on green corn.

* * * * * *

Lieutenant Percy drew off his white gloves for the duration of the attack. He placed them in his breast pockets. The Yndian capital now swam into his sight. — Up colors! he cried, & Captaine Scott did his duty. At once, good Captaine West did fire his pistol. The massacre began.

The houses of Paspahegh were like unto squat grey turtles. But when they got burnt, then they resembled beehives with the bees rushing out of them. As the Yndians came a-crawling through their low doors, Pearcie's Soldiers butchered 'em before they were half-born into the sunny World, piloted 'em out (pulling by the dead hand or bleeding scalp-lock), then kicked 'em left or right to make room for others. So the English revenued themselves with blood. Whether their victims did screech or whether they fawned with utter subservience, judgment damned them down into the bleeding ooze. To Lieutenant Percie, who stood with his hands on his hips, o'erseeing the vengeance, 'twas as if these murthered carcasses were Servaunt-men giving respectful way to my Lord De La Warr, who slid in & out of doorways 'pon his litter in much this fashion. Each panick'd Salvage whom Fate (or the people behind him) impelled from that low, mat-hung opening became for a twink invested with the unstinting attention of many men — until their unstinting sword-points had reduced him from Lord unto the gaping yokel of a corpse. As the heaps grew inconvenient, .2. Soldiers did roll 'em into the fires 'neath fish-smoking platforms, or hurl 'em into the pyres of houses with which Lord Delaware's business had already been concluded. Bloody-haired skulls cloven open like oyster-shells, lopped limbs, mounds of excrement, strutting flies, dancing flesh Maypole-garlanded with its own guts, all these were the gifts of the English. And Lieutenant Pearcie smil'd frozenly upon it all. His own cares ceased to sting him as the performance continued. Until the last Yndian was dead, the suspense would distract him. What if e'ery spectacle on which he'd turned his eyes in life were conducted by GOD with the sole purpose of conveying some meaning unto his soul? The reek of stupidity assail'd him here as elsewhere, but could it be that stupidity was GOD's instrument? I've already said that George Percie possessed the soul of the Artist. Since he painted & sculpted not, why then, he saw Art in e'erything. GOD decorated this Undertaking of His (call'd the World) in flesh. Cut the flesh away, & maybe we'd find *Theme,* or *Moral,* hidden in a murthered bratling's eye-socket. Or (as might be more logical) did GOD's Word incorporate itself in *sound?* The screeches of the Yndians & the half-crazed shouts of their slayers did comprise the songs in this entertainment, the parts of viols & drums being play'd by the creaking, crunching sounds of swords turning inside womens' breastbones & smashing through childrens' skulls. (The men they generally spent a bullet on, those being more dangerous to their executioners.) Roasted trees sprang apart; bark-plates & reed-clumps whirled into flaming incoherency. — *Victory!* cried the Soldiers. — Dead Salvages offered up their bellies to the light.

Maister Percie recollected how **.3.** years since, on his **.1.**st visit here (in company with Sweet John & Captaine Newport), he'd found himself very nearly ravish'd with delight at the sweetness of the mullberry-shade. So he went & stood beneath a tree, with his arms folded on his breast. And the shade refresh'd him not. Soon he'd give the order to set this tree alight. Reader, doth this seem strange to you? Pearcie lay full awearied from **.3.** years of the *twinkling fear.* These Salvages ne'er did cease to betray us. They seemed always in a rage. The King of Pasapegh had essay'd to subvert the Fort from the very **.1.**st. He deserv'd to die. Can we blame George Percy, that he made himself the subject of e'ery scene? When *he* died, the performance would be ended. But these broken-skulled Yndians striped with their own blood must be no more than decorations (or symbols & revelations at best), for altho' they'd been butchered, no curtain came down upon Percie's own eyes. By that very token, *nothing was his.* Nothing could refresh him. These mullberries here, why, they were but artificially fashion'd out of pasteboard, like unto the bones of these skeleton-puppets now beating out their bleeding dooms for the sake of his witness.

A Salvage head sank its teeth into the toe of a Soldier's boot. The Soldier screamed. Captaine West ran up & shot the head with his pistol so that it fleered into red & grey pieces. 'Twas a neat job! They dragged that corpse out of the doorway, then rolled it clear. Kemps sat sobbing in the bloody dust.

Now the Salvages denied to come out anymore, so they set the remaining houses afire regardless, flames shimmering nimbly 'twixt the reed-joinings which rapidly writhed out of parallel like unto the tangles of bloody legs sizzling all around. Once the walls had been substantially shrivelled away, the remnant Salvages exploded outwards, leaping thro' the flames when they could, falling into them when they couldn't. Most were now women with babes in arms, their more active predecessors having been the door-crawlers now dead. Now 'twas their turn to be reduced from persons down unto ancient rumors of history. The Soldiers jested lewdly as they spitted those females on their swords, frigging 'em with the bloody blades. Oftimes the soles of their feet drew together as they died, so that their knees pointed right & left; then they lay like unto frogs. The Soldiers hardened themselves with laughter. Childrens' heads they plucked off like fruits.

Lieutenant Pearcie judged their tactics to be ill-tuned. In Ireland he would have led 'em house to house at the very beginning, lined up all the inhabitants in the main square under some sweetly snickling pretense, & *then* (they being all safely put to death) return'd to fire the empty houses. But these dregs he commaunded, these Cut-purses & Stable-grooms, they were passing disorderly for any such method. — Well, no matter; he uttered no commaunds. He stood nerveless, desolate, unable to gratify his understanding.

Had he been the same in Ireland? Reader, I'll tell you this much: His service was well-desir'd, for his mind being oft embark'd into dreams, he rarely disciplined his troops, no matter what their misdemeanors. Crawling Yndians, screeching Yndians, bleeding & gutted Salvages, headless Naturalls, dull-eyed & groaning child-knaves with their limbs hewn off for a jest, all these did signify the success of his commission. They twitched; they sighed — dying, dying, dying! They died as insects die, nonsensically writhing. The women prattled in their barbarous dialect when their infants got slaughtered before they did; 'twould be too unfair if GOD's Word ensconced itself in their bleeding mouths, for the only phrase he remember'd of their language was **.1.** Sweet John had taught him when they attack'd the Chickahominies: *Mowchick wayawgh tawgh noeragh kaquere mecher* — which signified *I am very hungry. What shall I eat?*

He heard a Salvage singing from inside a burning house. The song ran: *Whe, whe, yah, ha, ne, he, wittowa, wittowa.* O yes — that too he remember'd. 'Twas something about the unmanliness of our English. Infuriated by the defiance implied, Lieutenant Percy strode to that spot (round which Soldiers were already congregating), uprais'd his sword, & lopped through several wall-saplings so that the fiery mats sprang apart. In that twinkling instant he glimpsed a quiver of arrows hanging from a rafter; & then he saw in the rear, framed by flames as scarlet as a heap of bears' tongues, an ancient-looking warrior squatting, drawing back his bow, with his face painted red & black. That instant, just as an English House-wife kills a spider in her kitchen — with loathing, disgust & fear enhancing her violence, Lieutenant Percy shot him with his pistol.

Hurrah, Generall! cried the Soldiers, longing to believe that he was **.1.** of them, & loved 'em.

Now thro' the corn-leaves a carven monster gibbered at them from a post. What was he? Like unto a dragon, perhaps, or . . . To his left stood another post, with another hobgoblin on it. And then there was a long, long house. 'Twas the entrance to the Temple of O K E U S, Who could not or would not save His People. (Dear Pearcie, Sweet John had once said, I've observ'd that their sacred buildings do e'er face eastwards, as is the fashion 'mongst the Turkes. — 'Twas most interesting to learn. Sweet John might be a vulgarian, but he usually spoke true.) The priests were singing songs within, at which a Soldier cried out in terror. Lieutenant Percie knew he'd better go there, to form up his heroes' hearts. With his accustomed courage he enter'd the Temple before all others, his sword snickling elegantly through the darkness as he went. Long torches were burning bright. He snatch'd the nearest, & fir'd the wall. Ahead loom'd a bulkhead of reeds. He cut a window with his sword. Peeping in, he found the next chamber like unto a Blacksmith's forge, all high & dark, but lit by eerie flames. Instead of anvils they had torches & altar-fires. Hideous statues stood against the walls; 'twas most unholy. (No plunder tempted him. In Virginia dwelt no gold — none — never. That Gambler's dream was finally perisht.) Hacking that wall aside, he advanced thro' that room & into the chancel, which stank most evilly; those mat-shrouded bundles on the shelves were doubtless dead Werowances. Well, let the Soldiers uncover what they would, before the flames did.

The priests had withdrawn into the rearmost hollow. Summonsing Captaine West, Percy gave the order for a volley to be fir'd. Could King Wowinchopunck be amongst 'em? He directed the shooters to aim low, percase their prey did lurk upon the floor, or in some secret vault as Sweet John had once told him. Afterward a lone Salvage voice was still screeching. Could G O D mean to address him thro' wordless cadences of torment? (Behind him the Soldiers were yelling: *A prize, a prize!*) Pearcie commaunded another volley. Now was all happily silent. He stript the screen aside. He brusht a fleck of dust from the silken butterfly at his left shoulder. He laugh'd.

Hark, Soldiers! he cried. There's naught to dread, unless you fear **.2.** skinny old fools painted like unto Merry Andrews — dead fools, moreo'er! If you want pillage, best hurry ere the flames fall on your heads!

Above the corpses, O K E U S leered in his face. Altho' 'twas but a wooden statue, Pearcie was surpris'd to find that he dreaded it. Crudely sinister was O K E U S's visage, watchful, with shiny copper disks for eyes in

which the reflections of the advancing fire did crawl like unto consciousness. The mouth gaped angrily, studded with fangs like unto a *Sharke's.*
Lieutenant Pearcie stood appall'd.   This DEMON, or DAGON, or
whate'er it was, embodied the sinful corruption which he'd always loathed.
He could not look away, for he knew that it would haunt him as much as
his own death. He'd never 'scape it more.

Then Captaine Davis was at his shoulder. Pearcie turn'd on his heel. He
departed the burning Temple.

✳   ✳   ✳   ✳   ✳   ✳

The Soldiers were full thrilled to see fair wenchen as common as Church
yard lilacs. Reader, what they did with them before they slaughtered them
you can well imagine.

What snap* d'ye find, lads?

Naught but green wheat in the houses, & some dried roots—

Take 'em, take 'em — I'm ahungered!

Lookee here, I've found more of their idols!

Lieutenant Percy stood dreamily a-brushing walnut-crumbs from the
hole in a smooth mortar-stone. The walnuts were bitter. He knew now
that the fruits of this Adventure would taste likewise unworthy in his
mouth. How could he have imagined otherwise? 'Twas the same as when
we went a-burning corn & decapitating Salvages at Roanoke a quarter-
century before. *Remember Roanoke,* Captaine Radclyffe had always
fleered. To Percie this echo now resembled the veriest Oracle which sighed:
Remember that all is ashes. And indeed, Paspahegh-Towne was now well
on its way to becoming coals & embers. Wowinchopunck had misfortunately 'scaped; ye Governor would dress him down again. Pearcie cared
not. He'd performed his duty to his uttermost. Percase that King had fled
to Powhatan . . . Flames hissed and curled from the bark-plated houses
with a noise like unto many bullwhips. Pearcie's **.70.** Soldiers ran happily
to and fro, like unto a Fire-brigade compris'd of children.

Captaine West came to him & said: Beg permission to report, Sir.

Granted.

All Canoas destroy'd, Sir.

And your men?

Nary a scrape, praise GOD!

Good. Help Captaine Davis.

---

*Plunder.

Lieutenant Percie brush'd a fly off **.1.** of his golden shoulder-stripes. He lifted a tiny silver bottle to his lips & kissed its mouth. He drank, but only a little.

At his feet an old beezum lay dead & naked with her skull mushed by gun-butts, & a stake cramm'd up her womb. The sight made him melancholy, but 'twasn't politick to blink. Soldiers must have their games.

The performance being nearly ended, at Lieutenant Pearcie's commaund the bugle did sound. All the butchers came a-running to the colors.

Now we'll make those who 'scaped us pine for their food, he said. Behead their corn. Fire it; raze it.

But, Sir, mayhap our Colonie will need it this winter—

Whose voice do I hear? Surely not mine own.

All the corne, Sir?

Filch what can be carried. Now begone, varlet. Do thy duty.

He heard them laughing like unto children as the **.1.**st stalks did catch fire. He laid his head in his hands.

Lieutenant Percy!

What tidings?

We've captured the Queen & her brood! And this Salvage here did plead for quarter so piteously, that I preserved him alive unto now. Shall we put 'em all to death?

Percie glanced up from his glorious dreams. He said: By my authority, man, I do depreciate thee, for having spared these Salvage cowards.

Captaine Davis stiffened. He said coldly: Having them now in your custody, Sir, you may do with them as you please.

So. Take this Salvage cullion & — you know not his station?

No, Sir.

Hew off his head.

The Salvage gazed at them, eyes glistering with hate. The merest twink, & his head went bouncing in the dust.

Where's Kemps?

That varlet sought to mislead us, so I beat him. I have him now under guard. Shall I slay him, Sir?

Nay, we'll need him another time. Where's my Lady Paspahegh?

Ha, ha, Sir! 'Tis a droll dignity you dress her in! She—

Hale her here.

The Soldiers march'd her up to him, waving their swords at her just as a Coach-man flares the whip above his horse's head. They stoppt. She stoppt. Somehow she'd found leisure to put on her crown of red-painted deer-hair engross'd with rodent-bones. Her children sheltered tightly in her armpits, just as e'ery night at darklins 'tis the custom for each ship in the fleet to sail under the lee of her Admirall, to salute him. They were all of them nearly naked, as is the custom with Salvages in their tender years.

In truth, this woman was merely a certain wife of Wowinchopunck, for these Salvages (not being utterly capable of reason) scarcely have Kings & Queens in any well-conceiv'd sense. But how could a mere Soldier understand this dinstinction? Better to preserve their faith they've spoil'd something valuable, thought Percie to himself. Award 'em their baleful happiness. A Queen? Why not a Queen? Doubtless Argall in his Roman conceit would have call'd her *Boadicea*. With a purple-feathered mantle thrown o'er her shoulders, & her hair loose & long unto her waist, she made a passing brave show.

Now the Soldiers began clamoring that *all* these Salvages be kill'd. At this, Lieutenant Percie remember'd his noble nature, which was not subject to the whims of any rabble.

Secure 'em on the pinnace, he said.

But, Lieutenant Percy, Sir!

Have you dispatch'd e'erything, Captaine West?

Aye, Sir. Not a corn-stalk unbroken, no house unburnt. Nothing alive, 'cepting only these prisoners—

I'll deal with them presently. Board 'em on the pinnace.

But, Sir, 'tis more convenient to kill 'em here—

Curs'd disobedience! Take 'em to the pinnace, I said.

Aye, Sir. We all of us mislike this —

Cross me again, & you're as dead as that hag you tread on. Trumpeteer, sound your horn. Drummer, to thine instrument! Captaine Scott, raise the colors. We'll instantly embark.

Trarintra-rarara.

The old hag groan'd. Lieutenant Pearcie's face flickered. He stabbed his sword into her breast & twisted. She groan'd again, then sighed.

Form up!

For'ard march! To the pinnace, double-time! Let no man forget his booty; we're not a-comin' back!

Aye, Generall!

To the landing, damn you! You're all damn'd!

Indeed, they appeared the part, being all stain'd with blood, & blackened with soot & their own spent gunpowder. Moreover, just as come Judgment

Day we'll all be clutching our war-medals, preferments, love-letters, gold-pieces, captur'd maidenheads, & other trophies, in hopes of pleading our case to the DEVIL, so Pearcie's good fellows form'd in ranks, each with his own plunder. Some carried wilting bundles of *Tobacco*-plants pluck'd whole, with dirt still pingling off the roots. Others grasped men's scalp-locks hack'd out, with the roots bloody. The most sensible fellow had wrapt up a skin full of fresh mullberries. The Soldier behind him had looted several copper crescents from somewhere — probably the King's house, or the Temple of OKEUS. Men came bearing women's skin-mantles shagged and fringed — & gore-splash'd, naturally, but without gore how could they have gotten them? They had skins of leather all carven and colored with the shapes of Virginian beasts, all adorned with copper beads. They'd grabbed puccoon roots in their fists, thinking for to sell them someday at Gravesend. They'd filched fishes from the smoking-platforms, & strings of dried mussels. Evidently they'd disremembered the corn. Well, 'twas not so glamorous a spoil ... A Soldier clown'd about with a fan of turkey feathers; another cherished a leathern-loop'd cradleboard. A pair of Soldiers had hacked off .1. of those wooden heads within OKEUS's temple, but Lieutenant Percie commaunded 'em to cast that idol into the river, which they did full sullenly.

Captaine Davis, report!

All well, Sir. Soldiers form'd up & ready to embark. We did slay round about .16. Yndians by the sword, & .50. or .3.score more by shooting.

Which signifies .70. or .80. persons?

Aye, Sir.

How many 'scaped?

No more than .3. or .4., Sir.

I'm satisfied. Now thank you for your pains. Get our jolly murtherers aboard, & accompt 'em all the way to .70., so we're sure of 'em. Then we go.

Pray, not yet, Sir! Our Queen hath suitors for to kiss her with their swords!

Damn you, Davis, for you mock my authority! I said you nay!

Aye, Sir, I'll count the men.

On that narrow crescent of beach, the cracked & shallow barges of Indian canoes lay all hacked to ruins now by a pile of frog-legged corpses, & the fish-weirs broken, with their diminutive palisadoes all ablaze. Soon the oncoming flames would crowd all unto death. Lieutenant Pearcie inhaled the dismal triumph of his aspirations, & Lord Delaware's. The stench of

burned & disembowelled people mingled with the ordinary smell of burning wood & the luxurious odor of roasting corn. Now a bees' nest caught
fire, & he fancied he could smell the cooking honey e'en before the swarm
came crazily a-buzzing through the smoke.

There was a certain moon-faced pond of algae-jade with dead leaves
fixed upon its shallow disk like insects in amber. He knelt beside it to wash
his hands. For a long time he stared down at the weed-grown double of
himself.

He march'd his prisoners up the gangplank, with Sentries before & be-
hind. He heard a Soldier sneer: *Just as trulls get squired home from the
Tavern-house!* . . . 'Twas not the time to take notice of such insults, or the
Queen might 'scape.

Her face was well-pounc'd with the likeness of a phantastickall fish upon
each cheek. She wore a necklace of shell-beads. He disremember'd whether
he'd seen her back in 1607, when the Salvages had serv'd 'em up with venison, cornbread & puccoon-painted wenchen for to frig. (Was she the very
same who'd solaced Captaine Newporte? That **.1.**-arm'd old Pirate had returned from the mullberry-grove with his ruffles red-stained by puccoon-
paint . . .) Poorly enough did Pearcie recollect any Yndian's face! And
now his ruffles likewise were attainted; the Tailor back at Jamestowne
could surely draw the blood out. Nodding heads on knife-blades, dead
girls, murther's masterships all crowded the bygone damsels out. Mayhap
she was a new addition to Wowinchopunck's harem, **.1.** of Powhatan's
castoffs. But nay, she had these **.4.** children, so Wowinchopunck must have
gotten several years' use out of her . . .

She spake unto him, but he knew not what she said. Kemps could tell
him. But, seeing how piteously that Kemps did gaze upon her, he grew enraged with that insinuating churl.

Now came the rest of his horde, strutting up the gangplank with their
high, wrinkled boots all caked with blood, shit, brains & soot. They stank
more of woodsmoke than of their butchery, that odor proving the stronger.
Somewhat awearied, yet anxious for to trade their spoils **.1.** with the other,
they laugh'd full sunnily — but, seeing the Salvage Gentry, they fell back
upon their anger. To name 'em repulsive or evil might be an error, for they
wore those selfsame expressions an hour earlier, when they were doing their
duty to the Governor, but their severity was bloodshot with menace, their
grins questionable, their frowns still more so. They were carnivores.

He caus'd his prisoners to be seated, ring'd round by Soldiers grasping
naked & bloody swords. Laughing, Captaine West raped away the

woman's crown. Her disheveled hair fell down. Now her gaze seemed most like unto a pond seen darkly through Spanish moss.

All present, Captaine Davis?

Yes, Sir.

Then let's depart.

Anchors aweigh!

Up spritsail!

Flood oh!

On the water they could see the reflections of flames crawling like unto a blonde woman's wind-blown hair. He heard the Soliders laughing about *Bone-fire Night.*

Captaine Davis, station a Sentry fore & aft. We know not whether the Salvages may seek to ambuscado us as we pass, for their revenge.

Yes, Sir.

And you, Captaine, keep to deep water insofar as you're able.

Aye, Sir.

Captaine West, reward the men with a dram apiece.

'Twill be most welcome to 'em, Sir.

A long low line of skittering bird-silhouettes came o'er the river, speeding toward Paspahegh.

He heard the men muttering about my Lord De La Warr's sickness. He was *riding 'twixt wind & tide,* as they put it. They thought he might perish. Lieutenant Percy rubb'd his forehead, longing for to take a little doze.

Now it had come into Lieutenant Pearcie's mind that if any meaning or signification could be imparted unto him, it had to come from his prisoners, who indeed were all that remain'd of Paspahegh-Towne. So he unwrapt his gaze from its cerements, & sat staring moodily into their faces. Was that infant in the Queen's arms a boy or a girl? He smil'd upon it, but it smil'd not.

One of the little boys look'd on him, then went to hide behind his mother. (A Soldier shook a dagger in his face.) For a fact, this was a sprightly little lad! Couldn't he be educated in England? The action being successfully o'er, Percy conceiv'd it untoward to harm any more Salvages, for now. This was the real reason he'd spared Kemps (no matter that he'd prov'd an unfaithful instrument). And the young Prince pleased him. Perceiving somewhat in Lieutenant Percy's countenance that he misliked, he commenced to weep, which Percie discovered to be a pleasant sound, like unto the gurgling of a turtledove. The boy's elder brother & the baby remain'd both *Yndian-fac'd,* as we do call the unreadable expression of those

Salvages. As for the little girl, she was clutching a half-eaten ear of green corn. Why not? Trulls in brothels, they say, relish stewed prunes above all other food. Foul & filthy trulls—

The girl whisper'd to her mother & pointed toward the north shore. The woman essay'd for to smile. Percy whirled to see why she did thus, & spied a fat deer a-browsing in a marsh of some .20. acres.

Lieutenant Pearcie, Sir?

Looking back at the bend he saw in memorialization of Paspahegh a mound of smoke arising up as dark as ooze. He said: What, they demand more grog already?

Sir, we beg leave to drown these children at least, for their evil eyes do pain us. And since they be DEVILS, 'tis no sin—

Be not so bloody-minded, he said, but then they did all commence to mutter against him.

At last .1. tall old Soldier with deep-sunk eyes did say: Lieutenant Per-cie, if you grant us not this favor, we mean to mutiny, for these children may 'scape to bear witness against us.

To whom?

To Powhatan, Sir. Lieutenant Percie, we're monstrous afeared—

He was silent. Then his old enemy, *Revulsion of all things,* did com-mence for to press him down. — Slay 'em, then, he said at last. I'll take no joy in it. May all your souls sink into Hell.

Then with ecstatic curses they broke the ungrown Salvages from their mother's grasp. (She pled in a mingle-mangle of words.) Snatching off their copper ornaments, in case they might be gold (for, Reader, most Sol-diers are a monstrous hopeful tribe), they shouted down their own con-sciences. (The small girl did shrill, for they'd ripped the earrings right off her ears.) Shouting, kicking, slapping, striking, they did hurl 'em into the river. Their Generall turned away. (For this Lieutenant George Percie was a very honorable man.) The babe immediately sank, as if 'twere weigh'd down with ornaments, & now the Soldiers did complain anew, lest some treasure had been there conceal'd. The other .3. children bobbed ('twas ac-tually a wonder to see how well they swam), until the Soldiers took aim & began to shoot, loud death-balls skipping & thundering on the water until e'ery little head was exploded into blood. It took time; they screamed & screamed. The eldest boy dove deep, & they had to shoot into the water to bring him up. As for their mother, she gazed upon it all with her arms folded tight across her heart. Pearcie compelled his gaze unto hers, which continued fix'd upon him. He could not pretend to himself any longer that she was base & vile like unto that frightful wooden head (now burn'd) which had glowered upon him outside the Temple of OKEUS.

Then sand sped downstream through the Hour-glass, like unto the sickening blur of pine trunks on either side.

Lieutenant Percie, Sir?

What now?

Now we'd kill the Queen, for our better security.

Well said, my bold Stable-groom. Do you venture to touch her, I'll blow out your brains. I care no more for your mutiny or your revenge—

Comprehending his sincerity, they slunk aft. For a long while the little corpses bobbed behind, face down, the otter-dark hair on their heads all rivelled with blood.

Two miles downstream, they came upon another pretty Yndian Towne, which they did stop to burn together with its corn. (Inside the shrine of OKEUS, there came a sound like a dog's rapid gnawing.) Percie stayed aboard with the Pilot. He sat beside the Queen, smiling bitterly. No plunder tempted him except her. GOD's word on her lips could save him. There were no other words 'graved upon some tablet.

When the Soldiers were finish'd there, the only thing left standing was a circle of poles where dancers had once exulted with uprais'd rattles, long-haired & bead-earring'd girls dancing on .1. leg, their tattooed breasts shaking above the wrappings of their deerskin mantles. Perhaps there'd been a dance there only yesterday. When would they dance again?

Captaine Davis, who was a kind if over-familiar sort of man, said: Dear Generall, are you melancholick?

Aye . . .

May I tell you a tale, Sir? Back in *Gloriana's* time I once embark'd me northwards on the seal fishery to Greenland.

I never was there.

Well, 'tis a Kingdome of seals! There those yelping brutes do lie .1. on t'other, like so many brown ballast-bags half full of sand. And when we clubbed 'em for our living, why, the same way they did lie!

So?

These Yndians, Sir, when we slaughtered 'em, I comforted myself by thinking *They're wild like unto seals.*

Thank you, Captaine Davis. Yet I—

Walruses & sea-lions do likewise heap 'emselves up—

Lieutenant Pearcie smiled sarcastically.

They resumed the voyage thro' that wide & ripply river, dwindling down unto Jamestown's ochery oozy lowness. All the time, he heard the Soldiers laughing as they told o'er the antic death-writhings of those little Princes & Princesses (or *Hell-brats* as they call'd 'em). Their blood weighed within his bosom, he knew not why. 'Twas necessary to remember how pernicious Powhatan had prov'd—

The Yndian woman was smiling faintly. She uttered a few gentle-sounding words like unto earth-clods shifting off a Sexton's spade.

What did she say, Kemps?

She said, *My husband will avenge this.*

The men were almost sleepy now, but they could hardly forbear to o'ergaze the Queen now with their squinting eyes. They rubbed their hands together, discussing her in low voices which prov'd not so low that Lieutenant Pearcie fail'd to hear them. He took another drink from his silver flask.

Poor Maister Percy! He remained e'er like unto some Gentleman who wore armor engraved on e'ery plate with the proof-mark of his hired War-smith. His armor was his gutted heart. His proof-marks each proclaim'd how strangely he long'd to lay his mouth on hers before she died, & breathe her Virginian breath! The Soldiers were already calling her *his cocka-trice.* — O, & will he *Adventure* that? they sneered.

He said to Captaine Davis: When Lord Mountjoy was Viceroy in Ireland, he forgave O'Neill and all those swine. He e'en restored all their titles & estates. All he demanded was that they make the knee to him.

Yea, Generall, 'tis true they had to humble themselves . . .

Perhaps yonder Queen . . .

But Captaine Davis kept sternly quiet.

Now they did commence to come in sight of Jamestowne. The Lookout shouted for delight. The Soldiers discharg'd a dozen shots in token of victory, & within the Fort the Church-bell 'gan to toll. (At this sound the Queen did upfling her hands strangely, like sea-foam riccocheting off sharp shoals.) Casting their rope around a tree, they disembarked. Lieutenant Percy had no word for any of them. (Being on his trial, so to speak, before his own Countreymen, he'd best remember that speech is less constant, hence more incriminating, than silence.) He carried his prisoner with him, so that no man might do her mischief while he was out of sight. Two Soldiers bound her hands behind her.

Shall we pluck off her head now, Sir?

Nay, said Percie wearily, we should see her handed over safe to y^e Governor. Captaine Davis—

Lieutenant Percy, Sir?

Nay. I mistrust you now. Guard the prisoner.

Maister Pearcie hailed the Wherry-man & was rowed straight to that long black ship. (In truth he had no great stomach for this visit.) He stopt not to refresh himself; his ruffles were stained with Yndian blood. The Sunne glared low on the cool water. He would sleep. Closing his eyes, he seemed to see the childrens' grinning heads ribboned with their own blood.

The Governor invites you in, Lieutenant Percie.

My Lord, I'm come to report—

What news?

May it please you, Sir, we did raze their capital.

In thy fawning face, *Cousin,* I seem to see some crookedness. How many on our side dead?

None, my Lord.

What then?

I did preserve their Queen alive—

O coward! I charg'd thee to destroy 'em all. I'm full ashamed. Now, to thy duty.

But should we treat with Powhatan—

Powhatan hath denied to be reform'd. Shame me no more.

And yet his daughter did feed the Colonie—

Do you censure my policy?

Never, by my faith!

Powhatan I mislike less than you this moment. For I'd thought you manly, *Cousin.* I'll say nothing of your recreant brother in the Tower, but look you to yourself. It may be there's a strain of treason in your blood, which disorders you unto contrariness. Or percase Virginia's langors hath softened you. Shall we examine you for womanishness?

Nay, I swear I've demeaned myself justly—

Burn her, said my Lord De La Warr.

'Twill be done, Your Grace. But since she hath already suffered so, to see the slaying of her children, methinks the sword wouldn't be untowardly—

You incite my discontent. So be it. Give her the sword. But know you've lost much glory in my sight—

Then, by your leave, I'll resign my commission.

Get out, untrue *Yndian-lover!* To think I must suffer this, when I'm already taken up with distracting news —

Upon his return to Jamestowne landing, Maister Percie saw that his Soldiers' exhilaration had already sunken into doldrums corresponding to his own. Their plunder wearied 'em now. They trampled it, or threw it into the river, or half-heartedly essayed to give it away. They complain'd that it stank.

At his commaund, .2. Soldiers took the Queen of Paspahegh into their grip. One was that tall old Soldier with deep-sunk eyes, the man who'd threaten'd mutiny. His face was like unto a wall. Lieutenant Percy could not cease thinking: *I am too good for this.* He dispatched Captaine Davis to insure 'twas fittingly done. Then he secluded himself in his quarters, where he drank himself stuporous. In his dreams, corpses drifted like unto dark clots of seaweed.

Captaine Davis & his men led the Queen into the tall grass, which was hissing & shuddering in the evening wind. The strawberries & raspberries were full ripe. 'Twas no use to take her very far. — Soldiers, do your best duty now! Captaine Davis choked out. For a prize they did snatch away her purple-feathered mantle. She blush'd for modesty, to be stripp'd thus bare (which Captaine Davis thought very seemly in a Salvage). Her breasts were wet with milk. They ripped the strings of shell-beads off her throat. Then they unscabborded their blades. And so they killed her with the sword, *Trarintra-rarara.*

RED SKIES (1610)

Those temporizing proceedings [of ours] may to some seeme too charitable, to
such a daily daring trecherous people: to others not pleasing, that we washed not
the ground with their blouds, nor shewed such strange inventions in mangling
murdering, ransacking, and destroying (as did the Spanyards) the simple bodies
of such ignorant soules . . .

CAPTAINE JOHN SMITH, *The Generall Historie* (1624)

*M*eanwhile, where was Argall? My Lord Delaware had dispatch'd
him to Bermuda, so I gathered me no gawp-seed when I learnt that he was
a-fishing off Cape Cod. They say 'twas because his Admirall, *Sir George
Somers,* had lost the way, & that's as may be. Percase 'twas because Argoll swirled hither & thither according to his own superhuman mercurial-
ity. Lieutenant Pearcie was but Death's Waterman. Argoll was — what
was he? Argall as counter-trend, Argull as the tablet of the Recording
Angel, Arkill as Captaine Fortune — 'tis all wrong. Just as a good ship's
scupper-leathers do let out all the bilgewater, but prevent the sea from entering in, so Captaine Argoll's strange jests (for, dear Reader, that is all they
were) found means to discharge their venom unto the World, but thro' their
obscurity prevented the World from marshalling any counterattack until
he'd already sail'd on. Where was he? Why, he'd sail'd on! He might have
wisht to explore a trifle (altho' our Histories never indicate he felt the same
pleasure-thrill as did Sweet John, to discover new Countreys). Was it now
that he completed his task of proceeding unfried thro' the Torrid Zoan,
thus disproving Ratcliffe's terrified fantasies? Forging friendship-shackles,
grinding victims in his rancorous palms, he flitted unknown ocean-heavens.
Codfishes fraughted his hold; *Cassius & Brutus* stood fast in hopes of Salvage plunder; the Lookout's glance was glued e'er to the Horizon, for
(faithful Christian that he was) he hoped for an earthly reward, & feared his
Captaine.

Admirall Somers sail'd for Bermuda alone, & died there from o'ereating
of roast pig. Argoll said in his report that a diabollickal fog had divorced
their **.2.** ships. Who are we to say otherwise?

Discovering & naming *Delaware Bay* (a Governor-pleasing strategem, of which mirthful *Machiavell* would have approv'd), chaffering to great advantage 'midst the new Yndians there, Argoll humm'd bland songs. What Adventures did he secretly Undertake? Historie will not tell.

On about September y^e .1.st, with Sol yet abiding in the House of Virgo, he reef'd sail at James-towne, & got rowed by *Casca & Octavian* to make his report within the long, dark, floating coffin-ship wherein Lord De La Warr did lie. His seclusion now partook of a still more funereal character. He reclined most of each day & night in bed, bulkheaded in, with the scarlet curtains drawn o'er the single porthole, & only .1. or .2. most favored Servaunts in red livery allowed to disturb his feverish agonies. This miserable old man, in more dread of death the more he inflicted it, had reach'd the stage when all his suspicions did incorporate themselves as hallucinations, & sit e'er on his chest: .I. George Pearcie meant to undo his Government through leniency — hadn't he sav'd the Queen of Paspahegh from burning? .II. Reverend Bucke preach'd double-bottomed sermons whose meaning was secretly poisoned 'gainst his authority. .III. The Colonists were all rebels. .IV. The Yndians were gathering a flotilla of their Canoas from which to shoot him with envenom'd arrows.

He was not so far agitated in his mind as to actually believe all these things, but *felt* them, & in his most sleepless hours a Death's-head came swimming through the air. From all these jealous anxieties he exempted only Captaine Argoll, whose presence infused him with a conviction of his own Gambler's luck.*

Raise me up, he said.

Yes, my Lord.

Now send for him.

Yes, Sir. The Governor permits you inward, Captaine Argoll.

I'll find my way. — Your Grace, a fair morning to you, & you're looking well recuperated. I'm come to report.

Captaine Argoll—

Aye?

---

*Dear Reader, I might have hinted that Captaine Argoll was scrupulous to keep aloof of *Historie, Posteritie, Friendship, the Publicke,* & all that rabble. But the methods in which he most relied was an unobtrusively iron cheerfulness, broken at intervals by hints of exorbitancy. O, he sang many an uncanny song, but only his Sailors & some Salvages knew him (I mean, knew the back of his hand) sufficient to fear him.

Ring that little bell, would you, please? Ring that . . . Jonas, a glass of sack for the Captaine & myself.

Yes, my Lord. Here 'tis, my Lord. And good refreshment to you, Captaine—

Shut the door. Now, Captaine Argoll, tell us of your new discoveries.

This request the euerworthy Argull perform'd, in words of sunny force, so that my Lord De La Warr enjoyed to be fraughted along to the strange Countrey now nam'd after him, whose Salvages (having not yet been much disturb'd) remained loving & obedient. Because this *Delaware his Bay* lay so far afield, 'twas easy for the listener to pretend it into Paradise.

I thank thee, Cousin-in-law, for thine love. 'Tis a comfort to me to be thus engrafted 'pon a map. Now then. More sack?

No need, my Lord.

Captaine Argoll, I would ask you — doth Lieutenant Percy continue loyal?

Pearcie's braying of his own graces again! (Thus the softspoken Captaine Arkill, who hadn't yet seen Maister Percie since his return.) Dear G O D, I fear to decipher still more Pearcie from his legendermain of boasting!

But he's loyal?

The loyalest knave that e'er did dance beneath the gallows-tree! — Nay, your Grace, I but jest! He doth feed himself too much on moonbeams to be hale; he's no threat—

I . . . And what think you of the Colonie?

All doth thrive, replied Argoll carelessly. (He thought otherwise.)

My jewel-soul'd Argall, I must believe in you, for 'tis now difficult for me to take myself about. Now, did you hear about our raid upon the Paspaheghs?

Ha, ha! I've learnt the quarrel was decided in our favor, Lord—

Altho' Percie prov'd weak . . .

Ah, but she was a pretty wench, if I may judge by her skull affix'd to Jamestowne Gate—

I'm told that some do contemn our policy 'gainst the King's children—

For instance, Reverend Bucke?

Nay, I'll name no names, whispered the sick man, gazing on Argall with anxious eyes. — But Captaine John Smith did come to grief for that they said he was too hard against the Salvages, & should my enemies in London-Towne hear of this, why, they might misrepresent my necessity, in order to do me mischief . . .

Nay, Your Grace strikes e'ery soul with admiration, mouthed Argoll. But you know I was once indicted.

Nay! cried Argall, who knew all about it.

'Twas for some misfortunate friendships, which link'd me most spuriously unto the Essex rebellion—

After which you got your pardon, Argoll soothed.

Despising the Governor's flutterings, Argoll cloak'd his own pitilessness behind an exaggerated regard. He said: Never fear, my Lord. Should weak souls prate about those Yndian whelps, I'll say to 'em, *O, let's not besmear ourselves again with that vice called virtue, that dung-thickened slop!*

I wonder how many Salvages did slyly 'scape, to tell Powhatan of our conquest. Methinks he'll gnaw at our heels . . .

We'll not be surprised. I swear we'll ruin all his fortunes, his foul fortunes of fairness never to be found again, dwindling like drought-water. Powhatan's a *superannuated quantity,* your Grace. Let's see *him* win the consent of birds to disinherit the eagle!

Dear Argoll, my mind's mazed by sickness. I comprehend not e'ery word you say—

Then, Lord, the substance is this. Give me your commaund, & I'll issue out to fight! I'll compell 'em to accept your peace!

Your arrival presages the improvement of my fortunes. Captaine Argall, I would send you to Warraskoyack in company with Captaine Brewster.

Aye, my Lord?

Burn the Towne. *King Tackonekintaco* seeks to 'scape his promise of corn. His nephew leapt o'erboard—

Ha, ha! I remember! Yes, with his ankles all fettered! I misdoubt me not his skeleton bobs below us now. Sure I'll burn that Towne right down to the last screeching brat . . .

* * * * * *

See Argull & Brewster at Warraskoyack. Being appris'd of the doom of the Paspaheghs, the Warraskoyacks have all fled. No matter. Soldiers burn this Towne & the next. The corn's all ripe, so burn it! We may be ahungered, but so shall be yᵉ Salvages! Let Powhatan feed 'em! (Thus calculates Captaine Brewster, whose father had been murthered by Yndians near about .3. years since.) Argall merely smiles, torch in hand, & sings:

> Red sky at night, Sailor's delight.
> Red sky at morning, Salvage's warning.

And for half the night the sky shines red with burning.

* * * * * *

An Yndian enters the Fort, seeking for to chaffer corn for blue beads. Lieutenant Pearcie doth cause him to be held under arrest, until the Governor's pleasure be known.

Strike off his hand, said my Lord De La Warr.

A COMEDY (1610)

Fie, fie, unknit that threat'ning unkind brow,
And dart not scornful glances from those eyes,
To wound thy lord, thy king, thy governor.
SHAKESPEARE, *The Taming of the Shrew,* V.ii.136-38 (*ca.* 1594)

*R*eader, Right Honourable; I warn'd you that this Book of mine doth drag me down toward the worst. For now all Virginia's Gravesended with doom. How can we get beyond that now? Must e'ry maidenhead become a grave? Nay indeed, for good men may shrug off their Warres at any time for to go a-wenching. They'll sheathe their swords in Yndian cunts! Don't you agree that such a device might speed as readily as Lord Delawarr's for to reachieve the peace? (O dear — I hope I'm not being lewd!) E'ry Sweet John craves his Pocahontas. Captaine Fortune's sure to be the pimp.

The curtain jerks creakily up. A Virginian river's a-flowing o'er the Proscenium. Let's call it the *Iames*.   To stage left, a family of whitetail deer are browsing & waggling their rumps. Startled by our applause, they flee crashingly thro' the dead leaves, but stop again well within sight. Now to other prey: Thro' the windows of the double-pillar'd Back-stage I spy some red-shoulder'd beauties peeping, eager for to launch *Cupid's* ambuscadoes. (Is it true that the lips of their secrets resemble a dog's black-leather gums?) Well, well. 'Tis to be a pastoral Comedy, then. We'll not need the sophisticated shop-constellations of London-Bridge. There's but .1. commodity to vend.

See a shipload of English Adventurers a-searching for iron-mines. What greater good can they now expect for their London-Towne Undertakers? (For Captaine Newporte's gold-mines prov'd phantastickall.) We need not uncase the souls of these lusty Actors; on with our Comedy! (Reader, don't you despise delay's dribblements?) The point is: They're thinking on those fair diamonds call'd *Women*. Now, were canny little Sweet John amongst 'em, he'd chirp out many sage admonishments not to pleasure their prick-heads at the price of their brain-heads, but Sweet John's so extravagantly

absent & disgraced, that all his wisdom's not worth the shilling we did pay
to sit here a-throwing our nut-husks & bread-rinds at the Actors we disfa-
vor. Enough! 'Tis all jolly! Percase our good Pricksters feel sad or e'en
guilty about what their Governor hath caused to be done at Paspahegh-
Towne. Call 'em *Love's Ambassadors.* (What would my Lord Delaware
say, if he heard of their endeavor? O, he'll but never hear! They've sworn
to haven the secret in their hairy bosoms.) So where's Captaine Fortune?
Calling all hands! As they draw nigh unto Appamatuck-Towne, .2. Salvages in a Canoa come bearing an invitation from *Queen Opposuno-*
quononuske for a feast & a dance. This royal damsel's the very same who
wash'd Sweet John's hands in an ewer of bark when he was prisoner at
Werowocomoco. In short, she's courteously disposed. Let's have a twitch at
her! 'Tis rumor'd that her Hand-maidens be passing fair.

And so the English go ashore, all proud & huftytufty. Indeed, it's as if the
happy summer of 1607 were back again, for **.I.** the idolatrous Salvages
wail & scritch-scratch in the dirt with their fingernails, as they e'er have
done to honor Christians coming into their Townes; **.II.** Queen Opposunoquononuske herself advances with many a simper, for to welcome
them to the envittlement she hath promised; **.III.** the Yndians dance, &
.IV. afterward the maidens are waiting with red-painted shoulders.

O yes: Venison, bread, dancing, then quim-holes — that's how the order
will infallibly go. Reader, you can lay your coppers on that!

(And if I may by your leave insert a little discourse on venison, 'tis meet
to note that *Belly-timber's as apposite as prick-fuel,* perhaps e'en more so,
for during Lord Delaware's epoch, more than **.150.** Colonists have perisht,
some for lack of vittles.)

Happy to disprove the need for Lord Delaware's cruelties, the Adventurers oer'night amongst their innocent trulls, who've forgiven e'erything.
Who needs Turnbull Street in Clerkenwell, where the whores are all be-
pox'd? Virginian damsels embrace us all night without pay, whickering so
sweetly in our ears: *Love you not me?*

Just before dawn, while the Englishmen sleep full stuporous in their
wenchens' tight-lock'd arms, the Queen's Bravos creep in & club them all to
death, excepting only *Thomas Dowse,* Laborer, who doth hide behind the
rudder of the empty ship . . .

And, patient Reader, here's proof for you that GOD & malignant
OKEUS are .1. & the same: This young man who got spared was of all
that crew most deserving of murther at the Yndians' hands, for 'twas he

who'd musicked his tambourine for a doom-lure to the Salvages of Kecoughtan-Towne. I myself can but scantly believe this coincidence to be more than a truthless Elizabethan tale bewrit by Anti-moralists. But 'tis *Historie*. Well, 'pon my faith, I'm passing sorry. And so down with the curtain.

VARIOUS PROCESSIONALS (1611–1613)

. . . hitherto our Colony hath consisted (as yt were) but of a handful of men, and not stored with desired victualls fytt for such Eaters as the English are . . . but now, the Commodityes of our owne Country being thither in some goot quantety transported, . . . and the first ragged government nowe likewise prudently chaunged into an absolute Commaund . . . yt cannot be doubted but that all things shallbe so forseene, that the best Courses shallbe taken . . .

WILLIAM STRACHEY (1610)

*N*ow 'tis the season for another Argoll-errand. He's in the thick of History now, in thie fair year 1612. Our torch-lights glister 'pon his countenance. He's weirdly storied according to his own orderly musicke. He's bound for *E'erywhere*. See that euer-worthy Captaine set forth to grasp the gunnels of the *Treasurer* (**.130.** tons' burthen), in which he's bought an interest, with his Salvage antimony-profits. He's getting rich now. He'll be in commaund of **.60.** men, for each of whom he's already dream'd up a Romanish appellation. He's ready to make himself a golden-coin'd name. O yes, this *Treasurer* is auspiciously call'd! Argoll loves her. Short-masted for long voyages, solid-hull'd, bowed in perfect proportion for speed, she'll carry him safe thro' life. Sweet John would have Adventured anything for such a chance. Argoll need only continue brave & steady to win any number of *Treasurers*. Why doth GOD serve up lives this way? Reverend Hunt might tell us, did we go to Jamestowne, but I've already told *you* that Reverend Hunt's perished of the Virginian flux. *Memento mori.*

O, kind Sir, another ha'penny! groans the Waterman. Your baggage doth break my back!

'Twas already broken by all the trulls who rode you for their whore! Give o'er.

Kind Sir!

Distrain thy mouth, or I'll see thee hang'd. Brutus!

Aye, Captaine!

O'erwatch this rogue. Doth he venture any mischief, duck him in the river.

Aye, aye. Cicero, come hither!

Here am I, Lieutenant.

Help me study the villain.

Good Argoll crows: Ah, lads, how it joys me to see you execute your office!

He hums a tune. Already they're quit of London-Towne's spires & stink. They pass the clatter of the Armorer's shop at Greenwyche. 'Twas in this Cittie that our late Queen Elizabeth was born. Here, too, Argall got his chestplates bordered in calfskin like unto my Lord De La Warr's. For the South Virginia Companie's awarded him a new & worthy commission — which he carries roll'd under his arm. (Reader, would you know what it says? It commaunds & authorizes him to *expell foreign interlopers*.) From London's Tower Bridge to Gravesend 'tis full **.22.** miles, but the wherry-voyage speeds by in a twink, so happy is he.

They board the *Treasurer* at **.16.** bells. The Trumpeter sounds *Trarintrararara*. The **.1.**st Mate turns o'er commaund to his Captaine, who asks: All well, Cassius?

Aye, aye, Captaine Argoll! E'ery plank is newly oakum'd & pitch'd, as you did commaund.

Were they pitch'd directly from your substance?

Sir?

For you're a blackish Hell-DEVIL, dear Cassius, & so I misdoubt me not you sweat pitch from your uttermost pores!

I know not how I'm pitch'd within, Sir, but my mother pitch'd me full carelessly into the World, & then I —

Cassius, 'tis unmannerly to caulk thy Captaine's jest with **.1.** of thine own. But I'll forgive thy vulgarity, seeing that all's well. All hands ready?

All hands ready!

Ho! Pompey!

Aye, Captaine! shouts the Quartermaster.

All cargo stowed?

All stowed, my Captaine!

Ready at the helm? Who's Helmsman?

'Tis Caligula, Sir! Ready at the helm!

Sails to the yards, lads!

Aye, Captaine Argoll!

Forward your main halyards!

Halyards for'ard!

Hoist sail!

Half-mast high, Captaine!

Cross yards, lads! Cable to the capstern!

Aye, aye!

Octavian!

Aye, Captaine!

Fetch your anchor aboard!

Anchors up, lads! Pull! Pull! Pull, you bloody bastards!

Heave ahead! Men to the tops!

Men to the tops, he said! You heard the Captaine!

Men to the yards!

To your stations, boys! All in their places, Captaine Argoll!

Anchors aweigh!

Down foresail. Hale off the sheets.

Helmsman, *touch the wind & war no more!*

And down the Thames they sail at good speed, rounding the coast of Kent, which may or may not be mysterious Argall's home Countie. The Mate sings out: Why, there's Swalecliffe! I know a wench there who try'd to father a bastard on me! But when the Under-sheriff came, guess what I told him? I says to him, I says, if 'twere my brat 'twould be monstrous strange, because I did nought but bugger her! Ha, ha! And then the Under-sheriff did say—

South of Hope Bay, contrary winds cause Argal to curse & commaund the Helmsman to *have a care of the Lee-latch.* They glimpse a crowd on the Small Downs. Argoll will not stop. At Sheldon they pass some manner of festival. Argull will not stop. They pass by Oxney, & Saint Margaret's at Clyffe. At Dover Haven they drop anchor, for to ship more supplies. The flag flies as e'er at Dover Castle.

The Pilot craves too high a wage. Altho' he gestures with hand-cunning as perfect as of some Salvage who can strike a fish with a pointed stick, Argoll dismisses him, & guides in the ship himself, nestling beneath the platform-guns. Argull can do anything.

D'ye see yon castle, Brutus?

Aye, Captaine. 'Tis **.120.** steps to the Tower there. And from that Tower I've seen all the way to *Callice** in France—

*Calais.

And what went ye a-seekin' in Fraunce, sweet Brutus? French pastry-puddings?

Nay, Captaine, I sailed not there.

All day the Sailors do cry their *Amaine!* and their *Strike!* as they lower casks into the hold.

Three villains desert. Poor Argall must bide until *Cassius* can catch **.3.** new ones. He names 'em Latinishly, altho' they're the merest sub-Argalls scarce tinctured with his substance. He treasures up much patience. Much as a Werowance plays on a reed-flute, wearing his copperplate & deer's head crown, so Argull charms himself with tuneful song. The Sailors agree they've never serv'd under so *Melodicke* a Captaine! Why, unassisted he might well have summonsed those Kecoughtan Salvages out of haven, simply by humming! Argall kens *Deneb* and *Regulus, Vega* and *Arcturus* — all the **.57.** Navigational Starres, in fact. And he kens e'en more notes of the Musickall Spectrum than that! Argall's perfect; Argoll's as terrifying as OKEUS.

Just then the *Trial* drops anchor. She hails from Virginia, & on board is *Lieutenant George Percy,* fled from the Government of that unhappy Colonie.

Beshrew my heart! laughs Argoll. And how stands Jamestown?

In parlous state. Where go you?

To feed your Colonie, & displace the French. And you?

To spend my days of resistless unrest.

Quaintly said! Yet I misdoubt me not you're more excellent than I in birth & position, murmurs kindly Argoll, enjoying himself. Indeed, Sir, you're as ornate as a ship's beak . . .

(See this Argall smile! See so beautiful a whitish-blue when the foam-striped waves join the mountain fog! Argoll's wearing the Changing-Shirt; he can shimmer himself 'twixt **.2.** anythings . . .)

Yea, Maister Percy, I've seen your coat of arms. As for me, my only ensign's *Whitecaps on the blue.*

And now he commenced for to jest with this feeble Percy, who conceived himself to be *a Gentleman of great parts.* 'Twas **.1.** of Argall's dearest pleasures to refresh himself upon his own observations of human nature — **.1.**st drinking in what he spied, with roundly innocent eyes, then getting intoxicated with his own keenness, at which point he began to strut and sneer a little; finally, in that inevitable **.3.**rd stage of drunkenness, he'd howl & lean forward to vomit out the ale of that day's faces, deeds & words — the ale having been changed, of course, through peristalsis, to *Insinuations, Libels,*

Slanders, & other such mush with a sour & beery stink. This rite, accompanied by much finger-pointing and empurplement of his visage, was mirthful for all idlers — for all, I say, who did not themselves fear to be regurgitated in bile that day.

A quickly expert heart-stab, punctuated by a twist — but 'twas all words. (I weary of this, chuckled Argoll from the other side of his mouth. I need a cure.) And soon Lieutenant Percy sat all wilted — *snerped up* as Sweet John would have said.

Just as a Lady gathers her cloak at a play, to be sure that her neighbor doesn't sit on it, so the trembling Pearcie, who feared no Salvage, did lust more than e'er now to array himself within his good boundaries, & therefore he avoided Captaine Argoll e'er after.

Where away, Maister Pearcie? Argall shouted after him.

* * * * * *

And so in September (having made his course .50. leagues northward of the Azores), there sailed upon the Virginian scene our sharp-hearted Captaine Argall, laden with guns & news. What hap there? Well, kind Reader, let the trumpet of History sound, to form up our worthy Adventurers into a procession in time. — Nay, did I say worthy? I meant *everworthy;* for they're all Argolls to me. *Captaine Fortune* leads the ranks, of course. That doughty old Gentleman thumps his stick, & his mortals march on to their rewards for the year 1611, to wit:

.1. Good *Captaine Newport,* sailing northwards on a voyage of discovery for the Russian Company, got shipwrecked by ice, but not fatally. .2. *King James* raised English & Scottish goldpieces by .2. shillings in every pound. .3. In Lincolnshire, my Lord *Robert Willoughby* played host to that sefsame King James at Castle Grimsthorpe (and where lurked Bartty I cannot tell). Queen Anne was there; I know not what she did. No doubt Robert kiss'd her hand with his usual sad courtesy, hoping for some additional preferment to come of all this. .4. *King Wowin-chopunck,* the Werowance of Paspahegh, whose wife & children, as we've read, met their reward at the hands of our mild English, was slain in battle by the same. .5. *Kemps,* our tame Salvage at Jamestowne, did perish of the scurvy. .6. *My Lord De La War,* sinking e'er deeper into the ooze of sickness, took Argall's advice at last, & departed in explicit despite of his commission. Still, he reassured himself that he'd taught the Countrey people to respect authority. A little more pressure, & they'd become utterly tractable & friendly . . . He saved himself in the West Indies by eating *Or-*

anges and *Lemonds*.   **.7.** And so *Lieutenant George Pearcie* (faithful enemy of John Smith, & moreover pale, with a small dark moustachio) did resume the Government again, for not quite **.2.** months, until **.8.** *Sir Thomas Dale* arrived on y^e **.10.**^th of May 1611, near about the time that the Salvages were planting their pumpkins.

* * * * * *

He too hath ridden his horse o'er many Irish corpses. Moreover, he's young. He'll never sicken. He's the man for Virginia. No matter that he's but Deputie Governour of that Colonie, & Sir Thomas Gates is Marshall. Sir Thomas Dale it is who'll be remembered. O, indeed, he's more strict than any Virginia Generall before . . .

* * * * * *

On pain of punishment he commaunds all the Undertakers to plant corn right away, since they've prov'd otherwise too stupid & idle to do it.

He makes new laws, with spinier penalties.

Just as at a cockfight the Gamblers get to sit closer arond the dais than the penny-paying spectators, so his new Counsell draws itself in close around its Undertaking, shutting out the rest from the Church, which is where it meets, Ratcliffe's Palace being now an utter ruin, & Wingfield's manse rotted & creepered to the core. (To Maister Percie, everyone's a shadow. No matter.)

Look you, dear Gentlemen, says Sir Thomas. Do you know why Mountjoy succeeded in Ireland?

Nay, my Lord . . .

Scorched earth. 'Twas a needful policy there. And so it shall be here.

* * * * * *

His executions of runaways began. — He's hired to be our Hangman, all did whisper.

They toll'd the Church-bell for each legal death.

Three Laborers who'd essayed to rob the Store-house of vittles he did commaund to be lashed unto treetops & left there to groan for food & drink, until they starv'd.

A hungry Soldier sought to desert to the Salvages. Sir Thomas commaunded that he be burnt alive.

A fellow was late to Church without excuse. Sir Thomas had him flogg'd.

All his Convicts he had variously burned, hanged, broken on wheels, staked, shot, or starved.

* * * * * *

He set out to view the River of Nansamund, where Sweet John himself had been troubled with Salvage treachery. No matter. The Indians tried to attack him there, so he burn'd all their houses.

* * * * * *

A message from Powhatan: Release your .2. Indian prisoners, or I'll poison you.

Sir Thomas laughs, sends back counter-threats of death.

* * * * * *

Then he sail'd up *James his River* to the Falls, .50.-odd miles away, near-abouts to Sweet John's failed Cittie of *Nonsuch*. (Indeed, the place was like unto the highlands or champion Countrey of Lincolnshire herself.) Here where Lord Delaware had likewise failed (his men suffering assassination at the hands of Yndians), he decided to plant a new Garrison entitled *Henrico*. Before his Soldiers had well quarter'd themselves, Powhatan's warriors attacked. He cared not. They went back for supplies; and (come September), up the coils of that Riuer *Iames* they did go, all the way to the very falls where Powhatan's Countrey endeth and the Countrey of the Monacans begins. These latter being Powhatan's foes, he plotted to make alliance with them.

On a high promontory they palisadoed .7. acres. Comprehending full well now that all Salvages are like unto those worldly Midwives, who will smother an inconvenient bastard as soon as it is born (& therefore well deserve the capital penalty), Sir Thomas did drive his men to the strictest speed. 'Twas the *twinkling fear* which impelled him thus (altho' he would have call'd it *prudence*). They rais'd up a Watch-tower on each of the .4. corners & manned it, so that no infidel could surprise 'em. His steady Enclosers now 'gan to dig away a channel, to translate Henrico unto an Islande.

He'd garrison the whole Province in time. That was the way to defeat 'em. As for Powhatan, Sir Thomas had now resolv'd to bid him come kneeling, & make formal submission; otherwise that murtherous old Salvage could expect to be hang'd.

* * * * * *

At Christmastide they did annex to themselves the Towne of Apamatuck, together with all its corn-fields, *without the losse of any, excepting some few*

Salvages, as Sweet John's *Generall Historie* doth put the case. Queen Oppossunisquonuke, who'd staged that comedy of treacherous trulls, was wounded, but misfortunately escaped. Her Towne became *Bermuda Hundred.*

* * * * * *

When Argoll arrived, he found himself oft summonsed by Sir Thomas for supper, in order to look into the characters of others. What quality rendered him such a *Politick Jewell?* Well, Argull being disappeared unto darkness, I cannot say; yet here's a maxim from an old sea-book which might apply to his mind-hatchings:

> *As touching those persons that are meete to take charge, that is to say, to be as maister of ships in Nauigation, he ought to be sober and wise, and not to be light or rash headed, nor to be fumish or hasty . . . he ought not to be simple, but he must be suche a one as must keepe his company in awe of him (by discretion) . . .*

> *And furthermore, the maister ought to be such a one, as dothe knowe the Moones course, whereby he doth knowe at what time it is a full Sea, or a lowe water . . .*

* * * * * *

See him snatch Yndian corn, burn Townes, burn fields together with Sir Thomas Dale. And so they begin to bring their Virginia into good order & array, no matter that the Salvages unceasingly raise up *the hue & cry* against 'em, singing: *Whe, whe, yah, ha, ne, he, wittowa, wittowa!*

* * * * * *

Again and again Sir Thomas did summons him. Good Argoll swore that soon they'd be able to sail e'erywhere in trade-trimmed boats. All the while he was smiling & thinking: To the DEVIL with you, you freshwater Soldier! — Not kenning his mind, Sir Thomas thanked him for his courtesy.

O, 'tis my innatest virtue, yawned Argoll.

When the Servaunts were out, Sir Thomas whisper'd about events at the Earl of Exeter's house, & a new Charter of greater greed. Argull nodded, smiling divinely.

Sir Thomas had it on good authority that the King would soon do such & so.

My Lord, I do admire your discreet & provident government.

Now 'twas the hour for the same old inquisition. Without Argall, they'd never learn. With Argoll, they'd improve e'erything.

Dear Captaine Argull, hath Powhatan brothers to be surpris'd at our pleasure?

There's our fine feigned friend dear *Opechancanough,* King of Paumaunkee. He hath .4. Palaces like unto Powhatan's. Each one's a hundred foot long. He hath likewise a hundred houses, all in Menapacunt-Towne. 'Twould pain him, did we crown the lot with flames—

Let's hang him!

Aye, my Lord, as soon as 'tis *politick*.

Whom else doth Powhatan value?

Why, his daughter, upon my life. (Argull felt so ennui'd & contemptuous that he could scarce resist whisking off Sir Thomas's head. How long must he hold the watch for these twanglers?)

That's *Pockahunta?*

Aye—

Let's have at her!

Indeed, my Lord, so soon as we can find her—

*   *   *   *   *   *

Sir Thomas sends good Argoll to *Patawomeck* to smooth o'er that little misdeameanor of Captaine West's .III. years back (in which some Pattawomeck Salvages had lost their heads). Those Salvages have proved testy e'er since. Should that caress be accomplished, dear Argall is charg'd to chaffer blue beads for corn.

'Tis said their King stands tall & stern like unto a Tower. 'Tis said he ranks as great as Powhatan. How much doth Argoll care? Not a cheeseparing! He's ready for anything.

Be careful & discreet, good Argull! For remember Ratliffe's fate—

This Yndian's a River-King, isn't he, my Lord? Then let him river-swim or sink according to his craft! Should he disconvenience me, why then, I'll make him lick my arse—

See Argall's steady grabbling. Following Captaine John Smith's chart he doth sail exact & easy. (Altho' he'd complained to ye Governor that no soul could tell how many miles answer'd to .1. degree or rule upon that sweaty little yeoman's map, 'twas only out of his own sportiveness that he'd thus marr'd Sweet John's honor; for, as he well knew, this *Map of Virginia* actually prov'd exceeding workmanlike. Here's double-palisadoed

Patawomecke-Towne, just where it should be. With Brutus
he doth troll the ale-bowl to Sweet John's memory.)

See him a-trading 'mongst the Pattawomecks in their softwood Countrey of green
which bleeds into red at summer's end, the
moist breath of summer commencing for to
stale, the trees a-crawling with sweaty ivy.
Argull introduces his Sailors to them thus:
We're your follies' foes. In December of 1612
he concludes an inalienable peace with those
Salvages.

He enriches himself mightily with hemp,
cod & antimony. Sir Thomas will never have
the wit to gainsay him. Then for yᵉ Colonie's
sake he gains near about **.400.** bushels of
corn. O yes; these Pattawomecks keep corn
enough for e'erything.

In 1613, refresh'd near radiantly by the wet
smell of spring, he ups sail again for Pattawomeck,
for to snickle some corn. He lingers, hunting bison for
his sport. 'Tis near about then that a certain *Pocahontas* sets off for the
same Kingdome, to get antimony for her father . . .

THE GRAMMAR OF KIDNAPPERS (1613)

A captive girl brought Naman to the Prophet. A captive woman was the means of converting Iberia . . . GOD makes the weake things of the world confound the mighty, and getteth Himself praise by the mouth of babes and sucklings.

REV. WILLIAM SYMONDS (1609)

Behold the fish, that even now was free,
Unto the deadly hook how he is tied!
So vain delights allure us to the snare,
Wherein un'wares we fast entangled are.

JOHN DENYS, *The Secrets of Angling* (before 1613)

*N*ow it came to Captaine Argall's ears, by means of a skinny Salvage, that Pocahuntas was residing at Pataomecke, keeping company with her friends while they did trade skins for face-paint & suchlike trash, for they were but Salvages and knew not what they did. This intelligence seemed to Argall to show the way to a princely opportunity (if, indeed, such royal words be fit towels for this fellow to wipe himself upon — but yes! "princely" will do; and in fact puts me in mind of a proper proverb sown by our friends the Turkes: *There are no ties of kinship between Princes.*). So he spoke a word in the ear of Sir Thomas Dale, who clapt his shoulder & cried: In GOD's name, good friend, get you hence ere she flits! hearing which, gentle Argoll strode aboard the *Treasurer* to commence stamping, shouting & railing at his mutchado'd Sailors (or *Whoreson Negro dogs* as he call'd 'em), until they raised sail with such speed as has scarcely been seen, faring more rapidly than the current itself (altho' that partook of the genus which in Lincolnshire they like to call *living water*). Down *King James his River*, once Powhatan's River, they sailed, right to the entrance of the Virginian Sea where the winds were whivelling & veering almost treacherously, then they rounded the cape after Kecoughtan (whose unmusically Salvage name we now render Hampton-Towne) and so turned into the wide and foggy Bay of Chesapeake, ghosting thence northwards past *.2.* river-mouths (*Pamaunkee* and *Toppahanock)* until they reached the wide gape of the River *Patamomeck*. Then in a steady seashell-sounding wind upstream they did course. — Shorten sail! cried Argoll. — Yea, Captaine, 'tis done. — On the .5.th inlet to the starboard lieth the village *Cecowocomoco,* where Spanish moss sways in the wind like scalps; this Towne they passed in quietude; next without remark they browsed across *Potapaco,* & then the river jaggled south where to the larboard good Captaine Argall spied ancient *Patawomeck* ...

'Twas a cool day near stark calm, with a bone-white fan of cloud behind the pine trees. And the Master, .1. Samuel Argall, did stand on deck spying in his sand-glass, until they anchored off the fishy bank, employing the stream anchor only, lest they must away again in haste. And for the same reason they refrained from taking in all sails.

Charge your bow pieces & stand ready.

Aye, Captaine.

Is all ready?

Aye, aye!

Brutus!

Dear Captaine!

Stand in for me here.

My dagger-hand's ready, Captaine Argull!

To slay me, or Salvages?

As you commaund, Captaine.

I'd prefer to fall 'pon my *own* sword, if it please you. — Octavian!

Aye, Sir?

Any *Canoa* that doth approach without an Englishman within, fire on her.

With pleasure, Captaine.

Know'st thou thy namesake?

I'm told he did turn Emperor, said the Sailor with a grin.

Too true! But he didn't conspire 'gainst his Maister to do it. D'ye comprehend?

No, Sir.

Good. Who's on watch?

Cassius & Marc Antony, Captaine.

Bid 'em ne'er blink their eyes, not for the merest wink, 'till I'm returned, & our squaw's battened down. All you wolf-dogs, stand ready now!

Aye, aye!

At this Pataomecke there dwelt a good and craven Salvage, well painted with antimony, by name .1. *Iapazeus,* whom by presents Argoll had tricked into adopting him as a brother; this being something that Salvages often do, in order to create obligation which might flower into profit. 'Tis writ by some Historians that John Smith was Argall's pandar, he having been as he put it *an old friend* of this selfsame Iapazaws. No matter. Good Argall, quick to follow the maners of any Countrey, got himself as many brothers as he could. — Down shallop! he commaunded, and his Sailors in their blue baggy trousers planted knives back in leather scabbords and lowered away with a splash; he leaped in; so did a quartet of them (to wit, *Sulla, Pompey, Cicero* & *Cataline*); then off they rowed, smartly dodging fish-traps and skinny black sapling-legs marooned in water, watching for Salvage mischief, until they came to land in a discreet spot walled in by immense blond rushes, where rotten leaves were decaying into black muck. — Sleep not, lads, ordered Argall. Neither make any noise. Be not so ignorant as to go a-hunting Salvage quim. D'ye remember the tale of *John Smith's* men, who got broiled for their pains? Then those suicidal pricksters retold the tale at Appamatuck! Hark to me & mine errand; be ready to push off fast. — And without further word he leapt audaciously ashore, where walnut-oiled Salvages cried him treacherous welcome.

Just as in a sea-battle the *Admirall* finds himself singled out alone before all others, to make the choice which will save all his fleet, so e'erworthy Argoll did now stand isolate betwixt himself and GOD, being charged to help his Countreymen get their living by whatever means; and my Lord Sir Thomas had willed him not to fail. How he joyed in it! O, he did laugh & laugh, calculating that *some strategem was likely to serve* . . .

Their corn did well, as he could see. 'Twould be serviceable to the Colonie. He saw some women weeding, & murmured cheerily: Bosomy buttocks & buttocky bosoms, 'tis enough to draw my vomit-sweat!

Behind an ancient midden of oyster-shells, little boys & girls together were playing some game with a leathern ball. Argull stopp'd to gift 'em with a few beads, scattering happiness in the dirt before them, as if he were feeding corn to chickens. They shrieked gloatingly. No doubt their parents would love him. Then yonder piddling wench, that squat & pockmarked *Pokahuntiss,* might toddle to him of her own accord . . .

Now breathless from the hot wet corn-fields a-crawling with snakes ('tis here that men take their pleasure with squaws) came his good little *Ensign Swift,* whom on a previous occasion he'd left for a hostage and spy. Argall's pet name for him was *Casca,* after another of Julius Caesar's murtherers. The boy's aspiration (as the Captaine well knew) was to possess a pocketful of solid gold nobles. He who sets sail toward wealth above all things oft employs an improvidently greedy heart as his Helmsman. The heart sings out: *Fair soundings!* A new coast gleams ahead, & the heart sees Sunne-specks — nay, golden nobles! — And so the lad's sojourn amidst Salvages hadn't spooked him; he'd improved the time with speculations of future trophies. — Good! thought Argall to himself. They've neither roasted him, nor sawed off his fingers with mussel-shells ... — Awarding Casca a jocular pinch, he gave him leave to visit his Countreymen in the shallop. — But meet me without fail in Japjaws's house, he commaunded. And bring a copper kettle, do you hear?

(For in England the *Redheaded white worm in a dock root* is the best bait for trout; and in Virginia a *Copper kettle* will hook most any Salvage.)

Passing within the double palisadoes of the Towne, replying to the greetings of all (they unrolled mats for him, & were commencing for to dance, but he turn'd his back), to the lodge of this Iapazeus he went forthwith, and (having been most courteously feasted on turtle stew, soft-shell clams & smoked sturgeon) expressed his desire.

Iopassus hesitated. Then, taking Argall's hands in his, he said in an earnest voice: Brother, it befits not my affection to traduce her by whom I'm also call'd brother.

Tell me, *brother,* laughed silky Argoll. Do you count my brotherhood worth the cherishing?

E'erworthy! the Salvage hastily exclaimed. I believe you know our word *Mufkaiuwh,* by which we signify *A Flower of a fine thing.* And I mean always to do you good service—

Ha, ha, ha! Brother Japjaws, how I love thee! Dear brother — you *are* my brother, I trow?

If you would have me so, replied Iapazeus, frowning.

Good. Now, *Brother,* you must look to your policy, and choose which *Mufkaiuwh* hath the sweetest scent, for today .1. flower shall be plucked up from your garden of brotherhood. And you shall find me equally constant in my hatred as in my affections. Betray not Pocahontas, and you'll not be my brother anymore, nor friend. If you would thus forbear my love, why, fare you well, good Japjaws. First come my lads to fire your house; next we'll spoil this Towne entire. And this wife of yours (where did she grabble those fine white beads? They date back from Sweet John's time!), damn me if the old doxy's not yet young enough to serve my turn—

Now I begin to see how variously beat the hearts of Tassantasses from our own, Iapazeus said, for when you pledged brotherhood to me and left your son Casca in my keeping, I little dreamed your love was no fine ribbon,

but an arrowpoint worked into my flesh. I advise you not to comport yourself so in our Countrey, Captain Argoll, for you bereave us of our pride.

In this vain world all must sooner or later sink to ooze, laugh'd Argoll.
Pride's the merest weed, like love; *Mufkaiuwh's* a weed; all weeds do wilt,
but ne'er mind; upon the slime new weeds will grow.

You trouble too little to respect your friends—

Dear *Brother,* you speak a passing merry gale.

I must to my Werowance, replied Iapezus most curtly, & he departed,
while Argull, not wishing to bide alone like some naughty Cabin-boy who's
about to get whipped at the capstan, went out from that lascivious Towne &
returned unto the waiting shallop, where his Sea-dogs discreet and sly
(good Slaughtermen all) rowed him back aboard the *Treasurer,* singing
with him his favorite ditty:

> Red sky at night, Sailor's delight.
>
> Red sky at morning, Sailor's warning.

'Twas almost .6. bells. Brutus relinquish'd commaund. All well, he said.
They agreed to lock Pokahuntiss in the Gun-room, should they catch her.
High-hoping Argoll disappeared within his Cabin. Just as in this his own
history he mainly lurks, clinging unseen to his own inner darkness, until
the strike of Policy's clock doth invoke his next maneuver, so on the *Treasurer* he liked to encoffin himself most secretly, aweing the Crew with his
aloofness.* (Brutus had once surmised to Cassius that could their gazes
penetrate that Cabin at such times, they'd discover no Argull there, nothing
but night-air double-varnish'd unto itself. Cassius replied: Good King
James would drown such superstition with fire! — But he said it uncer-
tainly, in a voice attainted by eeriness.) The ship lay still & warlike, studded
with e'ery martial appointment; the Towne likewise became passing still,
for our Yndians deemed it more than strange that the Tassantasses delayed
to chaffer. (Tell 'em it's 'cause we respect their King too greatly not to await
his commaund, chuckled Argoll.) Only Casca came & went, being familiarly tolerated by all. He'd stashed the copper kettle already inside
Japzaws's house. In a languid hour when they calculated that Argall slept,
he helped his Countreymen barter moldy sea-biscuit for venison, on condition that both sides render him a tithe. No more capable of repose than

---

*Methinks 'tis the way we confide all rarities to our best security. Don't these Salvages hide their
precious corn? Powhatan's subjects bury it in pits. These Patawomeckes store it in their houses
in high cribs; 'twas in the shade of one of those that Argoll had dined with Japzaws just now.

some buzzing beetle, he bustled & spied about so much, 'twas as if he owned .12. eyes in his head!

The Sailors fish'd yawningly for sturgeon. They play'd Tick-tack. — Draw — shuffle — cut! . . . — Come on, .8.! — Come on, .9.!

At last a Salvage paddl'd up with Casca on purpose to invite Argoll before the *King of Pastancy,* who filled the office of Chief Werowance of those parts. 'Twas the same with whom dear Argall had qualified his famous peace. O, *Blessed are the Peace-makers,* &c, &c, &c. Down shallop! — *Casca, Cato, Curio* & *Crassus* rowed their Captaine out of ship-shadow, each man sporting the .2.-fisted sea-pull. Brown mirrors of creeks offered skyward dear Argall's image. The shallop grounded; his Bravos leapt out, standing ready with their snaphaunces at half-cock. Brown water oozed betwixt stumps & bloody tree-hands. Tawny Salvages crept round barefooted, with leaves and feathers in their hair. At least their evil bows stayed un-nocked. Now Casca trembled a trifle, comprehending at last the grandeur of their undertaking. As for Argoll, he humm'd a Moone-tide song, then ceased, smiling as silently as an egret folding in its wings. *Tick again* & *tick again.* Where lay the Palace? — O yes: Yonder. The King would remember him. 'They'd been acquainted .3. years. — Thereto strolled merciful Argall, accompanied by the aforementioned Ensign Swift who bore blue beads for all Salvages of quality *(O, may they not drop 'em into their mouths,* prayed Casca, *for then the bluing might be dissolv'd!).*

The King wore a dead rat on his head. His face was silver-painted, as indeed were all those of his Counsell-men, for this *Antimony* mine of theirs did lie conveniently by. Each of these Nobles did greet their guest with an oration. (Argull longed to make of 'em all the merest by-word.) Somewhat blasted by his cares appeared this King today — compass'd in by Arkill's *Politick,* no doubt. Indeed the silvering of his face could not mask the blackness of its anger. (Did the Salvages blacken their countenances for just that purpose when they went to war — to shew their honorable rage? *Wowinchopunck* the King of Paspahegh had e'er adorned himself so. Argall joyed that he'd been killed.)

And now the King did proffer a pipe of *Tobaco* to all to smoke, which they courteously accepted. Casca seem'd monstrous addicted to that habit. As for Argull, he liked to beguile himself in building small smoky cumuli, but should this herb die utterly out of fashion, why then, he'd take no accompt of it. When this ceremony had expir'd — 'twas near about as wearisome as .1. of the Governor's dinners — he purveyed round a handful of crimson beads — the latest style of trash. Then those old Salvages did say: *Nowamatamen!* which signifies *I must keep yt.* To the King himself he presented a brass bell, which should have made him monstrously contented. (The King wrinkled up his tattooed face.) *Tick again* & *tick again.* And *now* before this Salvage Counsell (full secretly, so as not to frighten his victim out of Towne) did wily Argall give oath that should they do his will & in consequence fall into broils with Powhatan, then, why *then* e'erworthy Argall would join with them against the aforesaid Powhatan to the very death, deploying demiculverins, murther-shot & trundle-shot until all enemies lay piteously bereft of flesh — all *bloody,* in short (whispered kindly Captaine Argall), entirely *perish & stinking,* dismembered carcasses *stretcht & twisted into serpents,* childrens' hands *hacked off* in Lord Delaware's old fashion, e'ery tattooed Bow-man *boil'd alive in lead,* Powhatan himself *slowly roasted 'til his brains exploded from his ears,* all his wenches (including Pokahuntas) *split open, and their guts haled out through their arseholes,* and his Townes *black-burnt down to Hell.* Clapping their hands unto their mouths, the Salvage Counsell glared at him in terror.

✳ ✳ ✳ ✳ ✳ ✳

So they went aboard, the .3. of them, Iapazeus, Pocahontas (that precious instrument) & Iapazeus's wife. In their Canoa came stripling-Casca, for after this caper 'twould be perilous for him to bide amidst the Salvages. (Pocahontas's ladies advised her not to go. She smiled, commaunding them to wait without fear. Then she wash'd her face in the river & painted her shoulders. She donned a new deerskin mantle decorated with shells and bones; the Werowance had presented it to her. She hung chains of pearl from her ears. She donned a cougar-tooth necklace which her husband had given her. — Reader, this girl was always o'er-quick in what she did. More than once she'd made a pot too hastily, so that it shattered in the fire. Then there was that time when her impulse-vagaried heart did move her to pluck away Sweet John from the chopping-block . . .) The SUN descended; soon OKEUS would be out. A white SUN-trail grazed the river. Japzaws's wife (whose breast was prick'd & pounced with a fish's likeness) inquired whether they ought to bring a nice sturgeon or a basketful of mussels to the Tassantasses, for everyone knew them to be weaklings who could scarcely feed themselves. Laughing anxiously, Casca assured her that his *Dear father* Captaine Argoll possessed enough dainties for all. And Japzaws said: Woman, you've caused enough trouble by insisting on this. Now be silent. — For the spouses had lured Pocahontas unto this Adventure by pretending that the wife desired to see the ship, but dreaded to go unaccompanied by Powhatan's daughter. And how unwilling stood their friend to be persuaded? I conjecture she longed to feast again 'pon strange foods. She giggled & chattered with her Servaunt-maids whilst she sat painting herself. And there was, perhaps, someone among the Tassantasses whom she looked for, or at least wished news of. Did she seek that changeling call'd *Fortune?*   We would all of us improve our days — wouldn't King James himself aspire to conquer Fraunce & Spain? Argull's fresh in, & fraughted with eternal happiness! Come drink, girl, & satiate thy perplexities forever!

The masted rigging which loomed before her was conical, like unto a giant fish-trap. In this it reminded her most deceitfully of her Countreymen. Just as a Glass-blower must twirl the molten bubble on his rod, so good Japzaws did most carefully cozen her, turning his assurances ever about as the many-flagg'd ship enlarged herself ahead. The hot, heavy air turned clammy once they entered the shadows of the sails. Look! E'erworthy Argall himself now stood with his hands upon the gunnels, softly singing. *Policy's clock hath strook.*   The Sailors becked her to the Waist-ladder (whose wooden rungs are easy for Landsmen to mount); Argoll rais'd his forefinger, & the Trumpeter did blare *Trarintra-rintrara.*   And so now that ship did live up to her name, the *Treasurer,* for she bore the very *Non-pareil of Virginia,* who'd soon enrich our Colonie.

✳ ✳ ✳ ✳ ✳ ✳

Amonute, running her hands half-discreetly down those string-rank'd cougar-teeth to smooth the points unto bristling symmetry upon her bosom, was happy but a little anxious to meet the Tassantasses again. Japzaws had told her that the Tassantasses longed to behold her, for the sake of old days. (And when she looked about her, it seem'd that he'd spoken veraciously, for all these bearded Sailor-men were gazing on her almost gloatingly, as if she were some prize. Their whiskers gave them a strangely self-satisfied appearance.) She feared her father's displeasure. After the obliteration of Paspaegh, he'd begun to say that the Tassantasses meant to ruin him & drive his people utterly into the darkness. But could she get some worthy present for him, or (better yet) persuade the Tassantasses to desist from burning Townes, he'd be content. She knew how to bend him back to love.

In any event, 'twas pleasanter to play Tick-Tack & Lurch with some dapper little Captaine than to go home for to weed the corn-fields . . .

Argoll smil'd upon her, & extended his hand, for which she thanked him.

Meanwhile, his Sailors were already swinging down a wooden baffle o'er the top of the Waist-ladder.

* * * * * *

Pocahontas, my delight! I see you're plaited-haired no more. (Casca, tell Brutus & Cassius to stand behind her.) You've shaved your head, love! 'Pon my word, you look quite ravishable in your Salvage fashion—

Thank you, Captaine Argall . . .

Tell me, Cassisus, my ruddy co-conspirator, which Roman Emperor got o'erthrown by virtue of a woman?

I know not, Captaine Argoll. For in school I did learn me that they—

Then I'll tell thee. His name's *Powhatan*. And you know which wench it was? Behold her yonder!

Amonute comprehends but **.3.** or **.4.** words of this. Her smile unfurls itself nervously.

* * * * * *

And now, a tour of the *Treasurer!* Japzaws's wife gazes amaz'd upon the Bread-room, whose walls do glister with tin, to guard against rats. Thro' a scutter-grate they can peep down into the hold whilst Cassius holds a torch for their eyes' conveniency. None of 'em wish to go there — for to them it partakes of the lightlessness within the eyesockets of certain fishes. Next for the *Murtherer-guns* & kindred ordnance slung by iron chains behind the loopholes. ('Tis politick to affright Japzaws with these, Reader, for when he tells his great Werowance of them, what Yndian will dare attack an English ship?) In the great Cabin where the Helmsman must stand throughout e'ery voyage, Argoll uplifts the lid of a wooden box (& this lid is carven with our late Queen's likeness), to shew these Salvages how the Compass-dial doth fritter & fleer most eerily in the swells, whilst the needle points always straight. Amonute remembers that Sweet John once presented her Uncle Opechancanough with exactly such a gift. All her People feared it. They said that it held the secret of the Tassantasses' magic. When word came that Paspahegh had been burned, and the People there all slain so pitilessly, Opechancanough buried that souvenir in a marsh, for fear that its Power might otherwise draw the Tassantasses to Menapacunt.

* * * * * *

Her heart flushed with uneasiness. Japzaws and his wife were so shrilly merry, almost as her own People became on the day before the Sacrifice of the Black Boys, when mothers lose their sons forever. Flogged, drugged, long secluded, terrified halfway into madness, these children return home changed unto warriors, with their boyhoods scarcely more visible to them than clouds through a smoke-hole. The past falls away; their names are changed; they're divorced from all save manhood, which mainly signifies honor and death. Yes, her heartbeats pained her and a bad taste crept into her mouth. Her friend Captaine Argall also displayed overmuch gaiety, so she thought. Indeed, he resembled some sly *Crane-bird* with a fish in his mouth. As they sat down to table together, Japzaws giggled & goggled at Argoll most slyly, as if that pair shared some jest; but in reply Argull kicked Japzaws's shin with his pointed boot. They were in the Gun-room, deep under the Quarter-deck. The tiller groaned overhead; the ship herself did ever stir and creak, moving as did Amonute's own house in a wind; but while her house would have danced sideways, this hard-walled stinking chamber of festivity crept up & down until she commenced to get queasy. A breeze trickled through the Gun-port; she strained for to drink it in. She could not comprehend why the heavy oaken door to the Lower-deck had been closed in upon them (Captaine Argoll said 'twas to keep those bother-ations of Sailors out). Peering down thro' the Floor-hatch into the Bread-room, she spied the upturn'd gazes of several Sailors. What were they about? And now a Cabin-boy came a-rapping on that arch-shapen oaken door, & Casca leapt up to open it. The Cook entere'd, bowing unto Amonute. He set before her a bowl of stewed salt beef, for which she thank'd him in a whisper. After Japzaws' wife received her portion ('twas strange how she look'd so sadly pallid!), their companions got served in turn, courteous Argull last, whilst they all watched her. The Cook & the Cabin-boy withdrew at last, bowing again. — Now we're in haven, mut-tered Argall. Casca darted up to lock the door . . . Betwixt Japzaws & Cap-taine Argoll the tablecloth moved as if secrets were getting committed beneath it; then Japzaws paled and began to laugh louder than ever,* at which Amonute took full alarm at last. Casting staccatto glances about her, she commenced for to wonder whether 'twas but accident how she'd been

---

*According to Hamor's *Relation,* which glances over almost every Salvage with contempt, be they enemy or tool, Japzaws was *secretly well rewarded . . . with a small Copper kettle, and som other les valuble toies so highly by him esteemed, that doubtlesse he would haue betraied his owne father for them.* Captaine Smith in his *Generall Historie* doth likewise call this Japzaws *the old Jew, who for a Cop-per Kettle would have done any thing: and thus they betraied the poor innocent Pocahontas aboord.* Methinks he pitied Pocahontas! Could his pity have been (as so many Commentators and ill-starred Novelists do pretend) the sign of a secret love? For 'tis otherwise strange that this pillager and enslaver of Salvages would abused "his old friend" Japzaws, and by extension the e'erworthy Argall, who but did what was politic for the Colonie.

stationed in this corner, with her back against a bulkhead. Lieutenant Turnell sat across from her, gazing moodily at her puccooned shoulders. He
suffered from *the forest weariness*. Like unto his fellow Englishmen, he
was dining on sturgeon from hereabouts; in Virginia, that bully beef was
serv'd up only to Salvages, for a novel treat. English Sailors loathed it.

Once some Monacans had entered her mother's house by night, for to
slay them all; but the walls shook, and so her mother awoke in time to cry
out. Her uncle's sons had caught them before they could flee. Next morning, everyone helped torture those enemies to death. Amonute had been so
small then that she could scantly remember the occasion. But full well she
recollected waking to her mother's screams as the walls moved. Seeing the
tablecloth's twitchings reminded her of that. The ship lurched . . .

Goodly Argoll did pray aloud. Then they fell to. When they ate, they
threw nothing into the fire at first (indeed they had no fire here), nor left
any morsel for the POWERS. This neglectfulness scarcely amazed her, for
it had been the same in Captain Smith's time, but now that she stood in her
full womanhood & married, it seemed selfish, evil, dangerous.

Beside her sat Captain Argall, pretending to devote his uttermost attention to Japzaws, but it now began to seem that his left elbow might be
ready-cocked to pin her against the wall should she attempt to rise. More-
o'er, Casca with .3. other Officers sat at the next table. Could she 'scape
them she'd not find herself in any wise advantaged, since that oaken door
stood lock'd. Beyond it, Tassantasses guarded the Lower-deck, from which
only by ladder & after-hatch could she have gain'd the Upper-deck, itself
well-paced by other Sentries; meanwhile the baffled-off Waist-ladder was
ruled by its own Guard; so she decided to make no remark, hoping that
these leering faces were not leering after all, now fearing above all things
her father's sorrowful wrath; and she returned to her English supper with
downcast head, her eyes flashing like black swamp-water.

* * * * * *

But Captain Argoll served her a glass of well-sugared sack, & then another,
so that she felt happy, sleepy & queasy all at once. Silently she prayed for
good fortune. Sweet John had sworn to her that his Tassantasses would e'er
remain her friends . . .

. . . And then she was overtaken by the same feeling as when she'd been a
young girl and her aunt had through some grievous error let the fire go out.

* * * * * *

On that .1.ˢᵗ night of her new life, in the fashion of Revolutionaries, who grip the tightest immediately subsequent to their coup, Argall caused his dinner-tables to be folded away, & then lodged her in the Gun-room (which as we've learnt was both luxurious & well-bulkheaded against escapes); on the .2.ⁿᵈ, after her bitter gaze did ceaselessly exclaim against him, he judged it best to confine her in the hold-darkness below the beams of the first orlop, where smelly bilge would lap at her, & she'd hear rats and termites a-gnawing between the ship's ribs. — Nay, Reader, 'twas utterly unlike your piteous conception! The *Treasurer* being a fine, staunch ship, her pumps could suck up little more than sea-froth on e'en the stormiest occasion; our prisoner might wet her sandall'd foot, but no more. So lift up the hatch-rings rapid-like, dear Sailors, or Argoll in his sporting humor might lay about you with a rope's end! Indeed he's anxious for to haste her down. Why won't he leave Pattawomeck, then? Japzaws being weak-hearted, & the King of Pattawomeck being but a Salvage, 'tis possible that Powhatan could persuade 'em into some counter-treachery which might spring the *Non-pareil* loose! Better to flee unto Jamestowne, starry Argoll, now that you've caught your prize! — But Argall was not such as we. He stood stalwart 'gainst all contingencies. The *Treasurer* was loaded with powder & culverin-balls. Disclosing no anxiety, he'd abide here until his business with Powhatan had clos'd. Did any Canoas approach him untowardly, why then, at his whistle quick Brutus & Cassius would lead the men belowdecks to ready their ordnance from the loopholes.

Nonetheless, Captaine Fortune hath trick'd us all upon occasion, & so 'twere yet politick to stash Pokahuntiss away! She'd have light from several of those grated scuttles he'd shewed her on her tour, & they'd bring all the water she listed. Yea, honorable Reader, fortunate she was against her apprehensions; for had his wise heart not sued him to treat her well, he might have clapp'd her in the *Bilboes,* where his miscreant Crewmen sometimes spent a week, until their ankles were galled & bloody from the tight cold irons. (Sweet John knew all about that.) But Argoll's gracious nature refrained from malice against her whom he could have shamed. E'en her reproaches he'd have endured for now (being capable of the most ingenious patience), but should she whine her way up thro' his Sentries, pleading she but wanted air, percase she'd leap into the river, and put Powhatan's war to further rage ... 'Twas thus prudentest not to gamble upon her obedient behavior. Sir Thomas Dale could spend her as he liked; Argall preferr'd to hazard her not, not 'til he delivered her complete!

O, but she made a doleful noise, laying herself down upon her face and scratching at the wood with her fingernails. Ere now, he'd always fancied that Salvages did that only for to welcome guests of quality. This here, well, 'twas the sort of bereavement which an English girl might have express'd, had she been betrayed by her lover, or cast of a sudden unto *Old Bailey's* dungeon-hole . . .

Altho' they'd received a kilderkin of ale, some of the Sailors sorrowed for her, and almost did contemn their own Captaine. But *he,* many was the time he'd seen piteous things, when carrying out his service. No one could translate him into an unsteady man.

✳ ✳ ✳ ✳ ✳

Lieutenant Turnell begged leave to express his alarm lest the prisoner take her own life.

I see your education was very tender, my lad Brutus (thus jocular *Captaine Argall);* no doubt your School-fellows were wont to hang themselves at the slightest touch of the Master's rod! And you yourself, old spark, O, didn't you leap onto your sword, when punishment for stabbing Caesar loom'd?

Lieutenant Turnell, sensing on the back of his neck the cold wet breath of danger, prov'd quick to apologize & excuse, but to no avail; by command of Captaine Argoll he was placed in a packing-case fraughted with eyeholes & lungholes and then lowered into **.1.** of the spurkets (as the spaces between the side-timbers are called); there he'd be privileged (said Captaine Argull) to spy upon the squaw at his leisure, as doubtless his solicitude desired to do; should he discover more than he knew what to do with, he had permission to rap upon his case-roof, but otherwise not. While his habitation was being thus emplaced by **.4.** cursing members of the Coxswain's gang (they not knowing that anyone crouch'd within, for Argall had no need to make his Lieutenant a laughingstock or buttstock of any contempt save his own), the Princess Pocahontas got herself entertained by Argall with good bread & cheese, and he deferred to her in e'ery matter, in order to confuse her the more concerning his intentions. He smiled, bowed & proferred her stony plaints half an ear, as the Coxswain's gang swore some more and called their *Amaine! Amaine!* and then the Coxswain yelled: *Strike!* by which he knew that Lieutenant Turnell was down. At that, he presented her most graciously to the ship's Marshall, a certain *Domitian* (so nam'd after the exceedingly merciful Emperor of that name), who led her to her place, vocally deploring the neccesity & raising the lid of each scuttle-hatch for her as she went deeper & deeper belowdecks. Then bidding her goodnight,

Domitian motioned her down the final ladder, and when he saw her safely in the bottom of that foul place he closed the last hatch over her as gently as he could, hoping (because the Marshall was a kind man) that she would not hear that final ignominious toggling of the wooden lock . . . Then Pocahontas was alone with Lieutenant Turnell.

* * * * * *

He heard her repeating something in a low moan whose syllables he could not entirely distinguish, but it might have been *Ahkeÿ vwwaap,* which means *It hurts me.*

* * * * * *

She knew that her husband, her father, her uncle Opechancanough and Uttamatomakkin would all be praying to OKEUS to release her from His further wrath. What evil had she done? Or was her capture intended by Him to strike at her father? How she pitited him now! She feared his anger no more, so high did tower his sorrow on his account. He must surely be in agonies now that he owned no power to take her whom he loved from the Tassantasses.

Now she saw that everything he said was true and perfect. The Tassantasses were treacherous. They were enemies.

She said to herself: I must be brave.

* * * * * *

It was passing dark. There was no smoke-hole.

* * * * * *

What if only this endungeonment could unforestall her freedom? That peculiarly divided life she'd led, 'twixt her People & the Tasantasses, was resolved fore'er. Sweet John was vanisht. In spite of all her services, the Tassantasses regarded her as a mere victual for their bloody pleasures. She could never number herself amongst them. She was a *Salvage,* undeniably, without recourse. And whose Salvage was she? Her father could not save her, nor her husband Koroum. Dead alone, like unto a drop of rain draining down within black earth, she collected darkness, washing herself away. OKEUS was full revenged on her for all her faults. She lay whimpering in Evil's hands. Her course must change. She must change. What would she be changed unto? Her doubleness was decaying into singleness. Mysteriously fortunate, she'd gained the chance while living to taste of death.

* * * * * *

There was a song which Sweet John had oft sung unto her when she visited him at James-towne. Until now she had never understood it. The words sang themselves thus:

> I am as I am and so I will be
> But how that I am none knoweth truly.
> Be it evil, be it well, be I bound, be I free,
> I am as I am and so will I be.

* * * * * *

As for *Brutus,* he too must be call'd happy. For, Reader (if I may let you in on the droll secret), this seeming imprisonment of his was but a game which oft got played 'twixt himself & omniscent Argall. Sweet John gamed at *Lurch.* Pokahuntiss gamed at her Yndian reed-game. For Brutus, the most exquisite game was an unsaid **.1.** in which he teas'd his Captaine unto whimsickall punishments which allowed him to play the spy. Now enacted down into darkness, he got enriched by her whimpering. In the faint light he saw her squatting & he heard her piss into the bilge. Suffering intensely as he did from the conceit that his fellow beings distorted themselves in consequence of his observation of them, he commenced here to obtain the joy of imagining that he approach'd *Truth.* She'd never have deigned to piss if she'd imagined an Englishman could see her at it. And that quiet, dreary moaning of hers, that brokenly repeated *Ahkeÿ vwwaap,* would her Princesse-pride have permitted her to disclose any of that before the Publicke?

Reader, you may perhaps remember the desperate moonings of *Lieutenant George Pearcie,* when he wherried the Queen of Paspahegh downriver to be put to death. Put to death, yes! Translated unto sableness! Slave to perfection, hence to death, Maister Percy might well have thought her less fair, had he not just previously caused her Towne & children to be murthered. But 'twas not just that. Could he only *know her soul,* then the signification of what he'd just done might somehow be compass'd. In the case of Lieutenant Turnell, no crime had been committed; this hour's sands were not yet accurst. For what had they done thus far, but detained a wench with the contrivance of her own peers? Still the *Treasurer* lay off Pattawomeck; 'twould be easier than dumb show to release her back unto the Werowance, with a few toys & candied words. *Kekaten Pokahontas patiaquagh niugh tanks manotyens neer mowchik rawrenock audowgh.* Bid

Pokahantas bring hither two little Baskets, and I will give her white Beads to make a Chaine. Therefore to our Brutus the question ran more discomfortably *generally* than for Maister Percy. This Pocahontas could have been anybody. She was human; hence from him she occulted herself. When would her inmost curtain rise up? What soul would stride forward then upon her stage? To learn this, poor Brutus, qualitied by infinite doubts about e'erything, would have watcht her thus in secret for eternity if he could —

* * * * * *

And I, William the Blind, do likewise love to grabble in the hold of *Historie,* seeking in bygone darkness certain pale glimmers which are o'er insubstantial to be spied in today's sunlight.

* * * * * *

Softly passed like rats the magical hours of her oppressment. Her blood did not dry up in her heart; she lay betrayed by the healthy fullness of her life. Her heart could strike no spark. No vaporous thoughts issued from her murthered mind. She'd fallen already so far down from what she'd lost that she never remembered it. Her countenance, now incapable of extremes, set like hard-baked clay, baked itself into dullness, until emptiness had eaten through to the outsides of her eyes. Next day, Captaine Argall comported himself yet more agreeably to Pocahontas than he e'er had been before, so that she wondered what new mischief he intended. But in his judgment there remained no further stroke to strike: he'd secured the booty full & fair. Therefore his cordiality sparkled noxiously, & he offered her the best from his larder, not excepting the brandy & other such spirits, which he thought best to withhold for the time. He'd considered debauching her, so that with her shopworn maidenhead the rest of her person might also be his: — marriage with a veritable Princesse would doubtless entail his advantage. But that this Argall was no mere *Self-server* is prov'd by the fact that he had already aborted this unhatched plan. For .1. thing, Sweet John had won no joy from the wench — indeed, he lay suspected of treason, for allying himself so intimately with Powhatan's daughter. More-o'er, certain facts about the human animal must be commended to its trainers. Reader, would you have some other soul leap thro' hoops of fire at your whistle? Then you'd best establish your authority at a slight remove, so that the victim fills in the terrifying blankness of your face with her own reflection. She may be able to withstand you, but how can she o'erthrow herself?

(If she does, then she likewise loses.) For this reason Argall would not take Pocahontas: in good time he'd give her unto another (but not to that merest Fensman, John Smith!); for bestowing a soul away can be a deeper & more hurtful mode of taking.

*   *   *   *   *

So he translated her up into the Day-cabin. With the scrupulous aid of that satellite call'd Brutus, he spied upon & discovered the poor creature's every change, with such care that his Sailors marvelled clamorously, understanding but little of such causes as would require him to count her footsteps in the Cabin by the hour, to weigh & inspect her chamber-pot with his own hands, believing as he did to follow the secrets of her moods by the quality of her excrement, which presented unto him the ocean-smell of a narrow rushing creek-marsh. He commaunded the Cook to write down what she ate, & in what quantity (then, calling him a noble fellow, distributed those unread notations to a Sailor at the beak-head, so the man could wipe his arse); he listened most courteously to her supplications that she be permitted to return to Powhatan, & kept like tally of those. (Dear girl, said he, what you propose is misfortunately discountenanced by your own virtue, whose love-light we English must all live by!) When the Sentry heard her pacing in the night, he had instructions silently to wake Captaine Argall, who then, in his quarters adjoining hers, listened with his ear against the wall until she moaned & lay down again (altho' perhaps this last precaution serv'd only to verify that she remained sure-enkennel'd). Excellent Argull! With the bread of his authority he'd wipe up all her sauce!

I've read in some pleasant Chronicle (altho' doubtless 'tis the merest fable) that he dress'd her as an English Lady, not only for to alienate her all the more from her Salvage self, but likewise to obtain extremer knowledge of her; for each Sunday when they required the girl to change her linen, dear *Brutus* carried the bundle into his State-room. Rapidly rifling her soiled petticoats, Argoll snatched the chemise she'd worn nearest unto her heart & dropt it in a pan of vinegar already commingled with certain questionable astringents & spices, most likely of Tartar manufacture (but for the recipe I must refer you to other printed Relations). As the scum of grease did surface, Argall crumbled up 'twixt his marble palms a dried leaf of the variety *Sassafrass* & drizzled the powder down upon the meditational solution, at the bottom of which lay Pocahontas's chemise like unto some burst Jelly-fish. Now he brought the heat of fire most gently to bear, in order that the Salamanders which inhabit flames would enforce the synthesis or *Chemickall embrace*. Unlocking his stony jaws, he leaned o'er the bubbling liquid to demand: *Whom does she love?* At his will the potion declined into calmness, respiring back its steamy vapors so that he could perceive himself reflected with great credit. Presently his image pretended to blush with rage or some other intemperance as the brew became rosy — and then (just as Halton Towne in Linolnshire doth own the letter H for a cattle brand) the tallow curdled suddenly into the letter S. — So 'tis Sweet John again! he laughed, not in the least discomfited. My misbegotten little lass, I don't much envy your fortunes . . .

That this relation is apocryphal can be most easily prov'd: .1.^{stly}, the aforesaid Argoll kept his prisoner not e'en a single week, let alone several spans of linen-chaunging Sundays. Secondly, only a soul as voyeuristically corrupt as Lieutenant Turnell's could have operated thus. And .3.^{rdly}, whiche'er Englishman had forged such a witchery would surely have been condemned to burning.

Argall, Argoll, Argull! Nay, I'll have none of it. Arkill's no multidimensional fellow; he's but a painted Sea-Captain on the backdrop of our faded stage. Why on earth would he concern himself with a squaw's moods? Why comment; why observe? He's the merest trade-grabbler, & she but consigned *Merchaundise*. O, Reader, it contents us to pretend that Captain Fortune's as deep as the sea, for then our child-siz'd triumphs & treasonous reverses must mean something. But Captain Fortune's not e'en a droplet's-breadth in his curcumference; nay, rises not so high as bonesmoke, nor sets so deep as Pokahuntiss in the hold. He's like unto the *Bullhead-fish,* which best flourishes in shallow brooks. He's only history; he's merely Captain Chance.

* * * * * *

And always the fear of what would happen in the end was with her.

* * * * * *

Again she requested his permission to bathe in the river (which she claimed to be her daily custom — but 'twas surely .1. of her Salvage freaks). Altho' he would have wished to oblige her, still he feared that his men must either outrage her modesty, or else (did they not o'erwatch her nudity) carelessly permit her escape. He had to deny her this. Anyhow, he somewhat relished her woodsmoked female smell . . .

* * * * * *

In his fine soft singing-voice, Argall summoned brother Iapazeus to get quit of his wages: that copper kettle already paid, & other such trash. Then he bade that pawn send off any rapid Salvage to Powhatan, to inform him that his daughter had been taken spoil by the English.

The rapid Salvage arrived in a *Canoa.* Argoll sent Cassius to invoke him up the Waist-ladder. The rapid Salvage came & scowled. He was nearly naked, wearing but some leaves & grass cinched round his loins. The Sailors jeered at his bestiality. Argull stamp'd his foot; they fell utterly silent.

And tell him that if he will send home our Countreymen whom he doth detain in slavery, Argall continued, *and with such arms & tools as the Yndians hath stolen* (here he glared at the Salvage), and also a great quantity of corn, then he shall have his daughter restored. Otherwise not.

You steal Great Powhatan's daughter, yet name us thieves, the Salvage said.

And you choose to be my hireling, sirrah. Would you presume to correct me?

The Salvage was silent.

Go then, jackanapes. Eighty miles to Werowocomoco, yes?

He bides now at Orapaks.

O yes, I forgot. You Naturalls are more changeable than serpents. And where's that?

The Salvage stayed silent.

I'll wait you here, said Argall. (He knew very well where Orapax lay.)

He humm'd, then uttered a phrase which he had learned of Captaine John Smith: *Utteke, e peya weyack wighwhip,* which signifieth, *Get you gone, and come againe quickly.*

(See Pocahontas sitting belowdecks on a mass of poles. She prefers darkness to the Day-cabin, she says, so goodly Argoll must humor her. 'Tis dark, passing dark, but she never moves.)

Two days, and Argall, well-embayed there in a salubrious spot, was figuring his Sailors' wages. Removing from his travelling-casket's copper-lipped maw the stag-engraved counters which, meant to represent coins, were actually as fat as slices of a great metal sausage, he'd begun to lay them out beside the opened ledger when Lieutenant Turnell knapped upon his tombstone-shapen door.

Bring him to the Gunner's room, my Brutus.

Aye, Captaine. What if the prisoner craves to return there?

She won't.

He rose, locked away counters & ledger, then strode to the meeting-place (memorial now to sweet domination o'er these Yndians) where the Salvage glowered at him as before & said: Great Powhatan is grieved.

Argall smiled merrily and sang:

> First rise after low
> Foretells a stronger blow.

The Salvage continued: Great Powhatan desires you use his daughter well, & bring your ship into his harbor—

Does he? chuckled Argall.

. . . And there he will give you your demands, which being performed you should deliver him his daughter, & you and he shall be friends.

Good,   Argall replied.   Here's your wages.   I send no reply.   That D EVIL can stew, while I squire his filly back to my Colonie . . .

✻ ✻ ✻ ✻ ✻ ✻

On that warmish pale blue day when the messenger came, Wahunsenacawh's heart began quivering like a fresh oyster shucked from the shell. His jaws slowly grinned a brownish-black grin, and perhaps nobody knew that he was heartbroken. His Cronoccoes remained likewise silent. Later he must smoke a pipe with them and decide what to do. Opechancanough was here to comfort him. He would feed the messenger and guest him well. Wahunsenacawh arose, and departed Orapaks. Behind him, his Cronoccoes were saying: Leave Powhatan to himself. He must clear his mind now. — A sudden echoing splash, and black entities burst up from the black water with cries of fright, vanishing into the treetops. He was far away now. He prayed for his dear daughter Amonute. He offered tobacco for her safety. He remembered how gently she used to cut his hair.

✻ ✻ ✻ ✻ ✻ ✻

Her first winter had proven very cold. Her little hands and feet were always blue. By custom he should have sent her back to Rapahannock with her mother almost at once, but she was an autumn's child, and so he kept them both through the winter. Uttamatomakkin reminded him of his duty, but, being married to Powhatan's daughter Mayachanna, he too proved more tender than religion approved. So Amonute stayed at Werowocomoco until the spring.

Her mother rubbed her body with puccoon-root mixed with walnut oil. With his own hands he'd enwrapped her in a deerskin adorned with roanoke beads, treasure from his best storehouse, for as soon as she was born he'd loved her. She came to him with her eyes open and gazed at him without fear, messenger from another WORLD. He took unto himself the sight of that child, receiving and possessing her completeness just as throughout his long and eerie life his glance had drunk up women just now enjoyed or foemen so fresh-killed that they twitched like fishes in the net. Each time, unmoved but seeking, he'd meant to harvest from the dark eyes at that moment of dying or orgasm some explication. He'd but rarely and provisionally received it. Now he possessed it, because the baby *knew* him. She was his, and she loved him. A flush surged through his ancient yellow face. That was why he'd told her mother (full needlessly) to keep her warm — but not too warm, he quickly said. Cold was one of the enemies. He wanted her to be strong. She became strong.

Why her, and not another of his multitudinous children? He never knew through what means she'd instantly ambuscadoed his heart.

Why her? He knew that the hearts of the Tassantasses would never be moved.

Dusk was draining like tarry water from between the ferns of swamps. Someday he'd set a snickle for the Tassantasses if he could; but for now he was the prey who'd been caught in the love he'd always feared.

* * * * * *

So they weighed anchor and sailed down the river *Patamomeck*, their bulk & wake erasing the maps which had been made by scum-trails in grey river-water. *Flooh oh!* cried the Lookout. All omens were good (as I may tell you without any heresy). 'Twas the **.100.**th anniversary of Machiavelli's political Bible. E'erworthy Argall did sing:

> Mackerel skies and mares' tails
> Make tall ships carry short sails.

He reigned his own figurehead with both hands on the gunnels, smelling the brown-green water and the delicious trees. Wind snapp'd at his fingers. So what if the Salvages were enraged against him? Their revenge could always be bought off by beads. — Heave ahead! he cried. Men into the tops! Down foresail! Down mainsail! — And away they did speed. No Salvages came treacherously after.

Where stood the Arctick Pole today 'tween horizon and zenith? He raised his astrolabe, blandly humming to himself . . .

He spied a rich grove of cedar-trees. How fine 'twould be to translate 'em all into lumber & sell 'em at Gravesend! He knew some Merchaunts who'd pay dear for such stuff. Noble families preferr'd cedar for their chests, bedsteads & virginals.

Low dunes paved with half-crushed shells announced the sea. Trees squeaked in the wind. Came the wave-horizon. — Bring her round! ran his commaund.

Yea, Captaine.

Now steady at the helm.

Aye, steady, Captaine Argoll!

Ease the shrouds.

'Tis done, Captaine, 'tis done! — and the Sailors ran to the lanyards, permitting the great ropes to slip a trifle thro' the blocks, or *Dead men's eyes* as they be call'd.

They tacked south to Hampton-Towne (all in good order); west up *King James his River* to Jamestowne Fort itself with its bare moat and then the blond palisade beyond which the Soldiers sat playing cards beside a demi-culverin. Down anchor. The Sentry opened the gate without even calling *Who goes there?* for so well did he know Argoll's ship. — I pray you come with me now, Miss, quoth Argull, and he led the aforesaid Pokahuntas into Jamestowne, whose houses' wattles showed through their dirt walls like bones.

She turn'd on him a face of purest rage.

Humming like unto a drowsy bumblebee, he regarded the young squaw. What was she to him, but a sackless straggler, marr'd by her very birth? He could compass her entire 'twixt *.2.* fingers! But now she undertook to get saucy with him, which irked his heart. Just as the Hunting-Hound doth snarl and strain his head when the Forester comes to let him off leash, so Argoll's murtherousness, which in its way was as inhumanly lively & luminous as fire, commenc'd to twist behind his eyes.

You'll bow the knee and kiss my salty hand, he murmured.

* * * * * *

Two rows of houses now hath Jamestowne — some *.2.* storeys in height, and e'en a garret storey higher. The darling *Pokahuntas*   must therefore come to acquaint herself with such progress. And so she was conveyed back inside that triangularly palisadoed Fort each of whose vertices English cunning had reinforced with a crescent-shaped Tower studded with demiculverins. *I've caught her!* shouted e'erworthy Argoll, & in a twink the Church-bell clanged most gloatingly, while the trumpets did blare their *Trarintra-rarara.* The patched tents which had danced in the wind like her own People's houses, those were gone forever. There squatted a horde of steep-roofed little huts on the stinking, muddy ground. Everything was more crowded and decayed than when she had played there, yet more immovable.

A horde of Tassantasses helmed their heads, to make a show, as she supposed. Then they march'd out the Crooked-gate where Sweet John used to wait for her. Some wore red robes, whose brilliancy reminded her of sliced fish-flesh. Were they brothers, to dress the same? She understood them not.

The Governor, Sir Thomas Dale, was himself on hand to greet her, to which honor she did reply with meek declining gestures.

He becked her to a seat within his house. She whispered thanks. This house was all of wood. Through the window she could spy his Attorneys, Deputies, Officers, Ministers, Factors & Servaunts all staring at her. She craved to die.

'Tis a sorry hap, kind Princesse, that we must meet in these circumstances appointed. Yet great Powhatan your father will not give us leave to live else. We guest you solely to deflect his malignancy, which our own sovereign, King *Iames,* forbids us to tolerate. For what insults us, doth speckle with tarnish his own luster which sent us here, & that he will not suffer.

She wearily replied: I know not—

Nor need these matters concern your sex, Princesse. For now you'll remain our guest. Fear not any hurt from these Slaughtermen in the towers. And if you'll swear on your honor not to escape, we need not fetter you like unto some felon . . .

To which agreeing, she laid her hand upon her heart, then lifted up her hand to the SUNNE.

✳   ✳   ✳   ✳   ✳   ✳

Sir Thomas Dale wore threads of gold in his clothes, horizontal stitches of them like celestial porcupine quills. He was determined to lead her to GOD whether she would or no. In her pagan state he could scarcely repose any trust in her. The promise of self-imprisonment he'd just now gotten out of her, 'twas merely to try her temper. Sentries followed her everywhere.

Take her to the Block-house, he said. Princesse, pardon the necessity. 'Twill be but for the merest twink—

She denied to speak.

Come, Pocahontas, what do you fear? he said impatiently.

I fear naught, altho' you burn me as you did Wowinchopunck's wife—

Dear Princesse, we burn'd her not. Moreover, 'twasn't under my Government that the deed was done.

Then she lives?

Fear not for yourself, Miss. I promise we'll preserve you alive, so long as you demean yourself obediently to my commaunds.

They kept many Convicts & prisoners at James-Towne in those days. With the Virginian woman, Pocahontas, they held .2. Spanish spies, .1. of them, Señor Molina, a Spaniard by birth, & the other a runagate* Englishman, who must be kept alive only until 'twas convenient to wherry him homewards to the King's Justice. By August there'd be .15. Frenchmen also, thanks to a little exploit of Argoll's which we'll relate in its season.

But the inmates of fish-ponds cannot expect to swim round & round forever. 'Twould never do if our Slaughtermen enjoy'd no employment. Therefore, on the morrow of Pokahuntiss's arrival (& 'twas thought by Argull's men that this was done of purpose to afright that squaw), .1. idler, who'd thought by running away to the Yndians to escape all Christian discipline, got broken on the wheel, & so perished screaming. The next day a Cabin-boy for the same offense was by reason of his youth merely hang'd. *Trarintra-rarara.*

* * * * * *

Powhatan now returned .7. men and .7. broken muskets, pretending that he possessed no more English weapons. His Salvage mouthpiece swore that .500. bushels of corn awaited the Colonie, as soon as great Poughwaton but had his daughter back again.

Sir Thomas summoned a certain familiar of his, & asked: O what shall I reply to him, e'erworthy Captaine Argall?

Smiling, Argull quoth: Pray tell him that his daughter shall remain well used, but that we cannot believe the rest of the arms have been lost. Pray tell him that until he sends 'em back again, we'll keep the wench . . .

After that, Poughwaton sent no word.

* * * * * *

They had cows now at James Towne. For a dainty, Sir Thomas did serve up her a cup of milk, which she in her astonishment call'd *Hickory,* hav-

---

*Renegade

ing never before seen any white liquid which was uncomprised of nut-squeezings.   But she dreamed of leaf-wrapped venison barbequed in embers.

They hid themselves in their stinking houses whenever darkness came. — Well, well; she'd heard from her father that slaughtered game must be covered up from the MOON to avoid putrefaction.

They mix'd gentleness & frightfulness. They call'd on her to choose. But they'd already chosen for her, by raping her away. She hated them all.

When her uncle Opechancanough had captured Captaine Smith (as she now remembered), that shape-shifting *Father* of hers had affrighted her uncle by means of a magic needle in a circle. But she had no magic with which to affright the Tassantasses.

* * * * * *

Of a sudden her comprehension glimmered down into the bloodstained mystery of Sweet John's mind.   Dwelling captive at Werowocomoco, he'd made her all manner of promises solely so he could wriggle free. The Tassantasses felt no shame to behave thus, no matter what miseries they caused those to whom they pretended to be friends. She considered this course for herself. It might not be so arduous to feign loyalty and affection, until Fortune might grant her liberty. After all, the Tassantasses had dealt falsely with her. They upheld none of her rights, saving life and sustenance alone. But she was stricter with herself than that.   Among the People 'twas said that he who breaks his word once is forever dishonored — for, possessing not the practice of writing among them, they possessed of all sureties solely that of speech.

* * * * * *

As for dearly beloved *Captaine Argoll,* he, being quit of his prisoner, went forward with the building of the jury-masted frigate which he had left at Poynt Comfort, and finished her, caulkings & all. Hampton Towne did thrive most pridefully. New Colonists could scarce believe it hadn't always been there, little Gravesend as it was, with all England's distinctions, illusions & political troubles shrunk down behind sun-bleached rotten palings. Somebody had begun to rear up peach-trees. Argall thought 'twould soon be profitable for him to do business there. For a lark his Sailors grazed amidst the ruins of the former Yndian town near that spot, call'd *Kecoughtan* (a nest of diabolickall salvagery as I do believe). The ancient citizens of Hampton did swear that but **.5.** years since, when the very **.1.**st

Adventurers did disembark themselves here under Capaine Newport, Salvages used to swim out to the boats, bearing bows & arrows in their mouths!
O'er there they'd kept their weirs, & harvested their scallop-banks. The
houses had all been burn'd long since, & Virginia creepers o'ergrew the
charred places; but the Sailors spaded open a mound in hopes of treasure, &
discovered a throng of worm-eaten skeletons. How pleasant it was, to stand
there a-pitching skulls into the water!

Ho! Cassius!

At your service, dear Captaine Argall.

See how we've blotted the page white? Nary a blotch of darkness anywhere. And we'll do the same in all the other Townes. Then you know
what will befall?

What, Captaine?

Why, we'll be Noblemen. We'll be Lords. And then—

Yes, Captaine?

Then we'll be dead & perish'd. Hail Caesar!

* * * * * *

See Argoll discovering the Bay call'd *Chesapeack*. He retraces & deepens
Sweet John's map-tracks. He fishes; he chaffers with Salvages on ye Eastern
Shore. All do him honor. 'Twould be *Politick* to cut Powhatan off from
their shell-beads, or *Roanoake* as they call it. Then these Eastern Yndians
can be our friends — at least until England sees fit to send a stronger power
of men. He flitters up the still chocolate creeks of evening, which lie walled
by evening green. He discovers possibilities for making salt—

* * * * * *

Another miscreant was condemned to be staked. He was some vagabond
left o'er from the **.3.**rd Supply of 1609. The Sentry had caught him trying to
steal away, to the Chickahominies 'twas said. The Church-bell toll'd. For
fear he had the shits. Reverend Buck strove to comfort him. The wretch
durst not complain o'ermuch, for fear that Sir Thomas might increase the
punishment. When his doom came, the Virginian woman laugh'd & offered to assist in torturing him, at which everyone did revile her barbarity.

* * * * * *

They sent her **.50.** miles by water to Reverend Whittaker's, near Henrico —
a well-palisadoed establishment safe from accident, as was generally believed. Upon Argoll's advice (for this Mariner was famed for his subtlety

in such matters), Sir Thomas did commaund that the voyage be made by night, so that she'd not see the crusted black sores which memorialized the various Paspahegh Townes, the burned voids comprising the .2. former Warraskoyack Townes, the ashes of Appamatuck-Towne — for very likely (being a Princesse) this Pocahontas had enjoyed acquaintances among the royal families of those vicinities. Altho' Virginia creeper had fortunately embraced them all (since that weed loveth to feed upon the sites of fires), still 'twas needless to augment her bitterness. The only point at issue was *Security* (by which I don't signify the game which President Radclyffe used to play — & lost). Having discussed it o'er with his chief Captaines & Lieutenants, Sir Thomas was of the opinion that the Salvages all along the James were too weakened now to knap her off. Where could they strike from? And in this, as in most of his projections, the Governor prov'd correct. His investment in the Virginian woman would not be fritter'd away.

'Twas carefully timed, in the English manner. Darkness would cloak their doings with modesty shortly before they were to reach the .1.ˢᵗ scorched place. The escort lay under special instructions to comport themselves as agreeably as they could toward the Princesse, to distract her from what might otherwise be unpleasant reflections. Summonsing them all to a secret Counsell within the Church, Sir Thomas made it plain (exactly as he had unto her) that Pocahontas was not to suffer the fate of the Queen of Paspahegh, nor of the Queen of Appamatuck. Their own interest depended (he continued, & e'ery man now found himself subjected to the dark and watchful eyes in Sir Thomas's face) on preserving her in life & (to the extent that this prov'd possible) cheerfulness. Anybody who harm'd her would be burnt alive the instant he learned about it. They should remember that unlike these her kindred filthy rebels, Pocahontas had befriended the Colonie. They were therefore to act the part of pleasant English Gentlemen.

Amonute could hardly convince herself that she rode not through some alien dream. When she was a child in her mother's house the girls had sometimes frightened each other by forming uncanny shadow-shapes in the fire-light. Her mother warned them to take care, lest they make OKEUS angry with their mockery. Now the same sad strangeness pressed on her. The Moone stood already above the horizon, & today, that orb having declined northwards unto the House of Cancer, 'twas easily possible to calculate the hour of the day. Ensign Swift rode in the pinnace, on purpose for to guard her. (Thank G O D, nobody comprehended the *twinkling fear* which burthened his chest. 'Twould now be Powhatan's uttermost pleasure to murther 'em all . . .) Thinking to amuse his prisoner as he'd been instructed, good *Casca* did position his equinoctial card to cast a Mooneshadow 'pon his compass-dial, whereby he prov'd 'twas just past .**VII.** of the clock. For in this Arithmetick he'd been very well taught by Captaine Argoll (who whipped lads who made mistakes).   At this, the aforementioned Pocahontas much marvel'd, asking in her Salvage tongue (which after eating & frigging amidst 'em at Pattawomeck he well understood) why the hour should matter to any soul.

Princesse, in our own Countrey, she being so vast, the Citizens so numerous, & our business so serious, we must fix a time & place wherewith to meet.

She pityingly said: You Tassantasses do e'er plot out your future, as tho' you fear your own weakness 'gainst any sudden chance!

Whereat Ensign Swift did smiling say: Well, well, Pocahontas, Captaine Argoll plotted, & you did not, so who won *this* dice-throw?

. . . At which she fell silent.

*   *   *   *   *   *

And so in their proper course they arrived at Reverend Whittaker's. His Parsonage was well impaled, hence safe from base reprisals & rescues. Straight across the river from Henrico (which thanks to Sir Thomas lay now near pefectly enclos'd 'gainst Salvage thieves & rebels), 'twas hard by .**100.** new acres which the Reverend call'd *Rock Hall.*

They presented & preferr'd her unto him. 'Twas very late at night.

He was a careful man whose hair had been bleached by age, like unto wild oat seeds which the Salvages dry in the Sunne. Unsealing the letter which Sir Thomas had penn'd him (commending this woman unto his security), he gazed her o'er. Her escort had already departed. They'd sleep at the Watch-Houses.

Welcome, dear child, said he, and may your guesting here bring you profit. We're all but tools, which O U R   M A K E R doth take up in His hands, or not, as He lists. Do you ken your M A K E R ?

Powhatan made me.

Dear Princesse, I misdoubt me not your birth. And truly you may become a tool for good, deserving of a better Kingdome than you can now understand.

She turned away from him then. To a sharp-eyed Salvage Translator whom she saw ever in the Reverend's company (for as yet he could scarcely utter Salvage speech), she cried disdainfully: *Mowchick wayawgh tawgh no-eragh kaquere mecher*, which signifieth: *I am very hungry. What shall I eat?*

✳ ✳ ✳ ✳ ✳

This Reverend Whittaker, altho' of repute in his own Countie, had fared to Virginia — some say out of disappointment in the small success of his own affairs, & yet 'tis mealy-minded to assail the acts & motives of do-gooders such as our most excellent Minister. He'd heard that many things had fall'n into negligence in Virginia, especially the state of men's souls. All these he hoped to reform. But what gave him the greatest grief of all was the utter-most miserable & beastly *Darknesse of the Soul* in which dwelt e'ery last Salvage. With many groanings & tears, he spoke with Sir Thomas Dale, who replied: Take heart, Reverend; for so long as my Government endures, the reforms you desire shall be enacted, by persuasion & compulsion. More-over, as for the Salvages, if you but bide a twink, I'm sure we'll lead 'em also to the true path.

But when?

Why, dear Sir, we'll proceed as in Ireland: Tolerate any heathenishness, until all their greatness be crush'd. Then set 'em aright. So soon as we've knocked Powhatan off his feet, we'll raise a Church in e'ery shire. And me-thinks that won't be long a-coming . . .

My Lord, 'tis a nobly practical plan. Meantimes, how may I touch the Salvages' spirits?

You'll soon find satisfaction, I trow. Keep your commission dry.

And now his commission had come into its season.

✳ ✳ ✳ ✳ ✳

This chamber was tainted by OKEES and GHOSTS. She feared she'd never again see her husband's bark-roofed house.

What you see here, said this Reverend, hath been translated by English labor unto a sanctuary. And I hope that it refreshes you, child.

I was here before, said she. This ground once belonged to my brother Parahunt, before you took it.

Amonute, 'tis better that I not English your words for him, for I've come to depend on these Tassantasses, said the sharp-eyed boy. I dare not cross their will.

Do as you please, she wearily replied.

* * * * * *

He honored her at supper-time with a silver cup of aqua vitae, which she confessed did relish as well as anything she'd ever tasted. Moreover, some women came to her with tarts & little cakes which they had baked for her. Before she knew it, she felt easier in her mind. Again he told her not to fear. He asked her if there was anything she wished to say. But she knew that there was no reasoning with him.

* * * * * *

And now, dear Pocahontas—
    'Tis not my name.
    O?
    'Tis but a name my father calls me.
    But Captaine Smith doth say—
    What of him?
    Nay then, said he, waving his arms at her with the languid semi-liquid flowings of a sea-turtle's flippers as it swims, what shall I call thee, child?
    Amonute. 'Tis what I'm call'd in company.
    Ah. And how many names do you have?
    She fell silent.
    Feeling himself to be somewhat brave as he investigated her uncanny Salvage secrets, he inquired yet more insistently: And have you a name which you've sworn not to uncover?
    She flushed.
    Such names are passing perilous, my dear Amonute.
    Why?
    Know you whom SATAN is?
    Captaine Smith did tell me—
    In a low voice Reverend Whittaker asked: And 'tis true, child, that your DEVIL sucks young boys' blood from their left side?
    I know not—
    What do you call Him?
    She was silent.
    Whom do you worship?
    OKEUS.
    Ah! That's the .1. And why do you worship Him?
    So that He'll do us no hurt.

Poor child! He's the DEVIL for a fact! And does He suck the young boys' blood?

I know not. Please, I would rest myself—

From their left breast, as I did hear.

* * * * * *

He establisht her in a bed of her own, the room empty, lonely & fireless. Altho' the bedstead was a pleasurable novelty to lie upon (being much higher above the floor than in her People's houses, excepting her father's), she misliked the coverlets, for they near about stifled her with their weight. Moreover, they were flea-ridden.

Without the smell of woodsmoke, she could not escape the odors of these unwashed Tassantasses. Their heavy blankets pressed her against those cold, sickeningly smooth sheets. 'Twas like laying herself down in marshooze.

In the end she settled in. It scarcely mattered so much where she lived.

* * * * * *

I would wash myself.

But if you do, how might we be sure of you?

I gave my word not to escape.

Yea, child, but . . .

They brought her an ewer of water with which to cleanse herself, but 'twas foul. Moreover, she scrupled to ask them every day to labor thus. So she began to stink as they did. Dull-eyed, dirty-haired, she no longer cared how she looked or smelled.

* * * * * *

Sometimes she was permitted to promenade upon Henrico's **.III.** streets, but only in vigilant company, for fear she might rob the Plantation of her person. On the Sabbath they took her across the river to Church. On those occasions Reverend Whittaker spoke to the other Tassantasses, who listened in silence. They'd whipt off their caps when they came in; she knew not why. Sometimes they bowed their heads, as if they were humilated & sad. Reverend Whittaker uprais'd a CHRIST cross. Then at intervals they sang. She could not make out why they all must be present for those conjurations. Among her People it took **.6.** abreast singing to find the magic *Wesake root,* which conquers poison. At Uttamussack (so she knew from

Uttamatomakkin), .12. priests were required to speak with OKEUS. But at Henrico, it seemed, all the Tassantasses without exception must sit there. Reverend Whittaker explain'd unto her 'twas to beseech CHRIST for prosperity. It appeared that they desired to take more & more land, & cut it off from her father's power by means of palisadoes. Doubtless CHRIST would help them to burn away her People's claims. O yes, e'er the Tassantasses did swarm thicker around her People, encircling their Townes and burning them, just as the People hunted herds of deer, gathering them within hopeless walls of flame from which they shot them for their prey.

* * * * * *

Every day a smaller conclave did pray at Reverend Whittaker's, in much the same spirit as when the People cast coppers and other precious things into the river whenever they must pass near OKEUS' Temple at Uttamussack. Yet they threw nothing into the fire when taking up their food. She could not comprehend them.

Before you eat, child, render thanks to th'ALMIGHTIE.

I will not.

Then you will not eat.

* * * * * *

Good Reverend Whitaker spent himself abundantly in the service of his end, for which we his inheritors owe him much & should be content. He achieved it, of course. The ascendancy could not but have been his. His purpose being sharp and definite like a dagger, he had but to stab it into Pocahontas to pierce her as he desired. She enjoy'd no purpose in her dealings with him, save to escape him, which she could not do, so that her only avoidance was passivity, willful blindness; thus like Argall he sliced her open with her eyes closed. He had .5. potential means of exercising authority over her. I. The .1.ˢᵗ was *punishment*. This Argall had already used, in imprisoning her on the *Treasurer*. She was imprisoned here. Should Reverend Whittaker choose, he could deepen her misery to any degree, as well she knew. II. The next weapon he had was *reward*. It lay almost within his power to restore her freedom unto her, or indeed to raise her to various other heights. (If with all this raising and lowering, Pocahontas begins to seem like a noosed gallows-bird, 'tis hardly Reverend Whitaker's fault: he was "only following orders.") It fell now incumbent on him, by establishing fair rules for her conduct, that reward and punishment should be visited upon her not out of arbitrariness, but in accordance with Law — a grandly misty Law, preferably, which she would almost, but never entirely, be able to comprehend; that way he could fasten about her his .3.ʳᵈ string, which was **III.** *superior knowledge.* Could she not interpret the Law for herself, but required his wisdom, in order for her to receive reward and escape punishment, then she must invoke him. Once triply pinioned in this fashion, she could easily be tied with the .4.ᵗʰ hawser of **IV.** *identity,* in which he gradually become a greater exemplification of herself (particularly once she might be Christianized). Then at last the .5.ᵗʰ rope of his leadership, which was **V.** *legitimacy,* could adorn her throat like unto a pretty English ribbon . . .

He began by directing his Servaunt-boy to confiscate the necklace of cougar teeth which she wore so proudly. When he called upon her a quarter-hour later, her eyes were wild and wrathful, as he saw, much to his liking (the boy was soaking a black eye). — Princess, how I can calm you, I know not (said Reverend Whittaker). It is not I who commanded that your heathen idol by stripped from you, but rather Sir Thomas Dale, who is Governor of all Virginia —

Let me see him!

Who is Governor of this place, as I said, and also the Ministers, who cannot forbear that you be instructed. As to whether I have played the villain's part, I leave to your censures. Come, Miss Princesse, dry your tears. Would you like to see the sun? You shall come for a promenade with me . . .

She came, and they saw the Servant-lad, sullen, soaking his black eye, & Whitaker laughed & much against her will she laughed—

*   *   *   *   *   *

He lodged her with various of his parishioners in turn. At publicke expense (altho' she did not seem passing grateful), the Ladies dressed her as an Englishwoman. They brought her daily to visit with him; else he forsook not to come to her. He thought that if he but find the *Mithridate* (or *Antidote*) to her Salvage nature, 'twould prove passing convenient to the Colonie. Soon 'twas reported to him that she bowed her head full gracefully at table, without reference to her filthy OKEUS. Every Sunday morn, at .6. of the clock, he compelled her to go to Church like all the rest; for not only must his teachings there be a comfort & benefit to her, but also, should she bide alone, they'd have been forced to leave her chain'd & manacled. The Church-bell toll'd *Argall, Argoll, Argull.*

* * * * * *

She said to him: Captaine Smith promised my father to make him hatch-ets, & fashion bells for me; yet he lied.

And why made he so foolish a promise?

To save his life.

Ah. Then 'twas no sin—

What must I promise you to get free? I mislike it here.

I'm so sorry, dearest Amonute.

I would go to my father.

(Closing her eyes, she discovered that she could see him, in his Palace in Orapax where he sat in perpetual torchlight.)

O, child, 'tis natural you pine for your relations, but, you see, but I've promised Sir Thomas to stand Sentinel for your security.

Some discomfort in his face did make her wonder if he contemned the policy which had snatched her here.

* * * * * *

Distempered nigh to sullenness did she lurk alone, no longer hoping either to be rescued (for her father must surely be angered at her imprudency, in falling so easily into the Tassantasses' hands, and her husband seemed in-ept), nor to shame her captors, who bustled smug beyond shame. Reverend Whitaker's tallest dread was that some malady of sadness might carry her off. O, he did compassionate her! He therefore strove never to be back-ward in his kindness. She must neither drag about, nor brood.

Every day he conversed with her as much as he had leisure, both to learn more words of her Salvage language (which he'd surely soon require for the conversion of her brethren), & to teach her the King's English, which in truth she did swallow down like medicine, bitterly but swiftly, for she knew this would improve her. Her knowledge, already hatched before, thanks to the efforts of Captaine Smith, now quickly bloomed. Already they needed that Interpreter betwixt 'em but rarely. That she took satisfaction in these sessions he felt sure. Better thus than to sit with her face in her hands, hours corrupting after hours.

One morn he visited her at Goodmistress Cowley's & said: Princesse, I'm come to hear your pleasure. Do you care to learn the ways of letters?

'Tis dangerous?

No, no, young maid. There's nothing diabolical in it. Think you that our alphabet's akin to the rites of your OKEUS?

I know not—

Sir Thomas doth rejoice to hear how beautifully already your learning sends forth stalks & buds. Now I'll shew you a trifle, and if you be affrighted, why then, we'll cease.

He nodded to his Salvage servitor, who did bring in a palimpsetical device of the Reverend's own conception — to wit, a square wooden frame which he'd filled with floury sand at Poynt Comfort. Rolling a dowel across the grains to smooth them out, he next took up a stylus and carv'd:

$$A$$

Now let us call yon letter by his name, he said goodhumoredly. Do you know him?

Sir, I do not.

Well, Princesse Amonute, do you observe how he opens his mouth to speak with us? When I do the like, and sound out a noise without the help of my tongue, what issues out is plain *Ah*. Do you agree?

Ah, she said cautiously.

Indeed, and his name is A. That bar across his jaws, that's but to prop them wide, so that he doth always utter faithfully the same vowel. For you must know this: The letter's yet more faithful than the tongue. His virtue is precisely the warrant of his e'erlasting sameness. A knows and keeps his place. He's e'er A. Comprehend?

She nodded.

By my life! the Reverend laughed. I trow you do. And can you remember his face?

Yes—

Then, Princesse, kindly tell me his name, for I myself forget it—

Laughing, she said: A.

Then I would next introduce you to his brother, a strapping double-eyed lad named B . . .

* * * * * *

In the intervening weeks she became almost as pale as a Tassantasse, for she rarely went out. The magic of A and B did fascinate her, although she never entirely mastered it, for in spite of what Reverend Whittaker had promised her, A was sometimes $\mathcal{A}$ or even a. Throughout the remainder of her life she preferr'd to have others read aloud to her, rather than herself sound out those semi-treacherous letters — in part because she so rarely got leisure to practice. And yet she credited this *Alphabet* with a beautiful and near miraculous cunning, which prov'd to her that logic dwelled in the Tassantasses' doings, as she'd never until now believed for certain, fancying that they did not so much possess Science like unto herb-craft or bow-craft as dominate POWERS Which did their bidding. May-hap this latter interpretation remained true; for every day the Reverend told her of OUR REDEEMER, Whom he said was her Friend (altho' she never met Him), and Whose mysteries underlay the Tassantasses' every ac-tion, which drove her to conclude that for her own People's sake, and espe-cially her father's, she must bend the knee to Him.

At first she revolted against Him. 'Twas unnatural for JEHOVAH to allow His best-loved Child to be given over to his enemies. Her father would never act in such a way . . .

But where was her father now? He would not — nay, *could* not help her.

And again she fell to weeping. She wept until the MOON was reborn.

❋   ❋   ❋   ❋   ❋   ❋

Perhaps her father had perished. Had he now removed still further past Orapaks? His timidity increased in accordance with his age. Perhaps he feared that Argall would likewise knap *him* away . . .

Perhaps they had all perished.

❋   ❋   ❋   ❋   ❋   ❋

Is Captaine Smith dead?

Doubtless, child, for he's never sail'd back, as you yourself do see. I've heard his flesh was monstrous burnt & bloody—

She thought: There must be a magic song to sing for these happenings. Uttamattomakkin would know it. But I know it not.

❋   ❋   ❋   ❋   ❋   ❋

She knew it not. But Reverend Whitaker taught her to say these words: *OUR FATHER, Which art in Heauen, hallowed be Thy Name. Thy Kingdome come, Thy will be done, on Earth as it is in Heauen. Giue us this day our daily Bread, and forgiue us our debts, as we forgiue our debtors. And lead us not into Temptation, but deliuer us from Euil; for Thine is the Kingdome, & the Power, & the Glory, fore'er & e'er, AMEN.*

He showed her many wonders, hoping to render her as wide-eyed as .1. of the seals off the coast of Lincolnshire, but for many months she would not be reconciled.

* * * * * *

To worship the disgraced FELON, the VANQUISHED, seemed to her
beyond all words dishonorable. The Tassantasses claimed to follow His example, and yet they nominated themselves for victory. What could He do
to harm her, did she not propitiate him? Her People never troubled to
make offerings to AHONE, He Who'd made the SUN, for AHONE was
too good to hurt them.

But Reverend Whittaker said: Think not of Him as others proclaim
him. Consider only His relation to you yourself. You live solitary here; I
know full well you repine for your own people. CHRIST understands
you. He likewise pined alone, until he was tortured to public scorn. He sees
you now. He would comfort you.

He comforts me not.

Then you *see* Him not. Would you rather treasure up your wrath for
e'er? For I must tell you, Princesse Amonute, that should your father continue obdurate, we must keep you with us for e'er. I cannot comfort you by
restoring your liberty. But because I seek your good, I would comfort you
in another way, by telling tidings of Him. Believe me as you did about the
letters. You Salvages scarcely credit how we can speak to our Countreymen
at any distance, by means of writing. You yourself related to me how
strange-turned and soured with amaze *Prince Opechancanough's*
face did go, when Captaine Smith sent word to Jamestowne on a scrap of
paper. And if it be possible to read sounds you cannot hear, why not be
blessed by friendship with One Whom you cannot see?

But she withdrew into her own torment then, hunching her shoulders,
weeping, weeping, a sad girl whom he pitied far more than he could confess.

* * * * * *

Maister Whittaker did take such pains o'er the young Virginian woman's
case as to sail down to Jamestowne in a Soldiers' barge. As it happened, the
Governor had just return'd from a foray 'gainst the Nandsamund Salvages.
He was drest in his dark velvet cloak. He invited the Reverend to sup with
him, & 'twas a most jovial entertainment. The Servaunts did lay down silver platters which bore various Virginian birds roasted in sugar'd mustard,
the whole being nicely garnish'd with Yndian corn. They'd already un-
bung'd the ale-barrel. After this, the .2. men pray'd together. Sir Thomas
then inquired about his errand.

I have good hopes of Pocahontas's conversion, said the Reverend carefully, provided that we proceed with her in all kindness, examining our own motivations *in feare & trembling,* as the Scripture saith.

Which I rest sure that you shall do, replied Sir Thomas, stroking his dark beard, which was tapered all unto a point.

How long do you anticipate we'll keep the maid? For in truth she doth commence to pine. She asks me whether we mean to salt her away for e'er.

And what do you reply?

I must confess to you that I equivocate, for—

Good man! Look you, Reverend. Powhatan hath temper'd himself to treat with us no further. What can we do? Should we set her at liberty, his insolence will only be exalted.

Then—

Your task must be to improve her time, so that it speeds full pleasantly, for we have no quarrel with her as of yet. Should these Salvages continue to cut our throats, why then, to terrorize 'em we may be compell'd to do execution on her. But since she's gentle, 'tis better not to tax her with her peril.

'Twould be most woeful, should Policy require us to strike thus—

Aye, & it hath. Already we've ravish'd many a Queen down to death. Queen Paspahegh was the .1.st, Queen Opposunoquononuske the .2.nd, & I know not how many Queens Argoll & Brewster slew, or Sir Thomas Gates at Kecoughtan . . . Do you deny we had full cause?

Nay, my Lord.

'Tis good to meditate upon such things, said the Governor, relenting his sternness a little, for otherwise we proceed without justification. Now tell me, is your ward in danger of doing mischief to herself? For did she flee unto the grave despite our treasury of her, 'twould blacken our fame disadvantageously.

I believe she's tolerably comfortable, albeit she broods. I've commenc'd to instruct her in her letters, & find her of a ready aptitude. But she craves company—

Then set some harmless old biddies to take up her mind.

Indeed, several kind Gentlewomen have already befriended her. But women can't do everything for a woman who's been married—

Ha! Now you speak as earthy as a Soldier! So the trull lusts, doth she?

I hardly meant it in that fashion, said the Reverend with quickening horror.

Come, come, be not so o'er-delicate. You have a soul to save; she wants a man to complete her; find her a man. For many of our Colonists appear so wench-craz'd that they'd marry with previously deflowr'd Salvages such as herself. Such a marriage would serve us well. But it must be wedlock; I'll have no fornication in my Colonie—

* * * * * *

Dear Reader, to better assist you in apprehending the *Genesis* (so to speak) of the preceding conversation, I'd best likewise relate another **.1.** which had befallen some days previous in Sir Thomas's manse, beginning when Sir Thomas inquired: How now, Daemon?

My Lord Governor, our purpose might be well serv'd, could we get this Rolfe to bed her. Her maidenhead stripped, & little Englishmen grown in her belly, methinks she'd turn more dependent on our cause, & mayhap Powhatan would hesitate still more to strike . . .

But they say some greasy Salvage was already at blows with that maidenhead—

And mayhap John Smith before him. Ne'er fear, my Lord; a maidenhead's pearl'd and membranous, yes, but tissu'd largely of reputation alone. Let the London hucksters call her *Nonpareil,* & equal to a virgin's estate. Then the more shall yokels joy in her innocency. And this *Maister Rolfe* we're thinking of, he's a widower, so how can he care o'ermuch for **.1.**st fruits? Discretion hath the fame.

Much have I praised thee, Captaine Argall; yet sometimes I almost fear thy uncanny policies . . .

You know me. Have my policies yet accomplisht your hurt? You commaund corn of the Salvages, & I fetch it. You crave to snickle Pokahuntas into your Storehouse; I catch her with child's bait. What will you, Lord? Shall I away with my uncanniness?

Nay, I meant it not so—

Punish me not, whispered his guest with glowing eyes, utterly enjoying the little game.

Punish thee, Argall? I never thought of it. I keep note of my gratitude for you to draw from—

* * * * * *

GOD sends you a guest, the Reverend said.

Just as a dog might come scuttling in the loving hopes that those footsteps it hears are its master's — arriving to find (mayhap) a less exalted soul, the creature halts, noses down against the grass, and begins to scratch itself, as if it never intended to do anything else — so our darling Pokahuntas, being but a specimen of *Naturall,* did first in her laughable ignorance and vanity believe that Captaine John Smith stood without the door.

＊ ＊ ＊ ＊ ＊ ＊

Well met, Pocahontas!

She doth prefer to be call'd *Amonute.*

'Pon my faith, Reverend! Just when I learn'd to trick my tongue round .1. of her names, the lass goes & re-baptizes herself! Tell me, Pokahuntiss, shall I go & catch your father, so that he can be fairly hang'd?

Captaine Argoll, 'tisn't needful to torment the girl—

Pocahuntas, give ear, said her friend, playing with a stinger-like sword which hung at his left hip. (Yea, he's risen up before her in the same strangeness-oozing way as an animal putting on human shape in the forest. He's like her father, who sits ever inescapable at the center of the world.) — I come from yᵉ Governor. He bids me tell you that should you continue to wax in goodness, why then, he'll spare Powhatan from punishment, for your sake alone. Think on 't. Well, I must now haste myself for *Canada.* Darling, forget me not—

＊ ＊ ＊ ＊ ＊ ＊

One fine morn not long after Midsummer's Day* the Reverend did coax her to go a-walking with him in his bright green *Tobacco*-field. He thought that if he could not divert her, at least he'd put her to use. Off they went; Soldiers did open the Town-field gate; Sentiries cheerfully signalled her from the Watch-houses. All these Tasstantasses did crave to be countenanced as her friends. And indeed the girl did revive somewhat; it cheered her to squat and weed his field, which was quite large, he being seized of those .100. acres call'd *Rock Hall.* Presently there came to them .1. *Maister John Rolfe,* who was Undertaking similar experiments; he wish'd to try her knowledge, to learn how the herb might best be kept.

'Tis dried o'er a low fire, the girl said faintly.

I find your native tobacco somewhat biting in its taste, he said to her. Would it please you to try the herb from New Spain?

---

*24 June.

And he reached into his pouch.

In the latest English dress which Reverend Whittaker had granted her (a gift from Sir Thomas Dale, they say), this *Pocahontas* look'd nothing like her kindred Salvages, whose garish ornament e'er reminded Rolfe of a troop of Mummers or Musicians back in London-Towne: puffy red pantaloons or blue skirts chased with blue raindrops or black lightning-bolts, hats brimmed or unbrimmed, citterns or violins in hand, it booted not. In truth Maister Rolfe was wenchless, but Cupid's arrow had not transfixed him yet; more like, he was curious to learn what lore she might ken, regarding sot-weed.*

Amonute inhaled from the pipe which he offered her — for so one must do when hospitality is offered, even tho' amongst her People 'tis rare to present it unto women.

How doth it relish?

To her it seemed passing weak. Wearily she told him: You Tassantasses e'er own the best things . . .

Now essay this other leaf, Princesse, if it please you. Which do you prefer? This guards itself better than t'other 'gainst the hornworm. I've raised it up from Trinidad seed .2. years now, he went on, a little self-proud.

She kept silent. His face was as shallow & mild as a turtle's shell.

Princesse Pokahuntiss —

Ah-Mo-Noo-tay, interjected Reverend Whitaker.

Nay, Sir, I've grown different. Let him call me what he will . . .

Amonute—

Nay, truly it makes no difference.

Well, then, Princesse Pocahontas, my Almanacke remarks that when the Moone's in *Taurus, Cancer, Virgo* or *Capricorn,* 'tis most safe to plant new seed. Do you ken our constellations?

I understand you not, she said shortly.

Well, tell me this: Do you plant *Tobacco* by moonlight?

We don't talk of such things, she said.

O, you see, 'tis her barbarous religion! said Reverend Whittaker.

*   *   *   *   *   *

This Maister Rolfe hailed from Heacham-Towne in Countie Norfolk. As the crow flies, 'tis not much exceeding .30. miles from Willoughby-in-

---

*Tobacco.

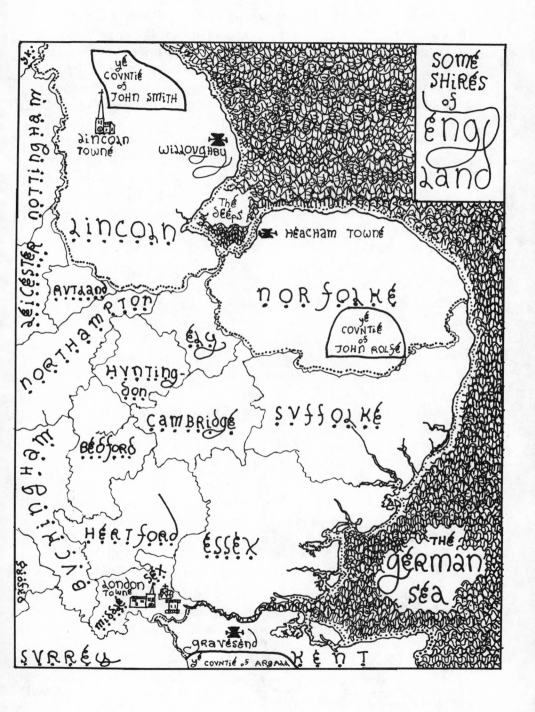

SOMÉ SHIRÉS of ÉngLand

yͤ COVNTIÉ of JOHN SMITH

NOTTINGHAM

LÉICÉSTÉR

BVCKINGHAM

OXFORD

LINCOLN

LINCOLN TOWNÉ

WILLOVGHBY

Thé DÉÉPS

HÉACHAM TOWNÉ

RVTLAND

NORTHAMPTON

NORFOLKÉ

yͤ COVNTIÉ of JOHN ROLFÉ

ÉLY

HVNTING-ᵈon

CAMBRIDGÉ

BÉDFORD

SVFFOLKÉ

HÉRTFORD

ÉSSÉX

THÉ GÉRMAN SÉA

LONDON TOWNÉ

MIDDLÉSÉX

SVRRÉY

GRAVÉSÉND

yͤ COVNTIÉ of ARGALL

KÉNT

Lincolnshire — but for that you must sail across *The Wash* & breast the muck, until the ground grows firm again near Boston. Peep with me into Speed's *Atlas,* dear Reader, & you'll see that this afore-mentioned Hicham (signified by but a single red house) lies beside a black creeklet which drains direct into Hicham Haven, altho' so sandy & oozy it appears to be there (indeed, Speed has mustachio'd the whole Countie about with stippled banks of ink-sand) that I know not how fair would be her havenage.

He was a member of the New Generation of Colonists. Sure he was an Undertaker like unto President Wingfield; but we cannot call him an Adventurer in Sweet John's style.*   He watch'd & waited, whilst the .1.ˢᵗ Colonists prepared the way. Those few who surviv'd became the Ancient Planters. He himself was call'd *Canny young Undertaker.* His ambitious obsequies would help bury Yndian Virginia a little deeper. But can we blame him? Otherwise he'd but Undertake his own funeral, poisoning himself upon the illusions serv'd up at Gravesend. We must act, dear Reader, & improve ourselves where we may. If others perish from that cause, why, then they must have been idle or Salvage loiterers! He long'd to husband the ground & become a good farmer.

There is an herbe called Vppówoc, wrote Thomas Harriot in a book which got publisht when John Smith was **.10.** years old. *The Spaniardes generally call it Tobacco. The leaves thereof being dried and brought into powder: they vse to take the fume or smoke thereof by sucking it through pipes made of claie into their stomacke and heade; from whence it purgeth superfluous steame & other grosse humors. This* Vppówoc *is of precious estimation amongst them, that they thinke their gods are maruelously delighted therewith.*

He **.1.**ˢᵗ tried to plant the accustomed English vegetables, such as *Pumpeons, Mellons, Cowcumbers,* &c. These prov'd successful, yet he wasn't assur'd that they could fill his coffers as it were. So then he essayed the *herbe called Vppówoc.* He long'd not to die poor.

✳ ✳ ✳ ✳ ✳ ✳

Sure Captaine Fortune must favor him, perhaps e'en in the person of this Pocahontas. Her *Tobacco* learning might well advantage him. He thought her an ingenuously hopeful young wench, altho' passing ugly.

---

*As the *Generall Historie* bitterly saieth: *This dear bought Land with so much bloud & cost, hath onely made some few rich, & all the rest losers. But it was intended at the first, the first undertakers should be preferred and rewarded, and the first adventurers satisfied, and they of all the rest are the most neglected.* No doubt Powhatan would have agreed.

* * * * * *

After a fortnight, he arrived with many Christian greetings, & ferried her
.5. miles down river to Bermuda Nether Hundred where he had his fields.
The Reverend accompanied them, for he had some business there with a
dying parishioner. (Moreo'er, 'twouldn't have been meet to leave tham
alone at this stage.)

Bermuda was a passing melancholy appellation for Maister Rolfe's
domicile, for his .1.ˢᵗ wife Anne, had been fatally distemper'd during their
shipwrecked sojourn on the Bermudas, or Devil's Isles, whilst giving birth
to a daughter named Bermuda, who also passed away unto HEAVEN.
Anne had lingered alive all the way unto Virginia, her upturn'd face seeming to shrivel day by day in the fetid ship-darkness. Altho' lucid in her
mind, she'd scarcely spoken to him. Perhaps the grief of the baby's death
had crush'd her down. He buried her in Virginia, where the branches of
great oaks subdivided the sky unto wheel-wedges. Thus *Bermuda Nether
Hundred* could not but remind him of his bygone state of matrimony.
Anne had prov'd a most honorable Goodwife, altho' somewhat shrewish;
whene'er they quarrelled she'd not scrupled to mention that by possession
of her hand he'd gain'd .2. tenements near about to Heacham, which he'd
sold to capitalize their voyage to Virginia. Of Maister Rolfe 'twas said, not
always admiringly, that he was very enterprising. But nobody could find
any unchristian act to reproach him for. Indeed, he was monstrous pious —
the harvest of a shadow-stifled childhood pass'd amongst his ancient
Kinswomen, who preferred never to go out. The boy's natural restlessness
being punish'd & henced corrected, he learned to bend his energies unto
practical affairs.

Certainly he felt grief when his wife & child expired — the more so since
little Bermuda died unbaptized. Yea, John Rolfe had become a Widower!
('Tis said that a man's sorrow o'er his .1.ˢᵗ wife is greater than o'er the .2.ⁿᵈ.)
He long'd for consolation, for an heir, & of course for a well-beseeming
partner in his labors. He concluded for to remarry as soon as he was able.
Howbeit, in Virginia very few English damsels could be found.

This *Pocahontas* now gave him very good advice about how deep to
plant his seed, & in what proximity. She was pale brown like buckskin. She
helped weed his fields, & the Reverend's, & those of the other English. They
call'd her *A good Saluadge*. Maister Rolfe commenced for to wonder how
'would be to have her helping him always. But he admonishd himself *Beware,* she being of the pagan sort, her soul all stain'd & confounded by the

most bloody errors. Moreo'er, good Reverend Whittaker had warn'd that she was somewhat cross-grained. — Altho' perhaps that befits her station, she being a *Princesse,* the Reverend concluded with a little laugh.

* * * * * *

Turning o'er the soil, he discovered arrowheads & other such trash. Some-one had told him (altho' he could scarce credit it) that merely .2. years since, this fertile *Champian-land* of corn-fields had been not only forested, but stained by the Townes of the Infidels. 'Twas easier, somehow, to pretend that this dirt which he impregnated with reddish-brown *Tobacco* seeds like unto sand-grains had been virgin for many centuries. Reader, haven't you e'er followed your civil path in all honor, laboring in the LORD's vine-yard, & then wondered whether after all this vineyard might not be yours? 'Twas hardly a fear which most of these Colonists would venture, for they'd grabbled so desperately to get their little strips of foreign dirt (& at what great charge to His Majestie!) that 'twould be half-witted to unhand them back unto Salvages. Nor did Maister Rolfe himself seriously entertain such follies. Howbeit, as his sympathy for the captive Virginian woman com-menced to flower tall & rampant (as doth all which grows in this strange Countrey's hot atmosphere), then by the same rule of logic so increased his sense of awkwardness when his spade disclosed Salvage relics. If she was worthy to be favored with his courtesies, why, what about these Salvage Townes now translated unto English farms? But he reminded himself that it was not as if the English wisht to dispossess the Yndians utterly, only to make their own living here while indeed benefitting these people by up-rooting their unlearned & perilous Religion. As for these late warlike meas-ures, self-defense enjoined those. All men were tired with Powhatan's perpetual oppressions . . .

* * * * * *

Wahunsenacawh heard through his spies that the Tassantasses were keep-ing her in close, so that she languished. Sickened with anxiety and grief, he went oftentimes alone to sit within the forest. He knew not what to do. He feared she'd die, but did he send all his best men to rescue her, 'twould yet prove fruitless; he'd never again undervalue the enemy's poisonous strength. Dulleyed and sickened, he stared. He could not bear to conceive of her suf-fering.

They said to him: It could be that *she was taken.* (They meant, *taken by*

OKEUS.) This might be true. If it was, then he could not have hindered it. This half-comforted him. But then he went with both his brothers to the Three Temples at Uttamussack. Wahunsenacawh cast many coppers into the river as they came. Opechancanough's people gave him a dance, but he took no joy in it. He scarcely touched his meat when they feasted him. His brothers saw that he could not be comforted, and fell quiet.

Ascending the blood-red sandhills, they entered the Great Wiochisan House where he would be kept after his death. Their father and all their grandfathers lay here enshelved, wrapped in snow-white mats now black with age and smoke. They prayed and conjured amongst the priests, but without result. Striving to hide his hatred for OKEUS, Who'd robbed and abused him, Wahunsenacawh gave great presents. His anger changed itself unto terror and back again. Everything must decay, he told himself. If not today, then tomorrow. But *she* was not dead and wrapped in mats. He almost would have preferred it if she were. Her captivity tormented her, and mocked his power.

His rage passed away now, he knew not why. He strove to quieten his heart.

It scarcely befitted him to mourn for her whom he cared for. Was he to permit all the People to behold his weakness? So he fixed a bitter smile on his face, but neither Uttamattomakkin nor his brothers were deceived. OKEUS had outstripped him.

Hearing of his arrival, his son-in-law Kocoum sent him a fat deer, for which he envoyed a runner to thank him with three blue beads. Kocoum was certainly a good man, an excellent hunter. Yet he could not bear to see him. Why had he not given Amonute to a husband who could have protected her?

He summoned one of Opechancanough's daughters and said to her: Cut my hair.

Pleased to be singled out, the woman squatted down beside him and began to grate away the locks on the righthand side of his head with two clamshells. Although she kept deferentially silent, he could scarcely bear her touch.

At the next day's dawn they were sitting in a circle with all the People at the river's edge, and then Wahunsenacawh rose up, pulled at the greyish hairs on his chin, and said: My brother Opitchapam will continue now. — The People grew mournful, for they comprehended that he could perceive his own death approaching. Opitchapam cried *Bowh, waugh* and the women lay down. The men thrust firesticks into the ground. Silently Wahunsenacawh made his own prayer of thanks to the SUN.

You are ill, dear brother?

Nay, he said unto Opechancanough, but in truth he felt weak. He wondered how soon he would perish and be carried here to Uttamussack. Opitchapam would not be Powhatan after him except in name. Wahunsenacawh had ordered it thus, but secretly, so as not to disgrace Opitchapam. These times required a Powhatan whose cunning could rush in everywhere like flooding rivers; otherwise the Tassantasses would devour them all. That man was Opechancanough.

Opechancanough did always support and comfort him nowadays. He hated the Tassantasses more than anyone. He said that when he was young, and went to spy on them at Roanoke, they'd brought sickness with them, slaying people by invisibly inescapable means, for which reason he believed they plotted to kill everyone and possess all the land. (That they used magic in this could not be doubted, for they did everything magically; and moreover, the physicians who sucked strings of sick blood from the bodies of the dying, in vain attempts to cure them, discovered the spoors of invisible bullets.) Opechancanough said that for this reason he'd comprehended the evil of the Tassantasses even before they'd destroyed Kecoughtan and Paspahegh; he'd seen it before they'd threatened him at Menapacunt; he'd known it always. He promised that someday he'd go forth to destroy them. So he comforted his brother; he strengthened him. In due course the People would be free of all this evil—

And Amonute?

Today we shall know, Opechancanough replied.

Putting on his accustomed crown of snakeskins and weasel-skins, Uttamattomakkin approached the Secret Temple alone. Wahunsenacawh sat by the fire in Opechancanough's house to wait, slowly painting his face black and silver. No one disturbed him until he was ready. Then he came out.

Opechnacanough and Opitchapam, who'd painted themselves long since, embraced their brother, singing many songs to clear his mind, but wearily, for 'twas passing rare that any man could move him.

He said unto them: Evil is watching

It does so always, dear brother.

Then they talked about the fish-weirs at Menapacunt. Opechancanough said that some repairs needed to be made. Indeed, soon the entire town would be consumed by age. Opechancanough asked his brothers to walk the ground with him, to help him discover a good site for a new town. They agreed, smiling a little, for even Opitchapam understood that this deference on Opechancanough's part was pure courtesy. Undoubtedly he would lead them here and there, and finally bring them to the place he'd already chosen, which they'd be sure to praise. Wahunsenacawh felt wearied with everything.

Then Uttamattomakkin returned, and in company they entered the darkness of the Great Temple, Uttamattomakkin first, throwing grains of corn into fires. Each of them laid beads and hatchets upon the crystal altar stone. Gazing into its translucent depths, Wahunsenacawh felt as if he were perceiving himself for the last time. Fears boiled variously in his heart.

When they came unto the pillars of smoke-blackened figures, Uttamattomakkin bade them wait again. He stepped behind the reed mat. He spoke unto OKEUS in the magic language, and OKEUS said: *She is lost.*

* * * * * *

Many times he went to the lesser Wiochisan house at Orapax, offering suet from the deer he'd slain, but never saw OKEUS.

* * * * * *

He summoned Uttamattomakkin most privately and said: Have I displeased Him, to have lost her so?

Uttamattomakkin gazed at him in pity.

Wahunsenacawh withdrew among the trees. When he was alone, he covered his face in his hands.

* * * * * *

Just as green gives way to orange on a half-ripe gourd, so the months and seasons changed their color at Henrico. To Amonute it now seemed that she had never dwelt anywhere but here. Sir Thomas Dale came for to see her & inquired most courteously after her circumstances. He said: We'd be friends with your father, Princesse, if you but help'd us. Then together in peace we'd rule Virginia.

How must I help you, Lord?

Become a Christian. Ally yourself unto us—

Why then bide I not free?

He spread his hands. — Because your father's the Virginian King; therefore you possess royal value, and so we must cherish you and be careful of you . . .

* * * * * *

With Reverend Whittaker's permission, her friend led her out thro' the pal-isadoes & along .7.-Mile Pale to the Corn-ground.

She smiled at him. After all his fieldwork under the SUN, his skin was golden like unto smoked oysters.

Nay, Maister Rolfe, you must plant the seed like this . . .

And with her hands she dug the earth, & shewed him.

He feasted her on bread & cream. (Her husband would have served her a raccoon stew. These Tassantasses could not hunt. She despised them.)

Maister Rolfe?

Ay, Pocahontas?

Can you fashion me some bells & beads?

Nay, dear Princesse, for I never fathom'd that art.

Your Countreymen cannot each .1. do e'erything?

Nay, for to learn a trade we must stand our Apprenticeship for nigh upon .1. years. How could we own enough life to do that for all services & manu-factures? Moreover, some businesses prove unseemly to wellborn souls?

Maister Rolfe, I construe you not.

Well, for an instance, Drapers & Butchers are rough-bred men. I pity not myself, that I've never kept a filthy stall in London-Towne for to sit plashed by carcass-blood . . .

Yet my father can do everything.

Ay, 'pon my honor, I misdoubt me not he's very clever . . .

He fashions his own arrows. Can your King do the like?

Now I must caution you, dear Princesse, to disallow your thoughts from venturing thataway; for many villains would be glad if they could tumble your innocency into some bear-pit of treason . . .

I care not for all that. Can he make arrows?

My dear, he requires 'em not, possessing demiculverins such as those yonder, in comparison to which your arrows are playthings!

Then can he make demiculverins!

Kind LORD, succor this soul in her dangerous ingenuousness!

*   *   *   *   *   *

She had nothing but her own blood to offer to OKEUS. In the night time, when she was all alone in her bed, she bit her arm until she drew blood. The table would be her altar-stone. Grating the wound hard against the corner of the table, so that blood ran more freely, she said to OKEUS: I im-plore you, save me from all this. I'll do nearly anything—

* * * * * *

That winter was not very cold. She heard the sound of running water under the snow. Yet she was cold, she knew not why. Mayhap 'twas the food the Tasantasses ate which sucked away her strength. She would have worn her embroidered deerskin mantle; as it was, she must make do with the Tassantasses' constricting clothes. Every day this Reverend Whittaker did dart & flitter around her, as if he were a snake in a warrior's ear-hole. As a girl she'd laughed to see those serpents swiggle round their masters' necks, or flickering their tongues in people's faces. But now she discovered no mirth in it. Maister Rolfe likewise paid her many a visit, quizzing her on how well she did say her Paternoster. And ever did his OKEE call'd JESUS haunt her heart. Just as the walnut-milk which she used to prepare in her father's house hath no odor, but tastes so richly oil & bittersweet, so this JESUS, who was but a word in the air, or a darkness near as dark as Captaine Argall's hold, took on an ever more corporeal semblance. The Tassantasses never failed to thank Him for her victories. Even Captaine Smith had done the like. Maybe 'twas true—

The Tassantasses insisted unto her that after her father died & got carried to the Temple at Uttamussack to be smoked dry and stored up with his pleasure, he would not live again in the west. How did they know this? They said that JESUS told them so.

They said that JESUS would come to punish her father, & drag him underground to be consumed by fire as he'd consumed his enemies. To this, Amonute proudly replied: Have no fear. He's brave enough not to cry out under any tortures.

'Tis not to the point, child. He may be passing brave, yet eternity will break him.

I know not why you insult my father's courage. I care not—

(She defies us, said Reverend Whittaker privily to Maister Rolfe. Yet why should she not, being most treacherously ensnar'd by Captaine Argall? That villain hath done more to damn her soul than Captaine Smith with all his licentiousness!

(Aye. But 'twill be a great comfort unto her to be saved.

(For which task I misdoubt me not you may prove fitted, Maister Rolfe . . .)

But look you, sweet child. Submit unto JESUS, and when you die you'll taste honey, I do promise thee.

And my father?

Once you're well CHRISTianized, you'll have the power to save his soul!

✳ ✳ ✳ ✳ ✳ ✳

Continuing unfree to work or even to walk unescorted (and she disdained to request the favor of a guard), she became sad and sluggish. At last she forbore even to lift up her eyes & hands to the SUN. Seeking for to comfort her, Maister Rolfe told her more about JESUS.

✳ ✳ ✳ ✳ ✳ ✳

Yea, just as the North Starre clings perpetually to the tail of *Ursa Minor,* so did Maister Rolfe stick to Pocahontas. The Reverend had taken him aside, murmuring that above all things it would prove worst for the Colonie, did this maid escape. For then she must be unreconciled beyond redemption; and with the secrets she'd spied out at Jamestowne and Henrico, she could help her father plot massacre. They must lock her friendship fast before they e'er let her go.

She resists me, he added bitterly.

Well, 'tis natural, replied Maister Rolfe complacently. The Irish do likewise hate all reformation.

He was growing surer of the Virginian woman's affection.

Had other brides been ready for the plucking, Maister Rolfe would have preferred to marry a wife with a portion equal to one-third of his value. But how does a body measure that, with Salvages?

✳ ✳ ✳ ✳ ✳ ✳

Smiling, he placed his hand on her arm.

When she was a young girl in Rapahannock, the winter cold had made a band around her forehead and chilled the back of her head. It sank into her naked chest so that the little boys laughed and tried to pinch her hard little nipples; she slapped their hands away.

She wanted his hand on her breast. 'Twas not e'en that she liked him, but she felt lonely, and some pleasure might have scared away her sadness.

Nay, she hardly wished to go with him. But it would soon be a year now; Kocoum must have forgotten her. How else could she e'er get free? (His shirt was torn. Meaningfully she said unto him: Had I some pemmenaw-grass I could make thread to mend it. But they disallow me from going out.) Perhaps the Tassantasses had altered her within her heart.

He took her hand in both of his. His grasp was as sticky as deer-horn glue.

* * * * * *

I would know how to call thee *Sweeting,* he said.

In my tongue? she asked shyly.

Aye.

Why then, 'tis — 'tis—

Maister Rolfe waited.

'Tis *Mufkaiuwh,* she choked out, & he comprehended not why she burst into tears.

* * * * * *

May I bathe in the river now? 'Tis the time of my uncleanliness. If you trust me not, send **.1.** of your women to watch me o'er—

Nay, Princesse, we trust you now, for you have practically promis'd yourself to our Maister Rolfe.

I'll 'scape not, I swear by the CHRIST cross & the SUNNE—

* * * * * *

Now they'd commenced for to call him *That lusty Widow-man.* For, having buried **.1.** wife, he already wooed another! He strove to explain to them that 'twas not for licentiousness, but they hooted until he blush'd.

It perturbs you not she's no virgin?

Nay, by my faith! What I've resolved on, I do not for myself but for the Colonie.

'Twas in his opinion a Turkishe action, to have raped the maid away from her kindred as *Argoll* had done — & yet a pleasanter maid could not be imagined; he thought very often upon her; he was glad to find her clapt up at Reverend Whittaker's!

She was the **.1.**st Salvage with whom he'd e'er made close acquaintance. Nor had he sought to befriend any of those people before, for, as all know, Salvages are good but for Wagon-drivers & Watermen. And yet he understood that e'en they had their Government, comprised (as is natural) of a Monarchy, & (as he supposed) some sort of rude Parliament like unto the **.7.** Electors of the Low Countreys. They were human beings, & above them as him lived the glowing Goodness of GOD — how marvelous 'twould be, if he could help her reach it! Already she had the Apostle's Creed & the **.10.** Commandments by heart. To be sure, he did not wish to be severed from his friends, but Reverend Whittaker enouraged him to keep on his course. And many others in that Colonie did say, in admiration or envy, that she'd bring him great good fortune. All the idlers of Henrico (such as there were, for they'd been distrained somewhat by Sir Thomas Dale's severities) cried out when they saw him: *I'd lay my last copper down on her!*

Granted, she was peculiar in some of her qualities, & yet she was warm; she was a woman; she could love. Why should he give her o'er? He cared not for the scorn of the envious who surrounded him.

'Tis said some pox-clapt yeoman kept her for a punk.

Maister Rolfe replied: I pity thy lewd-scarred soul.

Tut, man, you're foolish. E'en if you can effect this marriage, you'll be a laughingstock! And what gain could you get from that ugly little Salvage trull?

Enough!

O, I fear not *your* sting. Indeed, I mean but your good, Maister Rolfe. Keep on your course, & you'll suffer many a weary step.

In spite of all such insults, he long'd now for her to become his jewel. He commenced for to think her as clean as the water from black cherries.

Yea, he was now full resolv'd to marry with her, and through this marriage purchase title to some of her father's lands. In England he'd seen many a man or woman marry unwisely, & be forever after wretched. Nonetheless, having chosen to Adventure his life in the Virginian Plantation, Maister Rolfe kenned very well that the practice of husbandry would best advance him — and why not husbandry in both senses? This marvelous herb *Tobacco* might raise good money for him and the Colonie alike, perhaps before he e'en passed the prime of his age. Good Pocahontas seem'd fair for to help him in that, & be generally a good spouse (once she had made remission of her Salvageness, of course — 'twas utterly necessary that they worship his GOD together).

As for himself, he had no doubts about his capacity to be her support.

* * * * * *

Reverend Whittaker had assured them both that her cohabitation with the Salvage named Kocoum counted but as fornication, since she'd not been joined with him in a Church before GOD. And from that sin Rebecca stood fully now excused. GOD was not so unjust as to punish the ignorant defilements of .1. who had since rejected her own heathenishness.

But know full well, Maister Rolfe, that by Church law you may never divorce this maid.

Aye, said her Bride-groom in a whisper.

She, sincerely granting that they were both of them imperfect under GOD's sight, agreed to enter the matrimonial state.

Then the Governor of his kindness did present her with a jacket of white *fustian* (which is linen and cotton cloth), embroidered with starfish islands and foamy waves.

* * * * * *

But can such as she learn how to be a good wife?

Doubtless, your Grace — like unto the Sick-nurse who smothers her patient, in order to rifle through his clothes!

And the bell toll'd *Argall, Argoll, Argull.*

* * * * * *

She made public renunciation of idolatry, and for the first time, in a voice like unto a newborn babe weakly crying, revealed her secret name, to wit, *Matoaka.* Her eyes were as sad as last fall's leaves.

They baptized her *Rebecca,* for among the English as among the Turkes the custom is to conceal a slave's ancestry. (They were all as treacherous as the Monacans.)

* * * * * *

For I would bathe, she was complaining again, & yet they ne'er permit me near the river'd edge without a Sentry for to guard me.

He spoke to Reverend Whittaker, who granted her this favor. Then her face grew most strangely gleeful, almost licentious. Within his ear she whispered *Mufkaiuwh,* which is to say, *A Flower of a fine thing.* He essay'd not to reveal his disgust. Leading her to the river's edge, he turn'd his back, ready for to summon help did she try to escape.

Laughing & splashing, she call'd out his name, but he denied to reply until she stood decently drest beside him. For 'twas true what he told his enemies: He was not licentious.

She seem'd strange & sullen after that.

* * * * * *

Mild Argoll did laugh & laugh, when he heard 'twas prov'd that the Yndian wench had consented to become John Rolfe's cockatrice.

THE GRAMMAR OF HUSBANDS (1614)

Like barbarous miscreants, they quelled virgins vnto death, and cutting off their tender paps to present for deinties vnto their magistrates, they engorged themselues with their bodies.

Epistle of YUO OF NARBONA to the Archbishop of Bordeaux (1243)

*I*nto the frigate which Captaine Argall had built marched .150. men (for that subtle old Powhatan, as they well knew, could raise .1,000. warriors in .2. or .3. days). Sir Thomas Dale rode in Argall's ship. Six other boats kept them company on that fine spring morn when all the swamps were mirrors. And they set sail for Pamunkey River, *Trarintra-rarara.* With them was Pokahuntas — or *Rebecca* as I must now say. Dreading to meet her former relations, the maid stubbornly denied to take part in this voyage, until Reverend Whitaker did command her: Do it, *Pocahontas,* or else you must be damned. — And in thus employing .1. of her castoff Salvage appellations he expressed displeasure so well that the blood did rush to her face.

As for the men, they kept quiet. They did nothing unless they were commaunded, unlike Rebecca's kinsmen, who came & went as they listed when they worked together, making canoes or fastening sheets of bark to a new house's ribs. A good Soldier stands silent like unto a tree. He awaits his Captaine's commaund. Then, & not until then, doth he march, *.1. and .2.* Most of these *Jamestowne Helmsmen* had learnt in Ireland how to spoil a Countrey. Then they'd been Virginia-season'd. Some had burnt out that adders' nest call'd *Paspahegh;* others had conquered *Kecoughtan.* Some few had assisted Sweet John in his corn-raids upon the *Chickahominies, Nansamunds, Pamunkeys* & *Werowocomocans.* They sported souls & armor of varying quality. Sir Thomas's armor was even better wrought & gilded than my Lord De La Warr's; so that it sucked richness from the sun; while his inferiors mostly wore brigandine vests as rusty as Sweet John's.

Rebecca o'erstared the gunnels. The crown of a turtle's head rose slowly from tea-colored water.

* * * * * *

Why do you come? the messenger demanded.

I come to bring Powhatan his daughter, conditionally as he will render all the arms, tools and swords which have been stolen from us by treachery; secondly, he must return all our men, who have run away, and give me a ship full of corn, to amend the wrong which he has done unto us. If he will do this, we may be friends. If not, I shall burn all.

The messenger was painted head and shoulders with the root *Pochone.** The messenger said: I must send to Powhatan, to give him these tidings.

For a long time Sir Thomas stood gazing into his face. Then he said: Yes, yes, yes; I warrant he means to 'scape & defy our wrath. But tell Powhatan, pray, that our wrath can scarce be smothered up. I'll grant him .2. days. And 'tis certain that we possess Pocahuntiss; d'ye see her? (Kindly stand and shew yourself, Rebecca.) We'll not be dispropertied of her 'till her father serves our turn. I said: D'ye see her?

He smiled to see the Salvage's look of hate.

* * * * * *

The messenger said quietly: What dost thou think Powhatan is?

Ah, what do I think of his nicely trinketed slyness, his insubstantial complexion towards his friends — his malice, rather — his feigned affections like unto a cutpurse harlot? What I think's most easy to discern. But you know him better than I. You goggle up his leavings, the crumbs of his spoils got by treachery . . .

The messenger said: Powhatan is the King of the Head. Powhatan is the King of the Teeth. It is not Powhatan who's overturned the Countrey here.

After that they said little more to .1. another, save to arrange the exchange of hostages to preserve the truce 'til Powhatan should return answer.

* * * * * *

Two days passing without result (the Englishmen waiting on the ships, playing Doublets & Colchester Trump, both of which Pocahontas sought to learn — for it seemed that her woebegone mood was no more substantial than her other Virginian flitterings), Sir Thomas Dale concluded that they had better go ashore to serve further notice on that Prince of Wildness; but as soon as he got his men arrayed and began to lead them inland, then from pale lavender gullies of dead leaves the Salvages commenced for to shoot — almost silent

*Puccoon.

snipings with long arrows that whirled into the Soldiers' backs, the sharpened deer-shank arrowheads gripping flesh with double fangs. Tauntingly they called reminders of Ratcliffe's fate. Not to be behindhand with them, Sir Thomas gave the commaund to fire, by which they did kill some of the enemy & hurt diverse others, as they afterwards espied only by the blood (for Salvages never groan or cry out). He led them into the nearest Towne. The Salvages had fled. Sir Thomas gazed about him at the rounded wattled houses. — Like unto Swine-styes! he said in disgust. Well, let's make of this place a fine warm pasture . . . Thus he ordered his men to burn every house, which they did, having .1.st possessed themselves of the corn, to bring back to Jamestowne. Then they quartered themselves in the ashes that night, to show the Salvages that they did not fear them. Proudfaced Rebecca smiled, staring away.

Sir Thomas Dale said: As you love me, be not discontented. You can see the necessity—

I am content, my Lord, replied the trembling smile.

All night the enemy did keep them from sleep, singing: *Whe, whe, yah, ha, ne, he, wittowa, wittowa.*

The next day, just before the end of the Morning Watch, he led them back to the ships and they ascended the river further. (Tall black tree-soldiers stood at attention in black water — how could *they* ever be defeated?) Salvages dogged them from behind the trees. Sometimes the Salvages called: Where go you?

To burn all, if you will not do what we demanded, and has been agreed upon.

Now after these words a great grim Salvage rose up like a very *Whip-jack,* as they do call him, whose trade is to rob booths at a fair. He came striding toward them, making signs that he would parley, which Dale freely granted from within his wall of leveled arquebuses.

The Salvage said: You have acted contrary to custom, not we, for you have seized our land and made designs against us!

Sir Thomas Dale smiled thin-lipped at this folly.

The Salvage said: Hear me! Lay down your weapons for a day and we shall do likewise, for we do but wait upon Powhatan.

Tell him that his insolence deserves differently. Nevertheless I once again grant you the favor for which you ask. Go, begone.

* * * * * *

A Salvage came and asked: Why did you burn our houses?

Why did you shoot at us? queried Sir Thomas in reply.

Some lurkers did it, not us; we intend no hurt, but are your friends.

And we are in equal measure your friends, quipped Sir Thomas, at which Argall laughed so hard he must sit down.

* * * * * *

They sailed to a Towne call'd *Muscunt*, and he said to Pocahuntas that she must come ashore with him. She replied that she did not desire to, & wept until it wrung his heart. Nonetheless he was well enough used to her weeping that he could not set his own strategies aside because of it. As gently as he could, he told her that there was no help for it; she must come ashore. He heard her whisper: *It hurts me.*

He said to her: Have no fear. I would not be cruel with you.

O no, she said. You ever permit me to go where I please.

Take it as you will, he said shortly. You must come, and show yourself, but you may keep secret in your words. That is all I ask.

She accompanied him unresisting. Seeing her, the Salvages (of which there stood near about **.400.** armed men) sent up a shout of gladness, but she was as struck dumb. So far did she keep her bond.

Sir Thomas sat beneath a mullberry tree (for it was growing hot); surrounded by sentries, he took a sheet of foolscap and began to write a letter to the Virginia Company, saying: *The Kings daughter went ashoare, but would not talk to any of them, scarce to them of the best sort, and to them only, that if her father had loved her, he would not value her lesse than old Swords, Peeces, or Axes: wherefore she would still dwell with the Englishmen, who loved her.*

* * * * * *

I am the voice of Powhatan, the Salvage said. Open your ears. Powhatan says: Your swords will be returned to you in **.15.** days, and the corn likewise. Powhatan says: My daughter shall be your child now, and every day dwell with you. I grant this because I desire that we should be ever friends.

O, he *grants* it, smirked Argoll. That's so bloody good of him.

* * * * * *

Powhatan's brother Opachankano (or *Opechancanough* as we sometimes write it) came to Sir Thomas all the way from reed-wall'd Menapacunt-Towne and said with all the biting bitterness of Virginia tobacco: I desire that you will call me friend, and I you. I am a great Captain, and do always fight. Likewise you. And therefore I love you. Your friends will be my friends.

Yet for a greater confirmation, replied Sir Thomas, staring him in the face, I would that Powhatan send back to us our truant men, our arms, & the swords you promised.

Gnashing his teeth in hate, Opechancanough said: I know not why you again insult Powhatan's promise. In all Chesapeake there are scarce enough roanoke-shells to clear his mind of your ugly words. You speak like a child, without knowledge.

If I do repeat my demand, 'tis only for your good, that we forbear from punishment for all your treachery.

Treachery nourishes itself in strange places, it would seem. You Tassantasses took .1. whom we honored, and now you've gnawed up her mind, solely to give Powhatan grief. Have you in truth no women of your own, that you must ravish ours?

Sir Thomas Dale stood with his pale fist upon his hip and said: Now you begin to scorn me, fellow, Have a care. You understand not my power. And the worthy lady you mention, believe you she would begone from us? Rebecca! Ho, Rebecca! Come quickly! Child, do you know this Gentleman?

Yes, my Lord.

He is your relation?

He is my uncle Opechancanough.

Very excellent. Now do you tell him, Rebecca, that you dwell in our Colonie of your own pleasure.

It is so, she whispered dully.

So please you, Amonute, said her uncle dryly. And have you any word for Powhatan?

Say I love him; say I long for a good end—

A good end! laughed Opechancanough most grimly. Now I begin to understand you. And is it true that you worship OKEUS no more?

'Tis true, Uncle.

Now is your curiosity satisfied, fellow? Sir Thomas sharply cried, at which the Salvage turned upon him that steadily poisonous gaze, the eyes almost shut into black slits, like unto an *Alligator's*. And Sir Thomas suddenly thought to himself: This man will be dangerous to our cause until the very death. Would he might come to me again in war, that I could send a musket-ball through his head for mine own ease! How he hates me! And what a wicked snake he is . . . !

Opechancanough then said: Amonute, I sorrow for you.

Enough, fellow, get you gone!

Amonute—

Forget me, Uncle. I'm nothing now.

Speak not so, Rebecca. Opechancanough, get you gone, I said!

Now that evil Salvage ground his teeth in rage, then turned to go. He wore a rattlesnake's tail in his scalp-lock, & since his leave-taking proved passing abrupt, that dead ornament rattled. 'Twas an inimical sound, to be sure, & for a twink Sir Thomas felt transfix'd with eeriness. Nay, this man would never humble himself. Ominous, furious, stealthy & strong, he stood betwixt Sir Thomas and Virginia. Over his shoulder he did say in their Salvage dialect, so that Sir Thomas could not understand: Amonute, you and I are guilty together, for we each of our own accord did give *that knave* his life. Knowest thou whom I mean?

Yes—

I thought him a great Werowance, and you—

My Lord Sir Thomas, may I go?

I would you did, traitor-gulled girl! Go you to your Bride-groom, and speak no more to these Salvages . . .

* * * * * *

Had she married another Salvage, or kept to the marriage she'd had, she would have desisted in grating the forepart of her hair so close as do maids, but John Rolfe was wont to behold her so. The espousals having already occurred, came the publication of the banns*, & they sat on the rough long benches. Through the Church windows at James Towne Rebecca could see other steep grey-thatched roofs, then the sawteeth of the palisade. Her life smelled of Jamestowne — smell of smoke and dust.

I wish that I could say that her marriage was a splendid affair, with much jewelry and plate; that Pocahontas wore a dress embroidered with flowers & spiders in the best London-towne fashion; but I must make shift to tell you otherwise, for just as all sincere Navigators find it convenient to know the true *Meridian* or South, which they may accomplish either with a good compass or with a perfect magnetic needle, so you, sweet Reader, doubtless

---

*Yea, dear Reader — Just as when coming into England .1. must pay .4. pennies and then present .1.'s name to the Mayor & Magistrates, so when entering Matrimony's Kingdome 'tis generally meet to render up goods, & time, & various attentions to certain forms.

prefer to know the true *Wretchedness* of endeavors amidst those dull yellow houses of Jamestowne, with their twig-skeletons half sticking out. In fact she wore the christening-dress which Sir Thomas had gifted unto her. Some kind Ladies taught her how to stiffen it with starch . . .

Now there came to Sir Thomas .1. of the Salvage Werowances for an Ambassador, nam'd *Opachisco,* whose head was in accordance with their idolatry close-shaven on the right and long-locked on the left, & in his hole-bored ears hung a white bone stained scarlet and bloody. With him were .2. of his sons. And he said: I come at Powhatan's pleasure, to witness this marriage.

Perceiving these men, Rebecca came gladly flying, but they regarded her with a mixture of reserve and pity.

It is as Opechancanough told us, said the old man. The Tassantasses have gnawed up your mind, so that you'll serve their turn.

My uncle speaks as he lists. I must not contradict him.

Kocoum waits on your word. What shall I tell him?

That I divorce him, she whispered.

For ever?

Yes, for ever. It is no ruse. And he may have the house and grinding-stone; 'tis the law, and with my new husband I'll have no need of them.

Her husband lurk'd anxiously aside. She went to him, to see what he wanted. Sweating nervously, he said: Rebecca my sweeting, be sure they steal nothing, for I would not have 'em harmed. You know that your people are great thieves, & I heard just now from Sir Thomas that the very .1.st war we had at Jamestowne was when the Werowance of Paspahegh did steal some hatchets . . .

She gaped at him in dibelief.

In a low & childish rush he whispered on: You know how we requited *him.*

Aye. That none of my People will e'er forget. Especially the fashion in which they slew his wife & children. I knew them—

In my youth I saw a woman hang'd for breaking into her Master's house & stealing a flaxen sheet. O, Rebecca, 'twas a most pitiful sight—

She said to him: Think you these great men are yet so poor they'd steal your sheets?

And she turn'd on her heel.

Opachisco presented the groom with a pipe embossed by shark's teeth. Politely, Rolfe bowed & said: *Nowamatamen!* a Salvage word which his bride had taught him, meaning *I must keep yt,* or, *I love yt.*

Sir Thomas, who stood by, now turn'd his dark & watchful eyes upon

Captaine Argoll, & said in a low tone: I gave this *Opachisco* good courtesy
only for the sake of the peace. Be sure of it, Daemon, he's a spy for old
Powhatan.

No doubt, my Lord.

Still, it may be he's come to bring Rebecca her dowry.

I fear not, laugh'd Argull, puckering his lips. For in these semi-Tropickall
Countreys, a man gets no portion with his wife, but rather *buys her* as if she
were a cow!

Damnme! Think you Powhatan will use this occasion to extort more
from us?

He durst not, answered kindly Argoll, for if he doth try it, why, I'll pull
his cedar-bark Palace down around his ears!

And indeed the Salvages never asked Sir Thomas for tuppence. (Rebecca had whispered to 'em 'twas useless.) Moreover, Opachisco (once he
comprehended 'twas English custom) agreed to give her away in the
Jamestown Church, where Reverend Buck did marry them.

For Bridesmaids she had .2. of her Servaunt-girls from her heathen
time. The good Ladies of Henrico had fashion'd her a garland from Virginian creepers.

And so she was led out to be married, *Trarintra-rarara.** Virginian flowers had been strewn e'erywhere. For a twink she longed to flee like a straining deer, & then she no longer cared, & then she remembered her first
marriage, with her hand in Kocoum's as her father broke the beads over
them because Kocoum's father could not be permitted this dignity in
Powhatan's presence. No one would break beads over her this time, she
supposed for her Bride-groom's *Father.* Sir Thomas Dale would scarcely
agree to depart from the Tassantasses' customs to any such degree. All must
go English fashion. For a remembrance, Maister Rolfe gave gloves unto the
men; Rebecca presented them to the women. These gloves were another
gift from Sir Thomas, which sank them deeper into his debt.

Rolfe himself traipsed somewhat bashfully to the Church, like upon
some murtherer followed by a pair of ravens who wail and croak until his
guilt comes out. He feared lest he be sneered at again, for the crime of
Miscegenation. But then he cheered himself by reflecting that, after all,
he was achieving his good fortune. Look how far he'd already profited
himself since the day he'd .1.ˢᵗ gotten number'd 'midst the Undertakers

---

*'Twas so happily politic! For, as Thomas Nashe once wrote, *Fury is a heat or fire, & must be
quench'd with maid's water.*

and Adventurers who'd bide for good or ill within that half-raw Colonie . . . !

Good little *Casca* was there, he who'd help'd Captaine Argull in Pattawomeck so that this wondrous day could happen. No longer wench-chinned, the boy grinned at her, then jerk'd his gaze away, as if he spied some animal amidst the trees. *Reverend Whittaker* was there, of course, for her guidance & support, altho' Reverend Bucke must preach the sermon, since Jamestowne lay so to speak in his Bailiwick.   The *Ancient Planters* were all on hand to wish her well. *Brutus, Cassius, Octavian* & that breed came in as silent as sailing-ships creeping up Virginia's grass-walled rivers. The Salvages scuffed pebbles along the floor of the Church. For them & the rest, Sir Thomas had promised that a hogshead of ale would be opened at the end. Maister Rolfe had already feasted the company on love-wine at his own expense that morning — a gesture as prudent as 'twas GODly.

The Church-bell toll'd. (The bell-pull was near about as long as OKEUS's scalp-lock.) All the grass bowed before the wind as if some invisible Prince were running his carelessly caressing hand down the furry neck of that dog called *Terra*.   As for the English, they likewise bowed their heads; they might as well have been birds nodding their beaks for their marshy livings. Up to the altar now! Argall was all smiles.

Dearly beloved, said Reverend Buck, we are gathered here in the sight of GOD . . .

Maister Rolfe abode on Rebecca's right. In his hand he clutched a ring from his dead wife's hand.

(Brutus! Argoll did whisper-quip. See how comically she's decked out! That frumpy hat of hers, 'tis like unto some nosegay tied to an oxen's horns at May-day . . .

(Lieutenant Turnell sniggered appreciatively at his Master.

(Cassius!

(Aye, Captaine Argall?

(Think you this marriage shall serve the Colonie?

(Captaine, I fancy so, if Rolfe can tie her safe unto him. But if not . . .)

Silence in the Church!   the Marshal cried.

I take thee to be my wedded wife, to have & to hold . . .

They rais'd a CHRIST cross.

Reverend Buck sermonized thus, drawing from the Book of Judges: *They commaunded the children of Benjamin, saying unto them, Go, lie in wait in the vineyards. And if the daughters of Shiloh come there for to*

daunce, then come ye out of the vineyards, & catch you e'ery man his wife,
&c, &c., which all agreed to be most apposite to this occasion.

Then of a sudden Opachisco broke a string of shells over their heads, at
which Rolfe cried out & Soldiers seized the .3. Salvages, fearing harm, but
Rebecca quickly begged them to forbear, which they gladly did, seeing that
'twas but a Salvage custom like unto those of uneducated rustics in England. Then they all laugh'd . . .

* * * * * *

And now the bell did toll. (E'en in far Henrico this day they toll'd the bell
in jubilation at his prize.) She broke a string of beads o'er his head, at which
he smiled tolerantly.

Once the ale was gone, Sir Thomas uncasked some heady muscadine for
all to drink. The Ancient Planters commenced for to break bread o'er their
heads. (Rebecca hath woven treebark basket to gift 'em with, for which cu-
rios they express their laughing thanks.)

Now look you, Rolfe! cried Argall, dipping bread-sops in the wine, bed
your bride full valorously, or by J O V E I'll put horns on you myself!

What shall her jointure be, good Rolfe? dared *Cassius.* Do you have it
all writ down in your accompts?

Maister Rolfe smiled a little wearily. Such jests must be borne with on a
man's wedding-day.

He was safe now. He'd married her in a decent and comely manner.
'Twas his bounden privilege to unite himself with her. But all thro' the
marriage feast he felt affronted by dread. For his Goodwife seemed as flac-
cid as an Yndian bow in hot weather.

* * * * * *

In this lazy little book of mine I borrow wherever I can, to save myself the
trouble of thinking. Herewith, then, a summation of John Rolfe, as written
by one who met him, Ralph Hamor the younger. Hamor thought Maister
Rolfe monstrous steady, as we can see: *No man hath laboured to his power,
by good example there and worthy incouragement into England by his letters, than he hath done, witnes his mariage with* Powhatan's *daughter, one
of rude education, manner barbarous and cursed generation, meerely for the
good and honour of the Plantation* . . .

Read it again: *his marriage with* Powhatan's *daughter, meerely for the
good and honour of the Plantation* . . .

Those may be the saddest words in this book.

* * * * * *

Hearing of this golden union, e'en the *Chickahominies* saw which way the land did lie, and rush'd to become Englishmen & vassals of King James, just as in England herself do prudent rich men pay to get their Sovereign's name engraved on the handles of their ivory-handled kitchen knives. Perfect Argoll help'd 'em to it. (By his forehead he was clearly marked for noble things.) He mustered the men & upped anchor, upped sail. The cold, low, grey ugly river was foamed up with low grass, the horizons swollen here and there with more distant masses of trees. Brown grass & grey-green trees, these form'd the whole World. Somewhere herabouts that twangling little yeoman *John Smith* had gotten captured by Powhatan's desperados. Argall's Soldiers & Sailors accordingly were much afeared of the place. Several of Sweet John's men had gotten roasted to death here, 'twas said. But their Commaunder knew that the Chickahominies were harmless enough now. — Have the treachery on! humm'd Argoll thro' his famous *changeable smile*. We'll make 'em kneel for grace! — Reader, hast thou e'er seen the wrinkles between an *Alligator's* half-closed & sinewy eyes? Ancient Opechancanough was complected thus, as I've said; so too these Chickahominy Elders (who call themselves *Caw-cawwassoughes*); Argull stayed comfortably on his guard 'gainst their malice. Yet (trusting perhaps to his blue-eyed innocency), they covenanted & agreed to pay corn-tribute forever, in exchange for hatchets; and indeed their oath endured for a good **.2.** years, until Sir Thomas Dale sailed home with the Rolfes and some Spanish traitors, whom he did hang on the way. Once he was out of sight the Chickahominies revolted, pretending most insolently to have made their oath only to Sir Thomas, not to his Deputy, a certain *Maister George Yeardley,* who accordingly had to kill **.12.** and take **.12.** prisoner before they again turn'd loyal. Sailing home to Jamestowne with corn-laden boats (**.1.** of which sank), Yeardley's peace-makers chanced upon smiling Opechancanough, who gave them brotherly greeting and swore by the SUN that his good offices had compelled the Chickahominies to peace, so that our credulous English gave him copper and beads. — But let us not dwell on future ills; for the moment, in this year of OUR REDEEMER 1614, the marriage remained a brilliant stroke, which is why Sir Thomas (who kept a pretty wife in London-Towne) did send a lackey to Great Powhatan, demanding to marry another daughter of his, the youngest (of age **.12.** years), whom Powatan had already sold for **.2.** bushels of roanoke shells to a Werowance **.3.** days' marching from here.

He had remov'd to Maskunt-Towne by then, in hopes of being further out of their reach. That of course was fruitless. — Yes, here came the Tassantasses once again with new demands. His Cronoccoes spied their gleaming helms coming through his cornfields. (His wives were making mats out of marsh-reeds.) Slowly they came — O, they were far, far away! Holding a part-formed arrowhead in his left hand, he struck the edge with his wrist-guard, simultaneously squeezing his knees together, and detached another flake of rock. He remained perfect in that craft, at least. How ill it befitted him to be abused by these Tassantasses! But he was weary of fleeing.

Now his wives & children were all home. Ampotoike and Otterniske withdrew themselves to the menstrual lodge. He led the People to the river's edge to feed tobacco to the declining SUN. The Tassantasses were closer, but not much. The MOON arose. A baby began to cry. Yes, here they were. They were shouting for a canoe to bring them, as if they were Werowances here. He dispatched a canoe. To do otherwise was useless. Then he withdrew into his house.

In the quickness of his strategies lay his repose. From his repose grew quickness. He had always conceived his cunningest devices when he hunched in solitude. Now he possessed neither solitude nor cunning, so it seemed. All that remained to him was *caution*. He never forgot how the struggles of a speared sturgeon may drag the fisherman into the water . . .

He sat beneath strings of smoke-dried oysters and mussels, dreading to lose any more of his dignity. Winganuske dared to caress his shoulder; he threw off her hand.

Now the canoemen came into his presence. He asked whether the Tassantasses had presented any pearls, which they denied.

Upon Amonute's forced marriage he'd marked peace by giving them a chain of pearls, which Sir Thomas had promised always to invest upon his messenger's neck in token of truth; yet here they came without it. Doubtless they'd greedily sold the pearls; that was their fashion. Wahunsenacawh smiled bitterly.

What's their mood? he asked the canoemen. Do they come to make trouble, or do they come to annoy me with trifles?

We cannot tell, they said.

He sent his Cronoccoes to bid them wait. Had they been more worthy of his love, he would have come to the shore to meet them. Full slowly he painted himself crimson, and Winganuske set a string of beads around his neck. The MOON was much higher now. He hung a bird-claw in his ear, then powdered his face blue and silver.

When he came to the landing-place at last, he saw that Thomas Savage was with them. This boy had been given him by Captaine Newport; he'd played the spy's part, then run away without leave. As for his own Servaunt, Namontack, whom he'd given them in exchange, he'd never come home. No doubt they'd slain or suborned him.

Furious at this new insult, he approached the Tassantasses with rapid, menacing strides. He grappled his hands around their Werowance's throat, as if he meant to strangle him. Of course there were no pearls.

He led them into his house, with many bowmen following behind. Slowly he seated himself in his accustomed place, on the high bedstead behind the rearmost fire. His most beautiful wives were waiting there to comfort and adorn him — Winganuske at his head, Ashetoiske at his feet.

Sit down, he said. He smoked a pipe with them. He'd not honor them with a dance.

And how does my brother Sir Thomas Dale?

He does well, the Tassantasses said.

And my daughter and unknown son? How do they live, love and like?

Rebecca is so contented that she would not live again with you, they replied most insultingly.

Wahunsenacawh laughed, concealing his hate. He dared not do to them as he'd done to Captaine Radclyffe.

He'd told Uttamattomakkin to search everywhere in the Secret World, to find some weapon against the Tassantasses. But Uttamattomakkin said that OKEUS refused to allow this. Moreover, OKEUS had said: *She is lost.* Wahunsenacawh had no recourse. But he'd never forget the sweet smell of her head when she was his little baby . . .

Now tell me the cause of your coming, he said, percase a trifle curtly.

Immediately they began insisting that he annul the new marriage, so that the girl might be given to Sir Thomas.

Closing his eyes, he imagined his daughter's fate as the wife of Sir Thomas. He imagined what the Werowance of Nansemond would say, did he revoke the promise. These Tassantasses had no care for him.

He said quietly: I love my daughter as my life, and though I have many children, I delight in none so much as she. If I cannot often behold her I cannot possibly live. And how could I behold her did she live with you? For I have resolved upon no terms to put myself in your hands.

The Tassantasses sat woodenly. Belike they were too stupid e'en to feel the sting of his words.

Therefore, he continued, urge me no further. I need no additional as-surance of my brother's friendship; and for my part he hath Amonute as my pledge for so long as she lives. When she dies, he shall have another daugh-ter. Now you are weary, and I sleepy; thus we end.

The next day he came to the lodge where these Tassantasses had guested, and feasted them well. But already they presented new demands. Spying .1. of their Countreymen who lived with him as his servant, they asked most commandingly that he go back to Jamestowne with them.

Wahunsenacawh said: You have .1. of my daughters, and I am *content* (this word he uttered with sour irony), but you cannot see any of your men with me, but you must have him away, or break friendship.

The Tassantasses persisted, so he said: If you needs must have him, you shall go home without guides, and if any evil befall you, thank yourselves.

To this the Tassantasses replied: Without guides, then, we'll go, but here's somewhat for you to chew upon, great Poughwaton: Should we re-turn not well, you must expect a revenge.

At this, Wahunsenacawh withdrew himself in a rage, but Opechan-canough, *He Whose Soul Is White,* was there visiting. He never showed himself to the Tassantasses if that could be avoided. He whispered: Elder brother, speak mildly with them, and swallow your rage, which by OKEUS I swear inflames me as much as you. They have been striking us for o'er .10. years. Be patient, dear brother, and I promise someday we shall kill them all.

And so Wahunsenacawh returned to the Tassantasses, for supper to be their most civil host; and on their departure requested them to send him a shaving-knife, fishhooks, and other such. To each of them he gave a fine buckskin in remembrance, and by them sent .1. apiece to Amonute and her husband.

The Tassentasses said: What became of that knife we gave you?

The Tassantasses said: Have you no tribute to send to our high Werowance?

(Well, let that be as it would be. He had his women and his fire now; he was old. Let Opechancanough guard the People.)

They said: When will you come to Jamestowne? 'Tis your duty, great Powhatan . . .

＊　＊　＊　＊　＊　＊

In the rafters over his sleeping platform he'd concealed the cornhusk doll which Amonute once played with, the one he'd made for her. Now it was

brittle and rotten. It made him unutterably sad. He threw it onto the rubbish heap. And after that, never would he meet another Tassantasse again.

Nor did he and his daughter see each other, not ever. But don't mind
that, dear Reader — for Goodmistress Rolfe, they say, hath gotten her
piety's full reward: Her belly grows broad & round-roofed like unto an Yndian house.

THE GRAMMAR OF PILLAGERS (1613)

Yes, Virginia in the 1970s is close in spirit to Virginia of the 1670s: easygoing, friendly, old-fashioned, pleasure-loving, conventional, slow to rouse, moderate in religion, fond of privacy, respectful of precedent.

PARKE ROUSE, JR., *Virginia: A Pictorial History* (1975)

*S*ee Argall in *Canada,* which is a province of North Virginia now turn'd illegally French. — We'll pluck 'em down upon their knees! he chortles. Argoll *will* get his object. — Between **.9.** and **.10.** of the clock afore noon he spies *Saint-Sauveur,* a smallish Habitation of **.4.** French tents. He ups the red flag. His Trumpeteer blows *Trarintrararara!* Gunbarrels waggle carefully in the loopholes; then the ordnance begins to fire. E'ery concussion hath its echo, which the half-deaf Sailors can scarcely hear. But they spy their Captaine's lips a-fluttering in a soundless song. Smoke rises from grated scuttles & oer'hangs the ship. The Frenchmen seek to fire back, but they know not the use of their own cannon, for their Commaunder's run away!

Brutus hath a grin glued on his sadly pasty face. He hath swiped Pokahuntiss's pearl chain from when she was prisoner'd in the Gun-roome. He wears it secretly inside his clothes. (Just as pokeweed root smells excellently bitter-clean, so the idea of that young Princesse held captive afore his eyes doth perfume his fancy! In the sleepy darkness he loves to run those pearls betwixt his fingers.) Now he makes atonement for the theft by o'erseeing *Nero* (the Gunner), to ensure each murthering-ball's dead-aim'd.

Ha! A Frenchman falls slain by our blast! Well encounter'd, you broken animals! Give 'em another! Blood runs riot from a Frenchman's skull. 'Tis a shrewd leake!

Grace to peaceful Argoll, **.2.** perish outright, a **.3.**[rd] the next day, as meanwhile **.4.** more lie a-screeching in their own blood. They surrender. Argull loves himself.

He lands, commaunding Brutus to batten down all the prisoners 'midst the bilge, wherein he did once pickle Pocahontas. O'er the Habitation flies a standard of the *Fleur dy Lys,* which resembles the triple-mounded sub-lobe of a bloodroot flower. Argoll snatches it down.

A wounded Frenchman who can acquit himself of the King's English gabbles out: Your strike was unjustly misorder'd, & JESUS hears our grievances!

How sad! wept Argoll. Now I fall unto the shamefullest of pomps — or is it blissful disgrace? Domitian! Cassius, get me Domitian!

Here I am, dear Captaine!

And so you are. Now hark my words. Being Marshal, you're *Jurisprudence's vessel.* Upon this recreant I pronounce sentence of — what shall I pronounce?

Doom, Captaine!

'Tis affectionately wisht. Well, flog him senseless. Then chuck him in the hold with these other rebels.

Aye, aye. Come, lads! Who's got a rope's end for this knave?

With all the Frenchmen out of sight, he now enters the Generall's tent, giving his Roman Nobles full leave to pillage the others. (Look, dear Captaine! They sleep on goosedown pillows thick & soft as an English maiden's hair!) He sees a Popish Cross, but leaves it alone for the time being. He doesn't want the Commaunder's suspicions to be guided unto anything when he at length returns. What game's Argall a-gambling at, then? Oho! Here's what his *Policy* doth crave! He picks the lock of the Jesuits' treasure-chest, & lightfingers their commission utterly away. All the rest he forbears, e'en the golden livre-coins so ripe for pilferage & spending. He kens how to compass his Undertakings into guileful innocency. Down, chest-lid! Hold a funeral for the expir'd commission! Sole mourner, he mouths a hymn: *Red sky at morning, Sailor's warning.* Then he waits, playing *Security* with Octavian & Cassius. He waits all day, & all night.

Brutus hath taken Casca unto his charge, to teach him how to comprise an ambuscado, in case these Papists should come arm'd. — No fear, Reader! Such unworldly factionalists as they can but scantly feed themselves, let alone mount a peril unto true Christians! When their crestfallen Commaunder returns from his birch-barr'd lurking-place at last for to make submission, why then, Brutus lies asleep, Casca's disappointed to have no opportunity for ambush after all, & Argall winks his smiling tooth. He sings. He hums. He commences for to jest.

No doubt you enjoy letters-patent to this Countrey, he says, with his hands upon his hips. For, to be sure, you Papists strike me as most excellently scrupulous Gentlemen.

Monsieur La Saussaye makes haste to satisfy his demand, opening the treasure-chest for to save his people with a proof of their innocency signed by the Notary-Royal Notary of Paris. Howbeit — *sacré bleu!* the commission's vanisht!

How now, sirrah! cries Argoll in a heat. Are you imposing on us? You gave me to understand that you have an enactment from your King, & cannot produce evidence of it! Where's the parchment? Have you wiped your ass with it, you *Salvage?* Did you boil it for soup? You & your Colonists are *outlawful Pirates,* e'ery .1. of you, deserving death, which indeed my Maister, Sir Thomas Dale, hath commaunded me to give you —

Of a sudden he pauses, pretending to be kind.

But I'm much astonished that you others, you Jesuits, who are commonly regarded as Gentlemen of *Conscience and Religion,* abide here nonetheless in the company of these selfsame outlaws, Pirates & slack-souled French Gallants, who are men without law or honor. Certainly there has been some fault in the losing of your letters . . .

Sighing, he gives the commaund to burn e'erything. When the French Generall begins for to pray & beseech, he murmurs: You blow a great gale of wind!

Captaine Argoll, surely your good soul hath—

Dog, you heard me. Now would you feel the weight of my foot? I'm within .2. leagues of hanging you all!

When their Habitation's razed utterly unto ashes, he arrests some of those worms for to bring to James-Towne (where .3. will perish of sickness), maroons others on the sea, & leaves the remainder to subsist on Yndian charity.*

Some rascals do beg him not to abandon them thus to starve. He laughs.

Then he raises anchor, blandly singing.

✳ ✳ ✳ ✳ ✳ ✳

See Argoll at Jamestowne with his .14. captive Frenchmen. Safely toggling them within the Watch-house which Sir Thomas Gates had builded .2. years since, he begs leave to call upon yᵉ Governor.

Dear Captaine Argull, how well you've improv'd my heart by this! How dangerously had they entrench'd themselves?

Many thanks for your commendation. Nay, they were too dull in their strategems to pay us much harm . . .

---

*So I have told in the Second Dream.

Aye, well, their dullness shall not excuse 'em. Foreign traitors! My gallows stand ready for duty.

Good Lord, I'll fix the halters round their throats myself! But stay a twink! See how I've tamed 'em! If I snap my fingers *thus,* they'll make atonement for their idolatrous rebellion . . . Father Biard, come you hither!

Yea, Captaine Argall, doubtless your Governor longs to hear my adventures—

He longs for to strangle you, blockhead! Now quick! Wouldst thou preserve thy black-gown'd mummery of a life, & betray all t'other Habitations in Canada unto us?

For what purpose?

Why, for the purpose of our burning & pillaging 'em, of course! Now speak up quickly, for I would haste unto that business.

May it please the LORD, was the Jesuit's reply, that all the sins therein committed shall be consumed in the burning.

At this, Sir Thomas grew tempered unto mirth. He congratulated Argall's genius. The prisoners were reprieved. After that, you should have seen 'em eat out of Argull's hand! Weighing anchor & putting to sea in the name of GOD, Argull repaired with all speed back to Canada, guided by Father Biard,* & easily burn'd up .2. more French Colonies! *For whom the* LORD *loveth He correcteth,* &c.   (When he gets back to London-Towne, of course, he'll to go on his trial. But he's *Argull*; he's acting under orders; so they'll laugh it all off, & the French must go away remedyless . . .)

When all was ashes, he return'd unto where he did .1.ˢᵗ assault his enemies, & there dismantled the sole object remaining: a tall Popish Cross! Then on this spot he hang'd a Sailor for some unknown misdemeanor. The Jesuit prisoners were horrified to see the place thus desecrated; Argull said to 'em: Be thankful that I muzzled my Governor's restraint, good Fathers, else you'd likewise be a-dangle-dancing here! Then he flew away, with whirring dense-rigged wings.

* * * * * *

---

*About our liberator Father Biard did later write to Rome, in strangely glowing accents — but with Argoll e'erything's strange: *Certainly this said Argall has shown himself such that we desire him to have an opportunity of serving a better cause, and .1. in which his true nobility of heart may show itself, not in the ruin but in the support of honest men.*

See Argall landing at *Manhatas* *Island* in Hudson's River, where the Dutch hath erected .4. houses. — O, but do we truly see him? His ravishment of Pocahontas is attested; likewise his ruination of French Canada. But now he commences for to glimmer away again unto his unpetrified darkness. Reader, what can I tell you? I have at hand a letter from Charles T. Gehring of the New Netherland Project, which is an exercise in translation credited to the New York State Library. *Dear Mr. Vollmann,* he writes (March y^e .9.th, 1993), *This is a quick letter in response to your request for information on Samuel Argall's visit to New Netherland in 1613. As you will see by the enclosed pages from volume 4 of I.N.P. Stokes'* Iconography of Manhattan Island, *Argall's story about seeing Dutch on Manhattan in 1613 is a baseless fabrication. I know of no historians today who give any credence to Argall's 1613 experience. Unfortunately, there are works such as Fiske's* Dutch and Quaker Colonies in America *(1890) that use Argall's story in their narrative as if it were based on truth.*

Not based on truth? Reader, how could you or I e'er believe Argoll not to be e'erworthily himself? So let's continue the tale.

The Dutch hath erected .4. houses, as I said. — How Argoll blusters! He names 'em *Villains & inhuman miscreants.* But he cannot shout *Ho, Brutus!* for Brutus is presently bearing the Jesuits home unto England. No matter; good *Cassius* shall deputize Argull's grinning teeth! Summonsing their pretended *Governor* to him, he demands to know by what right they've taken root here. — Excellency, 'tis my mission to expel you & other alien intruders! he explains, enjoying himself to his uttermost. — I've done just that in North Virginia — d'ye hear? — and by the true Meridian I swear I'll efface you next, CHRIST be my witness!

But be reasonable, Mynheer; our late Henryk Hudson —

Your Hudson? Wasn't he pickl'd up unto sanctity within an English womb? So help me, Cassius, I know not what to do with this fine Gentleman! Pray burn his e'ery Undertaking, dear Captaine!

Graciously spoken. But put by your torch. — Nay, dear Excellency, you lie most nobly. Maister Hudson was a *Henry* and no *Henryk,* & therefore his discoveries belong to King James. Don't assemble his parts in your image, man; he'll *ne'er* be your Captaine Fortune! Now, make quick to answer: — do you submit, or do you not?

Ja, ja, we submit unto Virginia . . .

*Manhattain.

But they never paid any customs or tribute. No matter. 'Twas *Tick, tick & tick again;* in good time their claims would be extirpated. Anyhow, he meant soon to begone from Virginia utterly. He was now getting treble-rich from pillage & the Yndian trade; once a few more years had dropt, why, he'd tack about & land off . . .

* * * * * *

See him serving rum unto a Salvage (.1.ˢᵗ discover'd by Sweet John) who's call'd the *Laughing King*. Through his good offices, e'erworthy Argall forms a trade with all the Salvage tribes on the Eastern Chesapeacke, in order for to cut them off from Powhatan's Empire. They're mazed, poleaxed, stupefied. They're roll'd up under his arm. He mocks 'em in courteous song. He sluppers up their pearls & peltries. He's fulfill'd in e'erything. He kisses the chocolate cheeks of evening.

III

THE GOLDEN NUMBER

OR,

*HOW VIRGINIAN TIDES
BECAME ACCOMPTABLE TO
THE CLOCK*

THE GRAMMAR OF WIVES, .2.ND PART (1615–1616)

> Come, boyes, Virginia longs till ye share the rest of her maiden-head.
> GEORGE CHAPMAN, BEN JONSON and JOHN MUSTIN (1605)

*S*ee (from behind the window of an ornate frame whose metal is the deadened gold of autumn leaves) the darling *Pocahontas*. She sits looking out at us with a gaze of barely lowered mildness, while her little boy in his white ruffled shirt offers the same gaze, altho' barely upraised as he shelters between her arm & breast, holding her delicate hand in both of his. She does not draw him in to her because that would have spoiled the geometry of portrait, the .2. calmly lost faces arrayed side by side.

All agreed the child was handsome. (For yes, just as in Lincoln-Towne the Baker must prick his mark into the bread he's made, for the sake of accomptability, so Maister Rolfe found it most convenient to inscribe in his new wife that holy signature call'd *Progeny*.) By the time the portrait was painted (if indeed 'twas ever painted from life, which I misdoubt), the mother was finishing her life. G O D forbid we feel sorrow; she'd attain'd to the true knowledge of C H R I S T ! Her maidenhead had been shar'd to its uttermost. *Behold, thou art fair, my beloved* (saith the Scriptures), yea, pleasant; *also our bed is green.* Aye, dearling, a green grave shall be thy bed. Never mind; e'en Argoll shall also become dust.

Her dark hair cuts across her forehead in .2. widening diagonals before it falls behind her shoulders; beneath her Indian cheekbones her face narrows again, so that it seems she has a diamond face, in which her eyes are so meek and brown as to cut me to the heart (the boy's eyes, however, are brightly black). Beneath those shadowed eyes, her rather homely nose is similarly cut by shadow; her mouth smiles a little, but the longer I look at her portrait the sadder I conceive her to be, unless it's simply that (as would be logical) her illness already shows in her face as in the darkness around it, on it and in the heavy shadows round her neck, that Englishwoman's neck from which hangs the pearl necklace which her father apocryphally sent her at her .2.nd marriage, its white gleam matched forlornly by the glisterings of her earrings; then the widening angle of her shoulders and the narrowing cut of her pale red dress forms another diamond — because she's all diamond, the *Nonpareil of Virginia,* come to stay for a pawn!

Fraudulent simulacrum she may be (like unto that Caucasian angel of her Church-yard monument). No matter. She's tamed as is her original! She stares out, sick, gentle and queenly, & her son stares out with the guarded regality of children, & they wait, both of them, to offer themselves. Just as a dog when devouring some trifle leaves a puddle of spittle behind, so the fever which gobbled her life left an oozy puddle of sweat for her to lie cold in. But, after all, as she remarked to her husband from her deathbed: 'Tis enough that the child liveth.

*   *   *   *   *   *

When he was born, our aforesaid Goodmistress Rolfe insisted on cleansing him in the River James, altho' her husband came out against it (for, being on the verge of getting appointed *Secretary & Recorder of ye Colonie,* he conceiv'd it unmeet to hew to the customs of Salvages). They mock'd his manhood, that he failed to rule his wife. GOD knows, they mocked him in all things else! But, Reader, isn't scorn sometimes envy's earnest-mark? In such a case, there must be something to be envied. I seem to remember how Sweet John got o'erclouded by dissensions, for that he'd usurped a Gentleman's place, ignoring his own base birth. Maister Rolfe, who was somewhat better born, found many of neighbors turn'd against him, for that he'd become a King's son-in-law. But now to the counter-argument: Where scorn's most freely express'd, the expressers fear no punishment. Hence the Convict in the pillory, the Queen of *Paspahegh's* children facing Soldiers' guns, fair Virginia herself, & other such powerless presences, suffer scorn more publicly than doth King James. So it could have been quite simply that John Rolfe, while having few friends, was insufficiently powerful to be fear'd (as a Prince should be if he cnnot be lov'd). No doubt his now certain ascension to the office of *Secretary & Recorder of ye Colonie* indicated some regard for his character; yet perhaps there'd emerge some drudge-work in that sinecure, so that the general conviction of his aptitude for it might not have been so great a compliment as appeared upon the surface. However all that might have been (& we shouldn't forget that when our Planters get into a drunken humor, they slander all souls, merely to speed the time), the fact remained that the .1.ˢᵗ year or .2. of Maister Rolfe's marriage was spent in vanquishing the willfulness of his wife, she who used to turn naked cartwheels at her own pleasure. The months she'd passed at Reverend Whittaker's had already taught her that others' wishes must come before her own Salvage inclinations. Thus the possession of those last shreds of her pride's maidenhead prov'd a brief if not entirely pleasant task.

Sweeting, do forbear, said he. 'Twould be perilous to the child, for remember that he doth contain my more fine-compos'd blood . . .

When he tried to enforce his will, she grew hysterical, as women will, so that in the end he had to humor her (altho' at darklins, when the neighbors wouldn't see). But when she sought to bedaub the baby with walnut oil & red pucoon paste, he said her nay. Here he'd not back down, knowing his protestation to be well advised. Rebecca raged. He doubted him not her passions would cool, as they did. 'Twas wrong for an English infant, to appear thus. Rebecca wept: *Love you not me?* He smooth'd her hair.

Next, her father sent her bear-grease with which to anoint the child against lice, a practice to which Maister Rolfe at last consented, for it discolored not the skin to a Salvage tawniness. Rebecca thanked him & gave him a kiss. What did he conclude about that lineament? Well, in truth it did ameliorate his little son's sufferings, so that he wailed less, and learned to sleep through the night. Maister Rolfe took to using it himself. These Yndians did ken a few good tricks.

Not long after, Rebecca asked him to make a cradleboard for her greater conveniency; then she could dangle little Thomas from a nearby branch while she weeded the *Tobacco* fields. Maister Rolfe, cherishing her despite her baser quality, would have aceded even to this, but Reverend Whittaker bent his ear, to the effect that it was not seemly. We were not Naturalls, to hang our children from trees as if they were mere fruits! Rolfe nodded, repenting over his weakness. Nervously, Rebecca brushed a hayseed from her skirt.

* * * * * *

She is not quite as strong as the writings of Captaine Smith gave me to believe, said Rolfe to himself, while his goodwife sat weeping. (Like all the Salvages, she smelled of wood-smoke.) — That's too bad; 'tis really too bad. But I shall persist in religious fear, as I promised Sir Thomas Dale —

She turned her back. He arose, touched her not. At the threshold he said: Rebecca, my sweeting, I doubt not of your timely acceptance.

*   *   *   *   *   *

He'd become somewhat well to do, and had likewise enriched the Colonie through a trade in *Hawtorinkanusfkes,* which are black fox-skins. O yes, he was getting his reward for laboring in the LORD's vineyard! He had his good content. Somewhat to his own amaze, he saw the gloams & glisters of truly spectacular wealth not far ahead. His own labor had been careful, steady, & not devoid of shrewdness. Rebecca had assisted him yet more industriously than he'd expected (altho' that should have been predicted, so many Old Planters smiling told him, for amongst Salvages the women work unstintingly in the corn-fields, while the men do little but chase game like unto great Lords — or plot rebellions against our English). Truly she'd been a comfort. Fertile as the very ground, she'd conceiv'd before the .2.nd month of their marriage. He supposed they'd produce many more offspring in good time. She'd borne the child in the merest twink — & with hardly a whimper whilst she was deliver'd. (He could still remember the screams of his late wife Anne in Bermuda. Altho' he'd squirreled a piece of iron into her childbed for protection against DEVILS, that hadn't serv'd. When she'd perisht, my Lord Del La Warr had kindly consented to shoot off ordnance at her funeral.) Rebecca was sturdy, loyal, resolute. She prayed beside him morn & even. (Of course she'd already grown that habit, for e'en Salvages do pray at similar times, altho' only to the Sunne.) She weeded their property as rapidly as any rusticke wench from his own Countie. The hot Sunne harmed her not. Moreover, unlike Anne, she never complained, no matter how wearisome the task. Now *that* was a wonder in a woman! Her proposals about *Tobacco*-curing had prov'd mostly sound, for which he congratulated his own choice of spouse.

Sometimes her half-sisters or aunts came to help her in the fields — due to her father's filthy polygamous habits she had so many relations, particularly female ones, that Maister Rolfe resisted trying to catalogue them; but they worked rapidly & well — no matter that they went about nearly naked, a fact about which Rebecca had prevailed upon him to keep silent. In short, he enjoyed not only the presence of a number of unpaid Servauntmaids (many of them his wife's former "Courtiers," if we can allow Salvages so august a dignity), but also the *absence* of any hostile lurkers, for no Yndian would conceive of harming Princesse Pocahontas. Therefore, his holdings throve like none other.

Near every week, Yndians came to his house to chaffer their commodities for beads. He misdoubted him not 'twas a great comfort to them that he never took advantage of their brutish innocency. Seeing how his productions did flourish like unto the Biblical *Jacob's,* the Governor himself, & other Notables of the Counsell, had begun requesting that Maister Rolfe carry out their own trade, in exchange for a commission. Smiling, Maister Rolfe acceded. He thought to himself: *This is the service* IEUSUS CHRIST *requireth of his best Servaunts.* Everyone agreed him to be a good & faithful Steward. This circumstance (which I'd be unchristian to call a *Policy*) brought further benefits — not least, the consolation of his own goodness; &, not most, more property. If he had as yet little ready cash, no matter; he trusted that GOD would scarcely disremember him. Moreover, *Tobacco's* price had swollen to **.59.** pounds sterling for **.5.** hundred pounds, for the Doctors of London-Towne could no longer deny how sovereign a healer was that herb against *Ulcers,* the *Clap, Melancholy* & suchlike ills. 'Twas a considerable annoyance to the Spanish trade, & therefore a blow struck against Popishness. All hail *King Tobacco!* (GOD speed you, my Lord Vppówoc!) Even young lads & lassies in Lincoln-Towne now smoked pipes of it, such was the craze. (By 1696 it would be down to a pound and **.75.** shillings. Maister Rolfe was then sitting safely 'mongst the celestial Angels.)

For these reasons, Jamestowne, walled and moated like unto an old English Towne, had commenced to confine the Rolfes, as if 'twere a rotten little seedpod which could no more contain the sprout. (The other thing was that Sir Thomas Dale continued passing strict; 'twould be more pleasant to 'scape his grim shadow.) The new husband realiz'd he could dwell anywhere, Rebecca being his passport to tranquility in the very midst of Salvages. True Adventurer that he was — as much of **.1.** indeed as any Gentleman who drained and enclosed the Fens of Lincolnshire — he inspired himself not only thro' his mounting wealth, but likewise thro' the prospect of further self-praise. More than **.300.** Englishmen now dwelt in Virginia, building new Outposts, Plantations & Hundreds throughout that wilderness. Rolfe would fain choose his own domicile likewise — and doubtless Rebecca preferred to escape the shadow of her betters.

Regarding their intimacies, he lived likewise full contented. Having braced himself for the inconveniencies of marrying a *Strange wife* (so the Bible call'd her), he found them to be not much greater than those of any cohabitation. Rebecca lov'd him, as she did confess. She continued as ardent to live out life with him as if there were no going back. If she remain'd unripe in her mind, well, that would pass. Passing changeable she sometimes seemed, but weren't all women rul'd (as his *Almanacke* did say) by the Moone? No doubt she owned cause to thank him for releasing her from durance at Parson Whittaker's (for Maister Rolfe was hardly so stupid as to miss the favor which his proposal had proferr'd). He was satisfied. He'd devote himself to her care for as long as they both surviv'd. 'Twould form his greatest pleasure to see her grow in Christian understanding. Look how far she'd already outstepped her former bounds! Reverend Frankwell had said to him privily 'twas a wonder how earnest Rebecca remained in her faith, clinging to it almost with desperate execution. — Methinks the loss of her former life hath taught her the vanity of the world. 'Twould be well, Sir, if in your presently flourishing circumstances your soberness kept you to the remembrance of the same.

Reverend Frankwell sometimes spoke in barbs, so for a time Rolfe turn'd this saying over in his mind, to discover whether he was being accused of slackness. But in that respect he already watched himself, in all his Undertakings.

To be safe, next Sunday he made a larger offering to the Church.

On Sunday night she was giving the baby suck. The little eyes closed; the lips twitched slackly at the nipple. The father approach'd.

Rebecca, he said, are you contented that now you must depend on me?

Aye, she said, smiling a little.

And you comprehend how well I love you?

I comprehend your affection's degree quite well enough, she replied with that same strange smile.

They were not yet .1. — no, not even now. Reverend Frankwell said that unity came not all at once in marriage, particularly when somebody wed an outlandish woman. He must be patient with her. But Maister Rolfe thought he knew somewhat of the matrimonial state. Betwixt him and Anne there had occasionally arisen differences each as steep as the hill on which stands Dover Castle. But betwixt him and Rebecca he'd instead discovered a scorched place like unto those black & sinister clearings which remain after we've burnt a Salvage town — hot place, empty place, reeking of anger, guilt & murther.

I thank you, he went on (almost ashamedly), for our child.

Thomas had fallen utterly asleep. She laid him down in his cradle.

Truth to tell, husband, a cradleboard such as my People use would benefit me.

You ask'd me that before—

And you denied to please me.

Pitying her with all his heart, he knew not why, he said: Then by my faith you shall have .1. this very day.

But Reverend Frankwell did warn—

We'll say nothing to him.

Tears started to his eyes when she thanked him.

He went out & trimmed down a pine plank to size, boring a privy-hole in the middle, so that she could easily clean the child whenever he beshat himself. He'd seen how it was all done, when he visited his mother-in-law's reed-wall'd lodge. (He misliked it there.) Had he been o'er-strict with his wife (or *.2.nd self* as I should say)? Why then, he'd serve her more earnestly. The work went easily & well. One thing he lov'd about Virginia was that all things flourisht here. The climate being hot & moist like unto a womb, seed sprouted up from the mold near as quickly as a musket-shot. Any task to which he turn'd his hand had the like success. (Reader, 'twas merely on account of his youth & happy marriage, I'm sure.) That hole was augur'd out in a twink. Then he bepierced the board with other smaller apertures through which Rebecca could thread the lashings to bind the child on. Powhatan had gifted him with yet another deerskin, from which he trimmed some long soft laces, superior for this purpose to English twine. But the .2. holes at the top, from which the device would be hung, those he laced with some of Captaine Argall's stoutest hempen cord, for he feared lest the board come suddenly unmoored from ceiling or branch. Indeed, this was the reason he'd ever opposed the device. Reverend Frankwell's disapproval had likewise been but careful common sense, not the dark-sighted prejudice Rebecca deemed it. It still seemed to him near unnatural, to leave one's own babe all a-dangle like unto a felon on the gallows at Ty-burn Tree. But he could not gainsay the practicality of it. Rebecca's relations would be pleas'd (poor ignorant creatures). Moreover, seeing how Thomas did smile wide-eyed at the World as he hung and swayed so high, the father brimm'd with a happiness he scarce dared express.

✻ ✻ ✻ ✻ ✻ ✻

Clearing his throat, he said: Rebecca, my sweeting, I pray you swaddle him not so in English company.

As you will, husband.

Especially when Reverend Frankwell comes to call—

I must obey you, she replied, looking away.

Look you, Rebecca, he said somewhat sharply, are you discontented with my ways?

Have no fear, John.

He leapt up — he scarce knew why, as she'd comported herself in utter seemliness (well, mayhap the Mosquitors had been tormenting him) — and inquired of her: When you speak the name *John,* think you of me, or of him you call'd *Sweet John?*

She flushed. The baby shrieked (he was hanging on the cradleboard level with his father's face), but she paid no heed. Maister Rolfe confess'd that his voice had surely blared. 'Twas too late to whisper now. He felt shamed, to see how the babe did fear—

Well? he said.

Her wide face, with its bad skin & strange-shapen Yndian eyes, now struck him as passing loathsome.

Why must I endure this? she said quietly enough

You cannot choose now what you'd endure or not—

'Tis enough, .1. would think, that for all the help I gave your Tassan-tasses when they starv'd—

Come, come, Rebecca. 'Twas never as perilous here as that—

You were not here! If you believe me not, inquire of your Ancient Planters—

Nay, I grant you help'd us somewhat—

— That you .1. & all abuse me, naming me *lickerish wench* because 'tis not my People's custom to clothe their children 'fore they're ripe, & so when I, being but a girl—

I never call'd you—

'Tis enough your *Captaine Argoll* did knap me away, and how he did behave toward me I—

'Tis true, then, that he dishonored you? I've often feared it—

Dishonor's as you would define, merely so you can tame it from your thoughts.

Rebecca, I comprehend you not.

And what needs your delicacy on my account? she continued, raising her voice. You know full well you unhusbanded me, but e'en good Rev-erend Frankwell, who teaches that we must avoid divorce, cared not that I was already married when you took me. Does it grieve you, *Husband,* that I see your conveniency?

My heart had stronger reasons.

I hope it did, to cuckold my husband Kocoum, who's shamed and whom I'll never see more—

Whom do you love then?

My father. He—

That subtle old Salvage did—

He did as you did by him.

Whom do you love?

In truth I know not, nor who I am, nor what life I live, this life you *bought.* Stronger reasons, you say! GOD's wounds, I hope so!

Rebecca, use not OUR REDEEMER's name in that wise, for 'tis a sin.

O, and who taught me sin? And of which words do you pretend my ignorance? When your Colonists laugh before my very face in Henrico, which was wrested from my father, & when they make sport of my father's wives, whom I—

But those are of the vulgar sort, who—

— And when the Ancient Planters crow that in my girlhood days, I but playing in innocency of *sin,* they glutted their eyes on my Secret—

Who says that to you? I promise you I'll—

Some name it my *quim,* & others my *snatch,* while Argoll says my *cunt,* & my—

Rebecca, forbear!

Do I say it all rightly? Or doth my English continue defective, as our neighbors e'er tell me? Yet they speak not my language, nor do you—

Peace!

And now they've named me *the Tobacco Trull!* Think you I ken not what that signifies?

There is no help for your temper now, I see that. 'Tis passing tedious—

Kocoum would have avenged such slanders.

Then go to him.

E'en Captaine Smith, for all he was a liar—

Do tell, Rebecca. Now I see that for so long as you wish to chastise me, I must endure it; I will heartily accept it as a GODly tax imposed upon me . . .

Husband, I would ask you somewhat.

What would you?

Is Captaine Smith dead, as they say?

He—

Is he dead?

* * * * * *

LORD knows, he had taken advantage of her. He'd always known it. But he'd buried the knowledge in a grave. Yet it knapped upon its gabled coffin-roof, which was his heart-wall, and the only way to untune himself from that knocking was to devote himself to her without scruple, amending his affection & himself. She spoke true. He could not protect her from insult. What she suffered secretly he was unable to imagine. But if he continued to improve his position they'd dare laugh at her no more. It rankled him that they would abuse her thus, when she'd brought 'em naught but blessings. But that she amus'd the Parish he admitted did also affront *his* pride. Sometimes her presence shamed hm. What was he supposed to do? His guests sometimes look'd on her strangely, staying for but a little while, then hasting themselves away. How much Rebecca comprehended he'd never known until now. He long'd more than e'er to carry her back unto the wilderness which was her natural element. There her naivety would 'scape all censures. But did he settle out too far, then how could he conveniently be *Secretary & Recorder of yᵉ Colonie?*

Toward little Thomas his love flower'd entirely unconstrained, because Thomas possessed as yet no memory in which to engrave his faults, whereas his presence in Rebecca's heart — nay, call her *Pocahontas* — was as a festering Colonie which did rankle, & blight, & overgrow itself into grief. How could he appease her now, save with service and silence?

* * * * * *

He prayed: What should I do? I beseech you, GOD.

But GOD prov'd like unto OKEUS; He answered not.

* * * * * *

He went to her and said: I cannot bear it if you hold me disgraced. I *must* learn now, Rebecca, how painfully your soul dispraises me.

I dispraise you not. You've cared for me right loyally.

Thanks for that, sweeting, for I would not be uncharitable—

And if English compulsion raped me into your bed, she continued with a sarcastic smile, well, neither did my father ask me my mind, when he wed me to Kocoum.

Sorrowfully, he laid his hand upon her shoulder and inquired: *Love you not me?*

O, we get on well enough.

* * * * * *

All wise men agreed in despising those who wed for love. Yet he still hoped to discover love growing into their marriage like unto *Tobacco* seeds sprouting in the seedbed. (Well, of course love was there.)

He'd been told that no matter what the lips say, the hearts of those who live together beat in transparency to each other. If that was true, then her quiet rage revealed some counter-ugliness in him. What was it? Had they not both sought advantage from this union? Moreover, this principal of mutual responsibility could hardly be true as a general law; else any husband-poisoner's passionate hate must prove justified merely because it existed. For that matter (to extend the rule unto absurdity), until Argoll's famous wench-knapping, from which Maister Rolfe had so handsomely benefitted, the Salvages hereabouts had declined to reconcile themselves with the English, save by force & threat of force; yet what claims could their feathertopped Werowances possibly own, to commit all their sneaking murtherousness? So Rolfe reassured himself, & was soon amended. Yet, just as the Slaughterman bends his well-sharpened falchion 'gainst the victim's breast, so his own ever-swelling conviction that he'd done wrong unto her immediately began to re-oppress him. He dared not speak of it, not e'en to Reverend Frankwell. Rebecca perhaps imagined that he went about encased in a brigandine armor of sullenness, but the iron plates whose weight and bulk did alienate him were comprised of the metal call'd *Sadness*.

Calm-eyed, his Goodwife tied little Thomas unto the cradle board.

* * * * * *

The sun shone through the trees like an orange gourd. 'Twas the month of May — prudent season for transplanting seedlings of *Tobacco*. His Almanacke said 'twas best to do it when ye Moone was in Taurus or Aquarius ... Rolfe now stood legally seized of a certain parcel of land in the Countrey of Toppahannah* near James Cittie. Many new manses & hot dreary plantations were springing up there; farmers empaled all the land they desired, & ye Salvages kept silent, for, as the Bible saith, *God judgeth the righteous, & He is angry with the wicked e'ery day.* Two years since, when his Goodwife (or *Sweeting* as he call'd her) was knapped away from the Salvages, Sir Thomas Dale had returned unto the burnt ruins of Queen Opposunoquononuske's Towne, & there set his men to impaling ground for a new Plantation call'd *Bermuda Cittie*. This place did thrive. Last spring, e'en before Maister Rolfe's famous marriage had settled e'erything,

*Rapahannock.

they'd establisht *Bermuda Upper Hundred, Bermuda Nether Hundred, Rochdale Hundred, Digges Hundred, West Hundred* & *Shirley Hundred.* Now Virginia would only improve. In London-Towne the Companie was holding a Lottery, whose prizes did lure *Pocket-Adventurers* to underwrite the Colonie (O LORD, how simple 'tis to gull simpletons!). This would allow many new Soldiers, Blacksmiths, Milk-maids, Wives, Farmers, Tanners, Laborers & Servaunts to take passage here. (Hopefully they'd all learn to smoke Rolfe's *Tobacco.*) New Garrisons were arising throughout the Province. Soon 'twould be rendered more difficult for the Naturalls to rebel (as was already the case in Ireland). The intention of Sir Thomas Dale's canny Government was to distribute Powhatan's estates fairly betwixt the Adventurers & all loyal Salvages, just as soon as that cunning old Emperor should be undone. After that — the Monacans! Virginia was vast enough for every good soul to find its treasure.

Maister Rolfe, while justly proud of his own successes, hoped to coax many more favors out of Captaine Fortune, whose myriad green finger-shoots now strain'd up out of the furrowy mold he own'd forever. As I said, he was as contented as he could be; he expected the best, & Sir Thomas was proud of him. This new Church which had just been uprais'd hereabouts, what delight it was for him to hear its bell! Rebecca also seemed to joy in it. On Sundays, when it toll'd all Christians to worship, the baby's eyes open'd wider; then dear Rebecca smil'd as she took him up. (She left the cradle-board behind.) They had their own pew, of course, right behind Nathaniell Cleaton, his wife, & their **.4.** daughters. The youngest girls liked to play with Thomas when the service was finish'd. Rebecca laugh'd to see their sport.

'Tis said they're monstrous extravagant, whisper'd Maister Rolfe to his wife.

O, but their children seem so happy!

As is Thomas.

Of course, husband. I meant not to say—

Rebecca, beware of them, for they scruple not to slander me.

But those **.4.** girls—

They may play with Thomas, to be sure. And Maister Cleaton & his goodwife, why, greet them as befits a Christian on the LORD's day—

In fact, little Thomas had many admirers. For instance, Maister Rolfe's mother-in-law lived very near, altho' he disenjoyed to visit that ancient, smoky, bare-breasted beezum. On occasion he gave Rebecca leave to go. When he stayed home alone, he felt guilt & anxiety upon her account. For she gazed at him so sadly when she left his door! Sometimes the baby cried then also. (And once or twice he'd wonder'd whether she might fail to return to him. Hadn't she already abandon'd this *Kocoum?* Whene'er he imagined Kocoum, whom he was never to meet, he seem'd to see the long, naked strides of an Yndian spear-fisherman, young & perfect, carrying his silvery prey home to Rebecca from the blood-warm water.) But did he goad himself to be more Christianlike, & accompany Rebecca to Rapahannock Towne, why, then he moped miserably, being unable to speak more than a few words of their Salvage dialect, & they for their part regarded him but little. 'Twas as if Thomas had issued from her alone. Naked Salvage wenchen — her relations, he knew not exactly how — snatched up the child laughing, & carried him away 'pon their backs. Maister Rolfe feared 'em, but he must sit & smile. 'Tis true the Salvages played with the boy unceasingly, so that he gazed contented from his cradle-board. But they gave him of *Walnut milk* to drink, which was surely unhealthful.

His brothers-in-law were all good warlike Salvages with vambraces of fine wolf-skins. Rebecca said they'd once embroiled themselves in a battle with Captain Smith, but he'd compelled 'em for to be his friends. Maister Rolfe did seek equally to fulfill that commission of friendship, but he feared they despised him because he stayed at home & farm'd, like unto a woman. They smoked a *Tobacco*-pipe with him full politely whene'er he came; no matter that their breed of herb was bitingly inferior. In their broken English they ask'd how he did. He said he did well. Then they fidgeted; he could see they were eager to begone. Severed deer-legs lay on a bark mat, and he knew not why. He sat upon another mat, weary, angry, longing for to return to his labor. He resolv'd next to time to stay at home . . .

* * * * * *

Having some money now to spare, he hired Servaunt-men to raise up a larger manse — wattled & daubed to be sure, shaggy like unto Norfolk or Linolnshire houses, but inset with certain luxuries that he did write away for from London-Towne. (Captaine Argoll ferried 'em safely across the sea.) Moreover, he promised Rebecca that should their Tobacco-business thrive, he'd take her on a sail to England, to meet his kindred & buy whatever toys or jewels of London-Towne she did list. She chuckled like unto a shrewd Fish-wive & said: You Tassantasses are ever great liars.

Nay, sweeting, I swear it!

And do you swear by CHRIST or by the SUN?

Truly I swear it by CHRIST.

Then I must believe you, she laughed. He saw that she was pleased.

She made marsh-reed mats for their house, which he greatly relished, for they softened & eased the interior. Reverend Whittaker praising them, she made .3. more for him, for which he thanked her, calling her kind. Maister Rolfe felt a warmness in his breast when he heard. By my faith, she'd begun to make herself liked already on that Plantation. When a young wife died of *the seasoning,* Goodmistress Rolfe did advise the widower how to save the baby by feeding it on walnuts crush'd & boil'd, which he tried. The baby did thrive. After that, Maister Rolfe misliked walnut milk not nearly so much.

* * * * * *

And why must you keep the hearth a-glowing summer & winter? her husband inquired. Why, sometimes I feel myself half-smudged with smoke, & not a Mosquitor in sight to justify it! Tell me, sweeting, is this another of your Salvage superstitions?

'Tis better for the child.

Rebecca, what do you mean? He looks suffocated! Now tell me true. Do you reverence your OKEE in those coals? I know that He's a Spirit of fire, like all those other DEVILS & DEMONS ...

Husband, if you trust me not, why then, I'll not answer thee.

In a rage he crush'd the embers out, & dash'd water on them. She stood with her arms folded on her breast. The baby lay asleep in his cradle. Smiling angrily, she said: Now we'll get bad luck.

* * * * * *

At dawn she caught the locusts sleeping in the dewey grasstops, beating them down into the basket with a springy young maple twig. Her husband being already safely through the gate of his West Field as his *Almanacke* advised, he wouldn't see her. Many times had he chidden her for eating insects, but she relish'd such food & cared not for his meddling in matters unrelated to himself. Plucking off the unwholesome parts, she chewed up a handful of 'em and finger-fed the greenish paste into her darling baby's mouth. He smiled into her face; her heart joyed. Then he wanted to suck. Stripping off her clothes (for she much misliked the confinement of English dress), she lay back with him in her arms. If any guests came she would not answer. O, how she craved to sleep a little more! Last night Thomas had cried o'ermuch, which threw her husband out of temper. So many times she'd arisen to quiet him that she was worn out. Besides, she could not yet accustom herself to this English fashion of sleeping, in which she must lie head to head against her husband, so that his rank breath tickled her ear. Her People always slept head to foot, as indeed she'd done with Kocoum. But her English husband complained that her feet gave off an ill odor (al-tho' she bathed in the river morng & even, as he did not, nor would he pull the hairs from his private parts; this somewhat disgusted her). When she tasked him on his own uncleanliness, he merely replied that 'twas misre-spectful for the wife to thrust her feet in the husband's face. After that, she gave o'er. O, he was passing proud! And yet Rebecca had heard his own Countreymen make light of his pretensions — sometimes in the sinisterly satiric accents of Captaine Argoll (whom she loathed more than death), more often in the plainspeaking harshness of the farmers whose small crofts now sprang up all around her husband's Plantation. They seemed to regard him as a half-man; 'twas all strange; she herself felt contempt for many of her husband's qualities, yet when others hinted at his insubstantiality she felt — *fear.*   Reader, I cannot say that it was quite the *twinkling fear* that she felt; she suffered from no apprehensions about being massacred; but if her husband was no man, then how could he support & protect her?

He despises my feet in his face, she thought with sudden anger. Yet I de-spise not his, altho' they're unclean. He would be my Master. And yet he's no man.

* * * * * *

Still, she was not as unhappy as he thought her. For **.1.** thing, all the other women of her own Countrey must labor in the fields. She had more leisure now. Her *Father* Captaine Smith had spoken truly there, when he'd de-scribed unto her the lot of English wives. She'd grown a little fat, her belly now coming unto excellence in marshy pulsations & marsh-ripples. Her husband gave her leave for to lie abed late, & join him in the fields only when she'd put the baby to rights. Sometimes she pretended that it took a little longer to put him to rights than in truth it did. (Nor did he need her much. He'd purchased a bullock now.) Her husband had promis'd her a better life. Very well, then; she'd make **.1.** for herself. She thought it ab-surd enough that he insisted upon being her entire support. But if he was so foolish, why then, she'd permit him. She joyed in the times of gently, rhymthically slapping the baby's thighs, singing the songs her mother had once sung unto her, rocking him on her knee until his eyes closed. She whiled away the days. She'd learned to be an Englishwoman. She'd learned to be delicate.

Moreover, on those occasions when Sir Thomas Dale came by, he always made much of her, & ask'd her how she did. To have the Governor of the Colonie — a rich-drest man who scrupled not to slay evildoers by any number of ingenious tortures, yet a well-spoken man, a person whom all respected like unto a Werowance — inquire after her, e'en in her decayed estate, why, it made her glow a little. She'd planted her life among these Tassantasses; the better she could love them, the easier 'twould prove to shew she'd chosen aright. What other companions could she expect? Rejoicing in Sir Thomas's protection, she remained yet too proud to complain about the insults she received. When he was there, she scarcely thought upon them. When he was gone, she laid herself down on the bed, with her baby at her breast, & if she felt disinclined to weed or sucker *Tobacco,* she sent her husband word that little Thomas was sick . . .

* * * * * *

Thomas was getting eaten up by fleas. The dish of blood which her husband kept beneath the bed did trap some of the vermin, but not enough. Rebecca began rubbing the baby with walnut oil. When her husband objected, she gave him the backside of her tongue. Then he grew sad & said: Rebecca, my sweeting, I'm sorry to have trespassed on your affairs . . .

Then she pitied him, & sought to give him a kiss, but he shrank away.

* * * * * *

That night she opened herself unto him. To him she was always like unto the crimson scales of Virginian cedar-bark in the rain, or some green-mossed tree gashed bleeding red. That night he dreamed that he was running beneath beards of moss as grey-green as the sky. He awoke attainted by the words: *Strange wives.* Cypresses stood alone in isles of low plums, & the grass prickled on.

* * * * * *

Again she kindled a fire. She kept it going day & night. When he remark'd on it, she told him 'twas for Thomas's sake, after which he said no more.

* * * * * *

The baby was asleep. Her husband came quietly to bed. Feeling sad & lonely, Rebecca hoped that he would play with her. But when she opened her legs he roll'd against the wall. She lay there for a time. Then insistently, lustfully & angrily she did seize his hand, which she placed upon her secret.

Her husband pull'd his hand away. He sat up. He said her: 'Tis not my hungry appetite to gorge myself with incontinency.

✳ ✳ ✳ ✳ ✳

See Rebecca milking cows and tending her husband's *Tobacco*-crop. The taper'd ovals of the leaves do seem to grow greener 'neath her touch! See her suckle the child. 'Tis said that Great Powhatan with his own hands whittled a maple sprig, then sewed pebbles into a scrap of deerskin leather, which he lash'd unto the stick with deerskin thongs, and by a Salvage messenger dispatched this toy, which his grandson joyed at. Little Thomas was everywhere to be seen shaking his rattle most laughingly. But percase its origin was but a tale spread by John Rolfe himself, who e'er did seek (most tiresomely) to inflate this mixed marriage into justification, pretending that the Virginian King connived at it.

Truth to tell, now many envied him his choice. For she might be no very legitimate spouse, but in lands she was monstrous rich.

✳ ✳ ✳ ✳ ✳

But that tale was true, & the Salvage messenger (whom only she saw) was none other than her Uncle Opechancanough. He came by night, whilst her husband was selling *Hawtorinkanusfkes* for good profit far away in Jamestowne. He knapp'd at the door like unto an Englishman. When she let him in, she took in great comfort at his familiar tallness, his red-and-black painted face, his smell of puccoons & walnut-oil. Of course there was constraint betwixt 'em, not only on account of her choice in husbands, but also because amongst her People, as amongst the Tassantasses, women & men mix not so freely. For all that, he was her relation, & she must love him. Once she'd closed the door upon them both, so that no neighbor could see, she knelt down before him with her face to the floor, & began scritching with her fingernails, as she used to do at Werowocomoco when guests did come to her father's house. Gently he raised her up.

Pray seat yourself on the floor with me, Uncle, she said. As you see, we have mats here—

Very finely made, he said.

Thank you for that. Now would you taste my husband's new tobacco?

I cannot stay long.

The pipe lies ready here, & you see we have fire.

Indeed I see that he permits that now.

This tobacco hath a novel taste.

He said nothing, & she, knowing him so well, quickly prepared the pipe for him. He suck'd in smoke in silence. The baby opened his eyes & smiled to taste the fragrance of the smoke.

'Tis weak, he said at last.

Would you take another?

'Tis enough. Amonute, I came to see how you fared.

Well enough, Uncle. I have naught to complain—

I was much surprised to hear, he said, that these Tassantasses paid your father nothing when you were married.

'Twas at my word, she lied, with her head hanging down.

They value you not o'ermuch.

Amonute was silent. Then she said: That's old news. We married .2. summers since. And just last season, in *Nepinough,** you came to my mother's house. Surely you did hear—

I am yours to call upon by blood. I will always love you and help you.

Yes, she whispered.

Would you come away? I can bring you safe to Menapacunt, or farther yet beyond their reach.

And my child? she asked, feeling a sudden thrilling of hope.

Kocoum promises to love him as he does you, forever.

O, was all that she could say. I must think on it—

Now's the chance. Your Tassantasse husband's gone—

I know not—

Kocoum will pay your husband many *Hawtorinkanusfkes* to take you back to his house.

Why? Does he love me?

Uncle Opechancanough laughed, & would not answer.

He failed to protect me, so I love him not, she lied. (Closing her eyes, she saw again that pretty house beneath a mulberry tree where she had dwelt so happily.) Uncle, would you care for some food? I have bread and *butter,* & also some *milk* . . .

Remember, you married him for life. Your father gave you to him.

What says my father? she asked miserably.

I can scarcely tell you.

Amonute had always feared her uncle a little. Now she was also waxing angry at him. Most of all, she'd begun to pity him. Everyone knew that the Werowance of Quiyoughcohannock had lured away his favorite wife. So

---

*The season of "the earing of the Corne." — John Smith.

he comprehended the shame & loneliness of Kocoum, whom, moreover, was his nephew.

Uncle, I must tell you that I gave oath by the SUN not to flee.

I would you'd not done that, he sadly said.

They demanded it of me . . . I was afraid . . .

His eyes glittered into hers. She long'd to know what he meditated. She remembered how one winter's day when she was young he'd fallen sullenly asleep at her father's hearth, then awoken with a false smile. His gaze, where had it been? Above his smile, that gaze of his had terrified her, and she'd known not why. Wasn't *Argoll's* gaze worse? Well, that crawled & played with its own inhuman affections, whereas the glance of Opechancanough, human enough in truth, conveyed *hatred without forgiveness,* no matter that that hatred had never launched itself at her. The young men all loved him. They said he was both fearless and cunning, which doubtless he was. She must love him likewise, he being hers by blood. She knew that he loved her with all his heart. She loved him, but anxiously, without any tenderness. She was a traitress; he was a great man.

Clearing her throat, she continued: But I hope yet to help my father, you & everyone. In their Nation dwells a *Mamanatowick** like unto my father. My husband hath promis'd to take me. I would fain go there. I would meet him and say: Your subjects do always slay us, & steal our lands and corn.

Surely you look not for justice from him!

I know not, Uncle. But 'tis now the purpose of my life to learn how we can save ourselves. Should he prove unjust, why then I'll spy out his weakness.

'Tis sure, this voyage of yours?

He hath promis'd. Other than that I know not—

And what you discover you'll relate unto me?

Yes, Uncle.

Do you swear?

I swear by the SUN, she said, upraising her hand.

He rose, smiling grimly. — We shall all remember you, Amonute. I'll tell the priests at Uttamussack to sing songs for you—

She bowed her head, biting her lip so as not to weep.

From his buckskin purse he withdrew a pouch of puccoon-root, & another of antimony paint from Pattawomeck. — Your father sends you this, he said.

---

*Paramount chief. This was one of Powhatan's official titles.

I thank you, she whispered.

And this rattle is for your baby. Your father fashion'd it—

* * * * * *

One of her brothers kill'd a deer & brought her some meat & suet, for he much pitied her & her way of life. The next time she took Thomas to see her mother, she did secretly offer some of that suet to OKEUS upon the altar-stone.

* * * * * *

Thomas was singing unto himself, altho' he could not yet utter any words. He was growing up in her very arms. She could see his legs lengthening day by day. 'Twould not be long before she'd be standing on the river-bank watching as he went a-swimming for to hunt the fishes with a pointed stick, as children do. She'd throw a hunk of moss into the air & make him shoot it, to win his breakfast. Of course this husband of hers would never teach him how to make a bow. Her brothers would gladly do it. Could she grate away his rightward locks, so that they wouldn't get tangled in his little bow-strings? Nay, her husband would never permit that—

She clos'd her eyes. She sometimes thought that she could remember being at her mother's breast.

Rebecca, sweeting, could you grate away my hair in your Salvage fashion? 'Tis too long now in the back.

Aye, she said. I'll bring my clamshells.

She grated it left & right. When he was good & gone, she took her baby and went out to the woods, where, out of love and pity for her, her brothers had come in secret to raise up an altar-stone. Kneeling as if she were in Church, she laid down an offering of her husband's tobacco and quietly commenced to pray to OKEUS.

In the shadow, where the moss was still green and supple, she saw deer-droppings. She could see from the tracks that the deer was an older buck. Should she tell her husband? He relish'd that meat. — Nay, for what if he did discover the altar-stone?

And with a spiteful little smile (the expression of outraged powerlessness), she turn'd back to her husband's Plantation. Did he ask her where she'd gone, she'd reply that her relations had besought her to trade, but their commodities had prov'd inferior. O, she knew well what to say to him! She could already see herself there, & him laying his hand upon her neck in his distant, hesitating caress—

* * * * * *

She was lonely for Kocoum then. He at least would have caressed her the way she desired.

* * * * * *

See Rebecca scratching wearily with her hoe. She sets it down. She says the baby requires her.

* * * * * *

She made a cornhusk doll for her mother's child. Her husband said: Why not give her this doll? For 'tis English made, you know.

She thank'd him, wondering why she felt not more grateful. Doubtless the little girl would prefer the English novelty.

I would take it to her myself, she said.

Which sister is this? said her husband vaguely. Doth she dwell in Rappahannock-Towne?

Aye. Would you come with me?

Nay, sweeting, for 'tis time to be suckering our tobacco plants. Indeed I'd prefer it if you'd stay to aid me.

As you would, husband . . .

Nay, gaze not at me thus! If you must needs go to do your duty to your relations, I'll not confine you with me—

Have I angered you?

Not at all, he said.

I shall not go, she said.

When the day's work was done, each *Tobacco*-plant now well serv'd upon its little hillock, she took Thomas on her back for to gather strawberries from a burned clearing she knew. Her mother's aunts had once dwelled there with their families. They were all dead of a sickness. 'Twas evident that soon enough her People would be reduced to embers.

* * * * * *

Lacking the sunny Providence vouchsafed to the Welshman Arise Evans, who'd succeeded in marrying a lady on the understanding that she must never contradict him, Maister Rolfe gradually withdrew his concentration from his marriage unto his *Tobacco*-plants. Rebecca, squat & wood-colored like unto a veritable *Canoa,* likewise kept her own counsel. Sometimes he knew not whether he'd master'd her, or e'en what she thought. Month by month their friendship decayed, until it resembled the darkly sunken ruin of **.1.** of their Temples, which some late-arrived Rustickes did fear, calling it the *Goblin-hole*.   Such is the credulity of Servaunts & other natural inferiors.   When he **.1.**st survey'd his new property, Maister Rolfe had discovered the remnants of such an abomination.   Bidding his people utter no word of this to Rebecca, who lay at home a-suckling the shild, he assembled them all on that spot, & in a twink they'd spaded dirt o'er the gruesome old DEVIL-carvings, which some halfhearted Christian had charr'd long ago.   Before noon, e'ery mark of that Temple was vanisht.   Maister Rolfe did plant *Tobacco* upon that mound.

✳   ✳   ✳   ✳   ✳   ✳

The little boy having develop'd a strange ulcer on his leg, Rebecca made up a paste of the skin of the *Sassafrass-root,* which she patted upon the affected part, and 'twas a wonder how quickly he did heal.   Like all Salvages, she was very wise in such vegetable leech-craft.

Such of her doings as these made him trust her.   But then he return'd from battling hornworms and Rebecca in her wool cap was standing without their croft with the child in her arms.   Venus was already out, and the other night stars were gaining power.   Down Thomas's shirt filed an army of little buttons.   Sir Thomas Dale, after whom he'd been named, had granted him that gift upon his christening.

His pale brown Goodwife pointed upwards, and the child ceased his squirming long enough to peer up into the twilight.

Pummuhumps,   Rebecca was saying.

He revealed himself, inquiring nervously: Sweeting, surely you do not teach our son any Salvage idolatry?

She gazed at him in sad silence.   Then she turned and went into the house.

Rebecca, in the ALMIGHTIE's name! What means that word?

Pray address yourself to Captaine Smith, she returned in a rage, for unlike you, he did trouble to learn my language.

Captaine Smith is dead.

I misdoubt me not.   Then I'll tell you, if you would learn.

I —

I would but teach him how to say *Starres* in the language of his father. Does JEHOVAH forbid me that?

And then he was asham'd again, & sought again for to trust her.   She was good.   She was provident.   Oftimes he spied her drying their food on a bark mat. When she performed this, the victuals kept much better than any of the neighbors'. Rebecca never wasted anything.

* * * * * *

He went a-fishing in the reeds for to think. He caught a shad-fish & then a little sturgeon. Rebecca would be pleas'd. He fish'd some more. Then he realized that there remained nothing to think. Rebecca was his wife for good or ill. That was all.

* * * * * *

Behind a screen of shady trees, she smelled the wind that blew down from the hill-crest, ruffling the water into wrinkles like those of her mother's throat. She inhaled the odors of honey and pine resin. Thomas was a-singing on her back. Looking quickly behind her, she ascended a sunny rocky shelf surrounded by oaks. The water was very blue below. Again she listened and smelled. Then she went deeper into the forest. Before she knew it, she'd arrived at the bark-domed houses of Rappahanock-Town. Her husband would be angry; she cared not.

Her mother was picking inkberries for black pigment. The others welcomed her with many songs, some of whose words she disremembered. They feasted her on a fawn cut out of its mother's belly, and boiled still in the uterine sac. Amonute took pains to compliment the food. They made great exclamations o'er the English doll, & told Amonute how lucky she was, that such commodities lay e'er at her beck. She smil'd. She was happy to lie down again in a basket-bed by a fire maintained without questions.

When will you go to visit your father? they asked her. We hear that he's always asking after you.

Biting her lip, Amonute said: I dare not. For I've brought much trouble down on him. Besides, I fear my husband might not give me leave—

Her mother came rushing delightedly in. Caressing Amonute, she asked: Are you content?

I cannot say that.

Be brave, her mother said.

'Tis all you ever did say to me.

And what else would you have me tell you? If you mislike what I say, why then, hie you back home to your Tassantasses . . .

Sitting together by the river, they spun grass into rope upon their thighs. Her father continued well, as her mother had heard. Amonute begged someone to send him her love. They gave her a haunch of venison for her husband, & some People fraughted it homeward for her.

* * * * *

Bone-smoke comes down at last. There came an autumn, then a winter. Spring, silent and blue, narrowed Time unto the forest's green cerements, with long tree-shadows on the cool water. Maister Rolfe was in Myddle-Field, sun-roasting his *Tobacco* in little heaps & piles, as his Goodwife had taught him. A Servaunt came a-running. (He had **.2.** Servaunts now.) The Servaunt pointed. Here came guests, all of them helmed & halberded there in the shallop, with their muskets charg'd. What did they fear? Their tar-gets* lay ready at their sides. He misdoubted him not they'd been sent on some errand by Sir Thomas.

They came closer, hailing him. He smiled; he ever did joy to see his Countreymen. But Rebecca fled most sullenly into the house—

Go & fetch your mistress. Tell her to prepare our house for company.

Aye, Maister Rolfe—

Good content be yours, Gentlemen! What news from James-Towne? (Sweeting, bring my *Tobacco*-pipe.)

None, Maister Rolfe — except that Captaine Argoll hath return'd.

And doth he come in plenitude?

Which signifies, *hath he made a profit?* Your jewel of phrase grows famous 'mongst us all, Maister Rolfe! I believe he's turn'd a fine penny a-chaffering for beaver-skins with the Yndians of *New England*. But say, about his ar-rival I've got a risible tale. Once again the Sentry mistook his vessel for a warship from Spanish *Florida!* Ha, ha! Sir Thomas had him scourged—

As befitted such folly. Argull's on the *Treasurer?*

Aye.

Then I must quickly speak with him, for I have new bales of *Tobacco,* the primest yet, & I fear if I hie myself to him not hastily he'll fraught her hold with other men's commodities—

Do you never laugh, Maister Rolfe? Really 'tis passing humorous, the way we got so alarm'd, in case 'twas truly a Spanish ship—

How doth our Spanish prisoner?

O, he continues quiet. He can find no more traitors to help him, e'er since Sir Thomas punisht that other lot. Were you present for their burn-ing last summer?

*Shields.

Nay, for such sights displease me. But I gave Rebecca leave to go in Captaine Argoll's company, altho' she declined. 'Twas her kinsmen who track'd those Spanish pandars thro' the forest, before they'd made much distance to *Florida*—

There's more news. Sir Thomas would sail home to his Lady.

O, said Rolfe, a little alarmed. 'Tis news indeed, for he hath scarcely enriched himself as of yet.

Aye, well, mayhap the cooings of the turtledoves remind him that *There ain't no pockets in a shroud.* E'en *you* can't take it with you, Maister Rolfe—

And Yeardley is to be Governor?

So they say.

Well, well, 'tis *politick.* Now I'm full resolv'd to sail to Jamestowne.

Would you sail with him, then, Maister Rolfe? Your position's very high here; I fail to see why you should leave it, especially since you've now wed such a discreet Gentlewoman.

Staring into Maister Rolfe's face, another man remark'd: 'Tis said by all that you've gotten great fortune by her.

* * * * * *

Rebecca, sweeting, pray fetch our guests some cheer.

Looking his Goodwife insolently up and down, the .2.nd man sneered: *Mowchick wayawgh tawgh noeragh kaquere mecher.* Do you remember that jibber-jabber, Pocahontas?

My wife would prefer to be used by her Christian name, Sir.

How about you, Maister Rolfe? Did you e'er have occasion to learn that turn of phrase? Sweet John taught it to me, he did. Back in the days when he was President, we'd go & — *hah!* Well, Maister Rolfe, it signifies: *My empty belly pains me. What shall I eat?* And then we'd go, & Sweet John would bid us light the matches on our ordnance, &—

Sir, can't you understand that my wife mislikes your recollections?

I'm sure she's heard worse.

Gentlemen, what would you here?

We commence to grate on you, as I see. E'er did it go thus, when we'd guest ourselves at Werowocomoco or Kecoughtan. The Salvages soon slithered into a sadness, for we slupper'd up their victuals day & night. But they durst not 'scape their obligation, our matchlocks being charg'd.

Rebecca, shall I bid 'em to the door?

Without expression, Goodmistress Rolfe dipped her turtle-shell ladle into the stew and serv'd up portions. It befitted her not to acknowledge any of these persons. O, yes, good Reader; she'd learnt how to rule herself.

Nay, *Pokahuntiss,* you need not unstop your precious mouth. In fine, Rolfe, we're Captaine Argoll's new men. We sign'd his Crew-muster in a twink, for to *bing ourselves to Romeville* as they do say. And when we swore ourselves unto him, why, we also adopted his mirthful humors. He's named us—

I care not for your names—

Claudius ('tis me), & *Vespasian,* & that's *Aurelius* there. We're all later generations of Roman Emperors, if you do ken the jest—

I've heard it before. Rebecca, sweeting, I'm full sorry for their discourtesy.

For what? I must obey you all.

Captaine Argull hath spoken with our Maisters in London-Towne. The Company would invite you, Maister & Mrs Rolfe, for to come to England gratis—

For what reason, pray?

To raise subscriptions, while amusing the rabble with the person of Princesse Pokahuntas—

* * * * * *

See Maister & Mrs Rolfe at Hampton-Towne, which was once call'd *Kecoughtan*. Rebecca's brother Pochins was the last Werowance there, before 'twas conquered. White shell-shards abide, worked deep into the mossy dirt 'twixt those long, knuckled tree-roots which strain down into the river like piano-playing fingers. Rebecca remembers where the mortar-stone used to be. She denies to seek it out.

The baby (or *Breast-leech* as I should call creatures of that tribe) was asleep. Softly did she lay him down upon the grass. He slumber'd with a turtle's upturned neck and spread forelegs.

Sweeting, forbear me now. I must hie myself to Maister Shrewsbury there, for he's bespoken **.III.** hogsheads of my *Tobacco.* Would you refresh yourself with Mistress Shrewsbury?

Nay, husband, here I like it well.

English children are building Forts & Towers in the floury sand. A sea-otter swims close, raising his head to goggle with huge, sad eyes. The children commence hooting at him, & presently throw stones. But he will not depart. Rebecca wonders if he might be the SPIRIT of **.1.** of her dead kinsmen. Is he looking at her, or . . . ? After a time they give o'er their cruelty & ignore him. They're dragging monstrous kelp-weeds out of the sea, with which they would enchain in each other in their play. And always that sea-otter lurks sadly there.

Spy you that flipper'd vagabond, dear Princesse? 'Tis said that the Widow Jukes sometimes throws him scraps from her table.

O, replies Rebecca faintly, not turning round.

(The creature's head resembles a brown skull with charred eye-sockets.)

Do you remember me, Princesse? My name's Frauncis Stanwicke, & I was present at your nuptials.

How do you do, Sir?

Very fine, & 'tis a pleasure for to find you here. Where are you bound?

For Jamestowne, she says in her low & listless whisper.

Well, as for that otter there, some folks, seeing as how the Widow Jukes once said 'twas good luck for to feed him, did suspect he was her familiar. In England our good King James would surely burn her for witchcraft, they did say. But . . .

Rebecca gazes out at the shimmering, e'er breaking, e'er healing mirror of the sea.

* * * * * *

See Maister & Mrs Rolfe at James-Towne (which in spite of Captaine Fortune's pestilences hath become at last a fairly prosperous hive, complete with ropes, men, & nightmares of creaking boards). 'Tis high summer. Virginia presses dark green against e'erything, like unto *Tobacco.* Of this commodity, bye the bye, our Colonie now possesses on hand **.2,300.** pounds dry weight for to send to London-Towne. Much of it was grown in John Rolfe's wide Plantations, by Maister Rolfe himself, his Servaunts, & that ill-featured young Yndian woman they call *his cockatrice.* ('Tis said she goes in for bathing naked in the river, & other licentious sports.)

Tall, narrow clapboard houses begin for to rise outside the palisadoes. Nobody cares to fortify anymore. The Yndians continue friendly, thanks to this marvelous marriage. These houses have corn-cribs in their attics, & the cribs are full. Yea, dear Reader, finally our Colonists grow rich in corn!

(Whenever the SUN doth come out, the isle changes to green from grey.)

See **.2.** old Convicts surviv'd from the **.3.**^{rd} Supply of *Sweet John's* time. To them, Rebecca is an *autem mort,* a Churched woman, a wife. Disremembering not the bygone glory of her jewel-metalled maidenhead, they now fancy her to be fitter prey. They would *couch a hogshead* in her bed, discover her secret & *niggle* with her. What a lark 'twould be, to infect her with their pox! They stand idly around on what used to be call'd Smithfield, a-watching the married couple dwindle into the Fort. Then they watch Argoll's rapid-hearted Sailors careening the *Treasurer* on her side. She's already been unballasted. They've been commaunded to bream the sea-filth off her, & then tar her anew 'gainst barnacles. 'Tis needless work, some say, but they fear to cross their Captaine. The Convicts smoke *Tobacco.* Of a sudden they see a Sentry coming. They take to their heels, for fear of idleness's punishment.

See the Governor, Sir Thomas Dale, with his square pillow-epaulets on his long dark lace-sleeved gown. Beside him, worthy Argall stands tall & solid & grey-capped like unto his own ship's capstan, which is topped with lead to keep the wood from splitting. (Where hath he been? From March until summer of this 1615 he vanisht to no one knows where, chaffering or extorting, as I trow — he's stranger than a white moon-shape in a deer's dark coat. He returns to Jamestowne with a lullaby deep within his mouth.)

Dear Maister Rolfe, well met! Rebecca, 'tis my pleasure to discover you & my namesake both so hale.

Thank you, Sir Thomas, reply husband & wife in low & simultaneous murmurs.

And good day to you, Captaine Argoll, says Rolfe, stretching forth his hand.

Why, 'tis my gentle friends, my fine clasped souls! Poor Maister Rolfe! Could we but drown all the evil Tobacco-mungers in England, who e'er shrill that Virginian weed's the worst!

What do you mean? cries Rolfe, fading in his color.

Ha, ha! barks the Governor impatiently. Pay no heed to Captaine Argall's clownish humors. Dear Rebecca, you seem awearied. Would you care to sit yourself down?

Yes, Sir Thomas, if it please you.

Spoken lady-like! cries Argoll. But you weren't always a Lady, were you, *Pocahontas?*

Sir Thomas, this man doth make sport of my wife—

But you need him, don't you, Maister Rolfe? He wherries your *Tobacco* home for you. So defend your wife's honor yourself, if you've manliness enough to do it, or keep silent.

Oftimes I fear me I'm too gentle with 'em both, sighs Argoll, yet next minute I'd embrace 'em, for—

Sir Thomas hath turn'd upon his heel.

* * * * * *

Late on a honey-scented afternoon so still that the James River was but a blue blankness, the Lookout cried *Flood oh!* & the Trumpeter played his *Trarintra-rarara,* upon which they upped anchor in a ship built to the disgraced Sir Walter Rawleigh's proportions. This was the *Treasurer,* of course, site of Pocahontas's happiest hours, as she did well recall, & 'twas well-raked both fore & aft — a perfect-balanced ship, which could pursue her purpose without much fear of o'ersetting e'en in storms. — Sails to the yards! cried the Captaine (a certain *Argoll).* Stretch forward your main halyards!

They were well laden with *Sassafrass,* clapboard, & Maister Rolfe's *Tobacco.*   And (to turn to their living freight), Uttamatomakkin was there with them, on a mission from Powhatan to spy on and enumerate all the Tassantasses. (He cast a sprinkle of *Tobacco* upon the water, at which the Sailors did jeer at his idolatry.) His wife Mayachanna was there, looking passing fearful. Rebecca was there, of course, standing uneasily beside her husband. Her old Serving-maids were there, to the tune of near a dozen persons. Sir Thomas Dale was there, well busked up in his uniform. Having just now slain some Yndians who sought to resettle *Warraskoyack-Towne* (which is a fine portion of our Virginia), & likewise burn'd away diverse *Kiskiack* Salvages whose nearness threatened yᵉ Colonie, Sir Thomas felt that he had safely done his best endeavor, & was ready to return honorably homewards unto his Lady. Powhatan being ancient, & in the decay of his power, they but scornfully regarded his mischief. Yet Captaine Yeardley had sworn to erect new palisadoes, for the better security of the Plantation . . . — Of course dear *Cassius* was there, & *Brutus, Claudius,* & all the rest. That hispaniolated Convict, old Diego de Molina, whom they'd kept in durance since 1611, was there; & so was Diego's English Pilot, a certain Francis Lambry, who possess'd the doggish quality which is sometimes seen in a bear's face. Sir Thomas had told Maister Lambry that he'd be delivered safely to the Magistrates in England, but this was only to soothe his ignorance, for when they were far out to sea, Sir Thomas would read out from our Letters Patent these words: *They shall & may from tyme to tyme & at all tymes for ever herafter for their severall defences incounter or expulse repell & resist as well by sea as by lande by all waies & meanes whatsoever all & everie such person & persons as without license shall attempte to inhabit the preccintes and lymittes of the saife severall Colonies . . .*   and then they'd hang Maister Lambry from the yardarm and cast his corpse into the sea, to feed the *Sharkes,* which are a ruthless, dangerous species of toothed fishes most akin to Spaniards. But Maister De Molina himself they'd spare, to be deliver'd to the Ambassador of his Countrey.

Reverend Whittaker had come for to wish 'em all farewell. He upraised his hand most sadly there upon James-towne Dock. His destiny was to drown in the same year that his young convert was to perish.

It began to cloud up. 'Twould be a good fresh loom-gale they'd sail in. The river ran low and smooth and silver-blue. Rebecca on deck gazed up at the crow's nest, which resembled a sun-disk on a pole. One of the Tassantasses was crawling in it. She glanced ashore. The Fort with its bare moat and then the blond palisade with its points and its tiny square windows, wooden pegs holding it all together, pretended to be greater than everything. Certainly it had conquered & broken her. She hated it beyond accompting.

Just as cooling glass slowly darkens while simultaneously becoming transparent, so her Countrey faded from her forever. In Virginia Watson's *Legend of Pocahontas* we read that *during the long, starlit evenings, Rolfe told Pocahontas wonderful stories from English history. He recounted tales of heroes and recited lovely, romantic poems.* And I am sure that it was exactly like that. Soon she was drinking wormwood-juice against seasickness.

She raised the baby up, to shew him the strangely crawling blueness of the sea, but he gazed only at the gunnels, clutching his clumsy little hands around them.

* * * * * *

See Pocahontas sitting belowdecks on a mass of poles. Altho' her Serving-maids would console her, she never moves. Pitying her, Maister Rolfe hath taken up the child in his arms, for to give her rest. They come up on deck. The babe laughs at the Sunne. He clutches both his fists around .1. of the rat-lines, & uplifts his eyes toward HEAVEN.

* * * * * *

Every day Maister Rolfe did bring Rebecca to prayer, just as her father would have done. And e'ery day he smoked a *Tobacco*-pipe on deck with Uttamattomakkin, for that herb was sovereign against sea-sickness. He liked Uttamattomakkin passing well. Altho' that Salvage had scarce wit to speak more than .10. words of English, yet he prov'd better company than Rebecca, who mainly stayed belowdecks, complaining of qualmishness or else weaving a basket for to give the King. (See her on the foredeck, supported in her Servingmaids' arms as she weeps & pukes for seasickness. She resembles a skinny yellow corpse. Where's the child? Belowdecks with his father, I trow. Captaine Argull happens on her, &, swimming unto his clownish humor, sings: *Whe, whe, yah, ha, ne, he, wittowa, wittowa.*)

* * * * * *

Day & night the ship sped glibly eastward toward the SUN. Steadyyarded, with a goose-wing boom (which is to say a boom straight out), she fled that heathenish Countrey call'd *Virginia.* Being well-bowed, she made a foamy wake, which in the darkness sometimes glistered like unto fire. E'ery even, at .6. of the clock precisely, all hands did sing a Psalm. (Whene'er her husband was away, Amonute sang all the baby-songs which she could remember from her mother & her aunts. But indeed she remembered surprisingly few.) The Mates kept the tackle exactly trimm'd. The Carpenter stopt e'ery leak. The Corporal set each watch down to the uttermost minute of the glass. The Marshall smil'd, & wax'd a certain length of Hangman's rope for that unsuspecting English Pilot. He had it measur'd exactly. The Helmsman kept precise accompt of how many half-hourglasses he did steer upon each point of his course; for Captaine Argoll himself might well check his progress. In the dark cell where he stood, the compass-needle jittered & turn'd in its brass-ring'd box. All well! Grace to Captaine Argoll & his *Nauigation,* that hot passage home by means of *Moneta, Mevis, Guadalupa & Dominica,* which Captaine Newporte used to take in olden times, had been superseded, so that all fell into conveniency; & like writhing milk-foam on a beach, abandoned by its mother-wave, the Dominican course was left to Pirates & Amateurs.

This aforesaid Captaine Argull now sent courteous invitation to Maister & Goodmistress Rolfe, to shew them (did they care to see it) how he set his Globe to the elevation of the Virginian Pole, to find the proper Parallel for hasting homeward to England. Maister Rolfe did stand about with his arms folded, for in truth he found the entertainment not so curious, having already voyaged several times; as for squat Rebecca (who comprised the real target of Argoll's solicitude), she lay belowdecks with her screaming brat, sobbing & spewing into the chamber-pot.

Cassius, all well?

Aye, aye, Captaine Argoll!

Our course'll be perfect this time, or you'll answer to the contrary.

It shall be done, Sir.

Down foresail.

Down foresail, you rummy Salvages! Make speed, I said! — 'Tis accomplisht, Captaine.

Now, Cassius, sing me a song.

Sweet Captaine, with this Gentleman before my face I'm a bit afeared—

Ho — Brutus, Octavian, Cicero, Pompey! D'ye hear that? This cullion's *afeared* for to sing!

'Tis only that the Gentleman may regard me with disfavorable eyes, Capaine Argall, for I, being base, ken only vile harmonies—

Never mind our friend Maister Rolfe! *He* makes no distinctions. Look whom he married — ha, ha!

By the Dog-Starre, you're right, Captaine! Well, then (begging your pardon, Maister Rolfe), here goes:

> A queer cove of the Deuceville
> > Did dock a dell in Turvey.
> He gave her cheats & duds & lower
> > But his niggling was but scurvy—
> *Yet would he wap*
> *With a mort, with a dell . . .*

I'm not ignorant of God's heavy displeasure 'gainst such licentiousness, interrupted Maister Rolfe. Nor do I fail to see how you do twit me thus whene'er Sir Thomas sleeps below. Captaine Argoll, I have endured many private controversies with you—

And you'll endure many more, fellow. Wouldst thou learn the reason? Because *without me, thous canst ne'er vend thy* Tobacco *in England.*

Maister Rolfe turns away. He descends belowdecks. But soon all can hear a woman's angry cries, & a moment later he returns to forlornly pace the deck.

* * * * * *

Riding 'midst the *whitecaps* like unto thistleheads in this grey sea far beyond fields, she keeps monstrous silent, no matter which favors & privileges Argoll doth proffer unto her. She wears bird-bone beads in her ears. She's praying that what she discovers on this voyage will save her father.

* * * * * *

Taking soundings, they discovered cockleshells at **.80.** fathoms, then small sand at **.64.** fathoms, by which signs they knew to be near Ushant & the Lizarde. (The baby reached & cried out; he spied driftwood like a wooden octopus.) So by safe tackings they entered the Sleue where the Arctick Pole is elevated **.50.** degrees and a half, &, fearing not, arrived on the **.3.**rd of June, 1616 at a wedge-shapen harbor cunt-haired with ships' masts. — Good landfall! sang Argoll, for their reckoning had been perfect, as under him it always was. — Now shorten your sails! — Aye, aye, Captaine Agull!

The name of this place was *Plymouth,* & 'twas most anciently a nest of Pirates like unto Sir Walter Ralegh (who was now attainted of treason, as people did say). O, let us thank th'ALMIGHTIE that dear Rebecca got landed in Plimouth rather than ill-omened Gravesend! For, having 'scaped the terminus, the soulless throughway, she may be sure of coming to no harm. Plymouth-Haven's wedge-gape makes no grave-gape — for from it! 'Tis a monstrously visionary place, a Dream-Kingdome all of its own, altho' (to be sure) it in-gathers the very same bristling ships as Gravesend. From Plimouth no Adventurer hath e'er sailed & return'd poor! (I have this on authority from a most excellently rat-whiskered Waterman, who would do business with me there.) So come unto Plymouth-Towne, lay out all your riches on **.1.-in-.1,000,000.** Undertakings, & I swear you'll prosper! I swear your desperate life will die & be most goldenly encoffined! Nobody cares for Gravesend here. E'ery man-jack in Plimouth knows he will be King. Good Reader, have you been to Plymouth? In Speed's *Atlas* we discover that it lies upon the very boundary between Countie Devon (which is render'd most prettily in yellow) and Countie Cornwall, which the aforesaid Maister Speed made pinkish (as indeed resembles the earth of

those parts).   Now, in Plimouth-Towne they have many new edifices &
other wonders*, paid for with the spoils of their Scottish, Spanish, Irish,
French & Affrickan piracies.   And 'tis said they're a fantasying people for
that, e'er casting the dice of their safely landed wealth, in order to go to sea.
The Cornishmen across Plymouth Sound are more hard-headed.   They cast
their nets for pilchard-fishes, which they sell to the Plymouth dreamers —
or used to, before they found a richer & more gullible market in France.
But the men of Plymouth scarcely take note.   They're busy grabbling in the
air for pearls.   Say not that Plymouth's Gravesend — no matter that it owns
the very same wharf-stink, & counterpart wooden-wheeled carts hitched to
patient bullocks, the same rotting, bird-dunged mooring posts, the same
very urchins, Watermen, Oyster-wives, Tavern-keepers' touts, Drayers,
Sailors, Coachmen & idle trulls.

*   *   *   *   *

Uttamatomakkin had painted himself black & red for this occasion.   He
stood on deck with his knife & stick and commenced cutting notches,
counting every Sailor, whore & Waterman he did see.   Captaine Argall
laughed . . .

*   *   *   *   *

Possessing himself of her hand, her husband asked: Are you pleased, Rebecca?

   Of course I must be pleased to arrive in your Countrey, she said.

   Indeed she believed that her sufferings and humiliations in the Colonie
now lay so far from her as to be but particle'd of dusk and doubt.   Moreover,
since they e'er call'd her Princesse here, they'd surely now bring her to meet
her father's brother the *King of England* at last.   The basket she'd woven him
was finished.   She wished to embrace him as she would her father, then to
complain about how badly her father had been treated.   She wished to mention the doom of Paspahegh-Towne, & Argull's lies, & all the rest.   Resolved to
translate wrath into truth, she held her tongue against both husband and false
friends; only Uttamatomakkin knew her design.   He of course was glad.

   I see you do design to threapen me, kindly Argoll was laughing at the
Pilot.

---

*I am thinking here of their high Citadel & their long Arsenal, not to mention a certain house I
read of, which was builded all of white marble.

Nay, Captaine, I—

Brutus, give this yokel a shilling & then kick him on his arse.

Cables rattled slimily through the hauser-holes. The Sailors were all singing: *Now bing we all to Romeville* . . .

A Waterman skimmed up to them and cried: What! Still no novelties from Virginia?

Still laughing, the Captaine pointed out Uttamatomakkin & all the other Salvages, at which that Waterman fell gawpishly silent.

They hired a coach and went by road to London-Towne.

THE GRAMMAR OF CIRCUSES (1616)

A mask is treason's license: that build upon;
'Tis murder's best face when a vizard's on.
CYRIL TOURNEUR (?), *The Revenger's Tragedy* (1607)

*S*ee Argall pulling on a pair of perfumed gloves for to visit good King James! — Nay, not yet, they say; he'll not be knighted today, but soon. (I mistook myself; with Argoll naught is sure.) 'Tis said Sir Oliver Saint John hath been annointed Viceroy of Ireland. Sober Argull wonders whether he should haste to Ireland, to slupper up a plateful of the preferments & estates which are sure to be serv'd up in that Province. But stay! Dangers aplenty lie along that way. Unlike yᵉ Salvages, Irish rebels have guns, so 'tis a long & bloody chore to put them down. He takes futurity & divides it into .4. parts. There's the Muscovy Companie, where Captaine Newport hath served e'er since my Sir Thomas Dale pulled his beard in a fit of rage; there's the New England Companie (much o'errun by fanatical Puritans), there's piracy & there's the Virginia Companie. What can the Virginia Companie do for him? He knows their Directors, so he'll try them .1.ˢᵗ. He'll Marchaunt himself for the highest charge he can. — I can well direct mine own course, he says to 'em. — They praise his capacity; they beg him to stay. He's brought 'em *Pokahuntiss* (for all that the bitch doth stink) & the new short route direct from London-towne to James-towne. What quarter of the sky will his favors appear in next? Dear Reader, see Argoll at the Tide-gates of Fortune, dribbling out his own favors like unto an expert!

See Ralegh safely moated in the Tower behind triple walls (they'll let him out, then in again to get his death). See a scraggly band of robbers riding off to be hanged; see a recreant Earl's head on London Bridge. (Like everything the Tassantasses build, their bridges are solid & grand. Rebecca gathers gawp-seed in her gaping mouth; her husband laughs.) See the Night-watch & the Day-watch. See Queen Anne from afar, with her horse & jumping little dogs . . .

Four scaffolds now in front of the Tower, observes Argall, and a fine brace of siege-guns.

* * * * * *

Rebecca stares about her. She cannot make out why every street is crooked, like unto a deer's leg. Henrico's streets were straight, like Jamestowne's. (In her Countrey they have no streets at all.)

She wishes to play Tick-Tack, but her husband says that it's a vulgar game.

Just as OKEUS can appear directly from the air, so strange Towers loom at her upon sudden turnings. The air reeks of smoke. The men do not hunt, & yet there's meat.

See London's low coast of houses like a mass of crystals studding the Thames-edge, then across the filthy river (on which dance many gleeful-sailed ships) a higher coast of walls, steepled Churches, the squat, grim Tower where Ralegh awaits his doom. *Trarintra-rarara!* Yea, that trumpet will sound for him on the day he loses his head. But he hath already gone aside from himself, to dwell in dreams of old Piracy.

Just as at their dances the People all beat out the same time with their feet, whilst moving their heads & bodies full variously, so this London-Towne seems all of a piece yet contains many strange parts.

Of a sudden she laughs for joy, to hear e'er so many great clocks & Church-bells chime out the hour most beautiful & stately-like, with each singing its own musicke . . .

* * * * * *

See Rebecca at Saint Peter's Church, which is shapen like unto a grimy, ribbed stone book open & standing on its edge. Rebecca says: I would wash myself.

Here? In the Church?

Nay, husband. But I mislike the stink of London-Towne. I would wash. And our child likewise hath a stale odor . . .

O, Rebecca, 'tis but your Salvage fancy which impels you to that. For 'tis dangerous to bathe in cold water o'ermuch, especially now when the Moone's in Taurus. Besides, where would we do it?

There.

'Tis the fount.

Then in the river.

But see how dirty it is, Rebecca! And everybody would watch . . .

I care not. My women could stand around me.

But people might stand on a bridge and see. You are my wife, Rebecca. I forbid this.

When he utters the word *forbid,*   Maister Rolfe feels a thrill like unto pride.

✳   ✳   ✳   ✳   ✳

See John and Rebecca Rolfe at the Belle Sauvage Inn, just off Fleet Street, which folk call *the Stinking Lane* by virtue of its many turds & offals that squish underfoot, no matter how delicately the daintiest Gentleman might tiptoe along. (Well, well; Gravesend stinks worse.) Drunks stagger before her like belly-shot deer. Rebecca is as discontented as any Sailor whose surmises about Captaine Fortune hath not availed. The King refrains from sending word. The Virginia Company gives her but .4. pounds a week in old money. Moreover, altho' she strives to keep her promise to Opechancanough, to spy out the weakness of these stinking Tassantasses, her hope's nigh forespent. They're more dangerous by far than the Monacans, whom her father was never able to conquer. What further chokes her listless spirits is that hospitable Argall hath already taken Uttatatommakin to *New Prison,* the *Clink,* & *Saint Katharine's Hole,* for to terrify & to warn him. Success! Uttatatommakin is pallid, & his mind's much disturb'd. Torture is .1. thing, e'en torture unto death. But keeping men alive in filthy darkness to supplicate, gibber & rot, why, to witness it chills his heart. He whispers what she already knew: The Tassantasses are passing cruel. Moreover, 'tisn't easy to 'scape 'em.

I tell you, Amonute, they act contrary to all right.

Why are they thus?

Ask your *Husband.*

The young wife closes her mouth. Then she says: He tries to love me—

Good. For if he's like unto his Countreymen, his hate would prove an ugly quenchless fire—

Have a care. He comprehends more than he pretends—

He hears nothing — certainly not your father's voice. Think you he truly seeks our friendship?

I know not—

When I heard of their doings in Paspahegh I could not believe at .1.ˢᵗ.

I beseech you, speak not of that. When I think on Wowinchopunck's children—

I remember them well, especially the eldest boy, who was passing manly. I once saw him draw his father's bow—

I —

I heard that you told Opechancanough that you dwell among these people of your own pleasure. Or do you but dissemble as do I?

Look you, Uttamattomakkin. Revenge is now impossible.

You have made it so, by giving your person unto them. Now your father must abandon his defense for your sake—

I must not disagree with you, says Amonute in a low & woeful voice. Thomas awakes. He snuffles. He lays down his face on the other breast.

I'll tell you a thing now. I spoke with OKEUS. He's full angered with you.

Flames of horror enkindle themselves in Amonute's heart. Shuddering, she casts down her eyes.

He says you must die.

When did you speak with Him?

I went to Uttamussack before we came away.

She would be brave. She shrugs. She says: It must be as He wills.

I am sorry, dear Amonute . . .

But I would ask you something. When Captaine Smith lay in your power at Werowocomoco, you did conjure OKEUS, to learn whether the Tassantasses would be our friends—

And now you dare to call Him liar! 'Twas dangerous enough, *Matoaka,* when you revealed your secret name—

You deny to answer me?

Now I begin to pity you all the more. For 'twas *you* who spared his life. Otherwise we'd never have had these misfortunes.

I must not contradict you. Yet when you conjured Him, why did He not warn you?

I plainly see that you fear Him no longer, which is perilous for all of us. Well, well. And Captaine Smith was—

He never would have burned Paspahegh! 'Twas after his death that the town got devoured.

Amonute, your good friend Argoll did tell me a thing just now, & with much laughter. Captaine Smith lives. He dwells here in London.

If he lives, then why did they e'er tell me of his death? If he lives, why does he not come here to us?

These are questions which you may well ask of your loving *Husband.*

❋ ❋ ❋ ❋ ❋ ❋

She complains of a headache. Her husband shuts the gate against the feculent air & brings her cloves to chew.

When shall I parley with the King?

O, sweeting, if we could but sugar him into that, what an accomplishment 'twould be! But we must bridle our ambitious pride. How can I best tell you that His Majestie owns many subjects?

But *I*—

Rebecca, let us down upon our knees, to make our prayers.

I did pray many times today already, in the fashion you like best.

My poor Rebecca, you must not pray to please me, but to remember Him who—

Then if I pray no more, you'll not be displeased?

Now you mock me. O, 'tis too bad of you, my darling, to offend me thus—

I would not offend you—

The babe opened his eyes, and cried until his face sparkled freshly with tears.

Husband, is not my father King?

Aye, to be sure, but—

Is it not for that cause that Captaine Argall knapped me from my kindred?

'Tis true, although now I begin to fear me you nourish your wrath. Was it not PROVIDENCE which carried you to Jamestowne, so that you got both GOD and husband? But I almost dread to continue this talk, lest we open our old quarrels . . .

Mine own husband says it. But if my father is King, *where now stand his rights?*

You pluck down proudness and stubbornness upon your head. *Rebecca, Powhatan is a subject King.*

* * * * * *

Every Sunday & Wednesday in London-Towne they hold a bear-baiting or .2.; & so for lark Maister Rolfe did take his wife & all her retinue to see that sport. Rebecca clapt her plump little hands many times at the sight of the old bear, for she said that he reminded her of her own Countrey. Then a pair of Bear-men came to break off his teeth, at which the betting began, & at the *Trarintra-rarara* all the hounds came rushing in with their heads low. Rolfe did laugh now, for the bear gazed upon his tormenters with a ludicrous dignity like unto like some great Church-warden. Uttamatomakkin whispered into his wife's ear. Now the hounds commenced to bite & worry at the bear, who shivered in a palsy & could hardly even snap at them, so he could but endure. He wept when he was slain.

But 'tis percase a shocking sport, said Maister Rolfe, suddenly recollecting himself. Sweeting, did it cause you to feel woeful?

Uttamatomakkin said, still smiling: After all, your wife is Powhatan's daughter. Many times hath she seen men tortured so.

* * * * * *

Uttamatomakkin had been present when they burned Ratcliffe to death. He remembered how weakly & in what risibly unmanly fashion that Tassantass had died, uttering the sudden, open-mouthed screams of a baby cutting a tooth. It might indeed be true that the Tassantasses were more numerous, & even had more cunning minds for certain things. But the People were stronger. The People knew how to die.

* * * * * *

Thomas rush'd about. He outstretched his arms at all the Towers. He'd begun to speak. He did not speak his mother's language, but the tongue of the Tassantasses. Altho' she had expected this, her heart was grieved. She could begin to guess something of what her father felt for her.

* * * * * *

Every time they see a paper pasted to a post, Rebecca must learn what it reads. Her husband tires of that game, although he strains his patience to his uttermost. Anew she thinks on Sweet John, who once played Tick-Tack and Lurch with her as endlessly as she listed.

They go out .1. day, and pass by a Jeweler's shop. (Uttamatommakkin hath gone to be guested at Reverend Purchas's.) Rebecca would go in, which he allows. She spies a lovely jewel of gold. It shines more beautifully than any of the copper crescents which her People do bind up in their hair. Her eyes burn like greedy torches, and she whispers: *Mufkaiuwh*, which is to say, *A Flower of a fine thing*.

It is impossibly beyond our means, Rolfe says gently.

She rounds upon him. — You must always have your way, she says. She runs out of the shop and down the street. (O yes, she sobs many tears, just as rays of light do gush controllably from betwixt a lantern's chinks.) Rolfe colors, knowing his perfect innocency. But then his conscience stings him in the belly, because he led her past that Jeweler's without possessing means. And on account of his pangs he hates her as himself. How many husks & linings are nested in her heart? Must he in truth be reminded that beneath her discontent against him she yet reserves other claims? He goes into the street and waits, gazing at a Clock-tower, until she comes stalking back inevitably, just as the new moon always causes a flood at London Bridge. (Where else can she go?) For the remainder of that day she refuses to speak any tongue but her Salvage dialect, which he'd thought long since to wean her from. She slaps away his remonstrating hand and mutters: *Ahkeÿ vwwaap,* which signifies, *Something hurts me.*

* * * * * *

When she was very young she dwelt at Rappahannock, and when her mother pierced her earlobe with a sharp bone she screamed. Her mother withdrew from her then, disappointed. Amonute felt ashamed. One of her aunts comforted her. Now her mother returned smiling. She hung from the bleeding wound a jewel of shining copper which resembled a flower in shape. With her own hand she wiped away Amonute's tears. The child whispered: *Nowamatamen!* meaning *I love it.*

Where was that jewel now? Amonute had presented it to Japzaws's wife at Pattawomeck. Doubtless they still laughed at her there, for having been gulled into Argoll's hands. She'd never go to Pattawomeck more.

* * * * * *

Uttamatomakkin said: These Tassantasses give us nothing.

Uttamatomakkin said: Your husband is good for nothing. These Tassantasses are as nothing.

Amonute said: I am nothing.

* * * * * *

Uttamatomakkin said: Tell me why you had no fear, when you exposed your true name.

'Tis ever the same talk with you, she said wearily.

I would have your answer.

Why must you have it many times? About my name I told you: Before I revealed it, it helped me not.

Yes, child, and I told *you* that OKEUS must take His revenge.

I fear Him not, she said defiantly.

Uttamatomakkin keeps something in a bag of silk-grass which her sister Mayachanna wove for him. What it is he will not say. At her words he reaches in and touches it.

And what about this JESUS they would feed us on?

What about Him? He harms me not. But I must please my husband. Have a care, girl. You remain OKEUS's child.

And did He tell you true, when at His word you advised my father to slay all the Chesapeakes? 'Twas the *other* Nation from the East which we should have feared — the Tassantasses. Here we are in London-Towne. Look around you, Uncle. We are nothing in comparison to them. You know it!

Your father—

My father grows old, she returned with shrill contempt. He would den himself away from the world, & sleep out the winter of his days. He's lazy as a fat bear . . .

* * * * * *

See Uttamatomakkin with his long stick, which in obedience to the commaund of great Powhatan he still notches every time he meets a new Tassantasse. But there are too many. At last he cries out in rage, and hurls the stick away.

* * * * * *

At dawn, while John Rolfe lies sleeping, Rebecca and her people sit in a circle and gaze through the dirty windowpane at the SUN. They would wash, but cannot. Uttamatomakkin stands. Softly he murmurs *Bowh, waugh* and Rebecca and her women lie down. Uttamatomakkin taps his foot, but very quietly, so as not to disturb Maister Rolfe. He touches the floorboards with a stick. There are no river stones for him to beat with it, so he swishes it silently through the air. John Rolfe opens his eyes. Uttamatomakkin goes silent and mysterious, like a ball of clay souring in the ground. He craves for oil with which to rub himself, for in the Belle Sauvage Inn there are many fleas. But her husband will not give him any, for fear that the other Tassantasses might laugh. Rebecca sits up and faces him with her hands on his knees, her big breasts hanging down. Her husband sees. He turns away his face.

* * * * * *

Rebecca claps her hands in delight. Her name & likeness is pasted on the walls of Saint Paul's Church, for a wonder and for a lark! It pleases her to be made much of. (Certainly 'tis less dreary than her pine-girt prison of Henrico.) See how they've drawn a crown upon her head! (And 'tis diademed in English style, no hair-puff'd like unto Wowinchopunck's wife's.) She doth smile, winnicking for mirth in her somewhat low voice. Outside a Tavern-house, a blind man stands venting the selfsame broadside, crying out in a brazen voice: *Take home an Yndian Princesse!*   Rebecca giggles. The Tassantasses love her.

* * * * *

But now a very pallid, dirty, stinking man, with eyes shining like unto Uttatommakkin's at his raptures, comes a-running toward Rebecca. Her husband frowns, draws dagger. The man sobs: *Please, Maister, a ha'penny merely, for the love of CHRIST His sake!*

Get you gone.

The man leaps back, scanning her husband's blade-hand. Then full lewdly & horridly he commences for to smile at Rebecca. He snarls: Aye, but thou'rt *a bene mort.*

Husband, what doth he mean?

I know not, replies Rolfe, trembling.

The man flitters his tongue o'er his lips. Then he sings:

> Doxy O! Thy gaziers shine
>   As glimmer! By the Solomon,
> No gentry mort hath prats like thine,
>   No dell e'er wrapped with such a one.

Her husband runs at him with outstretched knife. The songster screams & bolts away.

Other men are laughing. They're all as dark to her as alligators in dark mud.

* * * * *

In bed beside her husband, she cannot sleep. 'Tis passing difficult to breathe. Upon her breast the baby kicks away bad dreams. She sighs out: Husband, I feel not well.

How so?

London-Towne's stink doth press upon my heart.

Aye, sweeting, but at least we go about not blackened by smoke as do your relatives—

I would bathe.

Tomorrow I'll find water for you, I promise.

You did promise yestereven—

In that respect I've sinned against thee, dear wife, for which I'm sorry. But tomorrow, I do swear—

Rebecca clambers out of bed, holding the baby at her breast so that he'll not wake. The hearth-embers envoy a richly bloody light. Believing her to be doing her business at the chamber-pot, her husband modestly closes his eyes. But she's looking for the walnut oil which her brothers did gift her with ere she left Tappahannock. They brought her a great gourdful of it, but (fearing the thumps of the sea-voyage) she'd translated it unto a fine jar of English earthenware which her husband had given her long since. She uncorks it and pours a little oil into her hand. It smells so perfect; 'tis the perfume of her home. Softly she rubs it on her baby's head. Then she draws her fingers across her nostrils several times, so that for a little twink she'll smell something more pleasant than the stench of her husband & this Belle Sauvage Inn . . .

✳ ✳ ✳ ✳ ✳ ✳

See Argall the e'er-worthy on a rainy November's day, striding into a Quarter Court held by the Virginia Company, where he's handily elected *Deputy Governor and Admirall of Virginia,* so that he need now brook no superior there, excepting the aforesaid Lord De La Warr, who continues too feveraguish to encoffin himself back westward in his long black ship. (A certain yeoman, by appellation *Captaine John Smith,* craves admittance to this Counsell. Kindly Argoll strides to the door to advise him: Your liver's ill-made for this fight, Sweet John, my fine knave — my *Prince,* I mean, my Prince of Milksops — of Cavaliers, was what I set out to say, when my tongue so unaccountably slipped upon your greasy vileness . . . — The yeoman shrills: Is this my requital then for all my pains? — Winking at Argull, the Marshal shuts the door.) As for John Rolfe, that laborer in GOD's vineyard gets elected *Secretary.* Captain John Martin (Sweet John's old enemy) is also there, and confirmed as *Master of the Ordnance.* How can such a sickly soul endure so long? Mayhap he's too feeble e'en to die!

Drawing off their gloves, Rolfe and Argall bid each other good morrow.

And now if I may question Secretary Rolphe, says Captaine Martynne, I'd like to be told how long you intend for your wife to live at our Companie's charge.

Your query's passing strange to me, replies Maister Rolfe. I'd thought the Princesse came at the Companie's demand.

(You see! chuckled Argoll into a stranger's ear. He names her *Princesse* now, to inflate her price. But at home she's but a drudge call'd *Rebecca. Passing strange* indeed!)

Martin says: I was not there when she got invited, Sir. (I speak sincerely.)

Nor were you, as I trow. But e'en if you construe the Companie accurately, I crave to know when this *Princesse* shall have fill'd her charge, & what charge she fills.

(*Bedmate* & *trull!* jested Argall. Nay, I forgot: *Wet-nurse* she is (nor an indifferent one, for her half-breed bratling doth thrive), & *predictable circus-beast*. And would you discover who made her so? Gaze upon me, O you clock-rul'd minions!)

Captaine Martynne, I cannot comprehend your displeasure, Rolfe returns. When have she, or I, contradicted the Companie? Can your mean wit o'erlook the humiliations of her life? And would you—

Methinks 'tis more humiliating that a husband cannot maintain his own wife. And meanwhile we turn no profit, & the Stock-holders bark at us—

For this I'll not be blamed. Whate'er revenue hath been discovered grows chiefly from the *Tobacco* which Rebecca shewed me how to cultivate—

And so the Gentlemen do make their debate like unto the legal Warres betwixt .2. English Parishes as to which must maintain a certain beggar. Where was he born? Where was he 'prenticed? Where doth he now reside? For such questions may well save the Parishioners several pence out of the poor-rate, can they but father him on the other Parish.

In the end, e'erworthy Captaine Argoll (whose quips & jokes Maister Rolfe had denied to hear) steps into the breach, saying: Full loyally hath Pocahontas served our turn. Bide your peace, Captaine Martynn. Yᵉ Companie had better secrete no spleen against her. Think you 'tis politick to present her to the rabble as a Princesse, then kick her down on her arse? I'd preferably array her in a tin crown like unto that toy we gave her father, & send her round with Mummers & Drummers for our street-stinkards to wonder at, because 'tis *they* we require to be our Servaunts in Virginia! Fear not, Martin; she's easily steered — and Maister Rolfe, being duteously endowed, hath surely engross'd our purpose in his heart.

Thanks for your word, Captaine Argoll. My wife & I do always honor you.

Their respective causes now being well achieved, Maister Rolfe doth invite the aforesaid Argull home to the Belle Sauvage Inn, to smartly *Tobacco*-scheme in private. A smile glimmers in the Captaine's eyes. Infallibly singing, he now wears golden stripes in his clothes. Rolfe's not taken by surprise; his uncanny partner doth unfailingly flourish in business, much as the fabled *Salamander* doth sport luxuriously in Hell's flames. No doubt he's divined certain new modes of trade. A Waterman in Gravesend hath hook'd him unto some richly dapper cousins of my Lord Salibury. Now, can the price but be held for a .12.month . . .

And how doth your little Princesse?

Why, in a quarter-hour you'll see her, Captaine Argoll, but I may as well tell you that she's been spiritless of late, as if she's caught some passing disease—

Aye, well, she hath not yet been *season'd* here. Bethink you, Rolfe, how many ill-season'd lads lie a-moldering in Jamestowne Church-yard.

I'd rather not haven my thoughts in that darkness. Rebecca's a strapping lass!

Nay, dear Maister Rolfe, I but jest! Strong & strapping bide we all, until the Church-clock strikes. Did you mark me? I said it's *Tick again* & *tick again,* till Time's lead clock hath boomed. — O, she'll thrive fore'er, no doubt.

Sometimes you confuse mine ear . . . Thro' this alley now.

Goodmistress Rolfe, it must be said, is nicely tucked up in a fair green dress, scotching any rumors of neglect on the part of the Company. She owns wondrous dark eyes in an otherwise unremarkable countenance. Argall proposes to buy for her a pair of the cork-bottomed shoes call'd *chopines,* for did she wear them beneath a long cloak, why, forsooth she'd appear taller, more like unto a Princesse which the Companie would have her be. But she sullenly returns him nay. — How about some rings for her fingers? E'en the naked-teated Mermaid in the Fishmongers' Companie's triumphal float wears those! This proposition also she denies. Argall grins, disdaining not to look her up and down. — To think of all the trouble she put me to! he muses, chewing, in delightfully rural fashion, upon a *Tobacco*-stem. — But then he turns to other subjects, for in truth it's hard to pay the wench any heed so far from Virginia. (Doubtless were some ill hap to take her off, he'd wish her back again.)

The *Frenchmen,* so he's heard, are making shift to recolonize North Virginia for their King; this is stiff news. And Lord Del La Warr's in his dotage; he'll destroy naught but paltry Salvages now. But could they raid the Spanish *Tobacco* Plantations of Hispianola . . . Argall longs to be full Governor of Virginia, not a mere Deputy . . .

The baby screams.

Where's Tomocomo? asks Argoll, remembering that sharp-eyed Salvage in the blue livery of a Servaunt.

Uttatatommakkin hath gone to shew his diabolickall dances again to Reverend Purchas.

And doth he write, *Tomocomo did such & such?* Or doth he prate more generally about antiquated Religions & other such quantities? Tomoco's a silly sullen fellow. 'Pon my faith, Pocahontas, let's kidnap his OKEUS! We'll marry him off to your husband's sister. Have you a sister, Maister Rolfe?

Afterward, Rebecca's husband escorts her to a vantage point for best admiring the coast of towers: *Saint Paul's Church, Bow Church, Saint Laurence's, the Exchange,* & *the Dutch Church,* but she most falsely and sullenly claims to have seen them all before.

* * * * * *

Oft he heard her mutter: *Maangairagwatonu,* but he knew not what it signified. So one day he did privily inquire of Uttamatomakkin, who chucklingly translated: *A great hole.*

* * * * * *

Indeed, as he'd told Argull, she was already gaunt from consumption by then, with her cheeks so hollowed-in that the bones beneath them started forth, & her dark eyes seemed to glare with sinister ferocity from their sockets. Even her chin had grown bony & hard. She was a wife, yet not a wife. A wife's the glass in which the husband should see himself, & yet altho' she smil'd on him & addressed him in becomingly low speech, he could not discover his likeness in her. Sometimes she fell as silent as Yndian bread-dough hardening on a stone. E'en the child shrank from him then, as if his blood could not persuade itself to yearn toward his father. Could it be possible they were both evil? — Nay, by his faith! Altho' his wife's mind had not yet broken free entire from its Salvage darkness, he cherished no fear . . .

* * * * * *

He conveys her to Heacham Hall, for to meet his family. In his new clothes he reminds her of a black cormorant drying his wings, the racks of his feathers hanging down.

They disregard her as if she were AHONE, Who of His own goodness makes the SUN to shine, & (being good) needs no propitiation at all. No matter. They're mischevious and evil, like all the Tassantasses—

Rebecca goes a-riding on a saddle-sore palfrey. Her Servaunt-maids stay at home with Thomas. Her husband rides ahead with his brother Henry, who's not been o'er friendly to her. Longing to return to the barn, her horse breaks into a canter, *Butter & eggs, butter & eggs,* until she draws alongside. Her brother-in-law is saying: I fear you've disremembered how the Scriptures do warn us to *despise the heathen.*

Rebecca comprehends his meaning full well. She fixes him with a glitering glare. She would hie her baby quickly forth from his house . . .

But Eleanor, her sister-in-law, is kind to her. Seeing the tears on her face, she leads her to the kitchen, shews her a cake, & says: Don't be scared to cut yourself a good breadth. Here's a knife, sweeting. Take what you like.

Thank you, *Sister.*

You're a good lass. Don't pay the others no mind. You're headed straight for HEAVEN.

Rebecca loves her husband again. She hates OKEUS. She loves the Tassantasses.

* * * * * *

See Rebecca in the bedchamber at Heacham Hall, gazing at a hanging: *Hope striving against the Idols.* Sullenly she draws on a long cloak of murrey velvet, almost as rich as that affected by our late Queen; then she picks up her new fan of swan's down. Her fable's like unto a deerhide with the hair half gone, as well she knows. Preparing for her sad AMEN, she ignores her husband's scoldings and commences culling the hairs from her armpits, using a pair of clamshells for her tweezers. He bites his lip; he calms himself. O, Maister Rolfe is acting wonderfully observant to her whims; he's a very obsequious husband. He's going to take her to see a masquing-show with many boats and lights; he's going to take her to see the King!

The Virginia Company has promised; belike also Queen Anne is curious to see the little Salvage maid; belike John Smith has written her some epistle on the subject . . .

Uttamatomakkin hath an eagle leg with fine talons, she says at last. Would you wish to borrow it of him?

What, sweeting, to wear in my hair?

Aye, for having married me you must partake now somewhat of my Salvage nature. 'Tis what the people say—

Which people?

Never mind, *Husband.* I must not contradict you.

* * * * * *

Yet now in truth she commenced to grow near about as happy as Sweet John approaching the cusp of some Adventure, for she'd never attended any of these affairs. Among her People she'd e'er joyed in dauncing round the fire. This masque would doubtless prove still more superior in sweetness, for whate'er the Tassantasses do fashion, its Salvage counterpart melts unto gossamer before it. Everybody said she'd have a treat. Moreo'er, the King would be there. 'Twas finally her opportunity to speak to him on her father's account. She knew enough now to keep silence about this with her husband, for he'd only warn & forbid her.

She feared naught. Hadn't she defied her own father before the People when she saved Sweet John? For the frowns of Tassantasses she scarcely cared.

Her Servingmaids entered in. They took Thomas away, for to feed & care for him. Sucking & reaching, eye-seeking for everything, he smiled on them for a twink. Then he commenced to cry. She heard the bleating of his desperate misery grow fainter as the women bore him away.

Come, come, sweeting, 'tis time to set forth.

Rebecca rush'd to vomit blood into the chamberpot.

* * * * * *

The King was already in his saturnal years, having waited so long & patiently for Elizabeth's demise that he was hoary when he came into England to be crowned. Her Slaughtermen had whisked off his own mother's head, and he'd kept silent, e'en toadied to slaughter's line for the sake of Kingship slimed and attainted by that acquiescence. So he rarely could enjoy his ease. Well, anyhow his mother had e'er disregarded him; she whirligigged upon her French follies, until she whirligigged down to death. Queen of Scots, she'd abated unto headless vassal of ooze. Her son wept out of .1. eye only. He feared to weep o'ermuch, for that would be treason. But did he distrain himself from any grief, they'd call him unatural. Leaden-tempered, he trudged patiently into his age. He forsook careless speech, & appointed for himself only the most furtive joys. Unable to doff the habit of scheming, he pleasured at foiling the schemes of others. 'Twas why he loved to examine witches, & hear 'em play strange tunes upon the trump. The men & women who got summonsed before him found him so round-eyed, so fearfully, flatteringly credulous, that they strove to amaze him e'en further with diabolical performances — no matter if they had to invent them on the spot. James must have his witches, & they had the grit to play along. 'Twas well worth the burning that came in the end. — But only infrequently could he play those brave games. Too much treason, after all, would bogeymander his sleep. Too many witches would affright the Kingdome. So he schemed on, & his thoughts swam joylessly on, just like those ships which come creeping through the night water to moor at the trees by Jamestown Fort.

Others, of course, did not live so. They must have their masques. He must show himself, must bring forth the living corpse of his soul & commaund it to smile thin-lipped.

They sat a-feasting at a long table covered with fine cloth, conversing most happily, their silken throat-wings flashing as they turned to gaze into .1. another's faces, whilst the Musicians sat at a smaller table, playing pleasant airs upon flute and cittern. What would Captaine Fortune gift 'em with tonight? (Amidst the witty smilings of Court ladies, a drunken libertine murmured: Can I but find Cupid, he'll save me, for that's his business; he'll take me far away . . .) The Banqueting Hall had been newly gilded, and adorned with pyramids & balls, some of gold, the remnant of silver.

Now came the Masque of a *She-monster* who birthed half a dozen Imps. She flew away, with whirring wings. She was off to make a plague.

A dyspeptic Gentleman whispered: Where's the *Sassafrass?* They always provide *Sassafrass* at these spectacles.

Now came the Masque of a *Talking cloud.* Now came the Masque of Aurora. *Trarintra-rarara!*

The miniaturist Nicholas Hilliard was there, on commission to paint a new portrait of His Majesty. Our late Queen had cherished his art, but rarely paid him; James was much the same. (Later, when he met Sweet John, Uttamatomakkin would complain: You gave Powhatan a white dog, which Powhatan fed as himself, but your King gave me nothing, and I am better than your white dog.) Maister Hilliard, himself near the grave, sat gazing into the King's eyes, hearing nothing of what was said, thinking over what colors he was to use; there is ordinarily a delicate and faint redness around the eyes, inclining slightly to the purple; in the King's case it was a shrill & ugly pink, and the whites of His Majesty's eyes were disturbed by throbbing red veins. On the morrow the King was to sit for the portrait. Maister Hilliard decided to paint his eye-whites full snowy.

Rebecca's husband had given her to understand that she must act just so, were she to avoid offending the Royal presence. He'd guide her through this even, like unto those Pilots who are wise enough to calculate precisely when & where a horizontal Moone doth make a full sea. She sat a-clasping together her perfumed leather gloves with the silver-gilt cuffs — a fine gift from the Virginia Company, as she did confess.

A Footman had carried off her velvet cloak. Another Footman had taken the basket which she'd woven to give the King. He'd sworn to see it deliver'd, but when he said it he laugh'd, so that Rebecca comprehended 'twas another lie. She cough'd into her hand.

She wore a silver tissue dress, the bust narrowing down to a curved point at her slender waist. She had once been nearly fat; she was slender now. Her neck was heavy with glass beads. Beside her on the .1. hand sat her husband, & on the other, Uttamatomakkin in his cape of dark brown turkey feathers — for while this marriage of hers required her to look civilized, the Ladies & Gentlemen of the Court might have been disappointed did he not play the Salvage part. He was nothing loath. He was an unregenerate Yndian.

Him they admired as they would have any new animal. Of her they said: What an ugly little Salvage! She appears unwell. But her manners are quite charming.

They said: What a pity that she is not an Englishwoman.

My word! Maister Rolfe has certainly taken a bunting for a lark! A very common-seeming Princesse his goodwife is . . .

How're their quims made? Are they the same as Englishwomen?

'Tis said they—

For a young woman, she appears to be a lame old jade.

'Tis true her father the King of Virginia wears a turkey-leg in his hair?

I did hear from Captaine Argoll that we crowned him with a bowl of tin!

Nay, that would be too ludicrous! Do you swear it?

'Pon my faith!

And who's that Salvage near her?

Tomocomo, he's named. The priest of her idolatry. Reverend Purchas claims the fellow can summon the DEVIL by means of a lodestone.

That's a lie. Otherwise we'd burn him.

My, but she doth look sickly! Are all their females made thus?

Apparently not, for a certain Gentleman of my acquaintance did whisper (in strictest confidence) that .1. day just past darklins when he got his opportunity—

'Tis said His Majesty was quite offended that Rolfe married with a foreign Potentate; 'twas near treason, he said . . .

Ah, but did ye hear the full jest? Apparently Pokahuntiss came not intact into his bed, for some greasy little yeoman had already sluppered up her maidenhead!

Well!

So when his Majestie was informed, he, realizing then that this *Pockahunta* was of no better quality than the basest Scullery-maid, did cry that the joke was on Rolfe!

Ha, ha, ha! (Don't let him hear.)

Now she glares upon us!

Fie! She does not!

She's ill at ease, no doubt, 'midst our sophisticated buzzing.

(When would she rise? When would she go to him & ask that her father's warrant to rule be respected? She long'd to lay down her head & rest. 'Twas strangely hot in this Palace; she feared she would vomit.)

Beside the King, the Queen sat brown, lumpy and shapeless like a flag-root.

Pocahontas, my joy! (Thus Argall, all doll'd up in a shirt embroidered with purled silver.) Or should I say *Rebecca*? Surprised to see me here? And do you still dislike me in all modesty? Tsk, tsk, what a bad name I must have! Come now; twirl about for my Lords & Ladies! The sooner you do, the sooner you'll be quit of 'em! (This last was whispered odiously in her ear.) 'Tis your task to stir up avarice in the browsing rump-eaters of this Cittie. Look, lassie (or shall I call thee *Sweeting* as your husband doth?) — there goes the royal Standard-Bearer, with his colors fresh & freaked; we'll make *him* wish he'd had the luck to marry with you!

Rebecca kens not all the fancy words he doth spew.

But say! You've neglected to paint your face either red or silver, as you were wont to do! Well, to be sure, your father's *Puccoons* & *Antimony*-mines lie at a considerable distance . . .

Dear Captaine Argoll, kindly respect my wife's innocency.

And what do you think your father's busy doing this even? Broiling offenders in the coals, I misdoubt me not.

(His eyes glow & glare like unto noonday-light through a pair of smoke-holes.)

Captaine Argall, I must remind you that my wife's no toy or pawn of yours, to torment as you list.

Oho, I'd disremembered. In me there's acid-stuff which etches away the past. To a pleasanter subject, then: Have you enjoyed her quim, Maister Rolfe?

Her husband reddens. He would spring at Argoll's throat, but — well, Argull can be simultaneously so kind . . . Besides, now that Argall's Deputy Governor, he'll soon be ruling o'er Maister Rolfe, who's thus all in a whirl. He fears to launch upon any action. He gazes anywhere but at his wife. (The King was watching catty-corner from his eyes, pulling at his spade-shapen beard. Gazing at him, Rebecca seemed to behold a bird's black neck in a grey river.)

La, la, *la*. Excuse my quips if they're too vulgar for your liking. I haven't yet had leisure to drink in piety at Reverend Whittaker's knee. Come, dear Rebecca, have you disremembered how to speak?

I forget nothing, Captaine Argall.

And when, pray, do you return to Virginia? I must up sail ere long, & it'd be my pleasure to fraught you homewards if 'twas convenient for you to keep your husband company—

I know not, replied Lady Rebecca shortly.

Good, for a female's conjectures should not be admitted.

Argall winked at Maister Rolfe, who sat so uncomfortably sluppered up in silks. — She *will* bring you back, you know, he said. Remember the proberb: *If you take a wife from hell, she'll bring you back if she can.*

She flinched, & Rolfe said: Good Captaine Argoll, 'tis not meet to speak so.

Playing with his own gold buttons, like unto a jaunty Musician who finger-flitters on a zithern, Argall replied: Come, 'twas but a jest. What silly faces you both do wear! You're stilted people, friends, like unto those Lincolnshire lozels that do strut wooden-legged 'pon dreary oze. Give o'er; 'tis *Merriment's* hour now. Be gay, Maister & Mistress Rolfe, for—

I crave pardon, Captaine, but d'ye see how she flinches from you?

O come, jeered Argall (evidently in his cups). You have no call to be afeared of *me*. I'm hardly of the same stripe as that father of yours, who as I said *broils offenders in the coals* . . .

Uttamatomakkin now smiled, remarking in his accustomed venomous whisper: But, Captaine Argall, among you Tassantasses, a husband-poisoner is burned alive, while a wife-poisoner is boiled alive in lead.

*　*　*　*　*　*

I see you commence to form fine opinions of us, Tomocomo. I would we'd never sailed you here.

(Reverend Purchas had examined him again. He'd refused to admit the self-evident superiority of the Christian doctrine. — Why, he's no wiser than Sir Giles Goosecap!* cried Purchas in amaze.)

I am the voice of my People, the Salvage said. I am likewise my People's ears. Powhatan will listen when I tell him of your Countrey . . .

Rebecca smiled then, fierce with pride.

No doubt, replied gentle Argoll. And 'tis true you can shoot fishes with

*A proverbial figure of fun.

an arrow on a cord? I know you can feed cornmeal to the DEVIL. So I've read in Captaine Smith's relation . . .

* * * * * *

Declining now in her resolution (for to rise & approach the presence now seems too awful, Captaine Argoll having suck'd out her substance), she whispers: Husband, stand you certain 'tis the King?

'Tis he without a doubt, dear wife.

Then I would speak with him. I would tell him my father's complaints—

(She knows that she will not, being weak now all the time. Can sea-grass deny to bow unto the wind?)

Rebecca, I dare not permit this. For I have it on good credit that he's much angered at our marriage. 'Tis treason, so he says, for a mere commoner such as myself to wed a King's daughter, & so I must not pretend—

Then you grant my father's a King.

O yes, but—

(She'd exposed him. 'Twas as if she'd scraped away the sand from a conch-shell & found the dark wet squirming meat within.)

When you murthered Wowinchopunck's wife & children at Pasapegh & then fired the Towne—

Rebecca, 'twas not I.

No matter.

No matter! You say this to your own husband! Moreo'er, here's not the place to embroil ourselves, since we can't 'scape jealousy's o'erhearing.

I do not comprehend . . .

These Gentlemen begin to listen. Prithee speak more softly—

What if I won't?

Rebecca, your father burn'd up Captaine Radclyffe & many others besides. Think you if you annoy His Majestie with the events of that Warre he'll be your friend?

And so she gave o'er her opportunity, & then they did depart the Palace, passing by the liveried Sentinels who stood as still and baleful as the Faces on posts outside any Temple of OKEUS. They went home to the Belle Sauvage Inn. They were o'ertowered by the clucking clocks of Policy.

THE GRAMMAR OF ENDEARMENTS (1616)

I, by love's limbeck*, am the grave
of all that's nothing.

JOHN DONNE, "A Nocturnal upon S. Lucy's Day, Being the Shortest Day" (1633)

*F*rauncis hath grey in his beard. His wool cap is become a part of his head, & he carries a long shepherd's crook, which their father never affected.

Anna suffers from a pain in her back, no doubt an affliction of the kidneys, so he strolls out to draw water for her from the well, for which she thanks him, but smilelessly. Feeling himself cumbered & distrained, he promises himself yet again ne'er to return to Willoughby, knowing that should he live long enough he'll come back again & yet again.

The Church-bell tolls. He'd prefer not to go, but durst not bring trouble upon his relations. Back 'neath triple-chamfered Tower arch! His prayers are casting umbrages on the floor.

Frowning at him, Anna clears ashes from the hearth. He remembers that amongst the Virginian Salvages, women are in charge of fires.

He suffers from an inflammation of his ankles where the Tymor's chains scarred them. Sometimes they swell, & he can scarcely sleep. But he'll not yet permit himself to be o'erwhelm'd by any bodily complaint. 'Twould make trouble for his relations. Setting his teeth, he pretends that he's sitting at his ease beneath a cherry-tree at *Nonsuch,* which was his Dream-Towne in Virginia. Just as some villains, pretending to be Gentlemen, do borrow horses from inns, & never ride back with them, so do his fancies frequently steal him away, & leave him in Virginia. He remembers that summer's day at Poynt Comfort when dragg'd their new shallop down the dunes' belly — but of course he was prisoner'd then on the *Susan B. Constant.* Closing his eyes, he sees Powhatan (who sports a turkey-leg in his hair).

The breeze plays with his hair; he pretends 'tis Tragabigzanda's fingers — nay, Pokahuntiss's — which touch him.

---

*Alembic.

They feed him on butter, cheese, curds & suchlike white meats. It rains & rains. Sweet John takes up his quill and commences to Undertake his *Sea Grammar,* penning: *A wet Docke is any place, where you may hale in a ship into the ooze out of the tide's way* . . . Willoughby is his wet dock. The fierce cold tides he once throve in now weary him; he craves to hide.

Anna rolls up her sleeves to work dough for a pie. Discovering those secret frayed white under-straps now tucked back around her elbows, her brother-in-law feels unaccountably sad & ashamed.

He remembers once spying Cicely in her blouse of bright red wool, with a dirty old apron slung carelessly o'er; 'twas when Mr. Reese Allen abode in life. She must have had some task to do in the kitchen.

*   *   *   *   *   *

He dines with kindly *Argall* in a red-latticed Tavern-house at Gravesend. He's pleading for a preferment, that he may return to Virginia, to get a place on the Counsell. Well, there's no Counsell anymore. Like unto my Lord De la Warr, he longs to be safely coffin'd in a ship. — I thank GOD all places are alike to me, he lies. — Argall hears him carelessly. Later he tells his Masters: Having spitted .3. Moorishmen, he's now resolved CHRIST owes him e'ery contrivance to hook him out of Hell. Three Moorishmen! Three fat Turkes who tripped over their own pajamas, & he 'fesses it modestly to the world! As well I ought to crow for wringing the necks of .3. trussed turkeys!

Do you attend my words, Captaine Argall? this tiresome *Smith* is saying.

Yea, Sweet John, but I must soon take my leave of you.

I crave not your charity, Sir, says John Smith so bitterly.

Welladay, what you crave not, I must not give. Now, fellow, knowest thou the distinction between a fair and a foul sea?

I —

Ha! Brutus, did ye e'er hear the like? This humorous upstart who would upraise himself from plough to paddle, kens not his own foul water that he pisseth forth in jets of eloquence! Sweet John, get thee gone to Lord Willoughby, and eat your preferments out of his arse . . .

*   *   *   *   *   *

See Captaine John Smith, now apprehensive, but using his best endeavor, as when he .1.st visited Miss Cicely Allen with his childish proposition of matrimony. He's off to visit Goodmistress Rebecca Wrothe, who now resides at Brentford in Middlesex. *Come back, come back, come back.*

Good even, my Lady, he croaks out, louting low on his knees. (Kocoum would have brought her many fat fishes.)

The baby sleeps, offering up his ear to the light.

I have a fine knife for Uttamatommakkin, he says. See? 'Tis sharp enough to carve out a flea's eye—

She covers her face with her hands, then turns away, gazing at the wall as tho' she were marvelous discontented. Captaine Smith in distress cries out: I repent myself to have writ the Queen she could speak English!

She's never merry now, saith Maister Rolfe. Best leave her.

So they turn & turn about in the garden for a good .2. hours, telling one another stories of Virginia (which is a strange and Salvage land scarcely yet marked on our *Mappa Mundi*). Captaine Smith doth most earnestly whisper how in departing that Countrey he forsook his best hours, locking them in with scruples. Such shady leafy joys he'd held level behind the walls of his heart! And now the ooze hath entered in.

To which Maister Rolfe replies: I'm passing sorry, Sir.

Excuse me, but what tidings had the Companie? You being Secretary, I had hop'd that had I grace sufficient to entreat you—

The time is not yet *Politick*.

O.

And now, Captaine Smith, I regretfully must—

Mayhap she disremembers me, ventures Sweet John, shipwrecked far from his vessel of ease.

If it be so, Sir, her forgetfulness arrived but today, for she ever speaks of you.

Why, 'tis kind of you to tell me so, Maister Rolfe. And I must congratulate you, on obtaining so rare a bride—

(Sweet John damned that deed of Argall's when he heard it, but age now begins descending o'er his soul's candle like an upturned glass; his flame flickers and struggles; he must earn his living.)

Maister Rolfe bows, uneasy with this tiresome guest.* Captaine Argoll, within whose assessments he treasures up his trust, hath call'd the man *A shining, crippled little soul*.

And your *Tobacco*, I hear that it doth thrive

So far hath Fortune serv'd me. Now tell me somewhat of your doings, Captaine Smith.

Well, .2. years since, I guess it's been now, I embarked myself for New

---

*After all, dear Reader, they're scarcely e'en fellow Countreymen, for *Boston Deeps* lies oozy — .3. hundred square miles of ooze! — betwixt Countie Lincoln and Countie Norfolk.

England as *Admirall of the Fleet,* but we took neither whales nor gold, so
I—

You made a map! cries Maister Rolfe with a bright blank smile.

Aye. So then I did hie me to Sir Fernando, the Governor of Plimouth-
Towne, with a project for a Colonie in those parts . . .

Scarcely paying heed (for he's thinking upon his Goodwife's sadness, wondering whether 'twould better ease her heart, did he dismiss this pest utterly
& forever), he inquires: What do you purpose to do now, Captaine Smith?

Sir Fernando hath promised me **.20.** ships, altho' I misdoubt me not I'll
find scarce half so many . . . And — But tell me this. You rest content in
Virginia?

'Tis our home, replies Maister Rolfe.

And sure your *Nonpareil* hath afforded you great help.

That she hath, says Rolfe with a weary smile.

The old Captaine approaches closer, whispering: O, what a great and
compassionate spirit hath your wife!

She means well, without a doubt.

I penned the Queen that *should she not be well received, seeing this
Kingdome may rightly have a Kingdome by her means; her present love to
us and Christianity might turn to such scorn and fury, as to divert all this
good to the worst of evil.* I beg you, Maister Rolfe, tell me 'twas not cunningly said!

You must hold her love & faith in scant regard, the husband frowningly
replies, do you truly believe that some reverse would impel her to hatred.

Nay, nay, Maister Rolfe, I aimed only at her good—

For that intention she and I both must thank you, saith his host. Now,
would you care to smoke a pipe of my latest *Tobacco?*

Aye, I think I would—

No doubt my wife was astonished, Captain Smith, that you forbore to
visit us before.

'Twas an unhappy accident which expell'd me from Jamestowne. I—

She speaks of you oftener than you might dream.

The guest rejoins in a rapid low whisper, as though he'd schooled himself against this very matter: You must understand that Maister Wingfield
has always hated me, because I deposed his dark schemes into the light.
And Maister Percy & he did always deal together, altho' I gave Pearcie Adventures & preferments in my time. Now, since my Lord De La Warr was
e'er attached to Wingfield by cousinage, it seemed bootless to—

Aye, thinks Rolfe to himself, mayhap this tarnished old Pirate's full adread, lest she mislikes him now, lest he's brought her remedyless unrest. Belike his years away have pained her . . .

(In truth, when he'd told her whom her visitor would be, her sallow face had frozen for a hideous long time, & then she'd hiss'd betwixt her teeth: *Your people are lucky in me. Do you know why, Husband?* Because 'tis my nature to drink down insults, & never vomit them up against you. My father & other relations are not constituted so conveniently . . .)

Captaine Smith, he says aloud, I pray you come with me.

* * * * * *

They entered Rebecca's budoir. Again he made a leg, clicked his heels, and whispered: *Your most humble Servaunt . . .*

Nay, *Father,* I remember you well, said she with an ironic smile. And do you remember the courtesies I did you?

Yes, my Lady. But I pray you call me *Father* no more, for percase it pains your husband—

Doth it pain you?

Nay, sweeting, I—

There, you see, it pains him not. You did promise Powhatan that what was yours should be his, & he promis'd the like to you. You call'd him *Father* being in his land a stranger. So for the same reason must I do you.

O, for you are a stranger here, he repeated stupidly. (She'd become so icily composed!)

You may well say that, *Father.*

I dare not allow you call me by that name, my Lady, you being a King's daughter with a well set countenance—

Were you not afraid to come into my father's Countrey, and did you not cause fear in him and all his people but me?

Yes, my Lady.

And fear you here I should call you *Father?* she shouted.

So I fear.

I tell you then I will, and you shall call me child, and so I will be for ever and ever your Countreywoman!

Pardon me, Maister Rolfe, I beseech you—

Nay, Captaine Smith, I'm not offended.

Her lip trembled as she said: They did tell us always you were dead, and (here she rounded on her husband) *I knew no other till I came to Plymouth—*

Captaine Smith did gaze upon her with woebegone eyes.

Yet Powhatan did command Uttamatomakkin to seek you and know the truth, she sobbed, because your Countreymen will lie much.

Pocahontas, my fine young dearling —

Prithee, *Father,* I like that name not. No one who respects my faith calls me by it anymore . . .

Was it not what thy father called thee?

Nay, not often, she said, turning away. She coughed into a handker-chief.

What did he call thee?

I shall not tell you. Ask my husband if you do not know.

'Tis true I know not.

Why did you fail you of your promise, to make me little bells, & my father hatchets?

Why, Princesse, because I did never learn me of that craft.

Tell me this then. What virtues do you own?

Well, child, I did learn me some Greekish, & how to read & reverence GOD, & how to serve my betters, acquit myself with arms, muster Soldiers, make maps, & make a brave show, & keep myself clean.

And 'tis a brave show you put on indeed, dear *Father.*

Lady Rebecca, pray what name did he call thee?

. . . And suddenly he remembered a summer's noon ever so long ago when he and Peregrine Bartty were boys together, a sparkling and pleasant day; Bartty had a new hawk, and so of course they went a-hawking. In the riverbank Sweet John found something — an elf-bolt, as people called it, or maybe a thunder-stone: some mysterious concretion of earth or rock in an arrowheaded shape — from fairies, Bartty said, but John Smith remembered it & 'twas nowise other than the flints that Pocahontas's people shaped to point their arrows with. And he wondered what else they had done that was buried now in the earth.

And she whispered to him that same word that she had uttered long ago: *Mufkaiuwh,* which signifies *A Flower of a fine thing.* But this time she whispered it in bitterness. And he never learned whether her father had called her this, or whether she meant it to apply to him as in the olden days. After that she withdrew & would not come out. When Maister Rolfe (having seen their guest to the door) peeped in to visit her, he found her weeping so wild as to be almost beyond the bounds of submission.

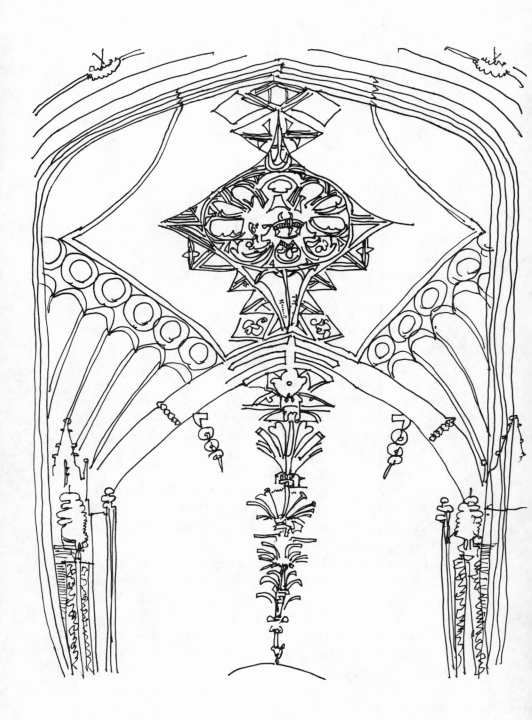

THE GRAMMAR OF CHURCHES (1617)

Harke! 'Twas the trump of death that blewe
My hower is come false world adewe
Thy pleasures have betrayed me soe
That I to death untymely goe.

WILLIAM STRACHEY (*ca.* 1620)

*S*ee Argall, now Deputy Governor of Virginia, at Pocahontas's funeral.
He sits beside John Rolfe on the men's side of the Church, chaunting his
Amens & *Hallelujahs* to the departed soul. Argoll's mutchado'd
Sailors likewise attend. Rolfe, pale and not quite weeping, stiffens as Rev-
erend Frankwell says:

Blessed is he whom Thou dost choose and bring near,
to dwell in Thy courts!

That verse I know pretty well, says Argull to himself. And what comes
after, I'll guess upon: We'll dump yonder wench into a hole to let her rot.
Ha, she'll be cosily lodged . . .

In the wilderness prepare the way of the LORD, says Reverend
Frankwell. *Make straight in the desert a highway for our GOD. Every
valley shall be lifted up, & every mountain and hill be made low; the uneven ground shall become level, and the rough places a plain.*

Now I must write the Companie to inform them of this, thinks Argall.
Rolfe will never have the sense to do it. And the brat on his lap is sick, they
say; how misfortunate for our claims if he too should kick up his heels —

The coffin lies proud, its gable roof like unto a single long breast beneath
the velvet pall. Uttamatomakkin & the other Salvages gaze upon it full af-
frightedly, paying the sermon no heed. Had she died at home, they would
have wrapped her in a cornhusk mat. But the Tassantasses do everything in
a more heavy, solid way. When will they commence for to toll the bell?
And why do they build no fire here? Menaced by the clammy dolor of this
Church, Rebecca's women weep more restrainedly than they would have at
home. Uttamatomakkin has already warned 'em that Maister Rolfe, sim-

pleton that he is, will fail to serve out beads afterwards. The women pity him, the baby, & above all themselves. They will weep for themselves still louder when they learn an hour hence that the Tassantasses have destined them to remain in England as Maid-servaunts. This moment they ken it not. They weep for the now remedyless misery of Amonute's life. They crave to set her high and safe on a platform — earth-holes are for commoners. But what do the Tassantasses care for their wishes? Moaning in fear, the women half expect the pall to commence magically fluttering and trembling as do the feathers of a bird's breast. After all, it must exist for some purpose, & the Tassantasses can accomplish strange things. But it lies moveless; nor comes the coffin to life. In a twink 'twill be let down upon slow ropes. How far beneath us constitutes fair soundings? (Reader, never fear. Rebecca will be safely berth'd.) Rolfe's lips are moving raptly, like unto a child's that will be punished if it does not remember what it's been told.

Now whom must I kidnap next to save our bacon? says Argall to himself. I'm passing wearied with these bunglers.

✳ ✳ ✳ ✳ ✳ ✳

That very same day, kindly Captaine Argoll, accompanied by Uttamatomakkin & the widower Rolfe, but not by Pocahonatas's bratling, whom Argall left in the care of Rolfe's brother Henry, boarded the *George,* a sleek if not over-commodious vessel, and set sail from Gravesend for Virginia, to take up his new office (a noble & fitting dignity, which I did not long since engross in parchment). It is written that his reign was very harsh.

End of yᵉ .III.rd Dream

GRAVESEND (1348–1996)

FURTHER HISTORY OF THE WILLOUGHBY DE ERESBY FAMILY
(1348–1995)

"... and more ought to be known about Lord Willoughby de Eresby's Eresby (Spilsy; L), once very large indeed."

NIKOLAUS PEVSNER AND JOHN HARRIS,

The Buildings of England:

Lincolnshire (1964)

*A*ccording to Pevsner and Harris, the site of "this lost great house," which, like John Rolfe's piece of Virginia, had been originally acquired by marriage, was to be found at the end of an avenue which began just west of the Church of Saint James (nowadays one must specify, for there are other houses of worship in Spilsby, too, all of them preparing us to die and become ooze). The avenue ran southwards from that spot, terminating at a "lonely but magnificent brick and stone quoined GATEPIER." Like an obedient voyager, I began at the beginning, which is to say the Church.* In the family Chapel I met the effigy of John, .1.st Lord Willoughby (died 1348), of John his son, the .2.nd Lord Willoughby (died 1372), of Robert his son (died 1396), who shared a tomb with his wife Margaret (died 1391), of William, the .5.th Lord Willoughby (died 1410), who lay beside his wife, of Richard Bertie, who died in 1582 and mingled his bones most romantically with those of his wife, the Baroness Willoughby de Eresby, who'd died .2. years before. In the top frieze I spied Peregrine Bertie, the .10.th Lord Willoughby, who was John Smith's landlord and who died in 1601. We know that his son, Sweet John's playmate, young Barty, held exactly the

---

*I am sad to report that the Willoughbys' antecedents do not seem to go back to that other beginning, the Domesday Book, where "in *SPILESBI*, *IRESBI* and *THORPE* (Saint Peter) Asketill has 6 curacates of land taxable. Land for 6 ploughs. The Bishop has 1 plough ... Value before 1066, 20 shillings; now the same." No Willoughbys anywhere.

same name. His daughter, who came to anchor in 1610, is represented "semi-reclining," as Pevsner puts it (without *him* I'd be lost).

Pressing on to the GATEPIER, I found that King Oozymandias had claimed most of their monument. In Willoughby, not far from Saint Helena's Church, there lie .7. bowl-shaped barrows in .2. rows, graves from the old time. Now they scarce come up to a man's knees, although they're monstrous wide. Thus diminish all material things, Christian as well as pagan. The GATEPIER was good for nothing now save but to pad out Pevsner and Harris's pages. But the Willoughbys had dwelt so long in these parts that the very soil had grown accustomed to them. 'Twas not so easy for time to slime over every trace. Why, they left relics at Willoughby, Tattershall, Edenham, and even Swinstead, where the .19.ᵗʰ-century tomb of Baroness Willoughby de Eresby remains (an ornate affair with her coloured coat-of arms, elaborate canopies with four little saints, *and .3. shield-bearing angels below*). Their history's near about as long as the fishhook with which we catch sturgeons in the River *Iames*.

In 1634, shortly after the death of John Smith, we find Peregrine Bartty, now long invested with the powers of a Country-Squire, at loggerheads with Sir Philip Lunden, who's now been granted almost every salt marsh in Countie Lincoln, to enclose & improve for himself if he can. King James commaunds Barty's brother (which is to say, Robert my Lord Willoughby) to arbitrate. Who do you think wins?* In 1641, we find Robert raising horses and troops to help King Charles fight the Long parliament. A year later, rewarded by a destiny as vibrant as the orange lichens along the topmost edges of the tombstones in Tattershall, he falls at the battle of Edgehall alongside .2. of his sons. Willoughbyship thus reverts to his boy Montagu, who's .1. of King Charles's pallbearers after the trial and decapitation. Half a century later, says the dustiest book on my shelf, *there emerged a decisive influence in county affairs in the person of Lord Willoughby de Eresby . . .* — namely Montagu's grandson, Robert, .4.ᵗʰ Earl of Lindsey & .16.ᵗʰ Baron Willoughby de Eresby.

In 1769, Eresby Hall burned down, but the family had already removed to Grimsthorpe long before.

The Willoughbys have their eponymous town as a memorial, but in death their lowly tenant trumped them long ago. Justice insists that we think of Barty and his father when we stroll among what Arthur Mee, with

---

*"Ignorant, or envious, if you be Readers: it is not to satisfie the best of you that I now wright." — Ralph Hamor.

his earnest would-be lyricism, describes as the "red-roofed cottages, tree-shaded roads, and a flower-bedecked station," which "all help to make the village attractive." But justice will not be heard. *Willoughby* has become a pseudonym for *Captain John Smith,* whom Mees, under the title "A Shining Place in History" describes as an "Empire-builder."

FURTHER HISTORY OF THE ROLFE FAMILY
(1616–1626)

Sleep is a reconciling,
  A rest that peace begets:
Doth not the sun rise smiling
  When fair at even he sets?
Rest you, then, rest, sad eyes,
  Melt not in weeping,
  While she lies sleeping
Softly, now softly lies
  Sleeping.
          ANONYMOUS, 1603

*N*ow it came spring at Jamestowne, and the waters rose very great, covering the grass with darkness which sparkled with innumerable question marks. Salvages of the better sort in their copper-embroidered mantles came most humbly to beg the boon of English friendship; while the commoner sort of Salvages who scarcely owned means to cover their secret parts with leaves or moldy leather emerged shyly from the wet leaves, hoping to indenture themselves, & turn more English. They'd become good Gunners now; Deputy Governor Yeardley kept a Salvage merely to kill fowls for his larder; and (until Argall's arrival) 'twas not uncommon to see a Salvage Sergeant-at-Arms drilling musters of Englishmen! Powhatan's brother Prince *Opechancanough* did also come frequently into Jamestowne, in order to extend his hand unto the palefaced breathren, preserving his sleepless smile, that did glare upon all alike, from the Governor down to the meanest pikeman. 'Twas said he could tame wolf cubs to be dogs. Why not believe he could likewise translate all his Salvage highwaymen & blackguards into loyal servitors of King James? Oft they did commaund him to remind Powhatan of his promise, that after Pocahontas died the English should have another Princesse to bring to bed, for the sake of unsundered alliance — to which he replied: 'Tis well. Great Powhatan hath no design against the peace . . . — and yet no shaveheaded **.10.**-year-olds came a-cartwheeling to shew their quims at Jamestowne anymore. And as for Powhatan himself, well, just as a ship hard-pressed by Pirates *strikes hull,* as we call it, which means to take down all his sails, in order (as he hopes) to sneak away by night without shewing any telltale pallid flutters, so King Powhatan stole e'er further away from the English year by year — which relished all parties well. So passed the sunny years. The Salvages begged beads, and cried: Give us good measure of cloth for our wives. Give us copper kettles!

John Rolfe was among those who, hanging up his armor & sword, be-friended these cutpurses (or *Yndians* as they are sometimes called), out of reverence to the memory of his wife. (After all, even Rebecca was born white; her mother had annointed her with a red ointment of earth & root-juice.) He got his family a Salvage Servant-maid, to whom he did show visage as tenderly generous as e'er was Lord Willoughby's to poor John Smith. But in 1617, not wanting to repeat his interracial experiment (which indeed might have lost him whate'er advantage he'd gained by union with a Princesse), he wed an Englishwoman named Joane Pierce, whose baby (born **.5.** years after the commencement of this union) soon loudly sucked, smacked its lips, grew into a womanchild. The language of Salvages spattered on her head like rain. From walnut-oiled Servitors as well as from her father, who'd grasped a few words in his previously married time, she learned to say *Ahķeÿ vwwaap,* which signifieth, *it hurts me.*   Just as spring snow finds itself speckled with dark dirt, so she dis-cover'd life & experience e'en as her father, beset by eerie memories of Re-becca, murmured in sleep: Away, sprite! — I cannot say why his dead *Nonpareil* should have affrighted him, except percase by the very Salvage-ness which she shared with all her wild kindred. Had he un-Englished himself with her? When he purposed to fetch him his son by that Lady, Joane (who was long-necked like unto a deer) answered that this would be a long score for her to bear, at least till little Elizabeth did thrive in years. Governor Argall likewise advised postponing Thomas Rolfe's return. And so the father felt it best to leave his son in fosterage a little longer, *for the good of the Colonie,* of course. Therefore he conveniently dreamed & delayed, until in the end they never saw one another again. Could Mais-ter Rolfe have wished to fan away from him the scent of Salvage flesh (e'en though it came from his own loins)? Of his **.3.** marriages, the union with Rebecca remained most problematic in his thoughts. When he dreamed of her, it was as a black swan that she returned to him: hissing, magical, inhuman.

But Maister Rolfe could not have been construed as being entirely discontented; for they now shouted for Virginia tobacco in the ale-houses of London; he'd increased his credit & to spare. His special variety, call'd *Varina,* was widely conceiv'd to be the best. Already he had .3. bullocks, .3. Servaunts, land in the aforesaid Country of Toppahannah (where he used to live with Rebecca), a red-sealed patent to a portion of Mulberry Island, and rents & profits from other seemly parcels. They call'd him *an Ancient Planter.* His house & lands were kept busked up most neatly. Every harvest season there came to his Plantation a graceful pinnace whose sails were dimensioned almost like sheets of paper; and this pinnace departed for Jamestowne laden almost to the water-line with hogsheads of his *Tobacco,* ready for sale. In 1618, when they finally put Sir Walter Ralegh to death in London Towne, the wiser sort said: There's immoderation's reward. He wanted to possess perfection at all points. Better emulate Maister Rolfe, who married a Princesse, but merely a Salvage one, so that King James became not too angry, as they say . . . — And indeed Rolfe's inferiors did imitate him, growing *Tobacco* in the very streets as they got leave, dreaming of shiny new Churchpence & Kingdomepence to enrich their pleasures. (No matter that about .300. souls did perish of *the seasoning* within a single revolution about the Sunne; no doubt 'twas worse in London-Towne.) In that year, England did smoke up more than .20,000. pounds of sotweed! And a mere .12. month later, 'twas said that England did import more *Virginian* than *Spanish* leaf. — Now 'tis Rolfe on the Counsell, quoth Argall, and all because his *Tobacco* doth thrive, and because he dragged that Salvage wench to bed. I should have tupped her myself.

That same year, Governor Yeardley did create a House of Burgesses for Virginia. *Trarintra-rarara.* And that House did decree to tax all freeborn men of greater than .16. years, the tax to be payable in tobacco (.10. pounds' worth). Good Maister Rolfe redeemed his tax with ease. Howbeit, shadows slept upon his fields.

Round about 1620 a Gentleman call'd *Thomas Lambert* (of excellent repute in that Countrey) did discover that the weed could be more effectually & safely cured, did the Servaunts but hang its leaves upon a line, instead of fermenting them all in a heap as did the poor Salvage Yndians. Maister Rolfe, altho' passing mortified that Rebecca had so barbarously instructed him, was among the .1.st to adopt Maister Lambert's method, by virtue of which his profits did arise yet further into glorious constancy. E'en King James himself had come around. Now he was a-taxing tobacco for his own profit; and his Agents fix'd each .20,000.-weight of the leaf which came into England with a Government stamp, so that fewer smugglers could cheat his revenues.

Maister Rolfe died most likely in 1622, either of sickness (which historians hold most likely) or of the infamous massacre of that same year, which was carried out by Rebecca's people. He died passing rich. They draped his coffin in a funeral pall of fine black silk, and lowered him into ooze. He was gone now; he'd reached the haven's mouth. Jane Rolfe soon became Mrs. Roger Smith.

His will survives, & divides the estate most impartially among the new wife, the English daughter, & the half-Salvage son, with his father-in-law being the executor.

As for Thomas Rolfe, the old records say that he'd entered that Countrey of Magick call'd *Virginia,* by 1635 at the latest. By then, I suppose, he was keen to make a name for himself, like any other masterless man who pastes to Saint Paul's door a paper bragging of his own rentable qualities. And why not? His patrimony had come justly due. He'd received an education of sorts from his Uncle Henry, who'd granted him leave to dip through many a primer & nautical book, from which he'd adorned his mind with such pearls as these:

Nowe for to make your instrumentes for the Sea with their vses, you shall repayre to the booke of Nauigation, made by Martine Cortis a Spanyarte, Imprinted by maister Jugge printer to the Queenes maiestie, which booke hath bene very chargeable to him, therefore it is not for me to meddle with nothing contained in that booke, or els I would haue shewed you the makinge of the Equinoctiall diall with his vse, which is very profitable to know the houre of the daie by.

Uncle mine, have you Maister Cortyss's booke in your collection?

That were a jest! Surely you don't think me eager to underwite Spanish commerce . . .

Uncle, pray tell me, what's an equinoctial dial?

Hang'd if I know! But should you desire to learn, why not take to the sea? I have a letter from worthy Captaine Argall remembering himself

to you. Misdoubt you not, lad; he'd fit you out — altho' I fear he's lately
perished—

Nay, I commit myself to you . . .

Your father died rich in Jamestowne, Thomas. And I trust that you
yourself—

Why sent he never for me?

Well, but you were passing young & delicate for sea-voyaging! Then,
too (as I confess), he doted upon your stepmother, who e'en now ranks her
offspring first. 'Tis natural in a woman. Never mind, lad; of your true
mother you need not be ashamed; she died a Christian, as I've oft imparted to
you . . .

From Billingsgate in London-Towne the fare's but tuppence to
Gravesend if you would ride in an open barge. That is how Thomas went,
in order to economize. How could he arrest his sacredly natural progres-
sion downward from *Nobleman* to *Gentleman* to *Citizen* to *Countreyman?*   (Would ye care to enjoy a spot of honest quim, Sir? quoth the
Waterman. I know a maid nam'd Joan Fortune, who's never yet been
mined. 'Tis but tuppence for half an hour of her company . . .) Thomas
comprehended full well that although he had patent to **.1,200.** acres &
more, his appointment to the Colonie remained equivocal.   His dead
mother (whose face, songs & everything he disremembered) counted for no
more now than the decapitated Queen of Scots who'd once given King
James suck. If the Counsell of Virginia yet pretended that the new Hundreds they were a-peopling throughout that Dominion required legitima-
tion through some Salvage bequest, why, then Thomas's mother would still
be call'd *Princesse,* & he himself would find sweet sinecure. But by now
the Colonie might be thriving so well (Jamestowne-Isle now partly mown,
bleached & corner-smoothed), as to disdain such self-abasing niceties, in
which case Thomas would be no more than what he was: an orphan whose
stepmother's father controlled his inheritance. And I've heard tell this man
delayed to render unto him his legacy. His half-sister was cold; she seem'd
most explicably to mislike him. We must not marvel, therefore, that like his
late father, Thomas Rolfe chose to cultivate his interests & allegiances on
both sides of the *Tobacco*-fence — or, to put it nicely, he kept himself exactly positioned, just as an astrolabe is held aloft such that sunbeams do
pierce both rule-sights. In 1638 a Colonist did wed his Salvage wench (by
name *Elizabeth*) — the **.1.**[st] such marriage since Pokahuntiss's. Did our
stripling Thomas attend? O, how he fear'd! He'd earn sniggers no matter

what he did! He went; congratulating M^r & Mrs Bass with reticent cordiality. That night in his bed, his cheek smoldered with shame. — But what *ought* I to have done? he asked himself. He thought to hear his Land-lady whisper: *That halfbreed . . .* In 1641 we find him entering the Governor's House with its smooth wooden table from England and its suit of tarnished armor; here a Negro Servaunt-man (or *Darky* as they've begun to call 'em here) doth pour him a glass of cordial, & he petitions Governor Berkeley to grant him leave to visit his aunt Cleopatre and his uncle Opechancanough, whose fame stretches all the way from reed-walled Menmend Town. — Reader dear, 'tis against them that Thomas must march a-warring merely **.3.** years hence, thereby following his duty to those who had victors' rights in him. But why drink up future sadness? Just as a Pick-pocket's accomplices do stall him from view, so that blackguard *Time* hides from us his oncoming murthers, plots & fiendish strategems, for he sends his best confederates — *This Year, Next Year* and *False Tomorrow* — for to crowd us about, whining for alms, plucking our sleeves, grabbling at our coattails and tripping us by our ankles, so that we never get sufficient peace to perceive the grave-pit that Time himself hath digged. Anyhow, in the Governor's manse it's already dim: the wooden shutters have been shut, to guard against Salvage arrows. *This Year* & his confederates leer at Thomas from under the Governor's desk. Very well; let them blind us. I myself, being William the Blind, see only that pleasant family visit of 1641, when *Opechancanough,* wary old Werowance that he is, sits copper-crowned & red-painted, smiling mirthlessly upon this nephew of his, passing the tobacco-pipe there at Menmend-Towne, with his Cronoccoes all about him. They're cunning and proud, like the Italians, 'tis said. They sport mantles of various animal-skins embroidered with white beads and copper. They reek of smoke. 'Tis cool beneath their cornhusk awning. Opechancanough continues silent. He's as ancient as Methuselah's corpse! Clad in a brain-tann'd deerskin faintly green, which gives off a faint scent of smoke, he gazes & gazes, unsmiling, gazes terribly, gazes & gazes, until Thomas would scream. Ever since the massacre he inspir'd (near **.20.** years since), it hath been a felony for Englishmen e'en to parley with the hated Salvages. No more puccoon-painted wenchen for a night's joy! Governor Berkeley's permission for Thomas's visit must not be construed as justifying a continued familiarity. Both Opechancanough and his guest know this. That's why the silence betwixt 'em seems as dark as the interior of a Salvage house. Thomas knows not what he ought to do or say. But mayhap (he consoles

himself) these hosts bear themselves no more coldly than his English stepmother . . . A half-naked, smoke-blackened old Salvagess is pounding fla-
groot by the creek's edge. (What an ancient beezum! John Smith would
have said.) Is that his Aunt Cleopatre, Queen of the Pamunkeys? He
knows not. A single long braid of hair, part black, part grey, trails all the
way down past her squatting buttocks. She stops, scratches her mosquito-
bitten bubs, and hawks into the water. And who's this near-naked young
wench who squats at his uncle's shoulder? (Opechancanough's favorite
wife, in truth. She was pregnant. By law, being now the Powhatan over all,
he must soon send her away.) Amidst the dark and humid trees, birds are
squeaking like unto new leather boots. Thomas hesitates. His hand seeks
the dagger at his side, but wills itself in all politeness to find it not. Am-
biguous it is to be Maister Thomas Rolfe. When Englishmen name him
Salvage, or Salvages *Englishman,* how should they be answered? And his
dead mother, he would know more concerning her, but from whom? All
he has of her is a basket woven from silk grass. He adores her shade. He
longs but to live honorably in the sight of her well-beseeming blood. They
all pretend to reverence her who'd brought the civil peace, but he spies contempt in their transparent hearts. (Pokahuntiss? he o'erheard a Cooper say
at Jametowne. She was but bird-lime to ensnare small prey . . .) Thomas
hath prepared many questions to ask Opechancanough; now the questions
wither within him. Still his uncle continues silent, until the tall tree-trunks
begin hiding the evening light on either side of him, drinking the radiance
like vampires. A warrior stands, commences singing, clapping his hands
together, & instantly the rest are dancing about him, howling, stamping,
striking their feet together. Thomas Rolfe knows not whether to sit or to
stand, for all that these Salvages are his relations. Is this dance meant to be
for him? He gazes at his uncle, who continues watching him most smilelessly.

He married with a well-to-do Englishwoman named Jane Poythress, on
whom he begat a daughter. What lands he got into his tenure, 'tis not written (altho' I've heard he did make a pretty little garden in the English manner). Some say that Powhatan bequeathed him many acres, but 'tis surely
folly to ascribe anything like akin to duty to such an ignorant old Salvage.
This Jane of his, the World remembers her not. Nor do we ken anything
about his daughter's moral color. I hope that her family continued to be of
such repute (at least on her father's side) that some gold-Adventurer took
her to wife. Of this I'm sure: Ready money cannot have been lacking to pay
her marriage-portion. But concerning her father, what were his doings in

that parish, & how his life and death turn'd out, are matters engross'd in many documents (I misdoubt me not) but all these got burn'd in 1865, at the end of the American Civil War. Hence no one even knows whether he remained alive after 1658, by which time it had coincidentally become illegal for Englishmen in Virginia to marry with Negroes, mulattoes, or Indians such as his late mother.

Further History of Pocahontas's Maidservants (1617–1621)

Crack the glass of her virginity, and make the rest malleable.
SHAKESPEARE, *Pericles,* IV.vi.142 (1609)

*T*he English kept these young Salvagesess in London-Towne for nigh upon .5. years, in hopes of translating them into Christian godliness. Meanwhile, they were profitably employed as Servaunt-maids & drudges in English houses. Their iron-pounced flesh, inked & branded with strange designs & the likenesses of beasts, did much excite their Masters. But when it became apparent that these wenchen remained hardened beyond redemption in their heathenish follies, the Virginia Companie, tired of maintaining them, shipped 'em off to Bermuda & married them with local Negroes, to keep them from telling bad tattle-tales back home in Virginia . . .

FURTHER HISTORY OF ARGALL
(1617–1626)

He filled the age he lived in with strange dreams;
Now the posterity gives him anathemes,
Detesteth his remembrance, and doth pray
He never rise more in the latter day.

WILLIAM DRUMMOND OF HAWTHORNDEN (before 1649)

The Governor tells ye Company in what a ruinous condition he found ye Colony by ye carelessness of ye people & lawless living and how he has improued almost euery thing.

He had transported .24. persons at his own expense, so the Company owed him .2,400. acres of wet blue evening light above the mud. The Paspaheghs had dwelt on that spot, until Lieutenant Percy slaughtered them together with their royal family. 'Twas all for the best. Of their burnt Towne not e'en the carven posts of OKEUS's Temple remained. The black ashes were richly becreeper'd. Argall was going to clear .300. acres of this dominion right away. Six hundred pounds it would cost. He'd settle his people on it, call it *Argall Towne,* and bind 'em to him by a bond to repay the .600. pounds within a politic time. Should they default, he'd kick 'em arse-end up!

His brother John held .4. shares. He'd buy John out or persuade him to relinquish all claims.

He crush'd a mosquito, scowled and wrote:

Indians so poor cant pay their debts & tribute powhatan goes from place to place visiting his Country taking his pleasure in good friendship with us laments his daughters death but glad her child is living so doth opachanko   both want to see him but desires that he may be stronger before he returns.

Knowing that Powhatan's good wishes must be fraught with hatred, he saw scant advantage in shipping the brat to Virginia too quickly. Make an Englishman out of him first! Then we can dispatch him forth, to spy on his grandfather, and learn his final secrets! Next, we'd establish him in Opechancanough's stead . . .

He call'd a greasyhaired Salvage messenger before his table and said: How does Powhatan?

Passing sickly, replied the Salvage.

Inform Powhatan that young Maister Thomas Rolfe likewise continues in feeble health. And tell him that the child doth repine for Yndian corn. Dost hear, my feathertopped friend?

I hear.

Damn me if you're not a sullen one! If Powhatan can envoy us **.500.** bushels, we'll fraught 'em to England so that the lad can thrive.

When comes he here?

In due time great Powhatan shall have his daughter's son before his eyes.

The Salvage said: Truly you Tassantasses are great liars and thieves.

Argall laughed & touched his shoulder, saying: If he bites the bait, he bites. If not, I'm content. D'ye ken why? Because Jamestowne's too well impaled for his malice! Now go.

(You gave me your oath he was dead, Pokahuntiss had complained to Captaine Argall when they met in London-Towne.)

(Smith? That dwarfish miller's-thumb? O, he may fleer & fly about to his soul's content, but who cares now for his buzzing? He might as well be dead, Princesse. Feed not your heart with him; you're a married woman . . .)

Singing most softly, he wrote:

Master Lambert has found out that Tobacco cures better on lines than in heaps and desires lines be sent. last summer a great mortality among us, far greater among the Indians and a morrain amongst the deer.

His Government was narrow & low in the water like unto an unrigged shallop. We may as well call it *Argall's ready Undertaking.* He wore real gold points & stitches in his clothes. Pacing round a blue and sun-pocked pond near the wet black pimples of fields, he well considered the Colonie's circumstances, then took leave of his tranquility. For the Salvages were too quiet! O, those whining Yndian beggars walking bare-legged down his dirt streets, he took no accompt of such trash, no matter how they shrilled. The Salvage cattle-tenders & corn-pickers, for them & their strangely half-grim (since half-shaven) countenances he cared not. The worst they'd do was get drunk and make noise. But Powhatan had withdrawn himself in recent months, which he misliked much, and Opechancanough — O joy, to let out *his* misbegotten blood! Sweet John had not prov'd so far wrong, to drill all men upon his pompously named *Smith Field, .1. and .2., .1. and .2.* But who'd have that now? They all thought that since Pocahontas had uncork'd her quim, her kindred must lie similarly disposed to be fecundated with Englishness. Argall planned infallibly otherwise. Was he the only soul in Virginia to be warn'd by the *twinkling fear?* He advised all Householders to bar and shutter the windows throughout the coming summer even on those sultry days when swamp-ditches slowly ferried field-blood the hue of charred emerald. He kept the demiculverins perpetually manned now, brooding within the Fort's broad walls. And they mocked & cursed his rigorous prudence from within the broad-gabled, thatch-roofed houses of Jamestowne. O, they spared not to censure him . . .

He hesitated and wrote:

> *desires another Governor be sent   all desire The Lord La Warr (who is our Lord Governor) to return to his Government where he'll find all things in good order & prosperity.*

Lord De La Warr would be perfectly easy to manage & soothe. Meanwhile, Argull could stand discreetly aloof within his own strangeness, secretly sluppering up the Yndian trade.

Some idlers threatened to rebel. He sent Brutus & Cassius to warn 'em: *Should any fellow seek to overthrow the life of our Governor, then he shall receive punishment by death.* They not submitting utterly, he had 'em whipt to the tolling of the Church-bell. He stood beside the Marshal counting strokes. Then to the assembled Colonists he proclaimed: I'll sing you a song about rebellion. Here's how it goes:

> When the wind shifts against the Sunne,
> Trust it not, for back it will run.
> When the wind follows the Sunne,
> Fine weather will never be done.

He'd scared & scarred yᵉ English. If yᵉ Yndians did rebel, he would be-gone well previous. To the DEVIL with his clownish Countreymen, who knew not how to play the game of *Policy!*

That was in March. He glowered wearily down, his beard upon his chest. His enemies sought to prefer up more Articles against him. In May he wrote a proclamation:

Every person to go to Church Sundays & holidaies or lye neck & heels on the Corps du Guard ye night following and be a slave ye week following 2^d offence a month   3^d a year & a day

A week later he wrote:

Against teaching the Indians to shoot with guns on pain of death to learner & teacher . . .

Uttamattomakkin was tattling to Powhatan that all English were evil. Argall longed to hang that Salvage. Howbeit, when Opechancanough arrived to receive his yearly present, he assured the everworthy Argall: Never fear, brother, for we know him to be an old rogue, whose mind's coil'd with venom. All his reports against you have been disproved. He's disgraced.

Then ask Powhatan why he suffers him to continue slandering us.

Powhatan lies awearied with grief for his daughter.

For Pocahontas?

Aye. So he reigns not.

That I disbelieve. He hath spawned so many others by all his concubines, why should he cherish her, but for a grievance? For you must know she came willingly aboard my ship, & e'en would have frigged me, but that I forbore—

I must not contradict you, brother.

So?

He reigns not.

And you?

O, I own no ambition to rule, *Brother,* said Opechancanough, smiling softly. 'Tis our brother Opitchapam who acts in Powhatan's stead.

The lame one?

You know him well, I see.

Well, keep Uttamattomakkin to his place. His falsehoods are vinegar. They corrode the civil peace.

This we comprehend already. And therefore, as I told you, we credit him not. He comes but seldom to Menmend-Towne—

And whom *do* you credit concerning our doings?

Stonily did Opechancanough reply: We believe you, *Brother,* for never yet have you lied to us.

Argall stared into his eyes. Then he said: You know very well that if it comes to war again, you'll lose more than your trullish niece—

Yes, *Brother,* you ever remind us of that loss.

'Tis my pleasure. I comprehend you love me not. Now begone.

He penned new commandments for the Colonie he ruled, to wit:

to go armed to Church & to work

Every man to sett .2. acres with corn (Except Tradesmen following their trades) penalty: forfeit of corn & Tobacco & be a slave a year to ye Colony

No man to shoot but in defence of himself against Enemies till a new supply of ammunition comes on pain of a years Slavery

No trade with ye perfidious Savages nor familiarity lest they discover our weakness

Strutting in his knee boots, with a tall hat upon his head, he knew that he was hated by all these Adventurers, Undertakers & Planters, because their greed hindered them from believing in the dolorous danger he foresaw.

The Counsell baited him, call'd him a *Cold spark,* & demanded to know when such martial regulations would be lifted.

So far as I conceive it, smil'd Argoll, we're already half betwixt Ushant & the Lyzarde, so to speak. We've crossed the .100. fathom line. We'll be in haven — afore Doomsday.

At this fine jest .2. Counsellmen did rise against him in rage, but he summonsed dear Brutus to lay 'em by their heels in the pinnace o'ernight, until they cooled. He intended never to lift the regulations, nay, not ever.

'Twas the last hour of the Morning Watch. He summon'd his minion.

Ho! Cassius!

Aye, Captaine Argoll!

How doth my ship?

Full well.

Is she laden?

With cedar-logs & Sassafrass clear up to her weasel!

And do they all fear me?

Aye, dear Captaine, by the very CHRIST cross!

Welladay, wept poor Argall in his infinite patience, how they do scheme & devise to get my love, sipping, pumping, draining, stealing it by the bucketload! And behold, my love runs *dry.*

Again he summonsed Opechancanough for to come to Jamestowne. He said: Tell your warriors to trespass no more upon English dominions.

They but chase down their prey. A deer kens not any boundary.

No matter. They must not come on private land. I've warned you.

Opechancanough smiled quietly. He said: We are not turkeys, *Brother,* to live but on tiny red acorns.

Argoll laughed. — I like your wit! said he. But 'tis not to the purpose. You heard my commaund. Now begone.

In a coffer he'd discovered Powhatan's ancient chain of pearls, which Sir Thomas Dale had promis'd that Despot would be e'er used for a token betwixt the English & the Salvages. Argoll thought 'twas more politick to hold the Yndians firmly to all their promises, yet flout his own. He accordingly gave the pearls to *Casca,* whom he was envoying back among the Pattawomecks for to trade.* Mayhap the boy could get a better bargain, did he wave that charm in the faces of those credulous brutes . . .

In 1618 he embark'd the *Treasurer* to the West Indies to pillage the Spaniards for his own profit, altho' in those days we were supposed to keep peace with those Infidels. (That's all **.1.**, quoth Argall. Let's hale 'em all down to kelpy Hell!) Among the booty captured by his pawns & haled back across the hot and crawling sea were some Negro slaves — the **.1.**[st] (so I believe) to appear within the Colonie. Black Salvages living & dying most miserably enchained, black flesh whip-mapp'd into riverine systems of blood, black carcases hang'd for essaying to escape — why, all these are the fruits of Argoll's far-seeingness. To wit, *that trade did thrive most CHRISTian-like.* And so we have yet another precedent to thank Argall for.

Argal, Argoll, Argull! History's instrument, America's votary, Pocahontas's Muster-Master, I already swore you'd die rich! But where are you? What are you? You glimmer, & again you're gone. Meanwhile, your atoms dwell within us all — as anyone can verify this very day by examining your signature, which lives circuitous and doubled, the S in Samuel grown spiky with treacherous vines, o'ergrowing all its channels, which have already narrowed like unto muddy creeks in grassland. As for the A, that's a true masterpiece of lines, as I must confess: We can see up its roots, which resemble spidery brooms, but then our vision rapidly gets lost in its excruciating tangles, from which Progress hides within the dark sideways pit of an alligator's eye. As it doth say in the Book of Proverbs, *All the ways of man are clean in his own eyes; but the LORD weigheth the spirits. Commit thy works unto the LORD, & thy thoughts shall be establish'd.* Glory be! Argoll hath enacted himself!

---

*Casca sat in the *Treasurer*'s rigging, a-scratching at himself. He was happy. Afloat, no one forbade him anything. Ashore, no Under-Sherriff chased him down. And he'd soon be away, back to the red-latticed Tavern-houses of Gravesend, which hath been call'd *Sea-gate of London-Towne.* He'd never again be compelled to go to Church! Already he was polishing up his lies. He'd tupped **.12.** young Salvagesses in a single go. Their quim-hairs were porcupine-quills. They spoke a dialect of Greekish. And for his labors they'd given unto him this *Sassafrass,* which it now occasioned him to sell for a shilling — nay, for a pound . . .

In 1619 Sir George Yeardley did arrive to take over the Government of *Iamestowne*. Altho' he called him *My singular good Argall,* yet our latter Hero withdrew into his bullet-shaped Captaine's chamber with its writing-desk & half-suit of armor standing ready. He was white-stubbled now, sporting the white spit-flecks which Sailors spy everywhere on the blue-grey sea. He knew what would happen. Indeed, Governor Yeardley did confiscate the lands of *Argall-Towne,* & require rent of the Towns-people, to prove that *they had been wrongfully seated by Capt. Argall upon that land.* But Argoll was vanisht. Taking the Sunne's shadow on his long & severally barred backstaff, he set sail down that clear-complected river call'd after our dread Soveraigne. *Flood oh!* — And so (after speedy vicis-situdes, he being e'er lucky there as in all else) he fell in with the English coast.

In London-Towne his enemies forced an inquiry of his doings,* but he was not found guilty upon his trial. (John Rolfe among others wrote him diverse letters of support. After all, without him how could Sour John have tasted his .2.ⁿᵈ wife?) And now for the rest of his life the euerworthy *Ar-goll* did have yet another tale to tell. — My foes bore false witness against me, lads, he'd say, but they got thrown out of court. You know why, Oc-tavian? Because when they gave their oaths, they swore by the SUNNE, like unto Salvages! Hah!

There came a drought in Virginia. The *Tobacco* was injured; prices fell. Argoll did not care. He sold *Sassafrass* for good revenue.

In 1620 he was made Captaine of a .2.-dozen-gun ship in an expedition against Algiers. In 1622 he was knighted — *Trarintra-rarara.* In 1624, when King James crumpled up the Companie's charter & took over

*Perhaps the wire-pullers, like John Smith, had read *Uncle Machiavell,* who teaches us how a certain Duke and Pope, wishing to drag the newly occupied *Countrey of Romagna* back to au-thority and reason, promoted a Governor of stern cruel excellence, who quickly brought Ro-magna to heel; this having been accomplished, the Duke, not wishing to become odious to the people, commanded that his Governor be executed and left lying with a bloody knife beside him. Machiavelli writes approvingly: *The barbarity of this spectacle caused the people to be at once satisfied and dismayed.* But the English wire-pullers failed. Was it because they had none among them stern & resolute enough to be Pope, or was it more simply that Argoll towered too great for mere humanity to end him?

Virginia as a Colonie of the Crown, euerworthy Argall did further business there, much to his own enrichment. Just as in a well-run ship all sheets & tackles get wisely belayed from kevel-pieces, so Argoll's schemes remained perfectly well-strung, ready for to swivel or catch the wind as he intended. To whom durst I compare him? Certainly not to a certain bustling little yeoman, who'd thought himself such a whopper . . .

In 1625, now a full member of King's War Council, he commaunded a fleet of .28. ships unsuccessfully against Cadiz. He muttered: *Islands and beaches, white and black* . . . These square-standarded monsters of his did gnaw & grabble at the enemy most remorselessly, while Argoll cloak'd himself in his Cabin. Some said that this e'er-growing reclusiveness came about because their Admirall was old, or sick like unto my Lord De La Warr, or indeed already dead & mummified (like unto my Lord De La Warr, now perisht .7. years since, off the Isle of Saint Michael); but the truth was that, most of his objects achiev'd, he lay on the brink of translation unto pure murtherous DIVINITY, needing no longer to incorporate himself e'en in shadowy smiles or bland sea-songs. Believe me, Reader, he continued to terrify all malefactors. Why didn't Cadiz fall to him? Demons such as Argall cannot die when success strews new flowers in their way. He'd done e'erything; 'twas time for him to become electricity, or a thunder-cloud, so he had to fail, break & die.

He perish'd in 1626, or perhaps 1633, some say from a fit of rage . . .

FURTHER HISTORY OF VIRGINIA
(1617–1622)

The remedy is to send Souldiers . . .
JOHN SMITH, 1624

*W*hen John Rolfe lingered yet in life, a certain Maister Richard Killing-beck and .4. other Englishmen, who went illegally to the Chickahominies to trade, received the reward of *murther*   at the hands of those Yndians; and on the very next Sunday, e'en as the bell toll'd, the Salvages slew .5. children whose youth had excused them from Church. So the Colonie raised up *the hue and cry,* but discovered not the poisonous vagabonds who'd done these crimes. Then people came swiftly running to Governor Argall, entreating his rapid action. At this, he did send a Salvage to Opechancanough at Menmend-Towne, for this pretense that Opitchapam was King o'er all the Salvages deceived him not. And when the Salvage did part the reeds of Pamunkey Neck, and come into Menmend, he uttered the following words, in faithfulness to Argoll's beck: You cannot undo what they've done, but I can undo your rabble, *Brother.*   So send satisfaction, quickly, ere I drown in my rage.

When the Salvage returned, he said to Argall: I am the mouth of Opechancanough. Opechancanough answers you once & twice that he is ignorant of the circumstances of this crime, and e'er seeks your interest.

O, does he? laughed that euerworthy Gentleman, gnawing at his beard. — Well, then, let him stay ignorant when I revenge my injuries upon the Chickahominies. If not, I'll send Slaughtermen to speed him. Tell him that, boy, with your most excellent expediency.

So the Salvage flew off to Opechancanough, who bade him come back with the following reply: The peace shall never be broken by me. I call on you not to avenge yourself upon the innocents of that Towne, which Towne you shall have, in token of which I envoy you this basket of earth. And I swear by the SUNNE to send you the murtherers' heads as soon as I do catch them. I have spoken.

Yes indeed, my *Brother* hath spoken his office. Tell him I'll be a-sharpening a brace of pikes on which to receive those heads —

. . . which never came.

And yet it seem'd otherwise so peaceful in the Colonie! Powhatan was dead at last, the Salvages announced. Nomore must they fear the plots of that crafty old Salvage. And it had begun to appear true for a fact that Opechancanough's elder brother, the aforesaid *Opitchapam,* or *Itopatin,* ascended to the cunning office of Kingship, for which e'erworthy Argall congratulated the lame man, thinking: We need but a generation more; then they'll all be subjugated, and Virginia entire will be labelled according to our will. — Truth to tell, he was gulled unto relief, that Opechancanough himself had not attained to that dignity. The Salvages tractably smiled upon e'erything. (In a word, they felt unceasingly terrorized by Argoll's greatness.) All men, Christian & Salvage, gave mouth honor to our most dread & gracious Soveraigne. And the Salvage Servauntmen discharged their places with utter faithfulness. Jamestowne's palisadoes stood most officiously around, but even after so many years they best resembled what John Smith of Lincolnshire would have called a *cradge,* meaning a quick dyke or embankment meant to hold off floods for the merest twink, until our Diggers & Bankers have time to solidify their work. Virginia creeper & Virginia rot did fecundate 'em unto crumbling skeletons.

When some new Colonists (or *Planters* as they'd now begun to call themselves) sought to break new ground at Waraskoyack in 1619, they sought the Emperor of the Salvages to confirm the bargain, but he arrived not at their summons. Nor did his brother.

Now Ophechankanough will not come at us, mused old John Rolfe. That causes us to suspect his former promises . . .

I'd prefer that you not discuss those Salvages o'ermuch, return'd his wife. For it reminds me of that *Pocahontas* of yours.

Rebecca was her name, as you well know—

See how you raise her up against me!

Nay, sweeting, I love thee best, thou being English after mine own fashion—

In 1619, near a dozen ships did come to Virginia, bringing .1,216. persons, including .90. young women to make wives. That was the year they started sending vagabonds & other dissolute persons to Virginia, to be rid of 'em; in 1619 they sent a full hundred. Thus their policy: Creeper down Virginia with many new human roots! Rape her, rob her, & use her for a cesspool! Vagabonds must die someday; then they'll fertilize the ground. Meanwhile, marry .1. another & bear me children of *Sassafrass!* And the Salvages continued content with these obsequies. Good Argoll, who knew everything, kept aware that in the woods on e'ery side of these Plantations dwelt boldly bitter knaves (remnants of the Paspaheghs & Kecoughtans, tools of Opechancanough, angry hunters, souls like unto those Servaunts at plague-time who at their very .1.st flush of fever find themselves cast out of their Maister's house). O, dangerous beyond all measure are such men, especially when they pretendingly smile, & kneel submissive on their marrybones.

(Argall knew that — but Argoll was gone now, sail'd back to London-Towne to face his enemies. And the Planters flattered each other thus: However so many they may be, they're not dangerous. For look you, they never took the Fort even in our *Starving Time.*)

Why wouldn't Opechancanough hie himself to yᵉ Governor? Perhaps he grew old; he must have own'd near about .4.score years by then. No English visited Menmend-Towne to spy him out. — O excellent, here he came again, half-smiling! The Counsell's secret *Instructions By Way of Advice* in the oakum-sealed box no longer warned them to be on guard against him. Indeed, our English from their generosity did e'en build him a Towne-house, with whose lock he spent many a happy hour playing, as if he were a child. He was very alert; he anticipated their e'ery courtesy. Thatching their homes with marsh-grass, like unto good hardy Adventurers, they laid by all distractions from Tobacco-profit. Their envy of Maister Rolfe inspir'd 'em just as love inspires us to our own Beloveds. Their ignorance was as comforting as an iron close-helmet toggled down over their eyes. New shops & houses sprang up like warriors out of ambush. Now even *Iapazeus of Patawomeck,* he who'd betrayed Pocahontas to his dear brother Captaine Argall, did come a-craving .2. English ships to sail up his river to trade — although when the English went there, the Salvages traded dishonestly, so that we took .800. bushels of corn from 'em by force. Meanwhile (in proof of our goodness), unknown Adventurers & benefactors did adventure near .1,000. pounds to bring up the infidels' children in Churchly courses, & thereby lead them out of wildness ... One Minister, 'tis true, did write home to London that *till their Priests and Ancients have their throats cut, there is no hope to bring them into conversion.* But (sad to say) no one listened, for Lord Delaware, George Percie & Captaine Argoll were all gone! E'ery year more men & women sailed unto Virginia, setting up their Plantations wherever they listed, without fear of the contemptible naked Salvages.

Another evil sign now glistered like unto foxfire in the darkness: *Maister John Pory*, the new Secretary of Virginia, being sent by the Governor to find the best place for establishing a Salt-works, did go to Mattapanient, where Salvages in a dense wood viny and cobwebbed did essay to ambuscado him; and later on that same voyage he heard from the *Laughing Kings* on the Eastern Shore that Opechancanough plotted some assassination. If only we'd taken these and diverse other warnings to heart, following the Bible wherein it saith: *Let us meet together in the house of* GOD, *within the temple, and let us close the doors of the temple; for they are coming to kill you; at night they are coming to kill you.* But the warnings all came from Salvages. And how can we scruple to believe Salvages?

In 1621 a tractable Virginian did warn that at the ceremony when Powhatan's bones were taken up and encased in leather to be betterinterred at Uttamussack (according to the notions of those barbarians), Opechancanough called upon the tribes to rise against our English, but when Governor Yeardley pressed him, he did most eloquently deny the same. Why should he turn against his dear *Brothers,* he inquired, who'd ne'er done him aught but good? And (since he spoke but simple truth) scarce any Colonist suspected his dishonesty. All were too greatly occupied in enjoying the new Cattle-Fairs; 'twas like unto Countie Lincoln or Countie Cornwall in some parts . . .

In the year of our redemption 1622 there did come to **.1.** Maister Morgan's house a Salvage who thanks to his mode of dress was call'd *Jack of the Feather* (known to the other Salvages as *Nemattanow),* a man so highly esteemed by his own, that 'twas said no English could kill him, he being courageous & magickall. In fell reversal of Argoll's doings he did entice Maister Morgan to Pamunkey to trade, & presently returned alone, telling the Servaunts that their Master was dead. In his baleful insolency he even wore the murthered man's cap. The Servaunt-lads therefore would bring him for questioning, but Jack of the Feather so far defied them, that they shot him. *Vanity, vanity,* saith the Preacher — for even as he lay dying, Jack begged those **.2.** boys to bury him in an English grave & keep secret the fact that a bullet had killed him, in order that his reputation for invincibility be preserved among the Salvages. What his killers replied I cannot say (perhaps they laughed, kicking his dying face). A splash, & birds began screaming like wild horses. Virginia grew sinister.

Now let me quote from Captaine Smith's *Generall Historie,* which doth read: *At the loss of this Salvage Opechankanough much gieved and repined, with great threats of revenge* (for Pamunkey, dear Reader, is

Opechancanough's own Kingdome, which means most certainly that Jack of the Feather was his henchman); *but the English returned such terrible answers, that he cunningly dissembled his intent, with the greatest signes he could of love and peace, yet within fourteene daies after he acted what followeth.*

Well (if I may up sail on our story), Opechancanough did borrow boats of the English, that he might conveniently assemble all the Salvages together in a place whose upside-down grey-green trees mirrored their ideals in a dull marsh lake, & he did exhort them to rise up all at once for the sake of their liberty, which treason being agreed, on the heavy clammy morn of the .22. of March, the Sunne now deep within the House of Aries, these selfsame Salvages did come under guise of friendliness to each Plantation in the Colonie, then fall upon e'ery Englishman & Englishwoman they could, yea, e'en every English child, bending over them, stabbing, their sweaty hairless arms upflashing and downflashing, the children screaming as their chairs crashed backwards and blood began whale-spouting from their hearts, their parents already retching & rattling down to death, closing their eyes upon the uplifted offerings of their childrens' dripping scalps; on that day the Salvages fulfilled their .15. years' yearning as best they could, hacking to death their dear *Brothers & Sisters,* oft falling .2. on .1. victim so that the .1.ˢᵗ Salvage could choke & gripe whilst the other did stab; and afterwards they further tormented the very carcasses, decapitating them as in England we do with felons, dismembering them, laughing for pitiless hatred, singing *Whe, whe, yah, ha, ne, he, wittowa, wittowa.* And so it went from dawn till darklins, in the houses and even the Churches. It was Opechancanough's aim to destroy the English entire, so that not .1. would remain in Virginia. At Jamestowne the murtherers did creep through shoulder-high grass which was channeled with milky brown, & presently they came within a shadow's length of the many-pointed palisade. Howbeit (for which we must thank OUR REEDEMER), some converted Salvages of good accompt did turn tattletale, out of pity for their Masters, or Machiavellian *Politick*; so that while many English did perish indeed, including half a dozen members of the very Counsell, yet throughout the Countrey .2. out of .3. persons were saved. And if I may once again quote Captaine Smith, *this massacre some will say will be good for the Plantation, because now we have just cause to destroy them by all meanes possible. Moreover, where before we were troubled in cleering the ground of great Timber, which was to them of small use: now we may take their own plaine fields and Habitation, which are the pleasantest places in the Countrey.*

FURTHER HISTORY OF CAPTAINE JOHN SMITH (1618–1631)

Or shall I tell of his Adventures since
Done in Virginia, that large Continent?
How that he subdu'd Kings unto his Yoke,
And made those Heathen flee, as Wind doth Smoke . . .

But what avails his Conquests, now he lyes
Interr'd in Earth, a Prey to Worms and Flyes?

John Smith's epitaph, 1631

'Twas at Reverend Purchas's abode that the question .1.st came up. Captaine Smith & the Reverend were entertaining each other in discourse upon certain new-found Countreys (which at that time Sweet John, with some sticky residue of optimism, still hoped to see again, altho' his youth was full taken off); when a Lady with a deer's round nose, who remember'd the Virginian woman (one *Rebecca,* as I believe, or *Pokahunta)* inquired: Think you she was well handled?

Why, madam, what can you mean? (Thus Captaine Smith, who'd just now accomplished the .37.th year of his age.) She was well married, brought before the King's presence, converted to reason . . .

And yet when I kept watch upon her at the King's masque I ever spied a sadness . . .

Those are feminine matters, madam, quoth the Reverend, clearing his throat most sonorously. Doubtless the sympathies of your sex enabled you to — to understand her, to—

Tell me, Captaine Smith, interrupted the unpleasantly determined Lady, by what warrant did we go to possess her Countrey?

Ah, but, madam, in possessing their Countrey we do no harm, Smith replied. In *Florida, Virginia, Newfoundland* & *Cannada,* is more land than all the people in Christendom can manure, & yet the Salvages culturate it not. And they believe themselves well used to sell you a whole Countrey for a copper kettle and few toys!

But *are* they well used?

Dear lady, as I told you, Pokahantas was converted to become as good a Protestant as you or I; she died a pious death. Surely that alone was sufficient reason to buy up her Countrey. But she well deserved our good usage, being the veriest *Non-pareil* of Virginia . . .

To this, of course, the over-tender Lady could reply nothing. But in after-years, John Smith found himself answerable many a time to these charges, an irritating conjuration of responsibility which ceased only in the Year of GOD 1622, when (as I have just now related) the Salvages put **.347.** Englishmen to death in a single act of rebellion. 'Tis wonderful how all moral luxuries drivel & dribble away once we've been counter-attacked! After that, they complained that he had oppressed the Salvages too much, or that he hadn't ruled them firmly enough; but nobody worried any longer whether we ought to be at James Towne where the pale tufts of white-tail deer go bobbing in the twilight. At least Frauncis & Anna, with their brass candlesticks they were so proud of, could spare no time to offensively accuse him about his doings in places they'd never been.

On his memory-stage, Pocahontas & Tragabigzanda alike grew dark, like Willoughby hedges at evening. Whene'er he thought upon the death of Pokahuntiss, his sadness savored of mild fittingness, for she'd perish'd a Christian, loving England. Safely dead, she could never turn against her newfound Countreymen. Didn't that make her the only Yndian of whom such could be said?*

He told Frauncis of the strangeness of the *Alligator* with his devil-teeth & his musk, but Frauncis did not care.

Frauncis was fat and rich now; he had lands & tenements now in Carleton. Frauncis e'en smoked *Tobacco!* Long ago now, Sweet John (essaying to speed his suit for Cicely's hand) had crowed to old Maister Reese Allen: *And I own .7. acres of good pasture lying in the territory of Charleton Magne!* But Frauncis had been seized of those .7. acres even then. Sweet John had signed 'em over. (Twas never any match, John

---

*Some folks claim'd that had Pocahontas survived **.5.** years more, Opechancanough's treason would have been prevented, but, Reader, you & I know as much as anyone how little influence our "Princesse" had actually enjoyed. Powhatan kept so vast a harem that whatever Princesses he bred were of scanter accompt than a crop of cabbages! What could she have done, to persuade her Uncle not to fight for his ancient dignities? Nay, her doom prov'd not so misfortunate for her; she didn't have to witness that Warre & its results.

against Frauncis.) Frauncis offered to give back the land, in longlast quittance for their father's farm; John accepted. He had no reason to refuse. Frauncis did not require his generosity anymore.

Then Anna came to him most privily, & said that whereas she & Frauncis had raised .4. children, of whom .2. survived & were well-married; & whereas he (the aforesaid Sweet John) had never gotten any children, why, then, percase he could sign the .7. acres over to those who could use 'em—

Anna was like unto some overfed lapdog, which turns a sad & disgusted nose to spoiled cheese. He'd heard her whisper to Frauncis: 'Tis plain his heart's soured with rancor! — O yes! Sweet John had gone sour like unto John Rolfe. Anna turn'd up her nose at him. He signed o'er the .7. acres.

Their house was passing dank, as he could not deny to confess. The Salvage dwellings at Kecoughtan had been warmer & drier, altho' smoky. Well, those were long gone, as he'd heard from gentle Argoll.

Had Sweet John attained the Gentleman's leisure he'd always craved, he might have return'd unto his boyhood's bower where he'd .1.ˢᵗ read Machiavelli — nay, Enclosers had seized that — well, *somewhere* he'd have reconnoitered high summer's tree-bulwarks dark green above emerald meadows, but he could not stay; his dreams remained unsounded yet; he must to London, even if only for a Soldier's pay. He must to Bristol & Plymouth; the fine Lords there would surely become Undertakers & Adventurers in his new Colonie in *North Virginia* (which we now call *New England*). After all, he stood no longer in his striplingdom. 'Twas high time to loose him into the pastures of *Sassafrass*. Yet when he finally discovered his opportunity, & sail'd to America, all fell into a shambles, for a wicked Frenchman seiz'd him, & locked him in durance — *him,* who'd done nothing! — in retaliation for Captaine Argall's destruction of Port-Royal. He returned home indebted & disgraced.

E'erworthy Argall had just now been knighted at Rochester, as he did hear. O yes. This Argoll did e'er feed himself fat.

Being invited to call upon the Willoughbys, he borrowed a horse of Frauncis and went a-cantering down mucky roads, *Butter and eggs, butter and eggs,* until he met the straight brickstone breast & upclenched arms of Tattershall Castle. He made his most respectful leg. Bartty was indisposed with an illness. Robert greeted him in good courtesy, & smilingly quizzed him upon his knowledge of *Machiavell.* 'Twas good sport. Yet all the time they sat there, Sweet John was hoping that Robert would send him on a mission. Robert forbore. The guest felt a creeping dread. What if the only Undertaking remaining to him were the cipherish .1. of hunting preferments to feed his age?

He wrote epistles to the King of Denmark, to propose sanguinary enrichments on whale fisheries. (He'd sunk somewhat further into debt.) He looked into going once more a-Soldiering in the Low Countreys, for (the .12. Years' Truce being expired), the *Contra-Remonstrants* were warring again with Spain. Why shouldn't he go? He kenned every aspect of the military art, from marching to drilling to murthering! Not an atom had he disremembered! His legs were near about as steady as e'er. Captaine Duxbury's face unsettled itself from Heaven, revisiting his brain to merrily shout: — O, Sweet John, were I stripped back unto your stripling years, what deeds I'd do in *Peru, America* & those places! . . . — Sweet John's place was .3.*rd from* Left, .21.*st* Rowe . . . But his friends advised him to take care, for he grew old, & the Spaniards might win this round. Besides, how would it profit him, excepting he pillaged some Netherlandish farm? (Flickeringly, from his long entombed boyhood, he remembered hearing the cry: Ralegh's seized the *Water-hound* of Brill! England's rich again, boys! — And he remembered his own sunny young piracies — *Trarintra-rarara!)* He did forbear.

He penned a plea to the skeleton of the Virginia Companie, a-hoping for silver pay. See the endless wrinkles of lamplight on the Thames at Tower Bridge, the water trembling, & ships groaning in the night. Someday, admired for his able & submissive patience, John Smith will be admitted to the upper orders. Nobility itself will count out coins and buy him passage to his dreams. Reprove that if you can! He *will* travel, even if only on that ominous black ship with a blood-red keel which now snickles through his dreams . . .

In the year 1623, altho' exports of *Tobacco* from Virginia now reach'd .500,000. pounds, there were bad times in Lincolnshire, and 'tis written that for many Fensmen, *Dogg's flesh is a dainty disch, and found upon search in many houses; and also such horse flesch as has lain long in a dike for hounds.* A sad sort of winter food, like unto the cheese parings and offal on which poor men subsist at Jamestowne . . . ! Sweet John dwindled further into debt, as might be expected from a Draper's 'prentice who'd run away rather than serve out his time. All through England, people were hounded by bankruptcies; & e'en though the Under-Sheriffs kept whipping home all unlicensed beggars, new vagabonds appeared in every Parish, imploring & threatening, grim like Salvages. The following year, just as the

plague returned to Lincolnshire (slaying his late sister's child Alice a fortnight past her engagement-day), John Smith published *The Generall
Historie of Virginia.* In the prospectus for that work he most bitterly penned: *These observations are all I have for the expences of a thousand pound, and the losse of eighteene yeeres of time, besides all the travels,
dangers, miseries and incumbrances for my countries good, I have endured
gratis . . .*

Frauncis said that the King's dragoons had come to Willoughby a-
searching for Popish Jesuits & other such trash. Frauncis said that the new
Beadle who paced Willoughby's dirt streets kept all the vagabonds away.
Frauncis complained about the tithes he had to pay the Rector. Down the
lane, a Milkmaid was a-calling her cows: *Cush, cush!*

Frauncis excused him from much labor on the farm that season. He assented. After all, the farm was not his.

At a Church-Ale to which he went with Frauncis he did meet Edward &
Cicely Bellowes, both of them passing yellowed and wrinkled with the
years. Neighbors call'd 'em *The Old Standards.* Maister Reese Allen being
long dead, the spouses dwelt alone on his estate at Belgreave. (For a long
time he star'd at Cicely, mazed. He'd forgotten that her .1.ˢᵗ husband
Ralph Nightingale had perished.)

Frauncis whispered that their children had all died of the plague. (He
himself had gotten touched by it, & altho' he lived, his face e'er after was
spotted like a measled hog.)

Frauncis spent many pence on beer that day, for which case his brother
laugh'd to see him fall sow-drunk. (Anna grew likewise a trifle flushed.)
Presently Frauncis invited him to marry with a certain ancient widow, by
name *Goodmistress Elizabeth Challoner,* who was seiz'd of a fortune, but Sweet John did smile abashed: Nay, brother, you shew yourself
too furious on my behalf. I have no craving to be wed.

In truth he hop'd yet to go for a Soldier, a Sailor, anything — & sooner
rather than later — for he remember'd well that wise saw of old *Machiavell,* that *Warre is not to be avoided, but is only deferred to your disadvantage.* In that same year when, wearied of faction, King James did say a
word, and the Virginia Companie was utterly dissolv'd, John Smith got
tricked by hope as in his youth, believing that every change must bring requital as he deserved. Soon he'd be a-speeding back to Virginia in a long-
beaked ketch. They say he haunted many a red-latticed Tavern-house near
Gravesend (and in particular *The Cardinall's Hat* on the bank side), asking
all Sailors & Watermen if any good Captaines were shipping men for *Vir-*

ginia, Florida, Canada or *New England,* but they advised him to keep out of the way, for he was entering further unto his age.

He said to them: I wonder that you mean to break my heart.

He penn'd a letter to the King direct, signing it *Your most humble Servaunt,* but never got any answer. (Maybe he should have writ *The Werowance of Capohowsick.*)

He heard from his good friend *Captaine Argoll* that the King had sent armor to Jamestowne, to crush another rebellion of yᵉ Salvages, but mainly it was rusty old brigandine vests in bad order. He essay'd to call on him, to request a preferment, e'en if it were but the office of Gunner's Mate, but Argall was already at sea.

In the year of grace 1625, when King James died, and .35,000. souls perished of the plague in London Towne, there came to England bitter, sullen tides whose wave-crests raised their angry heads higher than any Thamesman could remember. William Henry Wheeler in his *History of the Fens of South Lincolnshire,* written centuries after this event, records that when the tallest waves of all struck, *the sea walls in Kent, Essex and Lincolnshire were overthrown, and great desolation caused to the lands near the sea.* Are we authorized to assume that the inrush of bluish-grey water, which must have been as cold, filthy and familiar as death, did not swelter the wolds where Willoughby lay? (Frauncis said that the bing was full of corn, locked well away from rats, but some few ears suffered from a mildew. Frauncis said that their father's old horse-trees had broken. Frauncis said that the turf hive was in better order than ever. Lighting the *Tobacco*-pipe, Frauncis bade him stay, but not o'er warmly.) No doubt Stickney & Friskney became islands again, as they'd been in Roman times, but to the Willoughby people these misfortunes might have struck no more relevant a chord than classic erotic fantasies. Meanwhile the plague returned to Lincoln Towne. War came also. King Charles's deputies called out a muster in Lincolnshire; they wanted .400. volunteers to fight at Hull. John Smith was too old, they said. Melancholy becalmed his sails. Touching his beard, he said to Frauncis: When *Tobacco*-leaves on the vine just begin to turn grey, that's the time for harvest. — O, but Frauncis was grey now, too. He scarcely longed to hear that . . .

He lay panting in the swelter of malodorous air, uneasy, far from home, awaiting the attack. But his brigandine was rusted now beyond any hope of oiling & sanding away Time's bite.

He supped with his friend Peregrine Bartty, played with Bartty's grandchildren at table, admiring their pink & shining faces. He told 'em how Salvages can shoot a fish with an arrow on a cord. He told 'em how it had been when he was young so long ago and had wandered through *Affricka*'s markets: low, narrow, teeming places whose hot air rang & clang'd with scent-bells of fruit.

Sweet old John, I see you're in despond, says Bartty. But if you'd followed your humors to the Low Countreys, your case would be worse. Did you hear, man? Breda's fallen to the Spaniards! And Maurice is perished—

Maurice? Pray pardon, Lord, I ken not who—

Why, 'tis the King of the Contra-Remonstrants! Are you become such a desultory lozel that you listen no more to foreign arguments? And he—

Smith thought to himself (surely for the .1.ˢᵗ time): I wish to GOD I'd stayed for Tragabigzanda, and become a Turke!

Bartty's watch did chime.

Frauncis said that new Undertakers were leagued with Bartty & his brother my Lord Robert Willoughby to drain West Fen, but Frauncis was sure nothing would come of it. Parliament had passed a Bill of Enclosure not long since, but Frauncis said that 'twas treason to speak against the King. Frauncis said that some Dutchman or other was come to drain Hatfield Chase. In 1626, just as Robert was created Earl of Lindsey, the Dutchman began a-digging, and the Fen Slodgers threatened him & his works. That was the year that John Smith published his *Accidence, or the Pathway to Experience* — a treatise meant to teach sailors their trade. Robert had subsidized it, out of pity. The following year Sweet John cobbled together his *Sea Grammar* from passages in the *Accidence* now perfectly expanded into notability. Mayhap some canny Sea-dog might discover that volume, and hire him to be School-master for Sailor-boys who'd rapidly become Captaines (grace to his teachings), then carry him back to Virginia, gratis. He penned it all down most excellent, so that its crop of honest words might fill the mind's belly, like unto such fine potatoes of Lincolnshire* as *Spotted Lemons, Red Rose Kidneys, Magnum Bonums, Beauties of Hebron, White Elephants, Schoolmasters,* & *Reading Giants.*

Just as a Tapster grows worm-pallid from lurking always in his ale-cellar, so Sweet John, who e'er scribbled now to get his penny, took on a scribbler's hurried & pedantic manner (altho' he still reserv'd a twink of time to pray & sing a Psalm each morn). Frauncis proposed that he become a School-teacher in Louth. But John had no wish to end his days so tediously.

---

*Gracious Reader, pray forgive me this *Anachronism*.   Potatoes were never native to Lincolnshire, but came there of Virginia's womb.

He heard from Bartty that Argall had sail'd out of Plymouth Harbor as Admirall of .30. ships, & captured prizes worth at least .100,000. pounds. Argoll was no younger than he! And yet Argull had not offered him commaund of a single vessel. How bitterly his soul did smart! Everyone said of him: *He's a lost ship a-running before the wind.*

His mother's .2.nd husband was buried beside her now, in the yew-ridden Church yard of Willoughby.* Sweet John found leisure to sit beside her corpse while the bells did toll. He would not stay beyond the sermon, but rode away to pray at Grimsthorpe, where he hoped to beg new employment of Robert. Robert was not there.

Returning to London by way of Lincolne Town (longitude .20. degrees .28. minutes, latitude .53. degrees .6. minutes), he fell in with *Maister Brian O'Rourke,* a drunken Irish Prince who'd lain in the Gatehouse Prison for drunken brabbling & brawling, then took similar holidays in Marshalsea & Fleet. This worthy Gentleman would go a-whoring at Bishopsgate. John Smith denied to keep him company, believing himself now too aged for such follies, at which the said O'Rourke waxed angry, but Smith appeased his lickerish humor by relating to him all his trysts with Pokahuntas & Tragabigzanda (whom he claimed to have bedded near .100. times). — Then the Irishman commenced to guffaw, & said: Your pardon, Sweet John, but 'tis passing fierce to fancy thee a lusty lad who pulled .2. tigress's tails! For look 'pon thyself now! Ha, ha, ha! Know what thou art? Thou art but a *withered old Turke!* — Sweet John closed his eyes. His sadness dappled itself like unto forest leaves at James-towne. It was as silent as head-scarfed Tragabigzanda swimming elegantly through the rooms of her house. It signified no more than ashes in a forgotten urn. He had no pride now.

Laughing, Maister O'Rourke agreed to write a commendatory verse for his *Trve Travels.* Sweet John puffed it up with other poems & dedicated it to Robert, remembering well the admonitions of his *Machiavell.* Should he mention Bartty likewise? Nay, for those brethren gnawed e'er at each other's throats. (Besides, after all these years Bartty's experience continued as scatheless as a babe's! What battle or hurt had he seen? 'Twas

---

*History's best accretions and souvenirs are tombstones. Through wise use of this maxim we may console ourselves for the fact that poor Willoughby never got drenched in glamorous, violent blood as did Jamestown: People died there just the same, so why not call the place historic? "It was a lovely sunny day," writes the town's Reverend, Daffyd Robinson, "and the little band worked tirelessly for several hours, only stopping to exclaim on the many gravestones that were unearthed from their tangle of weeds and briars. I cannot remember the Churchyard looking so smart so early in the year." ("Wold and Marsh" newsletter, May 1995.)

hardly proportionate for Sweet John to admire him.) Instead, he added the Earl of Pembroke to the dedication, that worthy being passing rich; & squeezed in the Earl of Dover for good hap. Maybe the Publicke would finally realize how important he was (for certain fools, slaves to *Malignancy,* who could neither reckon the positions of Sunne nor Moone, nor say their Compasse, continued to deny him his desserts). But Maister Slaughter, the Printer, held up the *Trve Travels* for over .7. months, he said to see what might come of this new Colonie of Puritans in *Naumkeag.** Something extraordinary might yet transpire in the state and condition of that Colonie, in which case Captaine Smith (quoth Slaughter) might assay to add a few words. Sweet John raged himself into a veritable sickness, but failed to move that Printer's inky heart.

He heard that certain clever young Gentlemen had gotten letters-patent from the King to every part of Virginia he'd mapped. All this they'd divided into .20. parts, leaving none for him excepting some barren rocks they sneeringly call'd *Smith's Isles* . . .

He penned to King Charles the following petition: *I aske not any thing but what I can produce from the proper labour of the Salvages.* King Charles answered not.

In that Year of Our LORD 1630, which is to say the .50.th autumn of his age, he went to bide with Sir Humphrey Mildmay at Danbury Parish, Essex. Upon my life, but Sir Humphrey did like company! Gentlemen of leisure, most of whom had taken to wearing the new wider collars, entertained him with their philosphies, policies & trifles; Alchemists tansmuted his gold into empty air; & pretty Duchesses mingled with Countreywomen, as various as Powhatan's .100. wives. Not .1. of 'em mentioned the bad harvests. As Sir Humphrey once said, a man finds quite enough to do in providing for his guests & children. How many children *he* had I cannot tell, for by my faith I was not there; but doubtless Powhatan had out-offspringed him. O, but he was a ruddy, merry old man, who'd long since laid down his head in the lap of life! And a pleasant slumber he made of things. Phantasms entertained him, so that he dreamed wide-eyed, following their flitterings & mouthings with an attention all the more gracefully bestowed for that its objects were unmomentous. To John Smith, but lately escaped from the stink of turds in London's streets, Sir Humphrey's estate seemed at first to comprise a Paradise most excellent — nay, a veritable *Virginia,* in whose lap he too would have lain if he could — for who'd

---

*Cape Ann, Massachusetts.

offer herself to be his pillow now, excepting a .6.penny whore in Clerken-well? (Tragabigzanda had surely grown now unto motherliness or grand-motherliness. Did she spy him, no doubt she'd run at him screaming, with metal shining in her dagger-hand.) No matter. He made a leg; he said to 'em all: *Your obedient Servaunt.*

Smiling indulgently, his host granted him a chamber of his own, in which he stowed his *Trunk bound with iron barres* — a stout piece of life-ordnance, excellently lockable, for he always now he feared him lest he meet anew with .4. French Gallants. Full bashfully he lurk'd there, sitting upon his trunk, for he dreaded to cut a clownish figure 'midst those who guested him, but at last he hardened his courage, donned his best suit of apparel (of a tawny color videlicet, not unlike Pokahuntiss's skin), & forthrightly did exit.

The climate being passing fine for banqueting outdoors, the company disported themselves on the grass. Serving-men kept carrying new trenchers of roast beef, pies fashion'd of nightingale-tongues, &c to that long table on trestles, where Serving-wenchen stood sentinel against the flies. Lady Mildmay played most melodiously upon the virginals.

He tried to teach a young lad how to play Tick-tack, but the child said: I mislike me that game. That's a queer old game.

Everybody was smoking *Tobacco.*

Indulged by Lady Mildmay, who wore a gown of brocaded silk with decorative slits, Sir Humphrey, as I may have intimated, kept a dozen ladies near him, his favorites, as he sat in his chair of ease, swollen about the waist, like a generous tavern mug. John Smith stood alone in the grass and whispered: *Winganuske, Attossocomiske, Ortoughnoiske, Ashtoiske, Ponnoiske, Oweroughwough, Amopotoiske, Appomosicut, Ottermiske, Ottopomtacke, Appimmonoiske, Memeoughquiske* — for he could not disremember the names of Powhatan's wives. He was now attack'd by the name *Opposunoquononuske* — but nay, she was the Queen of Appatamuck, who'd courteously dried his fingers with a turkey-wing. We'd been compell'd to burn her Towne.

No one conversed with him. He smiled, clenching his scarred hands.

From a Florentine cassetta of gilt alder wood engraved with equestrian battles, Sir Humphrey took out none other than Smith's *Trve Relation!* — You see, lad, I keep by me the Tablets of the Law!

You are too kind, my Lord . . .

Not at all! And now prithee take you to your belly-timber, for I would have a word with some Gentlemen . . .

His host granted that he keep that private chamber of his, in order that he might pleasure himself with his studies. Indeed his mind & soul remained as busy as the shops of Lincoln High Bridge. Like unto that old *Almanacke* from Gravesend, which divideth the shining of the Starres into **.2.** equal partes, he thought to clarify everything. (This same *Almanacke* admits: *If you will describe the land true, then shal not the Sea be true.*) Flood oh! Full sail & happily did he scribble out his *Advertisements for the unexperienced Planters of New England, or anywhere, Or, The Path-way to experience to erect a Plantation.* Mayhap 'twould turn him an honest silver pound. Sir Humphrey, who found the writing crabbed, begged him to read it out aloud in easy afternoon scraps, which he was pleased to do.

The Warres in Europe, Asia, & Affrica, he began in a sternly brassy voice, *taught me how to subdue the wilde Salvages in Virginia & New-England, in America—*

Indeed, you need not trouble to inform us where New England is, said Sir Humphrey. We know that.

And some old Soldier sang out: Where'er *England* is not, lies our *New England.* Someday we'll rule the world!

(O, by the CHRIST cross! another Gentleman tittered.)

In America, *my Lord,* continued this freakish Captaine Smith, raising his voice, *which now after many a stormy blast of ignorant contradictors, projectors, and Undertakers, both they and I have been so tossed and tortured into so many extremities, as despaire was the next wee both expected—*

You dwell mayhap too much upon your ruptures & disappointments, said Sir Humphrey. Can you not entertain some commendations? Some pleasant tinkling little verse, for example . . .

O yes, some tinkling verse, my Lord, said Smith.

He retired beneath a leafless tree (it being late September, the Sunne having sunken into Libra) and scratched away with his quill. Returning to the company with a grim smile, he declaimed:

> Aloofe, aloofe, and come no neare,
> the dangers doe appeare;
> Which if my ruine had not beene
> you had not seene:
> I only lie upon this shelfe
> to be a marke to all
> which on the same might fall,
> That none may perish but my selfe.

Gracious! cried Sir Humphrey.

Shall I proceed to the next stanza? (Thus the grizzled Captaine Smith.)

Indeed you will not, said Sir Humphrey, whose white linen cap was embroidered with gold & silver threads. — Why, you write as if your hour were come! Come, drink with me now, man — cheer thyself in e'ery part that needs cheering! My sakes, a sullen season it's like to be . . .

And indeed a sullen season it was. The plague had returned to Lincolnshire. Essex too got attainted with it. 'Twas said that many families — Noblemen, Townsmen, yeomen, Fen Slodgers and all — were perishing of the famine.

Sweet John feared that he made Sir Humphrey restless, for the man now regarded him as if he were .1. of those stage-villains who gets booed at the Globe Theatre. Lady Mildmay grimaced at the sight of the unhappy guest. As for the other persons present, he scantly regarded them. Their conversation, strange to say, reached him only at a distance, & trivialities poisoned their words, so that to him they might as well have been frogs, or *Fen nightingales* as we say here in Lincolnshire. (O, he's in his mumps, they said. He's had reverses.) They could not succor him. As it sayeth in Shakespeare, *Would not the beggar then forget himself?*

Convulsively returning unto London-Towne, he accepted the kind hospitality of Sir Samuel Saltonstall. (Run, Smith, run.) In another room he heard a Gentleman say: He raves e'er on about his *Coat of Armes* with its .3. Turkes' heads. — Sweet John flush'd with chagrin. But 'twas not Sir Samuel he could blame for that . . .

Throwing over Maister Slaughter, he made an agreement with .1. Maister Haviland to print the *Advertisements,* but again there was much delay . . .

Frauncis was dead now, as he did hear. Ring the bell for him! Following this sad news, Sir Humphrey did invite Sweet John once again to stay, percase less for friendship's sake than because he was cousin-in-law to my Lord Willoughby's aunt (namely, Robert's aunt — for Robert still tried to help in his dry & fickle way). Sweet John declined the invitation. He feared the frowns of Lady Mildmay. (Listening suddenly, he heard a seagull crying in the fog.)

Sir Samuel gained him admittance to the wide, quiet, high-ceiling'd rooms where stripe-sleev'd, neck-ruffled Shipwrights did trace out shipshapes with their Compasses, then drew in orlops, ribs, mizzenmasts until their dreams lay full-boned upon the paper. He gazed upon the Shipwrights & blest them. He was not the man to benefit from their constructions. In his dreams he slogged through swamp water of a duller grey than an old silver breastplate. Rereading his dusty *Machiavell,* he discover'd no clue as to how he should best advance himself. He remained ready to hazard his body for any cause, Captaine of *.200.* and *.50.* horsemen, *Trarintra-rarara*. The Susquehannocks of Virginia had adored him like unto a GOD. Yet he owned not even a single Man-servaunt. *I am as I am and so I will be.* Again & again he stretched out his hands to find some friend, but many of his generation were perisht now. Meanwhile, 'twixt him and Virginia did the Kingdome now, the very State itself, raise up snares & snickles thicker than a Spanish galleon's wide fans of rigging, so that he grew rapidly awearied and encumbered.

Maister Haviland sent for him again. Upon his arrival, the Printer did begin (unpleasantly as he thought) with a *Good even, Sweet John.*

'Tis *Captaine Smith* to you, sirrah. You scarcely know me . . .

Captaine Smith, 'tis said you & I could get rich, did we rush out some penny broadside, detailing the *Romaunce* 'twixt yourself & *Princesse Pokahuntiss*—

Sweet John clapt his hat back upon his head. O'er his shoulder he did say: Sometimes the public baits blind old bears, but 'tis not much sport to do so.

Nay, Captaine, pray don't miscomprehend me—

He departed Maister Haviland's forever.

He could scarce compass his own Countrey's ingratitude. Why, King Charles had but lately pensioned that diabolickall Alchemist *Dr. Robert Fludd,* who sold a salve which, applied to the weapon which had wounded a man, would supposedly cure the wound. What trash! What Popish skullduggery! Yet for all his *Trve Travels* they did hardly e'en lodge him, let alone dress him in cloth-of-gold . . . ! Percy, Wingfield, Argoll & e'en Rolfe at the end, they'd all drest most brilliantly. Their dazzlements now tortured him as *False Starres* do the Mariner who's bereft of his course.

Rushing to a Tavern-house where rumor located Argoll's Sailors, he pled for a preferment from all strangers, until he was roundly expelled. (Tom Tapster shrilled: O, he affects to be accompted a *Gentleman!*)

A filthy Waterman clutched his sleeve & sought to inveigle him into some whore's oozy plaguish bed. He said nay. The Waterman pursued him. Sweet John bade him begone. The Waterman would not. He made his best speed away, yet the Waterman pursued him, grabbling at him. When he finally did 'scape, he was trembling; yea, Sweet John was afraid . . .

He receiv'd a letter that Frauncis had willed his lands & tenements half unto him, and half unto his wife Anna. *Pen and ink, pen and ink.* He did send to Anna, to ask her how they ought to settle this matter betwixt 'em, but she never replied. Wearied, he gave the matter over. He but scantly cared now to underprop his weak old age.

Maister John Tradescant, a certain companion of Captaine Argall's, did invite him into his study, where much to his surprise he found Powhatan's mantle, with which our good Captaine Newport had evidently not wished to remain encumbered (it was, after all, but a deerskin sewn with cowry-shells & other such trash). Land's sakes, .20. years ago now & more it was that they'd crowned that subtle old Salvage! 'Twas Newport, perhaps, who was responsible for all their reverses, for that coronation had permitted Powhatan to put on airs! O, & Sweet John had argued with the Counsell at the time, but the Counsell had said—

Following that visit, he felt obliged to summons Maister Tradescant to go with him to a certain red-latticed Tavern-House, where, trolling the beer-bowl one to t'other, they discoursed on all their ancient Undertakings, gilding failures into successes. (Did the Tapster watch 'em, to learn how much money they had?) Sweet John flushed, brushing back his long grey locks. He clenched his purse against his side.

And why did you never return unto Virginia?

Aye, well, they importun'd me, but I could not sit still for a lot of sheep-drunken coistrels. Now sometimes I regret it, for the lands & estates of Capahowsick Towne were deeded unto me irrevocably—

A drab would sit with him. *Your most humble Servaunt,* said he. (How Maister Tradescant did smirk!)

She licked her lips at him, then slowly blew *Tobacco*-smoke in his face. He explained to the pretty wench: I remember when that herb but drained our Treasury, & brought profit to Spain . . . — but she did not care.

His powers exhausted, he continued to bide at Sir Samuel's. In January he did celebrate his .51.st year, in March the *Advertisements* did appear, & in June he lay down upon his deathbed.

In Saint Helena's Church in Willoughby there is a plaque graven to the memory of John Smith. *He was first among the leaders of the settlement, which began the expansions overseas of the English speaking people.*

He is buried, however, in Saint Sepulcher's Church in London — which is itself a Gravesend or way-station for many other deathbound travellers, for there the condemned from Newgate Prison, being led out to be hang'd, do stop to receive a nosegay. Somehow, the fact that he did not choose Willoughby excites no surprise. Or, more likely, London-Towne got chosen for him; why should anyone ship the corpse of this unimportant drifter back unto Lincolnshire, especially when his nearest kinsmen lay already dead? I don't know who was at his funeral, but this I have heard: On that rainy day when they cut into the clay, making a square gulf in which to lower him, bone-water gurgled in from the other soft graves. He'd proved no Woldsman, but a Fensman, & a failure: they buried him in ooze.

FURTHER HISTORY OF THE PATAWOMECKS
(1622–1623)

In to that cuntery I would haue men geo armored of this sorte, for that they ar to deall with naked men . . .

Anonymous instructions for Sir Walter Ralegh (*ca* 1584)

*H*ungering for corn, which the neighboring Countreys could give them no longer (being pillaged, burned and spoiled), the English set sail for double-palisadoed Patawomeck, whose King had e'er been their friend. 'Twas he who'd allowed Japzaws & his wife to betray Princesse *Pokahuntiss* aboard Argall's ship, and during the massacre led by Opechancanough he'd done the English no hurt. So they requited him by kidnapping him, his son, & .2. of his relatives, whom they carried to Jamestowne and ransomed for corn. They also slew near about .30. or .40. of his subjects, male & female, like-wise children — for no Yndian's too young to be a traitor, & none's too young to die. Receiving the belly-timber they'd demanded, our Adventur-ers then kindly fraughted their captives back unto their Kingdome. — Why not blame sunny Captaine Argoll for the success of this strategem? For by haling Pocahontas back to yᵉ Colonie, he'd prov'd Salvage-snatching to be quite *Politick!*

Now, in several moldy old Histories I've read that in fact our English, rather than being tricksters, were in this case trick'd, for 'tis written that a wicked Werowance of the *Nacotchtank tribe* did persuade 'em that the Pattawomecks had fallen in league with Opechancanough. But, if trick'd, our merry English murtherers certainly lost nothing, so why not say they believed full well in the King of Pattawomeck's innocency? 'Twas but busi-ness, when they *Argoll'd* him! (Thus indeed's our habit in the Indies, the Azores, & anywhere else we go, when we must refresh ourselves. And indeed, since this King of Patawomeck had turn'd traitor to Virginia's in-nocent *Nonpareil,* how could he have expected to be advanced or even trusted by his new Masters?)

In the spring they needed corn once again, & sailed to Patawomeck in the *Tiger* for purposes of trade, but this time the perfidious Salvages did kill

all the Englishmen they could. (Well, again, possibly 'twas the Nacotch-
tanks, not the Patawomecks, but no matter, dear Reader, for a Salvage is but
a Salvage.) Accordingly Governor Wyatt sent a delegation of peace, who
hung out a flag of truce, coax'd 'em out of their double palisadoes & then did
offer up a toast of friendship — but the wine they gave the Salvages was
well and cunningly poisoned, so that the King & some .200. others of his
wise men, or *Cronoccoes,* together with his sons & warriors, did all perish in hideous torment.

Further History of the Patawomecks (1665)

> We have anticipated your desires by settinge uppon
> the Indians in all places.
>
> GOVERNOR WYATT to the Virginia Company (1623)

*A*fter this year they disappear from all records.

FURTHER HISTORY OF ALL
VIRGINIAN SALVAGES (1629)

And here might we have proceeded to the next point were it not for one scruple
which some that think themselves to be very wise do cast in our way; which is
this, in effect: The country, they say, is possessed by owners that rule and govern
it in their own right. Then with what conscience and equity can we offer to
thrust them, by violence, out of their inheritances? . . . This proposition, I confess, I never was willing to examine, considering my vocation is private . . .

WILLIAM SYMONDS, sermon on Virginia, 1609

*B*eing *so inclosed with Pallizadoes,* writes Smith, the colonists *regard*
not the Salvages; and amongst those Plantations above James Towne (a
place which I, William the Blind, found centuries later to be grassy and excavated, like a cemetery-island, a necropolis: indeed, in those parts many an
English skeleton still lies curled beneath the dirt), *they have now found*
meanes to take plentie of fish, as well with lines, as nets, and where the wa-
ters are the largest, heaving meanes, they need not want.

(That was the year the Colonie did export .1,500,000. pounds of
Tobacco into England.)

Upon this River they seldome see any Salvages, but in the woods, many
times their fires: yet some few there are, that upon their opportunitie have
slaine some few stragglers, which have beene revenged with the death of so
many of themselves; but no other attempt hath been made upon them this
.2. or .3. yeares.

And so we *Englishe* did reap the benefit of their defeated absence,
just as the Mayor and Burgesses of Boston Port in Lincolnshire retains by
ancient right all title to flotsam, jetsam, and the goods of suicides.

Further History of Opechancanough
(1622–1644)

The only real tragedy of those prosperous years occurred in 1622, when Opechancanough, who had succeeded his less warlike brother Opitchapan, led an uprising against the colonists.

Grace Steele Woodward, Pocahontas

Opechancanough's Salvages lurked & sniped after the massacre, so that by 1623 half the English were dead (many, however, had perished from hunger and the usual *Jamestowne sickness*). In e'ery Corporation of the Colonie, & back home in London-Towne, our great Lords, Generalls, Admiralls & Captaines did design revenge just as they would have done in Ireland (a most unruly Province, where we've learnt to hunt down rebellious Earls to death). — We are Soldiers of CHRIST, said they. — Relying on Sweet John's map, which had been full annotated & amplified by kindly Argoll, they gathered in & arrayed their helmed Soldiers, to commaund the most effective compassing of Virgina. At midsummer, when the corn was high, they fell upon every Yndian Towne they could reach, burning houses & crops, so that the Salvages would starve come winter. They also (praise be to OUR REDEEMER!) slaughtered diverse persons. ('Twas all for the betterment of those Yndians. Didn't they themselves beat acorns in water to remove the bitterness?) Altho' Opechancanough's painted Bow-men fell upon them in many a crescent-shaped ambuscado, English ordnance invariably won the field. So they knew 'twould be. (For the *twinkling fear* there's a remedy: We'll inflict pain.) 'Tis said that meanwhile King Opechancanough in his laughable ignorance did sow all the gunpowder he'd captured, expecting it to sprout and grow into gunpowderbushes which he could harvest without limit. For Sweet John had pretended to him, back in 1607 when the Salvages took him captive, that gunpowder was a species of grain rais'd in the soil of England. Wise Captaine Smith! *He* knew 'twas not fitting to teach the Yndians alchymickall secrets! It gave the Colonists many a laugh to imagine their enemies hunkered o'er the furrows of their corn-fields, waiting & waiting for that magick seed to grow. And the afterclap? In 1623 the English agreed to a truce, and sail'd up Pamunkey River to toast Opechancanough with spiced wine as they had done at Pattawomeck. How well would their purpose be achiev'd today? Thus debated the Gentlemen, standing at the gunnels while their inferiors did row. All of them were stricken with *the twink-ing fear,* but essayed not to show it. (And thus flows humanity through this Dream, cloaking fear & murther deep within its own soft-grown flesh.) 'Twas a humid, silent day, near about the **.3.**rd hour of the Afternoon Watch. Frog-croaks welcomed them into the swamp. Then they did see manlike figures a-running on the low shore to watch them, and presently came in sight of a Towne. — But no! All that lay in the past; no Townes

remain'd unburned within their reach; all Salvages ran away, never closer anymore. (They hide their lambs at tithing-time! laugh'd an old Soldier.) 'Twas but a charred clearing which they came upon, No-Man's-Countrey with Virginia creepers a-feasting upon the black ribs of Salvage longhouses. — Back water! cried the Captaine. Water was most monotonously glistering upon the Oarmens' blades. — Phew! said a Gentleman. This ooze doth stink like unto a Servaunt's breath! — Now here came their enemies with feather-crazed heads. Smiling, the Englishmen conveyed the wine-tub, clenching their weapons as they did come ashore. And King Opechancanough (that understanding Gentleman) did smile his own customary poisonous smile — who'd betray whom .1.st? — & then the Englishmen & the Salvages did all sit down upon mats of bark, orating of eternal friendship. Sobbing & begrimed, captive Englishwomen were released into their Countreymens' arms. Captaine Tucker most graciously did ransom them with beads & hatchets. At that, Opechancanough said a word, and the guests started in alarm; but 'twas only an invitation to start smoking their *Tobacco* out of long-stemm'd pipes adorned with copper. Now 'twas the Englishmen's turn to requite him. Opechancanough, however, did but sip, then jumped surpris'd at the taste, & grimaced, hesitating to drink deeper of the draught, so the English instantly let their harquebuses blaze, murthering & scalping a number of those deceitful Salvages (glory be to JEHOVAH the ALMIGHTIE) — indeed felling this *Opechancanough* himself, who yet crawled & slithered into the bloody grass, so that they could not discover him. Months later they learned that he had not been slain, but lurked at Menmend-Towne his capital, where his bullet-wounds healed but slowly, he being old. 'Twas said he'd physicked himself with a purge of *Lesser Sassafrass,* which is a *black drink* much relied on by those Salvages whene'er they need to vomit. No matter; some year they'd hunt him down. In 1624 they loaded their harquebuses, upped helms, & repeated their sanitary measures, against all Townes within reach. The anniversary of Opechancanough's massacre would be forever solemnized as a holy day, so that we'd never disremember the perfidy of those evil Naturalls (or *Virginians* as they were formerly call'd). Came another clash of arms at Pamunkey Neck; the English got the victory, and decapitated much Indian corn. Everywhere they raised up *the hue and cry* against the Salvages. In 1628, the aforesaid Apachankano sued for truce, which the English granted, & broke the following year, for there is no need to keep faith with perfidious Salvages. In 1632, he sued again for peace, and upon his most humble supplication received his readmittance into English affection. Why not another truce? thought our Colonists. For just as there is .1. quarter of the year when they hold no cockfights in London-Towne ('tis said the cocks' feathers then be too full of blood), so when the corn doth grow in Virginia, why, that's likewise a dangerous time for fighting. Lay in our crop, my lusty lads! Then it can be cockfighting season. And Opechancanough, he's passing ancient now; surely 'tis convenient to treat with him, & make him a broken old vassal, harmless, resistless to our new extortions of land. But, O, that snake! In 1644 he rebelled against his Masters once again! This time he killed about .400. souls; but the English had now grown so numerous that such a loss constituted only the .12.th part of their number. They swore then that having been gulled a .2.nd time, they'd nevermore let any defect into their vigilance. Tolling Chuch-bells, sending for all Brigades, they did scour the black swamp-channels of Pamunkey Neck, no matter how obscurely each water-way did twist (like unto London-Towne's unwholesomely slinking by-ways). Thus methodically they razed Opechancanough's outlandish Townes .1. by .1., & to pay the expenses of that campaign they sold many Salvages to be slaves, *Trarintra-rarara*. In 1646, having vanquish'd Menmend-Towne, they snatched that King Opechancanough by his long grey scalp-lock, & haled him to Jamestowne for to stand upon his trial. I've heard that his face was a terrifying mask of hate. While he lay in jail, on his heap of bloody straw, there came the sullen click of the lock. He denied to lift his head. Could OKEUS have told him? Nay, he needed nobody to explain the end. In rush'd an English Soldier, raging, & shot him in the back. Then that murtherer stopt for to listen. No sound! Only the sound of Opechancanough's guilt . . . No Jailer came a-running. The Jailer sat in the Guard-house, a-playing *Security* with the Marshal. Reader, that Soldier deserves our full commendations. For he (as I do verily believe) kept engraved on his heart's tablet this maxim from old Machiavell: *Such as Moses, Cyrus, Theseus & Romulus meet great obstacles in consummating their Undertakings, for all their perils lie in the ascent; yet when those are o'ercome, & those who envied them their success are exterminated, they'll commence to be respected, & shall continue e'er after powerful, secure, honored & happy.*

FURTHER HISTORY OF THE
CAROLINA SALVAGES (1709)

The plagues creep on the burning winds driven by flames of Orc,
And by the fierce Americans rushing together in the night
Driven o'er the Guardians of Ireland and Scotland and Wales. . . .
WILLIAM BLAKE, *America: A Prophecy* (1793)

*T*he botanically minded Adventurer William Lawson, whose destiny, al-tho' I'm sure he knew it not, was to be tortur'd and throat-slit ear to ear by Salvages, wrote of them that *the Small-Pox and Rum have made such a Destruction amongst them, that, on good grounds, I do believe, there is not the .6.th Savage living within .200. Miles of all our Settlements, as there were .50. Years ago. These poor Creatures have so many Enemies to destroy them, that it's a wonder .1. of them is left alive near us.*

The Nottoway Girls of North Carolina (1728)

Love is born of faith, lives on hope, and dies of charity.

Gian Carlo Menotti (b. 1911), notebook jottings for *Maria Golovin*

The famous Gentleman, Surveyor & rake-hell, William Byrd, whose occupation it temporarily was to determine where Virginia ended & North Carolina began, found these ladies *Wrapt in their Red and Blue Match-Coats, thrown so Negligently around them that their Mahogany Skin appear'd in Several Parts, like the Lacedæmonian Damsels of Old.* (Byrd appears to have enjoyed such tropes, for they often appear in his *Histories of the Dividing Line.*) Some of them doubtless had Nansemond blood, for these latter Yndians (who once held a high place in Powhatan's Empire, & annoyed *Sweet John, Lord De La Warr,* & *Sir Thomas Dale*) had by stages lost their lands to the English, until at last the remnant enrolled themselves amongst the Nottoways. We Colonists ought to take this extinguishment as a sign of GOD's favor to us, for 'twas none other than these Nansemonds who'd attacked us .121. years since, when we .1.ˢᵗ landed to commence the Colonie. Dost remember, sweet Reader? How could you forget the Nansemonds' *Whe, whe, yah, ha, ne, he, wittowa, wittowa!* as they shot Captaine Archer & poor Matthew Morton from ambuscado? O treacherous Salvages! And now they were gone & harmless, fitting toys for Maister Byrd as he inspected the charms of the Nottoway wenchen. (Death flies o'er, with whirring wings.) Their hair hung in a large roll on their shoulders (so he observed), & was braided with the customary white and blue "peak," or small cylinders cut out of a conch shell, drilled through and strung like beads.

— *It serves them both for Money and Jewels, the Blue being of much greater Value than the White, for the same reason that Ethiopian Mistresses in France are dearer than French, because they are more scarce. The Women wear Necklaces and Bracelets of these precious Materials when they have a mind to appear lovely. Tho' their complexions be a little Sad-col'red, yet their Shapes are very Strait and well proportion'd.*

*Their Faces are Seldom handsome, yet they have an Air of Innocence
and Bashfulness, that with a little less dirt wou'd not fail to make them
desirable. Such Charms might have had their full Effect upon Men
who had been so long deprived of female conversation, but that the
whole Winter's Soil was so crusted on the Skins of those dark Angels
that it require' a very strong Appetite to approach them. The Bear's oil,
with which they annoint their Persons all over, makes their skins Soft,
and at the Same time protects them from every Species of Vermin that
use to be troublesome to other uncleanly People.*

Think you, good Reader, that he would have delayed to take Pocahontas
unto his bosom? In his night-visions, her secret's like unto the white cup of
a puccoon flower.

*We were unluckily so many that they cou'd not make us the compliment
of Bed-fellows, according to the Indian Rules of Hospitality, tho' a
grave Matron whisper'd one of the Commissioners very civilly in the
Ear* (Maister Byrd was that Commissioner) *that, if her Daughter had
been but one year Older, she should have been at his Devotion . . . like
the Ladies that Game, they are a little Mercenary in their Amours and
seldom bestow their Favors out of stark Love and Kindness. But after
these Women have once appropriated their Charms by Marriage, they
are thencefourth faithful to their Vows and will hardly ever be tempted
by an Agreeable Gallant . . .*

*The whole Number of People belonging to the Nottoway Town, if
you include Women and Children, amount to about 200. These are the
only Indians of any consequence now remaining within the Limits of
Virginia. The rest are either removed, or dwindled to a very inconsider-
able Number.*

Forty-nine years later, Thomas Jefferson penned, *Of the Nottoways,
not a male is left. A few women constitute the remains of that tribe.*

FURTHER HISTORY OF THE POWHATANS
(1629–1787)

Soon their land became more valuable than their services as hunters, slave catchers, warriors and concubines.

J. ANTHONY PAREDES, *Indians of the Southeastern United States
in the Late 20th Century*

*V*ery *little can now be discovered of the subsequent history of these tribes severally,* wrote Jefferson in his *Notes on the State of Virginia.* To him, as to John Rolfe and John Smith, their vanquishment was as natural as the rule of husband over wife. Fate rides the tides, like the hideously spouting sea-hag off the coast of Lincolnshire in Speed's *Atlas;* and fated souls drown. Thus the Virginian Salvages, whom old chroniclers once described as tall, comely, strong and active, now sink beneath the mold. Someday, come Judgment, their murther-graves will gape anew, so that flesh now turned to earth may bleed again from its wounds. For now, *Archaeologists & Treasure-hunters* must do the job. Jefferson broke open an Indian mound and found skeletons, then dirt, then more skeletons, then more dirt, thereby proving that the original inhabitants of our Nation had indulged in periodic mass burials. Might they have begun dying in masses, too? Captaine John Smith had mused: *. . . It seemes* G OD *hath provided this Countrey for our Nation, destroying the natives by the plague, it not touching one Englishman . . .* Many there were who wished to help G OD along,* such as Virginia's governor, Sir William Berkeley, who penned a letter in 1666 which said: *I think it is necessary to destroy all these northern indians . . . 'Twill be a great terror & example & instruction to all other Indians . . . it may be done without charge, for the women and children will defray it.* No doubt several did perish as a direct result of such incitements, while others simply fled the Countrey, hoping to live out their generations before the English came further inland, garrisoning their conquests

---

*After all, this was the G OD Who slew all the .1.ˢᵗborn of Egypt, e'en unto the .1.ˢᵗborn of the Pharaoh's Servaunt-maid & the .1.ˢᵗborn calf of the cow she tended.

bit by bit, so that the Salvages must dwell **.1.**ˢᵗ under the
shadows of Forts, & then ring'd round by
farms & Citties. Of course they prov'd useful for to hunt wolves & fishes.

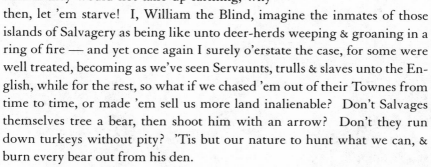

Now with right excellent speed we did
carve up old Powhatan's Empire, *Trarintra-rarara.* To those Werowances who
asked it of us in due submission we did
grant *Reservations* of land sufficient for
their dwindling numbers of Bow-men to farm.
And if they would not take up farming, why
then, let 'em starve! I, William the Blind, imagine the inmates of those
islands of Salvagery as being like unto deer-herds weeping & groaning in a
ring of fire — and yet once again I surely o'erstate the case, for some were
well treated, becoming as we've seen Servaunts, trulls & slaves unto the English, while for the rest, so what if we chased 'em out of their Townes from
time to time, or made 'em sell us more land inalienable? Don't Salvages
themselves tree a bear, then shoot him with an arrow? Don't they run
down turkeys without pity? 'Tis but our nature to hunt what we can, &
burn every bear out from his den.

Jefferson continues: *The* Chickahominies *removed, about the year
1661, to Mattapony river . . . This seems to have been the last chapter in
their history. They retained however their separate name as late as 1705,
and were at length blended with the Pamunkies and Mattaponies, and exist
at present only under their names.*

Capsized by all **.32.** winds, or points of the Compasse, the Salvages sank
and sank. The Colonists endured. They took the maidenheads of new
rivers & Territories.

For the new Virginians, such difficulties as Sweet John had fought now
were reduced almost to specters. In 1682 the Deputy Governor of Virginia
progued the meeting of the Assembly to a later date, *because until the Spring
time the Apprehensions of our Indian troubles are not great, Nor the Safety
& preservation of the Country against forreign Incursions in great hazard.*

In H.R. MicIlwaine's **.3.** immense volumes of the Council's transactions
from 1680 through 1774, one hunts nearly in vain for any mention of Pocahontas's memory, or Opechancanough's, or the Powhatan Empire's.
Brownish-yellow page-edges snickle the fingers like striated tree-bark.
Yes, Virginia must still be garrisoned, but they talked about that in the same
breath as when they defined merchantable tobacco leaves. They began to

sell their helms & brigandines to the Blacksmith for scrap iron; for 'tis passing laborious to clean one's armor in Virginia's corrosive breath; moreover, armor's out of fashion — for in Europe the guns have grown too percing strong; & in Virginia the Salvages dare not launch their arrows. (As Argoll said: Heaven gave 'em small capacity.) — Virginia's slipped beyond the verge; she's no more herself. Her insurrection's failed.

In 1682 they declared that Yndian Women-servaunts were tithable (which everyone already knew throughout the shire), and on that same day they repealed *a former law making Indians and others free.* In 1699, a Maister George Ivie did petition for the repeal of the Act of Assembly prohibiting intermarriage with Negroes, Indians and Mulattoes.* Had he found his own darling Pokahuntas? (Each to his own, they say. The shad-fish dwells in brackish waters, while bream & pike prefer the sandy depths of inland streams.) His petition was not assented to. For we must not call them unfeeling, these Burgesses. Indeed, they exerted the greatest tenderness upon their nursling Commonwealth! For instance, should a slave be put to death for disobedience, rebellion or other fault, the Burgesses made sure that his owner got fully reimbursed for his market value out of public money.

Gaze out, sweet Reader, upon the very fine grain of dark blue waves as you stand at Jamestowne! John Smith sailed here; for near upon a year 'twas his Presidential seat, or *con*ceit as his rivals did say. Here he got his memories, and blotted 'em down on parchments now rotten like his bones; those *Complete Works* he wrote keeps them afloat yet a few years longer. His voice drones hazily on, lower now than the slyest Waterman's whisper.

In 1699, the Burgesses of Virginia decide to remove from James Towne at last, & make a new capital at Williamsburg. They set sail, leaving behind 'em many graves marked & unmarked, whose festering contents will soon be eaten up by the river. The sun doth gleam & glister upon the ruins of the Glass-house furnace, which resemble half-melted rocks.

(Jefferson: *There remain of the* Mattaponies *.3. or .4. men only, and they have more negro than Indian blood in them. They have lost their language, have reduced themselves, by voluntary sales,*[†] *to about .50. acres of*

---

*William Byrd writes that "the poor Indians would have had less reason to Complain that the English took away their Land, if they had received it by way of Portions with their Daughters . . . Nor wou'd the Shade of the Skin have been any reproach at this day; for if a Moor may be washt white in 3 Generations, Surely an Indian might have been blancht in two."

[†]"The lands were your property," he wrote to Brother Handsome Lake in 1802, when he was President. "The right to sell is one of the rights of property. To forbid you the exercise of that right would be a wrong to your nation. Nor do I think, brother, that the sale of lands is, under all circumstances, injurious to your people. While they depended on hunting, the more extensive the forest around them, the more game they would yield. But going into a state of agriculture, it may

land, which lies on the river of their own name, and have, from time to time, been joining the Pamunkies, from whom they are distant but .10. *miles.*)

On Tuesday June ye .4.th 1706, having read them out .3. times, and amended them as needed, they passed the bills *An Act to prevent Indians hunting and ranging on patented lands* and *An act declaring the Negro, Mulatto & Indian Slaves within this Dominion to be real Estate.* On the .7.th they passed the bill entitled *An Act for prevention of misunderstanding between the Tributary Indians and other her Majestys Subjects of this Colony and Dominion & for a free and open trade with all Indians whatsoever.* In 1723 they read a bill entitled *An Act directing the Tryal of Slaves committing Capitol Crimes, and for the more effectual punishing Conspiracys and Insurrections of them, and for the better Government of Negros, Mulattos & Indians bond or free,* which passed after much dissension and amendment. Thus at last they categorized the Salvages with all other ungodly creatures scarce better than demons.

Another century of abuse was spaded upon the Salvages' living grave, and then another. Altho' Virginia yet in places remained utterly Salvage, which is to say disproportionate, yet many of us scarcely knew now what Salvages were. For where might we find 'em? Only in *Never-Never Virginia,* whose maidenhead is guarded by a lion in an airborne cockleshell. Between Leo's tassels & ribbons lies a miniature tempest in which a sailing-ship doth tilt. The storm supports itself on knobby feet — a chicken's? the lion's? — on the firm green ground of Virginia, thereby proving that we may as well take every vicissitude in life as no more than another stained glass window scene in Willoughby Church, where so much cool white spring light comes gushing in. Nor's a lion-footed sea-storm the only oddity you'll see in Virginia. For look! A feathertopped Salvage leans preposterously on his half-strung bow, 'gainst which he's slid an arrow in violin-bow in order to point out for us a grove of umbrella-handled vegetables which may actually exist somewhere in Florida, amidst the fantasies of .2.-headed anthropophagi. On the other lion-side of him, a Salvage in the stern of a canoe draws back his bow at a school of ducks,

---

be as advantageous to a society, as it is to an individual, who has more land than he can improve, to sell a part, and lay out the money in stocks and implements of agriculture, for the better improvement of the residue . . . I hope, therefore, that on further reflection, you will see this transaction in a more favorable light . . . Go on, then, brother, in the great reformation which you have undertaken. Persuade our red brethren then to be sober, and to cultivate their lands; and their women to spin and weave for their families. You will soon see your women and children well fed and clothed, your men living happily in peace and plenty, and your numbers increasing from year to year."

while another Salvage like unto a Thames punter mischeviously poles him *away* from his prey. *They disguise themselves in tawniness,* writes Captaine John Smith. For this Never-Never Virginia, the only one in which Powhatan still reigns today, is depicted on the title page of his *Generall Historie.*

FURTHER HISTORY OF THE PAMUNKEYS
(1676–1787)

*O it was a brave age then, and so it is ever, where there are offensive wars and not
defensive, and men fight for the spoil and not in fear to be spoiled, and are as lions seeking out their prey, and not as sheep that lie still whiles they are preyed on.*
THOMAS NASHE, *Lenten Stuff*

*I*n 1699 the Committee Appointed to Consider and Settle the Claimes &
Titles to lands in *Pamunky* neck and on the south side of the *black water swamp* did report to the General Assembly at James Cittie that *the
Queen of* Pamunkey *hath Complained that severall* English *have En-
croached vpon the Libertyes of her people, Contrary to the Articles of Peace.*
Why didn't those Salvages appeal to King Oozymandias? For he reigns
o'er all. He abridges his foes. He mercifully drowns all in his good time
(not excluding Captaine Fortune); he calls *Flood oh!* & the muck doth
come. He's been everywhere. (For example, they say the tide once lapped
all the way to Lincoln-Towne, back in Roman times before the Fens were
drained — altho' this may be a lie.) He'll return everywhere at his leisure,
as he doth plot the means. But for now we can always petition our Lords
the English. It passes the time. The previous Queen of Pamunkey had
complained before, back in 1676 during Bacon's Rebellion, when some English hotheads expelled her people from their Towne, hunting them in the
forest, murthering them & stealing their goods. ('Twas an old Towne by
then, full of rot & fleas. Soon they would have removed to a newer place.)
The Assembly return'd her lands to her the following year — well, most of
them — for fairness demands that we treat the Salvages near as well as our
English. (Ha! That Queen was so well treated she produced a half-English
bastard!) But the ooze rose higher around the Pamunkeys. I've read that
when they were compelled to abandon their Three Temples at Uttamussack, where Powhatan's bones lay wrapped in reed-mats beside his flimflam
English crown, they attempted to take with them the famous crystal altar-
stone. But it proved too heavy, so they buried it. Antiquaries of my own
race then tried to dig it up, but never did find it, which proves the altar-

stone, & therefore OKEUS, & therefore Powhatan & Pokahuntiss, & therefore all the Indians, to have never existed; unless we consider the other possibility that the altar-stone is sinking & sinking e'en now unto the bosom of that bottomless ooze.

No matter; the tale runs thus: In the end, the Pamunkeys had to sell off a trifle of their land, in order to pay their debts, then another trifle, &c. 'Twas passing convenient, the way those Salvages and their lands dwindled together! In 1699, good English farms began to spring up on Pamunkey Neck. (The reddish grass in that locality was a sea. A blue channel flowed through it, as if *Moses* had but lately come for the parting of the Red Sea.) The name of the Queen of Pamunkey who complained that year nobody remembers. What's the difference? She was but an ignorant Salvage. The Assembly conferr'd, and perhaps pitied her a little, or laugh'd for a good blink, and then the Clerk did scribble justice in $\mathcal{A}$s and $\mathcal{B}$s like unto the rope-fans and rope-webs by which Sailors do bridle those horses call'd *Ships*.*

Three-quarters of a century afterward, Thomas Jefferson in his survey of the Virginia-world did mark: *The* Pamunkies *are reduced to about* **.10.** *or* **.12.** *men, tolerably pure from mixture with other colours. The older ones among them preserve their language in a small degree, which are the last vestiges on earth, so far as we know, of the Powhatan language. They have about* **.300.** *acres of very fertile land, on Pamunkey river, so encompassed by water that a gate shuts in the whole.*

---

*Sweet Reader, shouldn't law be *practical*? In Lincolshire they drop all penalties for the crime of bastardy, should the child die. Why must there be penalties at all? Because fatherless children cost the Parish pence and tuppence and more pence for milk & bread! There's the reason. And if the babe's laid conveniently under ooze, the Parish saves pence.

FURTHER HISTORY OF THE POWHATANS
(1786–1984)

*. . . the Gull Groper takes him to a side-window and tells him he's sorry to see his
hard luck, but the dice are made of women's bones and will cozen any man . . .*

THOMAS DEKKER, *English Villainies Discovered by Lantern and Candlelight* (1608)

*A*nd yet the Pamunkeys did not perish, nor yet the Mattaponis, Rappa-
hannocks & several others. (Where are they, then? In Sweet John's day we
could easily discover Salvages on our river, coming out of the rushes & withes
to trap fishes. But now they've grown shy, that's all. They fear new strokes
of Policy's clock. Reader, no matter! See how the dogwoods bloom!)

The Nansemonds sold off their reservation in 1786. Twenty years later
all the sellers were dead of old age. Those Nansemonds who'd migrated
amongst the Nottoways of the Great Dismal Swamp years before continued
to survive, no matter what Thomas Jefferson thought; in 1890 there were
about .180. of them. But they were forgetting OKEUS. Just as among the
People each woman must use her own clay (for if she takes what another
woman's gathered, the clay might crack), so each soul, I believe, must needs
discover its own GOD. Well, well. But once Policy's clock hath strook,
why, then all souls must worship whate'er's Politick.

In the year of our redemption 1813 the descendants of the Laughing
King, who were now call'd *Gingaskins,* found their own reservation ab-
rogated out from under them, because their white neighbors (the *real* Virginians) feared mischief from Negroes & other vagabonds who'd begun
a-lurking there. Besides, 'twas prime farmland; why should it lie fallow beneath the Indians, who accomplisht nothing with it save beating the seeds
down from the golden heads of sunflowers? But in 1843 some Undertakers
who sought to abolish the Pamunkey reservation were foiled; moreover, on
several occasions the Governor himself upheld the right of Pamunkeys to
bear arms. In 1887 these Pamunkeys passed a by-law to prohibit marriage
with any non-Indians who were not white; for they saw how the wind did
blow against the Negroes. This measure prov'd advantageous to their privileges; for in 1900, when segregated coaches for whites & coloreds became

law in Virginia, Indians got license to ride with the whites. How could it be otherwise, when the greatest politicians of that State were proud to claim descent from a certain noble Yndian wench, by name **.1.** *Pocahontas?*

In 1901 the Chickahominy tribe incorporated most officially; in 1921 the Rappahannock tribe did the same. The Mattaponis had already split off from the Pamunkeys and subdivided into their own Upper and Lower territories. In 1924, all reservation Indians were made United States citizens. In 1975, Virginia's segregation laws were canceled from the statute books. In 1983 and 1984, the surviving Powhatan tribes gained state recognition. They dwell now in their separate allotments, awaiting (as do all of us) the arrival of Captaine Fortune.

FURTHER HISTORY OF AMERICA BRITANNIA (1584–1776)

For what is Fortune but a watery glass?
Whose crystal forehead wants a steely back,
Where rain & storms bear away all that was,
Whose ships alike both depths & shallows wrack.

FULKE GREVILLE, Sonnet CV (1633)

*R*ight honorable Reader, at the outset I did swear to you that I incline toward the best, & yet I must now confess the worst — namely, that these brave & noble-spirited endeavors of our English got no worthy reward. For just as Captaine Ratcliffe deposed Maister Wingfield, & Sweet John thereupon deposed Radclyffe, so our ungrateful Colonists composed a *Declaration of Independence,* then revolted against our dread Sovereign. Worse yet, the revolt succeeded. And so (just as Sweet John e'er did warn), Faction triumphed, & the Virginian Adventure went a-slithering down into ooze.

FURTHER HISTORY OF ENGLAND
(1568–1995)

A Prince ought to have no other aime or thought, nor select any thing else for his study, than Warre and its rules and discipline, for this is the sole art that belongs to him who rules . . .

MACHIAVELLI, The Prince (1513)

*R*eeking of mayonnaise, onions and cheddar cheese, the train sprawled beneath the roofribs of Paddington Station. Then it began to move. The gravel on either side of the track was stained dark with oil and other substances. Old ladies chewed and knitted, clutching their standard underclass tickets. Slowly we passed brickfronted factories, cranes, trees, the fields weedier and patchier than in France, everything a little out of order, like the ambergris under the armpits of an alligator. Why was it all so grimy? Methought the future of the Empire appeared to be as blackened as the old windowpanes in the Abbey of Bath. And yet those bright-eyed Enclosers, Undertakers & Adventurers had had their way! The Salvages were crushed, the Irish halfway govern'd, & the Spaniards long defeated. (For all these had warr'd rashly, so 'twas no marvel if some of 'em died poor.) The Fens of Lincolnshire were drained, more or less (no matter that the locality of Mabelthorpe, for instance, has been losing ground to the ocean since the .12.th century). We read that *several serious riots were caused by the Fenman, the successors of those who had so effectually destroyed the works carried out by Earl Lindsey* (which is to say, Sweet John's friend Robert) *and the former Adventurers. The enclosure was regarded by these men as an infringement of rights and privileges which they had long enjoyed. Very lawless excesses were committed in opposition to, and to the destruction of, the public works . . .* Two years after John Smith's death, the Fen Slodgers formed themselves into troops and rose against the Dutch engineers who served the Undertakers. No matter. Their fowling-pieces might as well have been Yndian arrows. They were defeated.

Perhaps the history of England is the history of Creampoke Sluice, of Maud Foster Drain (which dates back to 1568), not to mention the Black

Sluice Drain, Cook's Lock, New Hammond Beck which runs so miraculously, maliciously, drearily straight, Howbridge Drain and Median Drain ... We've changed ooze for grime. In 1855 the railroad came to Horncastle, and not much more than .2. decades later they closed the Horncastle Canal after a last load of guano from Boston. Then the highways grew, so that by the end of my century, the .20.th, Lincolnshire's skies could be periodically stained by the exhaust of little automobiles struggling for headway in the rain. Every road led everywhere. And the Undertakers continued triumphantly on. I've heard that in Anderby alone, more than **.9,000.** acres were outpumped in 1995, so that thick-bladed wet grass grew over the mire, and then the sheep began to graze.

Lincolnshire retains yet a few of her channels & sinuses, to be sure. But of late no Fen Slodgers have been reported. *The occasional riverside pub, a handful of bridges, and a number of anglers and swans are all one is likely to meet,* runs a treatise from 1976. *It cannot be pretended that the* Fossdyke and Witham Navigations *are particularly fascinating waters.*

A boy in knickers crunched mutton-flavored crisps, reading a picture magazine. Mayhap the mutton flavor in them was boiled out of Lincolnshire sheep, and their crisp-starch, well, why couldn't it have come from Lincolnshire potatoes? We may be sure that in any event the ingredients were English, given the wondrous superiority of England in all things (as hath been acknowledged e'en by certain Catholics). He finished the whole snack-bag, yawned, put down the picture magazine, and opened a comic book called *The Adventures of Captain Fortune.* At once he grew reverentially excited. He longed to ship on. (Sweet John's resurrected from his oozy rest!) He longed not to swither and swelter in his own life. He turned the page wide-eyed, as the train darted onward through the glaring clouds and screaming green meadows of England.

ADVERTISEMENTS FROM EAST LINDSEY

THE VIRGINIA MAPS IN
BLAEU'S GRAND ATLAS (1662)

Conjecture the rest; my words stick fast in the mire and are clean tired. Would I had never undertook this tragical tale.

THOMAS NASHE, *The Unfortunate Traveller* (1594)

*I*n this sumptuous work of **.9.** volumes, each of which was hand-colored and bound in gilt-tooled vellum whenever the Gentlemen purchasers could afford it, we find among **.600.**-odd maps more than **.1.** representation of Virginia. How many? By my faith, Reader, I cannot tell, having means but to purchase the **.100.**-map abridgement for which I paid more than **.40.** pounds sterling. But I'll tell you this: Here's Captaine Smith's map, resurrected and tinted to accord to the newest fashions. Where his version sayeth *Signification of these marks,* Blaeu's runneth *Notarum explicatio.* John Smith's trees, which resemble sunfishes standing on their tails, have been replaced by colored species of a modest oakish character, which generally lurk sole and reclusive amidst new eruptions of triangular white mountains, as if Blaeu's sheet were struggling to bring itself into the **.3.**rd dimension. (O, full confusing waxes the Virginian forest, so that we Adventurers know not what to hunt & whom to slay! How lost & darkened we'd be e'en now, were it not for Argall's gracious light!) Just south of Monacan territory, in the upper lefthand corner of that map, we find the over-famous representation of (to quote Blaeu's caption) **STATVS REGIS POWHATAN.** In his accustomed fashion, Blaeu has taken the image over and colored it. The grimy, murky smoke of Sweet John's map's longhouse has cleared, and the bent wall-palings of Blaeu's longhouse are a cheery vermillion, the fire-logs (which were drawn as straight as musket-stocks) orange like carrots, the smoke perfectly white, like the ivory nakednesses of Blaeu's Salvages. (In Sweet John's map, everything not black is white.) Far away, on the righthand marge, Blaeu has colored a Salvage who leans on his bow into a glowingly yellowskinned *Tartar,* or *China-man* (yea, Virginia's fill'd with fiery air!) and so the whiteness of the Powhatans seems all the more incongruous.

Dangle-breasted women sit langorously with tilted heads, necklaced with *Roanoke* beads. King Powhatan sits high over them on his platform, skin-colored & crown-colored so that he resembles some Brazilian chief with a bird-of-paradise headdress (in the serer map of Captaine Smith, he's obscured & skeletal even though his outlines remain exactly the same. Curious, what tinting can do!).

Well, well, 'tis all vanity, like unto the foundations of *James Cittie*, which now lie as uncovered as Lot's daughters, with replica bricks planted on top in order to piece out perimeters for our edification. James City, Jamestown, no matter; on this isle of old bricks and old trees utterly surrounded by the river's white mirror, a Dominion once had a capital, but I told you that the capital did remove. Reclose Smith's *Generall Historie* once again and turn o'er the leaf of Blaeu to the subsequent double-page spread, to wit, *Virginiae partis australis, et Floridae, partis orientalis,* where bat-winged cherubs rise from a turquoise wave-wash to offer us the scale of German miles. This map, our annotator tells us, derives from the 1638 edition of the atlas. But once again, with a few additions from 1621 and thereabouts, it's based mainly on .16.ᵗʰ-century scratchings, going back to John White and even to Le Moyne. After all, Blaeu was busy publishing maps in Amsterdam; he had no time to come to Virginia for new triangulations. White on white (or, as I should say, buff on buff), the long coast of America angles downward in a long diagonal from Powhatan's dominions all the way to Florida's final outposts of *Saturia, Seloy,* and *Cape Francois.* And within this unknown blankness of America (which hath the almost infernal brightness of rapeseed fields beneath a rainy Lincolnshire sky) we find flourishes, coats of arms to take up space, orange-tinted mountains here and there, .2. lakes as sullen as malachite.

I was in Florida once. I remember all the black dirt in the clutches of mangrove roots, and the strange curvy channels, green-walled, with blackness at the waterline. I saw my America salty and windy and bony with roots, the green mangrove-heads cut off from the water by a line of whitish-grey. Sometimes the water was green, and sometimes coffee-colored. I saw mangroves putting down new roots in air. I saw a bromeliad like a green puffer-fish cast into a mangrove's crotch. But Blaeu kenned only dotted borders, and apocryphal river-chitterlings shaded orange or green or blue to deepen the whiteness. His map's but fig-leaves strewn upon the incognita of the blank page.

Wander all the way back up the coast with me, and at the very top, just under the bordered braid of longitude .29.8., you'll find the name

P o w h a t a n. Ruddy Yndians gather about the title cartouche, some wearing red stocking-caps like unto *Father Christmas*. Well, but Werowances did wear crowns of red-dyed deer's hair. I suppose 'tis not so preposterous by half. But I wish that their Countrey were still alive somewhere even if only in antique books. I wish I could go to Virginia . . .

FURTHER HISTORY OF VIRGINIA (1996)

Wherefore, as they have merited, let them have a perpetual war, without peace or true; & altho' they have deserv'd it without mercy too.

THE COUNCIL FOR VIRGINIA (1622)

Boldness was one weapon that won Virginia for the English, but there were others as well, including good business judgment and a passion for freedom.

THE EDITORS OF *AMERICAN HERITAGE, Jamestown: First English Colony* (1965)

*O*n the freeway, speeding past pine trees and accidents, I listened to the radio singing "star-spangled, flag wavin' country classics" such as *Pocahontas lost her little smile* and *Dacker down, John Smith* and *I shore do need to tell her that I've thought the whole thing through.* I tuned to another station and heard: *Ah cain't git over the great work that GOD has done on mah behalf and is gonna do.* I changed stations again and heard: *When JE-SUS lived in the tombs & He was filled with demons & they tried to bind Him with ropes, Adam became a wild thing, but JESUS touched him & even though sin'll make you into a wild thing, a spellbound person, Adam did come to himself.* Another accident soon occurred, a fatal one immediately attended by police cars as sleek as the bronze lions in Trafalgar Square.

Old Virginia's heavy, weary afternoons once surrounded by green and stink now lie bled paper-white by English leechcraft. They live only in the void ground of old books. *Pen and ink, pen and ink.* Run, Sweet John, run. And the Salvages? Slaughtermen have cut them down. Welladay, New Virginia's afternoons are much the same as the old. How green can your fields be, O LORD? How rich your chocolate black fields are is written in the Gospels, which I do believe. I believe that you can bring us to the bright green and the dark green along the motor speedway, with sky-blue water-towers on every horizon, and pine trees guarding the dump. I believe in screen porches. *Trar-intra-rarara.*

ROAD SIGNS FROM FLORIDA TO VIRGINIA

Welcome to Florida

God's Free Gift — Eternal Life In Jesus Christ

Live with the Birdies, Grasslands

LAKELAND, NEXT FOUR EXITS

HOOTERS

WAFFLE HOUSE

Holiday Inn

GATORLAND—OUR DINOSAURS ARE REAL

ADULT CAFE — We Dare to Bare

PECANS 3 LBS $1.35

GATOR HEADS

Saint Augustine

RIPLEY'S Believe It or Not <u>UNUSUAL</u>

CAR SHOW

PLANET MEXICO!   348 MILES

If you want to save money, you're headed in the right direction.

Good Bee's Restaurant

Indian River Fruit

INDIAN MOCCASINS

International Golf Parkway, 1 Mile

GOO-GOO'S TAFFY LOG ROLLS

Jacksonville City Limit

La Cruise Casino

Do You Have The Health Care Plan You Really Want?

WORK HARD, DRINK EASY

Only GOD Can Fill An Empty Heart

Vacancy

Clean Restrooms

BAR-B-Q

Welcome to Georgia

WELCOME—We're Glad Georgia is on Your Mind.

99¢ Whopper

SUPER PLAYGROUND

BAR B QUE WOOD COOKED

Pigs for Sale

EL CHEAP FUEL STOP

Welcome to South Carolina

FIREWORKS CAPITOL OF THE USA

Sad Sam's Fireworks

HOBO JOE'S DISCOUNT FIREWORKS

Welcome to North Carolina

INDIAN MOCCASINS

JR Cigarettes—World's Largest

LOG CABIN MOTEL AND RESTAURANT

LIZ CLAIBORNE OUTLET SHOPS

BENTONVILLE CIVIL WAR BATTLEGROUND 1/2 MILE

Discount Cigarettes Next Exit

FACTORY STORES OF AMERICA Exit 95

(Pardon me, sir, how do I get to the Dismal Swamp to do some hiking?
(Go back thataway. Take a right at the traffic light. Take another right at the next light. That'll be forty-fifty miles. Then you can talk to them people.)

CIGARETTE WORLD 24 HOUR RESTAURANT

Entering Global Transpark Development Zone

Wolf Trap Drive

Cheese Steak

(and in this establishment we find every food-clerk arrayed in an absurdly polyped red cap like unto **.1.** of the fools on Shakespeare's stage)

AUCTION SALE

Wynne's Diesel Service

✠ TAKE UP YOUR CROSS ✠

DA-NITE LUNCH

Heritage Church Free Will Baptist

Madame Lurane

Leaving Global Transpark Development Zone

CRICKETS—LURES—WORMS

Sell Your Tobacco to Williamson

ROANOKE BODY SHOP

Shaw's Bar-B-Q House

GUNS AND AMMO REPAIR

Oysters in the Shell

BIG ED'S BAR

Manteo 19

Red Wolf Crossing

LOST COLONY 8

Fort Raleigh National Historic Site

Is America being brainwashed and degraded thru hostile sights and sounds?

Decoys

TOBACCO BARN

FIREWORKS

IMMUNIZE YOUR BABY

Old Swamp Road

WELCOME TO VIRGINIA

Radar Detectors Illegal

White Marsh Road

Great Dismal Swamp National Wildlife Refuge

James River*

Total Beauty Image Salon

HURRICANE EVACUATION ROUTE

NARA OF JAPAN

Steak & Seafood

Gods Holy Word Say No Peace In Middle East Until Jesus Comes

Jamestown Settlement

Pocahontas St.

---

*Approaching the James River from Suffolk one sees in springtime many trailers, farms and fields, the trees still autumn-striped and sere, except for the skinny pines with their monotonous green. I have always found pines to be monotonous trees, especially when there are many of them, because they all wear the same shade of green, a dismal, sickly hue associated in my mind with turpentine. Now it is close to sunset, and the weary light glares sickeningly on those bitter yellow-green needles.

. . . what if they have been more severe than [is] usuall in England, there is iust cause for it, we were rather to have regard to those whom we would have terrified, and made fearefull to commit the like offences, than to the offenders iustly condemned . . .

RALPH HAMOR, *A Trve Discovrse of the Present Estate of Virginia* (1615)

To see bright honor sparkled all in gore
Would steele a spirit that ne'er fought before.

BRIAN O'ROURKE, *To His Noble Friend,*
Captaine John Smith (1630)

CHRONOLOGY

GLOSSARIES

SOURCES

[AND A FEW NOTES]

A CHRONOLOGY OF THE THIRD AGE OF WINELAND

Many of the earlier dates in this Chronology are provisional.

III: THE AGE OF ARGALL

ca. 8,000 BC End of the last Ice Age.

Paleo-Indians arrive in Virginia.

ca. 100 AD Woodland culture (the precursor of the Powhatan one) established in Virginia.

ca. 500 King Arthur might have reigned, or fought the Saxons.

1348 Death of John, first Lord Willoughby.

1492 Columbus discovers the New World.

1513 Machiavelli writes *The Prince*.

1524 Verazzano probably sails past the Virginian coast. This incident is mentioned in Dream 3, *Fathers and Crows*.

1526 Possibly apocryphal Spanish settlement near Jamestown Island, with 600 residents, including black slaves. The name of this place is San Miguel.

1534 Henry VIII becomes head of the Church of England.

1535 Commencement of the dissolution of the monasteries. "All this upheaval and uncertainty must have caused dislocation and distress, and contributed to the great influx of beggars into the towns which was one of the most serious problems of the century." — Sir Francis Hill.

1536 Lincolnshire Rising, encouraged by local clergymen distraught over Henry's break with the Pope, put down by loyalists, including the Duke of Suffolk, who's married into the Willoughby family. Catholic traditionalists possessed enough power to express their anger a century later, after John Smith's death. "Obviously Cromwell did not crush ancient rites overnight" in 1649; "many images and relics were spared and in Exeter groups of women upbraided the iconoclasts. Yet in many areas of the south-east compromise was the norm. It was in Lincolnshire, the north, and to some extent the City of London where resentment flared into violence." — John Guy.

1540 Thomas More put to death by Henry VIII.

1540 (?) Wahunsenacawh (Powhatan) born.

1542   Mary Queen of Scots succeeds to the throne as an infant upon the defeat and death of her father, James V of Scotland.

1545   The Duke of Suffolk dies.

1547   Edward VI succeeds Henry VIII.

      In Russia, Ivan the Terrible becomes Czar.

      Probable trade encounter between English sailors and the Powhatans or their neighbors.

1550   Lindisfarne Castle built.

ca. 1550   Opechancanough born.

1550s   Wahunsenacawh becomes the chieftan known as Powhatan. So we will call him for the remainder of this Chronology.

1553   Mary Tudor succeeds Edward VI.

1553   Mary's parliament brings back Catholicism as the state religion.

1554   Princess Elizabeth (the future Queen Elizabeth) imprisoned on suspicion of having taken part in a plot against Queen Mary of England.

1554–55   Duchess Katherine Willoughby de Eresby, widow of the Duke of Suffolk, leaves England with her new husband, Richard Bertie, as a result of her public disagreement with Bloody Mary's religious views.

1558   Mary dies. Elizabeth becomes Queen of England.

1559 (?)   Spaniards kidnap a Powhatan chieftan's son. A Spanish ship carries off and proselytizes the son of a Powhatan chief. Another source gives the date 1561.

1559   Francis II becomes King of France. His wife, Mary Queen of Scots, takes the title of Queen of England.

      The Act of Uniformity reestablishes Anglicanism as the state religion of England.

1559–60   Elizabeth's campaign in Scotland ousts the French.

1560 (?)   Captain Christopher Newport born.

1560   Charles IX succeeds to the throne in France.

1561   Mary Queen of Scots returns to Scotland.

1562   Elizabeth intervenes in France on the Huguenot side. Her proxies lose, so that she must give up title to Calais, England's last territory in France.

1563   Witchcraft made a felony offence in England.

1567   Mary Queen of Scots abdicates.

1568–1648   Eighty Years' War in the Low Countries.

1570   Elizabeth excommunicated.

1572   The massacre of 13,000 Huguenots in France frightens Elizabeth into increased hostility to Catholicism and Mary Queen of Scots.

1576   40,000 African slaves in South America.

1577   Elizabeth equips mercenaries to fight on the Dutch side against Spain.

1579   The Spanish instigate or assist an Irish revolt.

1580   Samuel Argall born. But another source says: "Was probably born about 1580–85." And another: "Born ca. 1572."

John Smith born (baptized 19 January 1580, or 9 January 1579 Old Style).

"The real earnings of a worker born in 1580 would never exceed half of what his great-grandfather had enjoyed." — Christopher Hill.

Sir Francis Drake arrives in England at the end of his voyage round the world, having pillaged Spanish galleons along the way.

1580–81   Spain annexes the Portuguese Empire and the Azores.

1581   The Act to Retain the Queen's Majesty's Subjects in Their Due Obedience attacks Catholic recusants.

Christopher Newport sails to Brazil.

1583   Robert Bertie born.

Sir Humphrey Gilbert claims Newfoundland for England, but drowns in a sea-storm.

1584   Sir Walter Raleigh gets a patent to Virginia. He sends an expedition to reconnoiter. The explorers decide upon Roanoke as a good location for their colony.

1584   William of Orange assassinated.

William Parry, MP for Queenborough, caught scheming to kill Elizabeth.

1584–85   The Act for the Queen's Safety passed in Parliament. Between this time and Elizabeth's demise, 123 out of 146 priests put to death will be executed under its provisions.

1585   John Rolfe born.

First English settlement on Roanoke Island. The colonists burn an Indian village to punish the theft of a silver cup.

Iron discovered in North Carolina.

English ships in Spanish ports confiscated.

Elizabeth signs a treaty of alliance with the Dutch against the Spaniards.

Shakespeare moves to London.

1586   Sir Francis Drake attacks the Spanish in the West Indies and Florida. On his way home, he finds the Roanoke colonists very hungry; thanks to their brutal Indian policy, few "savages" care to trade with them. They return to England with Drake.

1586   Mary Queen of Scots put on trial.

Plague in Lincoln.

1587   Sir Walter Raleigh sends out the second Roanoke colony under Governor John White. Virginia Dare becomes the first English child to be born in North America.

White returns to London for supplies, leaving the colonists for what he believes will be a year.

Mary Queen of Scots beheaded.

Queen Elizabeth appoints Lord Willoughby de Eresby to take over the Spanish campaign in the Netherlands.

1588   White's relief expedition stymied by the war with Spain.

Defeat of the Spanish Armada.

1589   White reaches Roanoake at last, only to find all the colonists vanished forever.

Henry of Navarre becomes King Henry IV of France.

Lord Willoughby de Eresby sent by Elizabeth to fight for him.

1589   The Drake-Norris expedition against Spain and Portugal turns into an orgy of profiteering.

1589–91   English pirates take 300 prizes worth £400,000.

1589–95   Elizabeth sends 20,000 soldiers to France and 8,000 to the Low Countries.

1591   Sir Richard Grenville battles the Spanish fleet in a single ship for 15 hours. He dies at sea.

Sir Walter Ralegh secretly marries Bess Throckmorton, maid of honor to the Queen.

1592   Ralegh's deception is discovered by Elizabeth. He and his wife are sent to the Tower for several months.

15,000 people die of plague in London.

1593   Three Puritan separatists executed in England.

Spain loses the strategic northeast Dutch provinces.

Hawkins burns Valparaiso, but is captured.

1595 (?)   Pocahontas born.

John Smith apprenticed to a merchant in Linne.

1595   Sir Walter Ralegh searches for El Dorado.

Drake and Hawkins killed in an expedition against Panama.

1596   John Smith's father dies. Smith breaks his apprenticeship.

1596 (?)   Powhatan conquers Kecoughtan. Another source gives 1597.

1596   Elizabeth sends 2,000 soldiers to France to help Henry IV against the Spaniards.

Anglo-Dutch expedition storms Cadiz.

Spanish expedition against England destroyed by bad weather.

1597 (?)   Smith receives his inheritance and, probably with Lord Willoughby's help, serves under Captain Jos. Duxbury in France and Holland. (The chronology here is very confused.)

1597   English expedition against Spain dispersed by bad weather.

Lord Willoughby made Governor of Berwick-upon-Tweed.

1598   Hugh O'Neill, Earl of Tyrone, commences a rebellion in Ireland.

The Earl of Cumberland sacks Puerto Rico.

1598 (?)   John Smith home in Willoughby. Sets out to France with "Barty," is discharged by him, and gets shipwrecked off Lindisfarne en route to Scotland.

1599   Shakespeare writes *Julius Cæsar*.

Spanish expedition to Cadiz dispersed by bad weather.

Three hundred men sent from Lincolnshire to Ireland to help put down the rebellion there.

1599 (?) John Smith home in Willoughby.

1600 John Smith gets riding lessons at Tattershall Castle.

1600–1699 "By the end of the century the Powhatans were as oppressed as free Afro-Virginians . . ." — Helen Rountree.

"During the whole course of the seventeeth century, there were only seven complete calendar years in which there was no war between European states, the years 1610, 1669–71, 1680–2 . . ." — Sir George Clark.

1600 Captain Duxbury killed in battle.

Formation of the East India Company.

1601 (?) John Smith a mercenary in central Europe against the Turks.

1602 (?) John Smith captured by the Turks and delivered to the girl "Tragabigzanda."

1602 Bartholomew Gosnold explores Virginia. He names Cape Cod.

1603 Queen Elizabeth dies. James VI of Scotland, son of Mary Queen of Scots, becomes King James I of England. Sir Walter Ralegh is found guilty of plotting to dethrone him and sent to the Tower.

Martin Pring explores northern Virginia.

Gosnold's cousin Bartholemew Gilbert explores a little northwards of Pring, and gets killed by Indians.

James suppresses another rebellion in Ireland.

Plague year in London; 33,500 dead.

Shakespeare finishes *Hamlet.*

Samuel Champlain sails for Canada. See the Second Dream.

1604 James makes peace with Spain.

England establishes an unsuccessful colony in Guyana.

1605 (?) John Smith home again in Willoughby after a sojourn among the Turks.

Robert Bertie marries Elizabeth Montagu.

George Weymouth explores northern Virginia and returns with 5 kidnapped "savages."

An unknown European captain treacherously kills the Werowance of Rapahannock.

Gunpowder Plot to blow up King James and the Parliament increases anti-Catholic feeling in England.

1606 First Charter of the Virginia Company.

"Between December 1606 and February 1625, 7289 immigrants came to Virginia. During this period 6040 died . . ." — John L. Cotter.

1606 Jamestown colonists set sail from England (19 December). Included: Smith, Gosnold, Ratcliffe, Wingfield, Archer. Newport is "Admirall."

1607   Smith held as a prisoner for mutiny (21 February?).

Land sighted (26 April). First permanent white settlement in Virginia, at Jamestown. John Smith, pre-appointed to the council by the London puppet-masters, is finally released from durance and allowed to serve. To save the idle and quarrelsome colonists, he extorts food from the Indians.

Opechancanough entertains Captain Newport.

Wingfield, the first President, gets deposed by a faction including Smith. Ratcliffe becomes President.

(Late December.) Smith captured, and several of his men slain, during an attempt to explore the Chickahominy River. Smith taken to see Powhatan. The famous Pocahontas episode occurs (or doesn't).

1607   Captain Gosnold dies at Jamestown.

The House of Commons blocks James's attempt to unify England with Scotland.

1608   Captain John Smith's account of the Virginia colony is printed in London. This is considered the "first American book."

Smith explores northern Chesapeake Bay on two separate expeditions.

Smith elected President of the Council of Virginia.

Wingfield, Ratcliffe, Archer and Martin return to England.

The English crown Powhatan.

Starving for corn, the English (led by Smith) extort it from various towns and "Kings," including Powhatan and Opechancanough. Native resistance ends the Anglo-Indian "friendship."

1608 (?)   Powhatan exterminates the Chesapeakes and the Piankatanks.

1609–14   First Anglo-Powhatan War.

1609   Church of England made the official church in Virginia.

Samuel Argall sails to Jamestown for the first time that we know of, pioneering a shorter route from England. "He must have been regarded as a mariner of experience and ability, and I suppose that he had been to America before." — Philip Barbour.

Wounded by a gunpowder accident, John Smith returns to England. George Percy appointed President.

Seeking corn-trade with the Pattawomecks, Sir Thomas West is unsuccessful, so he lops a couple of heads.

Ratcliffe and most of his starving trading party get massacred by Powhatan. During the "Starving Time" that winter, the majority of the colonists die.

John Rolfe sails for Virginia with Sir Thomas Gates. Ship-wrecked off Bermuda. Rolfe's first wife and baby die there of sickness.

Rev. L. Sadler of Willoughby dies. His successor is Rev. J. Gart-side.

1609   Captain Archer dies at Jamestown.

Henry Hudson explores Chesapeake Bay, Delaware Bay, and the Hudson River as far as Albany.

Galileo sees Mars through his telescope.

1609–20   Twelve Years' Truce in the Low Countries.

1610   John Rolfe reaches Virginia, already once widowed. Lord De La Warr takes over as Governor (ferried to Jamestown by Argall).

In response to further Indian attacks, the English seize Kecoughtan and massacre the population of Paspahegh.

Some women of Queen Opposunoquononuske's town of Appatamuck lure 20 Englishmen into their beds, then murder them.

Argall and a Captain Brewster burn two Indian towns because a Werowance "acted falsely."

Argall explores the coast from Virginia up to Cape Cod, and later extends Smith's survey of Chesapeake Bay.

Pocahontas married by her father to Kocoum.

1610   Formation of the Newfoundland Company.

1611   Argall sails home to England, ferrying the sick Lord De La Warr. Percy becomes Acting Governor from March until May, when Sir Thomas Gates and Sir Thomas Dale arrive to take over. Dale quickly becomes known as the sternest, cruelest martinet at Jamestown yet.

The English burn Appatamuck and annex that territory.

The King James Bible is printed in England.

1612   Rolfe begins to experiment with tobacco.

Smith's map of Virginia published.

Argall sails from England in the *Treasurer* with a commission to expell foreigners from Virginia. (For a description of the boundaries of the new territory at this time, q.v., Glossary 3.)

Newport signs up with the East India Company.

The new town of Henrico is completed.

Argall concludes a peace with the Pattawomecks, who had been hostile since 1609 (q.v.).

The last heretics (who happen to be Unitarians) are burned at the stake in England.

1613   Argall kidnaps Pocahontas from a Pattawomeck town and delivers her to Dale at Jamestown. Dale sends her on to Reverend Whittaker at Henrico, who guards and catechizes her. Eventually he converts her.

Argall and Virginia colonists destroy a French colony at Mount Desert Island, later returning to destroy the houses and fortifications of that settlement. Tradition also has him stopping to intimidate the Dutch colony of Manhattan. He establishes trade with other tribes of the eastern Chesapeake, thereby weakening Powhatan's control over them.

Death of Edward Maria Wingfield.

In England, King James marries his daughter Elizabeth to Frederick, Elector Palatine.

1614   John Smith explores the northern coast of New England. For his pains he gets kidnapped by Frenchmen in retaliation for Argall's raid on Port Royal.

Argall sails for England on business. He considers joining the East India Company, but in the end remains with the Virginia Company.

Pocahontas marries John Rolfe.

1614   London cloth exports are "characterized by stagnation after the peak year 1614."

1615   Thomas Rolfe born.

Argall returns to Virginia.

1616   Pocahontas, her son and and her husband arrive at Plymouth, England, along with Argall and Dale.

A smallpox epidemic kills many Indians in New England.

1617   Pocahontas attends a masque given for King James. Before or after this, John Smith visits her for the first time since 1609. Apparently the visit upsets her.

Soon afterward, Smith attempts a colonizing mission to New England, but gets defeated by ill winds.

Pocohontas dies in Gravesend, England, aged twenty or twenty-two.

Argall appointed Deputy Governor of Virginia. John Rolfe sails there with him, leaving little Thomas behind in relatives' care. He soon marries Joane Pierce and has a daughter by her.

Epidemics among the Indians of Tidewater Virginia.

Death of Captain Newport.

1617   The practice begins of transporting criminals to Virginia as punishment.
Commencement of the Thirty Years' War.

1618   Powhatan dies and is succeeded by Opechancanough.

Charges of peculation, extortion, oppression and piracy brought against Argall, who remains Deputy Governor just the same.

Sir Walter Raleigh executed.

1618   Lord De La Warr dies.

1619   Sir George Yeardley appointed Governor of Virginia.

Argall sails back to England, where he's exonerated of all accusations.

Sir Thomas Dale dies in Java.

1619   The House of Burgesses meets for the first time in Jamestown.

The white population of Virginia approaches 3,000.

1619   A Dutch ship brings black slaves to Virginia. (These unfortunates were probably captured from the Spaniards by Argall's men.)

One hundred "dissolute persons" transported to Virginia.

1620   Argall sails on an expedition against Algerian pirates.

Sir Francis Wyatt appointed Governor of Virginia.

1621   At a memorial ceremony for Powhatan, Opechancanough calls for an uprising against the English.

Argall appointed to His Majesty's Council for New England (possibly this occurred in the spring of the following year).

1622–32   Second Anglo-Powhatan War.

1622   John Rolfe dies. Possibly (but not very probably) he is one of the 347 colonists massacred in the Indian uprising led by Opechancanough that year.

Samuel Argall is knighted.

English colonists kidnap the king of the Pattawomecks.

1623   After the Pattawomecks take reprisals for the kidnapping, an English "peace delegation" lands and poisons the king and 200 others with truce wine.

Opechancanough requests a truce. Since he rightfully mistrusts the wine, the English shoot him, seriously wounding him.

1624   King James withdraws the Virginia Company's charter; Virginia accordingly becomes a Crown colony.

Sir Francis Wyatt wins out over Argall in the competition for the governorship of Virginia.

Opechancanough loses a crucial battle with the English at Pamunkey.

John Smith publishes his *Generall Historie*.

1625	King James dies (aged 59), and is succeeded by Charles I.
	Plague deaths in Lincolnshire alone number 35,000.

1625–26 Argall commands a fleet of 28 ships in an expedition to Spain. He captures seven ships.

1626   Argall dies [Conjectural date. Some sources have him dying later, for he's said to have been a sponsor of the Trinity House, London, in 1633. He is mentioned as being dead in a document of 1641.]

Sir George Yeardley reappointed governor of Virginia.

Robert Bertie created Earl of Lindsey.

John Smith publishes his *Accidence.*

1627   John Smith publishes his *Sea Grammar.*

1628   Opechancanough requests a truce, which the English break the following year.

1628   First emigration of the Puritans.

1629   Official founding of the Massachusetts Bay Colony.

1630   John Smith stays at Sir Humphrey Mildmay's. He publishes his *True Travels.*

1631   John Smith publishes his *Advertisements* and dies.

1632   Opechancanough sues for peace, which the English grant.

1633   Argall dies [conjectural date].

1635 (?)   Thomas Rolfe sails to Virginia.

1638   A colonist named John Bass marries a Nansemond named Elizabeth — the first Anglo-Indian marriage since Pocahontas's. There will be only one more before all such unions are made illegal.

1640   War between England and Scotland.

1641   Thomas Rolfe obtains leaves to visit his uncle, Opechancanough.

1641   Rebellion in Ireland.

1642–46   Civil War.

1642   Robert Bertie dies in battle in the Civil War.

1644–46   Third Anglo-Powhatan War.

1644   Opechancanough launches his second major campaign against the English colonists, killing 400 people.

1646   Opechancanough (aged almost 100) is captured. An English soldier kills him in prison. Treaty of peace between English and Powhatans.

1649   Charles I is executed. Cromwell presides over the Protectorate.

1650   The English grant 50 acres per bowman to each Powhatan werowance for reservation purposes.

1652   The Irish revolt is put down.

1652–54   First Dutch War.

1653   An Englishman takes over Nansemond Town.

1654   English kill the Rappahannock Werowance in a land dispute.

1656   "By 1656 most Indians" in Virginia "were facing starvation," due to English population pressure on croplands and gamelands.

1658 (?)   Interracial marriage becomes illegal in Virginia. (But another source has this happening in 1691. I have not been able to resolve this matter.)

1658   Cromwell dies and is succeeded by his son Richard.

   Virginia Indians allowed to carry firearms on reservations.

1659   Richard retires in favor of the army.

1660   Charles II becomes King.

1661 (?)   The Chickahominies relocate to Mattapony River.

1662   Some colonists burn the Mattaponi werowances's house, probably to drive his people off their lands.

1665   Last mention of the Pattowomecks in the official records.

1666   Virginia's governor, Sir William Berkeley, proposes to exterminate "all these northern indians" [sic].

1669   An English census reports 50 Pamunkey bowmen. In John Smith's time (1608) there were 300.

1670   Nonwhites in Virginia are prohibited from having indentured Christian servants. All colored servants arriving by sea are to be slaves.

1671   Last mention of Moraughtacunds in official documents.

1676   English involved in Bacon's Rebellion expel the Pamunkeys from their town. Virginia's General Assembly rules that all Indians captured in war can be kept as slaves.

1677   The Treaty of Middle Plantation restores a tensely expedient peace in Virginia. Indian prisoners-of-war are returned, excepting those belonging to "loyal" English soldiers. Some of the Pamunkeys' lands are returned to them.

1677   Last mention of Chiskiacks in official documents.

1682   Virginia repeals "a former law making Indians and others free." All non-Christian servants are now slaves.

1683   Mattaponi Town taken over by Iroquois (Seneca).

1685   Mattaponis mentioned in the past tense in a land patent document.

1691   In a census, the Chickahominies are reported as having only 16 bowmen (there were 300 in John Smith's time).

1699   The Virginian legislature resolves to remove from Jamestown to Williamsburg.

Early 1700s   Some Nansemonds remove to Great Dismal Swamp.

1702   Powhatan Town on the James River vanishes from colonial records.

1704   Failing to get legal redress against white encroachment, 5 warriors of the Nansatico tribe murder a white family. All of them are hanged; the remaining 44 members of the tribe are sold into slavery.

1705   Virginian Indians lose most of their civil rights.

Many reservations suffer reductions in acreage.

1706   Virginia passes "An act declaring the Negro, Mulatto & Indian Slaves within this Dominion to be real Estate."

ca. 1718   The Chickahominies become landless.

1718   Queen of Pamunkey's last appearance in state documents.

1723   Colored people allowed to testify against slaves in capital cases.

1728   William Byrd meets the Nottoway girls of North Carolina.

1747   Saint George's church in Gravesend burns. Location of Pocahontas's grave lost.

1748   In West Virginia, Harper's Ferry begins carrying passengers across the Shenandoah.

1762   Repeal of 1706 "act declaring the Negro, Mulatto & Indian Slaves within this Dominion to be real Estate."

1769   Eresby Hall burns.

1776   American revolution.

1778   Thomas Jefferson successfully introduces a bill in the Virginia legislature to ban further importation of slaves.

1786   Only 5 reservation Nansemonds remain. They sell off their reservation.

1802   Free nonwhites in Virginia obligated to carry credentials of their freedom to avoid enslavement.

1806   Last of the (ex-)reservation Nansemonds dies.

1813   Gingaskin (Eastern Shore Powhatan) reservation terminated.

1831   It becomes illegal in Virginia to teach blacks and mulattoes how to read.

1843   Petition to terminate Pamunkey reservation as "anomalous" within the Virginian racial system is denied by the General Assembly.

1857   Pamunkey right to bear arms again upheld by the Governor of Virginia.

1861–65   American Civil War. Slavery abolished in the U.S.

1887   Pamunkey by-laws prohibit marriage with non-Indians other than whites.

1889   Population of Pamunkey reservation is about 100.

1894   Division between Pamunkey and Mattaponi tribes.

1899   Population of Chickahominy reservation is about 197.

Reputed population of Nansemonds is 180, Upper Mattaponis 40.

1900   Segregated coaches for whites and coloreds introduced in Virginia. Indians eventually permitted to ride with whites.

1901   The Chickahominy tribe formally incorporates, probably to avoid racial discrimination.

1921　The Rappahannock tribe incorporates.

1924　Virginia's "racial integrity law" classifies people with any amount whatsoever of colored heredity as colored. But a limited exception is made for whites with a little Indian blood, because some of them are proud to trace their ancestry back to Pocahontas.

Reservation Indians made U.S. citizens.

1925　The Upper Mattaponi tribe incorporates.

1950　Pamunkey population (including off-reservation people) is 119. Mattaponi: 163. Upper Mattaponi: 175. Rapahannock: 225. Eastern Chickahominy: 86. Western Chickahominy: 392.

1962　Virginian Indians permitted to hunt without a license.

1975　Virginia's segregation laws repealed.

1976　After a brief lapse, the Rapahannocks and Upper Mattaponis renew their respective charters.

1983–84　The surviving Powhatan tribes gain state recognition.

GLOSSARIES

I have tried to define every term which may not be readily comprehensible. (1) Because this is a novel, not a treatise in linguistics, the words are entered as they appear in the text, not necessarily in their nobly correct and inertial forms. In the text, however, their form is never the result of my own caprice, but of someone else's. (2) Sources for terms are not in any way exhaustive; they merely indicate where I have seen them in my reading. Thus, for instance, it is entirely possible that a term described as of Powhatan origin might have been Delaware as well. (3) The same word is often spelled a variety of ways in this book (e.g., "Pocahontas," "Pochohuntas" and "Pokahantas"; "Argall," Argoll," "Argull" and "Argal"). Every spelling is taken from a primary source. Rather than be a totalitarian, I have preferred to let the variants stand in all their charm.

1. GLOSSARY OF PERSONAL NAMES

Virginians all, by birth, emigration or love

2. GLOSSARY OF ORDERS, ISMS, NATIONS, HIERARCHIES, PROFESSIONS, RACES, SHAMANS, TRIBES AND MONSTERS

From Tymors to Werowances

3. GLOSSARY OF PLACES

All under the eye or claw of our Gracious Sovereign

4. GLOSSARY OF TEXTS

Relations, tracts, etc. most often mentioned in Argall

5. GLOSSARY OF CALENDARS, CURRENCIES, LEGALISMS AND MEASURES

For the convenience of wood-runners and merchants

6. GENERAL GLOSSARY

How to make enemies, or fetch Pocahontas for easy trade

1. GLOSSARY OF PERSONAL NAMES

AHONE [*Powhatan*] The "good" Power. Creator of the world, moon, sun and stars. Since He does no harm, He need not be propitiated.

Captaine Samuel Argall [*English*] "The euerworthy gentleman." — Hamor. "A man of ability and force — one of those compounds of craft and daring in which the age was fruitful; for the rest, unscrupulous and grasping." — Parkman. "The kind of fellow to have on your side in a fight, but who would be more helpful out of town when diplomacy was needed." — Ivor Nöel Hume. "Despite the career he seems to have stumbled into, he was far less aggressive than many of his contemporaries." — Barbour. "A subject of controversy." — *Dictionary of American Biography.* "The many references to Argall which show him up as a tyrant and a villain are based on these charges as written in the minutes of the Virginia colony by his bitter enemy Sir Edwyn Sandys; they neglect all the evidences which refuted the accusations." — *Dictionary of Canadian Biography.* "It has long been the fashion to regard [the kidnapping of Pocahontas] as an infamous act of treachery on the part of Argall, but the wisdom of his enterprise was proved by the English captives being restored and peace secured to the colony. As for Pocahontas, she regarded the abduction as the happiest event of her life . . ." — *Dictionary of National Biography.*

Bartty [*English*] John Smith's spelling for "Bertie." The last name (but evidently also the nickname) of **Lord Willoughby d'Eresby**'s younger son Peregrine Bertie. I have styled him as Smith does in the *True Travels.* Bartty and his older brother **Robert Bertie** both helped Smith in his projects. Since Bartty was the younger brother, and therefore unlucky regarding the primogeniture, I've imagined him as a slightly unhappy and foppish failure. No one knows for sure which of the two Berties helped Smith more. The Bartty I've imagined would have had less to do in life than his brother, and therefore be more inclined to, as my text puts it, "toy with this yeoman's desperate loyalty." [Also: "Barty."]

Robert Bertie [*English*] Eldest son of **Lord Willoughby d'Eresby**. [See **Bartty**.] One of John Smith's patrons, and possibly a friend. After his father's death, he therefore became himself Baron Willoughby of Eresby, and also the first Earl of Lindsey. He died in battle on the side of Charles I.

Sir Thomas Dale [*English*] Governor of Jamestowne after **Lord De La Warr**. (**Sir Thomas Gates** served briefly before him.) His first title was High Marshal. The governorship passed so many times between Dale and **Gates** that in this novel I've simplified by making Dale the primary character of the two. Energetic and ruthless, he established the new town of Henrico near the fall line, transformed the colony into a military machine, crushed disobedience and dissent among the colonists, and invaded Powhatan's heartland. It was he who presided over Argall's kidnapping of Pocahontas, and also dispatched Argall to destroy the French colony at Mount Desert Island. Strachey called him an "excellent old soldier." "In the context of his time Dale may have been cruel, but he was not unusual." — Ivor Nöel Hume.

Thomas West, Lord De La Warr [*English*] First Governor of Jamestown. Too sickly to be very cruel, except to the Indians, whom he dispossessed and massacred, he lasted less than a year before illness recalled him to England. Strachey wrote of his epoch that "the first ragged government" was "nowe . . . prudently chaunged into absolute Commaund." By Elizabethan standards of international law, he was no more than energetic at Kecoughtan and Paspahegh. By today's standards he was a monster.

Captain Joseph Duxbury [*English*] John Smith's commander in the Netherlands, *ca.* 1600. I presume that he taught Smith much of the latter's military craft. He died before Smith went to Virginia.

Queen Elizabeth I [*English*] "She was talented, engaging, and hard-working, yet cautious, conservative, imperious, and petulant in the face of change . . . her vanity was notorious, her tongue sharp, and, despite her declared intention to 'live and die a virgin,' sexual jealousy soured many of her personal relationships . . . Perhaps better than any other European ruler, Elizabeth mastered the political game . . . the reign of Elizabeth was the period when torture was used most in England." — John Guy. "The cult of Gloriana was skilfully created to buttress public order, and even more deliberately to replace the pre-Reformation externals of religion, the cult of the Virgin and saints with their attendant images, processions, ceremonies, and secular rejoicing." — Roy Strong.

The Reverend J. Gartside [*English*] Rector of the Parish of Willoughby from 1609 until 1644. I know almost nothing about him.

Sir Thomas Gates [*English*] Governor of Jamestowne after **Lord De La Warr**. In De La Warr's time he was Lieutenant General. He was also an original patentee to the First Charter, as was **President Wingfield.**

Gloriana [*English*] A fond nickname for **Queen Elizabeth.**

Captaine Bartholomew Gosnold [*English*] An early explorer (1602) of what was then the northern Virgina coast, he named several of its appurtenances, including Cape Cod and Martha's Vineyard. He was a moderate and, indeed, stabilizing member of the first council at Jamestown, but died "of a flux" before the first year was up.

Iapazeus [*Powhatan*] Adopted brother of **Argall**, and consequently his victim. His name may mean "Little Buffalo." Trading partner to **Powhatan**, Iapazeus was a **Werowance** [q.v.; Glossary 2] of the **Patawomeck** nation [Glossary 2], and related to the "King of Patawomeck." Apparently he had also been an "old friend" of **John Smith**'s. At Argall's urging, which was perhaps tinctured with intimidation, he and his wife lured **Pocahontas** aboard the *Treasurer* so that she could be abducted. [Also: Japzaws, Japazeus, Iapazeus, Iopassus, Jopassus.]

Kemps [*Powhatan*] Smith calls him one of "the most exact villains in all the Country." He was probably a Paspahegh, since Smith sent him to recapture **Wowinchopunck** in 1609, and **Percy** took him as a guide in 1610 when he massacred everyone in the town. I've imagined him as being an alcoholic, marginalized interpreter. Strachey, to whom he reeled off the names of some of **Powhatan**'s wives, calls him "a man made much of by our Lord Generall" (probably **De La Warr**). He "could speak a pretty deale of English, and came orderly to Church everyday to prayers . . ."

King James I [*English*] "He had through life that rather limited regard for truth which tended to characterise the sophisticated sovereigns of the later sixteenth century." — David Mathew. "No one was more skilful in stating objections and foreseeing dangers and difficulties; and the event gave, in some instances, a character of prophetic truth to his warnings which must have been the result of genuine sagacity." — Lucy Aikin.

Kiptopeke [*Powhatan*] Werowance of the Eastern Shore village of Accomac; brother to Debedeavon, the "Laughing King." [See **Gingaskins,** Glossary 2.] He was "discovered" by John Smith in 1608.

Kocoum [*Powhatan*] Pocahontas's first husband, about whom almost nothing is known. When Powhatan gave her to him, she was probably between 12 and 15.

Niccoló Machiavelli [*Italian*] Most famous and infamous as author of *The Prince,* which John Smith claims to have read with profit. "Machiavelli's program rests on the conviction that since one must start from the present state of things, one can work only with the material at hand. It is useles to say, only be good and you will all find better. The human material at hand (he saw and said) was bad . . ." — Jacques Barzun. [Also "Machiavell."]

Captain John Martin [*English*] One of the original Jamestown "Counsell-men" of 1607. He later returned to London. Distinguished for his sickliness and indecisiveness, he lingered on in the Virginia Company for years. [Also: "Martynne."]

Nantaquod [*Powhatan*] Half-brother to **Pocahontas. John Smith** was especially fond of him. Evidently he was kind to Smith during his captivity at Werowocomoco. [Also: "Nataquas."]

OKEUS [*Powhatan*] "The English called the Powhatans devil worshipers, but only in a very limited sense were they right. More accurately, the Powhatans were appeasers of a severe deity who policed their actions." — Helen Rountree. [Also: "OKEE," "QUIOCCOS," "CAKERES."]

Opechancanough [*Powhatan*] "He Whose Soul Is White." "This kind King." — John Smith, who was his captive and who later humiliated him by extorting corn from him at gunpoint. Half-brother to **Powhatan,** Werowance of Pamunkey, and in time Powhatan's successor. This cunning, dissembling enemy of the English orchestrated two massacres of the colonists, the first in 1622, the second in 1644, after which he was captured and murdered in an English prison. Had the Indians won, he would be remembered today as a freedom fighter. [Also: "Apachankano," "Ophechankanough."]

Opitchapam [*Powhatan*] Brother to **Powhatan,** shortly before whose death in 1618 he suppposedly assumed the Powhatanship. He was either a very weak ruler or else a deliberate front for **Opechancanough.**

Opposunoquononuske [*Powhatan*] The *Werononesqua* of Appatamick-Town [see G2].

Lieutenant George Percy [*English*] Fourth and final President of Jamestown under the First Charter. Elected after John Smith was forced to return home for medical treatment. Brother to the Earl of Northumberland; brother-in-law to **Lord De La Warr**'s first cousin. After De La Warr arrived to become Governor, Percy served under him, helping to massacre the Paspaheghs in July of 1610. He was then Deputy Governor in the spring of 1611, until Sir Thomas Gates and Sir Thomas Dale arrived. He seems to have been a tired, effete patrician. [Also: "Percie," "Pearcie."]

Pocahontas [*Powhatan*] Friend of the English, and subsequently their victim, at which time she was baptized Rebecca. "The word *pocahontas* means 'playful one' and apparently was applied to several of **Powhatan**'s daughters." — *Dictionary of American Biography.* "In the text of Strachey's manuscript, the name Pocahontas is stated to mean 'the little wanton.' The name is possibly to be connected with Strachey's 'pocohaac' — awl, penis." — John P. Harrington. "Pocahontas means in the Indian tongue, 'Bright stream between two hills.' She became the bright link of gold between two races." — Mittie O. McDavid. "There is also evidence that children were given secret, very personal names. Pocahontas's 'other' name of Matoaka became known to the English only after she converted . . . her formal name was Amonute, the meaning of which is unknown . . ." — Helen Rountree. "But of a certainty you cannot put faith in the absurd hocus-pocus of Pocahontas!" — James Branch Cabell. [Also: "Pokahuntiss," "Pokahanta," etc.]

Powhatan [*Powhatan*] Enemy of the English, and subsequently their victim. "All waited, breathlessly watching the face of the haughty Powhatan, and the destiny of an empire paused, wavered, and passed on." — Mittie O. McDavid. "Underneath his attentions [to the English] there was always the point: how to rid himself of these unwanted people." — Philip L. Barbour. "That **Capt. John Smith**'s pronunciation had the accent on the last syllable of the name Powhatan is shown by a poem contained in one of Smith's books, a line of which reads: 'Didst make proud Powhatan his subjects send.' That the etymology of the name Powhatan is not 'place of the waterfalls' is shown by Smith's giving the name 'Paquachowng' for the waterfalls at the upper end of the James river. This name sounds very different from the name Powhatan." — John P. Harrington. According to Strachey, he was also called Ottaniack and Mamanatowick, meaning Great King. Powhatan was his ceremonial or official name [see **Powhatan** and **Powhatans**, Glossary 2]. His given name, however, by which people usually addressed him, was Wahunsenacawh [variant; "Wahunsonacock"]; "Powhatan" was a titular or place-holder name (c.f. "Onontio" in the Glossaries to the Second Dream). (I have had the English address him as "Powhatan" since that is what Smith did; and on two or three very formal occasions I have had other Indians who fear or desire something at his hands call him "great Powhatan"; surely every culture has its obsequious persons.) He had three brothers and two sisters. [Also: "Poughwaton."]

Sir Walter Ralegh [*English*] Mecurial pirate, courtier, poet and gambler. He missed gaining a fortune when his Roanoke colony failed. After James I came to throne, his circumstances worsened. In 1618 he was decapitated for treason. [Also: "Raleigh," "Rawley."]

Captaine John Ratcliffe [*English*] Second President at Jamestown, after **Wingfield**. According to Smith, his real name was Sicklemore. Said by the same (hostile) source to have been craven and greedy. Murdered, along with most of his men, by **Powhatan** at Orapax in 1609, while trying to trade. [Also: "Radclyffe," etc.]

The Reverend L. Sadler [*English*] Rector of the Parish of Willoughby from 1576 until 1609.

Captain John Smith [*English*] Mercenary soldier, hireling of the Virginia Company, sea-captain, ambitious yeoman (whose dreams all came to nothing), accidental ethnographer and guller of **Pocahontas**. "Was Smith susceptible to a woman's charms, or was he immune? To the end of his days he remained a bachelor, and yet there comes out in his writings an attitude which I interpret rather as chivalrous courtesy than as amorous interest." — E. Keble Chatterton. "Some propheticall spirit calculated he had the Savages in such Subjection, he would have made himself a King, by marrying *Pocahontas, Powhatans* daughter. It is true, she was the very nonpareil of his kingdome, and at most not past thirteen or fourteen years of age . . . But her marriage could noway have entitled him by any right to the kingdome, nor was it ever suspected that he had ever such a thought, or more regarded her . . ." — Richard Potts. "Nor should we try to pontificate on the validity of the story of Pocahontas and that celebrated exaggerator, John Smith." — Ivor Nöel Hume.

Charatza Tragabigzanda [*Turkish Greek*] Smith's slave-owner, and subsequently his victim. According to Smith himself (our only source), she fell in love with him and sent him to her brother the **"Tymor"** to make him into an employable, marriageable

Janissary. Smith named a cape in Massachusetts after her. "This kinde Ladie." — Smith. "A distortion of a Greek phrase meaning 'girl from Trebizond.'" — Barbour.

The Tymor [*Smith's Turkish*] The brother of **Tragabigzanda**. He placed **Smith** under a very cruel discipline, either because that was the custom when turning POWs into Janissaries or because he wanted to punish his involvement with Tragabigzanda. Smith murdered him and escaped. [For discussion of his function, see "Tymor," Glossary 2.]

Uttamattomakkin [*Powhatan*] Priest of **OKEUS**, husband of **Powhatan**'s daughter Mayachanna [or Matachana]. Probably very close to Powhatan. He made a magical conjuration over **Smith** during his capitivity in January 1607, and erroneously concluded that the prisoner was harmless. Sailed to London with **Pocahontas** in 1616. Hated the English, for good reason. [Also: "Tomocomo."]

Wahunsenacawh *See* **Powhatan**.

Lord Willoughby d'Eresby [*English*] [Locally pronounced "Dearsby" in 1995.] His full name was Peregrine Bertie, Baron Willoughby of Eresby. He ruled the roost where John Smith came from. He rose high in the army and in politics under Queen Elizabeth. He and his sons **Robert Bertie** and [Peregrine] **Bartty** seem to have given John Smith considerable assistance throughout life.

Master Edward Maria Wingfield [*English*] First President at Jamestown. An Irish veteran somewhat past his prime, he apparently counted on his wealth more than his statesmanship to keep faction at bay. The result was his deposition by **Smith** and **Ratcliffe**.

Winganuske [*Powhatan*] **Powhatan**'s favorite wife, by whom he had a favorite daughter, possibly **Pocahontas**. According to Barbour, her name meant "Lovely Woman." I have followed Rountree, who supposes that Pocahontas's mother was one of Powhatan's more ordinary consorts, who got quickly divorced and sent back home after Pocahontas's birth.

Wowinchopunck [*Powhatan*] The Werowance of Paspahegh. In 1607, Jamestown took root on his land. He attacked the colonists almost immediately, quite possibly on **Powhatan**'s instructions. Strachey calls him "one of the mightiest and strongest Saluadges that Powhatan had vnder him, and . . . therefore one of his Champions, and one who had killed trecherously many of our men." In 1609 he attempted to murder John Smith, who subdued and imprisoned him. After he escaped, and Smith sent out two punitive expeditions against Paspahegh Town, an uneasy peace got reestablished. In August 1610, after some of Wowinchopunck's people had harrassed the colony, **Lord De La Warr** commanded that Paspahegh be destroyed, which it was, under **Lieutenant George Percy**. Wowinchopunck's wife and children were liquidated in the process. The following February (although Strachey writes 1610), Wowinchopunck was mortally wounded in a raid against the English.

2. GLOSSARY OF ORDERS, ISMS, NATIONS, PROFESSIONS, HIERARCHIES, RACES, SHAMANS, TRIBES AND MONSTERS

Adventurers [*English*] See **Undertakers and Adventurers**.

Appatamucks [*Powhatan*] A Powhatan group on the James River. Their *Weronesqua* or "queen," *Opposvnoquononuske,* washed John Smith's hands when he was captured by Opechancanough. Later she lured some Englishmen to her town and murdered them, for which cause *Sir Thomas Dale* [G1] burned the town and established English settlements there.

Caw-cawwassoughes [*Powhatan*] The tribal elders of the **Chickahominies**, who unlike core members of the **Powhatans** were not governed by **Werowances.**

Chickahominies [*Powhatan*] Tribespeople living on what is still called the Chickahominy River (a name which might signify, writes Barbour, "something like *tshikehämen*, a clearing"). Only loosely affiliated with the **Powhatans**, and as such potential rebels to **Powhatan** himself [q.v.; Glossary 1]. Powhatan thus wished to keep the English away from them.

Court of Sewers [*English*] The institution established under Henry VIII to render routine and perpetual the various ad hoc commissions controlling the water level in the **fens.** The Court of Sewers was empowered to order not only embankments, sluices, etcetera, in various localities, but also local taxation to pay for the same. Its ostensible mission of securing endangered villages from floods was augmented by hardheaded dreams of land reclamation and enclosure for the profit of speculators (**Undertakers** and **Adventurers**), most of whom just happened to be rich landowners.

Cronoccoes [*Powhatan*] Counselors to Powhatan. Later in the seventeenth century these would be called (by the English, at least) "cockarouses."

Fen Slodgers [*English*] "In isolated spots, scattered over the low, flooded fen part, lived the Fen Slodgers, the half amphibious beings described by Macaulay, who got their living by fishing and fowling . . . These men were violently opposed to any attempts to alter the state of the Fens . . . Although their condition was very miserable, they nevertheless enjoyed a sort of wild liberty amidst the watery wastes, which they were not disposed to give up." — William Henry Wheeler.

Gingaskins [*Anglo-Virginian corruption of Powhatan?*] The former Accomac and Occhannock Powhatan tribes first "discovered" by John Smith. Debedeavon, the "Laughing King," was a Werowance of one of these groups. Because the Gingaskins never actively resisted English settlement, they kept their lands longer than other Powhatan tribes. But by the early 19th cent., local whites wanted their land and expressed concern about their association with blacks. In 1813 the reservation was terminated.

Keyauwees [*Carolina Indian*] A tribe whose village was located near High Point, North Carolina. The early 18th century traveller John Lawson remarked on their men as sporting "Mustachoes, or Whiskers, which is rare; by reason the *Indians* are a People that commonly pull the Hair of their Faces, and other Parts, up by the Roots . . ." I assume that they would have been known to a well-traveled Powhatan warrior such as Opechancanough.

Mamanatowick [*Powhatan*] Paramount chief. This was one of Powhatan's official titles.

Monacans [*Algonquian?*] Enemies to the Powhatans. A Siouan group to the west of the fall line. Little is known of them.

Massowomeckes [*Algonquian?*] Enemies to the Powhatans; perhaps Iroquioans or even Iroquois [for definitions of these, see the corresponding Glossary of Dream 2]. They sometimes attacked Powhatania from the northern Chesapeake. John Smith had a superficial encounter with them in 1608.

Nanticokes [*Algonquian*] A nation in Delaware or Maryland. John Smith had a hostile encounter with them in 1608 during his first exploration of the Chesapeake.

Ningapamutla [*Powhatan*] "King of the Head." — Strachey. Meaning obscure.

Pamunkeys [*Powhatan*] A Powhatan group on the river then called Paminkey (now the York) headed by Powhatan's half-brother Opechancanough. The famous temples at **Uttamussack** [G3] were on their territory. The English treated them with special ferocity on account of Opechancancough's two "rebellions."

Paspaheghs [*Powhatan*] A small Powhatan group near Jamestown (which was in fact seated on Paspahegh territory). After various ugly incidents between the Paspaheghs and the English, in 1610 the latter fell upon the eponymous Paspahegh Town and massacred everybody they could, right down to the Werowance's wife and children. [Also: "Pasiphae," "Pasipha."] See Glossary 1, "**Wowinchopunck**."

Pattawomecks [*Algonquian?*] Uneasy allies of the **Powhatans** (to whom their language and culture was similar), former friends with the **Piscataways**, they lived on the south bank of the Potomac River. Possessors of antimony, a trade good used for face paint. **Pocahontas** [q.v.; Glossary 1] was in their town, Pattawomeck, when **Captain Argall** kidnapped her in 1613.

Piscataways [*Powhatan?*] A paramount chieftancy along the inner (eastern) side of the curl in the Potomac River, comprising the towns of Anacostan, Piscataway, Mattawoman, Nanjemoys, and Portabaco, respectively, as one goes downriver. "Apparently there was rivalry between the Powhatans and the Piscataways to extend spheres of influence, with the **Patawomecks** and other southside groups being caught between them . . ." — Wayne E. Clark and Helen C. Rountree.

Powhatan [*Powhatan*] Title of the paramount chief of the eponymous **Powhatans**. Wahunsenacawh, the father of Pocahontas, was accordingly ceremonially called **Powhatan** [q.v.; Glossary 1]. After his death, his brother, then his half-brother **Opechancanough**, became the next Powhatan.

Powhatans [*Powhatan*] "The Powhatan represented a well-developed chiefdom . . . of perhaps over thirteen thousand persons inhabiting slightly less than 16,500 square kilometers of the Virginia coastal plain . . . Chiefdoms can be considered kin-ordered societies characterized by ranked positions as well as centers which coordinate economic, socio-political, and religious activities. However, true economic or political class differences are absent . . ." — E. Randolph Turner. Through inheritance **Powhatan** himself [q.v.; Glossary 1] was nominal overlord of five other chiefdoms: the Arrohatecks, Appamattucks, Pamunkeys, Mattaponis and Chiskiacks. In about 1597 he gained the submission of the Kecoughtans for his people, and in 1608 he wiped out the Chesapeakes. The membership of the **Piscataways, Patawomecks, Rapahannocks**, Accomacs [see **Gingaskins**], Occohannocks and Nansemonds is for varying reasons plausible but not definitive.

Presidents of the Council of Virginia at Jamestown First Edward Maria Wingfield, then respectively John Ratcliffe, John Smith, Thomas West (Lord De La Warr), George Percy, Thomas Dale, Thomas Gates, George Yeardley, and Samuel Argall.

Rapahannocks [*Powhatan*] Probably one of the **Powhatan** tribes. Apparently they sometimes fought with other members of the chiefdom in defiance of Powhatan's own wishes. Little is known of Pocahontas's mother (we're ignorant even of her name), but I decided to imagine her as living in one of the two **Rappahannock** towns [q.v., next Glossary] because Pocahontas settled there after her marriage to John Rolfe. [For that same reason, I have assumed that her jilted first husband, **Kocoum,** did *not* live there.] [Also: "Tapahannocks."]

Salvages [*English*] Generic term used by the English to describe the American Indians; equivalent in connotation and denotation to the French "Sauvages"; not necessarily pejorative at the time.

Swart-rutters [*Anglicized Dutch?*] "Irregular soldiers in the Netherlands with blackened armor and blackened faces." — J.B. Steane. Something like "black riders."

Tassantasses [*Powhatan*] Strangers; white-skins; the English.

Tymor [*Smith's Turkish.*] A Turkish-born cavalry officer (called a *sipahi*) who ruled a small fiefdom (*timar*). A large domain was called a *zeamet*. According to Lord Kinross, these *timar*-holding *sipahis* were "a major part of the Ottoman army." A "Tymor" was commonly called a timariot. When called upon, he was required to lead into battle a number of soldiers proportional to the size of his holdings. See the Source-Note to page 103 ("Smith's sojourn with the 'Tymor'").

Undertakers and Adventurers [*English*] Entrepeneurs who paid for the enclosure of **fen** land [q.v., Glossary 3] in exchange for a share of the property; also used metaphorically in this Dream for any financial or emotional capitalist.

Vneghiawmdupmeputs [*Powhatan*] "King of the Teeth." — Strachey. Meaning obsure.

Watermen [*English*] Ferrymen, especially in the Thames reaches.

Warroskoyacks [*Powhatan*] One of Powhatan's subject tribes, based on the south shore of the James River, near Jamestown. John Smith found their Werowance friendly and agreeable to trade. In 1610, **Lord De La Warr** ordered **Argall** and Captaine Brewster to burn two Warroskoyack towns after a corn-for-hostages deal went sour. After Opechancanough's first uprising in 1622, the English attacked all the Powhatan groups they could reach, including the Warroskoyacks. Ten or fifteen years later this tribe had completely disappeared.

Werowance [*Powhatan*] "Commander." — Strachey. The feminine was "weronesqua." The ruler of a **Powhatan** town. Werowances were subordinate to the chief Werowance, or *mamanatowick,* of the whole paramount chieftainship. This man was called **Powhatan** [q.v., Glossary 1]. He was addressed, however, by his given name. [Also: "Vuarrarance."]

3. GLOSSARY OF PLACES

Accomack [*Powhatan/Algonkian generally*] Seat of the Accomacks, on the Eastern Shore of the Chesapeake.

Alba Regalias [*Smith's Latin*] Szekesfehervar, Hungary. — Barbour.

Appatmuck [*Powhatan*] "Capital" of the Appatamucks, on James River.

Argall's Town Townsite of 2,400 acres granted to Argall in compensation for his having shipped 24 settlers to Virginia at his expense. Located on former Paspahegh land, the town began in 1617. In 1619, Governor Yeardley claimed the area for himself, declaring Argall Town to be an invalid entity.

Axopolis [*Smith's Latin*] The place where our hero was auctioned on the slave-block, *ca.* 1600. Sometimes assumed to be Constantinople. Barbour believes that it was "near the site of modern Cernavoda, Rumania. A more likely place for a slave market, however, would have been Silistra, Bulgaria, 80 km. (50 mi.) upstream . . ." [Also: "Axiopolis."]

Caniza [*Smith's Latin*] Nagykanisa, Hungary. Captured by the Turks in 1600. — Barbour.

Chesapeake [*Powhatan/Algonkian generally*] "At or by the big river," or "Big-River People." — Barbour. John Smith was the first European we know of who explored and mapped vast swatches of this bay (1608). Two years later, Argall followed up his explorations. [Also: "Chisapioc."]

Fen [*English*] "A tract of low, peaty land," writes a drainage engineer, "with pools of water, or meres, in which grow reeds on the lower part, and grass on the higher part. The whole generally covered with water in the winter, except on a few high places or islands. The Fens were generally common land to the surrounding parishes" — that is, until they were drained and enclosed by rich **Undertakers** and **Adventurers** [q.v., 62].

Henrico A city meant to replace Jamestown as the principal seat of Virginia. Founded by Sir Thomas Dale through draconian measures in 1611, Henrico was located either 50 or 80 miles upriver from Jamestown, depending on which source you read. Pocahontas was kept on ice there after her kidnapping. After "Opechancanough's massacre" in 1622, the town sank from historical sight.

High Hungaria [*Smith*] "Mostly Slovakia." — Barbour.

Hungaria [*Smith*] Hungary.

Kecoughtan [*Powhatan*] An Indian town across the mouth of the James River from Jamestown. The Kecoughtans resisted joining the Powhatans until *ca.* 1597, when Powhatan conquered them, killed some, and resettled the rest *à la* Stalin. The town then was repopulated by Powhatan stalwarts. Powhatan's son Pochins became Werowance. In 1609 the English established Fort Algernon a mile away, and tensions between the two groups soared. In 1610, after one of their men was murdered near there, the English conquered the town by treachery, razed it, and forcibly annexed the land. The city of Hampton now stands on that site.

Lindsey [or **Linsey**] [*English*] One of the three administrative subdivisions of County Lincolnshire, the other two being Kesteven and Holland. John Smith was from Lindsey. Lord Willoughby's son Robert became the Earl of Lindsey.

The Low Countreys [*English*] The Netherlands.

Maskunt [*Powhatan*] Where Powhatan removed after **Orapaks**. Sir Thomas Dale's deputy, Ralph Hamor, visited him in 1614, shortly after Pocahontas's marriage to John Rolfe. Hamor's errand was to request the hand of another of Powhatan's daughters for Dale (who was already married to an Englishwoman). [Also: "Matchchot."]

Menapacunt [*Powhatan*] Opechancanough's residence in 1607–08. When John Smith was captured, he was taken to "a place called Menapacute in Paumunke, where the King inhabited." [Also: "Menapacute," "Menapacund" and "Menapacant."] This town lay quite near to **Uttamussack.**

Menmend [*Powhatan*] Opechancanough's principal town, on Pamunkey Neck. This name was recorded in the 1640s. Since Powhatan towns moved every 10 or 20 years, in John Smith's time Opechancanough would have had a different town with a different name. See **Menapacunt.**

Nalbrits [*Smith's transliteration of Turkish*] Possibly near the River Mantych, but no one knows for sure. Where Smith sojourned with the **Tymor** [q.v., Glossary 2].

Orapax [*Powhatan*] The "capital" to which Powhatan removed from **Werowocomoco** after hostilities with the English in 1609. He probably remained in Orapax for 4 or 5 years. See **Maskunt**. [Also: "Orapacks."]

Paquachowng [*Powhatan*] The falls of the James River at what is now Richmond; border between the Powhatans and their Monacan rivals.

Pamunkey [*Powhatan*] Opechancanough's "Kingdome," in the marshes and sand-hills between two streams which met at what was then called the Pamunkey River (now the York River).

Pattawomeck [*Virgianian Algonquin*] Capital town of the **Pattawomecks,** on the eponymous Potomac River. It was from this town that Argall enticed Pocahontas in 1613. The name probably meant something like "Trading Place." [Also: "Patta-womeke."]

Powhatan [*Powhatan*] The town where the paramount chief Wahunsenacawh, called **Powhatan,** was born. It lay on the James River.

Rapahannock [*Powhatan*] Capital town of the **Rapahannocks** on the river of that name; a fairly large town, comprising about 100 warriors. [Also: "Tappahannock."]

Roanoke [*Virgianian and Carolinian Algonquin*] Island in North Carolina's Outer Banks. Site of England's first colony in the New World. [For etymology, see **Roanoke** in Glossary 6.] Strachey plausibly blames its disappearance on a mass murder orchestrated by **Powhatan.**

Sander, Screwe &c [*Smith*] Stopovers on route to **Tragabigzanda**'s brother. "It is evident from what follows that Smith was only vaguely aware of where he was . . ." — Barbour.

Scandaroone [*Smith*] Iskendurun.

Trebizond [*Turkish*] **Tragabigzanda**'s name [q.v., Glossary 1] means "Girl from Trebizond," so I assume she was from there. Now known as Trabzon, this eastern Turkish port lies on the coast of the Black Sea.

Tsenacomacohe [*Powhatan*] Powhatan's dominion.

Uttamussack [*Powhatan*] Site of the greatest Wiochisan House, or temple to OKEUS. Famed for its crystal altar-stone. The bodies of Powhatan rulers were also kept in this place, in a second building where some of their treasure was stored. A third building had an unknown but probably religious function. Hence I have imagined them respectively as the Great Temple, the Great Wiochisan House, and the Secret Temple. Seven priests regulated these temples. Uttamussack, which lay in Opechancanough's dominion of **Pamunkey,** was off limits to commoners.

Veristhorne [*Smith*] "Red Tower Fort." Verestorony, Hungary.

Vinland [*Norse*] "Vine-Land" or "Wine-Land"; North America. The Norse thought of it as a promontory, and I have imagined it as being the Great Northern Peninsula of Newfoundland.

Virginia [*English*] Like Canada [see my Second Dream], a territory of uncertain extent. Named after the "Virgin Queen," **Elizabeth** [q.v., Glossary 1]. The English explorers and colonists did not know how far westward America, and therefore Virginia, extended. It was bordered on the south by the Spanish territory of Florida, and on the north by Canada (then called New France). The patent of governorship first granted to **Ralegh** in 1585 defined Virginia as extending 200 **leagues** [q.v., Glossary 5] north and south of **Roanoke**. The charter of 1606 recognized boundaries of 34 to 45 degrees of latitude. "In real estate terms the charter's wording annexed the entire continental coast from Cape Fear north to Eastport, Maine, on the modern Canadian frontier." — Ivor Nöel Hume. Strachey defined the Virginian coast as extending from "Cape Florida" to Cape Breton.

Werowocomoco [*Powhatan*] "King's-House." Powhatan's original "capital" at Purtan Bay on the York River, where John Smith was taken after his capture in 1607 and where the famous and possibly apocryphal "Pocahontas episode" occurred. After he and John Smith threatened each other there in 1609, Powhatan got tired of his proximity to the English and moved to Orapaks. [Also: "Weracomoca."]

Youghtanund [*Powhatan*] A town on the Pamunkey river, upstream of Opechancanough's various towns. It comprised about 60 warriors in John Smith's time. Nobody knows where Pocahontas's first husband, Kocoum, resided. But he could plausibly have lived at Youghtanund, out of reach of the threatening English and conveniently close to his bride's doting father.

4. GLOSSARY OF TEXTS

The Domesday Book [*English*] A census of the population, land boundaries and tax base of every English shire, compiled for William the Conqueror in 1086 (that is, twenty years after the Norman Conquest). John Smith's home village of Willoughby appears here.

The Generall Historie of Virginia, New-England and the Summer Isles: with the names of the Adventurers, Planters, and Governours from their first beginning Anno: 1584 to this present 1624 [*English*] John Smith's opus, part compilation and part original memoir of his two years as a founding member of Jamestown. Although Smith first wrote about his capitivity in the abbreviated *True Relation* of 1608 (which might well have been edited or altered without his knowledge), it is only here in the *Generall Historie* that we find the famous "Pocahontas episode" related. For further discussion, see below, p. 721; Source-Note to p. 224, "Smith's alleged rescue by Pocahontas."

The Historie of Travell into Virginia Britania [*English*] William Strachey's unfinished manuscript offering an eyewitness description of Jamestown and the Indians in 1610–11, not to mention a few plagiarisms from John Smith. Strachey proposed to kill all the Indian priests and civilize everyone else.

Pocahontas [*American*] Grace Steele Woodward's biography, published in 1969. This pleasantly written, painstakingly researched monograph, which was published by a reputable academic press, is as fascinating as any official product of Stalinist hagiography. Woodward has Pocahontas and John Smith becoming friends on the very first summer of his arrival (no primary source mentions her before the famous rescue of that winter). The atrocities committed by the English are either not mentioned or else toned down. The fact that Pocahontas was already married before she was kidnapped and married John Rolfe also gets avoided. The net result is that the tale of Pocahontas becomes more passionate, more romantic, and above all less disturbing to the descendants of the English conquerors. There are dozens of books in the same vein, especially those written for children.

5. GLOSSARY OF CALENDARS, CURRENCIES, LEGALISMS AND MEASURES

Aspre [*Turkish*] A unit of currency worth 49 florins (gold pieces) in 1488. At that time the income of a **Tymor** (see Glossary 2) in **Trebizond** (see Glossary 3) ranged from about 3,000 to 14,000 aspres.

Bartlemew-Tide [*English*] 24 August.

Carucate [*Norman English, used in* Domesday Book] Approximately 120 acres.

Cattapeuk [*Powhatan*] Spring.

Chichqueenes [*Smith's Italian*] "Venetian *zecchini* were gold coins worth seven to nine shillings . . ." — Barbour.

Cohattayough [*Powhatan*] Summer.

Copyhold [*English*] "Freeholders owning their land . . . might prosper . . . The position was different for copyholders, men who held their land merely 'by copy of the court roll.' The heir was liable, on succession to a copyhold, to pay an 'entry fine' normally fixed by custom, but which the landlord might try to raise arbitrarily. Copyhold was thus an insecure tenure . . ." — Christopher Hill.

Darklins [*Lincolnshire dialect*] Twilight.

Ducatoon [*Anglicized Dutch*] A silver coin in Holland, equivalent to about 5 shillings sterling. According to Barbour, the 1,500 ducats of gold received by John Smith as back wages from Emperor Zigismond Báthory were "well over 500 pounds at the lowest valuation for the ducat."

Fathom [*English*] 1.83 meters.

Glass [*English*] One glass was 1/2 hour. According to Smith, a seabord watch lasted for 8 glasses.

Hock Tuesday [*English*] The second Tuesday after Easter.

Kaskete [*Powhatan*] The number ten.

Lady Day [*English*] March 25.

League [*English, Spanish, French, Portuguese*] Four Roman miles at sea. Leagues on land varied considerably by nation.

Michaelmas [*English*] September 29.

Midsummer's Day [*English*] June 24.

Nepinough [*Powhatan*] The season of "the earing of the Corne." — Smith.

Ningh [*Powhatan*] Two. — Smith.

Noble [*English*] A golden coin worth about six shillings eightpence.

Pag-Rag Day [*Lincolnshire dialect*] May 14, when servants pack up their rags to leave their master's service.

Popanow [*Powhatan*] Winter.

Quintal [*English*] A hundredweight.

St. Stephen's Day [*English*] September 21 in John Smith's time; now December 26.

Taquitock [*Powhatan*] The season of "the fall of the leafe." — Strachey (parroting Smith).

Warp [*Elizabethan English*] Four. ("A warp of weeks" = 1 month.)

Watch [*Nautical English, still in use*] A spell of duty of 4 hours. The night watch, however, is divided into a pair of 2-hour "dog watches."

6. GENERAL GLOSSARY

> Note: Because it can be found in standard reference works, most nautical terminology has not been glossed.

Accompt [*Elizabethan English*] Account.

Ahkeÿ vwwaap [*Powhatan*] "To hurt, or a thing hurts me."

Amkonnmg [*Powhatan*] "The blossom of a black Cherry deadly poison." — Strachey.

Athurt [*Lincolnshire dialect*] Across.

Autem mort [*Elizabethan underworld slang*] A married woman. [Dekker.]

Beezum [*Lincolnshire dialect*] An old hag.

Belly-timber [*Lincolnshire dialect*] Food.

Bene mort [*Elizabethan underworld slang*] A fine girl. [Dekker.]

Bilboes [*Elizabethan English*] Sliding shackles affixed to a long iron bar; used most often to confine miscreants on a ship.

Bing [*Lincolnshire dialect*] A rat-proof box used to store corn.

Bing we to Romeville [*Elizabethan underworld slang*] We go to London. [Dekker.]

Blob [*Lincolnshire dialect*] "To catch eels with a ball of worsted and worms."— Campion.

Brigandine [*English*] A light armored vest, comprised of iron squares riveted to cloth. [Also: "Bringantine."]

Brimming [*Lincolnshire dialect*] A sow in heat.

Busk [*Elizabethan English*] A corset.

Caddis [*Lincolnshire dialect*] "Colored woolen braids used to decorate the manes and tails of horses." — Campion.

Caliver A kind of arquebus.

Canoa [*Elizabethan English approximation of Algonquian*] Canoe.

Cat-lap [*Lincolnshire dialect*] Bullshit.

Chamber-lees [*Lincolnshire dialect*] Urine, used to fertilize onions.

Charmings [*Lincolnshire dialect*] Paper, etc., chewed into bits by mice or rats.

Couch a hogshead [*Elizabethan underworld slang*] "Lie down asleep." — Dekker.

Cly the jerk [*Elizabethan underworld slang*] To get whipped. [Dekker.]

Cockatrice [*Elizabethan underworld slang*] Prostitute. [Dekker.]

Copesmate [*Elizabethan English*] Vile or vulgar companion.

Cradge [*Lincolnshire dialect*] A temporary dyke or bank.

Cuffewh kenneaunten mata mechik [*Powhatan*] "I understand you a little but not much."

Dacker down [*Lincolnshire dialect*] To slow up.

Flood oh! [*Lincolnshire dialect*] "An exclamation used on noticing the tide coming up a river." — Wheeler.

Gawp-seed, to catch [*Lincolnshire dialect*] To gape one's mouth in surprise.

Glister [*Elizabethan English*] Glisten.

Gudgeon [*Elizabethan English*] A kind of freshwater fish.

Hawtorinkanusfke [*Powhatan*] "A black fox skin or an overgrown sables."

Hufty-tufty [*Elizabethan English*] Swaggering.

Ka ka torawincs yowo [*Powhatan*] "What call you this." — Smith.

Kedge [*Lincolnshire dialect*] Paunch.

Kekaten Pokahontas patiaquagh niugh tanks manotyens neer mowchik rawrenock audowgh [*Powhatan*] "Bid Pokahantas bring hither two little Baskets, and I will give her white Beads to make a Chaine." — Smith.

Lurch [*Elizabethan English*] A board game which like **Tick-Tack** was probably similar to backgammon; its rules, however, have been lost.

Maangairagwatonu [*Powhatan*] "A great hole." — Strachey.

Maddocks [*Lincolnshire dialect*] Maggots.

Mamanatowick [*Powhatan*] Paramount chief. This was one of Powhatan's official titles.

Marowanchesso [*Powhatan*] The worst of enemies. [Smith.]

Marrapough [*Powhatan*] Enemies. [Smith.]

Marybones [*Elizabethan English*] Marrow-bones (or marrow).

Morion An eggshaped soldier's helmet, often with a ridge at the top.

Mowchick wayawgh tawgh noeragh kaquere mecher [*Powhatan*] "I am very hungry. What shall I eat?" [Smith.]

Mufkaiuwh [*Powhatan*] "A Flower of a fine thing."

Musquaspen [*Powhatan*] "A roote of the bignesse of a finger, and as red as bloud. In drying, it will wither almost to nothing. This they use to paint their Mattes, Targets, and such like." — Smith.

Mutchado [*Elizabethan English*] Moustache.

Muttusk [*Powhatan*] "A woman's Secret." — Strachey, who amusingly enough lists this term under letter "C" but dares not write the Anglo-Saxon word.

Neckaun [*Powhatan*] A child. — Strachey.

Netoppew [*Powhatan*] Friends. [Smith.]

Niggle [*Elizabethan underworld slang*] To copulate. [Dekker.]

Nouwmais [*Powhatan*] "I love you."

Nowamatamen! [*Powhatan*] "I must keep yt or I love yt."

Orlop [*English*] The first interior deck above the hold of a ship. — After Smith.

Pawcussacks [*Powhatan*] Guns.

Pilliewinks Thumbscrews.

Pot-noddles [*Lincolnshire dialect*] Tadpoles.

Primero [*Elizabethan English*] A gambling game involving four cards per player. Each card has three times its face value.

Puccoon [*Powhatan*] A root (probably bloodroot) used to dye skin red. I once tried to do this, following the procedure as Smith described it, but had no success.

Pummuhumps [*Powhatan*] Stars.

Punk [*Elizabethan English*] Whore. [Dekker.] [Also: "Punquetto."]

Roanoke [*Powhatan*] Wampum; shell-beads.

Rome booze [*Elizabethan underworld slang*] Wine. [Dekker.]

The RUFFIAN cly his nab! [*Elizabethan underworld slang*] The DEVIL beat his head! [Dekker.]

Sea-mark [*Elizabethan English*] Beacon for ships.

Secret [*Elizabethan English*] The female pudendum.

Snickle [*Lincolnshire dialect*] A running noose.

Spaughtynere keragh werowance opechancanough kekaten wawgh peyaquaugh. [*Powhatan*] "Run you then to the King Opechancanough & bid him come hither." — After Smith.

Tassantasses [*Powhatan*] Strangers.

Tawnor nehiegh Powhatan [*Powhatan*] "Where dwells Powhatan?" — Smith.

Tavululcu [*Turkish*] A kind of drum.

Thacgwenymmeraun [*Powhatan*] "I give yt yo^u gratis."

Threapen [*Elizabethan English*] To contradict.

Tick-Tack [*Elizabethan English*] A board game very similar to backgammon.

Tockawhoughe [*Powhatan*] "The chiefe root they have for food . . . It groweth like a flagge in Marishes. In one day a Salvage will gather sufficient for a week. These roots are much of the greatnesse and taste of Potatoes . . . Raw it is no better than Poyson." — Smith.

Trarintra-rarara [*Elizabethan English*] Sound of a martial trumpet fanfare.

Trull [*Elizabethan English*] Whore.

Undermeal [*Elizabethan English*] Afternoon nap.

Ussawassin [*Powhatan*] "Irone, Brasse, Silver, or any white mettall." — Smith.

Utteke, e peya weyack wighwhip [*Powhatan*] "Get you gone, and come againe quickly." — Smith.

Vambrace [*Elizabethan English*] A wrist guard, used especially in archery. (I have also seen the word used to describe the counterpart piece of metal armor.) The Powhatan vambraces were made of tanned wolf, raccoon or fox skins.

Vdafemeodaan [*Powhatan*] Go softly. — Strachey.

Vppówoc [*Virginian & Carolinian Algonquin*] Tobacco.

Wenchen [*Elizabethan English*] Archaic plural of "wench."

Wepenter [*Powhatan*] "A cookold." — Smith.

Whe, whe, yah, ha, ne, he, wittowa, wittowa! [*Powhatan*] A derisive chorus accusing the English of being unmanly enemies.

Wighsacan [*Powhatan*] "A small root which they bruise and apply to the wound." — Smith.

Wiochisan House [*Powhatan*] A temple to OKEUS. Every Powhatan town seems to have had one. The greatest, where the bodies of dead Powhatan rulers were kept, was in Pamunkey, at Uttamussack.

Yggdrasil [*Norse*] The world-tree, which may still exist somewhere, but it is as difficult to discover as the Tree of Knowledge because after Eve ate of the fruit and then Adam ate of it they threw away the seeds, which bloomed up into a whole forest like the wilderness called **Virginia.**

Zurna [*Turkish*] A kind of trumpet.

NOTE ON POWHATAN ORTHOGRAPHY: This language was no longer spoken by the beginning of the nineteenth century, but John Smith and William Strachey did each leave a list of Powhatan words. Smith's is two pages; Strachey's thirteen. The following remarks illustrate sufficiently the wretched confusion and paucity of our knowledge. (1) Strachey's ms. exists in three versions, and the Powhatan words are not spelled consistently in each. In an Appendix to Strachey's *Historie* (which is sourced in the Notes), the Rev. James A. Geary, Catholic University of America, writes that "the reliability of Strachey's citations of Indian words is very variable, mainly because of the variability of English spelling at the beginning of the seventeenth century" (p. 214). (2) John P. Harrington, introducing one version, notes: "The Virginia Indian words published by Smith are spelled entirely differently from those later recorded by Strachey" (Anthropological Paper #46, "The Original Strachey Vocabulary of the Virginia Indian Language," in the Smithsonian Institution's *Bureau of American Ethnology Bulletin 153,* Washington: 1955, pp. 194-95).* — In the Glossaries to this Dream, unattributed Powhatan names are taken from the Smithsonian version of the Strachey ms.; otherwise I have cited Smith (whose vocabulary occurs in the *Generall Historie*, between Books II and III). In two cases of Powhatan proper names I have cited Harrington for conjectural meanings.

*Harrington does hasten to put on his best bedside manner and reassure us (loc. cit.) that there is some common basis for these names: "The Virginia Indian language is now known to belong to the Algonquian linguistic stock . . . [and] is merely a dialect of Delaware . . . Almost every word can be found in the standard dictionary of the so-called Delaware language (Siebert, 1931, pp. 288-303)."

SOURCES

[AND A FEW NOTES]

Don't let your mind wander, for if you think
of several things at once you don't pay
proper attention to anything. And if you do
strike the truth it's only by accident.

FERNANDO DE ROJAS, *La Celestina* (1499)

It may be of interest to the reader to know what use I have made of my sources. My
aim in *Seven Dreams* has been to create a "Symbolic History" — that is to say, an account of origins and metamorphoses which is often untrue based on the literal facts
as we know them, but whose untruths further a deeper sense of truth. Here one
walks the proverbial tightrope, on one side of which lies slavish literalism; on the
other, self-indulgence. Given these dangers, it seemed wise to have this source list, so
as to provide those who desire with easy means of corroborating or refuting my
imagined versions of things, to monitor my originality,* and to give leads to primary
sources and other useful texts for interested non-specialists such as myself. I have
tried to do this as fully as seemed practical.

ARGALL

General Epigraph

page xi William Symonds epigraph — *Virginia, A Sermon Preached at White-Chappel*
(London: 25 April, 1609), as excerpted in the Encyclopædia Britannica's *Annals of
America: Volume 1: 1493–1754: Discovering a New World* (Chicago, 1968), pp. 32–3.
page xi Samuel Butler epigraph — *Erewhon*

*For two explanatory cases, see METHOD EXAMPLES 1 and 2 in the Source-List for Volume I., *The
Ice-Shirt*.

Argall-Text

page 5 Yachtsman's manual footnote — Jack H. Coote, *East Coast Rivers from South-wold to the Swale: A Yachting Monthly Pilot* (London: Yachting Monthly, IPC Magazines Ltd, 1993, 14th ed.), p. 76.

page 8 "I dug wells & drank foreign waters . . ." — 2 Kings 19.24. Unless otherwise noted (once or twice I used the original King James version), my Bible is the New Oxford revised standard version, 2nd ed. (1971). I have frequently archaized quotations for this book.

page 9 Types of ships in the "dead forest" at Gravesend — This is but a list of the most common ships mentioned in the various primary sources I've sourced throughout these notes. For more on ships and especially shipbuilding, see John Smith's *Sea-Grammar,* in Philip L. Barbour, ed., *The Complete Works of Captain John Smith (1580–1631) in Three Volumes* (Chapel Hill: The University of North Carolina Press), vol. 3. Henceforth this set will be referred to as "Smith" to distinguish it from other Barbour citations. After all, Smith wrote most of it. For schematic drawings of most of the ships cited here, see Ivor Nöel Hume, *The Virginia Adventure: Roanoke to James Towne, An Archaeological and Historical Odyssey* (New York: Alfred A. Knopf, 1994), p. 58.

page 10 The "fence" who dwells at the Sign of the Three Doves at Newgate Market — Inspired by a mention in David Beers Quinn, ed., *The Roanoke Voyages 1584-1590: Documents to Illustrate the English Voyages to North America Under the Patent Granted to Sir Walter Ralegh in 1584* (New York: Dover Publications, 1991 repr. of 1955 Hakluyt Society ed.), vol. 1, p. 155 (High Court of the Admiralty records, seizure of a French ship by one belonging to Ralegh; deposition of 8 June 1586).

page 11 "Up sprit sail!" — "Water sail now," writes Eric Reid (note to author, 1995). "This is usually spelled spirtsail now or called watersail, to distinguish it from an unreleated fore and aft sail whose peak is supported by a diagonal sprit."

page 11 The Almanacke's aphorism on tides at Gravesend — After William Bourne, *A Regiment for the Sea,* 1574, 1580, ed. E.G.R. Taylor (London: Hakluyt Society, second ser., no. CXXI, issued for 1961), p. 63 (*Almanacke for Three Yeares,* 1571, Fourth Rule).

page 11 Calculation of high water time at Gravesend as related to Dover and Harwich — Jack H. Coote, p. 97 (table of tidal constants).

page 12 "Your Grace's faithful and devoted servant, John Smith" — Dedication of *The Generall Historie of Virginia, New-England and the Summer Isles: with the names of the Adventurers, Planters, and Governours from their first beginning Anno: 1584 to this present 1624,* in Smith, vol. ii, p. 42 [p. 1 in original edition's pagination].

page 13 "Idlenesse and carelessnesse . . ." — *Generall Historie,* 4th Book, answer to "his Majesties Commissioners," question 1; in Smith, vol. ii, p. 327 [165].

page 14 "Just as the first ship in a convoy to descry land must shoot off his ordnance and raise his flag . . ." — After Richard Madox, *An Elizabethan in 1582: The Diary of Richard Madox, Fellow of All Souls,* ed. Elizabeth Story Donno (London: Hakluyt Society, 2nd. ser., vol. 147, 1976), p. 283.

page 15 "North Carolina, which was but lately (1662) Virginian territory" — North Carolina received her first charter in 1663. In John Smith's day, Virginia ran from Florida to Canada [see entry for Virginia in Glossary 3].

page 15 The states "lopp'd off" from Virginia — As related by William Byrd, *Histories of the Dividing Line betwixt Virginia and North Carolina* (1728, 1st pr. 1929; New York: Dover, 1967), pp. 4–11.

page 15 Yield of Carolina wheat — John Lawson, *A New Voyage to Carolina* (1709) ed. Hugh Talmage Lefler (Chapel Hill: The University of North Carolina Press, 1967), p. 80.

page 16 "No traces have been found." — Ivor Nöel Hume, *Here Lies Virginia: An Ar-

chaeologist's View of Colonial Life and History (Charlottesville: University Press of Virginia, 1994 exp. repr. of 1963 ed.), p. 46.

page 16 Oysters "as thicke as stones" — Philip L. Barbour, ed., *The Jamestown Voyages Under the First Charter 1606–1609* (Cambridge: published for the Hakluyt Society by Cambridge University Press, second ser., no. CXXXVI, 2 vols.), vol. 1, p. 134 (item 28: George Percy's discourse, *ca.* 1608). Note: Henceforth this compilation will be cited as "Barbour (Jamestown)."

page 16 The *Map of Virginia* — This appears in vol. 1 of Smith's complete works.

page 16 Footnote on South Carolina — Lawson, pp. 61, 10.

page 16 The tale of John and Amy Harris — Charles Harry Whedbee, *Legends of the Outer Banks and Tar Heel Tidewater* (Winston-Salem: John F. Blair, 1966), pp. 151–56 ("I Shall Love Thee Better After Death").

page 20 Contents of vol. 1 of Smith's complete works — After the items listed in the text comes .3.ʳᵈ the *Map of Virginia,* where our Countrey of Magick gets herself accuratedly array'd; then .4.ᵗʰ the well-turned *Description of New England.* Nor should we disremember .5.ᵗʰ the letter to Sir Francis Bacon, .6.ᵗʰ the *New Englands Trials* in both versions — everything with its textual and bibliographical note composed by that faithful editor and subscriber of stained glass windows already mentioned.

page 23 "Kekaten Pokahontas . . ." — from Smith's vocabulary list in the *Generall Historie,* in Smith, vol. ii, p. 132.

page 23 Footnote: Title page of vol. 3 of Smith's complete works — I've no time to delineate the Italian cypresses and Transylvanian mountains which also bedeck this book-Virginia (doubtless that magnifying glass of mine could spy out a unicorn or two in the distant Carpathian passes), but it would be treasonous to omit mention of the cameo portraits of Elizabeth, James and Charles suspended in Heaven. Their likenesses guarantee the Englishness of it all.

page 25 Distance from Gravesend round the world to Gravesend again — Bourne, p. 108 (*Almanacke for Three Yeares, 1571,* Fifteenth Rule); actually given for London to London, which ought to be pretty near the same.

page 26 Description of Gravesend — From a visit in January 1989.

page 27 Guidebook facts on the church: Built *ca.* 1485, destroyed in the fire of 1727 (at which time the location of Pocahontas's remains became conjectural, for the English were not relic-addicts and bone-grubbers like the French), rebuilt *ca.* 1732; chancel rebuilt 1892.

page 28 Pocahontas as Caucasian angel — I've since discovered that this is a common observation about Pocahontas representations. In the *Handbook of North American Indians,* for instance, one reads in a section on cigar store Indians that "females were called Pocahontas, Squaw, or Maiden. Pocahontases and Maidens, embodying the Indian Princess theme, were usually smaller than Squaws, and had more Caucasian or infantile features and wore classical or romantic dress. Squaws were more likely to have exposed or prominent bosoms . . ." (Washington, DC: Smithsonian, 1988, vol. 4, pp. 594–5).

page 28 "You shall not go!", etc. — Virginia Watson, *The Legend of Pocahontas,* retold by Karla Dougherty, ill. by George Wharton Edwards (Avenel, New Jersey: Children' [sic] Classics, Random House Value Publishing, Inc., 1995), p. 78.

page 28 The searches for Pocahontas's skeleton — Philip L. Barbour, *Pocahontas and Her World: A Chronicle of America's First Settlement, in Which is Related the Story of the Indians and the Englishmen — Particularly Captain John Smith, Captain Samuel Argall, and Master John Rolfe* (Boston: Houghton-Mifflin, 1970), pp. 237–38.

page 28 The rumor that ooze can actually give birth to serpents and crocodiles — Shakespeare, *Antony and Cleopatra,* Act II, Scene VII, Lepidus's first and second speech.

page 29 The pub at Gravesend — In this spot I composed my own definition of a genius: one of those people who when you say *the Land of Warm Beer and Warm Cokes* knows instantly that you mean England.

page 29 Theme of this Dream — And now to the moral (reading which, sweet Reader, thou may'st save your hours, closing this book forever to grabble no more in its textual ooze). In these **SEVEN DREAMS** of mine I wish merely to tell what was given & what taken betwixt *Adventurers* and *Salvages*. (Well, ahem! And what could we possibly take from vile, barbaric Salvages? Tobacco, yes, and possibly syphilis — or did we get that from the Turkes?) — **.1.** All gifts being writ in the jewel-decked Book of Generosity, I learned from its sky-blue leaves how the *Norse* folk bestowed ice and an axe upon the People of KLUSKAP, otherwise called *Skraelings*. These Salvages threw the axe most ungratefully into the fjord, having an aversion (so it appears) to the magical properties of iron; but the ice they could not so easily dispose of; indeed it bit them as harshly as any weaponhead, as it will do forever. 'Twas told in our First Dream, when Freydis Eiriksdottir overthrew the wild grapes with frost. In echo of those days when our continent was Wineland the Good, we find that in 1584, when Sir Richard Grenville discovered Virginia, "they found their first landing place very sandy and low, but so full of grapes that the very surge of the Sea sometimes overflowed them: of which they found such a plenty in all places . . . that they did thinke in the world were not the like abundance." **.2.** Next the *French,* not wishing to be thought lacking in the prosecution of their love (as IESVS surely knoweth), brought Crosses and arquebuses in scores. By these means the *Wendat People* were converted safely to destruction, as recounted in the Second Dream. **.3.** Meanwhile we *English* had invited ourselves to the banquet, too. Why not? America's as great and square as the Bed of Ware, which can sleep five persons! Just as scalp-lice and crotch-lice keep to their respective territories, so we and the French dwelled apart (as you, Reader, can well imagine), the new continent not yet having been mapped to a smallness requiring competition. (True, we destroyed the French nest at Port-Royal, but that was merely the act of a lunatic, *Argall,* who deserves no place in any book.) However that might be, what treasure did we convey to *our* appointed People, that is to say, the *Powhatans?* — We might inquire of the sovereign giver, King IAMES, whose friendship surely satisfied the utmost residue of their demands; but I prefer to ask the recipient *Pocahontas*. Her answer: *Argall*.

page 33 "As I sat amusing myself in the grass . . ." — quoted in the Encyclopaedia Britannica's *The Annals of America,* vol. 1: 1493–1754 (Chicago, 1968), p. 367. "The song has been sung in many versions, usually to the tune of "Down in the Valley"; this one was taught to one of the editors by his grandmother, who had learned it from her grandmother, before the Civil War.

I: Several Compass Circles

The Grammar of Princes　　　　*

page 37 Euerworthy epigraph — Ralph Hamor, *A Trve Discovrse of the Present Estate of Virginia, and the Successe of the Affaires there till the 18 of* Iune, *1614 . . .* (1615) (repr. 1957, Richmond, Virginia State Library), p. 2.

page 38 "I passe by the benefits of peace in those parts . . ." — Hamor, p. 36.

page 40 For many small details of English life, language and social organization during our period I am indebted most of all to Shakespeare, next to Smith himself, then to Madox, to Thomas Nashe, 1567–*ca.* 1601 (*The Unfortunate Traveller and Other Works,* ed. J.B. Steane; New York: Penguin, 1972); to Thomas Dekker, who chronicled the plague year of Elizabeth's death, and wrote from experience about life in debtor's prison (E.D. Pendry, ed. *Thomas Dekker: Selected Prose Writings* [Cambridge, Massachusetts: Harvard University Press, 1968]; henceforth cited "Dekker"); to the anonymously penned *Arden of Faversham* (*ca.* 1580), ed. Martin White (New York: W.W. Norton & Co., New Mermaids ser., 1982), to Molly Harrison and O.M. Royston, *How They Lived: An Anthology of Original Accounts between 1488 and 1700,* vol. 2 (Oxford: Basil Blackwell, 1963), and to Richard Gough, *The History of Myddle,* written in 1700-1702 (New York: Penguin Classics, 1988). Gough was born in 1635, four years after the death of Smith (Rolfe and Pocahontas were of course already dead). My assumption is that country life might not have been too different between Smith's time and Gough's. A few phrases emblematic of the Elizabethan ideology of cosmological order I've stolen or twisted from a certain dagger-bearded alchemist, to wit, William H. Huffman, ed., *Robert Fludd: Essential Readings* (Hammersmith, London: The Aquarian Press / HarperCollins, 1992). Henceforth this book will be cited as "Fludd." For general information on the powers and duties of officials in seventeenth-century Lincolnshire I have sometimes leaned on the long and helpful introduction in S.A. Peyton, ed., *The Publications of the Lincoln Record Society Founded in the year 1910,* vol. 25, *Minutes of Proceedings in Quarter Sessions held for the parts of Kesteven in the County of Lincoln 1674–1695,* 2 vols. (Lincoln: J.W. Ruddock & Sons, 1931). For clothes, furnishing, etc., I have made occasional use of notes taken in 1998 on artifacts on display in the British period rooms of the Victoria and Albert Museum, London. Here I have been stricter, and limited the subjects of my note-taking to items from Elizabethan and Stuart times.

page 40 Oath of the Secretary of the Virginia Company — King and Privy Council, Oath of the Secretary of the Colony Administered by Governor and Council in Virginia, in Susan Myra Kingsbury, A.M., Ph.D., ed., *The Records of the Virgina Company of London* (Washington: The Library of Congress: U.S. Government Printing Office, 1933), vol. 3, p. 6, no. III.

page 40 Smith's life and adventures before Jamestown — based on his *The True Travels, Adventures, and Observations of Captaine John Smith* (1630), in Smith, vol. iii. The incidents I relate will be found in pp. 153 [1] — 167 [9], 170 [11] — 179 [18], 184 [22] — 189 [24], 200 [31–32]. (Note: Page references in brackets relate to the pagination of the original edition, as supplied in Barbour's pretty margins.) I have also made use of Barbour's "Brief Biography of Captain John Smith" in vol 1, pp. lv–lxi.

page 40 John Smith in context — "The chief trouble (the ignorance I have mentioned) is that historians have studied Smith's career and Smith's writings without (or with little) reference to the atmosphere John Smith breathed. Even disregarding the improbable behavior known to have been characteristic of princes, prelates and politicoes, the whole *style* of the day was inflated — in writing and in living. The people were childish, 'for all their gifts and all their ability.' Attractive personalities were rare . . . Religious cleavages split society one way; a caste system cut across in another. Wealth could bridge gaps, to be sure, but that was acquired by cut-throat business, toadyism, blatant racketeering or piracy, when it was not inherited . . . John Smith ranked but little higher in Elizabethan society than a Hindu 'untouchable' in Akbar's India. Perhaps because of this, he was by nature tolerant of everything but intolerance, and by this token he lacked both the background and the ruthlessness necessary to forge ahead in the field of money-making, or in his chosen field of building an English colonial empire. As a result, for all that he accomplished, he was a failure as a colonialist. This fact is of course remembered; that no man succeeded is forgotten." — Philip Barbour, *The Three Worlds of Captain John Smith* (Cambridge, Massachusetts: Houghton-Mifflin, 1964), p. x. When I visited Willoughby in 1995, I was touched to find that the church's stained glass windows commemorating Smith's life had been donated by Barbour. [See the Textual Note, p. 11.]

page 40 "The greatest Merchant in Linne" — Smith's own words, in vol. 3, p. 154 [2].

page 40 "I sold my books and satchel . . ." — loc. cit., almost verbatim.

page 42 Authority of the Rector — The clergy received tithes of ten percent of all profits and produce, and could punish people for nonattendance at church, etc. See Christopher Hill, *The Century of Revolution 1603-1714*, rev. ed. (New York: Norton, 1980), p. 63. However, Sir Francis Hill in his *Tudor and Stuart Lincoln* (Stamford: Paul Watkins, 1991 repr. of 1956 ed.) suggests that, especially in John Smith's time, compulsory church attendance might well have been unpopular.

page 43 The noise made by a cantering horse's hooves — G. Edward Campion, *Lincolnshire Dialects* (Boston, Lincolnshire: Richard Kay, 1976). To appropriately color John Smith's speech I've made frequent phrase-borrowings from this pleasant book. And I have tried to render his speech slightly different from that of most of the other Jamestown colonists, who were not from County Lincoln. Hence in this book Argall, Wingfield, et al. tend to speak in "Shakespearian English." A twentieth-century historian writes: "Most of Jamestown's founders either died in their new homes or speedily returned to England." In the middle of the seventeenth century, when large scale immigration to Virginia began, the colonists came not from Lincolnshire or thereabouts, but mainly from the south. (See David Hackett Fischer, p. 226. This author continues in a footnote that "gentry families who survivied the early years of settlement included Archer" and Wingfield.) I have relied on Campion a little for some phrases of John Rolfe and his kinsfolk, they being not over far from Lincolnshire.

page 43 Life and character of Queen Elizabeth I — Primarily I made use of the excellent and impartial biography by Anne Somerset, *Elizabeth I* (New York: St. Martin's Press, 1991); Lucy Aikin's *Memoirs of the Court of Elizabeth Queen of England,* 6th ed., rev. (London: Alex, Murray and Son, 1869), which contains a number of extracts from contemporary documents; and Roy Strong's *The Cult of Elizabeth: Elizabethan Portraiture and Pageantry* (London: Thames and Hudson, 1977).

page 45 "Ah, silly pug . . ." — Although this poem is certainly addressed to Ralegh ("Wat" is short for "Walter"), the exact date of its composition is not known. (It was first published in 1960). I found it in Emrys Jones, ed., *The New Oxford Book of Sixteenth Century English Verse* (New York: Oxford, 1991), p. 185, no. 109.

page 45 Ralegh's complaints upon the scaffold — After Quinn, vol. 1, p. 231 (petition of Sir Lewis Stukely to King James, 1618), italicized phrase almost verbatim.

page 45 Enclosure — "The smaller man might . . . be evicted when the lands of his village were 'enclosed'; at least he risked losing his share of the commons and waste lands, so essential to provide fuel and maintain the animals and birds on which his sustenance depended. 'Enclosure' meant that land held in scattered strips in the village open fields was consolidated into compact holdings, which the occupier might hedge about so as to protect them against other people's cattle. He was then free to experiment with rotation of crops . . . The great age of enclosure for sheep-farming had perhaps come to an end by the seventeenth century; but enclosure and consolidation for improved arable farming, to feed the expanding industrial areas, was proceeding apace. Enclosure had long been attacked on the ground that it led to eviction of tenants and so depopulated the countryside. Tudor governments had tried, less and less effectively, to prevent it." — Christopher Hill, *The Century of Revolution,* p. 13. According to John Guy's lengthy *Tudor England* (New York; Oxford University Press, 1988), "the opinion of pamphleteers and preachers that the active land market nurtured a new entrepeneurial class of capitalists grinding the faces of the poor is hyperbole. Yet it is fair to say that not all landowners, claimants and squatters were entirely scrupulous in their attitudes: a vigorous market rose among dealers in defective titles to land, with resulting harassment of many legitimate occupiers. Most distress sprang, however, from inflation and unemployment" (p. 37). Guy presents in tabular form the work of economic historians which indicates that from 1451 until 1600 prices almost quintupled, and purchasing power of craftsmen and laborers declined by half (p. 38). As Guy notes, this gives "a sober impression of the vicissitudes of Tudor life." He sees the increase in population from 3.01 to 4.10 million (p. 32) as the main cause of these difficulties. An economic-ecological case can be made that the freedom of the commons brings ruin to all; hence enclosure is a positve good. See Garrett Hardin, *Exploring New Ethics for Survival: The Voyage of the Spaceship* Beagle (Baltimore: Penguin Books Inc., Pelican, 1973 repr. of 1972 ed.), pp. 118–19. I have elaborated on this in the eco-terrorism chapter of my long essay on violence, *Rising Up and Rising Down*. And here we might quote from the very pro-enclosure William Henry Wheeler's *History of the Fens of South Lincolnshire* (Stamford, Lincolnshire: Paul Watkins, 1990 repr. of 1896 ed.). Wheeler was a drainage engineer; his views are in line with his profession — which does not necessarily discredit them. About the enclosure of Tydd Saint Mary's Marsh in 1632 he writes (p. 132): "When the marsh was inclosed about 600 acres near the village were left for the householders to use in common, no limit as to the number of stock to be put on by each inhabitant being reserved. The commons were consequently stocked so heavily that hardly a blade of grass was left. Thistles and nettles grew luxuriantly, as it was nobody's special duty to keep them down. Sheep and lambs were frequently lost among them and were worried to death by maggots." My question would be: Were the villagers selfishly improvident, or were the 600 acres set aside for them simply too little?

page 46 Undertakers *vs.* Fen Slodgers — Wheeler, op. cit., throughout, and esp. pp. 30–36.

page 46 "All these for any thing I could perceive differ little in language" — Smith, vol. iii, *Advertisements for the Unexperienced Planters of New England, or Any Where* (1631), p. 279 (ch. 6).

page 48 "His father's line is anciently descended . . ." — Smith, vol. iii, p. 153 [1], almost verbatim.

page 48 "Cicely is well tucked up . . ." — The apparel she wears is based on a description of "A Farmer's Daughter" in Allardyce Nicoll, *The Elizabethans* (Cambridge: At the University Press, 1957), p. 34.

page 49 Smith's inheritance — after Smith, vol. iii, Document ii: "Last Will of George Smith, Father of Captain John" (1596), and Document iii, "Inventory of George Smith's Property" (1596/7), pp. 377–83.

page 49 Copyhold — See Glossary 5.

page 49 "The head of the Dragon . . ." — Bourne, p. 168 (*A Regiment for the Sea,* 1574 ed., ch. 23).

page 50 The fire at Cicely's house — Partly inspired by a story in Gough, pp. 107–108.

page 51 "Such oft is the share of fatherless children" — Smith, vol. iii, p. 154 [2], verbatim.

page 52 Lord Willoughby's repute: *"earnest in matters of religion"* — Sir Francis Hill, p. 98.

page 52 The "evil Popish practices" of lighting candles on Candlemas Day, etc. — For a general account of which practices were prohibited, how stringently, and when, I have followed Christopher Haigh, ed., *The English Reformation Revisited* (New York: Cambridge University Press, 1987), pp. 114–38 (Ronald Hutton, "The Local Impact of the Tudor Reformation").

page 53 Lord Willoughby's campaign in France — Guy, p. 344.

page 56 Wages of harquebusiers and pikemen at the end of Elizabeth's reign —

Thomas Bartlett and Keith Jeffery, ed., *A Military History of Ireland* (Cambridge, U.K.: Cambridge University Press, 1996), p. 149.

page 56 Ten shillings a quintal in Spain for salt fish — Smith, vol. iii, p. 415 [213].

page 60 The longitude and latitude of Gravesend — Bourne, p. 97 (*Almanacke,* Thirteenth Rule).

page 60 Footnote on the drainage of Wainfleet parish — Wheeler, p. 76.

page 61 Extract from the Domesday Book — John Morgan, gen. ed., *Domesday Book* (Phillimore: Chichester, 1986 repr. of 1783 printed version of 1086 ed.), vol. 31: Lincolnshire, ed. Philip Morgan and Caroline Thorne, part 1 (there are 2 subvolumes), p. 24: 355 b. My rendering lies between the entirely modernized facing text and its original referent.

page 62 Wheat prices in 1598 — Sir Francis Hill, *Tudor and Stuart Lincoln,* p. 224 (Appendix III: Corn Prices Returned by Leet Juries, 1513–1712). Hill's book has been a source of understanding of day-to-day life in Lincolnshire, and I've profited from it throughout the England sections of this text.

page 62 Friskney, Stickney, and the roster of Fen-towns which once were islands — Wheeler, p. 22. The parenthetical note on Sibsey's jurisdiction is taken from the same work, p. 77.

page 62 Varieties of cannons as explained by John Smith — *The True Travels,* in Smith, vol. iii, pp. 104–05 [64].

page 65 History and description of Lord Willoughby's family — A descendant in the fourth generation, *A Memoir of Peregrine Bertie, Eleventh Lord Willoughby de Eresby, Commander-in-Chief of Queen Elizabeth's Forces in the Low Countries, and in France; and Governor of Berwick* (London: John Murray, 1838). [Note: The man whom Smith called "Paragrine Bartty" was Lord Willoughby's second son. Lord Willoughby was himself the "Peregrine Bertie" of the *Memoir.* See Glossary 1: "Bartty," "Bertie," and "Willoughby."]

page 65 Description of Lord Willoughby (Peregrine, 12th Baron Willoughby de Eresby) and of his son Robert (13th Baron Willoughby de Eresby and first Earl of Lindsey) — After portraits reproduced in Tim Knox's pamphlet *Grimsthorpe Castle: Bourne, Lincoln* (U.K.: The Grimsthorpe and Drummond Castle Trust, 1996), pp. 6–8 (unnumbered).

page 65 Description of Saint Helena's Church in Willoughby — from a visit in May 1995.

page 65 Extract from the Psalms — Book V, Psalm 107, verse 19, in the New Oxford Annotated Bibe, rev. ed. I have slightly archaicized a few words.

page 65 The removal of the Willoughbys from Eresby to Grimsthorpe — Sir Francis Hill cites this family among others who established new residences to the south or southwest. Hill remarks (p. 8): "The relation of most of these seats to the north road is obvious. [Here] were the points of contact between Lincolnshire and the outer world."

page 66 Description of Lincolnshire in Speed's atlas — *The Counties of Britain: A Tudor Atlas by John Speed,* published in association with the British Library, introduction by Nigel Nicolson (London: Pavilion Books Ltd. 1995, a partial and rearranged repr. of the 1616 ed.), pp. 118–18 ("The Countie and Citie of Lincolne Described with the Armes of Them that Have Bene Earles Thereof Since the Conquest").

page 67 "Frauncis would soon have a wife, being engaged to the sluggish girl of his fancy, one Anna Oseney" — She is mentioned as Francis Smith's widow in the confirmation of John Smith's will (1631), when, "scornfully absenting herself" from the legal summons, she found herself cut off (Smith, vol. iii, pp. 387–89; auxilliary documents: document no. v). Otherwise not much is known of her. Barbour never even mentions her name in his *Three Worlds of Captain John Smith.*

page 67 *The Adventurers' Drain* — after Wheeler, pp. 250–51. The order to commence this drain (now [1898] the New Hammond Beck) was given, says Wheeler, in 1601.

page 68 Barty, Smith's guardians, Hume, etc.: order of events — This is very confusing, even to Babour, who has reconstructed Smith's syntax, vol. 3, p. 154, fn. 10. Smith's original leaves it unclear as to whether Smith went with Captain Duxbury to Rouen and then the Low Countries after his service with Barty, or else made a number of briefer and unsuccessful trips; I've supposed the latter. For further discussion, see Babour's *Three Worlds,* pp. 9-14. The business of approaching the palace is something that a desperate Smith could well have done, but I've made it up.

page 68 George Mettham's *Almanacke* — actually, Bourne, p. 60 (*Almanacke,* Third Rule).

page 70 "I had thought of proceeding farther . . ." — A descendant in the fourth generation, p. 92.

page 70 "None of these helping hands can be identified in documents . . ." — From the Biographical Directory entry for Robert Bertie, in Smith, vol. i, xxxi (Barbrour's preliminary matter).

page 71 "The Fens have obtained a world-wide notoriety . . ." — Wheeler, p. 2.

page 71 "Great rakes forwards on . . ." — *A Sea Grammar,* ch. XI, in Smith, vol. iii, p. 97 [53], almost verbatim. Eric Reid comments here (note to author, 1995): "Rake of the stem (now called overhang) does not contribute to weatherliness as far as I know, but of course Smith may have thought it did."

page 72 The procedure for securing the ship against a storm — After *A Sea Grammar,* ch. IX, in Smith, vol. iii, p. 87 [41]; and also ch. VII, p. 79 [29]. [Note: I draw so often on the *Sea-Grammar* for nautical terms that I will not cite small individual borrowings in these notes.] Throughout this book, I have also had occasional recourse to Peter Kemp, *The Oxford Companion to Ships and the Sea* (New York: Oxford University Press, Oxford Reference, 1988 corr. paper repr. of 1976 ed.).

page 72 The Almanacke's aphorism on tides at Holy Island [Lindisfarne] — after Bourne, p. 63 (*Almanacke,* Fourth Rule).

page 73 Description of the Mountains of the Sun and Moon — Smith, vol. iii, p. 211 [39], almost verbatim.

page 73 Description of Lindisfarne — after a visit in May 1995.

page 77 The sail from Gravesend to London — after Symonson's map of Kent, 1596, reproduced in Bourne, fig. 2, facing p. xiii.

page 77 Description of Queen Elizabeth — after the Rainbow Portrait (*ca.* 1600).

page 78 "There are people who feel the dead level of the Fens depressing . . ." — Arthur Mee, *The King's England: A New Domesday Book of 10,000 Towns and Villages in 41 Volumes,* unnumbered volume: *Lincolnshire: A County of Infinite Charm* (Carlton near Barnsley, South Yorkshire: The King's England press, 1992 repr. of 1949 ed.), p. 5.

page 79 Wheat prices in 1599 — Sir Francis Hill, loc. cit.

page 82 Description of Tattershall Castle — From a visit in May 1995.

page 83 Footnote on the marshy character of Willoughby and St. Helena's church — Nikolaus Pevsner and John Harris, *The Buildings of England: Lincolnshire* (1964), p. 422. "Perpendicular" refers to a period of English Gothic architecture covering roughly from 1335 to 1530.

page 84 Death of Captain Duxbury — Mentioned in *Three Worlds,* p. 17. However, Duxbury, like Shakespeare in the jest, may have been someone else by the same name.

page 84 Clausewitz on obedience — Carl von Clausewitz, *On War* (New York: Penguin, 1968 repr. of 1832 ed.), p. 259, almost verbatim.

page 86 Description of the Willoughby chapel and manor in Spilsby — From a visit in May 1995.

page 88 The swordfight with "Cursell" — It seems that Courcelles was only wounded, not killed.

page 90 The procedure for securing the ship against a storm — Again, this closely follows *A Sea Grammar,* ch. IX, in Smith, vol. iii, p. 87 [41].

page 91 Descriptions of fancy period armor, here and throughout — After a few color plates in Helmut Nickel, *Arms and Armor from the Permanent Collection* (New York: The Metropolitan Museum of Art, 1991). For technical information (cleaning of armor, etc.) I have relied on Charles Ffoulkes, *The Armourer and his Craft from the XIth to the XVIth Century* (New York: Dover, 1988 repr. of 912 ed.), esp. pp. 30–33, 40–41, 49, 70–71, 79, 139.

page 92 "We gave her a broadside, my Lords . . ." — Very loosely after the *True Travells,* ch. III, in Smith, pp. 160-61 [5].

page 94 "'Twas murtherous hard to render satisfaction both to Soldiers and people . . ." — Niccolò Machiavelli, *The Prince* (1513), in Robert Maynard Hutchins, editor in chief, *Great Books of the Western world, vol. 23: Machiavelli-Hobbes* (Chicago: Encyclopaedia Britannica, Inc., 1952), ch. XIV, "That Which Concerns a Prince on the Subject of the Art of War," p. 27 (ch. XIX); abridged, archaicized and "retranslated" somewhat.

page 95 Father Parsons and the Papist "traitors" of Lincolnshire — See, for instance, Sir Francis Hill, p. 107.

page 96 Various cattle brands of south Lincolnshire (described intermittently throughout this text) — Wheeler, p. 36.

page 96 "The Sunne was declining out of Libra." — Barbour *Three Worlds,* (pp. 53-54) dates this battle as sometime between 23 September and mid October 1602.

page 97 Description of the crag-islands en route to Axopolis — after an engraving by William Bartlett, in J.C.H. Pardoe's *The Beauties of the Bosphorus* (London, 1839).

page 98 Description of the bulging mosques of Axopolis — after a sketch by Melchior Lorichs, 1606, in Lord Kinross's most pleasantly illustrated *The Ottoman Centuries: The Rise and Fall of the Turkish Empire* (New York: Morrow, 1977), plate XIX.

page 98 The grand festival called *Coochick Bayrum* — Barbour (*Three Worlds,* p. 58) suggests very plausibly, by considering the various recorded and inferred dates pertaining to this episode, that Smith was bought by the Basaw Bogall for his sweetheart as a holiday gift, the holiday being Küçück Bayram, which I have transliterated as Smith might have had he known about it.

page 99 Description of Tragabigzanda — after a sketch of a woman by Gentile Bellini, reproduced in Kinross, plate XXII.

page 100 "She recollected some few *Italian* words . . ." — After a reasonable surmise in Barbour, *Three Worlds,* p. 58.

page 101 "She fed him on *Samboyses* . . ." — Smith, vol. iii, p. 189 [25].

page 101 Various descriptions of Tragabigzanda's house, furnishings and adornments — early seventeenth-century pieces on display from the John Addis Islamic Gallery, British Museum, London, 1998.

page 103 Descriptions of the branks, heretics' forks, and deadweight collars — after text and photographs in Robert Held, *Inquisition/Inquisición: A Bilingual Guide to the Exhibition of Torture Instruments from the Middle Ages to the Industrial Era, Presented in Various European Cities* (Florence: Qua d'Arno, 1985), pp. 150, 79 and 112, respectively.

page 103 Smith's sojourn with the "Tymor" — According to Franz Babinger (*Mehmed the Conqueror and His Time,* trans. Ralph Manheim, rev. ed, with preface by William C. Hickman [Princeton: Bollingen Series XCIV, Princeton University Press, 1978], pp. 6–7), "Murad [II] took a particular interest in his army. It was he who from about 1438 on organized the selective conscription of Christian boys in the territories of state as replacements in the Janissary corps and to serve in the imperial palaces. In Murad's own lifetime this levy of boys (*devsirme*) opened up the highest posititions in the state to Christians thus impressed into service. For nearly a century and a half these converts set their stamp on the conduct of Ottoman military and civil affairs . . . As late as the sixteenth century, . . . German and Venetian ambassadors reported with amazement that the wealth, administration, strength — in short, the entire ruling apparatus of the Ottoman empire depended on and was entrusted to men who had been born in the Christian faith but had been enslaved and raised as Moslems." From this one can deduce (as does Barbour) that Tragabigzanda sincerely meant well in sending Smith to her brother — and also that (because the upward mobility of Christian-born slaves endured only "as late as the sixteenth century") the social mechanism in which she placed her hopes was becoming obsolete. What had happened? Lord Kinross suggests (op. cit., p. 280) that the *sipahis* ("Tymors" — see Glossary 2) who used their soldier-vassals for field-work most of the time, were accustomed to a short season on the battlefield. The lengthening time demands of more modern war, combined with the terrifying new accuracy of German fusiliers, caused many "Tymors" to refuse to fight with material inducement, or, worse yet, to desert, as many did in the Battle of Mezo-Keveszles (Hungary, 1596), which Smith may well have participated in or heard about. As a result of their defection, 30,000 "Tymors" lost their rank. "To replace the dwindling feudal *sipahis,*" says Kinross (p. 285), "the government was obliged to increase the strength of its regular forces . . . That of Christian-born captives . . . was no longer sufficient . . . It was necessary for the first time to enlist into the armed forces on a large scale Moslem subjects . . ." If this is correct, and if the trend against the "Tymors" was going strong during the period of Smith's captivity, then it is easy to imagine Tragabigzanda's brother as a struggling, preoccupied man, worried about losing his own domain, and perhaps less than patient with a new charity case. He might well have been harsher than necessary with Smith. Perhaps he even thought that by so treating him he was doing him a favor, giving him the opportunity to be exemplary. In a study of some "Tymors" who lived in the place that Tragabigzanda called home, Christiane Villain-Gandossi found, as one might expect, that the annual revenue of these petty lords varied enormously, from about 3,000 to 14,000 aspres. An aspre was equal to 49 florins (gold pieces). ("Les Éléments Balkaniques dans la Garnison de Trébizonde à la fin du XVe Siècle," in Jean-Louis Bacqué-Grammont and Paul Dumont, ed., *Collection Turcica III: Contributions a l'historie économoique et sociale de l'Empire Ottoman* [Leuven, Belgium: Éditions Peeters, 1983], p. 129.) I imagine that the same situation of inequity prevailed in Smith's time a hundred years later, as it always has and always will. There is no knowing whether Tragabigzanda's brother was one of the well-off "Tymors." In short, in making my reconstruction of him I believe that I am entitled to a lot of latitude. (By the way, based on my own experiences of sundry Muslim countries, the appellation "brother" is very generously applied; it seems to me quite possible that the "Tymor" might not have been Tragabigzanda's biological sibling at all, but a family friend or a relative through marriage.)

page 103 Seyyid Lokman's lyric — quoted in Kinross, pp. 423–24.

page 105 "I am as I am and so will I be . . ." — attributed to Sir Thomas Wyatt, pub. 1815 (Wyatt died in 1542). This poem appears in Jones, p. 97, no. 54.

Argall

page 106 Angel-devil epigraph — Alastair Fowler, ed., *The New Oxford Book of Seventeenth Century English Verse* (New York: Oxford, 1991), p. 75 (Sir Francis Hubert, from "The Life and Death of Edward II").

page 106 Footnote on "Arkil"— Barbour, *Pocahontas and Her World,* p. 67.

page 106 "Just as air may invisibly contain within it clouds, lightnings, rain, storms, &c . . ." — After Fludd, p. 242.

page 106 Description of "Bristow" in Speed's atlas — Op. cit., pp. 82–83 ("GLOCES-TERSHIRE contriued into thirty thre Seuerall hundreds . . .").

page 107 Description of Kent in Speed's atlas — Op. cit., pp. 106–7 ("KENT with her Cities and Earles described and obserued").

The Grammar of Backstabbers

page 109 Charismatic setting epigraph — Arthur Schweitzer, *Big Business in the Third Reich* (Bloomington: Indiana University Press, 1964), p. 523.

page 109 Smith's coat of arms — After the color reproduction of it, frontis to Smith, vol. i.

page 110 The longitude and latitude of London — Bourne, p. 97 (*Almanacke,* Thirteenth Rule).

page 110 London as shaped like a bent bow — G.W. Groos, trans. and annotated, *The Diary of Baron Waldstein, a Traveller in Elizabethan England* (New York: Thames and Hudson, 1981), p. 3.

page 110 The ubiquitousness of tobacco in London in 1603 — Mentioned in Dekker's *The Wonderful Year,* which was written then. Indeed, throughout Dekker's writings tobacco seems to be a fact of life. Poor people set up tobacco-shops; crooked horse-traders blow tobacco-smoke up their animals' runny noses to make them seem healthier; prisoners yell curses when their tobacco's no good. In his *Gull's Horn-Book* of 1609 he defines the famous herb as "thou beggarly monarch of Indians and setter up of rotten-lunged chimney-sweepers" (op. cit., p. 75). My claim that in 1603 tobacco was not much to be seen in the small towns of Lincolnshire is a mere supposition, but, I think, a plausible one.

page 111 Life and character of King James I — David Mathew, *James I* (London: Eyre and Spottis-Woode, 1967); and Lucy Aikin, *Memoirs of the Court of King James the First* (London: Longon, Hurst, Rees, Orne and Brown, 1822), esp. vol. 2.

page 111 King Henry VIII on the beastliness of Lincolnshire — From a letter ordering the rebels of the Lincoln Rising of 1536 to submit; quoted in Sir Francis Hill, p. 45 fn. In my citation I've interpolated the word "shires" of necessity, having truncated the King's sumptuously wrathful pronouncement.

page 112 The great flood in the East Fens — "Shortly after James the First's accession to the throne [1603], a series of destructive floods burst the embankments of the Fens on the East Coast . . . drowning large numbers of people and cattle" (Wheeler, p. 30). To help me visualize the flood's topography, and Smith's travels through it, I have referred to the same book's reproduction of "A Map of the EASTE and WEST FENNE 1661 (Dugdale)," opposite p. 206 (fig. 8, chap. 6).

page 114 Wheat prices in 1605 — Sir Francis Hill, loc. cit.

page 117 The Charter of Virginia — *Annals of America: Volume 1,* pp. 15–16.

page 117 The tract of Richard Hakluyt [sometimes attributed instead to Sir John Popham] — *Annals of America: Volume 1,* p. 20.

Letter from a Lefthanded Man

page 120 John Stubbe's letter to Lord Willoughby (15 November 1585) — abridged from Quinn, vol. 1, pp. 222–23. For the capsule biography of Stubbe I am indebted to fn. 3, loc. cit.

page 120 The tale of Julius Caesar's centurion, Scaeva — Told in Lucan [Marcus Annaeus Lucanus], *Civil War,* trans. Susan M. Braund (New York: Oxford, 1992; orig. unfinished Latin version A.D. 66), pp. 110–113 (VI.144–261).

page 121 The sheep-rot of 1586 — Sir Francis Hill, p. 86.

The Grammar of Navigators

page 122 Epigraph on the "naturall inhabitants" — Thomas Harriot, *A Briefe and True Report of the New Found Land of Virginia* (New York: Dover Publications, Inc., 1972 repr. of 1590 ed., Rosenwald copy), p. 24.

page 122 Arthur, Malgo, Nicolas, Madock and the others — First Book of the *Generall Historie,* in Smith, vol. ii, pp. 61–96 [1–20].

page 123 English colonial and military policy in Virginia — In addition to the writings of Smith et al, I've also relied a little on books which discuss Tudor and Stuart actions in Ireland. Grenville, White, Wingfield, Percy, De La Warr, and others all had considerable experience in Ireland, and the policies there of scorched earth retribution for "rebellion," combined with disorganized indolence and graft during peacetime, seem compatible with what we know about Jamestown. I've made special use of Bartlett and Jeffery's *Military History of Ireland* (already cited), and of Charles O'Mahony, *The Viceroys of Ireland: The Story of the Long Line of Nobelmen and Their Wives who have ruled Ireland and Irish Society for over Seven Hundred Years* (London: John Long, Ltd., MCMXII).

page 123 "A certain northern Countie of Virginia not yet call'd Canada" — Here I'm speaking almost metaphorically. By the time John Smith went to Virginia, even the English equivalent of a militant pan-Germanist might have hesitated to lump in Canada with Virginia. And yet Argall did burn out the French settlement in Maine in 1613. Gilbert did erect that pillar in Newfoundland (which today remains an Anglophone province). The Elizabethans wanted Virginia to extend as far northward and southward as they could get away with.

page 123 Description of Newfoundland — After a visit to that island in 1987. For further description, see the First Dream.

page 124 The erections of pillars in 1583 and 1584 to denote English possession of the land — Quinn, vol. 1, p. 94 fn (Arthur Barlowe's Discourse of the First Voyage, 1584–85).

page 124 ". . . that did assure their Master of the goodness of the soil." — Quinn, vol. 1, p. 91 (Holinshed's Chronicles, notice of 1584 voyage).

page 126 Ralegh's commissions granting him the right to impress sailors — Ibid, p. 145 (draft commission from Queen Elizabeth to Sir Walter Ralegh to impress mariners, *ca.* January 1585), p. 151 (articles of complaint, State Papers Foreign, re: impressment of foreign seamen), p. 156 (10 June 1585 signet letter).

page 126 Piracy on the voyage of 1585 — Quinn, pp. 169-83 (editor's summary of events).

page 126 Loss of leg to a "Sharke"— Ibid, p. 230 (Sir Richard Hawkins, *Observations,* 1593).

page 126 Roanoke Inlet's "draw" of 10 feet of water — So claimed by Lawson, p. 71.

page 128 Sir Richard Grenville's burning of an Indian town (1585) — Smith's abridgement of Hakluyt, in 1st Book of the *Generall Historie,* Smith, vol. ii, p. 69 [5]. The town was called Aquascogoc. For Grenville's account, see Quinn, vol. 1, p. 191.

page 128 Grenville's spoiling of the Spanish viceadmiral — Ibid, p. 177 (Holinshed's Chronicles, notice of 1585 voyage).

page 129 "The bounds thereof on the East side . . ." — Second Book of the *Generall Historie,* Smith, vol. ii, p. 100 [21].

page 129 Suggested prohibition against any soldier's harming the Indians — Quinn, vol. 1, p. 138 (anonymous notes for the guidance of Ralegh and Cavendish, *ca.* 1584).

page 129 Extract from "Saint Machiavell"— Machiavelli, p. 9 (ch. VI, "Concerning New Principalities . . ."), archaicized.

page 133 White's statement of resignation: "Yet seeing 'tis not my .1.st cross'd voyage . . ." — Richard Hakluyt, *Voyages to the Virginia Colonies: A Modern Version, with an Introduction, by A.L. Rowse* (London: Century, The Century Travellers ser., 1986), p. 154 (White's relation of 1587), slightly archaicized.

page 133 Grenville and Ralegh's undertaking in Ireland — After Joyce Youings, *Ralegh's Country: The South West of England in the Reign of Queen Elizabeth I* (Raleigh: America's Four Hundredth Anniversary Committee, North Carolina Department of Cultural Resources [Division of Archives and History], 1986), pp. 46–47 ("Landed Proprietors").

page 133 "With curtains & flankers very Fort-like . . ." — Ibid, p. 163 (White's relation of 1590), slightly archaicized.

page 134 Footnote on the degeneration of "Humane Nature" — Lawson, p. 69 ("A Description of *North-Carolina*").

page 134 "All hopes of Virginia being abandoned," + the voyages of Gosnold, Gilbert, Pring, etc. — Op. cit., pp. 88–96.

page 135 "This we did to cause them to imagine some great power in us . . ." — Iames Rosier, a Gentleman employed in the voyage, *A Trve Relation of the most propserous voyage made this present yeere 1605, by Captaine George Weymouth, in the Discouery of the land of Virginia* (London: George Bishop, 1605), p. C [recto].

page 135 "These things considered, we began to ioyne them in the Rankes of other Salvages, . . ." — Rosier, p. C4 [unnumbered] [recto].

page 135 Smith's investment of nine pounds sterling in the Virginia Company; Captain Gosnold's relationship to Robert Bertie — Barbour, *Three Worlds,* p. 103.

page 135 Smith's visit to "Weymouth's Salvages"— No such visit has been recorded. However, it seems that Smith could communicate with the Powhatans better than the other colonists. Indeed, there must have been several occasions (such as his interview with Opechancanough after being captured in 1607) that no interpreters were present. I imagine that he had a minimal Powhatan vocabulary at his disposal (see Barbour, *Three Worlds,* p. 203), and so why not suppose that in his boredom and ambition during the year of waiting in England he learned from Weymouth's captives? According to Barbour (Jamestown), the appearance of these Indians in England "seems to have been the catalytic agent" of the Virginia undertaking (vol. 1, pp. 13–14). The same author (*Three Worlds,* pp. 98–99) suggests that he might have gained this knowledge from Thomas Harriot, whose work I occasionally cite in this Dream.

page 136 Smith's acquaintanceship with Henry Hudson — A plausible surmise detailed in Barbour, *Three Worlds,* p. 97.

page 136 "If there fall out any warres between vs & them . . ." — Harriot, p. 25.

The Grammar of Gentlemen

page 137 Agonies of America epigraph — Daniel Defoe, *The Fortunes and Misfortunes of the Famous* Moll Flanders, *&c, Who was Born in* NEWGATE, *and during of Life of Continued Variety for Threescore Years, besides her Childhood, was Twelve Year a* Whore, *five times a* Wife (*whereof once to her own Brother*), *Twelve Year a* Thief, *Eight Year a Transported* Felon *in* Virginia, *at last grew Rich, liv'd* Honest, *and died a* Penitent (1722), ed. Edward H. Kelly (New York: Norton, 1973), p. 236.

page 139 Descriptions of Tidewater Virginia (esp. Jamestown) — After a visit in 1990, and another in 1996.

page 140 Gosnold's pleasant memories of northern Virginia (which, by the way, is now Massachusetts) — Second Book of the *Generall Historie,* Smith, vol. ii, p. 90 [17–18].

page 141 The red copper crowns of Roanoke's werowances — Quinn, pp. 103 (Arthur Barlowe's discourse of the first Roanoke voyage, 1584–85).

page 142 "Be fruitful & multiply . . ." — Genesis 1.28, archaized a trifle.

page 143 Resemblance between "the white hilly sands" of Cape Henrico and the "Downes of England" — After the *Generall Historie,* Bk. II ch. 1 [21], in Smith, vol. ii, p. 101.

page 143 Newport's gold fever — After his letter to Lord Salisburie of 29 June 1607; given in Barbour (Jamestown), p. 76.

page 145 "Whey, whey, yah," &c . . . — William Strachey, gent., *The Historie of Travell into Virginia Britannia* (1612), ed. Louis B. Right and Virginia Freund (London: Hakluyt Society, 1953), p. 85. Helen C. Rountree suggests (*The Powhatan Indians of Virginia: Their Traditional Culture* [Norman: University of Oklahoma Press; The Civilization of the North American Indian ser., vol. 193, 1989], p. 84) that the Powhatans might have made this insulting song against the English because they did not die in a manly way. Strachey also hints at this (ibid, p. 86).

page 147 Role of Aunt Susie in getting Smith into the Council — See the Biographical Directory in Smith, vol. i, entries for Robert Bertie (Smith's "Barty"), George Metham and the two Wingfields.

page 147 Wingfield's "promise to betroth to them his best endeavors" — after Barbour (Jamestown), vol. 1, p. 228 (Wingfield's discourse). His "promise by the holy Evangelists" is based on the form laid down in the Orders for Council of 10 December 1606 (ibid, p. 47).

page 149 Gold threads in President Wingfield's clothes — After the discovery of gold threads found in the excavation of Martin's Hundred, presumably from the governor of that settlement, William Hardwood. See Ivor Nöel Hume, *Martin's Hundred* (Charlottesville: University Press of Virginia, 1995 rev. repr. of 1982 ed.), pp. 57–61.

page 150 "Were we in England I would think scorn . . ." — Barbour (Jamestown), vol. 1, p. 215 (item 34: Edward Maria Wingfield's discourse, finished after 21 May 1608).

page 150 Structure and fittings of the *Susan Constant* — after the diagrams in Brian Lavery, *The Colonial Merchantman Susan Constant 1605* (Annapolis, Maryland: Naval Institute Press, Anatomy of the Ship ser., no ser. no., 1988).

page 150 "They flew a flag in the main shrouds" — After the *Sea Grammar,* ch. XIII, in Smith, vol. iii, p. 103 [62].

page 150 *Instructions Given By Way of Advice* — Barbour (Jamestown), vol. 1, p. 49 (item no. 42, "The London Council's Instructions Given By Way of Advice," 20 November–19 December 1606). Note: Henceforth this compilation will be cited as "Barbour (Jamestown)."

page 150 "Well-waxed lines"— Used to mean that the *Instructions* had been sealed; cf. Cyril Tourneur, *The Revenger's Tragedy* (1607), ed. Lawrence J. Ross (Lincoln: University of Nebraska Press, Regents Renaissance Drama ser., 1966), p. 22, gloss to I.iii, line 93.

page 151 The use of fend-bolts — After the *Sea Grammar,* ch. II, in Smith, vol. iii, pp. 60–61 [5].

page 154 The Salvages' abandoned oyster-roastery — after Barbour (Jamestown), vol. 1, p. 134 (Percy's discourse).

The Grammar of Colonists

page 156 *"When You have made Choise of the River"* — Barbour (Jamestown), vol. 1, pp. 51, 50 ("The London Council's Instructions Given By Way of Advice").

page 157 Crushed nettles as a remedy for bleeding — Madox, p. 208.

page 157 *Archer's Hope,* pro and contra — Barbour (Jamestown), vol. 1, p. 138 (Percy's discourse).

page 157 Description of Archer's Hope — After a visit to that spot (now College Creek) in 1990.

page 157 Wingfield's banquet served on silver plate — Not as unlikely as it sounds. The leaders of these expeditions often travelled rather well. See, e.g., Quinn, vol. 1, p. 186, in which we read in the log of Sir Richard Grenville's *Tiger* that en route to Roanoke in 1585 they dropped anchor in the Spanish dominions of Hispaniola and "a sumptuous banquet was in serued by vs all in Plate, with the sound of trumpets, and consort of musick, wherewyth the Spaniards were more than delighted."

page 158 "As the circumstance of becoming a Prince from private station . . ." — Machiavelli, p. 8 (ch. VI); archaicized.

page 158 "Those who by valorous ways become Princes . . ." — Ibid, p. 9 (ch. VI); archaicized.

page 160 "The villages of Salvages in this order" — As they appear on Smith's "map of Virginia, with a Description of the Countrey, the Commodities, People, Government and Religion" (1612), in Smith, vol. 1, pp. 140-41. Indian towns which would not have been visible from the river, such as Nandsamund, have been omitted.

page 161 Marcellinus on the fens — Quoted in Wheeler, p. 8.

page 165 Sir Walter Ralegh's calculations of ammunition needed against the Spanish Armada — Youings, p. 54 ("The Defense of the Realm").

page 166 To "sleep my undermeal in a bawdyhouse" — After Nashe, p. 373 ("Lenten Stuff," 1599).

page 168 Elizabeth Hunt's "incontinency" with John Taylor of Heathfield — This seems pretty likely to have been a fact, given the drift of her husband's will of 20 November 1606, given in Barbour (Jamestown), vol. 1, p. 61.

page 168 Wingfield's complaint to Newport about harvesting of sassafrass on company time — Actually, after the letter from the Council to its English backers, 22 June 1607, as given in Barbour (Jamestown), vol. 1, p. 79.

page 169 Jamestown's first church — as described in Smith's *Advertisements for the Unexperienced Planters of New England, or Any Where,* in Smith, vol. iii, p. 295 [32–33].

page 169 Meetings of the Council in that church — Hume, *Here Lies Virginia,* p. 62.

page 169 Amount of gunpowder needed to fire a culverin — Hume, *The Virginia Adventure,* p. 152.

page 171 "On the second-and-twenty day of May . . ." — This and the next sentence follow Smith's abridged *True Relation* of 1608 fairly closely (Smith, vol. i, p. 29 [A3]), except that the date has been amended, after Barbour.

page 171 The portions of gold, silver and copper to be paid over to King James — Barbour (Jamestown), vol. 1, p. 28 (item no. 1: letters patent to Sir Thomas Gates and others, 10 April 1606). In one of the first surviving documents (perhaps the very first) relating to Virginia, we find the crown being granted the same share; see Quinn, vol. 1, p. 84 (letters patent to Sir Walter Ralegh, 28 March 1584).

page 172 *Instructions Given By Way of Advice* — Barbour (Jamestown), vol. 1, p. 50.

The Grammar of Emperors

page 173 Powhatan cruelty epigraph — Grace Steele Woodward, *Pocahontas* (Norman: University of Oklahoma Press, The Civilization of the American Indian series, 1969), p. 8.

page 173 English cruelty epigraph — Christopher Hill, *Change and Continuity in Seventeenth-Century England,* rev. ed. (New Haven: Yale Univerity Press, 1991), p. 75.

page 173 Description of Powhatan life and material culture — Above all I have used Smith's *Generall Historie,* especially the Second Book. Next I have referred to Helen C. Rountree's monographs (cited in these notes where appropriate).

page 173 Life and character of Powhatan as a politician — I have relied on the analyses of the various contributors in Helen C. Rountree, ed., *Powhatan Foreign Relations 1500-1722* (Charlottesville: University Press of Virginia, 1993) and in William Fitzhugh, ed., *Cultures in Contact: The European Impact on Native Cultural Institutions in Eastern North America A.D. 1000-1800* (Washington: Smithsonian Institution Press, Anthropological Society of Washington ser., 1985). Rountree in her introduction begins by making the point that Europeans imagined Powhatan to have powers of monolithic coercion equivalent to those of one of their own sovereigns. When he promised peace, and then a few of his "Salvages" attacked the English, they blamed Powhatan for treachery. In fact, "Powhatan probably had only limited power over his people's everyday lives, in spite of his wealth and rank and connections with the priesthood. This was true even in the loyalist heartland" (p. 181).

page 173 Powhatan's age — His exact date of birth is uncertain. He was probably in his seventies at this point. The skeletal evidence suggests that most Powhatans died before the age of fifty (Rountree, *Powhatan Foreign Relations,* pp. 57–66, 73: Douglas H. Ubelaker, "The Human Biology of Virginia Indians"). But then the average age of death in Elizabethan England was thirty-five — "and less for the poor," writes Christopher Hill (*Century of Revolution,* p. 19).

page 175 Names of Powhatan's favorite wives — Strachey, p. 61.

page 176 "He convoked a meeting in the Wiochisan house." — This word (meaning temple) was used by the Anglo-Virginian John Clayton near the end of the seventeenth century. I assume this important meeting — and there must have been one — would have taken place in the temple. See Rountree, *The Powhatan Indians,* p. 119. The same author suggest (p. 131) that only priests could actually see OKEUS, "and then perhaps only at Uttamussak," but since John Smith was the subject or object of an important conjuration at Werowocomoco when he was captured (*Generall Historie,* 3rd Book, in Smith, vol. 3, p. 149 [48]), I think it likely that the priests were speaking with OKEUS then and there.

page 177 History of Euro-Powhatan relations prior to 1607 — As usual, this is a vexed subject. I have relied on Rountree, on Hume, *The Virginia Adventure,* pp. 23–27 and (for the tradition that Powhatan helped murder the Roanoke settlers) pp. 95–96, 190–91.

page 178 "I have seen the deaths of all my people thrice . . ." — Closely after the *Generall Historie,* 3rd Book, ch. VIII, pp. 199 [76]. Powhatan was speaking to John Smith.

page 178 Moustaches of the Keyauwee tribe — Mentioned as a rarity by Lawson (p. 58).

page 179 "There is a king in this land called great Pawatah . . ." — Barbour (Jamestown), p. 102 (item 15: anonymous relation, perhaps Captain Archer's, 21 May–21 June 1607).

The Grammar of Virginia

page 180 Removal of obstacles epigraph — William Tecumseh Sherman, *Memoirs* (New York: Library of America, 1990 repr. of 1886 ed.), p. 365.

page 180 "The people used our men well . . ." — Barbour (Jamestown), vol. 1, p. 110

(item no. 18: Sir Walter Cope to Lord Salisbury, 12 August 1607). To make the meaning clearer, I have changed "vntill they found they began" to "vntill they found we began."

The Grammar of Lovers

page 181 Barbour epigraph — in Smith, vol. i, p. lix.

page 181 The events in this section are based on 3rd Book of the *Generall Historie,* pp. 142–50.

page 182 Machiavelli on over-easy Princes — Op. cit., p. 21.

page 187 Layout of Jamestown Fort — after John L. Cotter, *Archeological Excavations at Jamestown Colonial National Historical Park and Jamestown National Historic Site, Virginia* (Washington: National Park Service, U.S. Department of the Interior, Archeological Research Series Number Four, 1958), p. 11.

page 188 "What cheer, mates?"— I would never have dared use this line did not our protagonist himself utter it in his *Sea-Grammar* (Smith, vol. iii, p. 102).

page 189 The award of two hundred pounds to John Smith — Barbour (Jamestown), vol. 1, p. 223 (Wingfield's discourse).

page 189 Assault of 25 May and murder of Eustace Clovell — Barbour (Jamestown), vol. 1, pp. 95-96 (item 13: Captain Archer's [?] relation, 21 May–21 June 1607).

page 190 Opechancanough's gift of a deer as a Trojan horse — Interpretation suggested in Barbour, *Three Worlds,* p. 143.

page 190 The sickness at Jamestown — Malaria was the most likely cause, but it might also have been influenza or typhoid, according to Matthew Page Andrews, *Virginia: The Old Dominion* (Garden City, NY: Doubleday, Doran & Co., n.d.), p. 32. Hume weighs in for typhoid (*The Virginia Adventure,* p. 159), going on to say (p. 160): "The James Fort colonists' unwillingness or inability to work toward their own salvation remains one of American history's major mysteries. Percy speaks movingly of the daily ration of a small mug of barley soaked in water and shared between five men — while they camped beside a river brimming with fish."

page 191 The pall laid over Captain Gosnold's coffin — The archaeologist Ivor Nöel Hume (*Martin's Hundred,* pp. 77–83, 349–57) excavated what he plausibly conjectures to be the remains of gable-roofed coffins at Martin's Hundred. The gabled roofs allowed the funeral palls to be better displayed. Gosnold, if anyone, would have had such a coffin and pall — assuming that such were available. I've imagined that as the epidemic continued, they became less so.

page 191 Wingfield's foreknowledge of his own deposition — Barbour (Jamestown), vol. 1, p. 215 (Wingfield's discourse).

page 191 Dialogue during and after Wingfield's deposition — Barbour (Jamestown), vol. 1, pp. 218-21 (Wingfield's discourse).

page 192 "Good prize on all sides"— Barbour (Jamestown), vol. 1, p. 226 (Wingfield's discourse).

page 192 "I pray you be more sparing of law" — ibid, p. 224, almost verbatim.

page 193 "GOD *the patron of all good indevours, in that desperate extremitie* . . ." — Smith, *Generall Historie,* Bk. III ch. 2, [44], in Smith, vol. ii, p. 143.

page 194 Medicinal use of hellebore purges — Madox, p. 98.

page 196 Kecoughtan as a "convenient harbor for fisher-boats" — *Generall Historie,* 2nd Book, in Smith, vol. 2, p. 103 [23].

page 201 Emry's tale of the two thirteenth-century pallbearers — after Wheeler, p. 78.

page 203 Lavatory habits of the Dutchmen — Madox, p. 108.

page 203 Ratcliffe's illegal installation of Archer on the council — Barbour (Jamestown), vol. 1, p. 227 (Wingfield's discourse).

page 206 The Chickahominy River as *"The Back River of James Towne"* — After the *Generall Historie,* Bk. II ch. 1 [22], in Smith, vol. ii, p. 103.

page 206 Jehu Robinson — Actually a gentleman, not a laborer (Barbour, *Three Worlds,* p. 155). But I wanted to give Smith the ability to command all his men unequivocally in this scene.

page 208 Description of the Tymor's peaked helmet of iron — Seen by me in a museum in Istanbul, 1981.

page 208 "Master, let us breathe . . ." — After the *Sea Grammar,* ch. XIII, in Smith, vol. iii, p. 102 [60].

page 209 "Seminal worms" — after Albertus Haller, quoted in Angus McLaren, *Reproductive Rituals: The Perception of Fertility in England from the Sixteenth Century to the Nineteenth Century* (London: Methuen & Co., 1984), p. 23.

page 209 Jefferson on Indians' body hair — *Notes on the State of Virginia* (1787), Query VI, in the Library of America edition of his *Writings* (New York: Literary Classics of the United States, 1984), p. 187.

page 211 "That subtill old revengefull Powhatan" — Hamor, p. 2.

page 216 "That North Star which standeth upon the tail of Ursa Minor"— After Bourne, p. 87 (*Almanacke,* Eighth Rule).

page 221 Wages of tailors and drapers in Lincolnshire — after Sir Francis Hill, pp. 220–21 (Appendix II). Hill gives 26 shillings as the 1563 wage, so I've assumed some increase in the intervening half-century, since prices rose.

page 221 Strachey on Powhatan — Strachey, *Historie of Travell,* p. 57.

page 223 Smith's description of Powhatan — *A Map of Virginia,* "Of Their Religion," p. [35], in *Works,* vol. 1, p. 173; and also 2nd Book of the *Generall Historie,* in vol. 3, pp. 150 [50] ff.

page 224 Smith's alleged rescue by Pocahontas — This is a vexed subject. Did it happen? One difficulty is that Smith never mentioned the rescue in his first account, which is called the *True Relation.* James Branch Cabell (*Let Me Lie, Being in the Main an Ethnological Account of the Remarkable Commonwealth of Virginia and the Making of Its History* [New York: Farrar, Straus & Co., 1947], pp. 52–53) proposes that the tale is cribbed from a 1609 relation in Hakluyt, dealing with the Spaniard Juan Ortiz, who in 1529 was captured by the Hirrigua Indians near Clear Water Beach, and saved from execution by the chieftan's daughter. (As a matter of fact, many of Smith's pages are indeed plagiarisms.) Cabelll goes on (p. 60): "The *True Relation,* in short, compels any tolerably intelligent reader to decide whether John Smith lied, quite gratuitously, about Powhatan and Pocahontas in a private letter when he had nothing to gain by it? — Or whether Smith lied later, through rather more intelligent motives, during the touching-up of a book of travels which he was trying to make saleable? There can be, in the present low state of human nature, but one sane answer." E. Keble Chatterton, on the other hand, wrote: ". . . yet the truth of her saving Smith's life has been quite unreasonably doubted . . . In the first place we can rule out all sentimental sexual romance from the incident. It was rather a case where that natural human pity and abhorrence of death, which are characteristic of womanhood and girlhood, enter to stop the painful sight of suffering . . ." (*Captain John Smith* [New York, Harper and Brothers, 1927], p. 141). To my late twentieth-century ears, Cabell sounds polemical and Chatterton unconvincing; and generally the adherents on both sides of the argument do sound one way or the other. J.A. Leo Lemay, in his book devoted entirely to this topic, *Did Pocahontas Save Captain John Smith?* (Athens: University of Georgia Press, 1992, pp. 26–7), concludes that she did. The suppression of the whole episode in the *True Relation,* which would seem to be the most damning evidence against Smith, Lemay explains with any one of the following answers (take your pick): (1) Smith was embarrassed to have been saved by this girl-child, and in any case his life was so often in danger that the Pocahontas incident did not weigh especially heavy in his recollections. (2) Since his loyalty was often suspected (some persons, such as Ratcliffe and Wingfield, evidently believed, or pretended to believe, that he plotted to be King of Virginia), he may have preferred to avoid any mention of his ties with an Indian "Princess." (3) Describing himself as a prisoner of Powhatan might have made him appear less in control of the Indians. To me the most important thing about the *True Relation* is this: It was published possibly without his consent; it was edited definitely without his participation. In short, it is a corrupt text. The *Generall Historie,* on the other hand, was written at leisure, and published with Smith's involvement. As a professional author I am often shocked by the magazine versions of writings which appear under my name. For this reason alone, I would prefer the *Generall Historie* to the *True Relation* anytime.

page 224 The purpose of the rescue, if it did happen — A plausible theory is advanced by Barbour, in *Pocahontas and Her World,* pp. 24–5: "The ceremony of which Smith had been the object was almost certainly a combination of mock execution and salvation, in token of adoption into Powhatan's tribe . . . Powhatan himself was possibly his foster-father, but Pocahontas herself had been chosen to act in his stead. Relations with the dangerous Englishmen were still problematical, and Powhatan must stand aloof." To this Hume adds: "What better way could the idea of benevolence be transmitted than through a reponse to the universal language of a child's tenderness? The king's power had been demonstrated, as had the impotence of his captive — dramatized by his being saved not by strength but by the weakness of a female child" (*The Virginia Adventure,* pp. 179–80).

page 224 Character of Pocahontas — Much less is known about this famous heroine than most people think. Pocahontas and her millieu remain preserved mainly in a schematic sense. My try at realizing the "Princesse" as a character is thus a bit presumptuous. I have proceeded in a cautious, low-key and I hope respectful way. (By the way, as Rountree has pointed out in her *Pocahontas's People,* the belief of the English that Pochahontas was a Princess was partly erroneous. Descent among the Powhatans was in the female line. Powhatan's successor would be the son of his nearest female relative. This is not to say that Pocahontas had no status, but she was not a Princess in the sense that Smith understood the term.) From Smith's and Strachey's writings we get the sense of a privileged, socially engaged, playful and curious young lady — indeed, as her easy kidnapping proves, she was too curious for her own good.

page 225 Hair styles of unmarried (shaved in front, long braids in back) *vs.* married women (shaved to uniform length) — Strachey, p. 114.

page 225 Strachey's first reference to Pocahontas — Op. cit., p. 62.

page 226 Strachey's second reference to Pocahontas — Ibid., p. 72. Here James Branch Cabell comments: ". . . it is perhaps my duty to add that this alleged public display of the pudenda of Pocahontas has been afforded a figleaf through the assertion that Powhatan had, no doubt, two daughters called Pocahontas . . . I am deterred only by the reflection that neither Powhatan nor anyone of his contemporaries appears ever to have noticed this fact . . ."

page 228 "Kekaten Pokahontas . . ." and other Powhatan words and phrases in this section — from Smith's vocabulary list in the *Generall Historie of Virginia, New-England and the Summer Isles . . .* (in Smith, vol. ii, p. 132). See also the Orthographic Notes to the Glossaries.

page 231 "The *Lion's Taile* in Virgo"— Bourne (p. 100, *Almanacke for Three Yeares,* 1571) lists this star among other "notable fixed stars for navigation." An astrologer has explained to me that when the sun lies in a certain sign, the stars lie in the complementary sign — that is, halfway around the Zodiac. So it seemed reasonable to me that if the sun was in Capricorn, a bright star in Leo would be visible to John Smith.

page 232 *"O LORD, Thou hast brought up my soul from the grave . . ."* — Psalm 30.

page 234 "He is now the King's prisoner"— Barbour (Jamestown), vol. 1, p. 221 (Wingfield's discourse).

page 235 ". . . While I took my needless pleasure in discovering the Countreys around us . . ." — From here to the remainder of this sentence and paragraph is lifted, with a few minor alterations, from Smith's *Advertisements,* in Smith, vol. iii, p. 271.

page 235 fn The tale of James Read and the execution of Kendall — Barbour (Jamestown), vol. 1, pp. 224–25 (Wingfield's discourse).

page 235 Extract from the letters patent: capital crimes — Barbour (Jamestown), vol. 1, pp. 37–38 (item no. 1: letters patent to Sir Thomas Gates and others, 10 April 1606), abridged.

page 235 fn Wingfield's protest that he only roasted one squirrel — Barbour (Jamestown), vol. 1, p. 223 (Wingfield's discourse).

page 236 Navigability of the Chickahominy River — After Jefferson, *Notes on the State of Virginia*), Query II; op. cit., p. 129.

The Grammar of Tides

page 237 Grave epigraph — The exact date of its composition is not known. (It was first published in 1983). It appears in Fowler, p. 234, no. 281.

page 237 Differences in point of view between Europeans and Indians — This is of course a main subject of the entire *Seven Dreams* series, and cannot so easily be schematized. However, the following is a very good general statement: "A survivor also possesses a utopian attitude. This is not a reflection of any comfort orientation but is evidence of an artistic nature. He makes even the most miserable existence seem like millennial splendor. I have witnessed this in my best students. Their digging sticks are works of art, their deadfalls ingenious, and their camps miracles of compactness and industry. There is nothing crude in the primitive existence of these people.

"Stone Age living implies two things: first, an immersion within the affective domain of life and secondly, a life centered away from comfort and ease. Reasons for this may rest in meaning and time. Affective living places some of the meanings of life in the world of work — of doing. Priorities in a hand-to-mouth existence quickly force industry to an exalted plane. If not, existence would become unbearable. Activity and industry merged with increased spiritual insight form a union that may preserve life beyond the normal limits.

"Life on a higher plane than comfort and ease may seem strange in our culture, but it is an important quality of men who survive. This point has grave consequences for the comfort-oriented man lost in the wilderness. In Utah a man once died of dehydration beside a desert stream because the water was uncomfortably dirty." — Larry D. Olsen, *Outdoor Survival Skills* (Provo, Utah: Brigham Young University Press, 1973).

Of course most of the English were less "comfort-oriented" than most Americans (including Native Americans) are now. However, Wingfield and the other "gentlemen" were certainly an example of the type. Bred to expect service rather than to serve themselves and each other, they could not have survived in Virginia without the Indians' help. The Indians were not necessarily "better," but survival was their business. In this volume I have sought to begin with the details of that business as the foundation for any superstructure of reconstructed Powhatan personalities.

page 237 The sun ceremony — As described in the "Relation of Captain Gosnold's

Voyage into the North Part of Virginia . . . (1602), Delivered by Gabriel Archer, a Gentleman in the Same Voyage," in Rev. Samuel Purchas, *Purchas His Pilgrimes. In Five Bookes . . . &c. The Fourth Part.* [v. 4] *Unus Deus, Una Veritas* (London: Printed by William Stansby for Henrie Featherstone, and are to be sold at his shop in Pauls church-yard at the signe of the Rolfe, 1625), p. 1662.

The Grammar of Maids

page 240 Epitaph on Virtue — Sir Thomas Wyatt, *The Complete Poems,* ed. R.A. Rebholz (New York: Penguin, 1978), p. 192 (Epistolatory Satires, CLI).

page 240 Pocahontas as gift-giver — "Contemporary accounts agree: the person who sent the food that saved the colony was Powhatan, not Pocahontas, as Smith claimed in 1624. Indians and English alike lived in a world in which prepubescent girls had little real power" (Rountree, *Pocahontas's People,* pp. 39–40).

page 246 Extract from the letters patent: deportment toward the Salvages — Barbour (Jamestown), vol. 1, p. 29 (item no. 1: letters patent to Sir Thomas Gates and others, 10 April 1606), abridged.

page 246 Machiavelli on destroying powerful princes — Machiavelli, p. 5.

page 246 Improvements in Jamestown's church — as described in the *Advertisements for the Unexperienced Planters of New England, or Any Where,* in Smith, vol. iii, p. 295 [32–33].

page 246 Smith's Almanacke on the rising and setting of the moon — Bourne, p. 69 (*Almanacke for Three Years,* 1571, Fifth Rule).

page 247 Navigability of Powhatan's river (the York) — After Jefferson, *Notes on the State of Virginia*), Query II; op. cit., p. 130.

page 247 Names of the gentlemen who went to Werowocomoco near the end of February 1608 — Smith, *Generall Historie,* Bk. III ch. 3, [51], in Smith, vol. ii, p. 155.

page 248 Description of Powhatan's country — From a visit to Purtan Bay, Virginia (site of Werowocomoco) in March 1996.

page 248 *Instructions Given By Way of Advice* — Barbour (Jamestown), vol. 1, p. 51.

page 249 The old Almanacke on the disadvantages of using forests as landmarks — Bourne, pp. 57-58 (*Almanacke for Three Years,* 1571, First Rule).

page 250 The bad blood between Smith and Newport — A thesis of Hume's *Virginia Adventure.* See, e.g., p. 193. Barbour makes a similar case.

page 251 Difficulties crossing the bridge; marching double file, etc. — Smith, vol. i, *A True Relation,* pp. 63–65 [C4^r-C4^v].

page 252 Gloomy saw from "Ecclesiasticus" — Ecclesiastes 7.24.

page 255 Comparison of Indians' "howling" to that of wolves and devils — Barbour (Jamestown), vol. 1, p. 136 (Percy's discourse).

page 256 "I see you envy my estimation among the Salvages"— Ibid, p. 154 [51]; slightly altered.

page 256 "Gold's tested by a stamp . . ." — Madox, p. 216.

page 257 The victuals needed by the English — Barbour (Jamestown), vol. 1, p. 228 (Wingfield's discourse).

page 257 Powhatan's speech to Newport — almost verbatim (with a few abbreviations, clarifications and flourishes) — Smith, *Generall Historie,* Bk. III ch. 3, [52], in Smith, vol. ii, p. 157.

page 257 The hospitality of Pocahontas et al to the English: drawing off socks, foot-washing, cooking — Inspired by Quinn, p. 107 (Arthur Barlowe's discourse of the first Roanoke voyage, 1584–85). Obviously one must be cautious about imputing Carolina Algonquin behavior to Virginia Algonquins, but even a superficial student such as myself quickly becomes impressed with the cultural and linguistic similarites between the two groups. (Both, for instance, acknowledged werowances, and used that term.) The account my few sentences are based on deals with the hospitality to the English of Grangyno, "the king's brother's wife." Quinn remarks: "This is one of the few intimate glimpses we have of domestic ceremonial hospitality for this region."

page 257 "Women fresh painted . . ." — After 2nd Book of the *Generall Historie,* Smith, vol. ii, p. 121 [34].

page 257 Powhatan bed-hospitality — "Dignitaries staying the night were finally conducted to a private house, where they were provided with beds and also with female bedfellows . . . Sexual hospitality on the part of a town's women was fairly common in the Eastern Woodlands. The Powhatan case has already been mentioned, though there is no record of the marital status of the women involved . . . married women generally were permitted to have affairs as long as their husbands consented" (Rountree, *Powhatan Foreign Relations,* pp. 40–41: Rountree, "The Powhatans and other Woodland Indians as Travelers"). In 1700, Lawson observed (pp. 35–36): "The *English* Traders are seldom without an *Indian* Female for his Bed-fellow, alledging these Reasons as sufficient to allow such a Familiarity. First, They being remote from any white People, that it preserves their Friendship with the Heathens, they esteeming a white Man's Child much above one of their getting, the *Indian* Mistress ever securing her white Friend Provisions whilst he stays among them. And lastly, This Correspondence makes them learn the *Indian* Tongue much the sooner, they being of the *French*man's Opinion, how that an *English* Wife teaches her Husband more *English* in one Night, than a School-master can in a Week."

page 258 How Powhatan was gulled by blue beads — After 3rd Book of the *Generall Historie,* Smith, vol. ii, p. 156 [52].

page 260 Menapacunt as "pleasantly seated upon a high hill of ancient soft sea-sand" — Somewhat after Smith, vol. i, *A True Relation,* p. 51 [C$_1^r$].

page 260 The visit to Menapacunt — Ibid, pp. 75–77 [D3^{v-r}].

page 262 Footnote: "New England got pared off from Virginia by letters patent" — Stolen from Byrd, p. 4.

page 263 The swords-for-turkeys affair and its aftermath — *The Generall Historie,* 3rd Book, pp. 159–60 [54].

page 267 Calculation of interval since the creation of the world — After Madox, p. 70, corrected for interval between 1582 and 1607.

The Grammar of Explorers

page 268 Angelic Angli epitaph — Strachey, op. cit., p. 6 (dedication).

page 268 Shark epigraph — Quinn, vol. 1, p. 230 (Sir Richard Hawkins, *Observations,* 1593).

page 268 "If you live thirty years, my boy . . ." — almost verbatim from a descendant in the fourth generation, p. 95 ["On Oeconomy: An Address to His Son, by the Author of the Memoir"].

page 269 Footnote on Catharine Lady Watson — Mee, p. 349 ("Echoes of Famous Names": Spilsby).

page 270 Lord Willoughby's passing mention of Deeping Fen and Crowland monastery — after Wheeler, pp. 314–15. Wheeler is in part quoting from Camden's history of England.

page 272 The expulsion from the council of Captain Archer — Barbour (Jamestown), vol. 1, p. 228 (Wingfield's discourse).

page 273 "God send us all to do for the best" — After Madox, p. 81.

page 273 Procedure of measuring the "Arctick Pole" with the astrolabe — After Bourne, p. 84 ("Almanacke for Three Yeares," 1571).

page 274 The dragon of Castle Carleton in Lincolnshire — A.E.B. Owen, ed., *The Me-*

dieval Lindsey Marsh: Select Documents (Bury St. Edmonds, Suffolk: The Lincoln Record Society, The Boydell Press, 1996), p. 33 (document 15: "Castle Carlton: The Extent of the Seignory, 1424–25").

page 275 Discovery of Accomack, tale of the dead children, etc. — After the Third Book of the *Generall Historie,* in Smith, vol. ii, pp. 163 [56] ff. Kiptopeke's direct question to Smith as to whether the English caused the epidemic in his country is interpolated. Barbour in *Three Worlds* (p. 201) contents himself with remarking that the werowance's tale "may have had some hidden motive."

page 277 Smith's ditty about the doxy dell — Actually, a "canting song," from Dekker, p. 301, verse 3. This author "Englishes" the song (which he probably heard in debtor's prison), on p. 302. If I were to re-English it into a later form, it might read:

> This bouncing whore can fancily speak;
>   And fuck well for a penny,
> And snatch and steal most admirably
>   From every country town she passes.

page 277 Remainder of first voyage in the Chesapeake — Smith, loc. cit., to end of ch. V. (p. 169 [59]).

page 280 Footnote: the English chaplain's diary entry — Madox, p. 274.

page 282 Smith's difficulties on the voyage — "Even with the benefit of John Smith's training course in guerrilla warfare, wearing a heavy helmet and at the very least an iron breast- and backplate, he remained the equivalent of a tank in the jungles of Southeast Asia" (Hume, *The Virginia Adventure,* p. 208).

page 282 Navigability of the Potomac River — After Jefferson, *Notes on the State of Virginia),* Query II; op. cit., p. 131.

page 283 Description of Patawomeck Town — After the *Generall Historie* (as cited above), and also after some basic facts and hypotheses spelled out in Stephen R. Potter, *Commoners, Tribute, and Chiefs: The Development of Algonquian Culture in the Potomac Valley* (Charlottesville: University Press of Virginia, 1993). Potter has little to say about Patawomeck Town itself, but his remarks on the contents of middens, trash pits, etc. are helpful.

page 283 The double palisadoes of Patawomeck Town — Potter writes (p. 207) that two protohistoric Potomac sites in this area were fortified thus. Therefore, Patawomeck Town might have been.

page 285 Medical properties of antimony — After Basil Valentine (fl. 1604), "Triumph-Wagen des Antimoni," in Henry M. Leicester and Herbert S. Klickstein, *A Source Book in Chemistry 1400–1900* (Cambridge, Massachusetts: Harvard University Press, 1952), p. 29 (discussion of antimony oxide and oxychloride).

page 287 The second voyage through the Chesapeake — Following 3rd Book of the *Generall Historie,* ch. VI.

page 288 "Yndian bread made of guinea wheat" — After the culinary description of George Percy, who visited Kecoughtan in 1607; Barbour (Jamestown), vol. 1, p. 135 (George Percy's discourse, before 12 April 1612).

page 289 Signs of hatchet use in Susquehannock territory; Susquehannock adornments — 2nd Book of the *Generall Historie,* Smith, vol. ii, pp. 105–6 [24].

page 291 *"The* LORD *bringeth the Counsell of the heathen . . ."* — From Psalm 33 (abridged).

page 292 "A people come from under the world," etc. — This dialogue taken near verbatim from 3rd Book of the *Generall Historie,* op. cit., p. 175 [63].

page 293 "You have assaulted me . . . make me satisfaction." — Near verbatim from 3rd Book of the *Generall Historie,* op. cit., p. 177 [67]. But Smith said this in a previous incident.

The Grammar of Blackguards

page 295 Epigraph on the evader of destiny — Nashe, p. 72.

page 295 Description of the council's seal — Barbour (Jamestown), vol. 1, p. 27 (item no. 1: letters patent to Sir Thomas Gates and others, 10 April 1606).

page 295 "He'd stay the building of Ratclyffe's Palace," etc. — After the 3rd Book of the *Generall Historie,* ch. VII, in Smith, vol. ii, pp. 180–81 [66].

page 297 Dining with Duke Humphrey — After Nashe, p. 58 and fn. ("Pierce Penniless his Supplication to the Devil," 1592).

page 300 Machiavelli on colonies — Op. cit., p. 4. Here and elsewere in my citations of this text I have sometimes "archaized" and "Elizabethanized" the spelling, synonymy, etc.

page 300 Machiaveilli on injuries — loc. cit.

page 304 Coronation of the Master of the Poor in Lincoln — Described in Sir Francis Hill, pp. 89–90.

page 305 "We'd have Powhatan's favor much better only for a plain piece of copper!" — Loosely after the 3rd Book of the *Generall Historie,* ch. VII, in Smith, vol. ii, pp. 181 [66].

page 308 Ratcliffe's assertion that Powhatan murdered the Roanoke colonists — After Strachey, p. 58.

page 308 "Full .14. miles" from Jamestown to Werowocomoco — Figure given in the *Generall Historie.* But in the *True Relation* (Smith, vol. i, p. 61 [C3$_v$], we're told that it's "but 12. miles."

page 308 "The season of their feasting & sacrifice" — After the *Generall Historie,* Bk. II ch. "Of their Planted fruits . . ." [28], in Smith, vol. ii, p. 112.

page 309 "The palisadoes of Werowocomoco" — This town might or might not have been palisaded. Rountree writes that towns such as Pattawomeck, which were in locations liable to attack, were thus fortified; and I would suppose that given Powhatan's defensively suspicious nature he would have walled in his home town.

page 310 Saint Matthew's Day as the date of the annual Cattle-Fair "for white meats & for young heifers" — Gough, p. 266. This author was writing about Shropshire, and County Lincoln may well have done things on different dates. But one would think that the seasonal nature of cattlebreeding would require the various fairs for calves, etc. to be at roughly similar times of the year throughout England.

page 310 "Ramsay, the rich of gold and fee . . ." — Wheeler, p. 23. The rhyme, from which I've lifted half, refers to old monasteries in Lincolnshire.

page 311 The Soldiers' fears of being poisoned by a black cherry blossom — After Strachey's vocabulary, sheet B, wherein I find "Amkonnmg," translated as "The blossom of a black Cherry deadly poison."

page 312 "From experience I know that most of their courage proceeds from others' fear" — Near verbatim from Smith, vol. i, *A True Relation,* p. 63 [C4^r].

page 312 The "Virginian masque" — After Smith, *Generall Historie,* 3rd Book, ch. 7, [67], in Smith, vol. ii, pp. 182–83.

page 314 Powhatan's speech to Smith — Near verbatim, from the *Generall Historie,* 3rd Book, ch. 7, [68], in Smith, vol. ii, p. 183.

page 316 "By this, let no man think . . ." — abridged from the *Generall Historie,* 3rd Book, ch. 7, [69], in Smith, vol. ii, p. 185.

page 319 "Captaine Ratliffe is now called Sicklemore . . ." — *Generall Historie,* 3rd Book, ch. 7, [72], in Smith, vol. ii, p. 189.

page 320 "You cannot excuse yourselves . . . come into your river" — Closely after the *Generall Historie,* 3rd Book; in Smith, vol. ii, p. 191 [73].

page 322 Smith's decision to raid the Indians to save the colony from starving — The ethical error made by the English, in my opinion, was their assumption that they were justified in defending terriroity which did not in fact belong to them. For general discussion of this all too common abuse, see the chapter "Defense of Ground" of my unpublished monograph *Rising Up and Rising Down.*

page 322 The "King of Paspahegh" as "counterfeit-faced, Janus-faced" — After a phrase used in another context in Strachey: "He borroweth but a countorfeit face from *Ianus,* to turne to the penall Edict . . ." (p. 8).

The Grammar of Walnuts

page 324 Epigraph on Powhatan's affection — *True Relation,* in Smith, vol. i, p. 67 [D₁ʳ].

The Conquest of Pamunkey

page 325 Epigraph on Smith's forge — Dedicatory verse by Purchas, in *The Generall Historie,* in Smith, vol. ii, p. 48 [A₁ʳ].

page 325 Events of this chapter — *The Generall Historie,* 3rd Book, chs. VIII–IX, pp. 192–207 [74–83]. Speeches of Indian leaders, and Smith's replies, are often near verbatim, with additions.

page 326 Sweet John's procedure for "guesting himself upon Salvages" — Closely after the same, 3rd Book, ch. XII; in Smith, vol. ii, p. 168 [58].

page 327 "The King did throw a morsel into the fire, for a sacrifice to their DEVIL." — After Strachey, p. 98. This practice was limited to "the better sort."

page 327 "What may move the mouse to bite the bait . . ." — George Gascoigne, *The Adventures of Master F.J.* (1573), in Paul Salzman, ed., *An Anthology of Elizabethan Prose Fiction* (New York: Oxford University Press, World's Classics ser., 1987), p. 11.

page 330 The displayed scalps of the Piankatanks — Mentioned by Strachey in 1610. If they were on exhibit then, it seems likely that they would have been in 1609 as well, when the "triumph" was fresher.

page 336 Machiavelli's advice: Attaching Opechancanough to Smith "through baubles & favors" — An interpretation of Machiavelli, p. 11 (ch. VII, "New Principalities").

page 342 "There's no such dangerous service ashore, as a resolved resolute fight at sea." — Closely after the *Sea-Grammar,* ch. XII, in Smith, vol. ii, p. 100 [58].

page 343 Machiavelli on enemies — Op. cit., pp. 4–5.

The Grammar of Oceans

page 345 Dismissed fancies epigraph — Sir Walter Ralegh, *Selected Writings* (New York: Penguin Classics, 1986), p. 28.

page 345 Argall's calculation of the tide — after Bourne, p. 63 (*Almanacke,* Fourth Rule).

page 346 Soft ooze at 140 fathoms — Rosier, p. A4 [recto].

page 346 Soundings for Cape Henrico — Strachey, p. 51.

page 346 "I will not prefer it before our riuer of Thames . . ." — Rosier, p. D3 [recto].

page 347 Argall's service at Berg — Barbour, *Pocahontas and Her World,* p. 70. "Now Rheinberg," notes this biographer.

The Grammar of Gravesend

page 348 Epigraph on malignant times — *Generall Historie,* 5th Book; in Smith, vol. ii, p. 393 [202].

page 348 Events of this chapter — Ibid, 3rd Book, pp. 208–227 [83–94].

page 349 "A ship must go e'er contrary to her helm" — After the *Sea-Grammar,* ch. IX, in Smith, vol. ii, p. 85 [37].

page 356 Definition of Pag-Rag Day — after Wheeler, Appendix IV, p. 11.

page 356 Smith's speech to the "drones" — Abridged from pp. 213–14 [86–87].

page 357 "By so precarious a tenure is the fen land held . . ." — Ibid, p. 39.

page 358 "He is double mad that will leave his friends . . ." — Almost verbatim from the *Advertisements for the Unexperienced Planters of New England, or Any Where,* in Smith, vol. iii, p. 287 [23].

page 360 "And now I've redelivered to all parties their former losses . . . Thus all are friends." — After the *Generall Historie,* 3rd Book, ch. XII; in Smith, vol. ii, p. 223 [92].

page 361 Smith's accident with the gunpowder — After the *Generall Historie,* 3rd Book; in Smith, vol. ii, pp. 223–24 [92–93].

page 362 Ratcliffe to the Earl of Salisbury — 4 October 1609; in Alexander Brown, *The Genesis of the United States . . .* (1890), repr. Russell and Russell, 1964, vol. 2, p. 334.

page 363 "It is written that Pocahontas ceased her visits . . ." — in Thomas De La Warr, *A Short Relation made by the Lord De-La-Ware, to the Lords and others of the Counsel of Virginia . . .* (21 June 1611), facsimile copy, unnumbered, 20 copies from Heliotype Co.; after A.W. Griswold, repr. 1867.

II. Changes of the Moon

The Grammar of Martial Law

page 367 Hobbes epigraph on fear — Thomas Hobbes, *Leviathan, or, Matter, Form, and Power of a Commonwealth Ecclesiastical and Civil* (1651), in Robert Maynard Hutchins, editor in chief, *Great Books of the Western world, vol. 23: Machiavelli-Hobbes* (Chicago: Encyclopaedia Britannica, Inc., 1952), ch. 27 ("Of Crimes, Excuses, and Extenuations"), p. 141. I have re-archaicized the capitalization a little.

page 368 Instructions concerning martial law — Kingsbury, *Records of the Virgina Company,* vol. 3, p. 15, no. V (instructions to Sir Thomas Gates, before 15 May 1609).

page 369 Smith's high catch of sturgeon — *Generall Historie,* 2nd Book, in Smith, vol. 2, p. 103 [23].

page 372 Description of George Percy — After an oil painting, artist unknown, early 17th century, original in collection of Duke of Norfolk.

page 376 The murder of Ratcliffe and his men — Briefly related in the *Generall Historie,* Book IV, no ch. head; in Smith, vol. ii, p. 232 [105].

page 376 Casualties of the "starving time" — Insisting that "the commonly cited number of five hundred English before the winter set in is probably exaggerated" (*Pocahontas's People,* p. 296, n. 171), Rountree, in contradistinction to others, believes that "by May 1610 only 100 out of some 220 English people remained in Virginia, sixty of them in Jamestown" (p. 53).

The Grammar of Daughters

page 377 Table in the wilderness epigraph — John Milton, *Paradise Regained,* II. 337–91.

page 377 Manufacture of bows and arrows — Saxton T. Pope, *Bows and Arrows* (Berkeley: University of California Press, 1930), pp. 3–61; Reginald and Gladys Laubin, *American Indian Archery* (Norman: University of Oklahoma Press, 1980), and Larry D. Olsen, *Outdoor Survival Skills* (Provo, Utah: Brigham Young University Press, 1973), pp. 112–133. These books do not deal specifically with Powhatan material culture. However, these procedures were somewhat generalized. In any event, I have sought to Powhatanize them as much as possible. Thus, for instance, Rountree mentions that "English records say nothing of sinew backing or other devices" (*The Powhatan Indians of Virginia: Their Traditional Culture* [Norman: University of Oklahoma Press; The Civilization of the North American Indian ser., vol. 193, 1989], p. 42), so I have omitted that step. The illustration of the Powhatan man Eiakintomino posing with his accoutrements in Saint James's Park (facing page) clearly shows that his bow was tapered, so I have described tapering. The description of cutting the bow-stave from the tree is after a Leni Lenape method described in Laubin, pp. 56–57; the Leni Lenape were culturally related to the Powhatan.

page 379 Kocoum's courtship and marriage of Pocahontas — After the general procedure described in Rountree, *The Powhatan Indians*, p. 90.

page 388 Effectiveness of Indian arrows in killing deer — "In general," says Pope (p. 59), "it may be stated that aboriginal arrows are inferior in make and shooting qualities when compared with those of higher grades of material culture." However, "from the experience derived from . . . many . . . hunting episodes, I am covinced that an arrow that enters either the abdominal or chest cavity of a large animal does as much damage as a bullet, and even seems to cause more hemorrhage than most rifle bullets" (p. 61).

The Grammar of Wives, .1.ˢᵗ part

page 389 Tribute to Powhatan — According to Strachey (p. 87), Powhatan took 80% of all his subjects' skins, beans, grain, etc. for himself.

The Grammar of Hogs

page 391 John Donne epigraph — Jones, p. 638, no. 458.

page 391 "My elder brother Richard was Standard-bearer to a Captaine Scott in the Low Countreys." — Based on Barbour, *Pocahontas,* pp. 262–63, notes 4, 16.

page 394 "I earnestly entreat you all . . .", etc. — Somewhat verbatim, from *The Generall Historie,* 4th Book, p. 235 [107].

page 396 "The heathen rage . . ." — Second Psalm.

page 396 Machiavelli on the dangers of conquering free cities — op. cit., p. 8.

page 397 Distinction between "High Virginia, & Virginia's Low Countreys" — After Strachey, pp. 32–33.

page 398 "He discovereth deep things out of darkness . . ." — Job 12.12 (old King James version).

page 399 "Marriage brings you into cousinage with me." — See Barbour, *Pocahontas,* p. 76.

page 399 "A good Mariner, & a very civil Gentleman." — Barbour (Jamestown), vol. 2, p. 281 (Gabriel Archer to an unknown friend, 31 August 1609).

page 400 The Spanish rumor that Powhatan sends spies to West India and Newfoundland — Barbour (Jamestown), vol. 1, p. 154 (item 31: Francis Magnel's relation, 1610).

page 402 "The Sassafrass call'd *Rhubarbum album"* — After Strachey, p. 39.

page 402 Date of the attack on Kecoughtan — I have followed Rountree's use of 9 July (*Pocahontas's People,* p. 54). Barbour (*Pocahontas,* p. 77) gives 10 July.

page 403 fn "This grass-silk is said to be of the same substance from which the Chinese make their damask." — Loosely after Strachey, p. 36.

page 408 Lord Delaware's exhortations to the officers before the massacre at Paspahegh — If there were any, they've not been recorded. In my opinion, Delaware's administration marked the transition from the hit-or-miss imperialism of Wingfield,

Ratcliffe, Smith and Percy to the methodical destruction of Indian elites and noncombatants for the purposes of terror. The conquest of Kecoughtan was as coldblooded and treacherous in its conception as Powhatan's murder of Ratcliffe and his men. To be sure, it proved less cruel in the execution. No one was tortured to death, and quite possibly fewer Indians were killed than the number of Ratcliffe's unhappy crew. Yet the result of Powhatan's self-defensive treachery was only that the English became enraged. The result of the raid on Kecoughtan was that an Indian town was obliterated forever, and its territory lost to the invaders. The destruction of Paspahegh comprised an escalation of these tactics up to the threshold of genocide. The murder of the "queen" and her children, together with the destruction of the corn on which the Paspeghs depended for the winter, seems to me unspeakably wicked. It prefigures the actions taken against the Indians on a much wider scale after Opechancanough's rebellions of 1622 and 1644. For this reason, I have for moral reasons, if no others, based Lord Delaware's speech on Himmler's infamous remarks to an SS gathering on 4 October 1943: "Most of you must know what it means to see a hundred corpses lie side by side, or five hundred, or a thousand. To have stuck this out and — excepting cases of human weakness — to have kept our integrity, this is what has made us hard. In our history, this is an unwritten and never-to-be-written page of glory . . ." (quoted in Lucy S. Dawidowicz, *The War Against the Jews 1933-1945* [New York: Holt, Rinehart & Winston, 1975], p. 149).

page 409 *"Yet have I set my King . . ."* — Second Psalm.

page 410 Percy's previous attempt to capture Wowinchopunck — Strachey, pp. 66–67.

page 411 Order of the "Yndian Townes" encountered by the murderers between Jamestown and Paspahegh — After inspection of the *Map of Virginia, with a Description of the COVNTREY, the Commodities, People, Government and Religion* (1612), in Smith, vol. 1, pp. 140-41 (1st state of Smith/Hole map).

page 417 Eastward orientation of Powhatan temples, and their general layout — Strachey, pp. 88–89.

page 420 "Tis the custom for each ship in the fleet to sail under the lee of her Admirall . . ." — After the *Sea Grammar,* ch. XIII, in Smith, vol. iii, p. 103 [62].

page 422 Ruffles stained with puccoons by sexual activity — A detail stolen from Byrd, p. 120.

Red Skies

page 430 Epigraph on English forbearance — *The Generall Historie,* 3rd Book, p. 206 [82], written by William Box.

page 430 Argall's explorations; the raid on the Warraskoyacks — After Barbour, *Pocahontas,* ch. 7.

A Comedy

page 436 Queen Oppussonoquonuske — Rountree (*The Powhatan Indians,* p. 108) believes that she was not the same "Queen of Appatamuck" who washed Smith's hands at Werowocomoco in 1608. Barbour believes that she was.

Various Processionals

page 438 Epigraph on the virtues of "absolute Commaund" — Strachey, pp. 90–91.

page 438 Nautical commands — *A Sea Grammar,* ch. IX; in Smith, vol. iii, pp. 85–87 [37–40].

page 438 A few of Argall's phrases in this chapter have been lifted from "A Letter of Sir Samuell Argoll touching his Voyage to Virginia, and Actions there: Written to Master Nicholas Hawes. June 1613" (Purchas, iv., pp. 1764–65).

page 439 Argall's commission and meeting with Percy — Barbour, *Pocahontas*, pp. 96–97.

page 440 Description of Dover — After a picture in Christopher Morris, ed., *The Illustrated Journeys of Celia Fiennes 1685-1712* (London: Macdonald & Co., 1982), p. 122.

page 441 The sailors' cries as they lower items into the hold — *A Sea Grammar*, ch. VII; in Smith, vol. iii, p. 82 [33].

page 442 "The Countrey people . . . tractable & friendly . . ." — After De La Warr's relation; quoted in *The Generall Historie*, 4th Book, p. 238 [109].

page 443 Sir Thomas Dale's authority — For much of this period he was technically only Marshal, while Sir Thomas Gates was Governor. But Dale became Governor, and it seemed tediously unimportant to go through all this while compressing time here anyhow.

page 444 Henrico founded in part "to make alliance with Powhatan's enemies the *Monacans*" — After a hint in Strachey, p. 107.

page 444 Distance to the site of Henrico — See citation to "Fifty miles by water to Reverend Whitaker's, near Henrico," p. 734, for the section "The Grammar of Kidnappers."

page 444 "Without the losse of any, excepting some few Salvages" — *The Generall Historie*, 4th Book, p. 242 [111].

page 445 Qualifications of a "maister of ships of Nauigation" — Bourne, p. 170 (*Regiment for the Sea*, 1574 ed., ch. 28).

page 445 "And furthermore . . ." — Ibid, p. 171.

page 446 Argall's visit to Pattawomeck — Barbour (op. cit., p. 87) writes that it occurred at Christmas. Rountree (*Pocahontas's People*, p. 57) puts it during "the fall."

The Grammar of Kidnappers

page 448 Fish epigraph — J.D. Esquire [John Denys], *The Secrets of Angling: Teaching the Choicest Tools, Baits and Seasons, for the taking of Any Fish in Pond or River: practised and familiarly opened in three Books*, in [Prof. Arber], *An English Garner: Social England Illustrated: A Collection of XVIIth Century Tracts* (New York: Dutton, n.d.), p. 215. I have made occasional use of Denys in my fishing similes and metaphors throughout this book.

page 448 The abduction of Pocahontas — Told in Hamor, pp. 4–6. It is also very possible that Argall kidnapped the "Princesse" on his own initiative, not on Sir Thomas Dale's orders. The sources seem unclear. Barbour, who somewhat admires Argall, writes in his *Pocahontas* (p. 103): "Whatever colors one chooses to paint the picture of Argall's action . . . nothing more vicious was in his mind than acquiring a hostage worth a great deal by ransom. The caution he employed in carrying out his plan furthermore reflects, for all its calculated callousness, a quick and active mind, not by any means lacking in knowledge of human weaknesses or, on the other hand, in kindness." I imagine him to be a little less kind.

page 450 Respective locations of Japzaws and Pocahontas — Barbour (op. cit.) had Argall proceeding "directly to Pastancie — whose location we no longer know" (pp. 103–04). This was a "satellite town" of the capital, where Japzaws lived. Rountree (*Pocahontas's People*, p. 58) has Argall go straight to Pattawomeck Town. Smith's *Generall Historie* says the same (4th Book, p. 243 [112]). Strachey (p. 101) writes that in 1610 Argall had traded with Jazpzaws near the town of Mattchipongo. For the sake of simplicity I have followed Rountree and Smith.

page 456 The Waist-ladder — I had originally imagined that the sailors would throw down a rope ladder, but Smith's *Sea-Grammar* says the "the entering Ladder is in the Waist, made formally of wood" (ch. II, in Smith, vol. ii, p. 64 [9]). One would think that in those piratical days such a ladder would make it too easy for a ship to be boarded by enemies, but I trust Smith, who was there when I wasn't.

page 456 Structure and fittings of the *Treasurer;* and especially the location of the gun-room — Again I have relied on the diagrams in Brian Lavery's *Susan Constant.* Smith's *Sea-Grammar* also guided me here.

page 457 Footnote on Iapazeus's reward — Hamor, p. 5.

page 457 The same footnote: Smith's remarks on Iapazeus as "the old Jew," &c — Cobbled together from *The Generall Historie,* 4th Book, in Smith, vol. ii, pp. 243–44 [112].

page 458 Pocahontas's silent resentment — Here I recall the observations of John Lawson as he trekked the Carolinas in 1700: "Amongst Women, it seems impossible to find a Scold; if they are provok'd, or affronted, by their Husbands, or some other, they resent the Indignity offer'd them in silent Tears, or by refusing their Meat" (op. cit., p. 43).

page 459 "Her pumps could suck up little more than sea-froth" — Somewhat after the *Sea-Grammar,* ch. II, in Smith, vol. ii, p. 63 [9].

page 459 Pocahontas's doleful noise and fingernail-scratching — after Barbour (Jamestown), vol. 1, p. 134 (Percy's discourse). Percy is describing a custom of the Powhatans whereby they scratched the earth with their fingernails upon the arrival of the English. The significance of this act is unknown.

page 461 Pocahontas in the hold — This probably never happened. The historical Argall would have feared to increase her resentment through such treatment. Why then did I feel impelled to envision it? Years after my first conception of the scene, I came across the following passage: ". . . a Sadeian view of the dream suggests that the dreamer fortunately — *felix culpa* — finds herself in prison, cut off from green life, isolated and therefore on a path toward a deeper, darker way of imagining" (Thomas Moore, *Dark Eros: The Imagination of Sadism* [Dallas, Texas: Spring Publications, Inc., 1992], p. 85, "Isolation and Confinement"). It would be offensive to imply that anybody subject to literal imprisonment, as indeed was Pocahontas, was fortunate, and when I call her that in the text passage to which this citation is keyed, some sarcasm may be involved. But my own experience of suffering is that if I try very hard, and gain luck or guidance, I may be able to derive a little meaning from it. Who was Pocahontas and what did she become? Surely the kidnapping must have been one of the most transformative experiences of her life. She became coverted or brainwashed into Rebecca. I am angry and sad for her that it had to happen, that she couldn't have been left alone. But let's do her the credit of supposing that her sea-change, although it must have maimed her, was not entirely unaccompanied by what we now call "personal growth."

page 466 Argall's negotiations with Powhatan — It is unclear to me (and, I think, to everyone else) whether Argall actually dealt with Powhatan himself, as I have assumed, which necessitates the further assumption that he waited before bearing his prisoner to Jamestown, where Sir Thomas Dale would surely take over all negotiations; or whether in fact he did go straight back to Jamestown, which is how Barbour imagines it in his *Pocahontas* (p. 108). I prefer the former scenario, because Argall explicitly says in his letter of June 1613 (cited earlier) that "having received this answer" from Powhatan's emissary, "I presently departed from patowomeck, being the 13. of Aprill . . ."

page 468 "Heave ahead! Men into the tops! Down foresail!" — After Smith, vol. iii, p. 85 [38] (*A Sea Grammar,* ch. IX).

page 469 Description of shrouds and dead men's eyes — Ibid, ch. V, p. 71 [19–20].

page 469 "Two rows of houses now hath Jamestowne . . ." — Description after Smith's *Generall Historie,* 4th Book; ibid, p. 242 [112].

page 469 Description of Jamestown fort — after a painting by Sidney King for Colonial National Historical Park, reproduced in Charles E. Hatch, Jr., *The First Seventeen Years: Virginia, 1607-1624* (Charlottesville: The University Press of Virginis, 1957), 2nd illus. in front group (bef. p. 1).

page 470 "Attorneys. Deputies . . . and Servants" — Quinn, vol. 1, p. 87 (letters patent to Sir Walter Ralegh, 28 March 1584); spelling modernized, capitalization rendered consistent.

page 471 "Pray tell him that his daughter shall remain well used . . ." — Partly verbatim from *The Generall Historie,* 4th Book, in Smith, vol. ii, p. 244 [112] (who in turn is cribbing from Hamor), but I have made Argall's version slightly more stinging.

page 472 "He, being quit of his prisoner . . ." — almost verbatim, from Argall, "A Letter from Sir Samuel Argall, Touching His Voyage to Virginia . . . , Iune 1613," in Purchas, p. 1765.

page 473 The capital punishments under Sir Thomas Dale — Hume, *The Virginia Adventure,* pp. 320–21. Barbour likewise mentions the gallows, whipping, and shooting "almost daily" (*Pocahontas and Her World,* p. 151).

page 473 ".50. miles by water to Reverend Whitaker's, near Henrico" . . . — For some quibbling with this seventeenth-century estimate (the current distance "would be about fifty-five miles, though differences in the river-channel could add something"), see Babour, *Pocahontas and Her World,* p. 118. Hamor likewise says "fiftie miles" (*Generall Historie,* 4th Book, p. 242 [112]). One source says "eighty miles."

page 477 Reverend Whittaker's imputation that OKEUS sucks young boys' blood — Barbour (Jamestown), p. 149 (William White, fragment published in 1614, wr. *ca.* 1608).

page 486 Life and character of John Rolfe — Derived from his letter to Sir Thomas Dale requesting permission to marry Pocahontas, from his will, and from Babour, *Pocahontas and Her World.*

page 487 Powhatan lore mentioned by Pocahontas: drying of tobacco over a fire — Rountree, *The Powhatan Indians,* p. 47.

page 488 Rolfe's tobacco "which I've raised up from Trinidad seeds . . ." — After an inference in Barbour, *Pocahontas and Her World,* p. 117.

page 488 Virtues of planting with the moon in Taurus, Cancer, Virgo, Libra or Capricorn — After Bourne, p. 51 (*Almanacke for Three Yeares,* sec. "For setting, sowynge and Planting").

page 490 Speed's depiction of "Hicham" in Norfolk — Op. cit., pp. 130–31 ("NORFOLK, A COVNTIE FLORISHING & POPVLOVS, DESCRIBED AND DEVIDED WITH THE ARMES OF SVCH NOBLE FAMILIES AS HAVE BORNE THE TITLES THEREOF").

page 490 "There is an herbe called Vppówoc" — Harriot, p. 16 (my abridgement).

page 490 The list of English "vegetables" planted by Rolfe — Culled from Strachey's list of experimental produce, p. 39.

page 490 Footnote: "This dear bought Land . . ." — *Generall Historie,* 4th Book, p. 255 [119].

page 491 Rolfe's dead wife Anne — Actually, her name has been lost. See Barbour, *Pocahontas and Her World,* p. 116.

page 493 Description of the temples at Uttamussak — After Strachey, p. 95.

page 494 The invisible bullets of English disease — Opined by the Algonkian people near Roanoke in 1585–86, according to Harriot, p. 29.

page 495 "Uttamattomakkin spoke unto OKEUS in the magic language, and OKEUS said: *She is lost."* — According to Rountree's *Powhatan Indians,* (p. 131), priests were uniquely good at finding things, which is why I brought Uttamattomakkin into it. Moreover, only priests could speak directly with OKEUS. The "magic language" is mentioned on the same page. Rountree describes the temple interiors on p. 134.

page 500 "As clean as the water from black cherries" — After Nicholas Hilliard, *A Treatise Concerning the Arte of Limning,* ed. R.K.R. Thornton and T.G.S. Cain Manchester, U.K.: The Mid Northumberland Arts Group, Carcanet Press, 1992 repr. of *ca.* 1600 ed.), p. 53.

The Grammar of Husbands

page 502 Epistle of Yuo epigraph — C. Raymond Beazley, M.A., F.R.G.S., ed., *The Texts and Versions of John de Plano Carpini and WIlliam de Rubruquis, as printed for the first time by [Richard] Haklyut in 1598, together with some shorter pieces* (London: Hakluyt Society, M.DCCCCIII).

page 503 "I come to bring Powhatan his daughter . . . If not, I shall burn all." — almost verbatim, from Dale, "A Letter from Sir Thomas Dale . . . Iune 18, 1614," in Purchas, p. 1769. The whole account of this parley and its aftermath is based on Dale.

page 504 "Where go you? . . . and has been agreed upon." — Verbatim, loc. cit.

page 504 "Why did you burn our houses? . . . in equal measure your friends" — Almost verbatim from *The Generall Historie,* 4th Book; in Smith, vol. ii, p. 244 [113]; after Hamor.

page 505 Dale's letter; speech of Powhatan, speech of Opachankano — Purchas, loc. cit., almost verbatim.

page 507 Footnote: Payment of four pennies, &c when entering England — Groos, loc. cit.

page 508 Divorce: "And he may have the house and grinding-stone; 'tis the law" — After the procedure described in Rountree, p. 91.

page 509 Simile of Rolfe and the murderer with two ravens — After a tale told in Gough, p. 122.

page 509 Footnote: "Fury is a heat or fire . . ." — Nashe, p. 85 ("Pierce Pennliess").

page 510 Reverend Buck's sermon — Loosely after Judges 21.

page 510 Rolfe's mariage with Pocahontas — For procedure involved in seventeenth-century marriages which followed Church of England style, I have relied on Emily Pearson, *Elizabethans at Home: A Complete Picture of a Way of Life* (Stanford: Stanford University Press, 1957), on Alan Macfarlane, *Marriage and Love in England: Modes of Reproduction 1300-1840* (London: Basil Blackwell, 1986), and, with caution, on David Hackett Fischer, *Albion's Seed: Four British Folkways in America* (New York: Oxford University Press, 1989), pp. 281–86. (The caution comes from the fact that the Virginian marriages described by Fischer were based on the lifeways of south England, not on the lifeways of Lincolnshire or of nearby Norfolk, where John Rolfe was from. The observances, at least, are likely to have been fairly uniform; Anglicanism at this time had little tolerance for dissenters.) Macfarlane claims (p. 310) that until 1753 no religious coloring was required of an English marriage; Fischer implies the opposite.

page 511 "In a decent and comely manner . . ." — Wording used by John Rolfe himself in his will (but relating to his burial), as reproduced by Jane Carson in *Virginia Historical Magazine,* vol. XXX, p. 61.

page 511 "No man hath labored to his power . . ." — Hamor, p. 24.

page 511 Intermarriage as policy — In 1728, William Byrd wrote admiringly of the French practice in this respect in Canada. "Had the English done this at the first Settlement of the Colony," he went on, "the Infidelity of the Indians had worn out at this

Day, with their Dark Complexions, and the Country had swarm'd with People more than it does with Insects . . . I venture to say, the Indian Women would have made altogether as Honest Wives for the First Planters, as the Damsels they us'd to purchase from aboard the Ships. It is Strange, therefore, that any good Christian Shou'd have refused a wholesome, Straight Bed-fellow, when he might have had so fair a Portion with her, as the Merit of saving her Soul" (op. cit., pp. 120–22, *History*).

page 514 "And how does my brother Sir Thomas Dale? . . . if we return not well, you must expect a revenge." — After *The Generall Historie,* 4th Book, pp. 248–50 [115–16], some of this almost verbatim, but abridged. The vassal of the Tassantasses was Ralph Hamor.

The Grammar of Pillagers

page 517 Virginia epitaph — Parke Rouse, Jr., *Virginia: A Pictorial History* (New York: Scribner, 1975), p. 18.

page 517 A certain interesting theory about Canada — According to the French lawyer Lescarbot, who spent some time in Acadia, since the flies of Canada are red like foul blood, then they must breed among rotten wood.

page 519 "How now, sirrah . . ." — almost verbatim from Père Biard's *Relation* of 1616, in *The Jesuit Relations,* ed. R.G. Thwaites (Cleveland: The Burrows Brothers Company, 1896), vol. 4: Acadia and Québec 1616–20 (1897), p. 11.

page 519 "But I am very much astonished . . ." — Ibid, p. 13.

page 520 "For whom the LORD loveth . . ." — Proverbs, 3.

page 521 Argall's transactions among the Dutch — mentioned very briefly in an article by H. Ludwig, *Collections of the New York Historical Society,* second series, vol. 1 (1841). Ludwig cites a few hints by Beauchamp Plantagent, Esq., *A Description of the Province of New Albion* (1648), a book which I have been unable to locate. Ludwig suggests that one good reason for the paucity of information about Argall's raid on Port Royal and also his threatening mission to the Dutch was that the English were publicly embarrassed by them, at a time when relations with France and Holland were already strained. As for the letter from Charles T. Gehring which I have quoted, this is accurate and verbatim. Even spectacle-loving Parkman in his *Pioneers of France in the New World* allows, somewhat wistfully, that the story might be untrue.

page 522 Argall's trade on the Eastern Chesapeacke . . . — After Rountree, *Powhatan Foreign Relations,* p. 139 (ch. 6, Thomas E. Davidson, "Relations Between the Powhatans and the Eastern Shore").

III: The Golden Number
The Grammar of Wives, .2.ⁿᵈ Part

page 525 Description of Pocahontas and her son — After the Sedgeford Hall portrait (1615). Many biographers believe it to represent Pocahontas. Barbour writes: ". . . I was able to inspect the painting and to convince myself that it has nothing to do with Pocahontas. Dr. Sturtevant believes that it may represent an 18th-century Iroquois mother and child . . ." *Pocahontas and Her World,* p. 235.

page 525 "Behold, thou art fair . . ." — Song of Solomon, ch. 1.

page 526 Pocahontas's care of her newborn child: washing in the river, painting with puccoons, oiling with bear-fat, cradle board — After the general procedure described in Rountree, *The Powhatan Indians,* p. 94.

page 529 "This is the service IEUSUS CHRIST requireth of his best Servaunts." — Rolfe's letter to Sir Thomas Dale, repr. in Barbour, *Pocahontas,* p. 250. This paragraph and the proceeding one contain many shorter phrases from the same letter, often altered for my purposes.

page 529 History and procedures of tobacco-growing — I have relied a little on Joseph C. Robert's *The Story of Tobacco in America* (New York: Alfred A. Knopf, 1949). Indian tobacco was *Nicotiana rustica.* Rolfe tried *Nicotiana tabacum.*

page 529 Severities of Sir Thomas Dale at Jamestown during 1614–16 — In his *Pocahontas,* Barbour writes (p. 146): ". . . while it is certain that peace still reigned with the Indians, the peace that reigned within the colony may have been the peace of a detention camp."

page 529 "More than three hundred Englishmen now dwelt in Virginia . . ." — Barbour, *Pocahontas and Her World,* p. 152.

page 533 "I will heartily accept it as a GODly tax imposed upon me . . ." — Rolfe's letter to Sir Thomas Dale, repr. in Barbour, *Pocahontas,* p. 250.

page 535 "Rolfe, now stood legally seized of a certain parcel of land . . ."— After wording used by John Rolfe himself in his will, *Virginia Historical Magazine,* p. 62.

page 535 Virtues of grafting with the moon in Taurus or Aquarius — After Bourne, p. 51 (*Almanacke for Three Yeares,* sec. "For setting, sowynge and Planting").

page 535 *"God judgeth the righteous . . ."* — Seventh Psalm.

page 539 "She thought it absurd enough that he insisted upon being her entire support" — A common Powhatan sentiment about English husbands. See Rountree, *Pocahontas's People,* p. 156.

page 541 " 'Tis not my hungry appetite . . ." — Rolfe's letter to Sir Thomas Dale, repr. in Barbour, *Pocahontas,* p. 251.

page 544 "She did secretly offer some suet to OKEUS upon the altar-stone." — After Strachey, p. 96.

page 545 Arise Evans's marriage of non-contradiction — Related in Christopher Hill, *Change and Continuity in Seventeenth-Century England,* p. 53.

page 546 Pocahontas's treatment of Thomas's infected leg — There is no record of his suffering any such ailiment, but he plausibly could have. For her course of curing I have followed Lawson, p. 230, assuming that the medicinal value of sassafrass in North Carolina and in Virginia would have been much the same, and the curing procedures also similar.

page 552 Argall's pretended worries about "Tobacco-mungers" — After *The Generall Historie,* 4th Book, relation of Argall and Rolfe; in Smith, vol. ii, pp. 266 [126].

page 553 "Sails to the yards! Stretch forward your main halyards!" — After Smith, vol. iii, p. 85 [38] (*A Sea Grammar,* ch. IX).

page 553 Extract from the letters patent: Self-defense — Barbour (Jamestown), vol. 1, p. 29 (item no. 1: letters patent to Sir Thomas Gates and others, 10 April 1606), abridged.

page 554 Extract from Virginia Watson's *Legend of Pocahontas* — p. 196.

page 554 Drinking wormwood-juice against seasickness — Madox, p. 119.

page 555 "Being well-bowed, she made a foamy wake . . ." — After the *Sea-Grammar,* ch. 2, in Smith, vol. ii, p. 64 [10].

page 555 "Steady-yarded, with a goose-wing boom . . ." — After ibid, ch. IX, p. 88 [41].

page 555 The helmsman and compass — Ibid, p. 66 [12].

page 556 "A queer cove of the Deuceville" &c — A "canting song," in Dekker, p. 307, first verse; "Englished" by me (based on glossary on pp. 193-95) as follows:

> A yokel from the country
>   Did tup a whore in Turvey.
> He gave her goods & clothes & cash
>   But his fucking was but lousy.

> *Yet would he screw*
> *with a woman, with a whore,*
> *with a married dame with a trull,*
> *And not come away from the alehouse*
> *till he was drunk right up to his hat.*

page 557 Soundings for Ushant and the Lizard — Bourne, pp. 270–71 (*A Regiment for the Sea,* 1574 ed., ch. 22, which "treateth of the soundings, commyng from any place out of the Occident Sea, to seeke Vshant or the Lyzarde . . .").

page 557 Rendition of Plymouth in Speed's atlas — Op. cit., pp. 64–65 ("DEVONSHIRE WITH EXCESTER DESCRIBED And the Armes of such Nobles as haue borne the titles of them").

page 558 Plymouth as anciently a nest of Pirates — After the brief discussion in Youings, pp. 29–38 ("Fishermen and Privateers").

page 558 Footnoted attractions of Plymouth — After Fiennes, pp. 202–03.

The Grammar of Circuses

page 560 Masked murder epigraph — Tourneur, p. 110 (V.i.170–71).

page 560 Description of the Thames panaorama with the Tower — After an engraving by Claes Visscher (1616), reproduced (detail) in Hume, *The Virginia Adventure,* p. 115.

page 561 Description of Saint Peter's — After the colored engraving in Speed, p. 122 ("MIDDLESEX described with the famous Cities of London and Westminster").

page 561 Dangers of bathing with the moon in Taurus — After Bourne, p. 51 (*Almanacke for Three Yeares,* sec. "To Bathe").

page 568 "Half a penny for Christ His sake" — after Nicoll, p. 49 "Begging Bread for Prisoners" in "The Manner of Crying Things in London."

page 568 "Doxy O!" &c — Another "canting song," in Dekker, p. 303, verse 1; "Englished" on p. 304 as follows:

> O my chuck, by th' Mass I swear,
>   Thine eyes than fire do shine more clear!
> No rustling girl hath thighs like thine,
>   No doe was ever bucked like mine.

The meaning is, however, still more lascivious.

page 572 "She was already gaunt from consumption . . .": Circumstances of the one authentic portrait of Pocahontas — "That her drawn features were the product of a wasting disease and did not mirror her previous healthy appearance cannot be proved, yet it is hard to believe that any artist would have drawn the twenty-one-year-old 'poor innocent Pocahontas,' as Smith described her, in so unflattering a portrait had there been no reason to do so" (Hume, *The Virginia Adventure,* p. 348).

page 572 Pocahontas in Heacham — "No tangible evidence of a visit to Heacham exists. Yet where tradition is so strong, it would be futile to deny that it could have taken place" (Barbour, *Pocahontas,* p. 161).

page 575 Hilliard on the delicate pink normally to be seen around peoples' eyes — Op. cit., p. 103.

page 575 "You gave Powhatan a white dog . . ." — *The Generall Historie,* 4th Book, in Smith, vol. ii, p. 261 [123], almost verbatim.

page 575 ". . . When and where a horizontal moon doth make a full sea" — After Madox, p. 162.

page 576 Pocahontas at the masque — John Nichols, F.S.A., *The Progresses, Processions and Magnificent Festivities of King James the First, his Royal Consorts, Family, and Court, &c,* (London: J.B. Nichols, Printer to the Society of Antiquaries, 1828), vol. 3, p. 243

("Masques: Virginian Woman at Court, 1616–17; Mr. Chamberlain to Sir Dudley Carleton"). A footnote refers us to Birch's MSS (Brit. Museum 4173).

page 576 Costumes at the masque — For some of these I've drawn on notes I made during a visit to the Costume Museum at Bath in May 1995. I have occasionally used these elsewhere in the text as well.

The Grammar of Endearments

page 580 Epigraph on love's alembic — Fowler, p. 103 (John Donne, "A Nocturnal upon S. Lucy's Day, Being the Shortest Day").

page 580 Horse-stealers' tricks — After Dekker, pp. 223–27 ("Rank Riders" in *English Villainies Discovered by Lantern and Candlelight*).

page 581 "A wet Docke is any place . . ." — *A Sea Grammar,* in Smith, vol. iii, p. 57 [1]. I have modernized a few spellings.

page 582 "I repent myself to have writ . . ." + "And do you remember the courtesies I did you? . . . your Countreymen will lie much." — *The Generall Historie,* 4th Book, in Smith, vol. ii, pp. 260–61 [122–23], almost verbatim.

page 583 "Should she not be well received . . ." — From Smith's letter to Queen Anne, whose "abstract" is quoted in Barbour, *Pocahontas and Her World,* p. 158.

page 583 Smith's avowed reasons for not visiting Pocahontas: emnity of Wingfield, Percy and De La Warr — Ibid, p. 165.

The Grammar of Churches

page 587 Trump of death epigraph — Strachey, op. cit., p. 65.
page 587 "In the wilderness . . ." Isaiah 40.3–4.

Gravesend

Further History of the Willoughby de Eresby Family

page 591 Pevsner and Harris — These worthies also remark, noting the late arrival of the Renaissance in this district (p. 65), that "life in the mist-enshrouded Fens and the inaccessible Wolds must still have been feudal."

page 591 Domesday Book footnote — John Morgan, vol. 31, part 1, p. 3: 340 d. My rendering lies somewhere between the entirely modernized facing text and its original referent.

page 592 Description of Baroness Willoughby de Eresby's monument at Swinstead — Mee, p. 378 ("Cross-Legged Knight and Kneeling Duke": Swinstead).

page 592 Barty's marsh-quarrel with Sir Philip Lunden — mentioned in Wheeler, p. 101.

page 592 Footnote: "Ignorant, or envious . . ." — Hamor, p. iv.

page 592 "There emerged a decisive influence in county affairs . . ." — Sir Francis Hill, p. 195.

page 593 "Red-roofed cottages," "Empire-builder," etc. — Mee, pp. 417–18 ("A Shining Place in History": Willoughby).

Further History of the Rolfe Family

page 594 Sleep epigraph — Fowler, p. 157, no. 179.
page 595 Joane Pierce, Rolfe's wife — So spelled in Rolfe's will. Other sources list her as Jane Pierce.

page 597 "Nowe for to make your instrumentes for the Sea with their vses . . ." —
Bourne, p. 109 (*Almanacke for Three Yeares,* 1571; Sixteenth Rule).

page 599 Cunning and proud, like the Italians, 'tis said — By Nashe ("Pierce Penniless," p. 73).

Further History of Argall

page 603 Strange dreams epigraph — in Fowler, p. 223, no. 265. Untitled; first published 1976.

page 603 Argall's first four italicized paragraphs — Governor Argall. A letter to the
Virginia Company, March 10. 1617/18, in Kingsbury, vol. 3, p. 92, no. XLIII. Some
contractions are modernized.

page 603 Argall Town — described in Hatch, pp. 36–37.

page 604 Argall as governor — "A reign of systematic robbery." — Barbour, *Three
Worlds,* p. 328.

page 605 "Should any fellow seek to overthrow the life of our Governor . . ." — After
Madox, p. 282.

page 606 "Every person to go to Church . . ." — Governor Argall. Proclamations or
Edicts, May 10, 1618, in Kingsbury, vol. 3, p. 93, no. XLIV.

page 606 "Against teaching the Indians . . ." — Governor Argall. Proclamations or
Edicts, May 18, 1618, in Kingsbury, vol. 3, p. 93, no. XLV. This extract has been
abridged by me.

page 608 Argall's Negro slaves — If this account is true, writes Hume (*The Virginia
Adventure,* p. 359), "the dubious credit for the intent to introduce blacks to Virginia in
the seventeenth century belongs to Argall."

page 608 "All the ways of man are clean . . ." — Proverb 16 (King James version).

page 609 fn Machiavelli's tale of the Duke [Alexander VI and his son Cesare
Borgia] — op. cit., p. 11.

Further History of Virginia

page 611 "The remedy is to send Souldiers" — *The Generall Historie,* 4th Book ("Out
of these Observations it pleased his Majesties Commissioners for the reformation of
Virginia, to desire my answer to these seven Questions," question no. 5), in Smith, vol.
ii, p. 328 [165].

page 611 "He is ignorant of the circumstances . . ." + "The peace shall never be broken
by me . . . to send you the murtherers' heads as soon as I do catch them."— *The Generall Historie,* 4th Book, relation of Argall and Rolfe; in Smith, vol. ii, pp. 264-65 [125],
near verbatim, with additions.

page 612 "Now Ophechankanough will not come at us . . ." — Loc. cit. (Rolfe's letter).

page 612 "Near a dozen ships did come to Virginia, bringing .1216. persons, including
.90. young women to make wives." — Loc. cit.

page 613 "Till their Priests and Ancients have their throats cut . . ." — *The Generall
Historie,* 4th Book, relation of Master Jonas Stockam, Minister; in Smith, vol. ii, p. 286
[140], verbatim.

page 614 "Let us meet together in the house of God . . ." — Nehemiah 6.10.

page 614 "At the losse of this Salvage Opechankanough much grieved . . ." — *The
Generall Historie,* 4th Book, in Smith, vol. ii, p. 293 [144], verbatim.

page 615 "This massacre some will say will be good for the Plantation, . . ."— Ibid, p.
298 [147], verbatim, abridged.

Further History of Captaine John Smith

page 616 Smith's epitaph — in Smith, vol. iii, p. 390.

page 616 For the events of this section I am heavily indebted to Barbour's reconstruction (*Three Worlds,* chs. 25–26).

page 616 "By what warrant . . . a copper kettle and a few toys!" — These two paragraphs are derived in part from the first para. of chapter 4 of the *Advertisements,* in Smith, vol. iii, p. 276.

page 617 Frauncis's possessions from George Smith — taken from George Smith's will, in Smith, vol. iii, pp. 379-81.

page 619 Starvation food in 1623 — Wheeler, p. 394 (letter from Sir William Pelham). The same passage is quoted (with different orthography) in Sir Francis Hill, p. 142. To give some idea of how difficult life could get in Lincolnshire in this period I quote more of the extract (Hill version): "Our country was never in that want that now it is, and more of money than corn, for there are many thousands in these parts who have sold all they have even to their bed-straw, and cannot get work to earn any money. Dog's flesh is a dainty dish, and found upon search in many houses, also such horse flesh as hath lain long in a *deke* for hounds, and the other day one stole a sheep, who for mere hunger tore a leg out, and yet the great turn of scarcity not yet come."

page 619 Economic fluctuations 1603-31 — From Appendix D, appropriately labeled "Economic Fluctuations," in Christopher Hill, *Century of Revolution,* p. 277.

page 620 "These observations are all I have for the expences of a thousand pound . . ." — Smith's prospectus to the *Generall Historie* (1623); in Smith, vol. ii, p. 16 [A2, verso]. This sad paragraph continues with a plea for money.

page 620 The King's search for Jesuits — The order actually went out in 1612, according to Sir Francis Hill, p. 110.

page 620 Machiavelli on war — op. cit., p. 6.

page 621 The useless brigandine vests — Hume, *Martin's Hundred,* p. 123.

page 621 The plague outbreaks of 1625, 1630–1631 — Mentioned in Sir Francis Hill, pp. 134, 136.

page 621 The flood of 1625 — mentioned in Wheeler, p. 30.

page 621 Four hundred volunteers to fight at Hull — Sir Francis Hill, p. 118.

page 622 "Parliament had passed a Bill of Enclosure not long since . . ." — It had done so in 1621.

page 622 Barty's subsidy of Smith's *Accidence* — ". . . Robert Bertie, Lord Willoughby, Smith's personal friend, was in charge of an important expedition with few trained sailors and without any handbook for beginners. Smith wrote that he had 'beene perswaded' to print the *Accidence.* If the persuader was not Willoughby, some other person saw the need" (Smith, vol. iii, p. 7, Barbour's note to the *Accidence).*

page 622 Varieties of Lincolnshire potatoes (late nineteenth cent.) — William Henry Wheeler, *History of the Fens of South Lincolnshire* (Stamford, Lincolnshire: Paul Watkins, 1990 repr. of 1896 ed.), p. 399.

page 623 "Wold and Marsh" newsletter footnote — May 1995, p. 2.

page 623 The longitude and latitude of Lincoln — Bourne, p. 97 (*Almanacke,* Thirteenth Rule).

page 624 The "slaves to malignancy" who couldn't say their Compasse — some phrases borrowed from a sentence in the address to the reader of Smith's *Advertisements* (Smith, vol. iii, p. 264).

page 624 The sad tale of Smith's Isles — As told in the *Advertisements for the Unexperienced Planters of New England, or Any Where,* in Smith, vol. iii, p. 286 [22].

page 624 "I ask not any thing . . ." — Actually, not a petition to King Charles at all (although I imagine that Smith wrote one or two), but a pathetic interjection in *The Generall Historie;* in Smith, vol. ii, p. 307 [153].

page 624 "Powhatan's .100. wives . . ." — "The reported rapidity of turnover among Powhatan's wives is unequaled elsewhere in North America and is therefore a little suspect" (Rountree, *The Powhatan Indians of Virginia,* p. 112).

page 625 Smith's "trunk bound with iron barres" and "best suit of apparell of a tawny color videlicet" — Mentioned in his last will, 21 June 1631; in Smith, vol. iii, p. 383 (auxilliary documents, document iv).

page 626 "The Warres in Europe . . ." — *Advertisements,* in Smith, vol. iii, p. 269.

page 626 Smith's grim verse — Ibid, p. 265.

page 627 "Would not the beggar then forget himself?" — Shakespeare, *The Taming of the Shrew,* induction, scene 1, 2nd entrance, Lord's 4th speech.

page 627 The Lincolnshire famine of 1631 — Sir Francis Hill, p. 139.

page 629 Smith's plaque — From notes taken during a visit to Willoughby in May 1995.

Further History of the Patawomecks

page 631 Epigraph on naked men — Quinn, vol. 1, p. 130 (anonymous notes for the guidance of Ralegh and Cavendish, *ca.* 1584).

page 631 Events in this chapter — *Generall Historie,* 4th Book; in Smith, vol. ii, p. 309–14 [154–57].

page 631 "Since the King of Patawomeck had turn'd traitor to Virginia's innocent *Nonpareil,* how could he have expected to be advanced?" — A sentiment inspired by Ralegh (op. cit., p. 73, *Report of the truth . . . of the fight betwixt the* Revenge *and an Armada of the King of Spain,* 1591), who applies it less cynically to English to turn traitor to their country and serve Spain.

Further History of the Patawomecks

page 633 Epigraph on "settinge uppon the Indians" — Quoted in Hatch, p. 29.

page 633 Potter and Rountree of course detail their later history more substantially than I do here. Their summaries of events do not entirely agree. I have relied more heavily on Rountree for my version.

Further History of All Virginian Salvages

page 634 Smith extract — *The True Travels,* in Smith, vol. iii, p. 216 [42].

page 634 Perogatives of the Mayor and Burgesses of Boston Port — Wheeler, p. 344.

Further History of Opechancanough

page 634 Epigraph on the "only real tragedy"— Woodward, p. 189.

page 635 Events of this chapter — Based on Rountree, *Pocahontas's People,* pp. 56–88. Smith's *Generall Historie* covers events only up to 1624. For events of 1623, see the 4th Book, p. 315 [158].

page 637 The "lesser sassafrass" drunk by Opechancanough to purge him of the poisoned wine — A plausible interpolation based on the medical procedure described in Rountree, *The Powhatan Indians,* p. 127.

page 638 "Such as Moses, Cyrus, Theseus & Romulus . . ." — Machiavelli, p. 9 (ch. VI); abbreviated and archaicized.

Further History of the Carolina Salvages

page 639 Blake epigraph — William Blake, *The Continental Prophecies,* ed. D. W. Dörrbecker (Princeton: Princeton University Press, The William Blake Trust. Blakes Illuminated Books ser., vol. 4), pp. 112-13 [*America: A Prophecy,* plate 17]. The editor's text has inadvertently transcribed the plate's "of" for "or," which I have corrected.

page 639 William Lawson's remarks on Indian decline — Op. cit., p. 232.

The Nottoway Girls of North Carolina

page 640 William Byrd's account — Op. cit., pp. 114–116.

page 641 Population of Nottoways — Lawson, whose figures were collected presumably between 1700 and 1709, gives us the following data: "*Nottaway* [sic] *Indians,* Town 1, *Winoack Creek,* Fighting Men 30" (p. 242).

Further History of the Powhatans

page 642 Epigraph on the superior value of Indian land to Indian services — J. Anthony Paredes, *Indians of the Southeastern United States in the Late 20th Century* (Tuscaloosa: University of Alabama Press, 1992), p. 2 (introduction).

page 642 Jefferson — *Notes on the State of Virginia* (1787) in the Library of America version of his collected writings (New York: Literary Classics of the United States, Inc., 1984), pp. 221–2.

page 642 ". . . and it seemes GOD hath provided this Countrey for our Nation . . ." — *Advertisements for the Unexperienced Planters of New England,* in Smith, vol. iii, p. 275 [9].

page 642 "I think it is necessary to destroy all these northern indians [sic] . . ." — Sir William Berkeley to Maj. Gen. Smyth, 22 June 1666; quoted in Fischer, p. 387.

page 643 Jefferson — loc. cit.

page 643 "Because until the Spring time . . ." (1682) — H.R. McIlwaine, ed., *Executive Journals of the Council of Colonial Virginia,* 2 vols. (Richmond, Virginia: The Virginia State Library, 1925), vol. 1, p. 15.

page 644 Footnote (William Byrd on intermarriage) — Byrd, p. 4.

page 644 Bills of 1682-1706 — McIlwaine, *Legislative Journals of the Council of Colonial Virginia in Three Volumes*   (Richmond, Virginia: The Virginia State Library, MCMXVIII), vol. 1, pp. 41, 262, 464, 473.

page 644 Jefferson — loc. cit.

page 644 Footnote (Jefferson to Brother Handsome Lake) — Jefferson, p. 556.

page 645 Bill of 1723 — McIlwaine, *Legislative Journals,* vol. 2, pp. 689–700, 1045.

Further History of the Pamunkeys

page 647 Brave age epigraph — Nashe, p. 416.

page 647 The Queen of Pamunkey's complaint — McIlwaine, *Legislative Journals,* vol. 1, p. 262.

page 647 What transpired during Bacon's Rebellion — Rountree, *Pocahontas's People,* pp. 96–100.

page 648 The opening of Pamunkey Neck to English settlement — Ibid, p. 113. Rountree remarks: "The remaining reservation was insufficient from the outset . . ."

page 648 Jefferson — loc. cit., pp. 221–22.

Further History of the Powhatans

page 649 Gull Groper epigraph — Dekker, op. cit., p. 205.

page 649 Dates and events herein — Based on Rountree, *Pocahontas's People,* final chapters.

Further History of America Britannia

page 651 Epigraph on fortune — Fowler, p. 5 (Fulke Greville, Lord Brooke, Sonnet CV) slightly archaicized.

Further History of England

page 652 Machiavelli epigraph — op. cit., p. 20.

page 652 "Several serious riots were caused by the Fenman . . ." — Wheeler, pp. 260–61.

page 652 The riot two years after John Smith's death — Sir Francis Hill, p. 143.

page 653 Statistic on Anderby — *East Lindsey — The Secret's Out!* (newspaper published by the East Lindsey District Council, 1995), p. 17 ("2000 Years of History at Anderby," by Betty Kirkham).

page 653 Extract from the "treatise from 1976"— Andrew Darwin, *Canals and Rivers of Britain* (London: J.M. Dent & sons, 1976), p. 94; abridged.

page 653 Advertisements from East Lindsey — Selected from *East Lindsey — The Secret's Out!,* pp. 3, 10, 22; and from the brochure "SPILSBY Official Map and Guide" from the same year.

The Virginia Maps in Blaeu's Grand Atlas

page 655 Thomas Nashe, *The Unfortunate Traveller* (1594), in Salzman, pp. 278–79.

page 655 *[Joan] Blaeu's The Grand Atlas of the Seventeenth-Century World* (New York: Rizzoli, in cooperation with the Royal Geographic Society, 1990), pp. 168–71 (plate 73: New Virginia; and 74: Virginia and Florida).

Further History of Virginia

page 658 Perpetual war epigraph — Letter from the Treasurer and Council for Virginia, 1622; quoted in Barbour's *Pocahontas,* p. 210; slightly archaicized (since Barbour has probably modernized it).

page 658 Boldness and freedom epigraph — The editors of *American Heritage* (author: Marshall W. Fishwick; consultant: Parke Rouse, Jr.), *Jamestown: First English Colony* (Mahwah, New Jersey: Troll Associates, 1965), p. 7.

Third Dream Epitaph

page 665 Hamor on just causes — op. cit., p. 27.

* * * * * *

TEXTUAL APPARATUS

page 667 Gore-sparkled honor epigraph — one of several dedicatory verses written by Smith's friends quoted at the beginning of the *True Travels;* in Smith, vol. iii, p. 150.

CHRONOLOGY

page 671 Entry for 1535 — Sir Francis Hill, p. 65.

page 671 Entry for 1536 — Guy, p. 179.

page 672 Entry for 1580 from Christopher Hill — *The Century of Revolution*, p. 18.

page 675 Entry for 1600-99 from Helen Rountree — *Pocahontas's People*, p. 89.

page 675 Entry for 1600-99 from Sir George Clark — Geoffrey Parker and Lesley M. Smith, ed., *The General Crisis of the Seventeenth Century*, (London: Routledge & Kegan Paul, 1985 repr. of 1978 ed.). p. 57 (Geoffrey Parker, "The Dutch Revolt and the Polarization of International Politics").

page 675 Entry for 1606 — Hume, *Here Lies Virginia*, p. 44.

page 678 Entry for 1614 — Ibid, p. 32 (Niels Steensgaard, "The Seventeenth-Century Crisis").

page 681 Entry for 1656 — *Pocahontas's People*, p. 92.

GLOSSARY 1: PERSONAL NAMES

page 686 Entry for Samuel Argall — C.H. Coote, in Leslie Stephens and Sidney Lee, *Dictionary of National Biography* (New York: Macmillan, 1908), vol. 1. (Since the DCB and DAB are widely available, I have not thought it necessary to source their extracts in more detail.) Remarks of Ivor Nöel Hume — From *The Virginia Adventure*, p. 350. Remarks of Philip Barbour — From *Pocahontas*, p. 69.

page 686 Entry for Sir Thomas Dale — Strachey, p. 91; Hume, *The Virginia Adventure*, p. 320.

page 686 Entry for Lord De La Warr — Strachey, p. 90.

page 687 Entry for Elizabeth I — Guy, pp. 251-52; Strong [sp], p. 16. Last clause about torture, Guy, p. 318.

page 687 Entry for James I — Matthew, p. 625; Aikin, vol. 2, p. 397.

page 687 Entry for Kemps — Third Book of the *Generall Historie*, in Smith, vol. ii, p 210 [85]; Strachey, p. 61.

page 687 Entry for Machiavelli — Jacques Barzun, *From Dawn to Decadence: 500 Years of Cultural Life 1500 to the Present* (New York, HarperCollins, 2000), pp. 256–57.

page 688 Entry for OKEUS — Rountree, *The Powhatan Indians of Virginia*, p. 135.

page 688 Entry for Pocahontas — John P. Harrington, Anthropological Paper # 46, "The Original Strachey Vocabulary of the Virginia Indian Language," in the Smithsonian Institution's *Bureau of American Ethnology Bulletin 153*, (Washington: 1955), p 196; Rountree, *The Powhatan Indians of Virginia*, p. 80; Cabell, p. 51.

page 689 Entry for Powhatan — Mittie O. McDavid, *Princess Pocahontas* (New York: Neale Publishing Co., 1907), p. 27; Philip L. Barbour, *Pocahontas and her World*, p. 30; Harrington, pp. 194–95.

page 689 Entry for Captaine John Smith — Chatterton, p. 62; Richard Potts, in Purchas, p. 1731; Hume, *Here Lies Virginia*, p. 38.

page 690 Entry for Winganuske — Barbour, *Pocahontas and her World*, p. 5.

page 690 Entry for Wowinchopunck — Strachey, p. 67.

GLOSSARY 2: ORDERS, &c

page 691 Entry for Chickahominies — *Barbour, Three Worlds*, p. 151 fn.

page 691 Entry for Fen Slodgers — Wheeler, p. 35.

page 691 Entry for Keyauwees — Lawson, p. 58.

page 692 Entry for Piscataways — Rountree, *Powhatan Foreign Relations*, pp. 114–115,

131 (ch. 5, Wayne E. Clark and Helen C. Rountree, "The Powhatans and the Maryland Mainland").

page 693 Quotation-marked portion of entry on Swart-rutters — Nashe, p. 99 fn, ("Pierce Penniless").

page 693 Entry for Tymor — Kinross, p. 152.

GLOSSARY 3: PLACES

page 693 Entry for Alba Regalias — Smith, vol. iii, *The True Travels,* p. 165 [8] (Barbour's note).

page 693 Entry for Axopolis — Smith, vol. iii, Barbour's note to fragment prototype of *The True Travels,* p. 337.

page 694 Entry for Caniza — Smith, vol. iii, *The True Travels,* p. 163 [6] (Barbour's note).

page 694 Entry for Chesapeake — Barbour, *Three Worlds,* p. 430.

page 694 Entry for Fen — Wheeler, Appendix IV, p. 6.

page 694 Entry for High Hungaria — Barbour, *Three Worlds,* p. 64.

page 694 Entry for Menapacunt — Smith, vol. i, *A True Relation,* p. 51 [CIr].

page 695 Entry for Roanoke — Strachey, p. 58.

page 695 Entry for Sander, Screwe &c — Smith, vol. iii, *The True Travels,* p. 187 [23] (Barbour's note).

page 695 Entry for Veristhorne — Smith, vol. iii, *The True Travels,* p. 184 [22] (Barbour's note).

page 695 Entry for Virginia — Hume, *The Virginia Adventure,* p. 109; Strachey, p. 10.

page 696 Entries for Virginia settlements other than Jamestown between 1607 and 1624 (Argall Town, Henrico, etc.) are indebted to Hatch, who conveniently schematizes by place.

GLOSSARY 5: CALENDARS, &c

page 697 Entry for Copyhold — Christopher Hill, *Century of Revolution,* p. 13.

page 697 Entry for Chichqueenes — Smith, vol. iii, *The True Travels,* p. 161, fn. 8 (Barbour).

page 697 Entry for Ducatoon — Barbour, *Three Worlds,* p. 65.

page 697 Entry for Glass — Smith, vol. iii, *The True Travels,* p. 85.

Sources

page 703 Epigraph — Rojas, *The Spanish Bawd (La Celestina),* trans. J.M. Cohen (New York: Penguin, 1964), p. 34.

ACKNOWLEDGEMENTS

I would like to thank the very seaworthy Mr. Eric Reid of Ben Lomond, California, for commenting on some nautical usages.

In London, the eminent Robert Harbison and his most excellent consort, Esther Whitby, did kindly drive me to Gravesend. Esther also traveled with me to Willoughby and Holy Isle.

In Sacramento, Mr. Brandan Kearney loaned me some rare Elizabethan volumes. Lizzy Kate Gray kept me company on several library excursions.

I would also like to thank Janice Ryu, who came with me to Virginia and most of the English places mentioned.

In Albany, New York, Mr. Charles T. Gehring of the New Netherland Project responded as quoted to my query about Argall's raid on Manhattan.

In Alford, Massachusetts, Mr. George Minkoff sent me some pages of his own novel about John Smith. It was fun to chat with him about good old Sweet John.

I am grateful to Carla Bolte for her painstaking typographical work.